Folsom on Fire

a novel

by

Orlando Smart-Powell

PROLOGUE

In the grass *It* slid, winding its sleek, shiny black body across the ground. *Its* dead destination fixed in *Its* narrow eyes. As old as the stars themselves *It* was. *It* was father, mother, son, creator and destroyer.

It was ancient.

Its knowledge of what was to unfold upon Folsom, Mississippi in the Lord's year of 1890 was without limit. *It* had already seen Folsom's *tomorrows*.

"Oh yes! I *have* seen them," *It* hissed– or did *It* speak such words from a mouth that was not a mouth, which held a tongue that was not whole, but split asunder into two by a hand that was not a hand, but a living force?

The hardened heart of a man or woman was virgin clay in its grasp– especially when said hearts were already as stone and shaded dark, and open to its call.

It had come for a short visit– a collection of items. But *It* heard something that *It* liked. *It* paused and then changed its mind. *It* was in ecstasy as its stomach slid across the hot grass borne of blood spilt during many years of war. Even the trees were full of it flowing from root to trunk to limb to branch to leaf.

Man had been pitted against man, *It* knew, for *It* had been there. Blood had been let so freely. Souls once bright were now dark. Souls that had been shut in the dark were given light– but for only a short while.

It knew *It* was right– had always been right. *It* screamed as much to the heavens with a flicking of its forked tongue.

It swelled with pride knowing that everyone knew *It*, feared *It*, yet also loved *It*. They damned *It*, though called for *It* by every other name than the one they had given *It* ... pride ... jealously ... fear ... hate ... and yes, sometimes love. Flesh will burn and blood will coat that path upon which man walketh in Folsom. Man shall writhe in agony upon a pyre crafted by his own hands, *It* knew, for that *tomorrow It* had already witnessed.

Between trees, long grass, a garden, a field, *It* moved effortless– as if *It* possessed the feet of an angel– on until *It* made its way to the roadside. *It* waited for the wagons full of flesh to pass before winding up the dirt path to the porch where the old woman sat in her rocking chair– *Its* beloved daughter. The witch was calling for *It* yet again. Yes– *It* had so many daughters and sons, but she– the witch of Folsom, was ever dearest to its heart above all– at least for the time being.

It waited until she motioned for *It* to come closer.

It wound *Its* way up the two rickety steps that led to the porch. There was an empty rocking chair next to hers and the witch bid *It* to sit for a spell, which *It* did gladly. *It* wrapped its body around the rotten wood spindles of the chair, and then sat coiled upon the seat. The witch turned toward *It*. *It* raised its head to the height of hers. She smiled.

It saw no fear in the witch's grey eyes ... dull twin moons breaking through a misty night. *It* knew that she recognized what *It* truly was. But of course she did ... had she not called *It* forth from the ether and made *It* flesh once more?

The witch spoke her request.

It bargained.

She countered with a pound of flesh.

It was a give and take between one ancient and one old.

The witch was about to agree, but stopped abruptly. Her thin, almost nonexistent pink lips parted. There was but one more thing she asked for.

"Of course, my daughter," It agreed readily.

It knew she had not the wisdom to use what she asked for. No one of flesh and blood could. It would only drive her mad as it did the others before her ... many others ... long dead children of wicked fame and mythos. *It* granted the witch what had been asked for with foolish hope and desperation.

Damnation and salvation edged upon the horizon of despair ... it could not be stopped now.

Burning flesh and blood would soon shade the air black once again.

* * *

It left the witch and vowed to return once all was finished. *It* carried on with its journey west, to the town of Folsom. There was a friend of black, dead bark and bloody roots to visit once more.

"I am the beautiful one!" *It* proclaimed, with pride that only one who was truly beautiful could say and know to be true.

The Witch

The witch's head felt as though a white-hot poker had been jammed into it. She had seen far too much.

Death was coming . . . she had welcomed it, though she had not even been given a bag of silver coins for the dark deed she'd agreed upon with It . . . just flesh of her flesh. Though to her, that flesh was worth more than seven bricks of gold.

CHAPTER 1

The dead stirred restlessly in their graves of dirt and water.

Life was a struggle for whites and Negroes alike, though far harder and more difficult for Negroes.

It was near the end of spring in the year of 1890– the Gilded Age was gasping.

It was hot . . . dry . . .

Hate, lust and revenge were all in great supply.

Hope for a better tomorrow was like smoke– ethereal and easily disturbed.

Salvation was a dream– as was freedom. Any niggah– as all Negroes were referred to in Folsom, Mississippi, by whites– would agree to that.

The soldiers of the Confederate were either long gone, dead, dying or busily fading into a history of what could have been. What was left in Folsom was chaos as all struggled for survival . . . a way of life . . . a reason for living . . . even the slightest justification for being alive.

Reconstruction had failed.

A time ago, before the war, Folsom's lands had been bountiful– full of peanuts, sugar cane, sweet potatoes, wheat, and of course cotton which was king. Its river had once been a favorite place for young white boys to frolic in on the white side– but only in daylight, for who knew what lurked in those now black waters come nightfall? Perhaps the witch knew, though no one with a hint of common sense would dare ask her such a thing, for she might tell you the truth.

And once upon a time, there were slaves that numbered in the hundreds and thousands to work the fields, clean the homes, feed the chickens and cattle, plant the gardens, pick the cotton, dig up the beets and potatoes. Then, once all strength and will was stripped from them, they filled the graveyards with their broken bones from strong bodies that once were.

Although . . . some things never changed.

On the western edge of town, perched up high like Mount Olympus, there once stood a glorious, white mansion. The manor was the home of Mason Christianson, a wealthy land and slave-owner with more money than he could ever spend or bequeath to his heirs.

Not to be outdone, his rival, old man Monclair, a land and flesh-owner also, but a far more devious businessman, built an even larger home with twice as many rooms as the fifteen-room Christianson manor. It was on the northeast side of Folsom that Simeon Monclair I had erected his pride.

But the blessings had not stopped with the vast, fertile lands of the Christianson and Monclair plantations. The Folsom river that hugged the town flowed into the great fairway that was *Old Man River*. It gave a path for a better life to poor whites that came looking for such. Crafters, dockworkers, sailors and tradesmen came in droves.

The red-skin savages, as the whites called them with as much pleasure as chewing shit, were long gone from around Folsom and had been driven further west or effectively killed off. Thanks for their removal, by whatever form it took, was then given to Andrew Jackson and his Indian Removal Act many years earlier. *We bid thee say goodbye willingly—you of old who art Cherokee, Creek,*

Choctaw, Chickasaw and Seminole nations—lest we kill thee and thy
kin, for our guns are powerful and our desire for thy lands for our
'king' hath been stoked and made righteous by the will of God.

Folsom's center was growing year-by-year, but stalled slightly
when the talk of secession and war began. But truly, at that time
there was no real fear in Folsom that this would happen. Rumina-
tions of war remained whispers, and soon faded as daily life resumed and rumors of a battle with the north were said to be just
that. Plans moved ahead to keep the town expanding.

The cotton gin had tripled the Monclair and Christianson fortunes already– more land– more slaves– more cotton . . . then,
even more land and more slaves . . . God had been deemed to be a
very good God. The slave trade had been criminalized, but it was
of no matter to those who only needed a niggah-buck and a nig-
gah-bitch, which they had in great supply. Each newborn niggah
meant another coin in the coffer.

The Christianson and Monclair families began loaning money to
would-be fortune seekers in the growing town of Folsom. They
salivated in anticipation of future rewards to be made on their investments. Simeon Monclair I, never a man to be second to any,
with far greater dreams and more money than Christianson, decided to outdo him one better.

To those deemed a high risk, otherwise known as white trash,
he loaned money with a dangerously high interest rate. He was
confident that no man in town would dare cross him, let alone de-
fault on a loan– Folsom *was* his after all. He was buttressed by inherited rights of his father before him, who had exerted great
influence on those elected to govern the south . . . wealthy businessmen from Jackson, Peak Hills and other neighboring towns.
Simeon Monclair I reasoned he was too great to be challenged.

Unfortunately . . . or fortunately, depending on who one was,
war did arrive upon Folsom's doorstep. The two great families of

Folsom– the Christianson's and Monclairs' were effectively devastated. Their fortunes were but a singular weed in a tempest, and tempest it was that swept down upon them in blue.

The masters and the oldest male progeny of the two great estates joined the Confederate army as officers and never returned– alive that is. The Christianson and Monclair widows were somewhat comforted by the deaths of their husbands and sons, for if the war hadn't killed them, what they would have seen upon their return surely would have. The glorious mansions that straddled Folsom– gleaming white citadels of money, power, greed and self-proclaimed righteousness– were both reduced to ashes, but not before being plundered by the roving armies of the north.

Slaves also joined the blue juggernaut as the prophetic words of freedom sung in code by their long dead kin finally came to pass. The acres of crops that had provided the means for those two towering behemoths of white to exist in the first place were also scorched and rendered useless for years to come. The most damaged areas were carved up and given to the freed Negroes who'd been banished to live on the outskirts of the town across the Folsom river.

Many of Folsom's men had eagerly joined the Confederate army to protect their lands, their women, their pride, their sons' and daughters' futures. Most never returned home. Those that did manage to drag themselves back were never whole again . . . physically or mentally. Most bore badges of wasted courage for a lifetime of haunting dreams of death that often slipped into reality. It was the Age of Survival for Folsom, not the Gilded Age as it was for others. For once, the rich and poor whites of Folsom shared more than just white skin in common.

Mary Cole, however, cared nothing about white folks' struggle and survival, or their dreams of what used to be, especially since she had been scraping by her entire life. In fact, she was glad white folks were scared of what was to come. Now it was they who had to worry about their children's welfare day to day, struggle to put enough food on the table or wonder how not to lose their once well-built, now mostly raggedy homes.

Ain't heard about a good reason yet why I should give a damn 'bout white folk, she'd often thought, and told her husband, Lar.

She refused to be shaken from her belief that all white folks despised all Negroes. No one, not even Lar . . . especially Lar, could put a chink in that dam. Even those whites who appeared to tolerate Negroes, and there were very few of them, would have them all killed and never look back while they walked to church the next day, she felt. She often wondered what all those white folks at church were praying about anyway . . . *'Please Lord, heavenly Father, take these wretched Niggahs outta our sights and kill'em all dead. In your heavenly name we ask this. Amen,'* she mused.

Few days ever passed that she didn't reprimand Lar on this very topic. *But—Lar was Lar as he ever would be,* she thought. At night, he was barely able to keep his eyes open as he read the bible, which he swore held all the answers a man or woman ever needed in their lives. Mary had long ago decided to let him have and enjoy such delusions.

As of late, the nightly ritual of Lar reading scriptures from the bible had become goodnight stories for her and the child she carried. Lar sounded out the longer words, just like Enda Sully had taught him to, which chorused chaotically with Uncle Matty's door rattling snore just a few steps away in the other room. The closest thing Negroes in Folsom had to a preacher was Lar. He lived by the word of God and worked hard getting others to do the same. But, Mary knew he was no fool. She knew he was aware of what white folks were capable of doing to a Negroe. Still, she thought, it was that damned Bible that was always making him try to find one shred of good in people– white and Negroe. As far as she was concerned, the way white folks were, heaven was a place most white folks would never see, and that was fine with her. If white folks didn't want Negroes around them downstairs, then she'd gladly take heaven and an eternity without them upstairs!

* * *

Morning came earlier than usual for Mary.

Between dreams and reality she fought to awake.

She rubbed her swollen stomach and stifled a moan. The stretch marks seemed longer and deeper than the day previous. Moving her hands even lower, she massaged the hard nub that had once been her bellybutton. Now it was nearly flat and twice its normal size.

'Your chile gonna be a big'un,' every Negroe who thought they knew about babies would say. 'Well,' she thought, 'I'm a big gal anyway. It just make sense big gals have big babies.'

There was no use trying to go back to bed now, she figured. The roosters would be crowing soon and the child in her belly refused to stop squirming. She knew if she tried for a few more minutes of sleep, the child would start stomping on her guts again until she went to go pee. Though she pained from the stretched, scarred skin of her belly, she was determined to enjoy every moment, every second, day and week of it. This child was different from the others she had carried. She knew it. She felt it in her bones.

With this one, there had been no bleeding at all during the first few months. And this one was always kicking and squirming. Yes ... this one would live, she knew. The youngest ones, she remembered, if they were 'ones' at all, simply poured out of her in bloody clumps after a month or two of everything seeming normal. Without warning, after a few days of cramping they would slide down her legs like warm jelly.

The older babies, and they were babies at least to her, stayed in her a few months longer and had all stopped their wiggling right before they were born. The oldest ones were the hardest for Mary to let slip away into dreams. They all looked like babies but were far too small– their skin like gray, melted rubber, and their mouths open and lips curled up as though they had been in agony right before the light left them.

With her last pregnancy, had it not been for Enda Sully– a quadroon who could easily pass for white, she would have joined her babies in God's kingdom. Of that she was certain. The bleeding had refused to stop after she'd pushed the dead child out. Willa, a close friend and midwife from three shacks down, hadn't known what to do but to call the quadroon, which Mary hadn't wanted, but everyone . . . Allie Mae Brown, Uncle Matty, Lar, and yes, even she knew it had to be done.

Mary held no love for Enda Sully, simply because she'd always felt it was Enda's daughter, Maggie Mae, the old woman wanted Lar to marry. But come the quadroon did with her basket of herbs and mason jars clanging and filled with God knows what. The quadroon's icy, white hands had entered her . . . moved around in her . . . massaged and then pushed hard. Satisfied with what she'd done, the quadroon had wiped the blood from her hands on her tattered nightgown as if it were nothing but splattered goo from a carelessly cracked egg.

Halfway in the world of men and halfway on her way to the other side, Mary watched dizzily as Enda Sully went to the table and combined liquids, powders, and then some dried leaves in a jar. She'd shaken the small bottle until she produced a dead, brown liquid. This she'd poured into her cupped hand and then carefully, entering Mary once again, massaged it into her. A bitter cold flowed from the Enda's hands into her, spreading quickly and as far up as her breasts and as low as her feet. The wisps of Enda's unbraided white hair fell on her face as the old woman leaned over her and whispered to her in her strange, French accented voice . . . "I don't see no more blood coming, chile."

But now wasn't the time for such long passed nightmares, she thought. Too many things had to be done and a few things after that. There was cornbread left from the day before and a few eggs she decided to add some milk and water to and stretch it out for Uncle Matty, Lar and herself for breakfast. Out in the back, there were a few logs needing splitting. Everything was in short supply and high demand. She paid a long visit to the outhouse before making her way to the wood stump. Axe in hand, she began hacking away, knowing Lar was sure to fuss at her for even moving about. He wanted her to rest as much as possible, and not just for the baby's sake, but for her own also.

Well, he would just have to fuss about it, Mary decided. *'Ain't no sense having Lar do a thing I can do myself. 'Sides, if I wait on him to get stuff going round here, might as well wait on Lord Jesus come down do it hisself.'*

Mary had long ago come to the conclusion that a woman's body was built for working more so than a man's ever was. Why– just the hips, she reasoned, were made for hauling wood, holding babies and cradling pots. A woman's back was hearty enough for unrelenting bending and straightening to gather crops while the Mississippi sun scalded her neck black as tar.

She did indeed feel blessed amongst other women. She stood nearly eye-to-eye with Lar, who himself towered over other Negroe and white men alike. She could pump water, split logs and work a field with the best of men, if not better. And that no one would ever use the word pretty and Mary Cole in the same sentence did bother her when she was younger, but less so now. She knew what pretty looked like. And what she saw in the mirror, she knew wasn't that. She already guessed that Jesus wasn't going to come down and make her wide nose thinner . . . her tarry black skin lighter . . . her kinky hair straighter. And that was fine with her. So if folks said she was strapping, thick, sound and hefty, she would gladly take that as a pat on the back instead.

With their bed in the same room as the kitchen, the mixture of morning light and the aroma of eggs and cornbread was all it took to rouse Lar. She wished there was more food to slop on their tin plates. Lar had the appetite of three men and Uncle Matty, now far too old to work the fields anymore, needed all the strength he could gather to sit without teetering over.

She finished mashing the cornbread and milk together, creating a thick, white, lumpy mush that, with hard fried eggs, she hoped would fill their stomachs for a few hours at least. She set the plates on the bowlegged, wooden table that seemed to have once been a feast for termites– it was just old wood Lar had nailed together. "Lar– you come and get it now while it still got some heat to it," she told him. And still on beat, she walked toward Uncle Matty's room, the only true room in the shack, to get him going.

Lar grabbed her hand as she walked past him and stood up, pressing in hard behind her. He kissed her neck while gently rubbing her distended belly. "How you feelin' this morn', ol' gal?" He asked, sleep still strangling his husky voice.

She debated on whether to keep moving or to stop. She decided on the latter, allowing his hot, calloused hands to hold her. "Same as any other, I reckon."

He sat back on the bed with a plop and closed his eyes for a few seconds. HHe turned her around and raised her pink flowered dress up. "Lar, stop it now!" she demanded, playfully. "You actin' like a Billy Goat!"

"Hold on woman." He looked up and smiled. "I just wanna see my baby." He held her dress up to just underneath her breasts. With his other hand, he caressed her belly and then began kissing it. His touch warmed her throughout. His strokes said without saying– spoke without speaking– *you and my child are loved by me above all others.*

She let him kiss her belly a few more times and then pulled down her dress and feigned embarrassment. "Not now, Lar," she said, and then leaned in quickly and kissed his plump, brown lips. It was not just the touch of his hands that always evoked such passionate feelings in her. Sometimes it was a look from his dark brown eyes or the teasing alteration of his baritone voice to soprano. And at those moments, knowing that Uncle Matty was soundly asleep, her urge to lie next to his brown, now sun-blackened skin was nearly irresistible.

There was a lift and sway to her hips as she backed away from him and toward Uncle Matty's door. A weary moan answered her rap upon it. "You covered up, Uncle Matty?" He mumbled a reply in the affirmative.

He was sitting on the edge of the bed when she entered. The room smelled as he did– old and sick. HH e had an infection somewhere she was certain– it was called being *old and sick.* She walked to the window, which was nothing more than planks of wood nailed together then hinged to the wall, and opened it. She sniffed the warm air and judged that it wouldn't rain today– *again*– nothing new. She knelt down before him and grasped his feet. They were like chicken bones in her hands as she massaged and flexed them to break up the stiffness. She continued up his legs until she reached banged-up, gnarled pieces of round wood that served as kneecaps. She warned him before she began moving his legs out straight. With each crackle and pop of his joints, he grimaced. Had he any teeth left, he would have been gnashing them.

"Was' a time when I be doin' what you doin' for Massah Christianson," Uncle Matty said.

"What he have to be sore and achin' 'bout?"

"You know white folks back then," he said. "They always complaining 'bout somethin' o 'nother."

"And ain't ever seen a long days work neither," she huffed. "They still complaining about nothing and everythang."

"Massah Christianson would be sayin' to me," his gritty voice became authoritative, "Matty! Matty! My feets a'botherin' me . . .

come rub 'em. Matty! Matty! Fetch me a drink . . . I been out seein'
to niggahs all mornin' and I thirsty now! Matty! Matty! I just
blinked my eyes twice . . . come rub'em– they tired, too!" Mary
looked up at him and laughed. "Girl-chile, it be truth! You hear
me?" he snickered. "White folks couldn't pass wind 'cept with a
niggah to fan it away."

Mary kept on massaging his legs until he was able to move
them– stiffly, but freely on his own. She left him to dress himself
and returned to the outer room where Lar was just finishing up
breakfast. "You gonna ride the cart, right?" he asked.

She sighed, and then forced a smile. "Yes, husband . . . I gonna
ride it. Ain't no more walkin' to work for me . . . O.K.?"

"Just makin' sure you kept to your promise." He scooped the
last bit of meal in his mouth then wiped his lips clean with the
back of his hand.

"I ride it this day and the next until the baby comes likes I told
you," she said. "Now you gonna stop fussin' about . . . ."

He raised his arms. "I'm done."

"Good then."

She unwound the two frayed French-braids on either side of her
head and sewed them back tightly, and then braided the two ends
together. She scooped eggs and meal onto two more plates and slid
one down to the far end of the table for Uncle Matty. The meal
wasn't much to taste, but it was as good as it got for the times they
lived in. Dinner would be better she was determined. There was
still some pork in the smokehouse out back she was debating on
putting in with the turnip greens she had picked the evening before. Greens and a large pan of fried cornbread would be just as
tasty as anything, she reckoned.

Lar left and joined the caravan of other Negroe men and women
folk who had already begun their daily march to town. He fell in
line and would have blended in with the other dark, weary faces
had he not stood at least a head above them. There was not one

amongst the group who didn't greet him as brother, father and minister. Mary took great pride in that he was so admired; especially knowing that Lar was far too self-effacing to feel it for himself.

He had inherited the mantle of preacher from his father– that is if a gathering of Negroes in a clearing with a half-built church was a ministry. But also, Lar was not just their spiritual guide, but their unanimously appointed leader. Most Negroe folks like Lar were off to the fields to pluck cotton, beans, corn and sweet potatoes, or were in the process of prepping the fields to plant them. A few others, like Mary, were politely called housemaids and servants, as there still remained a few white families who could afford to be attended to by Negroes.

Once finished with breakfast, Mary went out to tend to the chickens. She'd thought it was odd that Lar was just finishing his breakfast when she'd returned from helping Uncle Matty. Lar was never one to pick and poke at food . . . any food. Table scraps, that were scraps of scraps from the night before had already been scattered on the ground and the chickens were in a frenzy over them. On the other side of the yard she saw six pig ears flopping about but not their snouts, which were buried deep in the trough to see who could eat their way to the bottom of it first. "That . . . that . . ." She couldn't find the right words to express her frustration *and gratitude*, so she walked away. "Lar know this be my chore," she fumed. She looked back at the animals once more before moving on. "That . . . Lord help," she whispered.

She walked back to the front of the house with her hands folded upon her belly. "C'mon, Uncle Matty!"

"What got you all riled up?" He grabbed the frame of the door for balance and stepped past the threshold. Years spent stooped over picking cotton and beans had ravaged his bones so, they now ground upon one another instead of sliding fluidly as they once had.

"Nothin', Uncle Matty," she replied, reversing her coarse tone when she saw how his bowed legs barely kept him aloft. "The cart be coming, is all."

"I ain't blind yet," he told her. "Hell– I can hear that raggedy mess comin' from way down yonder."

There was barely room enough for the two of them on the end of the pieced together planked wood wagon, though the others– the older men and women who regularly rode on it to town, had begun shifting around to make room. "Tail-end just fine for me," she insisted. "Uncle Matty can ride up there with ya'll." At her height, she barely had to lift herself to sit on the rear of the wagon. Uncle Matty, however, needed the assistance of two of the men, who had jumped off and practically lifted him on.

"Ya'll on?" Picken, the almost fourteen year-old driver asked.

"We on, boy," Mary answered. "Just don't be riding up over all them ruts in the road. If I fall off, I'm gonna come right up there and snatch ya backwards. Don't think you too old for my knee. Your frail-tail fit across it just nice."

Picken smiled at her. He loved it when she teased.

Mary smirked at him.

"Yes'm," Picken promised. He tagged the horses a hair too smartly, causing the two horses to buck and jerk the cart. Mary quickly grabbed hold of the bed with one hand and with the other, secured her belly from underneath. "Lord, have mercy! *Picken!!* What I just tell you, boy?! You be done shook this baby right out of me."

"Ooops! Sorry, Ms. Mary," Picken uttered quickly. "These be some hard-headed horses. My pappy says we still gotta learn'em to mind is all."

Mary raised her black, tattered lace-up shoes that again were beginning to lose their sole and said, "When Henry gonna get some horses that ain't as old as my ratty-tat shoes?"

"Don't know, Ms. Mary," Picken called back. "Sho' would like to have some more though."

She relaxed a little as the cart settled down. The ride was rough, but still preferred over walking. Despite not expecting to, Mary enjoyed herself. Perry Williams was there with his bright skin, yellow eyes and dark black, almost purple lips. Allie Mae Brown . . . *folks just called out Allie Mae if they wanted her to look* . . . sat across from him; she was the widowed mother of Willa, a midwife who lived down from Mary. Allie Mae was known to weave a cloth so fine, white women had even asked her to show them how to do it. It was a precious skill slave life had taught her. Thus having passed the skill on to her daughter Willa, and she having shown Mary, it resulted in Mary and Willa becoming sewing lovers who stitched and gossiped late into many nights. Allie Mae kept food on the table by spending half her day in the backroom of the Monclair general store as a seamstress and the other half going door to door measuring up white folks for britches, dresses and suits. Everyone . . . Negroe that is . . . gave Allie Mae credit and prayers for having to put up with Delilah Ford, who ran the Monclair store– but not as much as they gave Mary for having to put up with Simeon Paul Monclair II who owned it.

Joe 'Bruh' Evans sat on the far end close to Mary and kept a firm hand on Uncle Matty's thigh to keep him from tumbling away. He was the one Negroe who knew every story there was to know about anything there was to know about. "You gotta boy in there, gal," he told her.

"I told her that when she first got with chile, Bruh' Evans," Miss Ettie, the housemaid for the Johnson's family who was sitting next to him, said proudly. Above her right eye was a finger long, brown keloid that threatened to blind it. It was her badge for surviving slavery and the whip used to enforce it. "A chile ridin' up near your chest bone say he a boy."

"A big'un, too," Pete Baker added. Though his thin brown fingers had curled permanently inward and it pained him to hold a hammer and saw, he could still fix on a house or shack with the youngest of men.

"What say, Ms. Enda?" Rose Abby, another housemaid asked of no one in the wagon– but to another.

Mary looked around. She knew ears were pricked in anticipation of her reaction. All eyes watched her, except Uncle Matty, who looked away. Mary turned to her left and saw what had drudged up the name of Enda Sully– the quadroon witch. The wagon was just about to pass by Enda's piece of a shack she called a home.

Enda was on the front porch in her rocking chair. Instead of facing toward the road, she faced west, as if she shunned the light clawing its way up the eastern horizon. Her white folk, bone straight hair was once as black as Mary's skin, but was now white like the cotton she'd never picked in her life. It was in a single braid over her shoulder where her left breast had been before age pulled it down. If Enda Sully appeared near white– narrow nose, razor thin red lips, gray eyes and antique-white skin– then her daughter, Maggie Mae just looked white– at least to anyone who didn't know she had Negroe blood flowing through her.

Maggie Mae, the offspring of a more than half-white mother and a presumably white father made her way down the front dirt path of the home. No one, Negroe or white could deny the whiteness Maggie Mae tried hiding with long-sleeve dresses, like the washed-out blue one she had on. She could keep her wavy, near blond hair braided and bound under a black headscarf while in town amongst whites all she wanted, yet, how un-Negroe she looked was obvious to everyone. One look upon her delicate white face and shimmering autumn eyes speckled with drops of blue water, was enough to arouse insecurity in women and the passion of men. But behind her visage of perfection, Sandro Botticelli assumed could only come from paint and brush, resided not a woman Mary's age who was confident in her casing, but one who still ached for a man she once had and then lost.

Maggie Mae stepped upon the road just as the cart was nearing her house. Mary refused to look away from her, though Maggie Mae, seeing what rambled toward her had already bowed her head slightly. She greeted her elders and they chorused back theirs in return. And then . . .

"Mornin', Mary," Maggie Mae said. Her bluish eyes flashed upon Mary's black ones for but a moment.

"Mornin'," Mary replied just as politely. Her eyes locked upon Maggie Mae. A brief moment passed before Mary decided to speak again, but she had to nearly yell so that Maggie Mae could hear from the distance that had grown between them. "How's Ms. Enda these days?"

"She fine . . . she fine," Maggie Mae, hollered back, and began walking slow enough so that the dirt spun up by the wagon wouldn't choke her.

Though Mary always felt Maggie Mae still loved Lar, she managed to speak to Maggie Mae. Speaking to Enda Sully was another issue entirely. Mary was not alone in her feelings for Enda Sully . . . a voodooiene from further down south some claimed she was. All Negroe folk respected her and quietly shunned her unless they needed her skills. But all Negroe and white folk– whether rational or irrational– had fear of her. It was claimed by Negroes and whispered as a threat by white parents to their naughty children, that Enda Sully knew what coursed in the blood of man, woman and child, and could make it curdle if she wished. Some said she could tell when you were going to get sick . . . die . . . have good and bad fortune . . . a bounty of crops or vegetables rotting on their vine. And as far as Bruh Evans knew, for he knew most of everyone's business anyway, she had yet to be wrong.

The last time Mary had spoken to the witch was on the night she'd nearly died in childbirth and Enda had brought her back to the land of the living, but left her child in the realm of the dead. Enda had left her with words upon her ear as she laid half in sleep and half in death. Even now, Mary could remember the touch of those cold, pink lips and even chillier words uttered by her that night. *"Don't you have one . . . more . . . child. You hear me, Mary Cole? You do—and you both be dead."*

* * *

The cart spat out one occupant at a time as they drew further into Folsom. Each Negroe moseyed off to their respective employer. All the men were headed to either Monclair's fields further east or over to the larger one owned by Roman Meadows, which was east also, but southward on the dirt road. Sweet and field corn was almost ready for picking and the deposed king– cotton– would need his rows cleared so he could be planted, nurtured and ready to be picked come September. Though king cotton was more a pauper these days, still, a little bit of Yankee money was better than a chest full of Jefferson Davis likenesses imprinted on Confederate paper.

The few passengers that remained with Mary as they came up to the circular road fell silent . . . all Negroes did when in the vicinity of the old, dead tree. Day or night, the black bark never changed its crooked, vertical smiles. *It*– the black tree, lay within what had once been the town's park– a green land for whites to frolic, in accompanied by their slaves who were not allowed to enter unless they were called for ' . . . *change the baby's diaper, mammy . . . I need a drink, mammy . . . mammy—go fetch that scrap of paper over there and don't doddle!'*

The black tree– a two-story tall oak, had been planted by a forbearer of the Monclair's as a testament to his wealth and faux generosity he wanted witnessed and admired so that he could practice his act of modesty when it was commented on. Its scorching, however, had been just another victory to the Union soldiers who'd marched through.

Within a day of its torching, the park, its leafy trees, fat shrubs and hearty grass blended right into the dusty road that encircled it . . . all except the old dead tree that somehow had refused to turn to ash. Though it was scarred and would never show another color other than black upon its surface, it remained and stood strong. As care for the park was withdrawn and its grounds became worthless, folks didn't care if they rode their wagons upon it or let their horses shit on it. Yet, no one seemed to want to remove the old tree. Whereas whites sometimes found it useful, Negroes feared it and avoided it, for the tree sometimes produced dead things.

Mary slid off as they neared the west round of the street. She straightened her cotton dress that was not made for pregnancy and was far too tight. Because of the size of her womb, the front of her dress had risen a good five inches and allowed all who glanced down a look at her scuffed boots which she could no longer lace upon her swollen feet. But she cared not. She made her way down the road to the Monclair home which was a walk as familiar as knowing where to get up, step, turn and squat over the basin in the dark rather than trudging to the outhouse.

She left the kitchen door open after entering. She insisted that all white's had a peculiar smell– wet dog that is. Mary's thoughts didn't center on the kitchen that was slowly heating up, but upon Lar. She guessed that about now he was surrounded by a group of Negroe men preaching the Holy word before they started their day's work. Or was he already busy clearing fields? No man she knew of could handle a team of horses and a plow like Lar, who made it seem as if he were out and about for a stroll. She had a vision of Uncle Matty and his sore bones seated in one of Meadow's raggedy holding barns, counting out the bags of goods being loaded onto each wagon before it was sent over to Peak Hills for sale.

Though her work was no less hard and heat from the stove no less stifling than that upon the field of sorrow the Negroe men worked, she could let her mind wander, for her hands knew their duties well. She didn't have to think to reach for the eggs, flour or rendered pig lard and have them mixed, kneaded and rolled out into spongy biscuit. She could tell from the heat on her skin and the sweat on her brow when the stove needed another log or if it was just right. A glance at the frying pan that sizzled and popped with bacon told her when to turn them or let them fry a moment or two longer for that golden brown, ask for more, crunch-in-your-mouth taste.

Her mother, Sarah, had worked for the Monclair's since *she* herself was but a girl. Mary could only remember flashes and bits of the old Monclair life, for when they ruled Folsom from their citadel upon the hill, she was far too young to imprint such things in her mind. Her strongest memory was when the Union soldiers burned the mansion to the ground after looting it. That had stuck in Mary's head, for she remembered the Negroes celebrating the night the Monclair mansion smoldered red in the dark. As a child, she didn't understand why Negroes smiled and grinned– laughed and danced about a house burning– 'she did now.'

Sarah had made it a point to remind her of how the Monclair's once lived, with niggahs running around for every purpose and for no reason at all. She had taken Mary to what was left of the old Monclair house after finishing work at the new, but far smaller one. She'd showed Mary what once was a truly magnificent work of man. Sarah pointed to where steps had once led up to four white columns, and a little further in, two massive doors with round black knockers. But there was never a need to knock when there was always at least one niggah there to greet and announce you to the massah and mistress.

"Now– round yonder be what should been tore down to the ground first," Sarah had told her. They tromped through knee-high weeds, careful of setting their thin-soled shoes on glass or metal, or snakes whose kiss could bid one their last *good* evening of their life. "This be where us niggahs lived," she said, pointing to row upon row of wind beaten shacks, and others already collapsed under the ravages of rain and rot. "Don't recollect exactly which one me, you and Matty use to live in, but I 'member it be somethin' close to what they be now– everythang be all turned around for me. You too young to 'member, huh chile?" Mary nodded. "Holes so big in da roof, if it be rainin', it come straight in on ya, in ya sleep. And if'n it be cold that night, you gather close to ya kin to be warm, 'cause da walls had holes, too! And over there be them fields." She'd pointed toward the horizon, but Mary could not see them. "My mammy tell me she pick cotton sun-up 'til sun-down. Ev'ry day 'cept Sunday. When I still be on her titty, she said she just strap me close and let me draw while she kept on pickin'."

Negroe life, as far as Mary was concerned, had changed little since the iron shackles were removed. Though slavery was now a thing of the not too far removed past, it still existed in one form or another, and she witnessed it and lived it every day of her life.

Laws for Negroe advancement was nonexistent, no matter what the bureaucrats had said and wrote in their books of justice. Negroes that had sat in Congress after the war were all but gone, just as the right of Negroe men to vote, which had placed them there. The word of a Negroe had become as important as the squawking of crows. There was no salve for the gaping, oozing wounds from the war, Mary was certain. The northern blade had sliced through the south's chest bone, and the point of it now rested on its *da-thump—thump—thump—da thumping* heart.

And thus the dilemma of what whites were truly was presented to Mary in the form of a fair-skinned, and far too pretty, boy.

Simeon Paul Monclair III walked into her kitchen. His very presence brought a smile to her sweaty face. He was the sixteen-year old son of Simeon Monclair II– and also his greatest disappointment. He had many bruises, fresh and fading, to show his father's love of him. Mary knew first hand how deep Simeon's love for his son ran more than anyone, as she was the one who tended to the black eyes, split lips, bruised ribs or wherever else Simeon felt like striking, whether he had imbibed or not. She had always thought Simeon couldn't hate anyone more than he hated Negroes or his wife. But the boy, despite or because of Simeon's lackluster attention to him, had developed the sensibilities and emotionality closer to the softer sex. A boy he was, but his features were fairer than most girls. His eyes were a deep blue like his father's, but were nearly obscured behind a small forest of black lashes. His lips were plump for a white child– red and always seemed wet. His wavy, dense hair made soot pale in contrast.

"Come here, Paul," Mary called to him. Simeon had commanded that his son was never to be called by his first name, and so no one did. "Let me take a gander at ya eye." Mary wiped the sweat from her forehead with the rag tucked in her apron and blinked several times to focus her vision. She leaned over to observe the swollen eye. She held his chin in her hand and moved his head from side to side, 'mmm-humming' as she did. "Seems to be goin' down a tidbit," she assured him.

"It's still aching pretty bad, Ms. Mary," Paul said. "I thought if you get hit in the same spot more than once or twice it shouldn't hurt as bad."

"A hit gonna hurt no matter what," she replied.

She couldn't help but feel sorry for him. She'd changed his diapers, played with him in the yard, rocked him to sleep and cared for him when ill. Until the age of two, he'd suckled milk from her breasts meant for her second baby who'd died at birth just two weeks before Paul was born. And in return, Paul always had a gentle word for her or a helping hand if his father or sister, Beatrice, wasn't looking. And like now, he sitting on the very stool she'd sat on as a child watching her mother work, he would chatter until she could repeat back to him the shape, size and color of every pebble he'd seen on his way home from school. If it wasn't love she felt for him, it was as close as one got to it, even if he was just a white boy and all, she thought.

"You gotta learn to stay outta his way after he been near that whiskey-mess," she told him.

"I've been trying," he protested softly. His eyes looked everywhere but at Mary. "He came in on me when I was sleeping and started yelling at me. Saying things . . . calling me– names . . . you know?" Mary did know very well. "I pretended I was sleeping. I thought he would let me be. But then he hit me with his . . . his . . . hand . . . I mean the other one that doesn't have a hand. When I grabbed my eye he just stopped and left."

Though he was looking down all the while he was talking, Mary knew he was tearing. A black eye she could comfort and eventually it would go away, but she had nothing that could scrub the memory from his head. Isabel, his mother, could not protect him. She had seen the backside of Simeon's left hand and gnarled stump on the right enough to know not to step in front of him when he was itching to pound the boy's flesh. Mary's only advice was that which could not be voiced. It was something he had to decide on his own, and for his sake, she hoped he would and soon. He would have to leave Folsom, though she really didn't care to think about him being gone. Almost at an age where he could take care of himself, she hoped that if he ever did leave, that he could. But as he was right now– far too sensitive and fragile on the inside, she had little doubt the world would feast upon his bones in a week's time.

"Go knock on your pappy and sistah's door, if they ain't awake already," Mary told him. "Then you and your sistah can wash-up and come down and eat after your pappy done been fed." Paul grumbled, and then left and did as he was told.

It was not soon after Paul left that heavy footsteps descended the stairs and came dragging down the hall and into the dining room. Wood scraped upon wood as Simeon moved out his chair and then sat. She brought out his breakfast and placed it before him. There were no 'good mornings' exchanged between them and neither expected to hear it from the other. She waited for further instruction by the kitchen door, which was adjacent to the dining room. He reached for the fork with his left hand and cut into the bacon– scooped it up– balanced it– and then shoved it into his mouth. He gnawed the half strip of pork into bits and swallowed. Seemingly satisfied, he waved his stump at her and Mary gladly returned to her sanctuary.

Since neither tolerated the other's company well, she remained in the kitchen until she heard his chair sliding out once more and leaden footsteps from the previous night's alcohol grow faint. *'Off to suckle from your bottle some more, huh?'* Mary thought. Other than his daughter, Beatrice, his mistress and whiskey, the man's love of anything or anyone went no further, as far as Mary could tell.

Assured he was out of sight, Mary returned to clean the mess she knew he'd made like he did every morning. Biscuit crumbs were in the seat of his chair and on the floor. Some were mashed back into dough after treading on them to leave. Splattered juice from the runny eggs had already started to congeal on the top and edge of the mahogany table, and small bits of bacon were found as far down as the next table setting. It was a mess partly because he knew, she figured, it was his niggah woman's job to clean it, and secondly, he'd never adapted to using his left hand properly.

Niggahs were for cleaning, scraping, hauling, digging, picking–
she'd heard him say often from the kitchen as the family ate or entertained guests. And that was exactly how he treated them, she
knew from too much experience. To Mary, he was the epitome of
the white man's disregard for Negroes. Only, when Simeon Monclair spoke of the dark race, it seemed to come from a part of his
soul that no other white man dared rouse. It was the grit in his
voice that caught her ear when he said 'niggah'. Even other whites
paused when he said it. His eyelids were as wide as the edge of a
gutting knife when he preached of how dirty and prone to violence
niggahs were. And if he had been swiggin' from the whiskey bottle
. . . well . . . Mary shook her head as she retrieved the broom and
dustpan. "Even too hateful for hell to have him!" she said to her
child inside. She chuckled at the thought of old horn-headed, red-
skinned Satan with his bags packed and standing at the pearly
gates saying, 'Lord, I sorry 'bout everything I done to ya, but I can't
stay down there with that ol' crazy white man. He even too much for
me to handle!'

On her knees she went. She reached under the table to grab the
crumbs so carelessly dropped. She scraped the flattened pieces of
biscuit from the hardwood floors with the fingernails she hadn't
chewed down to the nub yet. The floors were still gleaming from
the cleaning she'd given it the other day, but there was already
dust accumulating on the claw feet of the table. She made a mental
note to get to it by week's end. It didn't take much to get Simeon
riled up. It was not as though he truly cared about the spotless
home she kept for the family. Negroe gossip said he usually spent
the morning in his office and in his fields, and the other half at the
tavern drinking liquor that was quickly drying up in all the coun-
ties around them. And if Simeon was not there, then he was with
her– and if not with his mistress, then at home in his study which

was off limits without invitation, which was rare, except if a white man came calling for help or need that had nothing to do with money.

Getting down on the floor was the easy part. Her knees were used to bending that way. Standing up with a near-term child was another job entirely. It was during times like these that she was glad to have thick thighs, because she needed every ounce of strength to pull back up.

"I swear you're moving slower and slower each day, Mary," Beatrice said, hanging on to each sound as they slid from half pouting, half smirking lips.

Mary turned and stared at Beatrice, who was leaning on the doorframe between the dining room and the hallway. *'Mary, is it now?* Mary fumed silently. *'Ms. Mary, to you, and its Mrs. Cole, if you knew better,'* she wanted to say. Instead, she continued to glare at Beatrice until the girl pretended as if something else had caught her attention and looked away.

"Ms. Mary, our food should have been set already. And look at the time." Beatrice dropped into the chair right of where her father had sat at the head of the table. Mary avoided following Beatrice's exaggerated request to look at the grandfather clock in the corner of the room. Already, her babbling was strumming a nerve that Mary was saving for the end of the day. "You still have to brush the tangles from my hair. You are aware of this?" she said, rather than asked, as she stroked her porcelain fingers through her waist length hair and only made it halfway through before getting stuck.

"You can eat your breakfast first . . . *chile*," Mary told her. Mary watched her as she walked towards the kitchen, almost daring Beatrice to look her in the eye. All Mary saw was a chubby girl with acne riddle skin made worse by her period, which she had just started to have regularly. Her waist-length, blond hair and beady blue eyes did nothing to enhance her looks as it might have another white girl, for Mary knew white folks loved such features in their children. Beatrice turned her head to the side and folded her hands in her lap and waited to be served.

'I can't tell who workin' my nerves more . . . this squirmin' child in my belly or these white folk?' Mary wondered. She was temperamental when expecting– she knew that much from experience. But if there was anything that got her cursing God, it was a snippy white child, particularly the one sitting in the next room. She didn't need to hear what Simeon told her about the world and her place in it . . . Beatrice wore it on her face always . . . it was in her screech of a voice. *'You're a Monclair woman! The world belongs to me!'*

There were many things Mary knew she had no choice but to accept. Scrapping for food had become second nature to her. A sore back and fingers gone stiff with ache before the hair on your head turned white, was to be expected. Walking out of the way for white folks was the law. Having a child be flippant at her, white or Negroe, was a pill she refused to choke down.

When she returned to the dining room Paul had already settled in his seat. He quickly raised his eyebrows and flashed her a toothy smile when Beatrice wasn't looking. She presented them a meal similar to their father's. Whereas Paul had the appetite of a dying bird, Beatrice devoured hers as quickly as she could while trying to maintain the poise of a proper southern lady. Though only twelve, she had already begun to take on the unflattering fullness of her mother at the hips and thighs. She would not be a petite lady, Mary guessed. And if gentlemen folk came knocking, it certainly wouldn't be for her intoxicating beauty or charming talk – for she lacked both– though still her suitors would say her cup runneth over with both, if they sniffed a few of Simeon Monclair's dollars in the bottom of it.

After returning to the kitchen, Mary had little choice but to listen to the Beatrice's chatter seeping in from under the door. Her idle yapping always dominated the conversation– dresses, jealous girls, and dreams of finding a handsome, wealthy young man were all that seemed to preoccupy her thoughts. She seemed convinced that regardless of Folsom's poverty, that somehow she would be cared for in the high quality manner she knew she deserved.

Just one day past, when Beatrice had walked in on Paul and her in the kitchen while she tended to his freshly bruised eye, Beatrice had carried on as though she hadn't seen it turning from blue to black, as it threatened to shut close. Beatrice had all but looked through her weeping brother with not a care that he was still shaking from the midnight beating or that he pained more inside than out. "Ms. Mary, I'm going to be late if you don't hurry with breakfast," Beatrice had uttered, before spinning around and exiting. She knew Beatrice had heard Paul's screams that night, as their rooms were next to one another and the walls thin enough to discern even hushed voices. 'She ain't care a lick at all,' Mary thought.

When Mary returned to the dining room, Beatrice sat as before – her mouth wiped clean and her eyes staring straight ahead. Paul had already scooped up his crumbs and deposited them on his plate next to his knife and fork, which he'd laid parallel to each other. Already he was on his way to his room to get ready for school.

"Ms. Mary," Beatrice said, eyes still forward, "Are you going to brush my hair now before you get too busy with all of those kitchen chores and cleaning . . . *and things*. I would rather not be late for school a second day."

"Go on up and gather your brush and ribbons, and I be right behind you," Mary replied, as she continued gathering plates.

Beatrice didn't move. Mary knew what she wanted, but asked anyway if it was going to make the morning go smoother and get Beatrice out of the house quicker. "Something else, missy?" Beatrice ignored her.

Mary was on the opposite side of the table in front of her. She set the plates down with just enough force to rattle them. "I said . . . something else you wantin', missy?"

Beatrice huffed– nearly growled.

Mary stifled her glee. She decided to smile about it later on the way home.

Beatrice stood abruptly and pushed her plate across the table, causing it to clatter and clang when it hit the other plates. "I'm finished. You may take my plate," she announced, with forced composure. She turned and marched away.

Mary figured it was too late for old white folks to learn the ways of this new world– that is, Negroes being free. White folks were going to have to face what they had done . . . so would say those Negroes who knew the sting of a lash and the uninvited penis of a white man. The old ones had predicted that one day Negroes would be free, and it had come to pass. Now a new prophecy was being whispered about from shack to shack. But Mary saw such stark denial of that prophecy ever coming about in every white face she saw. "They say, a niggah's day be comin'," she whispered to her restless babe and soothed it with a gentle, circular rub. "They say white folk be workin' for us one day . . . hummpf! I like to see that!"

Mary took her time getting up to Beatrice's room. She was sure the girl would be hot and furious by now. Mary figured it was a good way for her to start learning that the world wouldn't bow down to white girls forever. But Mary also knew just how far to push her, for surely her father would catch an earful of how the 'terrible Negra woman' treated her. And then reluctantly, after been scolded by her husband, Isabel was sure to come rolling in the kitchen, urging her to show some restraint with Beatrice. 'Pleading' to be more exact, as Isabel and Paul were the only ones in the house who seemed to value her presence anyway. Isabel always had, ever since they were children growing up in the Christianson manor when Mary and her mother were slaves and the former Isabel Christianson was then being groomed to marry a rich, influential gentleman from Peak Hills, not fifth choice Simeon Paul Monclair II.

'Why can't that damn gal be more like my Paul anyhow?' Mary wondered. *'She act like it be done killed her to be nice for a second.'*

Beatrice was seated at her small dressing table, her head held high and hands folded in her laps at the ready. From babe to young woman Mary had known her. She had been a beautiful child, Mary remembered. But Mary also knew that babies with big ears, button noses and doe eyes are cute as cute can ever get– that is, as long as they remained babies. Once those adorable features swelled and stretched as they grew, they weren't so irresistible and kissable. Beatrice's once web-soft, blond baby curls had dried and flattened like a stepped on worm, whereas Paul's black, wavy mop became thicker with age and wrapped his temples and cheeks in swirling locks of love. As Mary pulled the brush through the nest of blond weeds, she occasionally glanced at the young woman in the mirror and could see nothing of the child she had raised. And indeed it was she who had raised Beatrice.

As with Paul, she'd fed and bathed baby Beatrice . . . changed her diapers, and when old enough, taught her to use the outhouse on her own. It was to Mary that she'd run to when frightened, to have her nose wiped or when she just needed a hug. When sick, it was Mary's pregnant belly she clung to for comfort and Mary who cleaned the liquid stench from her rear end. Despite Mary's best efforts, a motherly bond had been formed. But what love she had for the child and the child for her was erased when Simeon lost interest in Paul continuing his bloodline. Simeon's only hope now lay Beatrice. And in placing all his dreams with her, he set her so far above anything and everyone, not even Beatrice could touch herself, though try hard she did.

But Mary's bond to Paul strengthened by the day. He was as dear to her as Lar, and though she often denied it, maybe more so. Lar was secure and could take care of himself. Strong willed– '*Yes Lord!*' – He could stand up for himself. It was why she loved him and had married him. But Paul would never be that type of a man, she sensed. He seemed to lack the determination and aggressiveness needed to survive in the south. Even more dangerous than that, was that his father sensed it also. Mary understood how dangerous it was to be a boy like Paul. She had known for a long time, and hoped Isabel knew also that Paul was in danger. Not just from his father, but from all who didn't tolerate boys or men like him . . . and there were many of them around in every color.

With vigorous strokes, Mary had finally given Beatrice's hair a hint of a shimmer. She pulled it back and braided it, and then affixed light blue bows in it to compliment her dark blue dress with frilly lace upon its sleeves. She appeared as though she were off to church rather than school.

Mary looked out the window and spotted Paul waiting at the entrance of the white fence that surrounded the modest property. He had groomed himself perfectly– as usual. His black hair had been combed back, but was so curly, it was already falling down on his face. Despite his black eye, he was still prettier than Beatrice who looked like a pug-mix next to him. Unlike the other boys his age, so far he'd been spared the blemishes and beet red splotches so prone to white skin as it approached manhood. He still did not look fifteen, but all of twelve, if that.

Mary watched them for a while as they walked off. Paul trailed in back. Mary figured he was trying to distance himself from Beatrice's chirping. She noted she would have to take all of his pants in pretty soon, as they were bunched around his ever-dwindling waist. But his exposed socks suggested he would need longer britches, and soon. She guessed she could stitch a pair or two together for him before the month's end. Sewing them was the easy part, getting her hands on fabric and thread to do so was the challenge. Even with the Monclair's, money was tight and only flowed when Beatrice was in need or Simeon was running low on whiskey.

Already Beatrice had cloth for three dresses to be made by Allie Mae and silk lace Beatrice was so fond of, to accent them. Had she the smallest care for the child, Mary guessed she too would have marveled– like ladies should with one another– at the fine linens soon to be made into dresses. But it was disgust and a helping hand from envy that stayed her hand from touching the cloth most folks could not even afford to dream about. Mary decided she would speak to Isabel about getting new cloth for Paul's britches anyway.

As Mary passed Simeon Monclair's room, she heard Isabel rustling about in her own room across the hall. She quickly made her way downstairs and back into the kitchen. Isabel would have plenty for her to do, so she decided whatever Isabel wanted, she would have to come to her domain to ask for it. She needed a rest anyway. The baby was on the move again, no doubt from her climbing and descending the flight of stairs.

Out of habit, she sat on the small barstool that was once hers, but now Paul's. The legs were uneven and allowed her to tilt-rock from side to side as she had done while watching her mother cook and clean and fuss. Remembering her mother's face, it seemed to Mary that she could see it clearer now than ever before. The lines of fatigue crisscrossing her mother's black skin– now Mary knew exactly how those grooves had been earned.

She remembered how her mother's dress clung to her with sweat from a woodstove that never cooled and unrelenting summer suns that never seemed to set for long. She vividly recalled her mother scrubbing out dirt; bits of food, blood, semen and shit from Monclair clothes with lye until they shone white once more and her hands were as tough as scales. Or was it that Sarah's ghost was more visible to her now because the sun was already blaring through the windows?

Mary had never known that the whites of her mother's eyes, which were yellow, had not always been that way. She never knew a mother who at one time had teeth, but only one who had calloused gums that could gnash meat and bread into pulp so that it could be swallowed without gagging. And still, though Sarah limped painfully, and it was just as painful for others to witness her move about, she always had a black-gum smile just for her, Mary remembered.

"Here, gal!" Mary remembered Sarah hobbling to her on her turned-in right foot. She would hold out a finger she'd dipped into her cake batter and bring it to Mary's lips to suck clean. "Ain't no taste like yo' mammy's– now is there?" To Mary, there *was* no better taste around than Sarah's, and the Monclair's– from Simeon Paul I to the III agreed wholeheartedly by scuffing her cakes down with nary a crumb for a mouse to find and pick over. *"White folks ought'a praise Jesus for this sweet bread tappin they lips! Hmm?"* Sarah was fond of saying.

"Mary!? *Marrrrry?!*"

The call of her name woke her from dreams of sweet bread and sweet mama Sarah. Mama Sarah faded into the sunlight that flooded the kitchen, but not before giving that good ol' black-lipped– black gum smile at her. Mary closed her eyes and tried to remember the sweet-sweat of her mother one last time. She hoped her own child would remember her as fondly.

* * *

Isabel entered the kitchen with company. The five black cats that followed sung out in desperation along with her. "Mary– didn't you hear me?"

"No ma'am." Mary was nary a second too late getting up from the chair. Having sat for just those few moments had stiffened her hips, and it showed as she limped toward the stove.

Isabel's pale green eyes scanned Mary from head to toe. "You feeling poorly today?"

"No, ma'am."

"Thank, God," Isabel sighed. "I know what you've been through with your . . . your . . . um . . . pregnancies." She smiled briefly and nodded, and then waited for Mary to agree.

Mary grudgingly shook her head. Mary was more concerned about the mammy feline and her four babies scouring the floor for scraps and leaving their trail of fur all over the place that inevitably wound up on every plate and in every pot she pulled out to use.

Isabel's head slowly swayed side-to-side and then up and down. "I know the Lord will let you keep this child. He *will* bless you."

"Yes'm."

"Oh no," Isabel whispered in alarm. "I nearly forgot about my sisters coming, and here I am sleeping late. And then, I wanted to see the children off. They did make it off alright, didn't they?"

"Yes'm," Mary uttered, as she continued cleaning the stove in preparation for the next meal.

Isabel walked over and stood next to Mary until she paused in her work. She looked up into Mary's eyes. Mary did find comfort in knowing Isabel actually saw her. "And Simeon?"

Mary resumed scraping at the bits of dried eggs. The coldness in which Isabel said his name did not pass her by. "He ate and left, like he do day-in . . . day-out."

"That's good then," Isabel replied flatly. She brushed at her green dress as though Mary had not just ironed every wayward wrinkle out of it just the other day.

Mary took note of Isabel's order while trying to ignore the felines darting about the kitchen. Something sweet was required of course. Mary knew sugar-laden treats sated Isabel's nerves once the initial rush was over. Some tea and crackers, Isabel added. "Fresh fruit, perhaps?" Isabel wondered out loud.

"No ma'am . . . you ain't got none, unless you wantin' me to take the cart down to your store," Mary said, though cringed on the inside at the thought of having to deal with Delilah Ford who ran the place.

Isabel looked toward the door and sighed. "No, no . . . not in your condition, dear."

"I send Paul when he get home from school. That way you can have your fruit with your supper tomorrow, or I can whip them up into a pie or turn-over . . . whichever you got a taste for." The suggestion, which was more of a statement, seemed to please Isabel. They quickly settled into their usual routine with Mary hovering over the hot stove and Isabel in the way helping to line up ingredients, pots and pans.

Just as Mary had started to make headway, a squeal snuggled out from underneath the backdoor. Isabel's hefty hips were already spinning around at the first peep. The plea for admittance and the saccharin cooing from Isabel made Mary's eyes shoot skyward.

"Mother's coming for you, baby," Isabel assured. "Back– back– back, Plyus . . . you have to let me open the door first."

Within moments, Mary's kitchen was a festival of fur. Plyus, the pappy feline was reunited with his wife and children, and all celebrated the reunion by running to and fro. The cats usually hid when Isabel was sequestered in her bedroom or were with her in the parlor while she read or sat staring at the wall, which was usually the case. But when Isabel awoke each morning, the parade of four-legged bodies would commence as they followed her from bedroom to outhouse, but somehow they always ended up in Mary's way. The constantly whining felines were what Mary hated most about the Monclair house next to Simeon and Beatrice. If she wasn't cooking, she was dusting– but that was part of the job. She knew it and had accepted it. But chasing down cat hair that rolled away when stepping near it was not. And if not chasing the tumbleweeds of hair across the floor, it was pulling the needle-like fur from the furniture, sheets and blankets– and then on the way home, trying to get the rest off of her own clothes.

Mary's patience ran out when one, of the kittens jumped up on the still hot stove and with a panicked squeal, pounced away and came so close to Mary's face, its fur brushed her cheek. Mary's foot slammed down on the floor and rattled the jars in the cupboard. *"Ms. Isabel!"*

"Did he scratch you?" Isabel asked quickly.

Mary turned away from Isabel to finish smoldering. "No ma'am, but . . ."

"Are you ok?"

Mary turned back. "I will be when these thangs be out from under my feet. That cake you want made gonna have more cat hair in it than flour, Ms."

Isabel reached for the broom. At the sight of their mammy coming for them, they scattered. Though Isabel would never have even entertained the idea of hitting them with the broom, a brushing of straw on their bottom was enough to get them moving. Isabel opened the backdoor leading to the flower garden, and seeing their chance, they fled into sun's warmth. William, the most skittish of the kittens hid under the pantry and required mother coaxing in order to emerge. Isabel cradled the kitten and walked him outside with reassurances that his mammy still loved him.

"Jesus– you gonna save me from these fool white folks or not?" Mary asked in a whisper. She watched Isabel through the window standing in the midst of the garden talking to the cats and kittens. Mary simply shook her head.

Hours before the sisters arrived, Isabel bounded from one room to another, and then off to the kitchen to tell Mary of some new catastrophe . . . dust on a table leg or the wrong color doilies laid out. After Isabel's second visit to sound the alarm, Mary insisted that she busy herself with knitting in the sitting room so that her sisters could see how far along she'd come in crafting more sweaters, which neither of the children wore nor wanted. Mary knew if she hadn't gotten Isabel out of her way, supper would never get started on time.

The two sisters arrived slightly before noon in wagons drawn by two young Negroe boys with clean, well-greased faces, pressed britches and stark white shirts. Mary had already opened the windows and shutters in the sitting room to keep it as cool as the summer sun would let it be. Just cooled butter-cake was sliced and fanned out on silver trays. Hot water was ready for tea leaves to relax and soak in for a spell.

Mary greeted each sister as she took their bonnets, scarves and gloves, and then showed them into the sitting room. As they walked down the narrow hall, Eliza, the second oldest of the sisters spoke to Mary as more of a friend, like they used to be when they were younger and thought themselves as just girls. Eliza was far more progressive than her older sister, Isabel, and younger sister, Catherine, who'd married Benjamin Watkins, a prominent lawyer from Jackson who had his sights set on becoming an even more successful politician– just like her mother had demanded.

But it was Eliza who was the first of the Christianson girls to say 'I do'. She married the reverend Ezekiel Davids from the small town of Goshen, just south of Peak Hills. At the just blossomed age of sixteen, and with her father away at war, Eliza defied her mother and married the man she had chosen. There were many reasons their mother had been against Eliza's marriage to the reverend. One being, the reverend was all of thirty-five and considered too old for her. But most importantly, he was deemed too poor for a Christianson woman to settle for. But of the three Christianson women, Eliza's marriage was the only one that was coalesced out of true love and mutual thoughts, not money and social advancement.

The fact was, the reverend Ezekiel was a pariah– white-folks said . . . and a honorable man– Negroes countered.

Ezekiel's version of the gospel soured in the stomach of most southern whites– tolerance of the Negroes and acceptance of them into society. It was a thought and a belief shared by his then child-wife, Eliza, now a woman, who had grown accustomed to disapproving stares of whites and cautious glances from Negroes. She refused to hold her tongue about her belief regarding slavery, women suffrage, Negroe acceptance and miscegenation . . . thorny issues white men thought were far too complicated for a woman to understand and form a sensible opinion about. Simeon held no love or even a semblance of patience for Eliza, or that 'crook-nosed, niggah-lovin' reverend husband' of hers, as he referred to Ezekiel.

Eliza took hold of Mary's hand as if preparing her for the whirlwind about to blow. 'How's the child, sister Mary? And you? How *is* brother, Lar? Has the foundation of the church been laid yet? Do you need more bibles or hymnals? Is there anything else that I or Ezekiel can do to help??'

"No ma'am," Mary lied. Their fledgling church was in need of just about everything from wood to build it to pews to sit on. "But Lar mighty grateful for all you and the reverend already done done."

Eliza moved closer. "We are all here for each other, Mary . . . we are all God's children. Why– even my boy, Jonathan has grown to have such a mind– praise be! He is so like his father, but more out-spoken– can you believe that . . . a sharper tongue than Ezekiel? Oh . . . and whites hate him for that." She lowered her head and shook it to and fro. "When the other boys call him that God-awful name– the you-know-what-lover . . . he smiles and says thank-you

– praise be! Now– I did have to pull him from school for his own safety. Some are just not ready to hear God's *true* word. But rest assured, Mary, God does have a plan for all of us– no?"

"Yes'm," Mary replied.

Eliza had always been kind to her, but Mary kept in mind that she *was* still white after all. What was to stop Eliza from becoming a snake like other white folks? Hadn't Enda talked about serpents one day slithering their way into Folsom? *'Ain't no need to go lookin' for them. They'll find you, gal,'* Enda had told her, Lar and Maggie Mae, when they were still but children. *'They say sweet thangs in your ear so you trust'em ... next thang you know, they done slipped into your bed and bit ya. And Ms. Enda ain't got nothin' in her jars on the shelf to keep you from meetin' the Maker or the devil who done bit you in the first place.'*

Mary went to the stables and brought sweet cake and tea to Eliza's almost teenage Negroe boys who, to the horror of whites, she was know to treat no differently than her own boy, Jonathan. She was often seen ... *gasp* ... pinching their cheeks and rubbing their heads in public, which had been quite the scandal in Goshen. But Eliza was Eliza as Eliza ever was and had been ... she paid the sneering white folks no attention, and upped the ante by occasionally kissing their chubby black cheeks when she felt the need for sugar-love.

Satisfied that the Christianson women were now satisfied, Mary took up company with her old friends ... 'brother' broom, 'raggin' rag and 'soapy' waters, and began cleaning the rooms upstairs. She hummed her spirituals low so as to be able to hear the soft and dreaded *'ting-aling- aling'* of Isabel's bell for help and assistance. The collard greens were already simmering with their side of salted ham-hock. Cornbread was already mixed and just needed milk, eggs and a hot oven to finish it. Chicken parts were battered and ready for the frying pan.

She checked on the collards now and again between mopping, wiping the walls, changing the sheets and getting the old ones ready for the wash. It was back aching work for two maids, or even three, but just a normal day for hefty Mary. It wasn't the old Christianson manor either, which required a cadre of sweaty-faced mammies to clean room after endless room, dust precious, imported furniture and scrub laundry that never ceased piling up. Yes – the age of gowns, mansions, and fancy ballrooms filled with a hundred guests, in Folsom at least, was dead.

* * *

Isabel came out and sat in the garden after her sisters had departed. She sat quietly on one side of the fence while Mary was on the other pumping water for the wash. Occasionally, Mary spied Isabel, but did not have to wonder where in her thoughts she was. It was Isabel's ritual each time her sisters visited, but left memories of the old days with her.

She guessed Isabel was preoccupied with the house and those in it, and *who* was not in it, but should have been had her dreams come true . . . had her beloved, Thomas Lang, not succumbed to gangrene during the war and forced her hand to join with Simeon Monclair's beet red stump. Though the Monclair's were white, had money and were influential, there was no happiness in their house as far as Mary could see.

When Mary looked up again, it was not Isabel who caught her eye, but Paul, who was crouched down behind a fat shrub no more than a few feet from her. He had his finger to his lips, pleading for silence. "Jesus, chile! What wrong with you sneakin' up on me like that?" Mary whispered, as she peeked over the fence at Isabel, who was still far away from reality.

"I need your help, Ms. Mary," Paul whispered.

"What wrong?" She pumped the water slowly so as not to arouse Isabel who was now smiling. She guessed Isabel was now talking to Thomas Lang's ghost. "Where your sister at?"

Paul rolled his eyes. "She's upstairs. She's fine . . . just fine. It's something else."

"Spit it out, chile."

"It's just . . . just that . . . I want to go swimming this afternoon."

"I'm sure your mammy let you go right after your chores done."

"I can't go later," he said, with a shake of his head. "Me . . . and . . . and the boys are all going now."

Mary's brows rose. *Friends?* she thought. *Somethin' ain't right. If Paul had any friends, it sure was news to her.* She let it pass for the moment. "And I'm supposed to . . ."

"You can tell her that we need some flour from the store and you sent me to get it, or else dinner won't be ready on time for father," he replied, without a pause or a skip. "I promise I'll only be gone for an hour at the most. I can be back for my chores before father comes home . . . if he comes home for dinner at all."

Mary stared him until he batted his blue eyes. Still, she just couldn't bring herself to deny him such a simple pleasure, though she knew Simeon wouldn't deny him a beating if his chores weren't finished. She whispered to him in a tone that she only ever used with Paul, for she knew he'd keep it secret– it was said with warm breaths, yet the words were cold and could be easily translated as a threat. "I know you and what you think 'fore you even think 'bout it, boy."

He bowed his head. "Yes, Ms. Mary."

"You be back here in an hour or less," she told him. "Your mother wants some fruits anyway, you hear me? So don't go off being simple and forget to bring some back neither."

Mary stood erect. "Ms. Isabel . . .? Ms. Isabell?!"

Isabel smiled at her and pretended awareness. "Hmm?"

"I gonna send Paul down to the store. I need some flour to finish off supper for Mr. Monclair– and get those sweet fruits you was wantin' earlier, too. You know how the mister get when his food ain't set up right when he be hungry."

"Oh– oh yes. You're right, Mary. Isabel looked around nervously and then began lifting herself out of the chair.

"Ms. Isabel– you go and sit . . . go on, now," Mary insisted gently. "Ain't nothing but a bag of flour is all. Paul be back 'fore we can turn around and call his name."

Isabel seemed to calm for a moment, but as usual, she could find danger in Heaven even if Jesus himself said everything was all right. "His chores, Mary! If Simeon comes home and found his chores haven't been . . ."

Mary smiled at her as she spun her lie. "He done already started on them– see now, Ms. Isabel? Mr. Monclair probably going to be late comin' anyhow. Children probably be sleep before he step through that doorway."

Isabel's brow furrowed. "Of course, of course." Somewhat reassured, she settled back into her chair and slowly drifted back away to dreams only dreams could conjure.

Mary gave Paul a stern warning about coming back late before releasing him with a nod of her head. She'd never seen him smile so as he ran half-crouched behind the fence, and then on the road, he began running. His black curls bounced joyously with each spring of his feet. She was unaccustomed to seeing him so . . . so . . . she had trouble even thinking of the word. *Happy?* she guessed.

Paul did return home in time just as he'd promised her. She was relieved he hadn't taken advantage of her goodwill, though truly, she had no facts to base a reason on that he might. He'd always been an obedient child– at least toward her. As long as Simeon wasn't stalking about like a drunken ghost, there was nothing she asked of Paul that he wouldn't do, and most time she didn't even have to ask before he was already doing it.

From the kitchen window, she watched him stacking up the hay, running around the barn to slop the hogs, and then finally, putting the chickens in for the night. When he slipped through the back, she caught hold of him by the shoulders to make sure he looked the same now as when he'd left. His hair was dry, but tousled. "Run a comb through that mess and get your tail back down here for supper," she said, with a mock look of disapproval.

He beamed and took off.

Mary paused. There it was again, she thought. *Paul be happy?* Hummpf! she snorted. Now she was certain something was going on with him.

Mary served supper, but the master of the house had failed to show, which wasn't unusual in the least. Unusual was that Paul was chatty and grinning as a boy was meant to be before the world showed him there was not all that much to smile about. He held an odd sway over court, much to the disapproval of his sister whose role he had uncharacteristically usurped. Isabel smiled politely at any and every comment he made. Beatrice brooded. But regardless, Paul continued on in his trademark, high-pitched voice, whether they were interested in what he had to say or not.

It was finally becoming dark and Mary was glad of it. The heat lingered, but the sun was finally sinking and the stove was cooling for the day. At least now with everyone fed she could sit for a while as she washed the dishes. The baby was still . . . sleeping she guessed . . . hoped. After so many babies who had squirmed inside of her and abruptly stopped moving, with this child, she'd become aware of its slightest move as she was her own breathing.

She was wiping dry the last pot and ready to depart so that she could catch the last wagon going back home, when she was surprised to hear a wagon approaching. She walked to the front of the house and looked out the front window, expecting to see Simeon pulling up, but saw no one. She hurried back to the kitchen and slid his already fixed plate that was sitting on the stove inside it anyway. At this hour, Simeon had likely already swigged down a half-bottle of whiskey and would be mad as hell if there wasn't food to cool the burn in his gut, she figured.

She started to call for Paul to come down and get ready to un-hitch his father's horse and put it in the stable, but stopped. The creaks and bangs of the wagon were approaching the back, not the front of the house. She looked out but didn't see Simeon. It was her own man. He was like a giant he was upon a cart that looked ready to be burned for heat. His hands looked as though they held thread instead of reigns. She was grinning as she walked out to meet him; only because of the toothy, prideful smile he was already wearing as he sat upon the barely held together cart hitched to two weath-ered horses. They knew each other too well and didn't need to speak before they both erupted in laughter. Mary's belly-roaring laugh was almost as deep as his.

Mary tried, but failed to smother her laughter. "What on God's earth you call yourself done got, Lar? 'Cause I sho' can't tell."

"Now look, woman!" he said sternly, but couldn't maintain the façade and began laughing anew. "This be our new wagon. It moves slow . . . but it moves. It can get us from here to there."

"Hummpf!" She walked around the wagon, moving her head slowly up and down in appraisal of it. The brown and white spot-ted horse eyed her, though the other that was solid black cried out when she approached its head. "These things as old as what they pullin', Lar. What they going to do for us other than fall over dead on the road?"

Lar jumped down from the wagon and stood next to her. He pointed from horse to horse. "You see this black one here and that one there– they called *'transportation'*, you see?" He reached for the black one's head, but it screeched and began bucking. "Damn fool!" he yelled at it. One firm hand from Lar on its harness and a solid jerk was all it took to settle the horse.

Mary stroked his arm from shoulder to elbow and began walking away. She stopped, turned and smiled. "You sure that ol' horse be the fool and not you?"

"Alright, woman!" he joked.

"You just wait down the road. I be finished here in no time. I don't need 'massa' catching you on his property. You know how he feel 'bout Negroe men by his house."

"I know, woman."

Mary had just turned around and was in the process of opening the backdoor when Paul came rushing out it, nearly running into her. "Hey– hey– hey– there, now! Slow down, youngin'! Where you off to in a rush?"

"Lar's got a wagon?" he asked, deciding to question her instead. She sighed. "Sho' look like it."

"How are the horses? Paul asked, but didn't wait for Mary to respond. "A mare . . . a stallion? What did he get?"

"Chile– I ain't looked underneath those thangs to see if they had a wanky."

Paul cupped his chin in his hand. "I best go check it out for you then, Ms. Mary," he offered. "We have to know these things."

Mary knew his ruse. It was not the horses he wanted to see, but Lar. The bond between them . . . a bottomless pit of adoration Paul had for him and one that Lar returned generously . . . was something she could never quite put a finger on. If Lar was near the house, then Paul was near Lar. They talked as though they were not men, but women after Sunday service desperate to catch up on the time passed since they'd seen one another. Neither one, as far as Mary saw, ever seemed to pause and think about the other's blackness or whiteness. *They be a strange pair*, Mary thought.

She went inside and finished settling Beatrice and Isabel down for the evening, and then returned to the kitchen and packed up the leftovers Isabel insisted she take. As she closed the door, she felt her child moving again. She sighed in relief. As she passed through the garden and the small yard, down the road she saw that Lar and Paul were now seated side by side on the cart. The reigns were now in Paul's hands.

"These horses be old, so you gotta take more care," Lar told him. "You can't just ride'em tough and hard, like you can young ones—see?"

"How long do you think they can work for you?"

The corner of Lar's mouth rose. "Long as they keep a'movin', boy! But I should have some younger ones by then to get breedin'."

Mary's presence interrupted their chat. She had been standing there for a few minutes already, though neither Lar or Paul had noticed her until now.

"Hey, Ms. Mary! Looks like you got some good transportation, now," Paul announced proudly, as if he had taken a part in it.

"I suppose I do, Mr. Paul," she said, and snapped her fingers at him ... code for get down and move your tail on back to the house.

"See ya, Lar!" Paul hopped down and began sprinting down the road. "Oh yeah! Thanks, Ms. Mary!" Paul called out as he faded into the darkness of the backyard.

"Thanks for what?" Lar asked.

She pointed her chin skyward and closed her eyes. "Chile wanted to go to swimmin' and had need of a good liar to do it."

"Lying about what?"

"Where he was," she said, matter of fact. "You know how that ol' drawed up sack of bones of a daddy he got be."

Lar gave the horses a snap and set them off. "Everybody know how that man is ... 'specially you." He glanced at her. "Mean o'l bastard– beatin' his wife and that poor boy like they dogs, when the dog be him. Wait 'til the Lord snatch him. He gonna see what a whuppin' really be like."

"Ain't coming no time too soon," she commented.

They rode on in silence, because no words were needed to express what was between them . . . love . . . exhaustion . . . respect . . . hope for a child soon to be born– though it had not always been that way. Maggie Mae . . . the beautiful one . . . the near-white one . . . she could tell that part of the story far better than anyone.

CHAPTER 2

An unseasonal heat wave was gripping the month of May, making each day seem to stretch out longer than the one before it. Even taking a simple breath in the humid heat was a chore. The ground was cracked and begging for moisture to soothe its wounds. But life in Folsom remained as it was . . . for now.

At the Monclair house, Mary was at it again– laundry– cooking – sweeping . . . But work provided a distraction for her, and any thought other than what was going on in her belly was welcome. She was already bigger than she'd been with the other babies who had died. And now, her feet were gone– at least that's what her eyes kept telling her every time she looked down. Her stomach was so bloated with child it hurt to move in any direction, but it was a good hurt, because the child was still moving inside. That was bearable. That was something to be thankful for . . . that and Fridays.

Fridays were an easy day for her and she needed one badly. It wasn't just that she would have two days of rest from the Monclairs, but that she would be able to work on her own home, her own cleaning and her own garden . . . and rest when she wanted to. For two whole days there would be no children to feed– just Lar and Uncle Matty. For two days there would be no Monclair clothes to mend– just Lar's and Uncle Matty's. For two whole days . . . She swooned at the thought of catching up on her rest, until she re-membered that . . .*Uncle Matty need a bath and Ms. Allie Mae wantin' me to run by stitch a spell and Lar gotta have his shoes tacked at the heel for Sunday morn' and then his suit need pressin' and . . . oh hell!* For two whole days, Mary figured she might as well be at the Monclair home working.

But right now it was imperative that Isabel's flower garden be watered, or else a quick, horrible death was assured– at least in Is-abel's eyes the situation was that dire. Still, Mary had to wake her from daydreaming and remind her that she was worried about the garden withering. Isabel startled and practically leapt into action. First they gathered all the buckets and pots they could find, and then began the arduous task of Mary pumping water into each container and handing it over the fence to Isabel, who then carted them to the plants that had been strategically scattered about the garden years ago when the Monclair's first bought the place.

Soft in the head Isabel may be sometimes, Mary thought, but when her mind was put to it, Isabel could nearly match her step for step– for a while. Mary had no doubt Isabel would take to bed for most of the next day with exhaustion, and that she would have to cart tea and water up to her. Mary knew she could have watered the plants on her own, though it would have been she who would need to be in bed to recuperate.

"We must break, Mary," Isabel begged, after hauling the twelfth bucket over to the elephant ears along the path leading to the backdoor of the house. She was dripping sweat from all three of her chins. Her dark, blonde hair adhered to her face, which looked more like one of Mary's just rolled-out biscuits that were ready for the oven. "Let's sit under the tree for a spell before we both pass out."

Mary silently praised Jesus that Isabel had some common sense.

Mary went into the kitchen and returned with a tray of tea that she had prepared that morning. "Come sit– please." Isabel motioned for her to take a seat next to her on the bench, which screamed when Mary plopped down on it. Both women paused and slowly turned to the other. Each quickly tried preemptively blaming the other should the wood bench go crashing down. They both began giggling so; they nearly toppled over and startled themselves . . . then began giggling anew.

A hot gust of wind blew over them, though on days such as to-day, it felt just as good as a cold breeze before a rain. Mary rolled up her dress and exposed herself to mid-thigh and let the heat escape. "*Mary!*" Isabel looked around in search of prying eyes. "You're near scandalous."

Mary ignored her and spread her legs even wider, and exhaled long and loud solely for Isabel's benefit. "Ms. Isabel . . . chile . . . it too hot to be actin' like a lady when you feel like an over-cooked chicken."

Isabel pushed herself up to get a better look over the fence. She scanned the yard and then the road. "If someone where to come . . ."

"They gonna see two hot women tryin' to stay cool in this here hell," Mary interrupted. "Children at school . . . Mr. Simeon at work . . . and we here by ourself. So ain't nobody got no business sneakin 'round here anyhow."

"True . . . true," Isabel agreed hesitantly, though was not fully convinced.

Mary closed her eyes and let her head fall back. "Go on and let those ankles cool a bit, Ms. Isabel. Only me, you and God gonna know about it."

Isabel looked around again. She finally dared and began raising her ground dragging dress. She rolled-up her dress until she was nearly as exposed as Mary. A breath named 'exquisite ecstasy' passed her lips.

"Now ain't that a good feeling, Ms.?"

"Exhilarating," Isabel moaned.

They sat quietly for a moment, both enjoying the balmy breeze upon their sweat beaded skin. Isabel broke the silence with a question that Mary did not expect. "Do you love, Lar?" She asked. Her eyes were still closed. Mary opened hers in surprise.

Mary thought for a moment, but not about the answer to the question, as that was simple. What made her hesitate was why such a question was asked. "Yes'm. Ain't no way I jump broom with a man I didn't love."

Isabel was silent for a moment. "He looks after you so well." She opened her eyes briefly and looked at Mary. "That was a silly question, wasn't it, dear?"

Mary decided against giving voice to despair and loss that was an ill-fitting coat Isabel refused to remove– so tight it was across her chest it was nearly choking her. Mary knew exactly where Isabel was going, for she was there with her in those days when she prayed that Stephen Allister would return to her. Only, Isabel didn't know then that his putrid corpse had already been buried, and was rotting in a field that held no glory for a Confederate soldier who had succumbed to gangrene. A mere scrape upon the sole of his left foot had become infected and then raged through his veins, and eventually poisoned his heart.

Next came the words of Belinda Christianson, matriarch of the Christansons who were now a dying breed. "You loved him, yes?" Poor Isabel nodded weakly as she lay in bed with grief– and in grief. Mary was there to hold Isabel's hand as a friend should. "So what!?" Belinda scolded her. "Do you think I married your father for love? God rest his soul, or the devil one," she added. "The south will fall, my dear child. I will also– but I won't let you. You *will* marry Simeon Monclair whether you love him or not . . . like him or not . . . even if you hate the very sight of him. Love is an option you no longer have, child." Belinda had turned to leave, but suddenly spun back around. "Now get out of that goddamn bed before I have you dragged out. *Mary* . . . bring down her wedding dress and make sure it fits properly. Look at the weight you've lost over that idiot, Allister. Just look at you! Your father will never stop turning in his grave . . . the war is lost, and now I must marry you off to that despicable, deformed excuse of a man to save you from a life upon the streets. We're Christianson's, for God sake!" she uttered defiantly, before she spoke her true despair. "What evil has befallen this house?"

Isabel's face was like a forgotten, wet sheet left to mold in the corner. "I'm sorry, Mary. I didn't mean to stir up . . ."

"Ain't no secret to anyone 'bout me and my babies– if that be what you talkin' 'bout."

"God rest their souls."

'Every last one of'em,' Mary thought.

And there had been so many tiny souls to rest. Miscarriages, half-borns, and then there were the full term ones who actually resembled babies. Memories of her dead infants were constant, sneaky and vindictive on good days, and vitriolic on bad ones. At the birth-death of her last baby, though she'd cried and beat her chest in anguish in front of those who were present . . . Lar, Willa, Enda, and Maggie Mae . . . it had all been for show. The reality of once again being denied motherhood was a crooked mouth jester mocking her from within, and there were no tears, passage of time or prayers that could soothe that pain.

"Don't you have one . . . more . . . child. You hear me, Mary Cole? You do—and you both be dead."

It was as though a child of her own was never meant to be, though she told no one she felt so, not even Lar. He'd wept for the dead children also. He'd held the last one for so long . . . a boy . . . it nearly had to be wrestled from him so that it could be buried out back behind their house with the others. It was fully formed– all fingers and toes present and accounted for. Its face was round and puffy, and would have looked so cute if it could have smiled a gummy smile. It had a head full of slick black hair, but its lips were as gray as its skin. It never knew what a breath of life was, only the drowning death of amniotic fluid that gushed out onto bloody bed sheets seconds after it did. *"You in heaven now, boy. Me and your mammy see you there soon,"* she heard Lar say to it.

"This one is going to live, Mary. I can feel it in my bones," Isabel assured her. "By the grace of God it will."

'God?' Mary thought with disgust. She didn't know Isabel's God or anyone else's who would allow all of her children to die. Was it the same one her mother and she prayed to when they were still slaves being treated lower than dogs, and only a smidgen better than Indian folk? That same God who did nothing when they hanged that sixteen-year-old Negroe boy over in Parsen County just last month? That God? *Him?* The same one that didn't give white folks sense enough to let a Negroe boy and Negroe girl just be a boy and girl? 'You sure 'bout that, Ms. Isabel?' She wanted to ask.

"Lar will be such a good father for your child," Isabel continued. "And you a good mother. You take care of my children so well– you always have. I just know things will turn out most fortunate for you and Lar this time."

Mary forced a smile. "I believe so too."

"Mary?"

This time Mary's sigh was audible, but it did nothing to deter Isabel from speaking. "Yes'm."

Isabel's façade of contentment had faded. Her eyes were overcast. Her head drooped so low Mary could barely hear her. "It's . . . just that . . . you have been with our family since you were a child. "You are very dear to me– you know that.

"I've always wished a better life for you. I know that is easier said . . . knowing how things are. I wish better times were upon Folsom," Isabel said. "All of us . . . white and Negroes, and especially we women. We need something better than what we have here. Don't you think, Mary? Remember when your mother– Aunt

Sarah– used to tell us how things were going to change for all of us one day? Hmm?" Mary remained mute. "She knew didn't she . . . about the war and slaves being freed . . . didn't she? Better times have to come . . . right?"

Mary had no plans of holding out for hope. Isabel would never understand that upon shelves southerners had crafted to keep order, she knew where she had been sat. From birth, her place had been pointed out to her by whites that refused to acknowledge that she was a human being at all. On the lower shelf were the Nigra dolls white children were allowed to toss about, kick and step on. These Nigra dolls were sullied, torn and then discarded, for they were deemed as unworthy as the stitching that held them together. 'Play with those first,' the white children were told. 'Have a care with the arms, legs and backs. If you play with them too hard, there shall be no one to clean and cook for us,' their white mothers told them. 'Listen to your mother,' white fathers would press home. 'Don't rip them apart– *yet!* For who will spread their legs for me when my urge grows great? Who shall open their mouths when I tell them– '*yes*' . . . that is what I want you to do with it??'

Slightly further up were niggah-boy dolls– just as tarnished as the Nigra from too many hands upon them. They sat down far enough where naughty white boys could run by with flailing arms and knock them from their perch. Their stitching was durable, but still worthless– though it was a challenge to see how great of a pull was needed to reveal their stuffing, even if one had to resort to using a knife to do so.

But who sits further up than the niggah-boy doll, than the white man doll. Out of reach he was to most hands that sought him. But . . . *ah* . . . the unreachable, porcelain white girl doll sat highest of all. She was deemed so precious; a rare, white marble pedestal was crafted for her, and her alone, for she was pure and virginal. Not even dust swirled up from the floor was allowed to settle upon her skin. She was the mother of white gods. She must be protected at all costs . . . *though* . . . *but* . . . the lie was . . . there were Negroes who walked about the store of southern life with brown, café au lait and white skin . . . hazel, green and sometimes even blue eyes, like Maggie Mae, who laughed at the precious white dolls, for they knew the truth of the white girl doll's vanity. Of course, white boy dolls would never admit such a thing, for they proclaimed self-righteously, 'for thousands of years, have we not ruled the world justly, built grand civilizations and spread the word of God? Are we not entitled now? Do not dare to judge us you white girl dolls. For you are where you are, because we are where we are. Now take a blindfold and bind your precious blue eyes.'

"The Lord will see us through– I'm sure he– "

"Jesus ain't seen to nothin' and ain't goin' to, neither!" Mary seethed through pursed lips. Her face was glistening from sweat. "Ms. Isabel . . . he done had his chance to set things right. If he ain't gonna do it, then it's up to me to see to it myself. The *Lord?* Hell!" Mary quipped.

Isabel's mouth fell open.

"Just 'cause we ain't workin' on some plantation no more, don't mean we so much better off. Well– that may be true some," she corrected. "But we still get beat and killed. I done seen that post-card that come for Mr. Simeon 'bout that lynchin'. The *Lord* ain't seen us through *that* mess yet, have he?"

Isabel clutched her chest. "And Lord . . . somebody help us all, too! That poor, poor boy . . . I can't believe somebody would even photograph that. I couldn't look at it."

"Well, I did– and hard."

Isabel gasped. "You didn't!"

"Yes, ma'am I did! Free ain't so free, huh? Free my . . ."

"Mary!" Isabel blushed.

"My ass!" Mary said proudly. She pulled down her skirt and stood up.

Isabel shook her head. "You and your tongue, Mary. And your Lar's a minister. He . . . he would just . . . "

Mary pointed her chin skyward. "That him, not me. I ain't got no time for no man to be tellin' me what to do– say– or act. Mary gotta see to Mary."

* * *

They all– Mary, Isabel, Paul and Beatrice, rode into town later that afternoon. Paul was doing his best to steer the wagon clear of ruts, but the ground, even where it looked smooth, was rough– the drought had seen to that. Mary was next to Paul up front, while Isabel and Beatrice lounged in the back under the cover of parasols. Mary tolerated going into the town's center by herself, or with Paul, but it was maddening having to accompany Isabel, who was forever undecided about what to buy, and Beatrice prancing about to advertise her meager goods.

Though Mary knew going to town meant having to call whites 'ma'am' and 'sir', it still irritated her . . . just as much as going into a store and being watched from entrance to exit. But if there was anything that made her clench her fists the tightest, it was being called 'niggah' or 'Nigra'. Folsom whites said it with such abandon, it was as though they thought her mother Sarah had declared at her birth . . . *niggah! That be a good name for my girl-chile . . . niggah . . . that sound good . . . even got a melody to it.'*

Paul had been just as enthusiastic as Mary about going into town. He begged Mary to help him slip away to go swimming, as he'd done for the past few weeks– off and then back, smiling over that delicious bird he'd swallowed and thought no one knew about. This time, the answer had been a resounding 'no'. Isabel and Beatrice both wanted to go venturing into town. Beatrice wanted to see if there was a new bauble to threaten Isabel into buying, or else tell father when he came home if she didn't. Of course, any Negroe boy or man could have carried and loaded packages for them for a few cents, but Simeon had forbidden it. *"Paul can do any work a niggah can do, and I don't have to pay him either,"* Mary had often heard Simeon saying when it came to work of any kind that could bring a Negroe close to his 'property' . . . his house too!

Paul had been close to an all-out, grand mal seizure in protest.

Beatrice was waiting in front of the house busily straightening her lavender bonnet for the fourth time, while Isabel, standing next to her, furiously fanned her moist face with a black and white laced fan. "I can't do a damn thing 'bout it, Paul," Mary whispered, as they hitched the horses. She tried not to be swayed by his dark lashes and a pouting mouth. "You been down at that river just 'bout everyday anyhow. One day not bein' wet ain't gonna kill ya. And you best mind what you doin, too. Beatrice been pippin' that you ain't even been down at the river. How she know your business– I don't know. But you know your sissy's mouth . . ."

"How do you know she's even telling the truth?" he snipped. Mary gave him a raised brow that she usually reserved for Beatrice. "Sorry, Ms. Mary."

"I can't lift those boxes by myself," she said. "I need a *man*." She blatantly eyed his slim frame while waiting for her ruse to work.

Paul shoved his hands in his pocket and kicked the dirt. "I hate 'em," he grunted.

"Hate who?"

"Them," he said, and then wiggled his head toward Beatrice and Isabel. "All of them– except you and Lar, that is."

"And take that to yo' grave," Mary told him. "Talk like that get me, Lar and a white boy like you whipped, too!"

"You mean white *man*?" Paul asked. A bit of levity had snuck back into his tone.

Mary smiled and displayed her big, white teeth surrounded by soot black lips. "Yes, *'mistah Paul'*! Man, I meant to say."

* * *

The center of town was nearly empty when they arrived. Before the war, it would have been a far different scene. Mistresses, missies and young masters could have been heard long before being seen as they picnicked and played in the park to pass the time. Weary eyed Negroes would have been standing on the outskirts of Folsom's little taste of Eden waiting to serve their owners. White boys could be seen running around the great oak or climbing its thick branches. And when mistresses and missies were bored from lounging in the park, they would stroll through Folsom's stores to see what new European fashions had arrived.

'Ba-bang! Ba-bang-bang-clang! Zip-zaw . . . and lift!!! Now nail it up there!' so said the *saw* to the *hammer*, as another daring entrepreneur pieced together his dream out of wood and tin in Folsom's bulging downtown. There was no time to doddle about if he were to make his riches in Folsom like so many others had. Fortune seekers swarmed Folsom like roaches after the last breadcrumbs on a plate, for new opportunities were to be had . . . so said 'word of mouth'.

Though when the Confederacy died, it took the hopes, dreams, fortunes and egos of many *Folsimians* with it. The grand park in the midst of town withered and returned to dust from which it had come. Shops were abandoned or looted– if lucky enough to have not been torched by Union soldiers and marauders. Those once optimistic entrepreneurs who joined the Confederacy to protect what was newly theirs, or thought might be, either departed Folsom or stayed and decided not to rebuild, for it was hard for walking, talking and breathing ghosts to accomplish such a daunting task. And besides, no one wanted their Confederate money anyway.

Time was patient, and vengefully reclaimed what belonged to it – 'I am eternal and as inescapable as my brother—he who rideth upon the pale horse. Curse and gnash thy teeth, for it shall be all in vain. I will not . . . I cannot . . . be denied!'

Rainwater eventually seeped through untended roofs– floors buckled and walls warped. Paint on buildings peeled away and advertised cryptic notes on their walls. Once, a pursuer of goods had but to walk out of one store and take two steps left or right to the next one. Now, they had to walk half a block from one store to the other in order to groan and complain about the lack of, and quality of goods offered, even though they lacked money to purchase the wares anyway. So it was indeed a surprise to Mary, Paul, Isabel and Beatrice as they were about to enter the store to see a carriage pulling to a halt not fifty feet away from them. They all wondered who would willingly come to Folsom. A few townsfolk stepped from their buildings . . . curtains parted from above and below. Shop patrons, town drunks and vagabonds, who happened to be on the road stopped and pretended to be busy with some mundane task, though their eyes were suspiciously aimed in the carriage's direction also.

The white driver slipped down from his perch and opened the door. A tall white man, whom to Mary wasn't worth attending to, stepped from the carriage. But what did catch her attention were two separate, almost smothered gasps that accompanied the stranger's arrival on Folsom soil. Mary squinted. It was not that her eyes were bad and she couldn't see him clearly– she just couldn't see what all the fuss was about. To her, he was just another white man in a wrinkled, brown suit wearing a straw hat.

The stranger turned and spoke with the driver, and then handed him money. Beside the rumples on the tail of his jacket, he was far too polished for a town like Folsom. Years ago, he and his fancy black shoes might have blended in, she thought . . . but not now. Upon closer inspection, Mary did recognize that he was that handsome type white ladies were want to swoon over, and lesser men gave respect to, even if they knew he didn't deserve it. He even moved with an elegance not seen since the Monclair and Christianson had real money.

Mary broke the trances that had befallen Paul and Beatrice by reminding them of the limited time they had. She looked over at the man once more before walking into the store. He saw her and seemed to smile almost. She didn't like that at all. She knew the most benign gesture from a white man could mean almost anything and rarely did it mean nothing at all.

Monclair General Goods was the best store left in Folsom. In the back room, off to the right of the sales counter was where fabric, the sewing machine and the seamstress, Ms. Allie Mae Brown, were kept. And always at the counter with the most unpleasant of smiles and manners, at least toward Negroes, was Ms. Delilah Ford – a widow by means of the Civil War. But Mary could remember even further back when she used to be *Mrs.* Delilah Ford. Mary passed by her as though she was not even there, but she knew Delilah's eyes were on her screaming *'niggah!'*

Time remembered when Mrs. Delilah Ford was about as low as a white could be in white society. For one, the words spoken on the coarseness of her backwoods drawl was as broken as that of the Negroes she so openly despised and felt far superior to– she did have white skin and the rights that came with it after all. Her life before venturing to Folsom was told by the grooves etched around her eyes, cheeks and lips, as if a blind child had taken hold of a knife instead of a brush and gotten hold of her face and mistaken its dry, paper texture for canvas. She was known to always slur her speech by speaking though a barely opened mouth to hide her golden, snaggled teeth, unless she was barking at some Negroe she didn't want in the store.

Delilah and her husband, Martin Ford, had journeyed from their home out in the eastern mountains to get their piece of Folsom fortune too late– war was coming. And being white trash, as other whites called them as easily as they said 'niggah' to Negroes, didn't help. But a small bit of luck– or so they thought at the time – did smile upon the Fords in the name of Simeon Monclair I. After pleading, begging and promising to work for next to nothing, Simeon Monclair I hired them both for less than that. Delilah, who was able to count, was put to work in the general store as an assistant. Martin was loaned money and given a few acres of lands to sharecrop and grow tobacco. He promised Delilah tobacco was going to be the next big commodity, and that finally, he was going to buy her one of those pretty dresses in Lorraine's shop next door to the Monclair store, and a tea hat to go along with it. But Lincoln spoke . . . the war came . . . and their lives changed, as it did for so many others. Delilah never got a chance to buy that fancy pink dress she had her eye on, or that pretty flowered hat that went with it. She did own three hole-ridden dresses of her own she could put on and pretend they weren't as raggedy as they were. Martin's hate for Negroes and the illusion to repay the high interest loan given by old man Monclair propelled him to volunteer for the Confederate army.

Alas . . . he never came home.

Though if there had been a way, which there wasn't, for his fellow soldiers to bring home what was left of him, they wouldn't have anyway. In formation and ready to march into battle, what befell Martin . . . some would say the wrong place at the wrong time . . . others called it just plain bad luck . . . most would say nothing at all, for he was but one of hundreds who died that day. While trying to load his rifle for the impending battle, his body was torn to shreds by a cannonball fired as a warning shot by the Union army. Delilah received a letter a few months later informing her of Martin's courage, but unfortunate death.

Delilah never had any love for Negroes before the war, but the murder of her husband, as she referred to it, fueled an unnatural hatred for them. Why– the sight of them– their big lips, wide noses and kinky hair– just looking at their *black* skin was enough to make her wretch. In their faces, she saw nothing remotely human, but something far closer to animals . . . monkeys and apes who could walk and talk who were ultimately responsible for her husband's death, and the life of servitude she led to Simeon Monclair II to pay on a debt that would never be paid off.

Once in the store, Mary left Isabel and Beatrice to admire the same old items that they had admired countless times before. Rarely was there ever anything new in the store, but still they looked about just in case something had shown up by chance. Paul was busy pretending not to gaze out the storefront window– but he was, and in the direction where the carriage that had brought the stranger to town. She walked to the backroom, knocked and entered before being given permission. None was needed.

"Hey, chile!" Allie Mae peeped. What little hair Allie Mae had was pulled back and twisted into a knot the size of a thumb. Gray hair was quickly replacing what had been black. Her face and fingers had not been smooth since she was five years old, though her smile still bore the innocence of a child's.

"Afternoon, missy," Mary replied. She saw out the corner of her eye that Delilah had come from behind the counter and was pretending to rearrange a shelf of neatly stacked preserves by the backroom door. Mary thought about giving Delilah a *'mind your own goddamn business'* scowl before slamming the door behind her, but settled on a firm shut. "She gonna have her ear down by the door-crack in a bit."

"You know that be truth," Allie Mae whispered. "That ol' nosy thang gotta know every lick and bit 'bout what goin' on. She worse than a chile up in grown-folk's business."

The room appeared to have no furniture or tables, as fabric was strewn across every available piece. On a table in the midst of the room, next to faceless, naked mannequins, was the sewing machine where Allie Mae was sitting and working her art. Mary moved the mound of cloth from the chair closest to the sewing table and sat down next to her. "Feet just as swollen," Mary uttered, as she stretched her legs out and grimaced as much from pain as she did from relief.

"How much longer you reckon?"

Mary rubbed her bloated belly. "A month or so . . . chile, I don't know. I don't even know my name half the time– tell you the truth. But I sure be one happy woman when this youngin' come," she lied. She loved the feel of life growing within her. Yet, she was anxious to meet the unborn and watch it take its first breath also.

They chatted for a while about everything and nothing of much importance to anyone but themselves. Catching up on the latest gossip of the day was paramount; Mary went first about the well-dressed gentleman who had just arrived. Allie Mae was next with news of even more strangers– white men, who had arrived hours before and were inquiring about Simeon Monclair. "Honey– these stump-jumpers I seen ain't like the one you done saw. These ones, I bettin' my life on can't spell 'gentleman'."

"Sho' nuff?"

Allie Mae looked as if she had just sucked on a lemon. "Mmm-hmm. And Delilah just laughin' up in they face. You know how she got that ol' choked-up laugh, like somebody done squished a frog." Allie Mae began jerking her head back and forth, and then spat out, "*huh-huh—huh-huh—huh-huh-huh-huh* . . . like she dyin'."

Mary squealed, and then quickly covered her mouth. She looked over and down at the door for signs of Delilah's prying shadow. "Girl, stop!" She told Allie Mae, and then giggled.

"Oooh . . . chile, you know that ol' tore-up mouth of hers. Every time she get the itch to open that mess, it make you wanna cry."

Mary successfully fought gravity and released herself from the chair that had felt like a well-padded throne. "Lord– Lord– Lord," Mary sighed. "Let me go and take care of these white folks. I got the whole mess of them with me this time. They be bangin' on this door here if I don't get my tail movin'. *'Mary I need this . . . Mary I can't find that . . . Mary—what you doin? . . . Mary—Mary—Mary!'"* Mary put her hands on her hips, looked up at the ceiling and slowly shook her head. "Hell! I'm talkin' like my Uncle Matty now."

"What?"

"Aw– nothin'. He was just tellin' me how white folks always actin' like they helpless when they get that lazy bone."

Allie Mae snickered. "Hummpf– I ain't heard Uncle Matty lie yet."

"'Fore I forget . . . you got that gal's dresses done yet?"

"Next week be a better time ta ask," Allie Mae replied.

"Ol' miss sassy-mouth out there can wait anyhow."

Mary opened the door, as Beatrice was just about to turn the doorknob. Without an 'excuse me', 'pardon me', 'hey, Mary', she stooped and slid under Mary's arm, and hurried over to Allie Mae. Her head could barely keep up with her eyes darting side to side. "Be ready next week," Allie Mae announced, before Beatrice could even open her mouth.

Beatrice rested her hands on her love-handles. "I hope you measured them right this time. I could barely fit into the other two dresses you made. They're practically useless now."

Allie Mae lowered her head and continued her stitching. "I do my best this time." Mary knew there was not a damn thing wrong with Allie Mae's measurements, but everything to do with Beatrice's fork to mouth disease.

"Not one of the dresses are finished?"

Allie Mae didn't look up. "No, missy."

Beatrice pouted, turned, and then followed Mary out.

Mary was barely out of the backroom when the hair on her skin bristled as Maggie Mae hustled into the store. Mary unconsciously pulled her shoulders back and her head up. She pursed her lips in preparation to reply in a courteous manner once Maggie Mae had. However, Maggie Mae didn't appear in the mood to say anything to anyone. She looked frightened. Her chest was heaving up and down too rapidly to blame it on the heat.

She was already pale, but what blood she did have that gave some color to her face, had fled. Her white headscarf had slipped to the side and a few locks of light brown hair had slipped out. She stood in front of the door clutching her wicker basket, as if to keep out what had disturbed her so. It was only when another patron, a thin, old white woman tried to gain entrance that she moved.

Mary went to her, forgetting what had made her straighten up in the first place. Mary did something she had not done since they both wore pigtails playing in the dirt under Enda's watchful eyes that never watched them, but were always on whatever lay past the horizon. She took hold of Maggie Mae's hand and led her away from the glare of whites that were staring at her.

"What be wrong with you?" Mary asked. Maggie Mae's hand was moist and shivering. Maggie Mae shook her head, and then re-alizing her hair had fallen out from her scarf, quickly tucked it back in.

Mary asked again, but Maggie Mae did not reply. Not having been so close to her for many years, Mary examined her face and saw that it had not changed . . . much to her disappointment. Maggie Mae's skin was still as white, clear and soft appearing as it had been when she was a child . . . not like her own which was taut, coarse from too much wind and sun-baked black. Maggie Mae's cheeks were still high and round, like her pink lips– not like Mary's flat cheeks and finger-thick lips. She remembered, grudg-ingly so, when she was a child and having wished she looked so pretty like Maggie Mae.

Maggie Mae eventually spoke, but in a hush. "I got startled is all."

Mary huffed at the lie.

She didn't have to think long to figure out what had likely startled Maggie Mae. Rarely was there a word spoken by whites that
Negroes couldn't hear. The Negroe gossip line from white Folsom
to Negroe homes was thoroughly intact and very reliable. White
men lusted for Maggie Mae. No– she corrected– they wanted her
like rabid animals. Maggie Mae looked white, but wasn't . . . and
because she wasn't, the taking of her virginity did not require permission . . . just opportunity.

"Stay way from here before it get dusk," Mary warned, as if she
were preaching yet again at Paul. "They less likely to mess with
you in daylight." But she knew that was only partially true. Evil
traveled as easily in the light, as well as in the dark. But it was the
best advice she had to give to her once friend. Mary began to walk
away, but stopped. "The woods, too, Ms. Maggie . . . ain't no telling
what be up in them neither. You know what your momma done
told us 'bout them."

Mary tried setting her mind back to the task at hand, but could
not totally dispel the dread Maggie Mae brought in with her. Hers
was a familiar tale known amongst Negroes . . . the white man's
craving for Negroe women. White flesh was satisfying and socially
acceptable, but Negroe flesh, or Negroe blood as was the case with
Maggie Mae, aroused a passion in white men that even frigid waters could not cool for long. To the white men of Folsom, Maggie
Mae was too unworldly a creature to be left unmolested.

She touched her belly to help calm her, because despite her best
efforts, she worried for Maggie Mae. Old Negroe women had
warned her that a pregnant woman was prone to do things she
never thought she would do. Or, had she went to Maggie Mae because she sensed another woman needed help that only another
woman could provide? She recalled Enda always saying that God
gave women a sense that a man was too hardheaded to use. If a
woman's child was in trouble . . . she could feel it. A woman could

spot a lie from the best liar . . . she could see it in a man's eyes– if she chose to see it. A woman could sense a man's lust . . . she could smell it in the air– almost taste it even.

Mary slid the empty wicker basket from Isabel's hands. Isabel, having had all the intentions of shopping had run into Abby Johns, who lived on the other side of Folsom, and seemed to have forgotten the reason she'd come to the store at all. Mary knew if she didn't start gathering goods now they would never be home at a decent hour for her to start dinner. But it didn't take her long to gather what they had come to get. Money was no problem since the family owned the store anyway.

Almost forgetting that she was having a fish fry this coming weekend, Mary set the basket next to Isabel and went back to retrieve cornmeal. She then got in line behind two middle age white women: Olivia Manson and Georgiana Riley. "Paul!" Mary called over her shoulder. He was still peeking out the window in the direction where the carriage had arrived earlier. "Carry your mama's basket out to the wagon. We 'bout to leave."

"Sure, Ms. Mary. I'll be waiting outside for ya'll then." He grabbed the basket and ran.

"Ain't been this busy in here for a long spell," Maggie Mae said, as she got in line behind Mary.

Mary looked to either side of her. Susan Miller and her second husband, Arlen . . . rumor had it her first husband left her, though she claimed he went off and was killed in the war . . . they were picking through vegetables. Horseshoe haired, Jimmy McCloud . . . and by coincidence, the town's blacksmith, was with his wife, Betty, stocking up on lye soap. "I was thinkin' the same thing myself. If I didn't know any better, I swear folks in this ol' dead town had a dollar or two still hidden off," Mary remarked, only slightly too loud.

Olivia and Georgiana abruptly turned around and glared at her – but Delilah's glower was the severest of all. The three white women stared long enough to send their message . . . that what Mary had just said would be repeated to other white ears. Any Negroe woman would have been chilled to her soul, as Maggie Mae was, and who'd immediately bowed her head. Mary, knowing she could not look them in the eye, stared at the grease stain on Delilah's dress by her right shoulder. She kept her eyes fixed there until the women turned back around– stiffly. Maggie Mae sighed in relief. Mary was never tense to start with. As far as she was concerned, her mouth was attached to her face . . . *hers* . . . not theirs . . . and she could use it when she chose to.

Olivia and Georgiana departed after setting up their deliver to be made by a Negroe boy later on that day. Mary, head held high, strode ahead as though they had simply said 'good day' and placed her meal on the counter. She reached into the pocket of her dress and felt for the two nickels.

Delilah's yellow fangs were bared. "Wait yo' turn."

Blood rushed into Mary's ears and began a rhythmic pounding. "If I ain't mistaken, Ms. Ford, I was . . ."

"I said wait yo' turn!" Delilah snapped. Olivia and Georgiana were but two steps to the door when Delilah bellowed. They stopped, turned and smiled unabashedly. Susan and Arlen, who were in the corner counting their change, paused and looked up. Jimmy McCloud who was not that far away from Beatrice, who was looking at new bows, both were practically salivating. Isabel, realizing that her friend, Abby Johns, was no longer paying attention to her tale of traveling from home to store, turned around. Even the backroom door where Allie Mae worked cracked open. "The mulatta is next."

Silence closed in around Mary.

She knew what was occurring had nothing to do with cornmeal and everything to do with the war and its aftermath. Folsom whites, like so many others, had placed their hopes in the strength

of the Confederacy and its tender. Neither they nor most southerners had believed the south would ever fall, and they were still
shell-shocked that it had.

Mary found her two nickels and laid them on the counter. "This
here bag of meal, Ms. Ford," she said flatly. Her eyes again studied
the grease stain on Delilah's shoulder.

Delilah picked up the nickels, jiggled them in her cupped hand
for a moment, and then threw them across the room. The nickels
played a jingle on the jars lined up on the shelves on the wall. "I
said that mulatta is next . . . *Goddamnit!*"

Isabel rushed forward and took hold of Mary's arm. "Ms. Ford,
please," Isabel whispered. She smiled and nodded to the white audience around her.

Delilah leaned over the counter. "This niggah is as disrespectful
as they come, Mrs. Monclair," she snorted. "I told her to move back
and let that mulatta come up, and she done gone and got mouthy
wit me– *again.*"

"A Negroe is a Negroe, no? Ms. Ford? No?" Isabel begged. "They
are both Negroe women," she said diplomatically, and then looked
at Maggie Mae, but suddenly performed a double take. "Oh my!"
she uttered.

"She black as tar standing next to that *thang* behind her,"
Delilah pointed out. "That make a difference here."

"Ms.? . . . Maggie? Please. " Isabel stuttered in defeat, as white
eyes now watched her every move. She motioned for her to step to
the counter. Maggie Mae sheepishly placed her wicker basket on
the counter and stepped back.

"Well take it out of the basket, you lazy mulatta!" Delilah
snapped. "Sa' wonder Mrs. Meadows keeps you workin' for her."

"Yes'm," Maggie Mae whispered. Her hands shook as she placed
each item on the counter. It had all become a show– Mary as the
center attraction and Maggie Mae the second act. Maggie Mae paid
for the goods and then hurriedly repacked her items and left.

Delilah folded her arms and lifted her pointy chin, waiting for the third act. But Mary did something Delilah did not expected. She smiled.

Mary walked to the counter with her head held equally high. She laid the sack of meal on the counter gently. "Here," Mary said benignly.

"Seven cent."

Mary held her smile for a second longer and then said, "no."

Delilah slammed her hand on the counter. "You ain't 'bout to bicker with me about the price of this meal now, is you?"

"No, ma'am."

"Seven cent, then!"

Mary pushed the bag of meal toward Delilah with a single finger. "I ain't needin' it no more." Mary swiveled on her swollen heels and walked away. There was no reason to look back . . . she knew what an ugly face Delilah already had and figured it just became uglier. "I be by the cart, Ms. Isabel, when you ready."

Outside in the balmy air, Mary was anything but warm. Sweat was soaking her dress, but provided a strange sense of cool relief. What she had done was dangerous, yet she felt no regrets about it.

She knew how to play the white's game, though most Negroes, especially Lar, told her she played it too dangerously. White-folks loved to hear a sound 'yes suh' and 'no ma'am.' They knew a good Negroe walked out of their way when they approached and never looked them in the eye when speaking to them. And talk back? Never! If a white said dirt was green, well just agree and say 'yes suh– you sho' right!' But Mary was always known to be the first to say, "Well . . . that dirt lookin' a bit more brown than green to my eyes . . . *suh.*"

"You all finished, Ms. Mary?" Paul asked. He was obviously bored now that the carriage was gone.

"'Bout five minutes ago we was."

Beatrice stormed out of the store, followed by Isabel who was scurrying after her. Her lips were moving faster than the words that came past them. "This will be all over town!" Beatrice cried.

Isabel nudged her toward the cart. "Beatrice, shush!"

"What happened?" Paul asked, but was ignored by all.

Beatrice's blue eyes darkened. "Mother . . . she embarrassed our whole family in there . . . and made a fool of you!"

"Fools stand in the street and carry on," Mary stated.

Beatrice turned to Mary. As if realizing her mouth was agape, she quickly shut it. The tension upon her face washed away and was replaced with a smug grin she had perfected the last few years. "I'd swear you just called me a fool."

"I don't call no one names. That wouldn't be Christian," Mary informed her. "I just let folks be who they be." Paul snickered– not only because it was funny, but because for all of her pretended worldliness, Beatrice didn't get it.

* * *

Cold, like a January morning was waiting for her, Maggie Mae knew. In Lar's arms, she would have felt safe. Even in fantasy, his thick, vein riddled black arms embracing her gave some comfort. She often wondered had God cursed her because her mother knew 'tomorrows' or could do things folks said were not possible?

Maggie Mae remembered a time when her mother was quasi-normal. Of course, her mother always seemed to know what others were thinking or were likely to do, but that was simply a trait of hers as common as making even the most bitter greens and stale cornbread delectable. Her prowess making gris-gris was pretty good, too. But when visions of the snake started coming to her mother just a few years back, her sound mind seemed to have left her, or so it seemed to Maggie Mae at first.

At first, Maggie Mae thought her mother had gone mad when she began talking as if she were someone else . . . men and women ... boys ... girls ... babies even. But truly insane? Far from it, Maggie Mae realized in utter horror. At the church's plank wood foundation that was only halfway finished, on one particular Sunday, she knew that if the other Negroes had heard what her mother said, they would have branded her as something far worse than a witch.

That Sunday, Enda had insisted they sit in the back away from the others. They had their sack blanket to sit on, but its thin skin was no protection from the pebbles that poked their bottoms. Still, Maggie Mae was engrossed in Lar and Lar's words, but that was no different from any other time Lar was near. And then without warning, Enda pulled her close. It was then she first heard her mother speak words that were not hers.

"... and the Lord came unto Moses ... can I get a witness?" Enda whispered to her.

" ... and ... the Lord came unto Moses ... can I get a witness?" Lar said to the congregation.

Enda continued. "... to Pharaoh you will go, and with thy rod, wield my might ..."

" ... to Pharaoh you will go, and with thy rod, wield my might ..."

"But I shall harden his heart," Enda said.

"But I shall harden his heart."

Maggie Mae struggled to break free of her mother's grasp, but those hands that held her tight did not belong to an old woman, but to something that should not have been sitting there listening to the Holy Gospel. "The serpent right up on his shoulder, chile," Enda told her. "I ain't got no root to get it off him."

From that point on, it had seemed as though her mother drifted even further into a realm not of this world, but to where few could go or dared to travel. At times her mother talked incessantly to no one, other times she would not speak for days. Each passing day she spoke less about the here and now, and more about the past and *'tomorrows'* to come.

'I already know what's behind the horizon! I've seen it!'

Maggie Mae left the Monclair store as quickly as she had barged into it. She could believe, yet could not believe Mary had done what she did. There had been a time when Mary would have simply obeyed the whites and gone about her business, she remembered. She'd known Mary, her first true playmate, all of her life. But as the years passed– the town saw war– people aging and dying– new lives sparking– Mary had changed also. *For the better?* Maggie Mae thought, *no*. She thought if only for self-preservation, Mary would be better off remaining the shy and scared child who would be the last to rile the anger of a white. But those were years past– slavery was gone. *It may be a new age, but not a better one,* Maggie Mae thought.

'I've seen it!'

Outside and away from the stares of whites folks in the store, she still didn't feel safe. She looked around for the man who'd caused her to flee into the store in the first place, but saw no sight of him. That was some good news. She knew he was not from around Folsom, for he never would have touched her or spoke to her in the way he did.

She had walked the steps in front of the Monclair Motel more times than she could count. Why she'd tripped over those warped planks that she knew were there had everything to do with Lucianna, her mistress, rushing her to get what was needed from the store and then back home. If her mind had been on what she was doing, she would have skipped over the rotten boards as usual. But she did fall, and not far from the well-dressed gentleman about to walk into the motel.

Without having to look, she could feel that some of the skin of her knees had been scraped off and was now embedded in the wood planks behind her. The basket she was carrying had tumbled away from her, and then was carelessly kicked even further away by a white lady too busy trying to walk around her. At first she struggled to get up on her own, but was aided by strong hands that effortlessly brought her upright. But the hands were as white as hers and she nearly screeched at the sight of them. She pulled away from them instinctively, as any Negroe woman would and should have.

"A bad stumble you had there, Ms.," he said.

With her head down, Maggie Mae nodded. She knew he was not from the south by the intermittent drawl on his words. She reached for her basket, but he was faster and his arms longer. He held it close to him at first, but then officially presented it to her as though she'd won an award. "Your basket, ma'am."

She reached for it, hoping to grab it and flee. But as she did, he bent his head down and glanced at her face . . . and gasped . . . a re-action she was used to from men who had not seen her before. While he was still stunned, she snatched the basket from him and made to run, but he caught hold of her arm and used her own mo-mentum against her to spin her around. Behind him, she saw that the coachman and two other white men had stopped to watch.

"Suh . . . please let go," she implored.

"But . . . your name, Ms.?" He'd asked. She offered nothing.

He let go of her arm, but the moment he did, she backed away. "Nicholas Barrons," he said and smiled, but that too was not re-turned.

"Hey, boy!" A man called.

Maggie Mae and Nicholas both turned. One of the white men standing behind them had his hands on his hips. His face spoke ev-erything but 'welcome' to Nicholas. "You need something with that Negroe gal?"

Nicholas' thick, black brows caved in. "What do you mean, suh? I was helping this young . . ."

The man cut Nicholas off with a throaty laugh. "That there is Roman Meadow's Nigra you messin' with."

Nicholas faced her and studied her anew.

"Get on outta here, Maggie!" the man barked, though he didn't have to in order to get Maggie Mae nearly sprinting down and into the Monclair store.

Maggie Mae surveyed her surroundings again. There was not a trace of the man– *Nicholas*– she remembered him saying his name was. She exhaled a pent up breath and then dashed across the street.

Being mistaken for white was an all too common occurrence for her, yet no less disturbing each time she crossed paths with some stranger wandering into Folsom. She knew why they mistook her for one of their own. As a child, she remembered staring into mirrors and wondering who or what stared back . . . Negroe or white? She felt like a Negroe, yet did not look like one. She looked white, but did not feel so.

Once on the other side of the street, she realized she was too close to the dead oak her mother told her and every Negroe never to go near. But it was either scurry past that dead thing or risk another confrontation with those white men– *and Nicholas*. And that was something she did not want this day or any other.

She hurried past the tree until she made it to the gravel road that lead out of the town's center. The sight of the Meadows' house was of great, yet eerie solace. Though Roman Meadows, the owner, had always been kind to her and paid her more than a fair wage for the times, his wife, Lucianna, was not. She knew Lucianna despised her, for she told her daily. Yet, for all her demeaning and threatening talk, Lucianna wanted her to stay. There were secrets to be maintained, after all. *Yes*– Maggie Mae knew that the threads entangling her could not be severed without cutting her own throat. But it was too late for 'what ifs' and 'maybes' . . .

'those tomorrows done already done past,' Maggie Mae could hear her mother telling her. Of the *tomorrows* yet to come, Maggie Mae had no desire to see any of them.

Elegantè Hostas, bright pink and blood red Crape Myrtles, surrounded the white shell of the Meadows' house– dark purple Jackamani clematises crawled up the lattices on its side. Ghosts of Babylon's hanging gardens would no doubt be jealous if they spied the plants draped like curtains from the second floor with leaves the size of a child's head. Such floral beauty suggested a home of peace and love, though Maggie Mae knew it was all but an illusion crafted by Lucianna.

She didn't hear any white men chatting or moving about the grounds as they usually were. They were sent almost daily from Roman's farm to provide upkeep to the house and his property. Roman's crops and lumber sold briskly, which afforded him the ability to keep the house and its oversized garden meticulously tended, even in the drought now upon Folsom. Lucianna, of course, insisted it would be no other way.

Maggie Mae knew little of Lucianna's past save the rumors that circled about her presently, which she knew more about than she cared to. But of the woman young enough to be Roman's child, she knew what everyone else knew– that Lucianna was a tempting feast of ember red hair upon a snow laden field, with emerald eyes that revealed nothing of the woman inside. She was the embodiment of primal, womanly sex without the warmth.

An almost suffocating aura came about Maggie Mae as she entered the dark foyer. Many times she swore she could feel her skin tingle whenever Lucianna was near. It was such a feeling of unease that she never had, or wanted to become accustomed to experiencing. She was careful not to drag her feet. Once down the hallway, and with a peek into each of the many rooms that broke off from it, she darted into the kitchen. At least among the pots and pans there was light . . . fading though it was; it was better than being in the other parts of the house that were almost perpetually in shadow. Lucianna's command was that all sheers and drapes remained drawn until dusk. "You know my skin cannot tolerate this southern sun," Lucianna would scold, when the drapes were not drawn quick enough in the mornings.

Maggie Mae quickly unpacked the basket and began preparing supper. Two and a half hours before dusk, supper would be steaming on plates in the dining room. One hour before dusk, she would be on her way home. That was the commandment of Roman himself to her *and Lucianna*. Lucianna had protested, complaining that Maggie Mae should stay until whatever chores needed to be completed was finished. But this time, Roman was adamant . . . "the Folsom sun will not set upon Maggie Mae coming from this house!"

Maggie Mae could not say she liked nor disliked Roman. He'd never been hateful or tried to molest her. He'd always insisted that she take leftovers home with her, and if she needed something extra, she was welcome to it. But the strangest thing to her . . . one she could not figure out . . . was that when he looked at her, he did just that. Practice had made her adept at detecting the carnal heat that flashed in the eyes of men when near them, even when her back was turned. She guessed it was a gift/curse from her mother. But never did she detect anything remotely like that from Roman. If there were a white in all of Folsom that she could trust– which she didn't, strangely, he would be the one, she figured. Compared to other white Folsom men, he was about as good as a white man got in these parts– though he wasn't really from Folsom, she remembered, which made her think slightly better of him.

Movement outside the kitchen door shook her back to the task at hand. The aroma of chicken dumplings must have aroused her mistress, she guessed. A quick glance out the window at the sun hovering above the trees in the garden signaled it was nearing time for Roman to arrive home. She retrieved the rose china from their sacred cupboard and the silverware from the drawers. After a few deep breaths to calm herself, she entered the dining room.

Lucianna was already seated at the dining room table. Maggie Mae averted her eyes from those of her mistress, but felt her mistress' gaze upon her. Maggie Mae's skin was past tingling– it was on fire. She went about setting the table, aware that her every step, move of her hand and head was being scrutinized. It was during times like these that she wished Roman would hurry home.

A familiar tapping sound broke the silence. It was Lucianna's nail upon the glass. It was her usual command when she was ready for her evening brew. "Brandy," Lucianna ordered. Her voice was low and husky, but all woman.

"Ma'am," Maggie Mae replied and fetched the contraband liquor. County after county was drying up. Wealthy whites, like the Meadow's, could still afford the best. Poor whites had to go down to Monclair's tavern to imbibe liquor more suitable for cleaning grease and grime off of metal.

She remained next to Lucianna, knowing she would tap twice more after quickly downing the first. Maggie Mae stole a few glances at that which so aroused men about Lucianna. Nearly pouring out of her plunging pink dress was a bosom that required no artificial support to defy gravity. Her milk white breasts still remained smooth and taut enough to deny crepe like skin from taking hold.

Tink-tink!

Maggie Mae filled the glass once again.

As if her prayers were answered for once today, she heard the front door opening. She set the bottle on the table and was about to go and assist Roman, but as she did, there came yet another . . . 'tink'. It was all but a game to Lucianna, Maggie Mae knew. She poured for her mistress again and waited. Instead of simply drinking it down, Lucianna sipped at it instead. Finally, she set her glass on the table and waved Maggie Mae away.

"Ma'am," Maggie Mae said in acknowledgement, and then quickly walked down the hall to meet Roman. "I'm sorry, suh," Maggie Mae mumbled, as she scuttled up to him. She took his wide-brimmed, black hat that and hung it on the wall hook.

"S'alright Maggie," he replied. "Where is she at?"

Maggie Mae turned her head toward the dining room. "At the table, suh." He glanced down the hallway. For a moment Maggie Mae caught sight of his eyes beneath their graying brows before they retreated back into their recesses. "Fresh shirt and britches laid for you on your bed, suh– if you need'em."

"Thank you, Maggie" he said, and walked to the landing of the corkscrew stairway. "I'll be down shortly. Tell her not to wait on me," he added, while ascending the stairs past imported tapestries of woodlands and lakes, where images of forbearers and children were usually hung.

"Yes suh."

It seemed like an eternity to Maggie Mae before Roman made his way to the dining room– especially being alone with Lucianna who had chosen to wait on him to eat. Lucianna tapped the glass again, and as she was about to pour her another, Lucianna caught hold of her wrist. Maggie Mae had to fight the urge to pull away from her. "Look at me, gal," she demanded. Maggie Mae reluctantly looked into those green eyes of hers. "Remember who I am. *You* know what *I* know," Lucianna whispered, and then released her grip, as well as the hardness in her face.

Roman entered the room shortly thereafter dressed in the clothes Maggie Mae had laid out for him. He appeared nothing like the gentleman who owned most of Folsom's best farm and woodland like he had moments ago, but simply as a man in gray britches and a brown shirt he hadn't bothered to tuck in. His closely cropped salt-pepper hair and beard he had trimmed weekly framed his face squarely, which at first glance appeared worn and rugged, yet gentle and warm if he smiled, though he usually didn't. He passed by Lucianna slowly, almost deliberately so, and sat opposite of her at the head of the table.

"A drink, suh?" Maggie Mae asked, trying to stop her voice from quivering.

"Wine please– of the red variety, Maggie– thank you."

Maggie Mae retrieved the bottle from the server's cabinet on the opposite side of the room and poured for him. "Whenever you please, supper is ready, suh."

There was a protracted silence, save the ticking of a clock down the hall. Maggie Mae knew he'd heard her, but his focus was clearly on Lucianna. She watched the watcher. His gaze– or what could be assumed as one beneath eyes hidden by folds of sixty-year old skin was upon Lucianna. "No," he said finally, never veering his line of sight from Lucianna. "Leave the bottle and let us be a moment."

"Suh," Maggie Mae replied, and then quickly walked into the kitchen. She pushed the door closed and pressed her ear upon it, connecting the Negroe gossip extension to the Meadows' home {dialing}. She wondered what she would hear this time. Would Roman admonish her for ordering more silks, linens, lavish dresses, furniture and costly paintings they didn't need? There was no one left in Folsom to impress, he would tell her as usual. So she listened, though she already had an idea what the topic was really about . . . the same one that cropped up every month or two.

"Why do you continue to be who you are?" Roman asked.

"Come now, Roman. What do you mean by *that* . . . suh?"

"You may play ignorant, Lucianna, but I won't– not anymore. Even that part of you refuses to change." His voice hadn't risen, but the tenor of it was like iron striking iron. "I've endured your ways more than any man ever would. Any other decent man would have had you whipped and sent away– if he hadn't cut your throat first just to be done with it all."

"Ahh . . . yet another rumor– eh, Roman?"

"History," he corrected her.

"Who's convinced you this time– Mrs. Barnaby . . . that hideous thing, Delilah Ford? Or was it Jimmy McArthur . . . yes? Maybe it was your right-hand, Wentworth."

"I won't move again– you hear me? You've already sullied my name once. If I have to, I'll set you out with the clothes on your back if you do so in *this* town– which shouldn't trouble you at all. We both know you've travelled that road before."

"You trust the word of your thieving foreman and some piece of white trash, mountain woman over me? Really Roman! I'm rather shocked you would believe such jealous gossip. You know how Wentworth looks at me whenever I'm around– or any other man for that matter. I really did expect more from you."

Roman sighed. "And I from you . . . my sweet, thorny rose. Obviously I have expected more from you than you could ever give. Let us just agree that we have made a horrible mistake– you and I marrying– and save our precious breath pondering the past. I never should've tried dressing up a she-wolf and passing it off as a lady– for a lady you *never* were and a lady you will *never* be."

Silence . . .

. . . and then a crash. Pity the china plate shattered upon the floor, for it was once beautiful and treasured.

Again silence.

Wood upon wood screeched in agony as a chair was shoved suddenly.

Footsteps echoed near and then retreated.

"Maggie!" Roman called.

Maggie Mae entered the room. Only Roman and the shattered china on the floor were present. "Suh?"

His voice remained as smooth as it was the first moment he'd walked into the house. Lucianna's murder of the china had not altered his pitch one iota. "You may serve supper now."

"Yes, suh," she said, and did as instructed.

After sweeping up the china and giving it a proper burial, she returned to the dining room. Roman ate in the same manner he always spoke . . . slowly . . . carefully . . deliberately. It seemed as if he didn't care that he'd just painted his wife as everything but a wife. But it was a poker face he wore, Maggie Mae was fairly sure. She remembered her mother saying how white men were so good at masking their true intent . . *'they smile when they angry on the inside . . . laugh when they 'bout to cut you . . . they sweet talk ya when they plottin' to do ya in.'* But . . . Roman was Roman as Roman ever was. With the closest lawman miles away past Peak Hills, the next town over from Folsom, it was Roman who mediated disagreements between farmers, shop owners or just about anyone who wasn't beholden to Simeon Monclair. His reputation for being fair was solid, whether it involved whites or Negroes, which before Roman came to Folsom, was unheard of for a white man to be.

"Maggie," he called, having finished his meal and two additional glasses of wine. He wiped his mouth, paying close attention to his meticulously trimmed beard and mustache. "Come around so I can see you."

"Suh?"

He folded his cloth napkin back into the triangle that it had been and rested his hands on the table. He leaned forward. "You are a gentle girl, Maggie– young, yet very naïve. But despite you running about here no louder than the mice, I think you are a smart child– no?"

Maggie Mae chanced a look at him, but did not see anger, but something that could quite easily be mistaken for compassion. She didn't know whether to nod or speak or move . . . so she looked down again.

"There are things I know that *you know*," he went on. "Actions . . . events . . . or whatever one would call the . . . let's say '*things*' . . . that are occurring in this house. Or– perhaps not happening– though I think they are. But who am I to say these– these . . .'*things*' are for certain when I have not witnessed them myself?"

She looked at him. He smiled. She shuddered.

"At least you are wise enough not to cross Lucianna. I know you heard what was said before supper."

Maggie Mae nodded.

He leaned back in his chair and seemed to drift away into thought for a moment. "I won't ask you to betray her confidence. I know it's not loyalty that keeps you silent. If you are indeed a smart child, you would have none for her. I know what she is capable of, Maggie. If you did betray her, who's to say that she would not call something down on you that I could not undo or protect you from?"

Warmth fled from Maggie Mae's blood.

He knows! But for how long? She wondered, feeling like she was now star witness for the prosecution and defense. She felt as though she were in yet another web just as binding and inescapable as the first.

"I . . . I can quit, suh," Maggie Mae said finally, half hoping he would fire here right then.

"And do what, child?" His almost nonexistent lips turned down slightly. "There are no jobs in Folsom for a gal like you. Most whites here can barely afford to eat, let alone pay to have someone cook what they don't have. Hard labor in the fields is all there is now, and even my hardiest men are beginning to break under this drought." He was silent for a moment. "Do you have the means to leave?"

Maggie Mae shook her head. "My . . . momma ain't well anyhow, suh"

"Hmm." He nodded. "Enda *is* up there in age, isn't she? I haven't seen her in years."

"Even if I could, where would I go? I don't have any family that I can speak of. And they say the country is goin' into a . . . a . . . ."

"Recession."

"Yes, suh," Maggie Mae agreed. "That means even less jobs for Negroes."

He almost smiled. "Maggie . . . Maggie . . . dear child. You have more options than any Negroe woman . . . if you were to leave." His brows worked their way up his forehead. "Understand, child?"

Maggie Mae didn't need him to elaborate on something she already knew. "Yes, suh."

"You choose to have less by staying here when you could have so much more. Your life would be a much better one if you left. You should think upon these things more," he advised.

"I 'spose once momma passes on, I could save a bit o' money and head north," she wondered out loud.

"Far north. And you wouldn't have to worry about money to get there," he added.

Maggie Mae smiled her thanks. "Negroes do say life in the north is a little better," she continued. "I could maybe find some housework or children to tend to. But I can't take care of both of us with no roof over our head or a scrap of ground to till."

"It seems you've been asked and answered this very question many times before. A husband would do you and your mother best," he suggested. "Surely you have many Negroe men calling upon you?" Roman paused. "*That goes without saying—no?* But you could find a young, sensible Negroe to provide for you. If you married a Negroe that had enough gumption, you wouldn't have to be where you are now."

"Negroe men 'round here ain't got more than what I already got," she replied. "Most likely, I end up takin' care of him."

Roman chuckled. "These are hard times for all." His solemn mood returned as quickly as it left. "Keep yourself as occupied as you can when Lucianna is near."

"Yes, suh."

She began to leave, but he waved at her to remain still. "I don't fault you, Maggie. This matter is between whites. She doesn't have any business putting a Negroe in the middle of it." With that said, he then gave her leave.

Alone and in the safety of the kitchen, Maggie Mae tried to piece together how such an ordinary day had turned so hellish. First there was Mary and her scene at the store, then Lucianna's threats, and now Roman who suspected dark deeds were being committed in his house, but could not prove them without her testimony. She felt bruised on all sides, except there were no physical marks to lay a cool cloth on and soothe. She felt out of breath, yet she hadn't run. She didn't even feel in control of herself, but more like other's hands had slid into her and moved her about as they wished.

With dusk fast approaching, she quickly cleaned the kitchen. Nearly sprinting upstairs, she turned down the *beds* . . . it had been years since Roman and Lucianna slept in the same bed. Next . . . with her hair securely tucked under her headscarf and every bit of her white flesh covered, she moved toward the back door, but paused. She wanted to fall to her knees, but instead squeezed her eyes shut so tight they hurt. "Dear Father . . ." she whispered, but realized she didn't even know where to begin praying. There were so many things that needed fixing, though one patch to one problem left other holes gaping wide. But there was one prayer, that if answered, it would make everything else bearable. She thought upon it, though hated herself for even thinking such a thing. "Forgive me, Lord," she asked. Even knowing he would never be hers again, she couldn't bear the thought of leaving Folsom as long as he remained here. The idea that she would never see him again was inconceivable to her.

Safely at home before the Folsom sun set, strangely, Maggie Mae still felt uneasy. Enda had prepared black-eyed peas, and as a surprise for her, put in a smoked ham-hock. But instead of feeling relaxed and at ease, she was as uncomfortable as she had been earlier standing across from Roman. It seemed to her as though someone was very close– almost standing right next to her. But there was only Enda in the house with her, and she was sitting in a chair on the other side of the room looking out the front window.

She had always assumed she didn't possess the gift that had been passed on for generations through her ancestral mothers, but sometimes she could sense things . . . a presence or a voice . . . a whisper . . . a thought . . . though never clear, it was present for certain. And in the vicinity of her mother, the sense always felt strongest, as if she were leeching some sort of essence from Enda.

It's gotta be momma, she thought. There was a familiar humming in her head like a fading echo. It was the unmistakable, low-pitched hum that had rocked her to sleep for many years. It was the reason, she figured, that memories she wasn't thinking about were suddenly coming to mind– and clearly. Visions of the past with Lar and Mary that she'd thought hidden were suddenly fresh again. But Potter Jackson, of all people, suddenly stepped in front of them as the others faded into mist.

Poor ol' Potter, Maggie Mae thought. She remembered how he had bothered Enda one too many times with his relentless attempts to woo her only daughter . . . showing up with an anemic bouquet of freshly picked black-eyed Susan, marigold and partridge peas, or whatever he could find on his way over, and then always finding a reason to sit by them at church so he could ogle her the entire time.

Finally, Enda told him exactly why he would never court her daughter, she recalled. *"It ain't because you're ugly as a wet rat . . . but you are!"* Enda had said out of the corner of her pink lips. "Ain't 'cause you sawed off at the legs neither. It 'cause you ain't gone *live* long enough to be any kind of a man for my gal. All you do is break her heart." And then, Enda's voice deepened. "You gone die badly, boy. I can smell it in your breath! And if you don't stop comin' 'round here, Enda make sure you die even worse than it gone be!" And poor Potter Jackson did indeed fall ill that following year and lingered in much pain for another, as his body rotted from the inside out.

Potter's mother, father and sister took what few dollars they had and could borrow, and took him to the closest physician who was in Peak Hills. The white doctor stepped out into the alley of his of his office– where he saw all of his Negroe patients– took one look at poor Potter, and then sent him home to die after taking their money, all for him to pronounce that there was nothing to do for Potter.

Ethillene, Potter's mother, who had no love for Enda the witch, as she referred to her, saw no choice but to call upon her out of desperation. On Enda's front porch in the dead of night, Ethillene pleaded with Enda to cure her boy. Enda flatly refused.

"I can't stop death when he already got the boy by the hand," Enda told her. "All I can do now is speed him to where he be goin'– up or down."

"You a witch, Enda Sully!" Ethillene screamed her grief. "You ain't nuthin' but a devil from hell, you bitch! You cursed . . . and I curse you again! And I curse that ol' white bastard chile of yours even more."

But . . . Enda's eyes suddenly opened, though not before her arm had risen and the index finger of her left hand, as though it had never even been bent pointed at Ethillene's chest. Ethillene shuddered, as though she realized she had gone too far in cursing a woman who might know, and possibly could alter her '*tomorrows*'. But instead of retaliating with her own curse, Enda said, "Chile– I been cursed since the day I opened my eyes. I already know where the Lord goin' to send me on judgment day, and that right there is curse enough for anyone . . . already knowin' where they goin' for all time." Enda left her rocking chair and walked toward Ethillene. For every step Enda took forward, Ethillene took two back.

Enda spoke as she walked. "You go and be with your boy. He gonna die quick enough as it be." Enda stopped suddenly and closed her eyes. "Mmm-hmm." She then continued her forward march. "He be gone real soon, Ethillene. You come and get Enda if you needin' him to go sooner . . . help *eassssse* his last breath. You don't want him lyin' twisted up in pain, do ya?" Ethillene was now backed out onto the road. "Pain like he gonna have make a man scream like a babe sometimes. You come on back when you need Ms. Enda, now."

All of these events Maggie Mae remembered with stunning clarity . . . frightened Ethillene . . . Enda's dead-on correct prediction of Potter's last '*tomorrows*' . . . her mother standing out by the road in a nightgown that swallowed her thin bones as she chased Ethillene off . . . herself standing in the doorway watching it all happen at only sixteen years old, and ignorant of the real world and the other world in which her mother lived in. Yes, it was *her* memory . . .

. . . but . . .

. . . she hadn't brought it to mind, she realized.

Maggie Mae began recalling other memories– mundane ones to bury those of Potter and shoo away her uninvited visitor. She recalled planting seeds in the vegetable garden last spring and how the black birds and squirrels dug them up almost as quickly as she had put them in. She remembered cooking a sumptuous meal last Christmas, complete with smoked ham, dressing, thick giblet gravy, baked pigtails . . . a lemon cake. She pulled forth a vision of just bloomed cotton-fields outside of Folsom and their vengeful touch to those who dared to try and steal their prize.

To her relief, she heard the bending of wood from her mother's rocking chair, where before there was silence. Enda had turned her attention elsewhere, she guessed. Maggie Mae dared not sigh in relief. She began to wonder what other of her secret thoughts and memories were being spied on. She hoped that her dreams, which were growing increasingly bizarre . . . red suns and roosters crowing three times and three times only . . . bleeding trees . . . could obscure her most precious memory from Enda.

She ate her dinner at the small table and then took five steps to the left and lay down on her bed. Sleep came to her slowly. Behind the shades of her lids lingered images of Lucianna and Roman– Lar and Mary– and of course, Enda. The darkness showed her the world as it truly was, and she did not like it at all. The darkness gave her visions of love that she would never have– deceptions she had too much of, and an ample amount of envy that she refused to relinquish.

Darkness was her truthful light.

Soon, reality blurred and was replaced with thousands of acres of burning fields and mile long chasms opening up in them. The sky was alight with ethereal flames of yellow, red and orange. She raised her arms and smiled as the conflagration of death barreled down toward her with its teeth bared– and engulfed her and all that was Folsom, Mississippi.

CHAPTER 3

Had she been a rich white woman, Mary figured she could sleep for another hour . . . the sun hadn't even thought about rising yet. If she were just a white woman, maybe she could squeeze in another fifteen or twenty minutes of rest– maybe. But she was neither a rich white woman, nor a white woman, or just a simple woman who didn't have chores to do. All she wanted on a Saturday before morning was to sleep a bit more.

Without having to open her eyes, she knew Lar had already risen and was outside. Though he'd tried not to disturb her as he got up and dressed, the absence of his heat and the sigh of relief from the mattress of its two hundred and thirty pound burden of black muscle, had shaken the last hope of more slumber from her mind. The baby was awake anyway. It was kicking and punching her in places she never knew she had.

She was unable to stop the world from creeping closer. Uncle Matty's light snoring was becoming more like the rumbling of an empty cart. Wood being hacked at the stump outside her window had already commenced . . . her mind's eye could see Lar perfectly – naked to waist as he cleaved the thickest logs in two with a lack-adaisical swing of his arms. Even her own breathing began to sound like a spent horse stung at the ear by its master's whip for a bit more work out of it. Yes– it was time for her to arise, she knew.

She rolled from bed and dressed. Uncle Matty was sure to sleep for a couple more hours at least. He needed his rest more than anyone, she figured. His voice was but a whisper of the steady tenor it once was, and his honey-brown eyes were now swirled with milk. 'Sleep on, ol' man,' she wished.

It was fore-day in the mornin', as folks called it, when she stepped out into the warm southern air. It was as cool as it was going to get today. She followed the sound of metal besting wood until she was around the side of their shack that Uncle Matty had built years ago, and Lar kept standing with a board here and a piece of tin there. She came upon him in mid-swing. Though a sea of just split wood surrounded Lar, his face and bare chest were just now starting to gleam with sweat.

She slowed her waddle to marvel at her ebony god. She questioned for the umpteenth time, why he'd chosen her . . . big, thick and black as tar– as kids used to tease her and some adults, too, she caught wind of . . . she of all women, he'd chosen to wed and bear his child . . . and to love.

She felt they were so different in almost every way.

Whereas he was handsome, beautiful even . . . Mary knew she was not even plain looking. She realized her shoulders and hips were too thick and wide to turn a man's head her way, unless it was for comparison. Lar's shoulders were striated muscle upon muscle, and his waist tight and slim from years of lifting, plowing and hauling at Meadow's farm.

Lar loved God.

She despised God most of the time.

But she never wondered how she could love such a man who saw the world so differently than she did. The question was . . . how could she not love him? When they made love, she always felt as though she was close to losing all sense of who she was. In the midst of ecstasy, she felt as womanly and as beautiful, and more satisfying than any woman who'd ever lived. It was that he looked at her in those sacred moments– never were his eyes closed in dreams of another. She never had a doubt it was she and she alone in his thoughts. And after– when they were too weak to even speak, she felt his eyes looking not at her, but disturbingly into her, for it seemed as though he saw her more clearly and deeply than she did herself.

She came close enough to draw his attention. Lar raised the axe above his head, paused and looked at her, and then swung. Mary didn't expect a warm greeting. Neither did she the night before when he arrived to bring her home from the Monclair house.

She had little doubt her spectacle at the Monclair store had already reached his ears. If Allie Mae hadn't spread the word, she was certain the whites that were in the store had already exaggerated what happened and spread it far and wide, as they normally did when a Negroe was involved. By the time the last white heard the story, if she didn't have Delilah pinned right down on the floor she would be surprised.

But Lar never mentioned anything about it. In fact, he never said more than a few words to her during the ride home. Only Uncle Matty, having just swallowed a mouthful of watery chicken broth, hinted about it as they ate supper. "So gal, anythin' happen your way today?"

She sneered at him, and then ripped her piece of bread in two before dunking it in her broth. "'Bout the same as the day before . . . uncle." And that was all that was said about that, that night.

But whatever Lar had thought about it seemed to have cured in his mind by the next morning, she figured, for suddenly, having cocked the axe above his head and ready to attack another defenseless log, he stopped and laid it to the side. Sensing the tide coming for her, she spoke before he could. "I'm just as much a woman as any white, Negroe or mulatta!" she proclaimed. "I ain't gonna let some craggly-face, white woman treat me like I ain't even there 'cause she still hot 'bout that piece of nuthin' husband of hers."

"That be neither here or there, Mary" Lar replied calmly, as she expected. "You and me know it ain't right, but that just the way it be."

"I ain't gon' live my life like that. You know that for a fact, Laurence Cole."

"No one sayin' you have to. I don't want you to neither. But you ain't gonna change the way Delilah feel 'bout Negroes neither. All you gonna do is stir up a hornet's nest."

"So what you want me to do then . . . huh? Be they slave again? What Meadow's pay you and Monclair pay me, it 'bout the same as working for nothing anyhow. So since things be the way they be– as you say, I just suppose to let Delilah treat me any ol' way?"

Lar shook his head. "It don't ever matter what happen, Mary. It never matter how it begin– only how it end up. And in Folsom, 'truth' never end up on a Negroe's side."

She folded her arms and rested them on her belly. "So do what then? And don't say pray, Laurence Cole!"

It was a sorrowful smile Lar gave her– one that nearly melted her heart. Instead of defending that which he loved and trusted the most, he took the log off the stump and sat down. The glow of the rising sun bathed his body from behind, making him appear as though he exuded light.

Her words had hurt him deeply, she realized.

It . . . *He* . . . *She* . . . *God* . . . she knew was his greatest strength *and* weakness. Standing before his aura of silence, she wished she could take back the words. She realized, as the silence lingered, that the wound she'd sought to inflict upon him was actually upon her. She loved him more than anything because he loved her for who she was. A good man he was and had always been, yet anger and vengeance had goaded her to lash out at him. She felt wicked.

Ashamedly, she could find little distinction between herself and Delilah Ford at the moment. Mary was about to step to him but stopped when he began speaking. The warmth of his voice, which she knew she didn't deserve, froze her where she stood.

'Be angry, dammit! Swear . . . curse . . . don't be kind, Lar!' she wanted to yell at him.

You can't change how the world be," he said softly, and then paused as he looked down at her belly. "I hate that you and the baby have to walk around with your head down from white folk . . . being scared to do what be right, and ashamed 'cause you have to do what you know be wrong sometime. Maybe I can't look a white man in the eye, but I sho' ain't gonna bow down to him . . . you know that, Mary," he said with conviction, "but I ain't gonna bring harm across the river tryin' to change a world that ain't ready to change."

When she replied, the edge of her blade had dulled. "Whether whipped or sent to the back of the line just 'cause I black . . . hell, Lar– it pain me all the same. Ain't no difference to me. If I can't be proud of Mary Cole, then I done lost everything."

"Well you ain't ever gonna lose me, gal," he replied, and then gave her a smug grin.

Mary wished that he would stop looking at her with those half-closed, brown eyes of his. She didn't want him to see her right now. She opened her eyes as wide as she could to dry the tears beginning to pool in them. Her hands began to shake, which she quickly placed on her belly and feigned caressing it. "I gonna see if those ol' hens done laid some eggs," she told him. Those few words were all she could muster before moving out of his line of sight toward the hen house.

She shooed the thoughts in her head away as gracefully as she did the chickens that flew hither and fro, and cried bloody murder upon her entry into their domain. "Just like white folk– cluckin' and flappin, and in the way doin' nuthin," she muttered at them.

And before she could fully right herself amidst the flurry of feathers and chickens running for their lives, the rooster crowed louder than she'd ever heard him crow before.

Mary collected the eggs into her pocket and returned to her own coop. Lar had already resumed splitting wood. Trying to submerge Lar's last words beneath a layer of mundane tasks was fruitless ... *'you ain't ever gonna lose me gal.'* Even as she cracked eggs into a bowl and whipped them fluffy, sliced the bread, woke up Uncle Matty and rubbed his legs down, Lar's words kept ringing in her ear. It was rage at white folks that had fueled her stubbornness that day in the Monclair store. What words she'd spoken were not meant solely for Delilah, but for all white folks– Delilah had only provided the opportunity. Delilah's disgust of Negroes was no different that most other whites in Folsom, she assumed.

How whites and Negroes could both learn from the same Good Book, yet see things so differently, bewildered her. Lar preached of the Lord's kindness and love, not man's judgments and punishments that were influenced with money, a powerful last name or white skin. *Ain't no tellin' whose bible those white folk readin' from,* she thought. Was it one that said grind Negroes into the dust? She wondered. Beat a Negroe if he looks you in the eye? Keep Negroes off the street at night? They best have a white man say so if we do catch them past dark. Make Negroes live on almost useless soil and sell them sickly animals to till it? Keep Negroes out of the front of your store unless with a white? Kill Negroes if you feel like it? All of these things Mary saw in almost every white eye ... *but ...*

"*Paul,*" she thought.

For the second time that morning it felt as though a weight had been placed on her chest. What she saw in the eyes of whites ... in the eyes of Delilah Ford ... she didn't in Paul's blue ones, which had been stripped of their innocence long ago. In her heart, she held hope that he would be a white who would always show kindness toward Negroes. Yet, she knew such kindness that would make him capable of showing compassion toward Negroes would also be his weakness. Simeon had already made it clear that Paul would never succeed him or inherit his influence over Folsom. Paul was to be left to his own devices unless he changed, and *that* she could not see happening.

A burst of sunlight through the kitchen window was a welcome sight– its warm, cleansing rays melted away dark, cold thoughts that she could not force from her mind. Each rising sun and moon meant one more day closer to seeing her child. If nothing else in the world changed for the better, there was always comfort that her child was still living inside her, and that hope was more filling than any meal that ever settled in her stomach.

She had breakfast on the table when Lar entered. He was finally dripping with sweat and found a rag to wipe down with before slipping on his shirt. She had just called to Uncle Matty to hurry up, but he had yet to emerge from his room. "Best go check on him," Lar said, as he sat down at the table.

"'Spose so," Mary agreed, and called Uncle Matty again before lightly rapping on his wafer thin door.

She heard ruffling on the other side and then heard him. "Can't seem to get down . . . grab for my britches."

Mary had no sooner opened the door before Lar was up and moving her to the side. They came unto the sight of Uncle Matty sitting on the edge of his dingy gray, flattened mattress with his pants still on the ground by his quivering ankles. His breaths were but wisps of air. Perhaps it was the sight of Mary and Lar rushing for him that drained what strength he had left, that made him suddenly begin to tumble forward.

Mary caught him with one hand on his chest and the other around his arm. She was strong enough to stop his forward momentum, but it was Lar's strength that lifted Uncle Matty effortlessly up and securely back on the bed. "Should've said somethin' sooner, Uncle Matty!" she snapped, though her face was contorted in concern, not irritation.

"Didn't reckon I couldn't . . ." He started and then lost his breath. " . . . pull'em up."

Mary sat beside him to catch her own breath. When there was no baby and swollen legs and feet that shrank and swelled day to day, such an exertion would not have even caused her to pause. But the rush of adrenalin and the quick step across the room to Uncle Matty was all it took to wind her. "You need to slow down, too, Mary," Lar told her. He kneeled down and began working Uncle Matty's legs through the pants and pulled them up. Mary leaned back and rested on the palms of her hand. She looked at Uncle Matty, who through exhaustion managed a toothless smile for her. She grasped his hand and felt it quivering, but somehow he managed to squeeze back.

Lar finished what Uncle Matty had started. As if handling a bundle of twigs, Lar lifted Uncle Matty to his feet and leaned him against his chest while he wiggled the britches up and secured them about his bony waist. Mary had moved to help, but Lar simply shook his head, telling her without a word . . . *'sit yore tail down!'*

"I give you a bath early today," Mary said. "I make it warm to soothe those bones . . . it draw out that soreness that done seeped up in'em."

Uncle Matty looked at her and blinked several times. "Ain't Saturday already, is it?"

"It past daybreak and you ain't out in the fields, now *is* you?" Mary sassed, feeling more herself again.

Lar sat Uncle Matty on the bed next to Mary and left to find a shirt for him. "Don't make me run out and find a switch and tear your rump up, gal. Hummpf! Been a day when *I* dressin' folk . . . massa and his chilin', and then you too!" Uncle Matty said. "Still 'member clear as day, um-hmm."

Lar returned with a shirt and slipped it on Uncle Matty. Mary's nose wrinkled. "That your shirt you just worn?" she asked.

"The other day," Lar replied innocently.

"Sakes alive, man!" Mary spat. "Why you ain't found a clean one? That one so strong it can get up and walk right out the door."

Lar ignored her part real and part feigned outrage at the malodorous shirt. He lifted Uncle Matty to his feet and held him until his arthritic knees found strength enough not to buckle. "I gonna pull in the washtub soon as we done eatin'. Ain't gonna matter what he wear now 'til then," Lar said.

Mary pushed off the bed to her feet. "Well, I 'spose I need to scrub some clothes before I wash him anyway. And that shirt you just put on him gonna be the first one in the tub, too."

Lar led Uncle Matty to the table where their breakfast lay cooling.

"You goin' on up to Allie Mae's after you done with Uncle Matty?" Lar asked, as he took his seat and took up his fork anew.

Mary surveyed her home . . . four walls and a large closet called Uncle Matty's bedroom . . . she shrugged. "If I get this mess here straightened up and swept out, and can pull those weeds stranglin' my tomato plants out back, I just might make it down there this afternoon."

"What you women be up to anyway?" Lar asked, as Mary sat down in front of her own meal. He even gave her a wink. "We ain't seen a drape or a robe one ya'll 'spose to be sewin' up. Ain't seen *a one!* So what ya'll call yourselves doing over there?"

Mary smiled . . . took a bite of scrambled eggs and chewed leisurely . . . looked at Lar and then spoke as she was now feeling *good and ready* to respond. "No man's business."

Lar shook his head. "Women folk always up to no good. Secrets and whisperin' and mess."

"You *men folk* ain't no better," she countered in jest. "Half the time we look out and ain't but a couple of ya'll workin' on that ol' church– the rest of ya'll standin' 'round jawin'. All I see is that floorboard you be standin' on every Sunday. *I* ain't seen a wall or window to hang a curtain from ... hummpf!" she snorted. "So while us women be cacklin' ... *as ya'll say* ... what you men be crowin' 'bout?"

"Ya'll boys do be flappin' ya'll lips a little too much," Uncle Matty added.

"Well you can stay up with the women since we be talkin' too much for ya," Lar teased. "But as far as I remember, you be doin' the most yappin' of all ... always got a story and ain't ever told the same one twice."

Mary laughed. "Amen."

"Gotta make sure ya'll 'member who you be, where we came from and what we done been through to get here– alright?" Uncle Matty stated.

"My back tell me all that and more ... every single day," Lar said.

"Amen!" Mary added, though this time not so jovial.

Lar took hold of their hands. Mary and Uncle Matty did the same. A hush ensued and was broken only by Lar's prayer over their meal. He asked for blessings for Uncle Matty, Mary, and their child. He begged the Lord to watch over *all* of the denizens of Folsom– Negroe and white. He pleaded for understanding and awakening of the soul to be his and all those around him. Mary only agreed with half of what he prayed for and felt that was good enough. She knew he took the Holy Word literally. If he hadn't, she knew there was no way she could love him as deeply as she did, for in her eyes, he would be no better than the whites who preached the same words as he did, yet acted contrarily. So she only prayed for the half she felt was right, and basked in the comfort of Uncle Matty's touch— and Lar's, the man who loved her.

* * *

The two windows in Mary's house had steamed up from boiling water on the stove. She opened both to let some of the heat escape and return from whence it had come, albeit in a different manner. Before heading into the garden, Lar had pulled the washtub in and brought buckets of water for her to heat on the stovetop. With the last pan of water heated and the bath water slightly hotter than tepid to soothe old, thin skin, she emptied the last kettle into a cauldron of lye-soap induced bubbles and called Lar in to lift Uncle Matty into the tub.

As Uncle Matty soaked in the tub, Mary went after cleaning the house. It was far easier to clean than the Monclair's, as her entire house could fit into two of the Monclair's smaller rooms. It took but a few minutes to sweep the kitchen and a few more sacred moments to scare the dust bunnies out from under Uncle Matty's bed. She was cautious when it came to the few *nice* pieces of furniture that had once been *nice* furniture in white homes. After being discarded by whites and then repaired by Lar, they became her *nice* furniture. In a cabinet set as far away from the cast iron stove that often billowed black smoke when clogged, she kept her precious linens, needles, thread and yarn.

A freestanding closet Lar had proudly crafted kept dresses, shirts, britches and his two Sunday suits. Both black suits, made by the skillful hands of Allie Mae, were still in good condition. After ten years of wear, they should have been rags by now, but Lar only slipped them on when necessary— Sunday sermons, funerals and weddings— and immediately shucked them when he had finished relaying God's words. Though the church was set in the shade of the woodland it buttressed, the southern heat drove an unceasing river of sweat from him and yellowed his white shirts that only boiling them in lye could clean. It was just the way things were– as everything was– as everything should be, she thought.

"You 'bout ready for a scrubbin'?" Mary asked, as she pulled up from her knees after wiping the floor clean beneath the stove.

Uncle Matty didn't answer. His mouth was agape and his eyes half-closed with only the whites showing. Low, steady breathing fluttered his lips like the wings of a weary butterfly.

She gathered a washrag, soap, a comb and a brush, and then pulled a chair up beside the dinged-up washtub. She leaned in close to Uncle Matty . . . waited and listened until she was satisfied he wasn't playing possum, and then leaned back and closed her eyes.

She grew fatigued easier each day. Yet, there were so many things left to do for a Negroe woman who took care of white folks and their children, a husband and uncle, and if she had time, her-self. With her eyes closed and ears pricked up, she could hear . . . Lar fighting with the horses to plow-up new ground . . . a wagon off in the distance nearing and then fading . . . women's voices as they walked past– faint, then loud, then faint once more. The sight of her mother, Sarah, walking toward her told Mary now that she was drifting away into sleep, and she welcomed it, if only for just a moment.

A gentle touch and even gentler voice woke her.

"Chile– scratch my head a spell for me," Uncle Matty mumbled, with eyes still half closed.

Mary wet the washrag and then his hair, loosening the bonds of his thumb size, curly gray locks. She lathered up her hands with the bar of soap and added the bubbles to his hair. She massaged his scalp gently. He cooed his thanks.

"I done told you some 'bout me . . . and you know lots cause I raised ya when my sistah' passed on," Uncle Matty said. "But there be a bit more you needin' to know. It be that time you know these thangs so you can tell yore little thang when it come."

"Did you go and ask *her*?"

Uncle Matty sighed. "I ain't got more than a spell more to work in them fields for Mr. Meadows. I can feel it– *I been told*," he whispered.

Mary stopped rubbing his head and leaned into him. Her voice, at first urgent, was now defeated. "It ain't right knowing your 'to-morrows'. It just ain't."

Uncle Matty ignored her and continued speaking. "My sistah . . . your mammy, Sarah. My Tira . . . she be dead now, too . . . my pappy, Joe Handy and my mammy, Sue– all done passed on, chile. Yes, Lord– Lord– Lord. It won't be long for the rest of us neither."

Mary's response was silence, but her mind lapped at the names of those she'd never known or was too young to remember. She parted his hair and slipped the teeth of the comb in it, and scrubbed lightly at the rows of hairs jutting from their follicles.

"My hair don't be as nappy as most Negroe, you know. And I ain't as dark as other Negroes neither. Used to be 'high yella' 'fore I start workin' the fields. It all be on account of who my pappy be. Not Joe Handy– though he be the pappy that raised me . . . but a mulatto . . . Judah be his name, though he ain't never once claimed me. I know this 'cause my mammy, Sue, told me when she knew it couldn't do nobody no harm. See . . . Judah be mistah Christianson's boy . . . heh– heh– heh!" Uncle Matty opened his eyes and looked at her. "Now don't be runnin' your lips tellin' Ms. Isabel who her half-brother be now . . . or her ol' Negroe nephew sittin' in this tub and you scrubbin his head– hear me, gal?"

"Sakes alive!" Mary gasped.

"Ol' mistah Christianson love him some Negroe women. Chile . . . what you don't know'll knock you for a loop– heh– heh– heh! Now, listen, chile. I ain't never done told you 'bout the beginnin' of our freedom, has I?" he asked.

"Chile– after the war ended, white folk went and paid ol' black tree a visit. Me, Tira and Sarah saw what nobody should ever see . . . but it was meant for Negroes to see, alright. We done seen what a man can do when the devil get up in him and stir up some hate. They had five, six, seven . . . I forget how many niggahs they had swingin' from ol' black tree, like rickety ol' branches 'bout to break off. Don't gotta ask why they killed them . . . just know white folk payin' back a Negroe for wantin' to be free and makin' a war that done nearly kill them all off. You be a Negroe woman– don't matter none neither . . . they have you swingin' in the breeze, too.

"But," he went on, "there be some true, God-fearin' white folk out there, too, ya hear? The kind Lar speak 'bout. And you know that boy don't lie. So you stop bein' huffy all the time and listen to him now and then. I know your mouth, missy!

"Well anyhow . . . we lyin' out in the backwoods one mornin', 'bout to get to fixin' some more on these ol' shacks we done put together, and your mama Sarah say, Matty, your Tira done gone leakin', and we know that youngin' be comin' real soon.

"We leave out quick with Tira, and I know only one place to go and that be to see Enda Sully, 'cause she know 'bout birthin'.

Uncle Matty opened his eyes slightly. He looked up at Mary who had become stone at the mention of Enda's name. "Ol' Enda ain't be like she be now," he added.

"I 'member first time I saw Enda Sully. Lord know I swore that woman be white. But she be what you call a quadroon– more white than just half. Ain't like that Maggie Mae of hers who look just like white folk– just *allllll* white. We figure Maggie Mae pappy be some white man."

"And who that be?" Mary asked, trying not to sound as interested in knowing as she really was.

Uncle Matty closed his eyes and mumbled.

"Who?"

"Enda Sully not say. Enda Sully never say nuthin' 'bout that gal's pappy– and ain't none of our business then . . . or now. So never you mind." Mary hadn't heard him talk that way to her since she was a child who needed a switch to the backside now and again.

His voice lowered and smoothed once again as he continued. "Enda always be right kind to us. When we need help, Enda Sully always been there for us . . . anytime!

"And even after Tira and my baby boy passed on, I ain't ever blamed Enda for it, 'cause I there when Enda Sully workin' on 'em, only can't nuthin' be done. If Sarah be here right now, she sho' give witness! Fever caught Tira a few days before my boy came. Enda try with that stuff in them jars and some mess she had Tira drink, but ain't none of that help none. Enda say when it all be over, it just meant to be that way, 'cause if it wasn't, she still be here. Don't really know if it meant to be or not meant to be . . . it just happened."

He sighed and then remained silent for a moment. And then . . . he smiled. "You should of seen you, though! I know how you feel 'bout Enda and Maggie Mae. Ain't always be like that though. You 'member, gal?"

"I try not to," she mumbled, as she rinsed the soap out of his hair.

Uncle Matty laughed deep, bringing mucus up from his lungs and began choking. Mary quickly leaned him forward and forcefully thumped his back until his voice cleared and his breathing returned to its usual, raspy rail. "What you mean you try not to? Huh?! Been a time you the first to say how much you love Ms. Enda."

Mary's was intending to wring the washrag dry, but ended up strangling it until her hands began to ache. "I don't remember any of that mess, Uncle Matty."

Uncle Matty looked at her and lowered his head. "Hummpf! You sho' is becomin' forgetful in your ol' age, gal."

"My mind be just fine– thank you."

"We owe a lot to that mulatta, only you can't see it yet."

"She ain't right and you know it too!" Mary countered. "You ask any folk 'round here and they tell you the same. Don't nobody know where she be from, how she got here, or what she be doin' up there fore-day in the mornin' in those backwoods she tell everybody to stay out of."

"Chile, all that mess don't matter!" he croaked. "Enda loved you like you her own. She learned you to read and write and how to talk like you got some sense in your head. You the one done turned your back on her."

Mary's fumbled to find words to respond, but when she did, they were too numerous and clogged her mouth. Finally two words did slip through. *"Uncle Matty!"*

"Uncle Matty, what?!"

"After what she done did?" Mary wasn't really sure whether she was asking herself or him. "She . . . that . . . she never wanted me to marry, Lar." She stared at the back of his head for a moment, and then rose from her chair and rounded the washtub to look at him directly. "You always say Lar be like a son to you . . . I be like a daughter to you . . . and you say this to *ME?* You know Enda wanted Lar for Maggie Mae. And if she had her way, they be married right now."

"Lord . . . you like your pappy more than Sarah when it come to thinkin' 'bout things." He paused. "Lar the best man here in Folsom. Lord God strike me dead if I be wrong 'bout it. He ain't ever gonna beat a woman, yell at her, or make her do somethin' she ain't want be doin'. He preach the word and live it like a man 'spose to– and that more than I can say 'bout other Negroe and white folk 'round here. That man work like a dog day in, day out, and ain't complained not a lick 'bout it. He just want you and me to be seen to. Roof over our head ain't leakin', is it? He done boarded up this ratty-tat shack best he can, and it keep the cold off our toes, too. And he don't mind none you speak like a man do!" he stressed. "Hummpf! Ain't too many mens gonna put up with a woman like that, neither."

"If Lar be so good, how can you say what you say to me?" Mary asked, as her voice followed her head and began to cool.

"Chile . . . I want you to be with the best man you can be with . . . and that be Lar. No other!" he told her. "Why you think it wrong for Enda not to want him for Maggie Mae then? Don't you think she want her gal to be loved by the best Negroe she can find, too?" he asked. "You think nothin' more 'bout Enda 'cept she be a witch doin' thangs that ain't right with the Lord, but you ain't think she be a woman and mammy to Maggie Mae, too! Enda know what kind of life that child gonna live the second she saw all that white skin on her. Ain't help none neither she be so pretty. She want the best for her chile, same as I. Now what 'bout that you ain't understandin'?"

"I understand that," she lied, hoping he couldn't tell that she had never thought of it that way. "But . . . but you know she meddled. I know she tried."

Uncle Matty laughed– and paired it with a smirk and a glare at her. "You be tryin' to talk 'round me, but I ain't that old, gal." He laughed anew as Mary's hands mounted her hips. "Enda ain't did what you think she done did, chile! I can see it in your eyes right now . . ." He then growled, ". . . *you think she put a root on Lar, don't ya?* Huh? A root for love."

There was no reason to try and hide her suspicions now, she knew. "You just said that mess 'bout Enda wantin' the best man for Maggie Mae and what she gonna do to have it."

"See now, if you listen to the gospel your Lar preach, you know you best never do what you talkin' 'bout," he said. "You don't ask the Lord to make a man want you– devil neither! 'Cause Lord won't listen . . . and if the devil do, it ain't goin' be right no way. Heartache and pain be all you get from thangs the devil give ya', 'cause it ain't natural. And believe me, chile, I done seen Enda do those thangs, and that why even white folk won't mess with her. They know she can do thangs and they scared of her. But chile . . . if Enda had put a root on Lar, we sho'nuff be sittin' here alone . . . just a you and me, gal . . . and your man be down there with Maggie Mae Sully– but they never be happy together."

The truth of it all seeped in quicker than Mary could sort it out. For years she had convinced herself that Enda had tried to interfere with her courtship and later marriage to Lar with roots and herbs, and all those unnamed things sitting in jars on her shelves. It never crossed her mind that it was simply a mother's love that drove Enda to do the things she did . . . which was nothing, if Uncle Matty spoke true. It was easier to hate Enda for things she knew the woman was capable of, and harder to forgive her for the things, she was now coming to realize, Enda had never even done.

"I best get you outta that messy water for dirt been done sank back on in," she uttered in defeat.

* * *

Uncle Matty nodded.

He realized he had said too much, but knew Mary had to hear it before it was all left unsaid. He could hear death calling his name every morning, and with each passing day, its voice grew louder and its presence closer. No one needed to know about the pain in his chest becoming more frequent, or how the heat nearly stole his breath whenever he moved about, he felt. Other than Mary's child being born, death was his most anticipated event . . . *his last* . . . and he smiled at the thought of it coming for him. But there was 'learnin' to do first. He recalled Enda telling him what he had to do for the child– Mary, before he left this world. And he had no reason to doubt the words of the only woman other than Tira that he ever loved.

* * *

Mary knew a bit of her mother and Uncle Matty's past, but many of the details, she realized now, had been purposefully hidden from her. While Negroes were building their homes on the outside of Folsom, Sarah had made her stay at the Monclair's to take care of the newlyweds. She had little memory of what happened in those days, weeks and months after most of the men came home from war. Her mother, Sarah, had died . . . yes . . . Uncle Matty had taken her in and raised her as his own daughter . . . yes . . . Enda saw to her while Uncle Matty was off working the fields . . . yes . . . no . . . yes? The search for answers to her past always seemed to come back to the same house . . . the same woman . . . Enda Sully. Still, the connection between herself and Enda was only slightly clearer to her now than before.

Her earliest memories of Enda were sitting at her table under the glow of candlelight with Maggie Mae, a toddler on one side, and Lar, the oldest on the other. Enda was at the head teaching from cracked and ripped books that had long since lost any color they once had. Amongst other gifts that she possessed, Enda was a learned woman of many things. How? Mary had no idea, and as far as she knew before this morning, no one else did either . . . but she had an inkling that Uncle Matty still possessed some knowledge of Enda that he was not willing to part with.

After washing and rinsing Uncle Matty, Mary went to the door to call Lar to come and help lift him out of the tub. *Ain't no reason to fool 'round and put my back out when I ain't gotta,* she reasoned. She opened the door, but didn't get a chance to holler for him– Picken, who drove the wagon in to town each morning was running straight toward their house and rousing up a dirt cloud in his wake. She was about to tease him for running like a duck, as his feet prominently angled outward, but the look of urgency on his face told Mary it wasn't the time for loving jabs.

"What be wrong?" she asked before he even made it to the porch.

Picken stumbled up the two steps of the porch. He walked over to Mary and grasped the frame of the door with one hand and rested the other on his knee. His dark brown eyes were the size of skipping rocks– his mouth hung open wide enough to swallow each whole. "Peak Hills . . . Ms. Mary," he sputtered. "There be trouble there last night."

Mary turned and spied Lar slowly walking off the fields toward them and waved at him to hurry. Uncle Matty called out his concern. "I don't know, uncle," she hollered to him. "Somethin' 'bout trouble in the Hills down over."

She grabbed Picken by the hand and sat him in Lar's rocking chair. The wooden chair swallowed him as he collapsed into it. "Sit a spell 'til Lar come– hear?!"

"Yes'm," he answered.

She waved with increased fervor to Lar again. "Hurry up, Lar . . . boy say they be trouble next town over!"

Lar's fast walk was suddenly transformed into a sprint. He had the porch creaking under his boots within seconds. In the distance, a few hundred feet away, the wind was heavy with Lar's name. Mary and Lar both looked in the direction of Terry Lee's house, their closest neighbor, and saw that he and his wife, Bertie, were hustling toward them. Lar, however, didn't wait for Terry Lee and Bertie to arrive before questioning a still winded Picken. "What be goin' on, boy?" Lar asked. His magnified silhouette shrouded Picken in shade as he stood in front of him.

"Niggah man came bucklin' through here to get a wheel fixed on his wagon at Mr. Pete's shop . . . had a whole load full of niggahs with him, too," Picken said, and then paused for a few quick breaths. "He say white folk done strung up a niggah boy in the Hills for stealin' chickens . . . but . . . he says white folk say now he done tried to push himself up on a white woman, too!"

Lar lowered to one knee and moaned as his bones creaked. Even kneeling, he was still more than a head above Picken and had to look down. "Which it be, boy . . . done stole chickens or the white woman?"

"Don't rightly know, Mr. Lar," Picken replied. "Ol' niggah say they even *ah-cusin'* him of settin' fires, too." He looked up at Mary. "Didn't stay long– that ol' man. He got his wheel fixed and tore off. He say he getting' his family folk outta the Hills 'fore they come for him, too."

"White folk!" Mary cursed.

The wind again brought Lar's name around.

Bertie made it up on the porch and was scuttling over to Mary. "Girl, what be happenin'?" Bertie asked. Terry Lee, her husband, whose hair was as vividly gray as Bertie's was black, eventually made his way up the steps and onto the landing.

"They done lynched some Negroe over in Peak Hills . . . from what the boy sayin'," Mary replied.

"Lord Jesus!" Bertie gasped. She took hold of Mary's hand and squeezed.

"What now?" Terry Lee asked, having joined the group late. "Say again. Who done did what to who?"

Lar moved Picken out of the rocking chair so that Terry Lee could rest his near sixty-year old bones. "Hell . . . that boy ain't done nuthin' to no white woman," Terry Lee proclaimed. "Ain't no Negroe in his right mind gonna do somethin' like that . . . 'les they *ain't* in they right mind. This be just a excuse for white folk. That all it be!"

"Mmm-hmm," Mary agreed heartily.

"What about the chickens then? Ya'll think he stole them?" Bertie asked. Her tearing eyes darted to Lar, Mary, Terry Lee, and then back to Lar.

Lar walked over and sat on the edge of the porch where Picken had taken up residence. "You steal a button from white folk, you be lucky to leave with your hand still on your arm. If the boy stole, it make sense . . . if you think like white folk . . . that a Negroe who steal done did other thangs too," he said.

"White folk gonna make a reason for it anyhow," Mary said. "Don't matter what you done did or if you ain't done nuthin' at all."

"Right– right– right," Lar chanted.

"Folk gatherin' at the church, Mr. Lar," Picken said. "They waitin' for you."

Lar didn't respond immediately. It was if he was still chewing on what had happened and was procrastinating about swallowing. "It be the same as last time . . . they ain't gonna hear nothin' new from me."

Bertie lowered her head and shook it side to side. "That poor– poor chile . . . Lord help."

"They need you, Lar," Mary told him. Still holding Bertie's hand, Mary raised it up. " . . . to hold they hand and let them know it gonna be alright."

Lar turned and faced Mary, Terry Lee and Bertie. He turned back around as Picken took hold of his hand and leaned his head on his chest. Lar looked down into Picken's large brown eyes and then hugged him tight. Lar stood and then began walking hand-in-hand with Picken toward the church. He looked up to the sky, but it was clear, silent and unmoving.

CHAPTER 4

The shade from the trees surrounding the wood foundation of the church did little to provide Lar comfort from the heat. There was no breeze to help evaporate sweat that dripped from his forehead and soaked his clothes. There was a mass of black faces gathering before him that was growing by the moment. The buzzing of the crowd was close to driving him insane. Mouths moved, hands waved and wrung . . . women cried . . . men scowled in anger. The same words rose again and again from the growing sea of weary waters . . . *Lar . . . Negroe . . . boy . . . lynched . . . murdered . . . Lar . . . again . . . white folk . . . rape . . .Lar . . . killed . . . again!*

Lar knew nothing else to do but pray for guidance and comfort. But how could there be?" he wondered. How could he tell his people that things would be all right, when he didn't believe it himself? He was feeling exactly what they were . . . despair and fear . . . anger and hopelessness– a *shade* called revenge wiggled its way through his thoughts at times. He felt ashamed that he was all they had as a leader and a man of God. Still, he held up his hand and hushed the crowd.

He was about to speak, but paused. He looked over the crowd and saw something he hadn't seen since he was a child. Making their way up the dirt road and across the small field were Mary and Maggie Mae . . . almost side-by-side . . . almost. Though sunlight distorted their figures, there was no mistaking Mary . . . tall . . . wide . . . looming– her dark skin glistening next to Maggie Mae's nearly washed out white skin. Their entrance into the crowd was enough to momentarily distract everyone, including Lar, from the reason all were gathered, for all knew of the love and hate that inextricably bound the two women and the holy man.

Lar waited until both women were settled in front of the crowd. Maggie Mae was blushing. Mary held her head high and smiled at Lar, and then surreptitiously nodded at him. Such a simple gesture of love was enough to strengthen his mouth, his mind, his will, which urged him to thank God for the thousandth time for having given her to him.

Lar raised his right hand once more. He bowed his head and began praying. "Our Father, who art in heaven . . ."

A man's voice pierced the air. "We don't need no prayers, Laurence Cole! We need some action . . . hear me! Ya'll best listen up! Ya'll hear what . . . "

Lar continued praying as the man kept ranting, and soon was joined by a chorus of fellow worshipers that drowned out the instigating voice, which had no choice but to diminish to a whisper, and then to nothing at all. When the prayer was ended, silence returned. *Death* was now the untouchable . . . unseen . . . yet present figure in their midst who struck fear in young and old . . . wise and foolish . . . *Destiny, Circumstance* and *Opportunity* stood in the back and waited to make their entrance.

"There ain't much we know for sure," Lar said, loud enough for the ones in the back to hear. "We do know a boy from Peak Hills done been lynched if what Picken and Pete Baker say be true."

A fellow field worker of Lar's, Jeremiah Lewis spoke up. "White folk been lynchin' more and more– Alabama, Georgia, Florida, and ya'll know they done gone crazy here in Mississippi doin' it. I believe it true, too!" The crowd agreed with boisterous rumbles of 'amens'.

"Ain't no way we can be entirely sure what done happened exactly 'til we hear from more Negroes out from there. We bound to know more sooner as more of them leave," Lar told them. "Ain't but a few ways outta Peak Hills, and comin' through Folsom be one of them."

"And ain't no Negroe foolish 'nough to go there now either," Esther Collins stated. She was a housekeeper at the Monclair motel when they had guests, which meant she didn't work there much at all.

"Amen, sister . . . amen," Lar agreed, with a fierce shake of his head. He pointed to the crowd and swept his finger back and forth at them. "Don't nobody need to be goin' there 'til all this mess be settled. Ya'll hear?! It too dangerous right now!"

Jonnie Ray, a young, handsome and moderately successful farmer with a home bustling and bursting with eight children, and another on the way, pushed his way to the front of the crowd. "Look now, Laurence Cole, I got bushels of beans and a whole cart of mess I 'spose to get there, and you know ol' man Monclair ain't gonna give me a fair price . . . Mr. Meadows ain't buyin' nothin'. I wait too long, they be done rot."

"Those few extra dollars ain't gonna do you no good swingin' from a tree!" Allie Mae said. She was standing behind Mary in the front.

"What I 'spose' to do then, Allie Mae?" Jonnie Ray snipped. "Ya'll know how long it take to get anything out this dirt they done left us with. *Shit* . . . this be the first year I can make a few good dollars."

Lar chanced that his words would convey enough compassion and authority to compel Jonnie Ray to see commonsense. "Wait as long as you can, Jonnie Ray! As long as you can if you dead set on goin' over to the Hills. But if not . . . sell'em to Monclair be the best for you *and your family.*" Jonnie Ray's reply was a wrinkle-inducing scowl. "Listen now, boy!" Lar urged a bit more forcefully.

"Knowin' white folk, they done lynched that poor boy for somethin' he ain't even done– and two, they could be lynchin' other Negroes over there just 'cause they can."

"Lar be right!" a man's voice flowed up from the crowd.

"We done seen it before, Jonnie Ray," Lar continued, " . . . *you, yourself done seen it!* White folk gonna lynch just 'bout any Negroe when they get hot and mad and they see we tryin' to do for ourselves. 'Member summer last in Lexington?" Jonnie Ray nodded reluctantly. "They lynched that ol' Negroe man, then went and strung up his whole family . . . children, too! And we still don't even know what they claim he done did!"

"Jesus, have mercy! Mercy Lord!" Abel Watkins begged. She was sitting on the side of the crowd with four of her grandchildren and an infant in her arms.

Jonnie Ray's anger seemed to subside a little. "Then we call the law on them crackers!" Jonnie Ray turned around and faced the crowd. "We get lawmen from Jackson down here," he said, to the black sea. "We get on down to the Freedmen's Bureau. It be there *for* us Negroes. We get some folk down to Freedmen's and . . ."

"They ain't gonna do nothin', fool!" a man hollered, cutting Jonnie Ray short.

"They just as crooked as the crackers here, Jonnie Ray!" another voice added. "And if you talkin' 'bout Freedmen's down in Jackson – they done shut the door tight on that mess . . . *clip-clap-slam! Go on home, niggah!*"

"Ain't no white gonna go against another white over some niggah!" another man cut in.

Lar waved his hand to the crowd again, but this time, it seemed as though there was no bringing them back to a semblance of calm. Mary got up and stood by Lar, and began waving her hands for silence along with him. But the din from the crowd continued to grow. Some agreed with Jonnie Ray, which only encouraged him to try and convert the others who wanted him to just shut up. But silence did eventually come . . . unexpectedly.

From the back of the crowd, the roar of silence began. It flowed forward, passing through the middle until it reached the front where Lar and Mary stood. With a better view than anyone else, Lar saw the crowd part down the middle and form an isle. With a cane in her left hand, Enda made her way though the crowd. Her limp was more pronounced than Lar remembered, but then, it had been years since he'd seen her walk any distance. Everyone knew she rarely ventured farther than the front road of her house . . . though the same could not be said about the back of her house, where the forbidden woods were. That she'd come such a distance on this day, at this time, did not bode well, he knew. As much as he loved seeing her, she was usually a harbinger of bad tidings and rarely of good ones.

She hobbled toward Lar until she was directly in front of him, and then slowly turned around. No one spoke . . . or dared to for that matter . . . *for the witch of Folsom had come.* Whether out of fear or reverence, respect in the form of silence was given to her. A dust devil sprang into life around her and swirled her hair about. As the wind died, it laid her gray tendrils across her white face and fallen shoulders. "Jonnie Ray!" she called. *"Jonnie Ray!"*

Though he was standing in front of her, her call was obviously meant to draw everyone's attention. She raised her wood cane that had been smoothed at its head by constant wear and pointed it at him without a quiver or shake to it. "You stay out of Peak Hills like Lar told you!" she commanded. Her speech was devoid of slave English she usually used, and more reminiscent of a French-Creole accent. "Are you a fool, boy? Or just a boy!? You stay out of there with those children of yours." She lowered her cane and leaned forward on it.

The crowd leaked whispers. Jonnie Ray's mouth opened wide. The crowd stirred like ants at the mound and then hushed and waited for her speak.

Lar looked around and wondered why no one else seemed bothered by how what happened, happened. Everyone was seemed focused on what Enda Sully had said, and he was glad she had said it and seemed to finally knock some sense into Jonnie Ray. But . . . he knew there was no way Enda could have heard Jonnie Ray ranting earlier about going to Peak Hills?

"All of you listen to what Lar tells you," Enda said, and then almost faded to a whisper, "crackers will kill all of you if you don't heed his words."

The crowd grumbled louder this time. From safely within the crowd a woman called out. "Tell us what you done seen, Ms. Enda! Tell us 'bout 'tomorrow'."

As if by magic, the crowd hushed instantly.

Then another voice called out. "What you seen in our 'tomorrows'?" And then another asked . . . and one after that. Like a spreading infection, they all began to chant. " . . . 'Tomorrows' . . . 'tomorrows' . . . 'tomorrows' . . . 'tomorrows' . . . "

Enda cackled in reply. She took hold of Lar's arm. "You walk me home now, chère," she told him.

"Ma'am," he replied.

The crowd parted again to let them pass, but they tried a new chant as Lar and Enda walked past them. "Tell us . . . tell us . . . tell us . . . tell us," they beseeched.

Enda let go of Lar's arm when they reached the back, and turned to face the assembly of Negroes. "I haven't seen anything," she told them. "It's just common sense I speak. Crackers don't know right and wrong when it comes to anything that means anything. Haven't your mamas and pappies taught you right?!" She paused, as if waiting for a response. "Crackers will kill all us niggahs if they have a chance. So you– Jonnie Ray," she said loudly, "you give them that chance if you want then. Black birds always looking for something to nibble on."

* * *

Lar and Enda walked in silence until they were in front of her small shack. She let go of his arm and proceeded to walk the rest of the way alone. However, he could not let her go away so easily. "Ms. Enda . . . wait a moment."

She turned and looked at him, smiling as she did.

Lar returned the gesture.

He'd known her all his life– and knew what she was capable of. "I'll ask what you already know I'm gonna ask," he said, with a chuckle, but then his tone turned grim. "I know you know about our *'tomorrows'*. You already done seen what gonna happen. So why not just tell that boy– Jonnie Ray? Why not just tell all of us?"

Enda walked to where Lar stood and pulled on his shirt. "Kneel down here, boy."

He complied without hesitation. His head was at the level of her chest. If someone happened to pass by and see such a sight– he, the holy man kneeling at the foot of the witch, tongues would have been wagging for sure, he knew. But to Lar, showing such respect to a woman . . . witch or not . . . who'd taught him to read and write, and who had practically raised him, was deserved. She looked down at him and took his head in her hands which should have been comforting to him on such a hot day were they not ice cold.

"You want to know how you going to die, Laurence Cole? I can tell you your *'tomorrow'* right here . . . right now. I can tell you it all." She displayed her gray teeth in a broad smile. "You want to know how Matty is going to die . . . crops going to grow tall this year or not? Hmmm? Rain coming soon or not?" She pursed her lips. "Sometime when you know something and you try to change it around, something far worse can come about. Sometimes good comes from it . . . most times not! There's a reason *'tomorrows'* are *'tomorrows'* and not *'todays'*, boy."

"I know all that, Ms. Enda," he said, "you told me when I was a boy. I remember."

She snatched her hands from his face. "Then why you acting like you forgot?! When Enda speak to you, you suppose to listen."

"Times done changed is why," he replied. "Folks nowadays . . ."

She raised her cane and swung it side-to-side like a conductor disgusted with his choir. "Nothing has changed, chère! Absolutely nothing!" She backed away as though to leave, but suddenly sprung back, startling him a bit. "Only thing different is there are different folks doing the same thing as before. Ten . . . twenty . . . thirty years from here 'til then, folks be doing and thinking the same way."

Lar's was blind to the meaning of her words. He shook his head in ignorance.

"Listen, boy," she said. Warmth had crept back into her crackled voice. "Day after day I sweep the dirt out of my house. Fifty years from now, some old woman will be doing the same thing. And a hundred years from now, another old woman will, too. Everyday you go to work and try to stretch your money as far as you can. And a hundred years from now, another Negroe will be doing the same thing. But are you happy? Satisfied? Mad? Angry? Huh, child?! Tell me, then?!" Lar didn't know how to respond, or if he should at all. "Having faith that the Lord going to take care of you is *your* salvation, Lar Cole. But most, who say they believe what you believe– don't– *they don't!*

You see, child, a man is going to live his life in a different way if he believes he's going to go on after dying. And a man– especially a white man, will do just about anything to live a happy life if he thinks he won't go on after death has grabbed him. And a woman – especially a white woman who doesn't believe what you believe, will scheme like a weasel to find a little joy in her life before she goes into nothingness. And how do I know this?" She raised her brow. "I *haven't* seen it– I've *been* it," she announced proudly. "I've been a white woman for a few years on the way up here to Mississippi. I've seen into the hearts of white men, boy. Sometimes I see too much!" She stopped as though her breath had finally run out. She gathered the side of her dress in her free hand and her cane in the other, and began walking up to her shack. Each blow of her cane on the ground stirred up a puff of dust in her trail. "Come by and visit 'ol Enda now and then," she told him.

Lar strayed from the main road on his way back home. There was no one he wanted to speak to, but he knew everyone would want to speak to him. They would assume that Enda had told *him* what she refused to tell them. Everyone knew Enda was all he had as a mother, as his own had died before he could even form a vague memory of her. His father– he too had passed when Lar was only a few days older than seventeen– had entrusted him to her care before he died. Enda was caring, he recalled. Beautiful . . . *yes* . . . once upon a time, long-long ago. Fiercely protective . . .? Definitely! Mysterious . . .? So, so true!

Mary would no doubt question him upon his return, he thought. Or would anger come from her first? He'd seen her disapproval the moment Enda took hold of his arm to walk her home. Though Mary showed no emotion about it at the time, it was precisely her lack of such a reaction that told him she was not pleased.

But truthfully, there was nothing he could tell her. Even he did not really understand what Enda meant about everything being the same and nothing every really changing. In a simple way, he could discern her words superficially . . . but years of being instructed at Enda's table told him there was far more to what she'd said. He was well aware that even a cordial 'good morning' from her was not to be trusted at face value. There was always more to it. Unfortunately, experience had taught him that the meaning of her words often arrived when whatever was set in motion could not be stopped.

His deliberate, slow walk home did nothing to clear his mind and help decode Enda's message. There was still the tragedy in Peak Hills to be handled, and it muddled his thoughts with images of a Negroe boy hanging from a tree, and other Negroes hiding in their homes, too scared to retrieve the body for fear they may be next just because . . . *'black birds always looking for something to nibble on'*. He found comfort that at least those words of Enda he understood. Within minutes after the lynching and when white folks had finished desecrating the body, black birds were sure to come and feast on whatever was left. He'd seen it before. He'd cut down burned, decapitated and bullet riddled bodies more than once.

Who gonna help us, Lord? Jesus . . . you listenin' to me? Who? he wondered.

He knew lawmen were of little to no use, especially since they were more likely to instigate the murders rather than stop them. And from what little he'd heard and read, politicians were equally guilty or ambivalent, which was the same in his eyes. He fantasized about choices Negroes could have to stop lynchings in an orderly, equal and just world that was disorderly, unequal and unjust. But he already knew any choice that could stop the lynchings was just a Negroe's dream.

Words of comfort for his people eluded him. He felt like he was trying to drink water from a sieve. For every inspiring and uplifting idea he could think of to use at the next sermon, there were ten dark thoughts to shadow them. He thought it easier and more logical to just tell everyone to run. 'Move north, ya'll'. Or for the young and foolish– like Jonnie Ray, *'get yourself a pistol, boy. 'Cause one day, white folks gonna come for you. And that ain't a 'if', but 'when''. Believe you me!'*

Lar understood that a fount of grief was feeding the darkness lurking in his heart. Only he, God, and the night were privy to his secret lust for revenge. In dreams, he reveled in dragging a white man, stripped naked, with a rope tied around his neck until he'd found a tree sturdy enough to support it . . . *pull—pull* . . . until the white man's feet no longer touched the ground, but danced a dance upon air, that if was performed upon a stage, it would have received thunderous applause for such deft talent. The eyes of the white man bulged from his sockets like a boil quickly filling with pus, as he sensed his doom drawing nigh. The white man would claw at the rope that was ripping the skin on his neck like wet paper. This white man . . . this faceless white man of dreams, would beg to be treated like a human being, as he lost control of his private bodily functions publicly in front of women and children, who would snicker at a grown man peeing and defecating in front of them. And the white man would say with his eyes: *look at me, Negroes, and see your eternal salvation denied for what you have done to me.* But Lar loved that the white man could see his own earthly salvation was not to be. The white man would be alone in his death. No one would come to his aid. His death would not be avenged, but celebrated.

A gentle breeze passed by him and his cheek felt cool. When he touched it, it was wet, yet his hands seemed on fire. He looked at his palms and saw nail marks dug into calluses from unknowingly clenching his fists. What should have been a steady thump in his chest felt like a rolling drumbeat. The beast he thought he'd bound and silenced long ago was viciously clawing at its tethers to be free again. The beast reminded him of those vengeful thoughts he'd prayed would never return . . . white skin covered in blood made to look as beautiful as the morning sun . . . white corpses hanging from trees as comforting a sight as watching children play on a summer night.

Lar quickly changed course.

It scared him to think such thoughts, and even worse, how good they made him feel when the beast reminded him of them. For a lesser man– a godless man, it may be normal to witness one's people butchered like animals time and time again, and wish the same fate for those responsible. But a man of God? He thought ashamedly. It was unforgivable!

The black shade of the forest along the river called to him. All knew many had died in the forest during the war. But that stink of death that still lingered was now his personal siren. Where the river crept along its shores, fishermen were sometimes seen waiting out their prey. Near the bridge and fully bathed in sunlight, white boys swam in its murky waters. But where Negroes lived, the forest and brush was much denser and required great effort to navigate through if one sought to hunt coon, squirrel, rabbit or gather wood. But if Negroes did venture in, it was always in daylight and close to the bridge where the sun was strong enough to break through the monolithic oaks shadowing the land below. "Those woods filled with haints and ghosts," Enda had warned. "They still angry! They ain't in a forgivin' way just yet. Ya'll leave them thangs in there be . . . let'em wander 'round a bit 'til they get tired and go to where they 'spose to be. Now Enda done spoke! And that be all Enda gotta say 'bout it'.

Lar gave no mind to Enda's counsel as he boldly made his way in to the forest. All he knew was that no one with commonsense would come looking for him in there. The ecstasy he felt imagining lynching white men haunted him as no nightmare could. The beast within him seemed insatiable. He knew it sensed his weakness growing. The beast was reaching into parts of his soul where lust, greed and envy resided . . . perverse pleasures that aroused him. He felt nothing physically, yet in that dark corner of his spirit, he felt alive bathing in fantasies of killing whites. How would a white man ever see his evil unless he was faced with it himself? He pondered. How could a white man every know the pain of knowing someone he loved was burned like a torch while others shouted in glee, applauded and photographed their job well done? Would it take a white man to have his child's four limbs tied to ropes, and those ropes tethered to four horses stationed in four different directions, and once branded and whipped, those horse pulling and bucking until they ripped their prize away . . . an arm or a leg?

Lar walked further, and quicker into the forest's depths, knowing he could not return home in such a vengeful, hateful state. Directly ahead, he could hear the river lapping at its shore. Birds whistled and screeched overhead, though he paid them no attention at first, but suddenly he stopped and looked up in search for them. *Those some blackbirds up there?* He wondered.

Unseen creatures crunched twigs and brush as they scurried away from the stranger who dared enter their domain. It was only when he was deep in the woods that he realized that day seemed to have become dusk, though the sweltering heat reminded him it was otherwise. At the river's edge, where trees close to the bank had their gnarled, finger-like roots exposed by constant erosion, the rippling reflection of the sun on the water's surface failed to bring him comfort as it usually had when he came here to contemplate. To his left, toward Folsom, and to the right as far as he could see, there was nothing but trees.

Without hesitation he marched into the water. The sun-warmed liquid quickly filled his boots, sinking and adhering him to its muddy floor. He waded out until the water reached his neck and then laid back into the waters with a prayer upon his lips. Light and sound disappeared as he sunk beneath the watery murk, as he prayed that his sinful thoughts would also.

He resurrected himself and discovered all *still* as it was– water *still* flowed past his neck, as the sun *still* continued to beat upon its shimmering surface. The trees were *still* a haughty green and their roots *still* dug firmly in the earth. He *still* remained Lar . . . the man . . . preacher . . . husband . . . Negroe . . . *sinner.*

But something had changed. He was no longer alone. A snake as dark as the waters it swam in, or as the Negroes called them–cottonmouths, shared the river with him now. Whether it was a trick of the sun in his eyes or the dirty water stinging them, it seemed as if the serpent was headed straight for him– its white mouth agape and tongue lashing out. Lar's thoughts sped, but his movements were cautious and slow. He was careful to breathe only when he needed to. He pushed lightly with his right foot and moved out toward the center of the river. He locked eyes with the serpent, whose own seemed fixed on him. He knew if he lost sight of it, the brown, nearly black serpent could easily blend into the water and swiftly be upon him.

But despite his maneuver, the snake still seemed to be coming right for him.

He moved to the right with a push of his left foot. The snake scrunched and expanded like an accordion and shifted in the same direction. Lar questioned the wisdom of his elders. Cottonmouths were not supposed to follow a person if they were given berth to pass, but would if they felt threatened, he remembered being told. But this one seemed to have forgotten such a rule. Further to the right he pushed. Yet again, with a coil and recoil, the black-faced, white-mouthed serpent came toward him.

No longer did the river's water drip from Lar's brow, but his own salty sweat as a sense of dread began drumming in his head, making it harder to think rationally. He pushed with his left foot and began moving back toward the shore. The pounding of his heart stole control of his feet and made him jerk instead of smoothly pushing off. His unconscious mind took command of his arms and haphazardly began propelling him inland. Rotting flesh from where the snake would strike and lying sick for months, if he didn't die right off, became a possible reality to him. Mary and the baby slipped into his thoughts, even as he pushed his feet to move faster in the thick mud– his movements were now just involuntarily twitching muscles. And then there was Enda . . . had she seen this? He wondered. But that image was quickly replaced with a Negroe boy who looked so forlorn . . . he was hanging from a tree by a rope around his broken neck with a chicken firmly in his grasp.

He chanced a glance at the shore and saw that it was now no more than ten feet away. Though his body was now only half-submerged, his soaked clothes and boots filled with water weighed upon him like a hundred pound child. Realizing that the black serpent was still closing in on him, he dashed for the shore.

Whereas his entry into the water had been smooth and without incident, his exit was far from it. His first attempt made him think it might be his last. His left foot slipped from underneath him, and with the weight of his body and soaked clothes helping gravity, he slammed face down into the river. A child's fright arose within him as he fought the water and grabbed at the muddy floor, which slipped through his hands like fresh clay. Several frantic attempts to grab hold of the riverbed finally proved successful, and with a lurch, he launched himself onto the shore. He was finally on muddy ground, but did not stop there. He scrambled on hands and knees until the ground he clawed at went from moist to dry. He spun around and looked for his serpentine nemesis, all the while coughing up and spitting out river water. But his would-be predator had already lost its passion for him and was already halfway across the river, he saw. He propped himself up on elbows and watched it swim further out and eventually blend colors, disappearing into the murky river. He was safe now . . . muddy . . . but unharmed. He could already hear Mary as he walked in looking as though he'd been playing in mud and dirt. She was already most likely in a fit at his extended absence and unknown whereabouts . . . but his piggish appearance, he knew, would just deepen the matriarchal tenor in her inevitable lecture to come.

He checked his surroundings. The trees were motionless, and the critters, which he knew were present but hiding, were silent. An occasional slapping of the river's hand onto the bank and a soft whistle of a winged creature were all that he could hear. He knew if by chance someone were to come upon him, it would not be a woman or a girl. Convinced this was true, he stripped from his wet, muddy clothes. Not as convinced of his isolation by the river's shore, he crouched as low as his long, thick body would allow between screens of waist high thickets. He watched for his slithering, brown-black friend– just in case it decided to pay him another visit. He dunked his clothes and boots into the river and washed them underneath the water, and then wrung them out, careful not to rip the stitches. He walked back into the woods, taking care to plant his bare feet only on moss covered ground or dirt until he finally found a sunlit tree with low hanging branches to hang his clothes and boots on. He lay down against the tree. His bedding was slightly uncomfortable at first– the sharp grass and sticks against his back and buttocks pricked him and crackled beneath his weight, but became somewhat soothing as his body relaxed upon them. The heat was now bearable, as his damp, naked body was free of its suffocating layers of cloth. Sleep fell upon him quicker than he expected. His dreams were of nothing he would remember later, just blissful unknowing.

A snapping twig woke him from his slumber. He opened his eyes, but lay motionless. It was mid-afternoon as far as he could tell by the sun's seat in the sky, which meant he'd slept for a while. A quick glance at his dry, stiff clothes validated his first assumption about the passage of time. Was it an animal? He thought. He listened for another sound to follow. That someone other than himself would be so far out in the shaded forest seemed unlikely . . . but not impossible. He waited some time before carefully reaching for his undergarments and britches, and cursed the sticks that crunched beneath him with the slightest movement. Having pulled them down, he speedily and haphazardly dressed his lower half, and once sufficiently covered, stood and scanned his surroundings. But all was still around him, save a wayward bird flying overhead. Was it a blackbird?

He finished dressing. Though his clothes were fully dried, his boots were still damp inside. Regardless, he knew he would have to have them washed and hung once more before they were fit for wearing and working in again. And that they were his only boots, there would be no work on the church done on his part this day.

"She gonna be one cranky ol' thang tonight!" he whispered. He'd been gone at least a couple of hours without having told a soul where he'd gone. Surely in that time someone had come by the house looking for him. But . . . here he was, in the forbidden forest wrestling with the *beast* once more.

"You a selfish man, Laurence," he muttered, as he remembered a child had been killed no more than a few miles down the road . . . his church was not even half-built and there were five Saturdays of chores left to be done. "Fine preacher you turnin' out to be Laurence Cole. Daddy be right proud, huh?" he said mockingly. "You 'spose to be leadin' a flock, and you, the shepherd, done ran off!" He picked up his pace, as well as his shattered pride, and ran out of the woods toward the one constant in his life, which was Mary, who was sure to be fit-to-be-tied upon first look and smell of him.

CHAPTER 5

That evening when Lar returned home, Mary let the matter of his running off drop with just one question. "You ain't gone over to Peak Hills, have ya?"

"No," Lar offered simply.

Though his unexplained absence had at first infuriated her, it now simmered in her gut like a pot of black-eyed peas and hamhocks. It wasn't like Lar to up and disappear as he had done. He usually told her he would be gone and she would just wait a few hours until he returned from who knows where. That he had done so without saying a word caused her to worry that he was more troubled by the events in Peak Hills than he'd let on. She'd seen how the pressures put upon him by the other Negroes at times wore him down mentally and physically. They looked to him as their leader . . . their strength . . . he who possessed the answer to a puzzle never meant to be solved . . . then lastly, as just a man like every other man.

Had he returned home just a few minutes sooner, he would have saw his front porch crammed with uninvited visitors waiting for spiritual direction. Mary was already fed up with their nervous, fretful chatter and inquiries of Lar's whereabouts the moment they started arriving after the brief meeting at church. Sensing that the tapping of her foot from dwindling patience was about to start stomping a hole in the porch, she abruptly stood up from her rocker and sent them all home with a promise of answers to come the next day . . . this day, which was Sunday . . . the Lord's day.

It was an early, balmy Sunday morning. She had just finished smoothing out Lar's suit when the picture of him returning yesterday came back to her. His clothes were a mess of wrinkles and stunk like he did– like a Billy goat who'd played in river water. She was ready to demand an account of his every lost minute, but after seeing his face up close, she decided against it. The near palpable aura he usually exuded had dimmed. Even confronted with the direst situation, it was Lar, if it there was anyone, who could find some good in it, if only a little. It was his God that always propped him up and carried him through the hardest of times. It was that same God that irritated her with *Its* preaching of forgiveness. But in that moment when he arrived back home, his drawn face and eyes bereft of their sparkle, it seemed as though that same God had reneged on *Its* word and left Lar in the Valley of Death.

"You all right?" she'd asked, surprising herself at the choice of benign words coming from her mouth. He stopped, obviously stunned himself. She smiled demurely.

"Fine, Mary Cole," he replied and kissed her lightly on the cheek.

"Don't be sittin' down in them clothes on for you get the whole house stankin'," she instructed, without a hint of anger. "You might as well go on and take yourself a wash."

She'd gone back to shucking peas, all the while sneaking peeks at him as he carried bucket after bucket of water into the house and filled the washtub. Though she had desperately wanted to know where he'd been for the past few hours, her wifely senses told her to just leave it alone. And what had Enda said to him as he walked the old woman home? She wondered also. She too knew Enda and her peculiar ways. Though her love for the woman had waned greatly over time, especially after the death-births of her

babies and Enda's warning about the one she now carried, her respect for the woman's ability to see 'tomorrows' had not wavered
in the slightest.

She often wondered how Lar reconciled his love for God with
his love for Enda Sully. She understood he loved Enda as a mother,
but could not make out what else exactly bound them despite their
differences. Enda was a woman more likely to stroll deep into the
forbidden woods to collect her roots and animals innards– doing so
boldly at night when no grown man was likely to venture there
alone during the day. Her attendance at church, which grew more
infrequent as the years passed, was only just for show, Mary assumed. She couldn't fold her brain around how Lar, a servant of
God, could love such a woman who stood for everything God was
against.

Yet ... he was far from alone in his love and need for Enda,
Mary knew. She could think of only a handful of Negroes who
hadn't gone running to the old woman when their prayers had
failed, hoping she would give them some root to hold on to ...
gris-gris or a jar with God knows what was in it to bury in their
backyard to compel those from the spirit realm to intervene on
their behalf. Yet, they were the same ones who were the first to
holler, dance and sing their love for God at church every Sunday.

Mary chuckled and dropped her hypocritical casting stones
from her hand, remembering she too had sought Enda's assistance
when God was too busy or indifferent to attend to her pleas for
help. Having pushed out her last dead baby, she'd screamed at Lar
and Willa– whose midwife skills had failed, for having brought
Enda to stop the bleeding that was draining away and taking her
life along with it. And though she'd recoiled at the touch of Enda's
healing hands, she was thankful that the woman knew and could
do such things that weren't natural. Mary realized she was alive
right now only because of Enda.

Mary held up the suit jacket and deemed it ready to wear. She called for Lar who was sitting on the porch with Uncle Matty. "Be that time now, ya'll."

* * *

"I lost count of how many folk got the Holy Ghost. You sho'nuff preached it today, Lar," Mary beamed. Her arm was snugly entwined around Lar's. "I don't think I ever seen Negroes jump so high, 'cept it be by the lash."

"Child, you ain't never seen no lashin' like they used to give," Uncle Matty chimed in. Lar was holding his arm on the other side as they walked back home. Lar, having thoroughly been seared by the mid-morning sun toward the end of his sermon, had removed his jacket and unbuttoned his shirt midway down. Mary was beside herself with pride at the ferocity in which Lar had delivered his sermon on receiving a place in Heaven for those who had lived a virtuous, Christ-like life. She really didn't care for, or believe for that matter, most of what he preached, but it had been a sight to see those around her shake and shout when the Holy Ghost came upon them. With every strike of Lar's fist to his open palm, 'amens' scattered up in the air like startled birds fleeing to the sky for safety. He drove home each and every point as though it were the most important of all. Women who'd caught the Holy Ghost danced a jig and stirred up dirt with their tattered Sunday shoes– if wearing their Sunday hat, it was more than likely flung away as others sought to restrain and fan them. Ersa Adams, who'd become *happy* and required three men to restrain and settle her down, suddenly remembered the reason why she was being fanned and started bucking and screeching, "*Jesus! Jesusssss!!*" as the Holy Ghost came upon her once again.

"It wasn't just 'bout me and my preachin'," Lar admitted, in his typical, yet genuine self-effacing manner. "It be the time we in right now."

Uncle Matty shook his head. "True, true, boy."

"Folks are scared and should be too," Lar continued. "Too many disturbin' things keep croppin' up closer to Folsom like it did after the war . . . it bound to come back 'round here soon enough. We Negroes be on our own right now. Ain't no congressman gonna help some Negroes. 'Specially when they ain't nuthin' but ol' massahs and massah's sons wantin' back what they lost after the war. They already done stopped givin' Negroes a bit of land to till. Now they wantin' us to sharecrop so they can rob us blind."

"So what we gonna do now?" Mary asked.

Lar looked at her for a moment, and then turned his attention upward to the eastern sky. "Ain't much we can do– is there?"

Mary squeezed his hand and smiled at him, hoping to draw him back to earth. She knew what and *whom* he sought in the clear blue skies. "I didn't mean it like that, husband– *preacher man!*" She sassed. "I know we got prayer . . . and we pray and pray. Can't no white man take that away. I just sayin', what else can we do then? The Lord love us for our prayers, but prayers ain't gonna make white folk treat us right. We got a right to have somethin' too."

"This be home for Negroes just as well as whites," Uncle Matty joined in. "We worked this land for free all those damn years . . . hell! Tearin' skin off a niggah's back to get their roads built quicker . . . fields cleared faster . . . houses built tall and wide. We belong right here where we at. This land be just as much ours as theirs. And more ours, if you askin' an ol' Negroe like me!"

"That's right," Mary agreed.

They walked in silence until they reached their shack. Lar helped Uncle Matty inside and put him down for his afternoon nap. When he returned outside, Mary was sitting in her rocking chair. Her eyes were closed and her hands rubbing her belly in circles. "You ok?" he asked with a hint of urgency.

"Child just movin' 'bout is all."

Lar squeezed her shoulder and then took up residence in his own rocker next to hers. He sat forward with his legs spread wide and rested his elbows on them. "You tell me, Mary . . . If God and prayers ain't the answer, accordin' to you . . . then what is? You always sayin' God ain't gonna help none, and prayers neither, so just what should we do then? Who we turn to ta' help us?"

Mary stopped rubbing her belly, which was actually paining her, though she dared not admit so to Lar. Every time they spoke of God's destiny for Negroes, he'd never asked such a thing– she usually did . . . *'what we do?'* It was Lar who always had the answer to such a question, which always led back to God being so mysterious; a simple man couldn't understand why God does what God does, when God does it. But now, he'd spun the questioning arrow in her direction. For all her opinions on the matter, she could come up with nothing more than . . . "I don't know."

Lar sighed and sat back in the rocking chair. He pushed off with his foot and began a squeaky back and forth rhythm. "Me neither, old girl," he whispered.

Mary resumed caressing her belly, which seemed filled with as much bile as it did with baby. The pain echoing throughout her womb was beginning to subside. "I know what I would like to do . . ."

"I think every Negroe knows what they would like to do," he said.

"I know it ain't right to think that way, but it's the way I think 'bout it. White folk and they ways." She huffed.

Lar smiled. "You know, Mary . . . prayer is only a part of it. We have eternal souls. And eternal mean . . ."

"Forever."

"Right! Right!" Lar turned his chair so that he faced her. The familiar glow Mary was accustomed to seeing about him was beginning to shine once more. His eyes widened and held a hint of a sparkle within them. "Now– you just try to set your mind to understand 'eternal'."

She lowered her head, but kept her eyes fixed on his. "Laurence Cole . . . I know what eternal mean."

"But can you feel it, Mary?" he urged upon a whisper. "Can you touch it with your mind . . . to go on forever and ever and ever after that? Try to see God as eternal, only he was never born like you and me. He always been when there ain't even been an earth, or even time for that matter. Imagine that, Mary . . . always been there . . . Alpha and Omega, the bible says . . . beginnin' and end. And the Lord done given us an eternal soul. So once we die and go to be with him, we don't ever have to worry 'bout dyin' again. We don't have to worry 'bout white man's laws, 'cause we got God's holy laws. We always be with him, and him with us– that what I mean by 'eternal'. To have that forever, a man can take a lot of sufferin'."

Mary lowered her eyelids until they were nearly shut. "Hummpf! Then all us Negroes goin' straight to heaven if sufferin' be what let you in those pearly gates," Mary replied.

"Be fine with me if it be that easy– but it ain't," Lar said. "You gotta do right by the Lord, too! Lots of folk suffer on the inside, but you can't see it 'cause they make themselves pretend to be happy . . . pretend not to see what right in front of they face . . . pretend– pretend– pretend . . . and suffer 'cause of it."

"So what you 'spose to say to that poor child's folk? 'Don't worry that your boy suffered . . . that they hung him up and strangled him 'til he dead, 'cause he gonna be with the Lord . . . be eternal?'"

The teacher in Lar beamed. "Yes!"

Mary laughed. "Lar– I love you, but ain't nothin' can soothe my achin' heart if a child of mine was taken from me like that." Instantly, Mary realized that she was not so very different from the lynched boy's mother she spoke of. Without expecting so, her own words quieted her. Thinking about all the infant souls she sent to God made her heart want to stop, but it was too ornery for that to happen.

Lar took hold of her hand. "That be how I handle *our* sufferin', Mary. I know where our babies be, and I know I'll see them again–every one of them . . . forever and ever."

Mary coughed to clear her throat, but her voice still came out strangled. "I figure if God see fit to love me enough, I see my babies, too. But if he don't, things just have to be the way they be."

Lar rose from his chair and walked to the door. "And that be our difference, Mary. I *know* I'm gonna see our children one day."

* * *

The Cole's shack smelled of deep fried fish that had been promised and delivered by Will Anderson and his wife, Lilly, not long after church had ended. The arm length fish were gutted and washed by the men and the two teenage Anderson boys, Lester and Thomas, while the women battered them with cornmeal and fried them in lard as quick as they were brought in. The fish were part of an ever-expanding trade between the two families that was initiated by the women and had been carried on for years. This time it was fish for two months of Sundays for a set of three britches each for Buck, the two boys, and a dress for Lilly, with the Andersons supplying the material and thread. With no money ever having to be exchanged, and only a bit of Mary's time at her sewing machine, it was mutually beneficial for all. And since Mary and Lar loved sitting on the porch into the late night with Buck and Lilly anyway, it was little more than an excuse to get together.

Mary had pulled an extra chair in the kitchen for Uncle Matty to sit on while she and Lilly fried the catfish until they were golden brown and crunched with every bite taken. Uncle Matty, insisting he was starving and couldn't wait, was already nibbling off of his second plate of tender catfish. After each piece he gummed until it was broken up enough to swallow, he licked his fingers clean of any remaining cornmeal and grease that had stuck to them. He swore to Mary and Lilly that it was the best catfish he'd ever had. They laughed, knowing Uncle Matty *always* said whatever fish he was eating was the best. "I ain't lyin' this time, ya'll," Uncle Matty professed. "This here be the best ya'll done ever fried up!"

"Ok, Uncle Matty." Lilly winked at Mary. "We see what you say come next Sunday then."

"I sure that be good, too– but this I know got it beat already." He popped another piece in his mouth. "Mmm-hmm! This fish here done been blessed!"

Mary was about to add to the banter when Thomas, the youngest of the Anderson boys, walked in with another bucket of cleaned fish. "Put on yon' table there, boy," Mary instructed. "How much more ya'll got?"

Thomas ran back to the door. "Daddy! Hey, Daddy! Ms. Mary wantin' ta' know how much more catfish we got left to do." Thomas looked back at Mary and smiled, displaying his prominent overbite. "He say, 'how much grease ya'll got left be how much fish we got."

Mary, who was standing over a bubbling pot of lard, cocked her head toward the door. "Ok now, Mr. Anderson! I make sure you get fed last then," she hollered, and then heard Buck and Lar chuckle in response. "Girl," she said to Lilly, "we gonna be here all day. I gonna eat somethin' soon, though. This youngin' been squirmin' and yearnin' for some fish since the first piece hit the grease."

"Gal!" Lilly squeaked. "Don't be lyin' on that helpless baby. That all you!"

"Sho' is," Mary admitted readily and then laughed. "But don't be sayin' nothin' to Lar. Girl– he think all this eatin' makin' the baby all fat and big, and all it makin' big is me! When this youngin' come out, I still gonna be big as this house and yours together . . . shoot!"

Lilly her hands on her hips and cocked the left one out to the side, displaying her own full-figure proudly. "You be same as me then."

Mary looked her up and down, and couldn't resist smirking as she spoke. "Lord– I in big trouble then."

Lilly's tiny nose and lips, and her rather large eyes nearly met in the center of her face as she giggled. "Oooh, chile– you didn't!"

Mary puckered her lips. "Mmm-hmm . . . I be wearin' the same size as you if I don't stop all this eatin'."

"Now wait!" Lilly wagged the long fork she was using at Mary. "Now I know– you was wearin' a bigger size than me even 'fore you got with child."

Mary looked up and studied her grease and smoke stained ceiling. "I don't recall bein' that big."

"*Mary!*"

Mary winked at her. She couldn't get enough of Lilly's girlish squeal. It was during these times that Mary knew joy family and friends brought . . . Lar's thundering voice out by the porch explaining another tale he'd read from the bible . . . chatter amongst the playing Anderson boys was a sweet, but haunting echo of what may come despite the words of Enda . . . Uncle Matty's feisty sass. The love flowing from Lilly and Uncle Matty in her kitchen and out onto the porch with Lar, Buck and the boys, reminded her why she stayed in Folsom.

Uncle Matty rose from his chair after twice rocking back and forth to gain momentum and with a firm pull from Lilly. Once steadied, he shooed Lilly back to the stove and waddled toward the front door. Mary guessed he was heading for one of the two rocking chairs on the porch so he could chit-chat with the men and scold the Anderson boys when their play got too rough, or when they were running too fast, or . . . just acting like boys were supposed to. He stopped at the door and called back to the women. "Ya'll invite more folk for fish?"

"No suh, Uncle Matty," Lilly answered. "I 'spect this fish done drawn'em here. I come on down too if I smelled somethin' as good as this. Invited or not, I'm comin' ya'll! Set me a plate and get outta my way!"

"Heh-heh!" Mary chortled.

Uncle Matty ignored them both. "These folks in a wagon loaded way down pullin' up here. I 'spect they ain't headin' up here for no fish."

Mary handed her fork to Lilly and wiped her hands on her apron. She joined Uncle Matty at the door. "What say, uncle?"

"Who it be, Mary?" Lilly asked, not daring to take her eyes off the filets that were fried light brown like the back of her hand and almost ready to take out.

Mary removed her apron and tossed it on the table behind her. "I don't know. Whoever it be, I 'spose ain't stayin' long though," she remarked. "They on the move."

Lar and Buck were already walking toward the road to greet the strangers who'd stopped. Mary helped Uncle Matty to a rocking chair and then proceeded down the path herself. "Ya'll keep cleaning," she told the boys.

"Yes'm," they replied.

Mary's walk was more of a waddle as she strode to catch up to the men. Her feet were aching and felt twice their size and six times heavier. But she moved quickly as only a woman her size and strength could.

She discovered that Uncle Matty was right. The wagon in front of their home was loaded to the brim. Two thick-legged horses pulled the wagon, though in a few more miles, they would realize they lacked the strength for the task they were charged with. Nothing had been loaded on the wagon with care. Pots and pans danced precariously on hastily tied ropes that hung from the side. A couple of chairs had wood-slat crates stacked on top of them and more pushed between their legs. A hoe, shovel and a pick stuck out the rear, and with the next bump, would most likely slip off. Shirts, pants, boxes of tin plates and jars rounded out the mound made over the weather beaten wagon. The front seat of the wagon was also full. A Negroe woman and two children– a boy no more than three and a girl almost in her teen years were huddled together side-by-side. All three wore straw hats that kept the sun off their faces that gleamed with sweat. Mary positioned herself between Lar and Buck. She shielded her eyes from the sun with her hand and saw three living people with dead eyes staring back at her. The woman, who had been talking to Lar and Buck, fell silent when Mary arrived.

"This be my wife, Mary," Lar told the woman.

"Ma'am," the woman greeted Mary in a dead voice, as the dead are known to speak in.

Lar looked at Mary. "She be, Ms. Freda, the mother of that boy . . ." he paused, " . . . from Peak Hills." He looked back at the slim woman still grasping the reins in her cold hands.

Mary's mouth parted, though just as it did, she felt a new strength come unto her. She pushed Lar and Buck to the side and squeezed past them as she reached for the young girl who was on outer edge of the wagon-seat. "Come here, child!" she demanded. "Get on up in here and eat some."

Freda quickly placed her arm across her daughter. "No ma'am!" she screeched at first, but then muttered, "no ma'am– no ma'am. It ain't safe for us *or ya'll.*"

"She be right, Mary," Buck quickly agreed.

"Laurence Cole!" Mary huffed in shock and disappointment.

Lar lowered his head momentarily. He looked into Mary's eyes and concurred with Buck. "She and those chillin' ain't safe here or anywhere– time being."

Freda began to weep. Her daughter reached across the toddler who sat in the middle and took hold of her mother's hand. The girl looked at Mary. Had joy, not sorrow, been touching her face, she would be such a pretty girl, Mary thought.

"They took my pappy last night," the girl uttered. "Got my brother the day 'fore . . . now my pappy. White folk say he in on it, too, what they say my brother did– only my brother, Casper, not do nothin'. My pappy ain't did nothin' neither."

"Goddamnit!" Buck spat.

Freda wiped away her tears. "My boy ain't stole no chickens or nothin' else," she professed. "White folk sayin' my boy been stealin' from 'em for a long time. They say my husband been doin' the same, but he been off sellin' crops for the same white folks who sayin' he done been stealin'. He ain't even been nowhere near town for God knows how long."

"They say that how he been stealin'," the girl added. "They say he ain't been out sellin', but creepin' 'bout stealin' with my brother at night. They say that how come we got plenty of food to eat and be down buyin' stuff at Moody's store."

"My husband, Danny, work hard on our farm– Casper too!" Freda's sobbing renewed with vigor. "Our dirt be good, Ms. Mary– real good . . . black– black– black it be, and hold on to water! We ain't stole nothin' from nobody!"

Mary scampered around the cart and grasped Freda's hand. "Girl, we know that!"

"Now white women say they done seen Danny peekin' in on them when they ain't dressed," Freda said, as sorrow and anger danced in her voice. "That ain't true, neither!"

"*Lar*," Mary implored again.

Freda shook her head. "No ma'am . . . *no ma'am*." She pulled her hand away from under Mary's and switched positions. "I ain't gonna bring that evil under your roof. No ma'am and no suh, I won't."

"Chile, now you . . .," Mary began.

"White folk tore my boy apart!" Freda cried. Her dull eyes looked through Mary. "*Apart!*" she hissed.

"God!" Lar gasped.

"Negroe men went to get his body night-before," Freda continued. "White folk left him in an ol' muddy gulch in the back woods when they were done with him. They brought Casper back to me in a sack! Torn apart! Lord Jesus! Dear Jesus . . . my child! *My child!*" she mumbled, more to herself than those around her. Her toddler began crying, but it was clear he didn't understand what his mother spoke of, only that she was very sad and that he should be also.

Freda's grip on Mary's hand was crushing, but Mary didn't pull away. She realized such pain was nothing compared to that of a grieving wife and mother, and gladly accepted it. She looked past Freda and saw Lilly just now running from the house toward them.

Freda continued. "Bunch of white men with guns came and got Casper right out of our field. Danny be right there, too, but they put they gun right at his head and told him to move so they can shoot'em. Danny couldn't do nothin' to stop'em from takin' Casper. Then they came back last night and took Danny! They knock down the door and just took him! They say Casper done told'em everythang! They beat Danny and roped his neck and took him off." Freda shook her head, imploring Mary to believe her. "I scream and scream, 'He ain't did it! He ain't did it!' But they took him 'cause they couldn't see me, like ya'll see me. I fall to my knees and pray and pray! And they still take him– 'cause they can't see me . . . and Danny ain't Danny to them no more– like my boy, Casper ain't Casper no more! They were just niggahs to them."

Mary felt her sorrow for her dead babies diminish under Freda's solemn gaze. Murderers had taken Freda's baby that she had born, raised, fed and loved. Such a tragedy seemed unbearable to Mary. And then to lose a husband . . . father of that child, was unthinkable. But . . .

"He could still be alive?" Mary asked Lar, who shook his head side to side. Mary already knew the man hadn't survived, though her heart had compelled her to hope for hope's sake.

"Too late," Lar sputtered. Both mother and daughter cried out in unison. "I sorry ma'am."

Freda began huffing as though she was trying to expel the last breath from her chest. Her deep, quick breaths seemed to draw a semblance of calm back into her limbs, her face and voice. Where such steeliness came from, Mary couldn't fathom, but watched so in awe. If Freda had jumped off the wagon running, screaming, and pulling at her hair and clawing at her skin, Mary figured she could've understood that display of emotions better. But Freda had stifled her pain, at least for the moment. When she spoke again, her voice was somber . . . mechanical . . . dead, like it was before. "Negroes here say I should come see you for what I need done," she said to Lar.

Lar walked over and stood next to Mary. He grasped her hand, and then laid his other on top of her other one which was still held strong by Freda– completing the trinity. "Ma'am," he said.

"You be a minister, folk say." Lar nodded. "Be it a month or a year . . . once they done laid Danny and my boy in the ground, and white folk done forgot 'bout them, will you go and see them on to God right? Give'em a decent prayer where they be? Pray for they souls?"

"Yes'm," he replied instantly. "I pray for them every day I here in Folsom, too. And soon as it be safe 'nough, I go there and do it right proper."

Freda sighed her thanks.

"Everyone bow your head before the Lord," Lar instructed. Even Mary promptly complied. Lar used his deepest voice and teased his words with vibrato. His cadence was the flittering of hummingbird wings. His pleas for comfort from Lord Jesus drew tears from every eye. His body trembled as he recited the Lord's Prayer with such vigor, that even Mary's stout knees began to weaken.

Mary broke the circle she, Lar and Freda had formed. "I . . . we . . ." she paused and cleared phlegm from her throat, " . . . help you on your way, Ms. Freda," Mary croaked. "You hold on right here." With her womb braced with an arm underneath, Mary strode toward the house as fast as her tree-trunk legs would allow, but not before taking Lilly's hand and pulling her along. "C'mon, gal!" Mary was calling the Anderson boy's names even as she strode up the walkway. She gave each boy a specific chore to be completed as quick as possible.

"What be happenin' out there?" Uncle Matty asked.

Mary stopped. Her mind raced to condense what Freda had told them. "Devil done decided to come 'round to Peak Hills," she explained, and continued inside. But she was halted once more, but this time it was by Lar who yelled for her. "The sock, Mary! Bring half the sock." Mary nodded.

Lilly gathered what fish was already fried and wrapped them in cloth as instructed by Mary. Before Mary disappeared into Uncle Matty's bedroom, she named off other staples– bread, canned beans and pigtails, to be packed for Freda and her children to take on their Trail of Tears. Lilly knew her way around Mary's kitchen as well as her own. It took only a few moments for her to find what she needed– wrap it– cry– grab some more food– and cry again.

Mary kneeled at the foot of Uncle Matty's bed. His mattress she had sewn years ago was flattened to the point where it resembled a thick quilt. She pulled back the covers and saw that the stitches were all still intact, save the small opening which she'd left purposefully– The Bank, she and Lar called it. Deposits and withdrawals were made in it via a hand with the thumb pressed tightly against the palm and four fingers bunched together. She reached for what a broken back, calloused hands, sun seared skin, aching knees and a mouth full of 'yes, suhs' and 'yes, ma'am's' were worth in the south.

She slipped the sock into the pocket of her dress and returned to the kitchen. Lilly had three bundles of food on the table and was wrapping a fourth. "C'mon girl, they gotta strike out now!" Mary barked. As they shuffled out of the house, they met Lester, who was carrying a jug of water toward the wagon, and Thomas, who had an armful of hastily picked cucumbers and tomatoes from Mary's garden out back.

"Where ya'll boys runnin' off to with my tah'maytahs?" Uncle Matty cried. "And . . . and . . . and where you goin' with all my fish, gal?" he asked in bewilderment, as Mary dashed past him and left a scented trail of fried fish in her wake.

"Hush now, uncle. We be right back," Mary snipped.

Lar and Buck had been just as busy as the women and boys. Buck was on the back of the wagon handing down furniture to Lar. He moved and adjusted what he could. Lar then handed the furniture and boxes back to him, which Buck stacked firmly and evenly. Mary, Lilly and the boys arrived as the last two chairs were being secured on the end of the wagon with rope.

"Got the food, Lar," Mary huffed.

"Give it to them up front so they can get at it and don't have to stop," Lar instructed.

Freda and her daughter leaned over to their respective side to receive what was being handed to them. The boy, likely having smelled the still warm fish, instinctively reached for it. The girl unwrapped one of the packages and took out a large piece of fish. With the sense of a mother, she carefully picked at the fish and felt for its petite bones before handing it to the toddler who gobbled it down. He smiled and looked up at her for more. She then broke off a large piece and handed it to her mother, who unashamedly stuffed the entire chunk into her mouth. Again the boy begged for more and was given it.

"You all set Ms.," Lar stated, and then gave the wagon a firm pat. "How far you goin'?"

Freda looked at her children, and then looked back at Lar. Her blank expression had already given the answer before she spoke. "Don't know, suh. I guess we just head north 'til cotton fields run out. We ain't got no family north, but we ain't goin' further south – *ever*."

Mary pulled the sock from her pocket and retrieved the contents inside. The small roll of dollars looked larger than what it actually amounted to . . . twenty-three dollars including change that she and Lar had been saving for the past year. There had been forty dollars, but seventeen of them was now standing out in a small paddock munching on grass.

"No ma'am. I can't take your money," Freda protested.

"Now this I ain't hearin' nuthin' 'bout!" Mary argued. "You gonna take this here for you and those chillin."

Freda's eyes welled with tears. "Ma'am, no. Your chile . . ."

" . . . be well looked after," Mary interrupted. She counted out twelve dollars and pushed the other eleven back into the sock.

Freda looked to Lar for help.

"No ma'am," he said. He took the money from Mary and handed it to Freda. "Lord done seen you to our doorstep for a reason. You take this here bit of money and get as far away as you can from here. You don't worry 'bout us none."

"But, suh . . . we ain't *ever* comin' back here."

"Don't 'spect you to," Mary interjected. "Go on take it now, Ms. It be gettin' dark here soon and you still got to pass on through Folsom to strike out north."

"Negroes can't pass through there at night 'cept with a note from a white man . . . even still it ain't safe," Buck warned. "Don't know how far word done traveled 'bout that mess in Peak Hills, but white folk round here talk real quick.

"Amen," Lilly testified.

Freda took the money and put it in her pocket. Mary forced a cough, and then patted her chest where her cleavage began. Lar and Buck instinctively turned around to allow Freda to squeeze the money into her corset and out of sight.

"You try and find a church before it get dark," Lar instructed. "Negroe folk gonna help you out. You just say Lar Cole done sent you and he say to look after you. And you tell'em what done happened, too! You tell'em! You trust in the Lord and he gonna give you strength, sister. You see you done made it this far already. Now that should already tell you somethin'."

Freda looked at Mary. "You see me . . . don't you?" Mary nodded. Freda sighed. "You do see me," she whispered, as though now convinced. "You hear me, too?" Mary smiled and shook her head again.

Buck stepped up to the wagon. "You do like Lar tell you now, Ms."

Everyone backed away from the wagon. Their goodbyes were tainted with the bitterness of needed medicine as the wagon pulled away and started the journey into a realm of uncertainty. Lar clung to prayer . . . Buck and Lilly to hope. Mary snuggled next to her old friend, anger.

Mary was the first to walk away. "God . . . you protect them now– hear!?" she demanded of the unseen deity. Her next words were for those around her. "She can tell everyone she see 'bout what done happened, but it ain't gonna change nothin'. Thangs gonna be like they is now . . . ten, twenty, thirty years from here on." Lar immediately swung his head at her and stared. "You all right there, Lar? You look like you just caught a chill."

"I . . . I . . . I all right. I all right," he sputtered.

"You sho'?"

"Mmm-hmm," he grunted. "What– what were you sayin' now?"

"I was sayin', ain't no one but Negroes gonna care 'bout a dead Negroe . . ."

* * *

. . . But Nicholas Isaac Barrons . . . as white of a man as a white man could be, did care.

Nicholas was the sole progeny of Abram Barrons, a philosophy professor and Sorane Barrons, an English teacher, who lived in the small city of Orion, not fifty miles from Chicago. Nicholas often had the sense that his destiny had been written even before he was born– and for that he was grateful. As the child of two well educated minds, soft hearts, yet steely dispositions, he found it hard to imagine being someone other than who he grew up to be. *But who exactly am I?* he pondered, while sitting at the desk in his small, fairly clean boarding room he'd rented in Folsom. He felt as though he not only suffered from multiple personalities, but that each one was in a constant struggle for dominance. *You're tempting fate,* he thought. Yet, going against fate had become such a familiar, nervous feeling, he was afraid he was actually getting used to it.

He'd been gone from his home in Orion for almost an entire year, travelling in and out of small, dusty towns of the south and journaling all that he'd seen. And much of what he'd witnessed so far made him emotionally and physically sick . . . ashamed to be white . . . embarrassed to call himself a Christian . . . a man . . . a human for that matter. That was until . . . except . . . ever since he saw the Negroe beauty that was actually whiter than he was. She had scarce left his thoughts since that day he literally ran into her.

She was making it ever so difficult for him to keep his mind on his mission. He dreamed of the day when he would return to Orion and finally just sit, relax and compile all of his notes into an article to be published at the small, independent press, The Chicago Chronicler, where he worked. His hope . . . his reason for coming to the south in the first place, was to be able to write an expose that would awaken . . . no, shock Washington and whites everywhere into commonsense and action against the vileness perpetrated against the Negroes in the United States of America; a place where all men were supposed to be equal and had spilled so much blood in a civil war to fulfill that creed.

Lynchings were an evil he'd heard tales of– thanks to and at the insistence of his mother. But to observe it firsthand . . . to hear screams that should never come from a human mouth was almost beyond believing, if it were not so true and so commonly perpetrated. He knew, had he known– truly known, the sound a human was capable of making as they were being flayed, burned alive and chopped up for souvenirs, he never would have come to such a place, for even demons hid in fear from ten– thirty– fifty– two-hundred white grinning faces in orgiastic ecstasy while committing such acts.

It was his mother, Sorane, who'd made sure that once his eyes opened at birth, they would always see the real world, not just the white one around him. And it was his father, whose insight to the blight of America's soul– which was slavery, that Nicholas had no doubt, had buttressed his will and helped set him on the course he was now on. At a time when so many Negroes had fled the south after the war, his family's choices had made them pariahs to many whites.

One . . . Sorane quit her job she held for many years teaching at an all white school on the east side of Orion to work at an all Negroe school on its poverty stricken west side. But the greatest sin of all that was committed, and the one that had forever morally separated the Barrons' from their white friends, relatives and neighbors, was educating him, Nicholas Isaac Barrons– heir to his grandfather's small fortune, alongside the very Negroes she taught. 'Nigger-lovers!' Was what whites uttered to them when being polite . . . yet . . . they also called them 'nigger-lovers' when they weren't.

Nicholas' grandfather, Harold Barrons, had simply thought his son mad, though in character, since Abram had long ago defied his wishes and became a man of utter unimportance in his eyes . . . a professor of all things . . . not a lawyer, doctor or businessman like himself. But Abram raising his only grandchild with Negroes was a sin he equated to sacrificing Nicholas upon an altar. Such an insult to the Barrons' name had been enough for the elder Barron to strip Abram of his inheritance and bequeath it all to Nicholas, who he'd hoped one day would exorcise himself of his parent's neuroses. Yet, despite his grandfather's ill talk of his parents, Nicholas still loved him– his father made sure of that, yet Nicholas despised the old man's views and his money.

"Eyes open, Nick!" Sorane often said to him, when she wanted him to use his noggin for more than just wearing hats or banging on the ground. She had made sure he knew what money could do to the purest of souls, and what those souls were wont to do to keep it, like his grandfather. Though his love for his grandfather was unwavering, he'd come to learn, sooner than he'd wished, that the money inherited by his grandfather from his father, and father before that, was tainted by sorrow and blood of whites, Negroes and Native Americans alike.

As an adult now, he understood being raised along side Negroes had been the greatest blessing his parents had ever given him, and one that all of his grandfather's money couldn't buy. Hearing tales of slavery from the parents of his Negroe classmates further nurtured the sapling branches of his mind that his mother religiously watered. Their accounts of plantation life were vastly different from such genial tales he'd heard from whites, especially those in the south he was now encountering. The cruelty inflicted upon

Negroes, he thought, was unthinkable . . . laughable as a tale that had been stretched far beyond the suspension of belief, if it were not so true. Though now . . . *now* . . . he sometimes wished he was still a boy who was ignorant and oblivious to the world and those who claimed dominion of it, and of others on it. To be born and raised with less care than a sow, horse or cow was the most contemptible of all injustices– a story old Negroe folk and his parents told him, and one he truly believed with all his heart. Having your sister, mother, daughter taken to the master's or his son's bed, was a wound to the soul, they said. The whip upon your back, which was already rife with keloid scars from the last time, was but a common occurrence. To be sold, or have your family sold . . . oh– but there were so many tales of devilry, Nicholas recalled. Each subsequent one seemed worse than the one before it.

But there was one more gift he had received from his Negroe playmates and their elders . . . their language. Like a faucet, he could turn it on and off– switching from his dialect of northern English to a southern drawl complete with dead on uses of 'gonna, fixin-to, sho-nuff, 'bout-to, ain't no and ya'll'. It was exactly what he needed to separate himself from the vile, opportunistic carpetbaggers the whites of the south despised and looked upon with less respect than vultures– unless the price was right and they could choke it down along with their fallen pride. Even he agreed carpetbaggers were little more than scum. Thousands of them had flooded the south with their northern money and purchased acres of land, homes, jewelry or whatever had been of value to whites, who if desperate enough, would saw off and sell their left foot, and offer to take off the other for a few dollars more.

But to the white southerners, he . . . Nicholas Isaac Barrons, was a glimmer of hope. He was his wealthy father's herald who was sent to galvanize partners in revitalizing the south with factories that would produce lumber, paper, textile, machine parts, sugar and most of all, money for those wise enough to invest quickly.

Whites were needed– he lied to them, to run the factories and mills as managers. But Negroes ... *ahhh* ... they would be needed in large numbers to work in the blazing sun and operate dangerous machinery, providing the critical 'niggah grease' to spin the rusty wheel of fortune back to where it was and should have been before the Yankees started meddling in their southern affairs. Even the most cynical whites smiled upon hearing his proposition put in such terms. Of course it was all a ruse. It was never the white man or woman that he cared to assist– it was the Negroe.

But subterfuge was needed, he found out quickly and almost to great harm, if not death. On his very first attempt to connect with Negroes in a small, rural farming community in Georgia, he promptly learned that a white man, southern or northern, did not simply walk and talk amongst Negroes, especially where they lived. Whereas the Negroes were wary at first upon hearing his true reason for being there, they were far more accepting and welcoming after weeks of carefully building trust with them. The whites had a very different reaction to his fraternization with Negroes. He was quickly labeled as a 'rights fighter' ... or as the town folk said, a 'niggah lovin' carpetbagger', and asked him none too politely to leave. *Well—the sheriff's pistol aimed at my head did help convince me,* he remembered vividly.

And so, thus was born his elaborate tale of plans to industrialize the south once more. Greed and a sense of once more being respected as a white man seemed to instantly overcome the whites' disapproval for his sojourns into Negroe shantytowns. "Your Negroes must be many and strong. My father will not even consider investing in a factory where whites will be in the way of harm, gentlemen," he lied, and they swallowed every bite. "And neither will my father tolerate strong willed niggahs who are trouble rousers and sink his investments. That he will have no part in, no matter how willing you southern gentlemen are," he stressed. "Money– my friends! It all revolves around money. Marauding Negroes in Florida ran my father from his textile business while the North continued their aggression upon us. He knows firsthand how these niggahs are and what they are like, and . . . how to deal with them."

Then Nicholas layered the lie even thicker. "He has schooled me in such things also. At the urging of my father, I will appraise your niggahs, and weigh their salt and temperament. My father, mother *and I*, seek to return to our home, which is the south, and be away from those niggah loving Northerners." And for the question that was always sure to follow, and had in every town he visited, he bought an answer after the first incident in Georgia. "I have no fear of niggahs," he always said with a smarmy smile. Then cockily, he would unbutton his jacket if he wore one, or if not, raised the left leg of his pants to reveal a small, silver-snout revolver strapped to a holster on his shin. "I'm no good at tying a noose, gentlemen. But I have a pretty good aim for coon," he would say proudly and self-effacingly, which generally brought a good laugh or two, and always seemed to strengthen his budding allegiance to their white brotherhood.

Gun or no gun, he realized the game he played was a dangerous one. Negroes he'd seen basking in the sun hung from nooses were more than enough to tell him so. But what was ingrained in the psyche of so many southern whites was what troubled him most. It seemed that the lynching of a Negroe was a festival to them. Businesses and schools shuttered their doors so that families would have time to prepare their lunches in time to witness the last breaths of a Negroe. *Animals are far kinder, even when they hunt for prey*, he figured. *At least they eat their kill, not gloat over it.*

Every Negroe . . . northern and southern he'd spoken to so far had had family members, friends or known someone who'd been lynched. Every time they spoke of it to him, it seemed as though he were talking to souls long since left the world. Yet silently, as he listened to grisly tale after tale, he could not help but rejoice and shout in wonder at the strength Negroes had to continue to persevere in a life that seemed to not want them to live. *They still* loved God and sang praises to Jesus. *They still* found the strength to till their fields, sweep their porches and learn to read, write and achieve as much knowledge as whites would allow. *They still* brought more children into a world full of despair, chance, injustice and hope. *They still* continued on . . . dead souls or not.

Nicholas, however, found his will to *continue* far more of a challenge. There had been many a white man he had to force himself to befriend who had been perpetrators of the very crimes he'd sought to bring to light. Many times he ached to reach for his pistol and exact revenge, for he felt that if God was truly just and Jesus the savior, surely they would not punish him for killing those who would lynch a man, woman and child, but applaud and pose with him by their corpses and smile . . . *flash-flash* . . . The urge to visit evil upon vengeful whites seemed to grow with each tale of woe he heard from Negroes. The ancient Hammurabi code of 'an eye for an eye' seemed not so primitive anymore to him, but a necessity.

Nicholas walked to the window and opened it. The warm evening air felt good upon his freshly scrubbed and shaved face. The sound of men and women's chatter, horse hooves and wagons created a meditative chant that helped him clear his thoughts. His wit and mental guard had to be sharp, he knew, as there were important men to be met with and fooled tonight. His seeds of subterfuge had not taken long to sprout and grow. They now only needed water and a sunny, honest face to make them thrive. An investor, a bit of a northerner but with southern roots, and one with lots of money had arrived in town, and many wanted in at ground level, especially the two gentlemen with the greatest influence over Folsom who had requested his presence. But there was yet another southerner that he was told he must meet, the boarding house clerk informed him. Another man was to arrive soon in Folsom with great news of a budding southern kinship, the clerk told him with unrestrained glee– but not tonight.

Tonight was for the men of Folsom. However, he wasn't looking forward to meeting Simeon Monclair or Roman Meadows.

CHAPTER 6

Paul Monclair's knees were aching as he kneeled beside his bed in prayer. *Why even bother,* he wondered. He felt as though the more he prayed the more intense his feelings for men became. Before going to bed and a short time after he finished masturbating, he begged God for forgiveness after the too moment of pleasure had passed. In the morning, like now, he prayed yet again for the feelings to leave him. Though, as if possessed– after pleading with God to give him the strength not to think those thoughts, he would relent and caress his privates until he climaxed in muted ecstasy ... and always afterwards, there came more self-hating for the beast he felt he was, which was so clearly reflected in his father's eyes for all of his sixteen years.

Why won't you listen to me, God? he questioned silently. *Help me. Do something ... anything.*

Paul opened his eyes and stood. The feelings were still there and had not lost their ability to arouse his already spent, though youthful and easily regenerated libido. One image in particular was causing him the most anguish, yet it was one his mind's eye made the most vivid despite how hard he'd wished it would just go away. He recalled all the lies he told Mary about swimming with the boys and remembered it was those lies that had presented the opportunity for such a stimulating image to be imprinted in his mind.

But Paul hadn't been swimming with *'the boys'*, but *a boy*– David Greenlee ... a schoolmate one year older who he'd bonded with, not as much by chance or want, but by process of elimination. David was almost six-feet tall, and come fall, would be well past that. Though David possessed a particular distaste for learning, which seemed difficult for him, he did learn to love food, which had given him a teddy bear like belly and rear-end that attached to wood-post size legs. Paul was already accustomed to the relentless taunting from his classmates, but such ostracism had been foreign to David.

In each other's company and confidence, they had at least some relief from the constant taunts, teasing and rancid gossip. *'Sissy'*– they would call Paul in greeting ... *'sodomite'*– when addressing him properly ... *'cocksucker'*– if they were on a first name basis. For David it was nearly the same, though all the boys and girls knew *'dummy'* had to precede their new names to differentiate which sissy, cocksucker or sodomite they were referring to.

Together, Paul and David restored some peace to their lives, which made them feel as if they actually belonged somewhere, even if it meant that where they belonged was where no one wanted them to be. The tribes edict was that they were deviants, and not only *that* which does not belong, but *that* which must be extinguished if given a chance. Just being around David and away from such unbridled vitriol by the other boys was a joyous respite for Paul. But after each time he was with David, his yearning for more time with him grew ... *and he knew why* ... as did God– every evening and most mornings, or whenever he could escape to the outhouse for a few minutes.

Their swimming escapades had started innocently enough. They had been forced to find their own swimming spot far away from the other boys who swam by the edge of the bridge that weren't cocksuckers, dummies or faggots. They had decided to hunt for their *own* spot where they knew their classmates would not follow and harass them. Across the bridge where Negroes lived and deep into the dreaded woods, they claimed a small clearing near the river's bank. At first they were terrified going so deep into the woods, for once in them, day was no longer day, but like dusk. But after a couple of tentative treks to their newly claimed hideout, it had become more of an adventure. Eventually they had learned the grass to stay bent down, forming a path that led them to their dirt and brush covered paradise. When they were deep enough into the woods, the sound of crickets, squawking black birds, scurrying coons and squirrels let them know they were far away from all those they wanted to leave behind, if only for a short while.

The first time they ventured into the woods and discovered their hidden alcove, Paul knew his life had changed for the worse. He had never seen another boy naked, and it scared him. The feelings aroused in him at the sight of David's pecker and butt made his fantasies of him pale in comparison. David was drenched in sweat from the walk through the forest and had been the first to strip off his clothing and run for the water. Stunned, Paul soaked in the wonder of David's body from behind, which had been shaped and thickened from arduous work on his father's ten-acre farm.

David had turned and smiled, and then waved for Paul to join him. At that moment, Paul could neither see nor hear anything, for the illusion of David naked he had conjured in his mind the night before had become flesh and blood before his blue eyes. He *did* however feel blood rush to his heart, and disturbingly, to his pecker– both which began to swell. Repeated calls from David for him to come into the water created more panic, for as hard as he tried to stop his penis from growing larger, it refused and expanded the crotch of his britches. But again, he felt as though God had finally listened to at least one of his prayers. With his back to David, he slowly fumbled with his pants to stall for time and accidentally brushed his crotch with the back of his hand, which was all the stimulation he needed to find relief and pleasure. After shivering from the unexpected orgasm and stalling for a few minutes more, the blood in his penis finally flowed back from whence it had come.

As their outings became more frequent, Paul learned a semblance of self-control over his body. Before the aroma of man-sweat oozed from David or the sight of his naked body could excite him– which David was always parading about in front of him with no shame– Paul learned to twist his thoughts to that which appealed least to him . . . Holly Ambel, the girl at school with large breasts all the boys talked about getting the chance to fondle. There were still times when he lay close to David or when they playfully wrestled when the sight, heat or scent from David's naked flesh threatened to fan a conflagration of lust within him. At those moments, even the most sickening thoughts he could imagine could not hold his passion at bay– only a spontaneous dash to the water could cool his rising fever.

But alas, nothing could have prepared him for what had happened only a few days past. What did happen pleasingly haunted his dreams, just like the sight of the handsome stranger he'd seen outside his family's store had. Yet, what he'd spied in the woods gave him a better understanding of what 'shameful' really meant.

David was stuck at home setting up fenceposts and so, to both boys' disappointment, could not join Paul for their Saturday swim. Rather than stay at home and have Beatrice running her nails across his ear drums, or chance being roped into some laborious, banal chore, he decided to venture to their secret place alone . . . only, it was not as secret of a place as he had thought.

He spotted Lar's head above a set of bushes near the small clearing he and David had already claimed as their own. But as he was about to call out to Lar– his friend . . . despite his father's feelings for him, simply because he was a Negroe . . . Lar began undressing. For the second time in days, Paul saw another man in naked glory, though this time a real man . . . black skin encasing a muscular giant only heard of in legend. He knew he should have called out to Lar, but the beast that was reflected in his father's eyes goaded him into bending his legs and slowing his breaths. Paul again felt that all too familiar, crotch filling sensation.

He cursed himself as he continued watching Lar at the urging of the beast.

The realization that he was staring at, and in turn becoming aroused by his friend made his stomach raw, yet he did not look away . . . the beast was too convincing. For minutes . . . hours it seemed to him, he watched the drops of river water sheeting away from Lar's body before he finally settled into a small niche and went to sleep. However, simply watching from where he was crouched was not enough for the beast. It desired to see more, but . . . the beast was nervous. It moved his foot too quickly and inadvertently stepped on a twig, snapping it and waking Lar in a panic from his slumber. Paul became a possum as Lar stood and scrambled to clothe himself. The reality of what might happen if Lar found him spying suddenly struck Paul's head like a rock to the temple. When Lar scampered off, he came so close to where Paul was crouched, if he had reached out his hand, he could have grasped Lar's leg as it swooshed by him.

Paul felt that at least for now his vile secret was safe . . . his lust for men . . . what the reverend Michael at his church called an 'abomination' . . . the sin that could only be redeemed in a bath of hellfire that would rage forever and ever and ever . . . *amen.* Yet, now in his room looking in the mirror, he knew God had long since forsaken him anyway, for he no longer recognized the person who stared back. Actually, he realized he never even knew who that boy had ever been.

He wanted to cry away his pain.

He wanted to purge his body of the beast that made all those thoughts so pleasurable to fantasize about. He could no longer see his thick, dark coiled locks upon his forehead and lying against his ears . . . or his rose-colored lips and long black lashes– only the eyes of a beast. He couldn't' see those things that made others call him pretty and lovely.

I'm . . ." he thought, *"I'm . . . a pervert. I'm just like they say I am . . . a pervert and a sicko—right? I* **am** *gonna burn in that Lake of Fire.*

His head dropped to his chest as if it suddenly had doubled in weight. He couldn't find the strength to face the thing looking back at him in the mirror. He whispered, "I wish I was just dead." Again he pictured Lar naked . . . *black skin glistening like polished marble.* "Just die! You hear me! You sicko– faggot! Just die!" *David's two-tone skin . . . brown up top and pale from the waist down . . . his generous round behind . . . his dangling penis always an inch or two longer after roughhousing, like his own.* He knew no matter how much he wanted or prayed to like women, it would never happen. Boobies and the holes girls have aroused as much passion in him as stubbing his toe against the dining room table, while even the musk of a man was enough to make him sigh in wanting. But peace and salvation was but a necktie, rope or a belt that could be hung from a beam out in the woodshed, he remembered.

He ran to his door and bolted it. Safely behind two inches of wood, he covered his mouth to silence his whimpering and freed the tide that was welling in his eyes. He cried for the boy he wanted to be, and was not . . . the boy he'd become and who would soon no longer be trapped by the evil thoughts of the beast within. He even thought of taking a trip into the woods with some rope to hang himself. *I can go in far enough where nobody would ever find me before the animals got to me,* he mused in his head. *But I gotta go deep. I can't let David find me—not like that.*

The idea that taking his own life would finally give him free-dom was enticing to him. Finally, he felt he could relieve his father of the son who repulsed him so much . . . the son he could barely speak to unless he was beating him. He could be away from his mother who seemed to simply tolerate him, and Beatrice who al-ways joined in taunting him at school as much, if not more than the others did. And David– not always aching to feel David's hand on his shoulder out of pure friendship would be a welcomed relief, especially when he constantly dreamed of so much more from him. He was determined not to expose David to the contagion inside him. Lar too, could be free from the sickening fantasies of a per-verted boy, he figured.

There was but Mary left for him to consider. For her, he could not think of what his absence would free her from. And search as he might, he could find no reason to leave her. He loved her so, which in itself, he knew, was looked upon as being just as damming as being a pervert. He wished he was still two years old and could crawl into her arms and snuggle like he used to, for it was there where he always found comfort in her kisses on his fore-head and cheeks that he had never known from the woman he called mother.

Paul's scale that weighed whether to gather the rope and trek off into the woods or to continue to endure such pain in his heart remained unbalanced. Never seeing Mary was the only reason he could think of to let the rope stay hung upon its rusty nail in the shed . . . at least for now, he resolved. *But you're gonna have to do it,* he thought. He vowed everyone would be free of him and the beast once he found courage enough. When he did take the rope on his last walk into the woods, he figured it would be apology enough to David, Mary and Lar for being such a sick, vile thing, and then just wait for the devil to welcome him home once he swung his last swing.

CHAPTER 7

Mary ignored Isabel's calls from out in the garden. Instead, she simply continued sweeping the upstairs hallway. It was mid-afternoon on Monday, and she was already exhausted. And right now, she hadn't the nerve to be around Isabel, or any white folks after what happened in Peak Hills. Memories of Freda and her children fleeing haunted her better than any ghost could– they were in the way at every turn it seemed, slowing her down as she swept and mopped around them. Freda's crying and her daughter's whimpering was as incessant now as it was in the kitchen when she got Simeon's breakfast fixed, and then served so he could, thankfully, be on his way.

As she guessed it would happen, word of the lynching in Peak Hills swiftly made its way to the ears of Folsom white folk. The only problem was that it didn't seem to bother white folks a bit. The way Mary saw it, it seemed to put white folks in a better mood than they been in for months . . . lips hinting of smiles . . . their steps seeming a bit lighter . . . their joy in referring to a Negroe as a 'niggah' all but seemed renewed. It was fear white folks wanted Negroes to always feel, she thought, but she was damned if she was going to just give it to them freely.

Can't bow my head no lower when my back be already broken, she thought. *Already gotta scoot to the side when they come by.*

Can't look'em in the eye when they speakin' to me, 'cause that mean I some uppity-ass niggah. Gotta do as I told to do! Mary stopped to catch her breath. She leaned on the broom handle with one hand and rubbed her belly with the other. "Child, you comin' soon or ain't'cha? You must gonna be a big'un like folk say, 'cause you wearin' your momma down! Hear me?" She felt a small kick in response and smiled.

"Are you *that* tired, Mary?" Beatrice inquired, after slipping out of her room into the hallway.

Mary summoned her will to refrain from turning and snatching Beatrice by the hair and swinging her about. Though she didn't like to pray– she did . . . *for restraint.* Beatrice was wearing one of the new dresses Allie Mae had finally finished. Her hair, which Mary had brushed into life and had put into two looping braids that attached at the nape, were decorated with pink ribbons to match her outfit. Despite being attired in such lovely linen that would have made most plain girls pretty, the dress had failed to work its magic on Beatrice, who appeared as though someone had stuffed her into it as punishment for a dastardly deed.

"If you ever be in my condition, missy, you gonna know what tired be," Mary replied, in the same dry manner in which Beatrice had asked.

"Oh– I will someday," Beatrice assured her. "I'm going to have lots of children. But I could never imagine myself working, let alone working *and with child.*"

Mary resumed sweeping. "Hummpf! Sometimes you never know what be comin' 'round the bend nowadays."

Beatrice giggled. "Mary, please . . . I already have many young men, from very respectable families– I might add, promising to call upon me once they and I have reached the proper age. I doubt if my future will ever be so bleak as you're trying to make it out to be."

"If you're thinking Payne Hallson or Albert Longfield are gonna call on you, I wouldn't hold my breath," Paul said, as he slipped out from his room. "They promised Holly they would call on her, too. They tell every girl that. Payne and Albert are both rotten anyway."

Beatrice's thin, almost nonexistent lips, slammed together. When they parted, they literally smacked. "Rotten only because they'll have nothing to do with you and your dumdum friend. How is Dumdum David anyway?"

Paul's black brows sunk at the mention of David's name. "I don't think 'dumb' is a word I'd use to talk down about others, Beatrice," Paul said.

Beatrice closed the distance between her and Paul until she was nearly nose-to-nose with him. She pointed her finger at his face, threatening to scrape out his blue eye. Paul instantly backed up, but found his closed room door blocking his retreat. "I know some words to describe you! Not like you and your '*friend*', Dumdum David, haven't heard them anyway." She smirked as she stepped back slowly, and then put one hand on her hip and cocked her head. "Would you like to hear one or two of them now? Hmmm?"

Mary saw Paul's face relax, though not in a good way, but in such a manner that begged, 'no . . . please.' She was sure her eyes weren't failing when she looked at his hands and saw them quivering. His lips slowly parted. "You're . . . just . . . just . . . horrible . . . mean and evil! You know that?!" He sputtered.

"*Meeeee?*" She squealed in delight. "Ha! Meeee? You are something, Paul. You and Dumdum David are the ones who are *eeeeeevil.*" She smiled as she stood on her field of victory. "*Paul and David . . . Paul and David . . .,*" she began singing

Paul looked at Mary and then quickly lowered his eyes. "Beatrice, don't . . . please?" Paul whispered.

"*Paul and David . . .*"

Paul grabbed a tuft of his hair and began yanking on it. When it wouldn't come loose, no matter how hard he pulled, he leaned against his door and dropped his hands to his side . . . and he began crying. "Stop it . . . please," he begged.

"*'Paul and David—Paul and David—wanna have a baby—wanna have a baby—bump in front—bump in back—pull down my pants and hump my back. Paul and David—Paul and David—who's the sissy—wanna be prissy—bump in front . . . bump in back—pull down our pants and . . .'*"

Mary felt as though someone had just stabbed her in the belly when she saw tears dripping from Paul's chin to his shirt. Again, she wanted to grab Beatrice, but not by the hair this time, but at her throat. "That 'bout 'nough, missy Beatrice! Why don't you go on down and help your mammy out in the garden?"

Beatrice displayed a wondrous smile for Mary as though she meant to dazzle her. "I suppose," she replied, and then spun . . . her braids followed moments after. "Or maybe I'll just sit in the garden and watch mother pick and preen. I have so much to think about now– like what shall I talk to father about when he arrives home this evening. Hmmm? Sing him a song? What do you think, Paul?"

"Just . . . p-p-p-lease? Please, Beatrice? I'm-I'm sorry for saying that about Payne and Albert– all right!? I'm sorry! I'm sorry . . . I'm sorry, ok?" Paul begged, as he wiped snot and tears from his upper lip.

"That be enough, Missy Beatrice!" Mary implored softly, in hope that a kinder touch would drive Beatrice away. "You done said what you want to say, now. Let thangs be how they be now."

Beatrice continued walking away, albeit slowly. "Hmmm? How about the other song? I think that *'rotten'* Payne Hallson– as you call him, Paul, made this one up . . . *'Dumdum David says he loves a girl—but it's just Paul with the black-black curls. He's gonna bend over—like he's picking clover—so tell me when it's over so he can take a turn. Sissy-sissy Paul-Paul wants to be a girl—but he's just a boy with the black-black curls. He's gonna bend over—like he's picking clover—so tell me when it's over so he can have a turn'."*

Paul lifted his head. His fists were clenched and his mouth quivering. ***"Shut up!"*** He screamed.

Beatrice smiled and shook her head in disappointment. "Awww . . . poor Paul and his friendly-friendly-friend, Dumdum David."

Paul pushed away from the wall and charged toward Beatrice. Mary reached out and grabbed his arm, but he pulled away with a strength she did not expect. "Tell father then and see if I care!" he yelled. "Tell everyone, you . . . you . . . bitch!"

"Oh Jesus," Mary whispered.

Beatrice's smile hadn't diminished at all.

Footsteps sounded below, right before Isabel's voice rang out in alarm.

"And I hope you do marry Payne, or . . . or . . . or Albert . . ." he said, "they're hateful and evil– just like you *and* father. It's just what you deserve."

"Paul, don't . . ." Mary begged. But it was too late . . . the damn had already been breached.

"You've earned everything coming to you," he hissed. "You'll end up just like mother– and it'll serve you right. That's right . . . *Beatrice* . . . Payne or Albert, or whoever is dumb enough to marry you is going to beat you in your fat face."

Isabel had reached the landing in time to hear every word and gave the impression that she hadn't. "Paul . . . Beatrice! What's going on here?! All this screaming . . . my God! " She was breathless, but trying to sound calm.

Beatrice quickly exchanged her smile for an expression of fear. "Mother! Paul was about to rush upon me. He was going to strike me!"

"Liar!" Paul screamed.

"Ms. Beatrice, that ain't true, now," Mary interjected. If anyone was going to strike Beatrice, Mary knew it would have been her.

"Mother, it's true!" Beatrice pleaded. Her voice lost strength, as though she was suddenly overwrought. "I was so scared. And Mary . . . Well, she tried to stop him . . . a little."

Isabel took Beatrice by the hands and bent down so that she was eye level with her. "Beatrice . . . darlin' . . . you know your brother would not have struck you . . . would you, Paul?" Isabel begged, not truly asked.

Paul was silent for a moment, and then answered with a grunt. "No."

"See darlin' . . . he was just mad about what ever you two were quarrelling about, which I'm sure was really about nothing at all." Isabel nodded her head, as if hoping Beatrice would soon do the same.

Beatrice snatched her hands from Isabel's and straightened her spine. "You always take his side, mother."

"That's not true. Sweetheart, you know that's not– "

"I'll speak with father when he comes home and he'll settle it all," Beatrice spouted, cutting Isabel off. Her orchestrated fear of Paul had vanished as quickly as it started.

Isabel gasped. Momentarily, her lips moved as fast as her fluttering eyelids, though nothing came out at first, but then . . . "How – how . . . dare you speak to me in such a manner."

Beatrice rolled her eyes and shook her head, as though she had just turned thirty years of age and Isabel was now the impudent child. "Mother, please." She looked at Paul and lowered the lids down on her blue eyes. "And you! I'm sure father will want to speak with you later . . . *Paul-Paul with the black-black curls. He's gonna bend over—like he's picking clover . . .* "

Before another word could be spoken, Paul ran. As he fled toward the stairs, neither Isabel nor Beatrice had time to fully part to allow him passage. As he slipped past Beatrice, he grazed her shoulder with his own. Beatrice's years of acting and feigning in-sults was put to use, as she half-spun and fell into the wall. She shrieked in shock and pain as only the best of thespians could.

Within seconds, the only sign of Paul was a door slamming downstairs. Mary dreaded what would await him upon his return. For his sake, knowing how Simeon was bound to react to what happened, she hoped he wouldn't.

* * *

"Lord, have mercy," Mary whispered, half-angry and half-shocked, at all that had transpired within an hour's time that now had her driving a cart in the midday heat.

Her sweat-soaked dress stuck to her back, breasts and thighs, as she drove the cart toward town with nothing on her head except the cornrows atop of her head. But it was either choose to look for her headscarf that was in the kitchen somewhere and continue to listen to Beatrice's tirade, or immediately leave for the Monclair farm at the behest of Isabel. "I want you to tell father now!" Beat-rice demanded, with tears that hadn't ceased since her feigned as-sault.

Reasoning with Beatrice had been pointless. After she and Isabel brought Beatrice down to the front parlor and laid her on the couch, Mary quickly exited and pretended to slip off into the kitchen, hoping Beatrice would eventually settle down and just let the entire matter drop. Mary closed the door and listened.

"Beatrice– you need to calm yourself," Isabel pleaded.

"I knew Paul would strike at me one of these days," Beatrice whimpered, more to herself than her mother. "He hates me so."

"It was an accident," Isabel suggested.

"Deliberate . . . mother! You saw it all, but now you're trying to defend him as usual."

"No . . . I . . ."

"I want father here now!"

Mary wasn't sure what happened next, but she guessed Isabel had attempted to soothe Beatrice with an unfamiliar touch of motherly comfort. "Don't touch me!" Beatrice screamed. "I am not going to live afraid . . . you may, mother, but I won't. *I will not!* I'm a Monclair more than I'll ever be a Christianson."

Footsteps padding toward the door were Mary's cue to quickly depart to where she was supposed to be. She was in the kitchen for no more than a few moments before the door opened and a droopy eyed, blanched Isabel was standing before her. Mary hadn't had a chance to grab a utensil or a pot to create the illusion of her working, so she simply turned and faced Isabel, who was standing half--in and half-out of the room. But then, Plyus, papa of the feline brood that stalked Mary's kitchen, strolled in behind Isabel and rubbed his back against his mistress' right shin. Isabel scooped up the cat and cradled it.

"All of this commotion has scared you to death, hasn't it, Plyus?" Isabel asked of the oval-faced cat, and then snuggled him close, rubbing her cheek against his and letting him lap at her cheek. Not to be left out, three more of the black felines scampered in and circled her feet to see who would be taken aloft and set in Isabel's arms next. Any other time, the sight of the cats and their ever present trail of hairs would have had Mary fussing about it, but she could see Isabel desperately needed her four-legged children, especially now.

"Mary . . ." Isabel paused for a moment, and then spoke as if *she* had come to a decision. "I want you to go out to the farm and find Mr. Monclair."

"Ma'am?" Mary was surprised. Simeon was adamant about not being disturbed at home, in town, after work, while he was sleeping, awake or reading the paper, or eating breakfast, or sitting, or . . . To bother him in town at night was especially taboo, because he was not to be found in his office at the farm, but because he was again enjoying drinks at his tavern before slipping away into the company of the widow, Earnestine Richards, his well known, but never mentioned mistress. But it was still mid-afternoon. There was still time.

"Tell him Beatrice needs him at home . . . and that she is very upset and wants to speak with him," Isabel instructed.

"Mr. Monclair ain't just gonna up and leave his work, Ms. Isabel," Mary replied, hoping she might change her mind. "He gonna want to know what done happened. And he ain't gonna take too kindly to me comin' to fetch him."

"Of course he's not," Isabel replied. "But Beatrice is going to brew all day long if he doesn't, and God knows what's likely to come out of her mouth then. Isn't it all already bad enough, Mary?"

Mary grasped her hips and lowered her head. Isabel was right. Beatrice had already bared her fangs and was likely to bite the next time. When Beatrice was still a toddler, her incessant screaming and uncontrollable temper-tantrums, during which she would yank her own hair out and leave strands of it on the floor, had convinced Mary that she would be nothing but a handful of trouble the older she got. But Mary realized she had been very wrong. There was no 'would become trouble', but 'have always been trouble'.

"He gonna want me to say what be a matter, Miss."

"Then tell him," Isabel said flatly. "I suppose what happened is better coming from you than her, though I don't suppose it'll make any difference. There's only one story he's going to believe, Mary. It's probably best if Paul didn't return."

"I know, ma'am," Mary responded, knowing full well whom she meant.

For a brief moment, it seemed as though Isabel was about to break down into a fit of tears. But she took in a deep breath and sighed before speaking, although shakily. "As soon as you return and tell me what Simeon has to say, I want you to leave."

"Ma'am? But supper . . ."

Isabel shook her head. "I don't want you around when Simeon comes home . . . especially if Paul comes home, too."

"I know how Mr. Monclair can be," Mary responded.

"No, Mary– you don't." Isabel's voice began to wane. She moved close to Mary. She whispered, as if the walls had suddenly sprouted ears. "You have no idea how he can be. All you've ever seen is what he has already done. It's how it's 'done' that stays with you . . . it's what I don't want you seeing tonight." She stepped back and resumed speaking in a normal voice. "Find him quick, Mary, before it gets too late in the evening and he fills up on drink."

"I will, ma'am."

"Find Simeon quick for Paul's sake . . . *and* . . . just . . . just find him."

And Mary did.

Simeon Monclair was exactly where Mary thought he would be; given it was not yet dusk. She entered the wood frame office and was greeted with a grunt from Wilshim Colby, one of Simeon's foremen. She had seen him around town before, and only knew his name because of Negroe folk talk about who was a decent white– nary none . . . a halfway decent white– only one hand was needed to count those folk . . . and a nasty, hateful white– more than you can shake at with a stick . . . Wilshim fell into the nasty, hateful white category.

"I need to speak to Mr. Monclair, if he be in, suh," she said.

Wilshim looked up from the stack of papers on his desk and grimaced. He eyed her up and down, and then lowered his head back to his work. "Who you?"

"His maid . . . Mary Cole."

Wilshim continued thumbing through his papers. "What you wanna see Mr. Monclair 'bout?"

"His children', suh," she answered simply.

Wilshim set down his papers and looked up at her. He squinted at her, and then curled his lips. He was just a bit of a man, no wider than the chair he sat in. His short black hair was spotted with gray all over, but not at the temples or crown that gave most men in their middle ages a distinguished look. His pale skin, having lost most of its plumping layers to age and weather, practically flapped as spoke. "You gonna say what you here 'bout or you just stand there like a mute niggah?"

Niggah? Me? Mary fumed silently, as she debated what response to give. *You sittin' there with your dirty-ass shirt . . . but I the niggah? Half your teeth done rotted in your head and the others done fell out—breath stankin', too . . . but I the niggah? You ain't even got a blade to shave your nappy beard . . . but you call me a niggah? You 'bout as dumb as a stump be thick . . . but I still just a niggah to you?*

"Ms. Isabel say only to speak to Mr. Monclair 'bout it," Mary decided to say. "That be his wife I talkin' 'bout . . . Mrs. Monclair—suh."

"Fine then," he replied, and then stood. "Stand there and I'll see if he feel like bein' worried wi'cha."

"Suh," she said, and then looked the other way. Though there were chairs in the room she could have sat in, she knew Wilshim would not offer her one to sit in. She was only a niggah to him after all, pregnant or not, she knew.

Wilshim knocked on the door behind him and opened it only after Simeon grumbled something Mary couldn't quite make out. He walked in and closed the door behind him, but was back out a moment later. He returned to his chair and stared at her for a moment. "Go on, gal," he said. "All I can say is, it best be important."

Mary walked over to the office door, which was ajar, and already her olfactory system, which was already sensitivity since being pregnant, was overloaded by the smell of processed liquor from Simeon's lungs being exhaled into the small room. She knocked lightly. She was hesitant to judge just how foul of a mood he was already in.

"Come in," Simeon ordered.

He was sitting at his desk. In his left hand, he was holding a piece of paper up in front of his face . . . his stump was hidden from view beneath the table. When he lowered the paper and revealed his face, Mary's heart quickened. Bolts of static, red lightning surrounded Simeon's blue eyes, which were still remarkably brilliant despite his fifty-some years of age. His lips seemed to hold no blood, but were more like the color of rainclouds. Mary predicted it would not be a bad night at the Monclair's, but a horrible one. Yet, despite his journey to intoxication, his blond, mostly gray hair remained meticulously parted on the left and combed back, revealing a receding hairline that had begun in his thirties. His clean-shaven face was as smooth as wet paper that had been crumpled up and then spread out to dry in the sun. She knew Simeon had only spruced up for one reason . . . and it wasn't for Isabel.

Praise be there still be some light out here, she thought. If it had been any later, Mary was positive he would have been in the company of Earnestine Richards, and that was a door she would not even consider tapping on, no matter how much Beatrice 'hooped and hollered' for her daddy, and Isabel begged her to. Dabbling in the business of a white man and his white whore could get a Negroe killed quicker than a Negroe striking a white man, or his white whore, she thought.

"Suh?" She asked finally, and then looked away as he looked up. "Ms. Isabel told me to fetch you home."

"Fetch me? Am I a dog?"

"No suh. I sure she ain't mean to say it that way, suh," she replied. "There be some trouble at home with Ms. Beatrice. Ms. Isabel told me to come out here and let you know. Beatrice say . . .

"What happened? She hurt?"

Simeon's change in tone from caustic to an uncharacteristic semblance of caring caught her off guard. "No suh. I mean . . . not really, suh," she replied. She could hear the rollers of his chair grinding on the wood floor. "Not the way you 'spectin'."

"Don't tell me what I'm thinkin', gal," he huffed. "What's this mess about?"

Mary chose her words carefully, knowing she was now charged to set the stage for the play that was to follow in the evening. The last thing she wanted to do was to set his temper simmering, only to have Beatrice's manufactured tears and phantom pains turn up the heat to an inferno and boil it over. But even the most delicately selected words, she knew, could not smother what Paul had done. She didn't blame him for doing what he did, especially after the nasty, humiliating words that had spilled out from Beatrice's mouth. But Beatrice was no ordinary girl that Paul insulted and had carelessly brushed past. She was Beatrice Monclair, the most beloved thing in Simeon Monclair's life . . . besides the widow, Earnestine.

"The children got to arguing . . . 'bout somethin' or 'nother, and it just all got outta hand," she explained.

"Arguing about what? And what do you mean got out of hand? And where the hell were you and Isabel during all of this?" Simeon rose from his chair. His stump hung lazily at his side . . . red with fury it was, and had always been since becoming a stump and no longer a hand.

Mary sighed silently. "They be talkin' so loud, I couldn't right hear what they be fussin' 'bout, suh. But . . ."

"Goddamnit– but what?!"

Mary couldn't see any escape from the corner she was in. There was no way around it, so she told it exactly like it happened. She hoped the truth would prevail over the lies that Beatrice had without a doubt formed and repeated to herself so often, that she probably now believed it to be the God's honest truth. Still, Mary left out what had started it all. Beatrice's taunting innuendos about Paul and his friend would not come from her, she resolved.

Simeon placed his shriveled stump atop the papers on his desk. "And you did nothing?"

"It happened so fast . . ."

He didn't let her finish. "Isabel did nothing as you let Paul hit Beatrice? Is that what I'm hearing?"

"He didn't hit . . ."

"You did nothing!" he shouted.

Mary quickly sidestepped out of his path as he walked to the door and swung it open with such force that it came back and hit him on his heels before he stepped into the other room. Mary followed and saw that Wilshim, who had been sitting at the table when she'd entered, had already risen to his feet. "Go to town and tell those gentlemen at the motel to meet me at my home tonight instead of the tavern," he directed.

"I can do that for you right now, Mr. Monclair," Wilshim responded humbly, like the servant he was paid to be.

Simeon glared at him. "Well, that certainly is preferable than doing it later now, isn't it?" Wilshim lowered his head as he scrambled for his hat and nearly ran out the door. Simeon then focused on Mary. "Gal– you best find that son-of-a-bitch before night's end . . . or I'll make sure he's found."

* * *

But locating Paul, however, was no easy task. Mary couldn't imagine him having run off for good. *He may be just 'bout a man, but he still be a baby to me,* she thought. As fragile as he was and ignorant of what really lay beyond Folsom's borders, she was certain he couldn't survive on his own. But if he hadn't run off, where could he be? She thought upon all of the places he might have gone or to whom. '*Who,* be right,' she whispered suddenly. She snapped the reigns, and with a jerk from the horse pulling the cart, she was on her way before the destination had a chance to settle in her mind. It was remembering Beatrice's words that gave her some hope of finding him ... '*Paul and David ... Paul and David*' ... Lester Greenlee's boy– David. She didn't know the boy or the family personally, though she did know *about* them. One– because they shunned the people of Folsom and kept to themselves mostly, and two– Lester was the only man around who rivaled Lar in height and girth. If Beatrice was right, and Mary had no reason to doubt her words that had clawed at Paul's heart so deeply, then if anyone knew where Paul might be, it would be the Greenlee boy.

Unfortunately for Mary, after enduring another bone jarring wagon ride– this time out to the west-end of Folsom, and after having spoken with David's mother, Francine, she discovered she had been half right. "No– Davey 'spose to be with some Patrick boy or 'nother," the slim-built woman replied to Mary's inquiry. "I sure it a Patrick, not a Paul. We don't 'sociate with them Monclair's. My husband ain't gonna have no part of nuthin' with a Monclair name. He barely let Davey go into town for schoolin' as it be."

Mary could tell from Francine's broken English that she rarely ever stepped off the farm, let alone knew what a schoolbook looked like. "Well ma'am, don't reckon you know where David and this ... *Patrick* ... might be, do you?" Mary asked, as she wiped sweat from her brow for the fourth, fifth, sixth ... tenth time.

"Swimmin' I 'spectin'." Francine scanned the horizon, as if she might be able to glimpse the boys frolicking in the water somewhere upon it. "You know boys come summah– always runnin' off to the river. You ask me, I wouldn't touch that filthy water ... all those dead soldiers they say stuck to the bottom of it– uh-uh."

"Yes'm," Mary replied.

"Davey been just itchin' to get to that cesspool everyday. Lester took a switch to'im for forgettin' his chores the other night and made him stay put here– so he couldn't go for a spell. Today was the first day he could, and he took off like a rat with a broom after him. That boy," she huffed. "You know where the boys be swimmin'?"

"Yes'm."

"Down off by the bridge," she said anyway. "That be what Lester told me. You likely find him there, I reckon."

Mary gave thanks and was about to leave, but Francine held up her hand and stopped her. "We got a well out back if you like a sip of water. The trough full too for that horse."

"Mighty nice of you, but I ain't got nothin' to drink from," Mary responded genuinely, as she was surprised that a white woman had even offered her such kindness.

Francine shut her left eye and lolled her head to the same side. "A cup? Cup for . . . oh hell!"

'Ahhh,' Mary thought– Francine remembered 'who' and 'what' she was.

"We ain't like that!" Francine blurted. "Lester and me and our people ain't ever *owned* nobody– it sick and unchristian. I don't care who know how I feel 'bout it neither. When folk started screamin' 'bout war with the north . . . we stayed right out of it. The south made they mess and gotta pay they dues. If people don't wanna let people just be people, then to hell wit'em. Now as far as those folks in Folsom, Lester always say, 'don't bother us and we ain't gonna bother ya'll.' Now you get 'round there and use *our* cup and get some cool drink in ya . . . you sittin' up there full as a tick with that baby. Go on . . . get 'round."

Mary drank greedily from the well, but not with as much passion as she did absorbing Francine's shocking and unexpected verbal tirade. She was relieved that no one had ever bet her that there was a white in Folsom who actually thought Negroes should actually be treated like people, for she would have wagered her home, clothes, chickens and pigs that there wasn't. She gave water to the horse that seemed equally as parched as she had been. With thanks once more to Francine, she set her destination for the bridge.

She made her way around the circular path and toward the narrow, heavily-worn wooden bridge. But it was upon that dusty road that she was suddenly aware of the near silence around her, save the rambling of the cart and occasional huffing from the horse. The great, dead tree suddenly seemed not so lifeless– its leaf-barren branches reaching for the sky. Its trunk was thick and would take at least five men a day and a half to uproot its many legs that ran deep and wide. The tree had stood for more years than she'd been alive, and more than her mother and grandmother, too. Yet having been torched by Union soldiers and was now seemingly dead within, it appeared as though it had not lost one branch or twig. Despite wind and rain, vicious thunderstorms and an occasional icy frost, the tree had not even bent, whereas other trees that appeared to be just as sturdy had been stripped of their arms or completely snapped in two. Yet now, as she gazed upon it, it still standing proudly in yet another year of southern heat, it seemed not as dead as folk had always told her it was.

Once past the Meadow's place where Maggie Mae worked, Mary could see the boys swimming and running about a good fifty feet before she came to the bridge– their white bodies were ghosts upon the black water and soil. But they were not carefree, innocent boys in her eyes, but the next generation of noose-makers. How many of their fathers had lynched a Negroe? She wondered. Whose families once owned slaves and raped the girls, women and boys, too? Whose father fought for the confederacy and mother prayed daily for the death of the Union? Which of these boys harbored revenge for their father's failed dreams behind smiles of boyhood joy?

No– they were not just boys. Though the south was decisively beaten, the war had done nothing to remove the privileges of 'white' boys whose legacy was to keep a foot on Negroe's necks when their father's feet grew old and weary. Beaten in war . . . they beat Negroes. Humbled in war . . . they stripped respect from Negroes.

She was closer to the edge of the bridge, but did not see Paul or David amongst the group . . . she didn't expect to . . . but she did recognize some of the others. She spotted the Anderson and Mitchell boys chasing each other by the bank and trying to throw the other in. Albert Longfield, who Beatrice had her eye on, was floating on his back ignoring the raucous from the shore that the others made. The Johnson, Gregory and Bartfield boys were there also . . . Payne Tressen, Beatrice's other hopeful paramour, was nowhere to be seen. Many of the boys, she knew, had lost their grandfathers, uncles and fathers in the war, such as the Johnson and all five of the Spader boys. The Collingwood boy's father had come home alive, but left his leg and right arm on the battlefield. Such deaths and maiming were tragedies for any family, but Mary felt not the slightest bit of empathy for any one who had fought to keep the south as it was. In a deep, dark place hidden in her heart that she didn't even share with Lar, she rejoiced in their suffering.

Forced to interact with them, she knew which face to put on. She didn't bother leaving the wagon. Girlish giggles arose when she asked if they knew the whereabouts of Paul or David. A few shook their heads and a couple of more said they did not. A voice, she couldn't see which boy it had come from, yelled out from the protection of anonymity, "We don't swim with girls!" A couple of the older boys began singing before they erupted in laughter . . . *Paul and David . . . Paul and David* . . . soon all were joining in. Some began running around poking out their small bird chests and pushing out their barely covered rears from the cut off pants they wore as swimming trunks. Others flapped their wrists and skipped as they raised their voices to a falsetto.

Oliver, the Johnson boy said upon stretched vocal cords, "Hey there, mistah . . . I'm Paul . . . ain't I just pretty."

The oldest Spader boy, Conrad, stuck his teeth out and moved his eyes side-to-side. "Duh!"

The boys who watched were giggling deliriously.

Conrad hunched his back and walked around in circles as if his feet had suddenly tripled in size and weight. "I'm . . . I'm David . . . I think?"

The audience cheered.

Oliver turned around, and with his back to Conrad, bent over at the waist. "Ooopsie! I think I just dropped somethin' on the ground," he squealed. "I best find it quick 'fore some big dummy come up and take my *beeee*-hind." He began shaking his rear from side to side. "Oh dear . . . oh dear, where it be?"

Conrad began thrusting his hips at the air only inches from Oliver's rear-end. "Duh . . . duh . . . maybe this'll help you, Pauly-Paul. Duh . . . duh . . . duh . . ." The crowd gave their rendition of a standing ovation by rolling in the mud in a fit of hysterical laughter.

Mary felt a strange thing happening inside. Her throat was tightening and her eyes were beginning to sting. The spectacle below revealed a place within her that she was convinced didn't and couldn't exist . . . her heart aching for a white. And though she knew next to nothing of David, she felt pity for him also. The fear and anxiety filling her was no less than if Paul was hanging from a cliff with no one but her to pull him back from the precipice. She suddenly realized how foolish it was to think he was safer away from home. She was always relieved to see him off to school, if only to be away from that damned house for a while. She realized now he was simply trading one problem– Simeon and Beatrice, for another– soul-beating persecution at school.

She disembarked from the wagon. The child in her belly weighed heavily upon her, but did nothing to slow her steps to the edge of the bridge. "Any of ya'll know where they *might* be?" She asked, struggling to get the words out of her throat that was threatening to seize up and strangle her.

The boys were still giggling from the impromptu production and ignored her, except . . . One child who seemed immune to the shenanigans did provide some help. He left the group and climbed up the embankment. His cutoff britches were caked with dirt from having sat on the ground after swimming. There was no smile upon his face, but nor was there anger– more like a hint of embarrassment.

He cautiously looked back toward the boys before speaking. His voice was in flux between childhood and manhood, and squeaked when he spoke. "I ain't seen where they be exactly, Ms. Mary, but . . ."

Mary was quite surprised that he knew her name. "Who you be?"

"Cal?" he replied– asked, as if he wasn't quite sure. Again, he looked around at the others who had already resumed playing. "Me and Paul *used* to run 'round togethah . . . when we was youngah."

"You Hendrickson's li'l boy? Your mammy and pappy live down the road from the old Monclair home?" Cal gave a semblance of a smile, and then nodded. "I ain't seen you in years, now. You and Paul always be together when ya'll was babies."

Cal's head drooped. "Yeah . . . I know. I . . . I think they on the other side," he whispered.

"Over there?" Mary directed her eyes toward the other side of the bridge. "You sure, chile?"

Cal's eyes widened in a silent reply of 'yes'! "The others throw stuff at 'em and say they gonna beat Paul and David up, so they'll stay away from 'round us . . . I-I-I mean *them*."

"How you figurin' they done gone up in there?"

"I kind of . . ."

"Kind of . . . ?"

Cal hesitated a moment. "I . . . I . . . saw David and Paul leavin' out one day togethah, so I try to see where they goin'. I only got far as those last row of houses back yonder," he said, pointing toward the Meadow's home and the others looming in its shadow. "I caught 'em zippin' 'cross the bridge and then down the hill into the woods. I 'spect they was guessin' no one was lookin', 'cause they kept peekin' 'round all scary like and didn't cross ovah 'til nobody was 'round."

"You be followin' them?"

"No!" Cal blurted loudly and then again in a hush. "*No . . . no . . . no*. I . . . I was j-j-just curious is all." His eyes swept his left and right periphery . . . once . . . then twice . . . then a third time for good measure. "I-I-I gotta go . . . Ms. Mary. I check there . . . ok? And I wasn't followin' them . . . ok?" His eyes were on the move again.

"Alright, chile . . . alright." Mary shook her head stiffly to let Cal know that she understood that– 'no', he was not following them, for following them meant rhymes about Paul and David would then include Cal.

"Damn it!" Mary exclaimed under her breath. It was foolish for Paul and David to have gone into the woods, but also a wise decision, she figured, for boys like them who wanted to escape taunts and threats. All the times she helped Paul sneak off to go swimming, she realized now, she had inadvertently let him go where no one with any sense wanted to go . . . except Enda. She mounted the wagon with one brief stop and one destination in mind. "Don't be tellin' no one what you told me now, chile." Cal bobbed his head in reply.

She checked the time with a glance up at the sun. Lar wouldn't be off for a few more hours. She knew without a doubt he would gladly trump through the forest with her to look for Paul. That was of course the most rational idea, only . . . it was a time for irrationality, she decided. Commonsense would only rouse up the devil more in Simeon if she didn't find him soon.

She figured Lar wouldn't understand anyway, and felt no need to tell him about what had happened. She would have to tell him something, however, but it could never be the truth. Lar preached against boys and men like Paul. She knew it wasn't right to lie about it, but still, she felt it was the right thing to do for both Paul and Lar's sake. Lar cared for the boy immensely. Whenever Simeon wasn't around, and Lar, waiting patiently outside their fenced yard to walk her back home, it was Paul who'd learned how to unlock the gate and free himself to Lar's open arms. Had it been any other white child that Lar bounced on his knee or played in the dirt with, she would have reprimanded him. But Paul was different . . . obviously.

As a child and even now as a grown boy, she had to constantly shoo him from the kitchen. As a toddler he was always tugging at the hem of her skirt until she picked him up and carried him about for a moment or two, which satisfied him for but a brief moment before he was tugging at her again. The older he became . . . old enough for his father to see in him what he now tried to beat out, the greater that hate grew within Simeon for him, and the closer Paul drew to her and Lar.

She pulled the wagon around the back of the house and tied it to a hitching post. She went to the well and drew water to drink and then splashed her face to cool it down. Off in the distance behind her home, the forest was waiting with Paul and David in there somewhere. Toward the east, the woodlands seemed to go on forever, but to the west, it came to an abrupt halt where the bridge to Folsom was.

She was wary about going into the forest alone, but knowing that Paul and David had foolishly– but bravely ventured in time and again, reassured her that a woman such as she could. But she was a grown woman and had to be wise about it, she decided. She went to the side of the house and removed the long handle axe from its resting spot in the stump and slung it over her right shoulder. It felt heavier than she remembered, but she had not used it for months ever since Lar was so quick to chop wood before she could find an excuse to. Before she was with child, she could swing the axe almost as deftly and half as powerful as Lar could, which was more than most men in Folsom could claim. Though she didn't have Lar's swiftness with the axe, her meaty shoulders and pork, collard greens and corn thickened muscular hips were enough to split wood with usually one swing.

After what seemed to her like a mile of trekking through her garden and then another past waist high grass Lar had yet to tame into farmland, she entered the woods and maintained a direct line from the back of her house toward the river. Once at the riverbank, she was close enough to the bridge to know that Paul and David were not to the west of her, but to the east. She commended herself for having the sense to take the axe with her. It provided not only protection from those things Enda said lived in the forest – though shouldn't, but also proved to be a useful walking stick in the face of dense brush and fallen trees that had to be scaled. Having been forced away from the river and back into the forest by felled trees by the bank, fortune– it seemed, had found her, or she had found it. She came upon what appeared to be the beginning of a path of trampled bushes, splayed shrubs and prickly brush that seemed to have been pulled to the side.

The path was leading her slightly to the east, but as she looked up ahead– briefly, lest she misstep and trip, it led back toward the river again. She hoped Cal had been right about Paul and David sneaking off into the woods. If Paul was not here, chances were, he was gone from Folsom. But that was an even more troubling thought. Times were still dangerous for everyone. Lawlessness was the law of the land, especially in small towns like Folsom. A Negroe or white's desperation for money, clothes and food, could easily lead to someone's death if they were like Paul– unwise to the real world, she thought. But the only other choice for him was going home, and the consequences that awaited him there were only slightly better than what might lay in wait for him in the world beyond Folsom.

Her hope for finding Paul came into view . . . unexpectedly and caught her by surprise, even though she now knew who Paul really was. What she saw rendered her motionless with fear for him and David, but it also warmed her heart to see him look so at peace . . . a feeling such as only love could conjure. Either Paul no longer cared or had just become careless, like he had been earlier with Beatrice.

She was certain neither Paul nor David saw her as she came upon them, for neither one moved– but she did. Looking backwards and seeing there was enough space, she turned and inched away as silently as possible . . . far enough away, so that even if they stood they could not see her, but close enough for them to hear her voice when she called out for Paul, and hoping that the sound of her voice did not betray what her eyes had seen.

* * *

Paul had ran from the house and only realized what a catastrophe he'd gotten himself into after he was in the light of day. But that Beatrice enjoyed doling out such hate to him was making it all so much worse. She would tell father everything, he had no doubt, and then it would all be over. There would be no turning back time now.

He was barely able to see through his tears as he ran and had nearly slammed full force into David, who was all but a blurry blob sauntering his way as he passed the gate. David's voice had stopped him in his tracks, yet he could not stop shedding tears. He didn't tell David what had happened, but pleaded with him, which he really didn't have to, to go the river– their place of safety and refuge.

His tears had waned and dried upon his face by the time they neared the bridge, but the pain and fear coursing through his heart was an unstoppable torrent. There were only three boys down by the river, but they were all preoccupied in play. Keeping with their protocol, they waited by the white gate of the Meadows' home and the melancholy willows that guarded it, which was perfect for staying out of sight of those coming or going across the bridge. There was only one wagon crossing the bridge when they arrived, and it was headed toward the Negroe side. After the wagon and its Negroe occupants were further down the road and nearly invisible to the eye, they snuck across.

Once in the woods, and having found their secret path that was becoming more visible with each endeavor, the reason why he was here shadowed all joy of being close to David again. The notion of continuing to live as he was terrified him. Each day alive made what was already bad seem even worse. But how could it be any worse than it was now? He wondered. *There's no place for people like me*, he thought.

He knew practically nothing about anything outside of Folsom except what was taught at school, which only what his teacher, Ms. Leland, taught through her thick lenses that saw God, Jesus and the Holy Ghost in everything that moved. He hadn't learned a trade and wasn't strong enough to work in the fields, which required endless hauling and lifting. He was ignorant of the family business, or how to run any business .. his father had made certain of that. The Monclair store, farmlands, the home and pittance of a fortune . . . his birthright as a Monclair male . . . would never be his. The inheritance to be had, he knew, and was always reminded whenever his father's fists struck him, would go to Beatrice and whoever decided to put up with her for the prestige of marrying a Monclair. No matter how hard Paul searched for an alternative, he could only come up with one means of escape from the beast within him and his father's unyielding, damming fists. Yet, each day, he hesitated to craft a noose from the rope hanging in the shed, though his intent to be free of his father . . . the beast . . . his life he no longer wanted to live, was not lessened.

After finally reaching their secret clearing and seeing David disrobe– removing his shirt and shucking down his pants and underwear in one swift motion, Paul knew making the noose and hanging himself from it was just inevitable. It was seeing him naked and realizing how absolutely beautiful David was to him . . . top to bottom . . . bulging belly to tree trunk legs . . . his smile– David's smile, that told him he was in love. Though realizing that made Paul begin to cry anew. They were tears of hate for his sister and father . . . tears for his mother and her ambivalent helplessness . . . tears for wanting to touch David, if only just once as more than a friend. He began to feel weak and started to shake uncontrollably. Hysteria was rising within him and he could not force it back from whence it came, but he welcomed the delirium as a reprieve from his world that was spinning out of control.

From behind, David's arms slipped under his own and wrapped around his chest. Instead of David's touch slowing his spiral into insanity, it hastened it, for such a touch was a sensation beyond pleasure to him. David's warm, moist breath upon the back of Paul's neck raised each and every hair erect. David's arms held him up as he began to succumb to gravity. He felt as if David was only teasing him with such a tender display of emotion, for he always felt a *'thing'* like he had never deserved such compassion.

Surprising him, Paul felt David's bare chest press against his back and David's cheek nestling in the crook of his neck. He began rubbing his hairless face against Paul's, but it only made him cry harder, for it was all he ever wanted from David, and it had become reality. David turned him around, but the weight of shame weighing upon Paul wouldn't let him look up.

"Paul ... tell me what's a mattah?" David asked in a whisper. Paul shook his head. "Please ... you scarin' me, Paul. I ... what can I do?"

"I just want to die," Paul blurted, not daring to look up. "I want ... to ... die. I-I-I can't take this anymore– I can't. It hurts too much." David began panting. Paul felt David's grip tighten and threaten to squeeze his breath out of him. A warm drop plopped on Paul's forehead, and then another, and then ... drip ... drip ... dap. He chanced a look up at David who was nearly a foot taller than him and saw that he was crying.

"You're the only friend I got, Paul. Please don't be sayin' thangs like that." David's eyes were becoming redder with each passing moment.

But Paul was ready to accept his life in this world was now over. The evil secret of his heart, his mind and thoughts would be no more, he determined. And as the years passed on, he figured no one would ever care that he, the sick, vile beast, had ever lived and then died. "They know about me ..." Paul admitted, and was surprised at his bravery for having spoken as much, " ... and what I am."

"What you *are*?"

"I *want* to die," Paul whispered as much to himself as to David. "You don't understand ... I can't live like this. It ... it ... all the time I'm awake, it hurts– even when I'm asleep, too, I feel it. It never just leaves me be. I don't wanna be this . . . this thing. I . . . I . . . I just don't want to hurt all the time."

"You ain't hurtin' now, is you? Huh? I ain't ever gonna let you hurt none." David's grip around Paul tightened even more. "Tell me what happened."

Paul continued speaking as though he heard nothing David had just said. "No . . . I don't hurt when I'm out here with . . ." he paused, as fear stole the words from his mouth. He knew his time alive was growing short, and now, there was nothing left to lose. "With you, David," he finished. "I feel good when it's just you and me alone. You ain't gonna ever really know what I mean by that, but . . . I-I . . . you make me happy . . . but . . . you're gonna hate me, too when you know why. All my family hates me for it. And when I die . . ." Paul couldn't finish, for his breath was pulled from him. His head swam in a blinding light, and all he could do was respond with all the power so much ache inside had given him for so many years. But now . . . he felt what he knew everyone else always took for granted . . . he felt alive. With David's lips upon his, he felt wanted.

Through such sudden and exhilarating confusion of not feeling dead anymore, Paul realized that his eyes were still open and so were David's– whose own stared back at him, and said to him those very same things that he'd been trying to hide from David for weeks. In dreams, Paul recalled, he'd fantasized how warm and unyielding David's lips would be as they encompassed his. Reality proved to him that he had not been wrong.

When David's lips parted from his, Paul paused for no more than a moment to look at him before reuniting them. When David responded with vigor, Paul started crying tears not of pain that were so familiar, but ones of joy that were completely foreign to him. He reached up and grasped David's round, chubby cheeks and dug his fingers into them until he finally gave up attempting to mesh David's flesh with his own.

A spark, which was now passion, spiraled into a brushfire that was fanned by gusty winds of longing. Their hands explored the body of the other. David pulled Paul's shirt up and over, and then off . . . then came down britches and underwear, and shoes tossed off carelessly to the side. David made his way back up, kissing Paul's tummy and chest and both sides of his neck until he found Paul's waiting, open mouth once more.

Standing chest to chest, their lips danced feverishly upon the others'. Their bodies produced oil that was a mixture of sweat and passion, which they massaged deeply into the others' thighs, buttocks and back. Against bellies, spastic wands dueled and cast magic neither had ever experienced before. First warm, now steamy breaths shared from one mouth to the other preceded pent-up passion that was finally released. They panted and shook in the afterglow, not knowing what to say or do next– but their bodies knew. Their lips caressed the others' gently and slowly before parting. And after . . . they walked to the river and bathe silently, then returned to where their clothes lay strewn about. Paul picked up his underwear and was about to step in them, but David stopped him. David spread out their clothes on the ground, then laid down on his side and tugged at Paul to join him– which he did gladly . . . just like he dreamt of doing in dreams of David wanting and loving him. "Lay down with me for awhile?" David asked . . . just like Paul had dreamt David would say in dreams he had believed would always be just dreams and nothing more. Paul snuggled his thin back into David's thick chest and let himself be cocooned again by thick arms, which despite the heat, were quivering.

Paul's world began to blur as exhaustion and exhilaration finally sapped what strength he had left. As he drifted toward sleep, he finally, in whispers, told David of the debacle that had occurred at home not more than an hour ago. He was succumbing to sleep from the heartbeat lullaby at his back and kisses upon his neck while David whispered . . . *"you all I got, Paul . . . if you die, then I gonna die, too . . . ok? But I don't wanna die. I . . . I love you, Paul. I been hoping you love me. I wanna be with you—I always did.'* The world that had never made any sense to Paul suddenly seemed a little less frightening . . . until a familiar voice woke him.

* * *

Mary remained where she was until the bushes in front of her began to move. Soon after calling out his name as though she were looking for him, not just having come upon them sleeping naked in each other's arms, she was confronted by two red-faced boys. They looked nervous, and with good reason, she thought.

"How did you find me?" Paul asked disappointedly. He finally broke through the overgrowth of shrubs and was now in full view of Mary. David stepped through next and quickly bowed his head.

Mary felt physically taxed and emotionally dizzy. She leaned on the axe. "The Hendrickson boy said ya'll might be in here."

"Cal," Paul uttered with disgust. He looked up at David who barely managed an eye blink of acknowledgement.

Mary saw worry growing within him. "That be the one."

"How . . . how did he know?"

Mary motioned for them to follow. "See this here," she said, pointing at the ground with the axe and then at the broken arms of shrubs as they passed them. "I ain't no woman to be messin' 'bout in the woods, and I followed ya'll right where ya'll done been. Good thang for ya'll, folks stay outta from up in these parts."

David then spoke. "Uh . . . um . . . Ms. Mary? How Cal reckon we be over here?"

"Lil' devil say he saw ya'll sneak 'cross the bridge one day."

"He been spyin'?" Paul's voice screamed silently beneath a layer of pretended calmness.

Mary knew exactly what they wanted . . . *what they needed to hear.* There was no doubt in her mind that if it had been anyone else who had come upon them snuggled together without a stitch of clothing on, hell would have broken loose upon both of their households and likely the entire town. She saw that the boys were waiting on her to assure them that what they thought was hidden remained so.

"He just knew ya'll cross the bridge is all," she replied. "Those other boys swimmin' in that ol' dirty river ain't know nuthin'– just the Hendrickson boy. *I* find ya'll 'cause ya'll got a lil' path goin' here. When it stopped back there where I was standin', I just fig- ure to start callin' out for ya. You know you gotta' go back, Paul," she told him. Her tone was suddenly less matriarchal, and instead, motherly soft. "Your pappy done sent me to fetch you back."

Paul walked in silence a few steps before responding. "He knows then? Who told him . . . Beatrice? She go running off to the farm . . .?"

"I did," Mary informed him, realizing there was no use trying to hide what would soon be known.

"You?!" He cried.

Mary stopped, spun, and with her momentum, whacked the head off a shoulder high bush with the axe. "Goddamnit, chile! What you 'spect I gotta do? That sistah of yours been hollerin' for your pappy, and if she didn't get what she wanted right then and there, ain't no tellin' what . . ." She stopped in mid rant. David had taken a step back and looked as though he was ready to bolt at any moment. Paul was frozen were he stood. Mary sighed and cooled her burning lips with a swipe of her tongue. She lowered the axe and walked up to him. "Chile– ain't you thinkin' right?" She asked. She bent down so that their eyes were at the same level. She searched his face for understanding but saw only fright. "I had to tell him what happen just the way it did. Chile– *I had to go.* Your mammy a mess. All she could do was do as your sistah tell her– have me go get your pappy . . . and he sent me on to look for you." Paul's lips trembled as he attempted to speak, but nothing came forth. "Boy, you done known me since you had a thought in that head of yours. I know you when you still in your mammy's belly. Folk may do you wrong, and Lord know, folk always gonna try– folk just like that. But you know, Ms. Mary ain't ever gonna do wrong by you. I ain't ever had and ain't ever will. I did what I did 'cause I had to . . . not to hurt you, chile, but to help you. Just like I be up in this mess now to find you, and here I is, big as God knows what. And you, too, boy," she looked at David. "Your mammy want you home now."

"He's going to beat me bad, Ms. Mary," Paul stated.

"Maybe just tan your hide," she lied.

David moved forward cautiously. "I ain't ever seen Paul without a bruise on'em."

"You know he will," Paul said.

Mary finally spotted the clearing that let out to her home. "I know, chile. I know."

After retrieving the wagon and receiving more than a few stares from Negroes as she boarded with her white boys, they set out for town with David up front with Mary and Paul on the back with his legs dangling off the edge. The boys who had been swimming by the riverbank were gone, and only a few white folk, mostly women, children and old men were out onto their porches as the greatest blast of the day's heat was now over. They were all silent as they rounded the dead tree, and as they drove past the Monclair store and on toward the road that led out.

The sun was heavy in the sky. Mary had an idea of what to ex- pect, but, having known Simeon Monclair for years, she never re- ally knew which way, or when, or upon whom his foul wind would blow. Lar would be by shortly to take her home. But she

knew she would not be able to leave until things were settled between Paul and his father, one way or another. She mulled over
what to tell Lar, who would no doubt find suspicion in her motive
to stay. He knew she never stayed late unless commanded by Mr.
Monclair, and those times had been rare occasions.

The oil lamps were lit in most parts of the Monclair house, including Simeon's study. "'Bout time you got off, David-chile," she
told him, but did not turn to say it to him in case a look or a touch
was given from one boy to the other that was none of her business.
The wagon leaned right and then snapped back with a screech as
David jumped out. He ran ahead of the wagon and meekly waved
his goodbye with a foot sized hand. "Paul!" He called. "Don't . . .
just don't! Hear me? Or me too . . . o.k.?" Paul nodded. Then off
David ran.

Paul moved up front and sat next to Mary. From the corner of
her eye she could see what skin and strips of muscle beneath he
possessed did little to hide his trembling bones. She was frightened
for him also. She felt as though she were leading a piglet off to
slaughter by giving Paul the impression that things wouldn't be
too bad, all the while hiding a knife behind her back. But there was
nothing she could do to stop it. She only hoped that Simeon had already drunk too much and had passed out in the study, as she usually did if he wasn't drinking in town.

But her wishing turned out to be like so many of her prayers to
God for a child that would live. There were two sets of wagons by
the stables, neither of which was Lar's. "Your pappy 'spose to have
company tonight," she informed him, recalling the meeting she
overheard him talking about earlier. "That be a good thing," she
suggested, but did not for a moment believe her own words, but
hoped Paul did.

After putting away the wagon and settling the horses in for the
night, they slipped in through the kitchen. Mary ventured in first,
cracking the door slightly and peering about the dark room. Satis-

fied no one was there, she entered with Paul nearly attached to the back of her skirt, like he was sewn on. They moved toward the door leading into the dining room, and again, Mary opened the door a hair and assessed the surroundings.

All was quite.

Simeon's study was down the hall from the dining room and off to the left, too far away to hear anything emanating from it, though the stench of pipe smoke was clearly in the air. "I go check the hallway and you keep an eye on me," she instructed. "You see me wave, you run real quiet like and make for your room and stay there. I have to tell your pappy you back, 'cause . . ." She paused. "You know I gotta tell him."

Paul shook his head. "I know, Mary. It's my mess anyway. I . . ."

"Shhsss!" Mary hissed. Paul grabbed the back of her skirt, as he too heard the heavy footsteps approaching. Mary reacted out of instinct and reached around and grabbed hold of Paul's wrists, all the while moving backwards until they were in the middle of the kitchen.

The thudding, graceless footsteps seemed to stop right at the door– it began to open. Light from the oil lamps in the living room crudely jumped in and posed as warped trapezoids, triangles and parallelograms on the floor and wall. Paul gasped as the door opened further. Mary tried to stifle her anxiety by holding her breath, despite the cadence of her heart doubling.

The door stopped halfway open. "Mary– that you?" A feminine voice whispered, to both Mary and Paul's relief.

Paul dropped his head against Mary's back. They both exhaled. "Ms. Isabel," Mary whispered.

Isabel's attempt to covertly slip into the kitchen was unsuccessful– her wide hips and full figured torso required great access to enter through the narrow doorway. Isabel closed the door and approached them with a small lamp in one hand and Plyus cuddled to her breast with the other. "I've been so worried about both of you," she said. Her voice was only a shadow of the shadow it usually was. She reached for Paul, but he retreated further behind Mary.

"Paul . . . are you alright, dear? Come here . . . please," she begged.

Paul stayed where he was and Mary didn't blame him either. She knew Isabel was helpless to protect Paul when she couldn't even protect herself from Simeon's open hand and occasional fist. For a moment, Mary felt as though time had spun back ten years, and Paul was that child again who reached for *her* even when Isabel reached for him . . . his thin nails digging into her flesh as he fought being taken away by the woman he had to call *Mother*. Mary tried speeding things along to dispel the tension between mother and son. "Ms. Isabel, we need to be gettin' Paul to his room 'fore Mr. Monclair spot him down here. He still be in his study room?"

"Yes," Isabel replied weakly.

"What he doin'? He gonna be there for a spell?" Mary asked. "Long 'nough to get Paul upstairs? He drinkin' heavy?"

"Slow down, Mary– I can't think. I . . . I suppose . . ." Isabel hugged Plyus closer to her chest.

"Is he *real* drunk?" Mary asked bluntly, dismissing Isabel's state of disarray. "He was swillin' that mess when I saw him earlier, but he was still movin' 'bout just fine."

"Yes-yes," Isabel replied, still a bit bedazzled. "He spoke with . . . um . . . um . . ." She shook her head, " . . . Beatrice! Yes . . . he was already pouring drinks before those other men came along. I'm sure he's quite full by now– I think."

Paul peeked from around Mary's backside. "What did Beatrice say?"

Isabel looked to Mary, as though she was afraid and ashamed to answer Paul directly. "I don't know. Simeon went to Beatrice's room and . . . God . . . she had been fine for awhile until he came home, and then she started wailing when she heard him down-stairs." She sighed. "He didn't even ask *me* what happened– just her. Then he went to his study, and that's when I saw him pouring a drink. Then those seedy looking men arrived. He's been in there with them ever since."

"Thanks, mother," Paul grunted facetiously.

"Now, Paul . . . what can I have said if he won't speak to me?"

"What you've always said . . . nothing."

"That be 'nough!" Mary snapped, but quickly lowered her voice. "This be the wrong time for ya'll to be fussin' and fightin' and car-ryin'on." They were all silent for a moment.

"I'll go see if Simeon is still occupied," Isabel announced, and then handed the lamp to Mary and walked out of the kitchen.

Mary turned to Paul and held the lantern up by his face, but lowered it when she saw he was crying. He fell into her bosom and sobbed. "Alright now chile– alright. Ms. Mary here . . . hmmm? I here."

A light rap came at the other side of the door, and then next, Is-abel peered in. It seemed as though she was about to speak but changed her mind when she saw Paul in Mary's arms. She cleared her throat. "Come now," Isabel urged weakly.

"Let's go, Paul," Mary directed.

Mary led Paul to his room. As she was about to leave, what she saw pained her, and made her want to stay by his side to hold and comfort him. His blue eyes seemed dull . . . his face was bereft of blood. And though he said nothing as she slowly closed the door, she saw that his lifeless eyes were telling her everything he feared was coming.

She peeked in on Beatrice, whose back was to her as she lay on the bed. Her hair was a web of blond threads upon frilly lavender pillows. Mary could just barely discern a slight rumble escaping from the girl's throat as she lay in slumber. She closed the door and headed down to the study.

Mary paused before knocking on the door. Isabel peeked around the corner from the hallway. Mary flicked her hand at her and whispered. "I come get you in a li'l bit." Isabel nodded and left.

There was a rumble of talk behind the door that ceased when Mary knocked. "What is it?" The voice was Simeon's.

As Mary walked in, the smell of cigars, cigarettes and someone's rotten feet nearly gagged her. The three white men present she didn't recognize. And true to Isabel's description of them, they were not the type of well-dressed men Simeon usually associated with. Their clothes were dusted with a light film of sandy dirt. Their hair and beards were neglected bushes. And in the midst of the adult ragamuffins was Simeon– bloodshot eyes with just a hint of his dazzling blues showing through, standing casually in Allie Mae's woven britches and a sweat stained white shirt. In his left hand he held a full glass of whiskey, and as usual, positioned out of sight behind his back– the stump.

"I done found Paul for you, suh" she said, not venturing in any further than past the doorframe. She could feel all eyes in the room appraising and dismissing her all at once.

"Where's he at? Here?" Simeon slurred. His eyes were fixed upon her with a dizzying intensity.

"He be in his room, suh– already sleepin'."

"Don't matter if he is or not," Simeon uttered. "It seems to me, you haven't been as truthful as you claimed you were . . . *Mary*."

"I just said what I know, suh," Mary replied innocently.

"Then you're tellin' me . . . *Mary* . . . that I or my daughter is now lyin'."

"No, suh." Mary struggled with all her might to hold back from saying more. She wasn't surprised that her account of past events was being challenged, but still, it infuriated her that her word meant nothing. She could hear Lar's voice in her head . . . *'Jus' shush, Mary. Jus' don't say nothin!'* But she did. "I not tryin' to . . ."

Before Mary could finish, one of the white men spoke up and cut her off. He was seated by the row of bookcases to Simeon's left. His stomach bulged and hung over his waist, threatening to rip the seams of his liquor, dirt and food stained shirt. When he opened his mouth, there was nothing white, gray or yellow to be seen, just pink gums. "Ya see, Mr. Monclair . . . ain't it like I told ya? They wanna make it like you can trust'em, but ya cain't. Now ya got this big ass, nappy-headed niggah standin' here callin' ya a liar in ya own fuckin' home."

'Leave it be, Mary!'

"All I know is what I seen, suh," Mary claimed. Suddenly, she remembered the lynching in Peak Hills and regretted having said what she said– almost.

Her response had definitely caught the white man by surprise. His face reddened as much as it could despite the dirt upon it. His eyes widened, and then quickly became slits as he struggled to lift himself out of the chair.

"Sit down!" Simeon barked, and then gave the man a steely glare of his own.

He slumped back in his chair. "Ya . . . jus' gonna let a niggah talk to me like that?!"

"I said shut up, Lucas!" Simeon spat. "This is my goddamn house and I'll do things here the way I see fit– and anywhere else for that matter. That is why you're here, isn't it?!" Lucas huffed and glared at Mary again.

A slender fellow, older than Lucas, but not as gray as Simeon, spoke up. "Lucas, ya do as Mr. Monclair tell ya– ya hear?" Lucas' pride completely vanished.

"I heard'em, alright, Artie! Fuck . . . I got ears, ya know."

"Then fuckin' use'em, ya slow-wit!" Artie snapped back. "Mr. Monclair'll tell ya when he want your fuckin' advice! Not the other way 'round. He say jump . . . ya move ya fat ass! He say shut the fuck up . . . ya shut the fuck up!" Artie then nodded at Simeon. "Sorry 'bout that, suh. It *ain't* gonna happen again."

Simeon ignored Lucas' attempt to become one with the chair, and completely dismissed Artie's second hand apology. He raised his right arm– the shriveled, red stump peeked from beneath his shirtsleeve and aimed in Mary's direction. "Where these men are from, you act like that and you'd be getting the black peeled from your back. Now . . . apologize . . . to your betters."

Mary felt as though her skin was blistering and popping, just as surely as if she were rolling around in a fire pit. Her first thought was to tell them all to go to hell. And the fat one– the one who seemed bent on meddling in what was not his business; she wanted nothing more than to spit in his face before slapping his blubbery jowls. But none of this would ever happen, so instead, she cursed God for letting things be the way they were. She was at their mercy. She didn't need them to remind her of her place in their world . . . she was not only a niggah, but something worse– a niggah woman. She apologized first to Simeon and then to Lucas, but of course, didn't mean one word that burned her tongue as she spoke them.

Simeon returned his stump to its resting place behind his back. "Men," he said, "it will take some time before I can fully act upon your request. But it will happen sooner than later, I assure you all." The men mumbled their pleasure. "So for now, I must call an end to this night . . . Arthur, Reginald . . . Lucas."

Reginald, the other white man in the room and the youngest of the three, replied first. "Obliged ya could see us, Mr. Monclair." Lucas and Arthur echoed his sentiment. They retrieved their hats and made for the door. Mary quickly moved out into the hall as they came toward her and let them pass.

She was about to leave, but Simeon snarled at her. "You've always been an indignant woman, Mary Cole. You're far too prideful. The only reason you're still in my employment has nothing to do with Isabel's family once owning you, or that she has a liking for you. It's nothing more than I don't have to see any more niggahs running 'bout my place when you can do the work of three . . . seeing to my children being one of those duties– but you failed today. I pay you to do what Isabel is incapable of doing. The only rights you have here are the ones I give you. A woman talking like a man may pass with niggahs 'cross the riv'ah, but not here. I *will* have order in this home," he stressed.

Mary stayed where she was as Simeon walked past her. She then followed him and paused when he stopped at the stairs. To her left, she saw a shadow lurking around the corner that was Isabel. As Simeon began his ascent, her heart beat in rhythm with each step he took. "Tomorrow, things shall be different– that I assure you, Mary Cole. And it will begin starting tonight."

"Suh," she acknowledged, and watched him ascend the stairs until he was out of sight.

* * *

Please God . . . please God . . . please God . . . please . . .

Paul sat on the edge of his bed and sped up his prayers as the shuffle of footsteps, which he had no doubt belonged to his father, neared his door. He'd been praying since Mary left him in his moonlit room, with only snickering shadows dancing on the wall to keep him company. He knew all his prayers were for naught, because *he* was coming. The shadows knew also and began hiding.

God . . . I know you hate me . . . but please . . . oh God, please . . . don't let him hurt me too bad this time. I'm begging . . . let it be over quick.

The doorknob creaked as it turned to the left.

God . . . why did you make me like this?

The door opened, and a new shadow entered the room and enshrouded him in darkness.

God . . . let father see I'm really, really scared this time. Make him know that it's enough that I'm scared. And . . . and . . . I'm sorry too, God. I'm sorry for everything that I do that makes you and father hate me. Please . . . just this once . . .

But Simeon did not go away. Paul figured he wouldn't.

He stopped praying when his father shut the door behind him. He hoped he could be brave this time– that he wouldn't cry out or try grasping at his father's arms while begging him to stop the beating. But his father was strangely silent, unlike the times before when he'd enter bellowing out curses and insults. Paul knew that meant something new was to come . . . for nothing, however, is forever.

Simeon took hold of Paul by the throat and pulled him to his feet. He gasped for air, but did not struggle. Paul wondered deliriously while his breath was being squeezed off and peeing his pants, how his own father . . . not some stranger or the boys at school, could be doing such a thing to his own flesh and blood . . . his own son . . . and seemingly with such pleasure.

Paul's eyes began to burn, and now there were six of his father glowering at him as his vision blurred. His neck felt moments away from snapping as the pressure his exerted began to increase exponentially. There was barely a passage for air to flow in and out of his chest; yet, he was able to sputter two words. *"Father,"* he choked out. *"Please . . ."*

* * *

Simeon stood in the doorway of the room and stared at Paul for a moment. The sight of the pretty, dark-haired boy sitting on the bed– scared and shivering, simply served to remind Simeon why the boy repulsed him. Paul was, and became more and more each day, exactly what he despised the most . . . a freakish abomination that was neither strong nor resilient, but just the opposite– soft and warm . . . he– with his long, black lashes and ringlets about his head. Simeon appraised him as nothing but a creature full of sickness. The boy, and Simeon used the term loosely, was to him, the worst a man could be. He was a reminder of a night long past that had stretched into years in his thoughts . . . a rotting albatross about his neck . . . a sick joke played upon him over and again every time he looked at Paul. That his own loins produced such a thing didn't shame Simeon as much as sicken him. Paul . . . *It* . . . should have been heir to the family's crown, but he was determined Paul would never have any of it, except the name of 'Monclair', which he wished he could take away also.

His thoughts were cloudy from whiskey, but his intent was as clear as fresh sprung water. When he grasped Paul by the neck, he wasn't quite sure why he hadn't just struck him. But as his hand grabbed Paul's soft muscle and felt it collapse in his grip, he was glad he'd decided to choke him first so he could watch him struggle to breathe. *Just what a thing like you deserves,* Simeon thought. He knew if he squeezed any harder, he could be done with Paul for good and rid the infection in his own soul. He stared into Paul's eyes and saw his own blue ones staring back at him, which made him squeeze even harder.

You don't deserve Monclair eyes, you sick fuck, Simeon seethed silently.

Paul mumbled something, but to Simeon's intoxicated ears that were now pounding his war drum, it was nothing but gibberish. Though, for a moment he thought he'd heard the word *'please.'* *'Please,' is it now?* Simeon wondered with incredulity. He now knew he was right about Paul all along. The boy had no strength and never would– no manly qualities . . . just cowardice . . . aberration and softness. *'Please,'* Simeon ruminated upon Paul's plea again, but now with added disgust. *Oh yeah . . . beg then! Turn over and spread yourself . . . like a woman. That's what you really want to beg for . . . just like a woman . . . like a bitch in heat. You wanna be on your knees and take a man in your sick mouth? Good, 'cause that's where you belong . . . on your knees.*

"You ever touch her again and I'll kill you!" Simeon spat, on hot breath that reeked of whiskey. "A *man* like you doesn't ever touch a *woman*. But you ain't too much of a man anyway are you? You're not a Monclair man; so don't ever let me hear you say you are to anyone. I don't care who asks if you are. If someone does, you deny it– 'cause you're nothing of mine. You'll never be. You say you're a Monclair and I'll kill you!"

Simeon kept his grip on Paul's neck as he took a step back. He raised his gnarled stump– though it looked red and angry, it was actually as hard as tree bark. He stopped as he reared it back. His eyes were drawn down to the front of Paul's pants, which were wet.

In the morning, Simeon would only remember that the first strike of his stump felt good, as Paul's lips popped like skin stretched boils being lanced, and that a womanly cry from him had followed. Other than that, only his swollen stump and scrapped off skin from the knuckles of his left hand would remind him of what had occurred. He would feel cheated that he couldn't remember any more than that.

* * *

Though far larger and heavier than Isabel, Mary still made it to the stairway first when Paul screamed from above. *It just a dog up there bein' kicked,* Mary thought, in an attempt to fool herself. *Folk don't cry like that . . . right? That ain't no human makin' that noise . . . that can't be Paul.* But another peal of pain from Paul rang out and jarred her consciousness back from delusion to reality. The ceiling above came alive with pounding and stomping . . . scuffling on the floor. Isabel and Mary looked at each other in disbelief that it was Paul screaming so ungodly.

Beatrice came bounding down the stairs . . . one . . . two . . . one and three stairs at a time. She ran toward them like a woman on fire with her hair plastered across her face with tears. Her white nightgown hung on by only one shoulder. She wrapped her arms about Isabel's waist. "Mother . . . mother, he's killing him! Paul's screaming so!"

Paul cried out again, but this time it was prolonged and chilled Mary's bones. It stopped as quickly as it began. But the rumbling from above continued on.

"Mother!" Beatrice shrieked, as though she too were being assaulted. "I didn't want this . . . I swear I didn't. I didn't think father would be like this." The ceiling shuddered again, causing Beatrice to squeeze Isabel even tighter.

Mary, knowing that she could not intervene, leaned against the wall for support. She felt as though her heart was leaking and her soul slowly departing. Every bone in her body said to go to Paul, yet a small, sensible part of her mind cautioned her feet not to move. It told her to accept what was happening to Paul, but hate it. The sudden absence of Paul crying out panicked her. Beatrice's assessment of Simeon's intent seemed not that of buyer's remorse, but of prophecy. Simeon, it seemed to all of them, was intent on killing Paul.

Mary glowered at Beatrice. "You the cause of all of this," she spat. Her words were as ice water in Beatrice's face, who looked at her dumbfounded. "Every lick that boy take, you 'sponsible! God gonna 'member ever thang you done did today, missy. So just stop your *cryin'!!* You got everythin' you wanted– hear me? If that poor boy up there dead, it all be on you then . . . not your daddy– just you!"

They all looked up as a door opened from above and lazy footsteps drew near the stairs. "Let'em pass on," Mary instructed, as she quickly ushered Isabel and Beatrice into the living room and out of sight. They waited silently as Simeon descended from above and walked down the hall to his study. He closed the door, and finally they all began to breathe again. Huddled and still silent, they moved as one and began making their way back toward the stairs, until a round of knocking from the kitchen startled them. Beatrice screeched and then quickly covered her mouth. Mary glared at her. Though she too had been taken off guard by the knocking, it only took her mind a moment to realize whom it was.

"Go on up, Ms. Isabel," Mary whispered. "I be right up with rags and water . . . I reckon he gonna be needin' somethin' cool." Mary shuffled quickly and quietly to the back door, hoping to answer it before Lar knocked again, but she was too late to stop him. She was shushing him and waving her hands frantically for him to cease before even reaching the back door.

Lar spoke as she opened the door. "What in God's name be happenin' here, Mary? What all that screamin' . . ."

Mary covered his mouth with her hand. "You hush, Laurence Cole! Right now!" She whispered. "Quiet! You hear me!?"

It took some effort, but Lar managed to pull Mary's hand down. "What all that racket up yonder?" He asked.

She shook her head. "Not here . . . you know better, Lar." She took him by the hand and hurried him through the garden and off Monclair property. She stopped as they passed the threshold of the small gate where Lar had tethered the horse and wagon with Uncle Matty sitting upon it.

Mary walked to the rear of the wagon and placed her hands on the back end, and then leaned over. She was utterly exhausted. Her stomach and the baby seemed bound together in knots– each taking turns pulling and twisting her insides like wet rags that refused to be wrung dry. Tears came first, and then the pounding of her chest combined with a sour stomach completed the trinity of emotions she hadn't the will to suppress.

Lar put his arms around her waist and pulled her into him– and she let him.

After slowly wiping away her tears, she told him what she needed *him* to know. The argument . . . the so-called push and shove . . . going out to the farm to tell Simeon what happened . . . finding Paul and then bringing him back home . . . and then the beating. Lar spoke from incredulity. "That was Paul hollerin' like that?" Mary nodded. "I thought that was that girl-chile of theirs. Lord Jesus!" He gasped. "How bad he done beat that boy?"

Uncle Matty chimed in. "I ain't heard tell-nothin' like that 'less a Negroe be gettin' lashed."

Mary dried her tear-wet hands on her dress and straightened up as best she could. Just having Lar near seemed to renew her fortitude. "I gotta go on, Lar," she said. "They ain't gonna know how to see 'bout him like me."

"What you wannin' me to do then? I don't feel right leavin' you here. And you ain't walkin' home if that be what you plannin' on," Lar replied.

"I be alright 'til mornin'," she assured him. She straightened her dress, pulling it down over her belly were it had ridden up, and exhaled loudly. "You come on by and carry me home for ya'll head off to work. I only gonna stay long 'nough to fix that ol' bastard somethin' to eat– then I come home."

Lar stared at her disapprovingly and grunted.

"Ain't nothin' more likely gonna happen 'round here." *'I'll cut his heart out of his old, white chest 'fore he come for Paul again,'* she wanted to say to Lar, and despite the consequences of such an action, she actually feared that she would. "Ol' Simeon likely done passed out by now anyway."

"You need to be layin' your tail down somewhere, gal," Uncle Matty admonished her.

"Soon 'nough," Mary answered. She was already stepping backwards. "Ya'll get on now."

Lar seemed as though he was going to speak, but stopped, and then started again in earnest. "I be back real early for ya then," he told her, though Mary knew those were not the first words poised upon his lips.

She didn't wait for Lar and Uncle Matty to drive off before walking back toward the house. But then she stopped and remembered the water and rags, and then went back to the well. Lar had just turned the wagon around and was headed off. His head was turned around as he was making his way down the road. She smiled as he waved. She in turn signaled her love back with a raised hand and then started pumping water into a small bucket.

Beatrice was sitting on the floor outside of Paul's room when Mary made it back up the stairs– bucket and rags in one hand and a kerosene lamp in the other. Beatrice's legs were drawn up and her head was resting on her knees. She looked up when Mary approached. Her prized white skin was splotched red and glistened with tears. Her too small of a mouth for her round face drooped on the left.

Beatrice spoke first. Her voice, though weak, still raked at Mary's ears. "Please tell him I'm sorry, Ms. Mary," she implored. "I didn't want it to be like this. I didn't know father was going to . . ." She stopped and began whimpering.

Mary still felt nothing but disgust for her. It seemed to Mary that no matter what happened in the house, Beatrice always seemed to find a way to center it on her, and this time was no different. She disposed of Beatrice's words from her thoughts like shit from her backend without bothering to wipe. She stepped into Paul's room, but Beatrice grabbed hold of her skirt and pulled.

"I didn't say anything about the teasing . . . or David, or any of that stuff," Beatrice offered quickly. "I swear I didn't, Ms. Mary."

"Little too late for all this-and-that and the-other now– ain't it, missy?" Mary replied dryly. She grabbed her skirt and snatched it out of Beatrice's grasp. "You go to bed. Me and your mammy take care of thangs from here on out." Beatrice reached for Mary's skirt again, but Mary stepped out of her reach and stared at her in wonder. She couldn't fathom where Beatrice had again summoned the audacity to try and touch her again.

"Promise me, Ms. Mary. Promise to tell him I'm sorry," Beatrice begged, with more earnestness than Mary had ever heard her use before.

But Mary's heart was coated in ice for all things Beatrice. And she was, Mary thought, an actress unparalleled. She didn't care that Monclair's golden haired princess was *now* sorry, or felt for the first time, a miniscule of pain that Paul endured day after day. Mary entered the room and closed the door as if Beatrice had not even spoken, or for that matter, was even there.

The smell of urine and feces immediately stung her nose and punched her gut. Isabel was on the floor moving her hand in circles. Mary set down the bucket and covered her mouth and nose from the stench that was as thick as the muggy air in the room. She moved closer to Isabel and saw that her eyes were threatening to bolt from their sockets as she wiped the floor with a rag. When she lowered the lamp further, she saw that the rag was not actually a rag, but one of Paul's white shirts that would never be worn again. It was pale yellow on one end and bloody on the other. Mary gasped in disgust. She shined the light on the bed where Paul was laying on his back . . . motionless . . . his legs nearly turned around in the opposite direction, as if they had been broken.

"He won't let me touch him," Isabel droned. "So I'm cleaning? Is that alright that I'm cleaning, Mary? I want to help, so I'm cleaning this mess here. And . . . and . . . oh, let's see . . . what else . . ." Isabel looked up and turned her head from side to side, focusing on nothing in particular. "Umm . . ." Isabel looked right through Mary before resuming wiping the floor, which was now just a concoction of smeared urine and blood. "I'll tidy up the room next . . . alright? That seems like it would be good. It's always such a mess in here . . . boys, you know."

Mary left Isabel to her compulsion and walked over to the bed. For the second time in mere moments, she inhaled uncontrollably. This time, however, it was due to shock. She knelt down– the movement came naturally, as her knees had suddenly become weak. She sought out Paul's eyes for a sign of awareness, but they were already obscured by swollen skin. His upper lip was split down the center and resembled raw meat cut with a bread knife. Mary cupped his face in her hand.

He jerked his body in reply. "*N-tock . . . eeeee!*" He gurgled.

"Paul?" Mary whispered.

"Dah-n . . . n-gok . . . nah tok . . . eeee."

"Don't touch me," Isabel translated, as she continued polishing the floors with blood and urine.

Mary put the lamp down on the nightstand. She grasped his head with both hands now, careful not to press too hard, but gentle enough for him to sense *her* touch. "It be me, chile– Ms. Mary."

He mumbled something Mary couldn't discern, but he seemed to relax at the sound of her voice, which gave Mary a glimmer of hope that he knew it was she, not his mother. "Ms. Isabel," Mary said, trying to remove all signs of alarm from her voice. "I need you to fetch a few more buckets of water, now. You understandin', Ms. Isabel?" Isabel didn't reply, only wiped. "Ms. Isabel!"

It took Isabel a few moments to track the voice calling her name. "Yes, Mary?"

"I need more water, ma'am," Mary said slowly, knowing that Isabel's body was in the room, but that her mind was further away than the stars in the sky. "And more rags too."

"Oh, I can do that!" Isabel replied eagerly, as though she'd been given some enjoyable task to fulfill. "And I'll straighten the room when I return, and this time I'll make sure to stay on him about it. You know, Mary– keeping his room tidy is not such an arduous task, now is it? Hmmm?"

Mary placated her. "No, ma'am it ain't." Isabel continued talking to herself as she left.

"It all be over now," Mary assured him, and ran her fingers through his blood wet, curly hair. "Ain't no more comin' your way." She stroked his chest, but he yelped in response. His body jittered on the bed. Such a light touch seemed to cause him excruciating pain. She could do nothing but watch as his body stiffened while he tried pushing the back of his head clear through the mattress. Without hesitation, she placed butterfly kisses on his ear and caressed his head until he relaxed and became limp once more.

She lifted his shirt and saw even more red bruises . . . they beginning their disappearing act and reappearing as purple, simply biding their time until they turned black– but that would be tomorrow. She wondered if he would ever come to realize the bond he now shared with those he did not share the same color with. She saw him as much a victim of hate because of *whom* and *what* he was . . . no more and no less than a Negroe. And like Negroes, there would be no one for him to cry out this injustice to, and to find justice from. No one would come to his rescue. No one would care for people like him, like no one seemed to care for lynched Negroes, she thought.

Mary took hold of his bloodstained shirt that was already ripped at the collar. She saw that he'd finally settled into a painful, yet peaceful state, only because the beating was over, and the worst . . . the memories of it . . . was yet to come. She winced at the thought of removing his clothes, knowing it would cause him further pain, but it had to be done. "This gonna hurt, baby," she apologized preemptively.

He did not reply or move.

She carefully ripped the shirt down the center and at the opening of the arms . . . he stirred slightly, because the worst was still yet to come. She pulled the shirt from underneath him. He growled. "That be over now, chile," she whispered.

She removed his britches without incident, but he groaned as she grabbed at the waist of his stained undergarments– his face contorted anew. His body again began to shake and threatened to start convulsing. She took greater care as she pulled down his underwear. His thighs were smeared with feces. What she saw at his groin reaffirmed her belief that mankind was little more than just an animal who could talk. She now understood what had caused him to scream like a banshee the last time.

Not being a man, she could only compare the testicle on the left with that on the right, and judged that it was double its normal size. Its skin was no longer loose like it should be, but appeared as though it was stuffed with strawberry preserves. It pulsed and practically grew the longer she stared at it. Paul's physical expression of manhood was without a doubt in her mind, deliberately targeted by Simeon. "Only the devil can do somethin' like this to somebody," she whispered angrily. She shook her head and began tearing up as she looked at the swollen sac again.

She dipped a rag in the bucket of water and gently laid it over Paul's groin. He moaned in reply. Realizing that she would not be able to clean the injury, at least not at the present time when it was still so raw, she cleaned what she could between his legs and scrubbed the sheets he lay on. She opened the window to let out the stench and to inject fresh air.

Isabel returned looking more like a weary servant than a well-to-do southern wife. She had a bucket in both hands and towels draped over both shoulders. She glanced at Paul spread eagle and naked, save the small wet cloths over his privates, and then quickly looked away. She went to her knees and began cleaning the floor again, but Mary absolved her of her sins. "You go on get some rest now, Ms. Isabel. I take care of it all 'fore morn'," she told her.

Isabel looked around disorientated, as if she had never stepped foot inside the room before. Her eyes roamed everywhere but where Paul was at. "But the room is such a mess . . . shouldn't I . . ."

" . . . go on to bed," Mary finished.

"Perhaps I'll lay down in the side parlor," Isabel said quietly to herself. Her eyebrows rose. "I can hear you better if you need something from there . . . right?"

"Yes'm." Mary nodded, knowing that the parlor she referred to was the furthest place in the house from Paul's room. "I call you if I need anythin'."

With Isabel gone, Mary finished washing Paul. For every place there was a bruise . . . to the top and right of his stomach . . . both lower ribs on the left– two of which looked broken to her . . . his swollen eyes and split lips, she laid a cool compress. His body was hot to the touch and she feared fever would soon come upon him. Looking at him– his thin frame draped in wet rags, she realized how much of a child he still was.

She pulled a chair next to his bed and sat down. With the pressure finally off of her feet, she realized how bad they hurt and resisted the urged to look at them, knowing they were swollen like Paul's lips, testicle and cheeks. But as she sat quietly, fighting at first and then loosing the urge to sleep, Paul began moaning again. But it was not in response to his injuries, she could tell. It seemed as though he was trying to say something.

His arm reached out as he mumbled through torn lips. She rose with and an exhausted sigh. "You try and stay still now," she urged softly.

But his voice grew louder.

She took hold of his hand and felt him squeeze a little.

She smiled.

"See now," she said, squeezing back, "you be fine– you comin' out of it. Just rest a spell, now." But he growled and squeezed softly again. Still not understanding his jumbled words, she leaned in closer, but as she did so, his voice grew louder. He tried to move his body, even though it seemed to cause him even greater agony. She sat on the bed next to him. His other arm reached up and grabbed aimlessly for her. She now understood what he wished for.

"Alright now, chile– hold on." She lifted him by the shoulders and laid his head between her bulging belly and her lap. He cried out and shook for a while before his sharp intakes of breaths slowed to a rhythmical pace. His muscles, which had tensed during the sudden change in position, became flaccid once more. Finally, and to Mary's relief, he murmured in pleasure.

Mary relaxed also and rested her head against the wood head-board. She knew, before sleep came upon her, that wet rags on the kind and number of bruises Paul had would be insufficient to heal them. There was no skill that she had that could help him, and she knew Simeon would never allow him be taken to doc Reedy, the sole physician in town. She was left with only one option, though the thought of it kept her from falling asleep quicker than she would have liked. Had Paul been a Negroe child, she would have taken him to *her* immediately. She alone, Mary knew, possessed the skill– good, benign or evil, or whatever it was– to provide the type of healing Paul required.

She made her decision and decided to think upon it no more. Lar would arrive in a few hours and she would just have to have him take her to the witch, no matter how she felt about Enda; it was not for her, she reminded herself, but for the child who lay within her arms.

"I gonna make sure you feel much better come tomorrow," Mary assured him.

* * *

Paul no longer felt pain, thanks to his mind separating itself from his physical trauma– at least for now. He was hovering above himself . . . able to see his body and sense his organs trying to right themselves, as healing fluids rushed in and swelled those places that injury had been given to. He was in a far better place now.

Mary's belly that he lay against was alive with a sound like flowing water and occasionally a push from the child within. A silly thought occurred to him as he lay there, despite his circumstance. He wondered what it would be like to be within her now . . . to trade places with the unborn child. He fantasized how different things would be, for to live the life of a Negroe– *as Mary's child*, was far preferable to him than being a white, male Monclair with all of the privileges that could come with such a name and lack of color. And as he lay swaddled in her arms and listened to her heavy breaths flow in and escape out, a beautiful dream took hold of him and carried him even further from his pain, anguish, shame and regret.

He no longer felt Mary's arms– but *his*. It was David who now held him close and whose breaths were a sweet song to his ears.

They were lying under their usual tree by the river. His head was on David's lap and he was gazing up into his eyes. The townsfolk of Folsom were gone. There was no one around for miles in any direction.

Finally, Paul felt free.

David, it seemed, sensed it also and leaned over.

There was no apprehension in the kiss he shared with David– no fear of prying eyes to cast condemnation or fear of retribution in the form of death for daring to love another man, like his heart dictated. It was a kiss free of anxiety and restraint, and full of passion that only freedom could foster.

The taste of freedom was a feeling Paul now knew he could never relinquish, no matter the consequences. He vowed he would die before he let that happen, but never, he promised himself, by his own hands. It would have to be taken from him– with a fight to death.

And in that long kiss he shared with David . . . his love . . . he damned God and his father.

With a kiss, he sealed his hatred for Beatrice and for the woman – his mother, who was not a mother to him.

With a kiss, he said goodbye to the illusion of a peaceful childhood that was beaten out of him.

With a kiss, he opened his eyes and finally found his soul, which had been waiting for him to see it and nurture it for so long.

With a kiss, he strangled the beast within him and stole its mask, revealing his own face.

With a kiss, the beast within him died, for he finally understood that there never was one inside him at all.

Yet . . . with a kiss, he knew there *was* a beast that actually existed, but it was external of him . . . that beast had blue eyes and a hard, red stump.

With kiss . . . such a kiss . . . an awakening kiss, he thought, *I was blind, but now I see!*

CHAPTER 8

Whereas Paul had sleep filled with pain, and Mary very little as she comforted his broken body and soul through the night, Nicholas Barrons roused that next morning long before the sun had. It wasn't a troubled slumber that woke him, though he had had plenty of those of late; it was the God-awful heat the town seemed unwilling to relinquish that had stolen sleep from him. He had hoped he would become used to such a hot climate after so many months in the south, but he discovered he was mistaken about that, as he was about most aspects southern. "You just have thick, northern blood, boy," he said to himself.

He dismissed the thought of trying to fall back to sleep. He rose and went to the washbasin on the dresser and sponged the sweat from his armpits, crotch and backside. He put on a pair of tan slacks and a white short-sleeve shirt, leaving only enough buttons undone as to not be distasteful, but enough for ventilation. He looked in the mirror and saw that his black hair, which he'd not washed for two days now, still glimmered from the oil built up in it, even after passing a washcloth through it several times. Still not satisfied with it, he bent over and scooped water in his hands and sloshed it through his thick, short hair. The result was less than what he'd hoped for, but far better than it had been before. "Must impress," he whispered, as he brushed through it several times until he was satisfied he didn't look absolutely destitute.

After coming down narrow stairs, he was greeted kindly by Edgar Williams, caretaker of the Monclair motel with his wife, Deborah, a petite and ragged-looking woman . . . one would say if one were kind. Every time Nicholas saw her, he could not help but think that through some horrendous miracle, the woman had died horribly from starvation and was then resurrected, albeit in a worse state than what she'd been in before.

Neither one impressed upon Nicholas that they were overly concerned about hygiene. Edgar seemed to enjoy wearing the same clothes for days on end, and Deborah, who did change her dresses slightly more often than that, didn't seem to mind the stale musk Edgar carried and perfumed every room with. Even Edgar's thick, chicken-scratched glasses, which he always looked over, not through, seemed to have a perpetual film of water spots and dust upon them. But despite their aversion for bathing, the motel was clean, much to Nicholas' relief. Then again, he thought, it wasn't so arduous of a task to keep tidy, especially since he was only one of four guests they had.

Many times over meals prepared by Deborah, he listened to Edgar's tales of how the motel had once been bustling with so many guests, they often had to turn people away. "Now that was 'fore the war hit and dried up everythin' but the rivah," Edgar had said. "We was 'bout to pay off our debts to Mr. Monclair and buy the place . . . but . . . you know . . . the war . . . *that fuckin' war.*"

Deborah, who would never have been accused of being a pleasant woman, had chimed in. "The war hit us hard, boy," she told him, with a sorrowful shake of her head. "You and those fellas that came the other week be the first customers we done had in months . . . ain't that right, Edgar?"

"Yeahup," he replied.

Edgar waved Nicholas over to where he sat reading a newspaper. His legs were up on a chair he'd pulled to the side of the table. Deborah was sitting across from him, and seeing Nicholas approach, did not bother to stifle her sigh of exasperation at his early arrival. "Breakfast?" She droned.

"Yes'm . . . please," Nicholas replied, turning on his most charming, polite learned southern accent. But it was a wasted effort. She stared at him momentarily as though he'd kicked her in the shins, and then left for the kitchen without a word.

Nicholas brushed the encounter aside and sat down. He was actually mad at himself for having said *'please'. 'Please' for what?* He thought, as visions of another plate of grits and flavorless, hard scrambled eggs came to mind. He was sick of grits and eggs, which was all Deborah ever served for breakfast, and on a couple of occasions, for lunch and dinner when they had run out of food. Collards, mustard greens and cornbread he could take since developing a taste for them at the homes of his northern Negroe friends his mother schooled and befriended. But grits he'd had his fill of. No matter how much salt, butter or sugar he added to them, they still tasted like mush mixed with sand to him.

He knew money was tight for most people. In small southern towns like Folsom, there was no economy or an infantile one at best. And if that meant eating grits every day or corn mush to fill the stomach, then that's what they did, as his gut and constantly bound bowels had discovered. *But grits again,* he growled silently.

"That wouldn't happen to be a current paper would it?" Nicholas asked hopefully, trying to divert his mind from the smell of eggs wafting into the room.

"Sho' is." Edgar smiled and displayed all six of his teeth . . . five of which rested on his bottom gums and were lazy in their posture. A moment of silence ensued, and then Edgar winked at him and began cackling. "I just foolin' with ya, boy! It the same as last month's. I just like goin' over what I done read to make sure I ain't missed a thang or two."

Smile, Nick, he thought, ' . . . just smile.' "I thought you were expectin' a new shipment the other day."

"Uh-uh," Edgar replied. "You see– you don't listen real close, now do ya? Huh?" Edgar looked over his glasses at Nicholas. "I say we *might* get a new delivery of mess in with some mail– but that ain't come neither. Ol' Timmy, the mail boy, be late sometime. And today, we can consider him definitely late."

"I see."

"Well you can take a gander at a page of this one. You might come 'cross somethin' you done missed, too!"

"No thank ya, suh," Nicholas replied, taking care not to sound condescending to someone who moved their lips while reading.

"You never did say how thangs went with Roman and Simeon Monclair *lah-dee-dah, da second,*" Edgar inquired.

Nicholas laughed. "Everythin' went fine."

Edgar lowered his voice. "So– what you think of Simeon? Huh? A piece of work that man is– I tell ya. He think he God or somethin', don't he? And boy– you ain't seen nothin'. Should've seen him when the ol' Monclairs really had money. He be struttin' around town here like he was grand emperor of the world. Hell . . . treated all of us white folk like we was the niggahs."

Edgar leaned in closer. Nicholas, feeling compelled to do the same, did, but resisted inhaling Edgar's perpetually foul breath. "Mmm?"

"Monclair's lost everythin' when the Yanks came through," he whispered. "Only way he got a bit of money now, 'cause he married that Christianson woman . . . Izzy . . . Itty . . . hell– start with an *"eh"* or somethin' o' 'nother. Anyhow, that how he got what he got now, and he still think he head cock." Edgar leaned back in his chair and beamed as though he'd just divulged the meaning of life.

230 / ORLANDO SMART-POWELL

"I didn't know that . . . I mean, no one ever mentioned that to me," Nicholas responded, as his curiosity began to peak.

"You be real smart not to go yappin' 'bout it either," Deborah warned, as she walked over with a plate of food in her right hand, and two more balanced precariously in the other and on her arm. She left and returned with thick black coffee for all, and then pulled up a chair between them and sat.

Great . . . grits and eggs again, Nicholas thought, but smiled at her, even as his stomach started to become queasy.

"We ain't got no butter for the grits this mornin' . . . just gotta do without," Deborah said unapologetically.

Great . . . dry grits and eggs, Nicholas added to his previous thought.

"Yeahup." Edgar continued, "Best not be sayin' what I done told ya to no one. Simeon Monclair *da* second ain't a man to go messin' with."

"Most buildins' he got a deed on, 'cludin' this place," Deborah told him.

"Almost had it paid off 'til the Yanks came down to hug up on they niggahs," Edgar assured him.

"We gonna have this place once business picks up again," she mumbled though a mouthful of eggs.

Edgar grimaced at her optimism.

"I know it will . . . God willin'," she insisted. "The fact you wantin' to start some real business and get this town goin' again tell *me* thangs goin' to be alright soon 'nough. Our Jeffy and Harry ain't died in that goddamn war for nuthin' . . . hear me?! We gonna be alright one day. God gonna see all this mess be put right."

"Now Roman Meadows be a different charactah altogethah," Edgar informed him. "He ain't like that ol' crackle-faced Monclair."

"Now he a good man . . . 'spite . . ." Deborah stopped and grinned.

Nicholas tried to appear as uninterested as possible. "Despite what, ma'am?"

Edgar straightened up. "Let's not go spreadin' gossip now, Debbie."

She glared at him. "It ain't gossip if it be truth."

Edgar ignored her. "He a good man– ya hear me, boy? I ain't never heard tell 'bout him doin' nuthin' mean-hearted to nobody. He runs his farms and mill jus' like they 'spose to be– fair and fair. Anyone 'round here tell ya', if ya sharecroppin' for him or owin' him rent and can't pay, he downright understandable 'bout it."

Deborah raised the left side of her singular brow that stretched from eye to eye. She wiped her mouth with the back of her hand and pushed her cleaned plate away. "But . . ." she uttered, and then looked at Edgar and waited.

Edgar sighed. He pushed his glasses up on his beak-like nose, but still looked over them as he spoke to Nicholas. "Don't suppose you met the Mrs.– Lucianna."

"*The* Lucianna Meadows," Deborah added with a wicked smile.

"Actually, no," Nicholas replied. "But I have a feelin' I will today. I wanted to speak with Roman this mornin' and thought since I was up early enough, I could drop by his home before he left. They've extended a suppah invitation . . . so I'm sure to meet her soonah or late'ah."

"Make sure Roman or that mulatta nigrah workin' for'em is there when you do meet her," Deborah warned.

"Sorry ma'am?"

Deborah smiled. "Ms. Lucianna be real popular with men folk . . . if you know what I mean?" She winked.

"Rumor and gossip say she do, and both be sins– good book say," Edgar countered. "The way I look at it, that mess ain't nuthin' but jealous women tellin' tales and men folk braggin'.."

"Don't seem like a tale if jus' 'bout everybody tellin' the same story," she replied.

"Shit . . . that ain't nuthin' but monkey-see-monkey-do," Edgar explained.

"How are the Negroes here?" Nicholas asked. "The factory my father wants to set-up needs hard workers who aren't indignant and full of sass."

"They gettin' a bit uppity if you ask me," Deborah said quickly.

"Oh– I wouldn't say that," Edgar disagreed.

"What do you mean by 'uppity', ma'am?"

Deborah smiled in response to her opinion being taken serious by someone in the room. She stretched her neck out toward Nicholas. "You know how niggahs be. Well, maybe you don't know too well, you bein' born up north and all. But your mammy and pappy can tell you right . . . that is what you said, ain't it? Your kin be from the south?"

"Yes'm– Georgia," he lied, with a poker face.

Satisfied with his response, she continued on. "These niggahs 'round here just gettin' more mouthy day by day," she said in wonder. "White women 'round here gots the feelin' it jus' ain't safe to walk 'bout 'less you got a man by your side. Ain't no tellin' what them niggahs do if they catch ya' alone. That why we stopped them from comin' in town past dark. We got too many little white gals 'round here for niggah-men to be roamin' here and there and everywhere."

Edgar dismissively waved his hand at her. "Ain't none of our niggahs done nuthin' like what Debbie sayin'."

"Yet!" She spat, and then glared at Edgar. "Just weeks ago, they caught a niggah boy stealin' right out of white folk's houses. And . . ." she paused, "come to find out, that ain't all he was up to. He and his pappy was sneakin' looks at white women when they ain't got they knickers on. And it ain't stop there neither– uh-uh." She pointed her finger at Nicholas. "And this is what I mean 'bout how you can't have a niggah 'round here past dusk and dark, and especially a niggah man. They lust got to 'em. *Lust!*" she seethed.

"Why– those two niggahs– father and son if you can believe that, took advantage of a white woman!" She sat back and sighed, as if her own words astounded her.

"And God's justice was done, too," Edgar said flatly. "And that be that and all that. But our niggahs don't act like that."

"Yet!" Deborah exclaimed.

"Justice as in . . . ?" Nicholas asked.

"Strung 'em up," Deborah told him, as though he should have known. "We ain't got no law 'round here 'cept fifty miles south. Ain't no judge 'round to help see thangs done properly, so white folk did what was right and needed to be done," she said proudly. "These niggahs gotta learn that jus' cause they *free*," she spat the word as if it were something profane only seedy men used when drunk, "you ain't gonna go rapin' and killin' and actin' like you still in the jungle."

Edgar slammed his hand on the table. Startled plates and tin cups ran for the table's edge for safety. "Good grief, woman! You makin' it seem like niggah's are standin' outside 'bout to do you in. It ain't like that, boy. Those folk keep 'cross the river, 'less they have to come work. And once the sun done set, they go on back to where they come from, 'less they got permission." He turned to Deborah, and for the first time, Nicholas saw a sliver of anger cross his face, daring Deborah to challenge him. "And that how it be here in Folsom!"

Deborah stood abruptly and left, abandoning the dirty dishes on the table that she usually cleared after each meal. Nicholas jumped as she slammed the kitchen door behind her. Edgar was oblivious to her tirade and gingerly sipped his coffee.

"You don't pay no mind to Debbie," Edgar instructed. "Niggahs here be real manageable. They works hard and they ain't gonna give you no trouble neither. Now if you put *good* white folk ta' work for ya, " he said, with a more than deliberate smile, "they gonna make sho' you and your pappy get a good return . . . hear?

Though– I can't see why a good lookin' young man like you need more money than what you got. You probably got pretty little rich gals crawlin' all over ya . . . huh? Huh? Heh-heh!"

Nicholas couldn't help but smile at Edgar, who was doing his best to burrow his crooked nose up his rectum. "Yes, suh," he replied. Nicholas stood up. Looking through the window, he saw more of the local town folk were up and moving on the wood walkway in front of the motel and in the streets.

Edgar began clearing the table. "Reckon I gotta do it all 'round here," he grunted. He shook his head and huffed. "Ol' shiftless bitch got the nerve to call niggahs lazy!" He balanced the cups and plates in his hands. "Oh . . . now if you don't believe what I done told ya, ask Roman Meadows. He'll tell ya' the truth. He got plenty of niggahs workin' for'em and ain't ever had a problem. You do that now– hear?"

Nicholas promised he would.

* * *

Wagons crowded with Negroes were headed off for the fields as Nicholas walked out of the motel. Though there were a few white women walking about, the majority were white men, who too, like the Negroes, were in their grungy work clothes ready for another day's labor under the Folsom sun. The few shops still operating in town had already opened their doors in hopes of a few sales. As Nicholas walked toward the bridge, as Roman Meadows had instructed him in finding his home, he could see the effects Reconstruction had on Folsom; which was none. The vast majority of the money spent on Reconstruction had gone to the larger cities before the whole concept imploded. What was left was what he'd seen in the past few months in the south . . . Negroes and whites struggling to recover and move forward, though not together.

The fact that people, having heard of his interest in revitalizing Folsom, stopped him, spoke with him, nearly pleaded with him to remember their name, spoke volumes about the gravity of the situation they were in. The first few days in Folsom he was regarded as a stranger, but more likely a carpetbagger . . . *God forbid.* The weight of suspicious eyes upon him walking from post office to tavern to trinket shop was palpable. Voices were not welcoming, but politely forced. It hadn't been until word of a new industry he was pondering to bring to Folsom spread that greetings became genuine and desperate. Invitations to dinners and lunches were extended. Men perfected ways to turn a conversation about the heat or draught, or hatred of the north into tales of their daughter's legendary beauty, though Nicholas knew such fabled beauty had only become legend when they realized what he was most likely well-to-do. Within a week's time, he had become the man to know.

Yet, he could find no other connection to these people who wore his same color, other than they were fellow human beings. The south was such a different culture than what he was accustomed to. The thought, that just a few short years ago, some of these same people bought, sold and owned another's body . . . fellow human beings . . . was disturbing to him. From pulpits, he knew it was taught that it was a white man's right to own Negroes. Even the government had validated the white man's right to wield the lash and rape Negroe women and girls, for they knew the lash could demand obedience as well as silence in all matters of the body.

"And what would you have done?" Nicholas remembered his mother asking him. He was only a few years shy of going off to college and was full of pride, knowledge and self-righteousness . . . the most dangerous mix of qualities one could possess, his father, Abram, always told him. He swore that if he had been raised in the south years past, he would have never owned a slave or treated a Negroe in such a manner as they were. That '*ugly*' word . . . '*niggah*', he'd told her, would never have crossed his lips.

"I would have worked to free them, of course, mother" he'd told her, as if there were no other option to consider.

He recalled his mother laughing in response to his bravado he never had to prove, but not in a patronizing manner. As he thought about it now, her laugh meant something entirely different than what he'd initially taken it as. It was a laugh that said, 'live life, grow old and *then* give me your answer– taste hard times, and then tell me.' He realized now that it was as a laugh meant to challenge his beliefs– even now it did– just as she had always wanted.

"My courageous, little abolitionist, eh?" She asked and cupped his face gently. "Imagine, Nick . . . pretend for a moment with me, o.k?

"You are born in the South and have a very good life– better than your one here. As a slave owner you are southern royalty. And all your life, from your very first memory, there are Negroes who work for your parents and they work for the parents of your friends. And before you've even learned to speak, you have heard . . . *rather*, you've been taught, that being owned by whites *is* the place of a Negroe. You go to church and the minister tells you the same, because he says God has told him as much. You go off to boarding school and your teachers remind you of this also.

"You grow up learning that the Negroe has the mind of a child. He doesn't speak like we do. He doesn't act like we do. You've learned that they've come from the wilds of Africa where they run around naked and do unspeakable things. But here in America, with God's will and by his right, you and your fellow whites have *saved* them from a life of depravity. You feed them. You clothe them! You've shown them how to speak English instead of some guttural, wild tongue. And in return for all that you have done for them they serve you. They farm your lands and clean your houses; they provide stability for your family, so that when you marry and have children, they too can carry on the tradition of helping the poor, ignorant Negroe. Symbiosis it's called . . . one helping the other so that both can exist.

"Now . . . tell me, Nick," she'd then said softly. "Would you have risen against all that you have been taught to believe? Could you have gone against your father and I . . . your friends and neighbors to side with the Negroe? Could you have seen the truth through the darkness that was the only world you had ever known?"

Nicholas remembered responding without hesitation and with blind conviction. "Yes!"

She had then smiled, he reminisced. "You are truly your father's son . . . stubbornly insightful," she complemented. "Which is why I married him. I wanted to have a piece of him to call my own."

Nicholas found the Meadows' house easily enough. It was the only one that looked as new as the day it was built, unlike its distant neighbor's, whose homes were beginning to tilt left and right as they sank into the ground, and their exteriors nearly bare of what paint that hadn't flaked off yet. The two-story home was startling white and shined like a beacon in a sea of gray despair. Its foundation was encircled with meticulously trimmed shrubs with fingertip long green leaves. Once he was past the white picket fence, large flagstones led him up and onto a wrap-around porch that was home to oversized ferns that hung from its ceiling. Tropical-like plants exploded from their painted planters, nearly obscuring them with leaves the color of blood, clear summer skies and pink autumn sunsets. The flora of the south never failed to mesmerize him with their almost otherworldly appearance.

Nicholas tried to dissect the motivation of the owners who maintained such a well-groomed manor in a dying, if not already dead town as Folsom was. What he'd heard from others in town about Roman– which wasn't much, other than he was a fair, sensible man, had already set him apart from other large landowners in Nicholas' eyes. Most businessmen he'd run into were preoccupied with having others sharecrop and rent from them at exorbitant costs, because for poor whites and Negroes, it was the only choice most had to survive.

Roman had remained silent for most of the conversation the night they met briefly, Nicholas recalled. Roman nodded when he seemed to like what was said, but never offered an opinion on anything. Nicholas had even offered to buy him a drink, seeing that they were standing in the tavern next to the motel at the time– if a small, oil lamp lit room with a few tables could be considered as such, but Roman politely refused and instead invited him for dinner.

Roman was, as the Williamses had told him, a stark contrast to Simeon Monclair. He found Simeon to be just as they'd described him . . . as cold on the surface as he seemed within. When he sat with Simeon only a few hours after meeting Roman, there was never a moment he didn't feel on guard. Simeon, unlike Roman, had peppered him with question after question. Simply explaining that his family was from Georgia wasn't sufficient for Simeon, who probed even deeper about his background. The man with cold, blue eyes wanted . . . demanded more. He wanted to know maiden names and other relatives who surely must still reside in Georgia. Simeon inquired about Nicholas' schooling . . . where, when, for how long? *"Where did your family's fortune come from?"* Simeon asked brashly. *Why come to the south now? What's your politics? How did your family support the Confederacy?* Simeon was relentless, Nicholas remembered, none too kindly. It was a blessing to him when Simeon finally fell quite, drank his last shot of whiskey and left stumbling out into the dark.

Nicholas pushed aside thoughts of Simeon and his red, calloused stump of a hand. He grabbed the shiny brass knocker and rang out to the inhabitants inside. He heard nothing stirring from within, even after repeated knocking on the fist thick, wood door. The small, slender windows on either side of it were shielded with drapes and were of no use to peek through. He was about to leave when he heard a sharp crack from around the back of the house. He debated whether to investigate. He couldn't deny that the Williamses had aroused his curiosity about Lucianna Meadows. He wanted to see what had provoked such jealously from Deborah. He realized he would meet her later that evening, but the idea of seeing her sooner was tempting. He followed the porch around the side and then down a small flight of stairs. When he rounded the corner to the back of the house, he stopped. He was tempted to rub his eyes, but he knew he was not in a dream, even though it felt as though he had just stepped into one.

The beauty of the exotic plants on the porch suddenly lost their wonder in comparison to the ones he now saw in the expansive garden before him. There were plants with stems as thick as his arm and leaves the size of a young boy's chest. Some leaves were striated with green and white; others with subtle and explosive hues ... pink and orange ... purples so dark they were nearly black. Miniature trees with glistening leaves, as though each one had been waxed and buffed, were scattered about. At the far edge, near the river that the property ran up against, a wall of towering trees rose mightily to the sky. Willows were scattered near the giant trees and lazily brushed their fingers on the ground. Even the grass was emerald green, but very much out of place in Folsom, which was suffering from a drought of rain and life.

The path of walking stones from the front of the house continued on into the rear, leading all who walked upon it into the magical realm. He heard movement and walked in further. He saw a woman with her back to him, and was about to call out to her when she suddenly dropped out of sight behind a wall of elephant ear plants. He checked to make sure that his shirt was tucked into his trousers securely and properly. He wiped away the sweat beaded on his forehead, but with no place to discard it, he used it to smooth his hair back.

He came up behind her. She was scooping spilled dirt from the stone walkway into a pile. A yellow flowered plant was sprawled out next to her with its roots exposed in another mound of dirt. A large, red clay pot, the source of the sound he'd heard earlier, lay shattered in a multitude of pieces around her.

"Mrs. Meadows?"

She jumped.

When she turned around, all thoughts that had been swirling in his mind moments before . . . his mother . . . Edgar and Deborah Williams . . . Simeon . . . the garden . . . all evaporated at the sight of *her.* The ivory Negra who had been haunting his thoughts since he first saw her was staring at him. Her very presence made him suddenly feel bountiful with life, yet insignificant next to her.

His body began to act on its own accord. He introduced himself, but had no memory of having told his mouth to move or to speak. It was the same when he bent down on one knee to assist her, and she, like a frightened kitten, backed away. In that moment, he didn't care that she was obviously troubled by his presence. Self-ishly, he acted on his need to be near her, if only to solve the kaleidoscopic puzzle that were her blue-hazel eyes.

"I ain't Mrs. Meadows, suh," she said.

Nicholas barely heard what she said; he was too focused on how pretty her pink lips were when they moved. He shook his head free of the delirium that was gripping him. "No . . . no . . . *you aren't,* Mrs. Meadows," he whispered, and then smiled. "You're that girl from town . . . the one who tripped. Maggie . . . Ms. Mag . . . Ms. Maggie?" He asked awkwardly.

"Yes, suh," she replied demurely.

"Let me help you– Ms. Maggie," he offered.

"Ms. Lucianna still sleepin', I believe."

"I didn't come to see her. I mean . . . um– I was hopin' to catch up to Mr. Meadows . . . Roman, that is," he rephrased.

She looked up and past him, toward the house. "He already gone."

"Well I'm glad I stopped by anyway."

Maggie Mae took another step back.

"To help you," he said quickly. "It seems I have come to your rescue once again." He chuckled in hope that she would also, but she was a doe transfixed by the light of his poor humor. He realized, as he saw her constantly looking behind him and fidgeting with her hands, that he was frightening her more than allaying her fear of him. He wondered what was behind him that so preoccupied her attention.

But more importantly, he was trying to figure out why he was behaving like he was. He had no good answer for his adolescent antics, other than he was a male who had come face to face with a creature he felt unworthy to share the same space with. He knew the game he played now was as dangerous, if not more so than the one that had brought him south in the first place. With the exception of New Orleans, which had once tolerated a white man taking a Negroe for a mistress, here and now it was absolutely taboo. Yet it all seemed so wrong to him that a thing such as color should deprive him of the opportunity to get to know her better.

Her natural beauty held him captive, for even in her headscarf and dirty, tattered yellow dress, she was far lovelier than other ladies who bathe in perfume and concealed their faces in paint. Her hesitancy made her even more endearing to him. She was a bright, wild flower in Folsom's dry wasteland of sharp and dull rocks. Yet, here in the lush garden, she blended in seamlessly with the exotic flora around her.

Nicholas slapped his hands together, knocking off the dirt and then stood. "All done for you, Ms. Maggie," he announced proudly.

"You shouldn't have done that," she scolded. Again she looked at the house and then at him, but promptly lowered her head.

He was taken aback by her words, but was emboldened by her brief connection. He looked at the cracked pot lying on the ground and spoke instinctively . . . truthfully. "And you shouldn't be doin' this," he replied. "That pot is far too heavy for you to be carryin' anyway."

"The gal can manage just fine, suh," a woman's voice said from behind Nicholas.

Nicholas turned around and lowered his head respectfully. "Beg your pardon, ma'am." She was standing in the doorway, but the shadow of the porch overhang cast a shadow and revealed nothing more than a silhouette of her. "Mrs. Meadows, may I presume?"

"Depends on who you are."

"Nicholas Barrons. Perhaps your husband has mentioned . . ."

"Ahhhh," she sighed. "Our honored dinner guest for this evenin'."

"Yes, ma'am."

An abrupt silence ensued.

"Maggie," Lucianna called. She waited for Maggie Mae to come to the steps of the porch before speaking again. "I see you've destroyed yet another of my belongings."

"Yes'm," Maggie Mae whispered with a bowed head.

"I wouldn't expect full pay this week . . . again. I'll have nothin' to show for any of my efforts with you fumblin' about and destroyin' everything of value."

"Yes'm."

Again silence.

"I do expect breakfast shortly, Maggie."

"Yes'm," Maggie Mae said quickly and disappeared into the house.

Nicholas only caught a glimpse of Lucianna as she stepped to the side and let Maggie Mae pass by. "I was hopin' to meet your husband this mornin'. But as Maggie Mae has informed me, he's already departed," Nicholas offered. Lucianna's shadow shifted.

Nicholas waited for some reply, but none came. Casually, she stepped out onto the back porch. Finally he saw Lucianna in the flesh– and flesh there was to be seen. He now had a better understanding of what Deborah and Edgar Williams were talking about.

She was little more than thirty years of age, he guessed. In contrast, he'd pegged Roman . . . gray haired and deep lines between his brows and on the outsides of his eyes . . . closer to sixty. She was wearing a nightgown with a white, and practically sheer robe tossed carelessly about her shoulders, which was open and revealed enough of her breasts to draw attention to them. Her fire-engulfed hair– bountiful and wavy, lounged upon the bloodless skin of her shoulders. Her nose and cheekbones were sharp, yet her green jeweled eyes and dainty jaw softened the total of her face.

Nicholas, embarrassed at her brazenness, forced himself to look only at her face– after quickly peeking at the cleft of her chest. He was attracted to her physically . . . what man wouldn't be, he thought. Only, there was something about her that pushed those thoughts away as quickly as they had come. Instead of her arousing a soothing and teasing passion within him, he felt scorched instead. Her white skin suddenly seemed as cold as it looked. And he did not care for her playful, smug grin, which presumed to suggest that she knew what he wanted. He had no doubt she'd played this game before and was often victorious.

"My husband," she finally said, "goes to work very early and arrives in the evening late at night."

"Of course, ma'am," he acknowledged, knowing exactly what she really meant and did not like it at all. Already she was casting charms, he observed with a large dose of caution. The words of Deborah Williams suddenly came back to him . . . "Ms. Lucianna be real popular with men folk . . ."

"Surely he told you this when you met," she said.

"He did mention it. Care for the fields in this drought has of course increased his workload."

"Then you are also aware that supper will be served closer to six in the evening, rather than at five . . . the time I believe he's told you to arrive?"

"No, I didn't know that," Nicholas replied. "I shall adjust my time accordingly then."

Lucianna smiled again. "Of course you won't, Mr. Barrons. You shall come and have a spot of sweet brandy with me . . . at five. "

Nicholas was speechless.

"I too would like to be privy to your interest in my husband's business" she told him. "And you need not worry, Mr. Barrons . . . I can see as much upon your face. My servant gal will be my guardian until my husband arrives and joins us."

Nicholas felt his face warming. He hadn't realized his thoughts were so transparent to her. *She's a wily one, Nick,* he cautioned himself silently. It suddenly occurred to him that perhaps it was not white men he should be most suspicious of, but their women.

"Do you fancy my garden, Mr. Barrons?" She asked.

"I've never seen the likes of it except in an arboretum. Compliments to you and Mr. Meadows are much deserved. It is exquisite."

"As it should be," she said proudly. "What you cannot see is all of the effort that has gone into maintainin' it. Roman chides me for keeping it so, but I cannot bear lookin' at dead things . . . withered plants where lovely flowers should be. He says that it's a waste of resources. But we're close enough to the river to draw from it. And being that it's so dry, his workers mill about doing nothin' at all. Idle hands and minds . . . You do know what is said about them . . . yes?"

Nicholas nodded. "The devil's playground."

"A learned man," Lucianna replied, as if impressed, that is if she had not turned her head slightly as she spoke. "I simply have them come here and work. They tend my garden instead of standin' in Roman's fields watchin' his crops wither."

"The efforts are certainly worthwhile," he commented.

"More than you know, Mr. Barrons," she replied almost imperceptibly. "I shall expect you at five. And you shall tell me of this enterprise you're suggestin' that has all of Folsom in a tizzy."

"It will be my pleasure," he lied.

"Mr. Barrons," she called out before he turned to leave. Her tone deepened. "I do have my husband's ear in all matters. A favorable impression upon me would be in the best interest of this industry you are considering here."

* * *

Nicholas made his way southeast along the road that bordered the river in search of Roman's farm and mill factory, but his thoughts were clearly elsewhere. In his mind, he was still standing in Lucianna's garden. It hadn't taken him long to decide that he didn't care for her. The manner in which she spoke to him, and even before that, so rudely and dismissively to Maggie Mae, had permanently ruined any hope of finding a redeeming spark of charm in her that could counterweight her brashness. And beautiful though she was, to him she paled next to Maggie Mae. It was Maggie Mae's sweetness and purity that held him in once her beauty had drawn him forth. Her being unaware of the mystical pheromone she exuded made him feel warmer than the Southern heat ever could. She had seemed so frightened on both occasions they'd met. Each time, he had to refrain from grabbing hold of her and shielding her from whatever unseen forces she seemed constantly threaten by. Truthfully, he admitted, he just wanted to touch her and make for certain that someone as lovely as she was real, not an illusion meant to haunt and taunt him.

He pinpointed the cause of the malady afflicting his heart, which was making it feel leaden, yet robust. He knew nothing about her other than she was a Negroe who didn't look like a Negroe, but was more beautiful than any white, Negroe, or mix of both he'd ever seen. But his thoughts shifted back to Lucianna, who, from what little he did know about her, seemed the opposite of Maggie Mae in every way. He wondered had she been a man and spoken to him with such forthrightness as she did, would he be feeling any different now. *Is that it, Nick, old boy?* He pondered. *Or . . .* he asked himself *. . . was it that she was both beautiful and bold?* He could see how most men could easily become enthralled with her and not realize what they had until she revealed the other, far keener side of her blade.

His legs walked on their own accord as he lost himself in thought over Lucianna and Maggie Mae– but more so Maggie Mae. He was almost a mile south of central Folsom, and the river that had been to his left disappeared behind trees and overgrown grass that was more brown than green. There was a house up on the hill and set far off the road on his right, which meant Meadow's farm was even further up the road. And it seemed to be getting hotter by the moment. "Just follow the road alongside the river south for a ways and you'll come upon the mill first," Roman instructed. "The cotton and produce fields are further back. You'll know the buildin' when you come to it. It's just about the only thing out that way." Still, there was no sign of what Roman had described. To be safe, he decided to save himself a walk in the wrong direction by stopping and asking the owner's of the house if he was indeed going the right way. He turned around and walked backwards more out of boredom than anything else, but did not expect to see anything– though he did see something– someone.

The sun's glare obliterated most of his vision. Even with his hand as a shield, he saw nothing more than a heat induced wavy figure approaching him. He changed direction toward the figure and picked up his pace. Walking in the heat with company was preferable than sweating it out alone, he figured. He'd been report-ing for only three years . . . interning as a researcher for other sea-soned reporters for two before that, but he knew enough already to realize that the most unusual circumstances usually produced the best stories. But as he neared the figure, it moved to the oppo-site side of the road.

He raised his hand and called out. "I say . . . hello there!" No re-ply or even a physical acknowledgement was returned. As they neared one another, he saw that the figure was a 'she', and not a 'he' as he first assumed. The large straw-hat obscuring her face was a giveaway . . . the ground-length dress also.

"Ma'am!" He called. "I was wonderin' if you could direct me to Mead . . ." He became silent. She peeked at him from below her hat and quickly hid her face. "An unexpected surprise," he gushed, and meant every single sound of every syllable of every word.

Maggie Mae looked at him. "Not for me. I know where you goin'." She kept walking. Nicholas turned and skittered to catch up to her.

Nicholas grinned and showed a few teeth. "Oh . . . so you *are* followin' me then?"

Her eyes widened. "No, suh! I been sent."

"By Mrs. Meadows?"

"Yes, suh."

Nicholas had to walk quickly to keep pace with her. He tried fo-cusing on what was in front of him, but a greater urge kept him sneaking glimpses of her from the side. "What's so pressin' that she has you out in this heat?"

"A message for Mr. Meadows."

"Oh," he said apologetically. "Didn't mean to pry."

He looked forward, but peripherally, he saw her look at him, and he quickly did the same in hopes of . . . *see me, Maggie Mae . . . keep looking at me . . . no—just let me look at you.* But she turned away and studied the road ahead.

What the hell is wrong with you, Nick! He thought. *Get a grip on yourself . . . right goddamn now. It will never, ever be . . . ever!*

"Ain't nothin' important," she commented.

All thoughts of what was wrong with what he was feeling instantly turned to mist and evaporated under the heat of the Folsom sun. *'Ever'* suddenly didn't seem so final. "No?"

"Mistress needin' a few workers to move things 'bout . . . haul water and dig up plants and that."

"Mistress? You make her seem as if she were the wife of an English Lord."

Maggie Mae scrunched her nose. "Suh?"

"A lady," he explained. "You know . . . Lord Roman and Lady Lucianna. *Mahstah* and Mistress of Folsom m*ahnah*," he said in his best replication of old English. She turned her face away from his, but not before he spied her smile. "And who is your Lord– my lady?"

She looked at him. "Only lord I got be the Lord, Jesus Christ. And I ain't what you call a lady neither. I just a maid."

Her answer both pleased and disappointed him. "Not a lady?" he asked. He held out his hand in front of her. "Wait a moment, please."

She stuttered to a halt.

"It is I who have not been *a gentleman . . . my lady.* Forgive me if I have forgotten my manners." He held his hand out. "Nicholas Isaac Barrons." Again he saw fear in her eyes. She was unmoving in response to his seemingly . . . he hoped it appeared that way, though he knew it wasn't . . . innocent gesture. He bowed his head and extended his hand even further. *Let me just touch you once,* he prayed silently. Tentatively, her hand rose and moved toward his.

He took hold of her hand and enveloped it in his. *So—so beautiful you are,* he thought, and fought his body's urge to gasp. Her hand withdrew suddenly and sharply, but its magic lingered upon him.

The road they walked began to incline. After cresting the steep hill, he saw traces of Meadow's farm. In the far distance, he spotted a great expanse of trees, though not nearly as densely populated as the woods across the river where the Negroes lived.

"I'm puzzled . . . why are you walking?" Nicholas asked. "Surely Mr. Meadows can spare a horse and wagon, or even two."

"Ms. Lucianna don't want me usin' it. She say it ain't gonna hurt none to walk." She sighed. "I ain't too good at managin' a wagon anyhow."

He nodded. "But still, you shouldn't be out here in this heat the way it is. Heat has a tricky way of makin' you sick before you know it."

She smiled at him.

Nicholas suddenly felt faint.

"Heat only bothers folk who ain't from down here," she informed him. "We may be hot as a pan of grease, but we get used to it real quick like– 'specially if you ain't gotta choice."

"So you've heard that I was raised in the north then?"

"No, suh," she said with a shake of her head. "Just . . . just that . . ."

"Maggie Mae," he said, as warmly as he could, "don't be afraid to speak with me. It's just as you said, I'm not from here. These ways . . . these southern ways are not *my ways.* Speak as you please."

"Well, suh . . ." She paused briefly. "It just that sometime . . . I guess . . . well . . . you sound like southern white folk sometime, then other . . . well . . ."

Nicholas grinned.

"Sometimes you sound more like other southern folk who ain't white."

"Really?"

"Yes, suh." Maggie Mae stopped and then started again. "It ain't just your word . . . it just the way you say them, and move your head and hands when you talkin'."

"You know– I can say the same thing about you."

"I know."

"I can tell you've had some schooling."

"So have you," Maggie Mae commented.

"Tell me . . . I'm curious now. How do you know that?"

Maggie Mae shrugged her shoulders. "All I do is just listen. My mammy say folk be too busy talkin' over one another, they don't take time to listen to half of what somebody gotta say."

Nicholas agreed. "Like me," he said. "I've been talkin' about me and haven't heard one thing about you. Do you live with the others . . . across the river?" He realized his question was a foolish one and didn't need the puzzled, almost angry look that Maggie Mae gave him to realize it.

"Of course, suh," she answered quickly. "I'm . . . I a Negroe."

No, he thought, *you're absolutely exquisite and you don't even know it.*

"I apologize," he spoke quickly and earnestly. "Like you said, I'm not from here. The ways of the south are, as you can imagine not the same in the northern states."

"I don't 'spose they are . . . *is,*" she stuttered, and then paused for a moment. "Down here there be just Negroe, white and Indian. And all the Indians been ran off from Folsom years ago. So there's just be Negroe and white now. If you got *all* white blood– you white. You got *any* Negroe blood– you Negroe. And if you Negroe, you live 'cross the river."

"Would you ever leave? Not just from over there, but . . . Folsom?"

"No, suh," she responded quickly.

Nicholas turned away and took his turn studying the road ahead of them. And as much as he wanted to, he couldn't hide the obvious disappointment gluing itself to his face. He hoped he could peel it away before it dried and stuck and she saw it. He tried to convince himself to feel relieved that she had said 'no' so quickly, putting an end to thoughts of fantasy that would never become reality. But her reply gave him no solace. It was just as his mother had always told him, but he never quite understood until now . . .

"You're a dreamer, Nick—like your father. This isn't the world you were meant to live in. Still, you're here in it. You'll learn to live with sorrow—like everyone else. You'll have to, if you want to live at all. You'll see what I mean one day, and you'll see you don't belong here. It'll hurt sometimes. Sometimes it'll hurt so badly, you'll want to cry and just give up . . . but . . . that's when you'll realize you're alive, and truly treasure those who are most important to you."

"From what I hear," he said, "young folks are leavin' Folsom as quick as they are of age. The town is dyin'. And still, even if you had the chance, you wouldn't seek a better life elsewhere?"

"Ain't that why you here? Folks been talkin' 'bout you bringin' work to these parts. You talkin' like you ain't?"

Ahhh, he thought. He hadn't assumed Maggie Mae was of a simple mind, but neither did he think she had known enough about him to cut flesh from the lie he had sat on Folsom's empty plate. She possessed both beauty and wit, he gathered. "But say that I did not invest," he persisted. "And that's not to say that I won't. But if I didn't, and no other man did also?"

"I have my mammy to tend to," she explained. "And my mammy ain't gonna leave Folsom."

"What says your father, then?"

"It just me and mammy. Always been," she replied, with a swift turn of her head, loosening her straw hat from her head. A wavy tuft of gold hair escaped. Feeling it upon the back of her neck, she quickly tucked it back inside.

Nicholas ached. How he'd wanted his hands, not hers, to be the one to touch those golden strands that had tumbled from her head. And not stopping there, he wanted to caress her cheek . . . brush his fingers across her pink lips and then part them ever so gently with his own.

Her voice startled him from his daydream. He knew he'd been caught staring at her, but he no longer cared if she knew how he felt or not. In fact, he wanted her to know, no matter how ludicrous and unfathomable it all seemed to her or him. He hated the south and their rules and customs now so more than ever, but especially because of her and how she was making him feel.

"We're here," she announced, rousing him from his other world where he was upon one knee with diamond in hand and offering . . . begging her to accept it.

And it was true . . . a small cabin was set off slightly from the road. Its rustic brown paint had worn well; its windows were clean and gave it the appearance of a family's abode, rather than an office. But in front of the cabin were six, large wagons led by hearty looking horses. Some were loaded to near capacity with wood, and others stacked with bundles of straw, and yet others holding puffy sacks of what he thought could only be cotton. Men– white and Negroes were on the move. The Negroes, most all of them, were stripped to the waist and were the busiest . . . hauling woman-sized sacks upon their shoulders and depositing them on the wagons a short distance away. And even as he watched, two more wagons, both empty, could be seen coming from behind the small cabin to take their turn to be weighed down with goods. It was then, as he and Maggie Mae walked further and the road finally started to level out, that he could see a far larger building that dwarfed the small cabin. He recognized the tell-tale red, swinging doors instantly.

Sensing his time with her quickly shortening, he said words he knew he shouldn't. His mother, who was sitting on the right shoulder of his brain, chided him. *"Foolish boy . . . wake up! This isn't your world, Nick."*

"May I come by and speak to you sometime? At your home, with your mother present of course?" he asked hopefully. But her demeanor seemed to harden at his words. He quickly added, "To learn about the Negroes here. For the business I am proposing, of course."

"I'm just a woman, suh. Why would you want to speak with me about things like that?"

He quickly thought of an excuse, but it was not a lie. "You seem to be truthful in how you speak. And that is exactly what I need more than anything. And like you have said, whether life or death comes to this town by me or another, you will stay regardless . . . that tells me you will tell me the truth in all matters, because it affects you either way."

He watched her most carefully as she looked up toward the cabin that was now so close. Her eyes sparkled. Even glimpsing them from the side they were as rare and precious as jewels stolen from an Atlantean crown.

"Lar Cole," she finally said, after an uncomfortable moment of silence between them.

"What?"

"Laurence Cole works for Mr. Meadows, too," she informed him. "He's the man you want to speak with. He knows every Negroe around here and just about every other around." She paused for a moment. When next she spoke, her tone was one of strength and conviction he hadn't detected before. She whispered, "And suh, you are in the south. What goes on up north doesn't have anything to do with what goes on here."

Nicholas whispered back. "Maggie Mae . . . wait." But she had already began walking toward the cabin. "You haven't answered my question," he offered, hope still clinging to his voice.

"Yes suh," she said, never stopping her advance away from him, "I did."

Nicholas knew that she had, it was just that he refused to accept her answer. In his heart, he knew the ways and customs that cast a shadow on his feelings were wrong. But he *was* in the south, nevertheless. And his reason for being here was not to become enamored with someone he could never have. But that was sensible thinking, and at the moment, he didn't want to behave as such. *Be quiet mother!*

Despite the shocked, if not disapproving looks he and Maggie Mae garnered from the Negroe workers who were close by loading the wagons and the white men at the helm preparing to leave, he moved ahead of Maggie Mae and up the steps, opening the door to the cabin for her. And though he was cognizant of the mores between whites and Negroes, he was not one of them, and vowed to do as he pleased and as his heart foolishly dictated.

With Nicholas refusing to budge from his gentlemanly position, his hand holding the door wide open for her, she entered first . . . reluctantly. He looked back at the workers before he too entered and saw that they were already buzzing around one another as they looked upon the spectacle he was causing. He refused to cower, and instead, tilted his head in respect to the whites and acknowledged the Negroes with a smile. They all, Negroe and white, responded without words, just stoic fixation.

Nicholas realized that besides Roman Meadows, who stood by an open window that faced directly toward the barn, he and Maggie Mae were not the only occupants. There were two other white gentlemen standing silently and close to Roman while he scribbled into a leather bound ledger he was holding.

The office was a reflection of Roman– clean and organized, Nicholas assessed. Ledgers, like the one he was writing in, were stacked neatly in a bookcase on the far wall behind him. On the long, wooden desk with baby sized elephant legs, his papers were in small stacks, each pile separated by mere inches and lined up perfectly along the edge. The smell of oak, of which the cabin was constructed, pleasantly aromatized the room.

The white men patiently waiting for Roman's orders were the first to acknowledge their presence, but it was to Maggie Mae that they spoke. Roman's writing hand seemed to stall at the mention of her name, Nicholas observed. When the gray haired man turned and looked at her, he did not like the feeling it aroused within him.

For an instance, Nicholas thought he saw the inkling of a smile from Roman. But if there had been one, it faded quickly, as the man's eyes returned to their cover beneath folded skin. "What does she want now?" Roman asked her, not bothering to acknowledge Nicholas.

Maggie Mae's head hung low, and before she could answer, Roman spoke again. "Why am I even asking such things? How many workers does she need today of all days that we finally have enough cotton and timber worth selling?"

"Just two, suh?" Maggie Mae responded softly.

"Two," Roman said flatly. "And why didn't she tell me this before I left instead of sending you all the way out here? I don't want you walking up and down these roads, you hear me?" He glanced at Nicholas who was standing behind her. "There's no telling who's on them."

"Yes, suh."

"I'll make sure of that this evening," Roman added. "Did she send you with him?"

"No, suh!" Maggie Mae replied quickly. "But, suh?" She hesitated. "Ms. Lucianna asked for the same ones who came the other day. She say they do good work 'round the place."

Roman's face took on the life of a corpse as he stared her. "I'll send whoever I feel like sendin'," Roman seethed. He turned away from them and spoke with the men at his side. After scribbling in the ledger once more, he closed it and dismissed them. Again, Roman's attention turned to Maggie Mae. "You can hitch a ride back to town on McMullen's wagon. They'll be some Negroe men on the tail-end with you," he reassured her.

"Yes, suh." Maggie Mae turned and left, but not before giving Nicholas a furtive glance, who, at the unsolicited gesture, drew his lips together to prevent a sigh from escaping.

Once alone, Roman finally acknowledged him. "A busy day then, suh?" Nicholas offered, in hope of resetting the tone in the room. Roman didn't respond immediately. Nicholas felt Roman's eyes weighing upon him . . . summing him up . . . measuring his worth.

"One of the few busy weeks that has come along this year," Roman replied.

Nicholas relaxed some. He was never very good with awkward silences. But around Roman, that was all there ever seemed to be. "I don't think anyone is havin' a good year."

"Doesn't that go without sayin'?" Roman replied, but not harshly.

Roman offered him a chair in front of the desk with a wave of his hand, which he accepted gladly. Roman sat behind the polished, oak desk. He tensed his arms and grimaced as he bore the full weight of his body upon them, and settled into the chair with a sigh of relief. "And you, my northern friend," Roman said, as the pain marking his face slowly subsided, "are out here for what reason? I thought we were to meet this evenin'."

"Yes, suh," Nicholas replied. "There's really not much to do in Folsom, so . . . I thought I might take a look at your operations."

"Well– you didn't have to come strollin' all the way out here on foot. I would have given you a ride or had one of my men provide one."

Nicholas thanked him for his thoughtfulness. "I had planned on travelin' out here with you, but as it were, I arrived at your home after you left."

Roman leaned back in his chair. "So you've met, Lucy?"

"Yes, suh."

"And of course, Maggie Mae."

"On the way here, suh," Nicholas offered without hesitation. "By accident." Roman's lusterless gaze didn't flicker. The air inside the room suddenly felt thick and unwelcoming to Nicholas. Again, he knew he was being studied– well. He was certain his every move and word was being deciphered and analyzed.

"Accidents are from carelessness," Roman commented. "I didn't peg you as a careless man, Nicholas."

Nicholas was bound mute. The beads of sweat forming on his forehead were unstoppable at this point. He fought the urge to wipe them away and reveal his nine of clubs, two of hearts, ace of spades, and a three and seven of diamonds. Already a droplet of sweat was coursing past his left ear on its way to his jaw.

"All my white and Negroe workers are fine folk," Roman boasted. "I've never had a problem. And Maggie Mae's a fine Negroe gal, too."

Nicholas offered a weak, noncommittal smile.

"Just because she's a Negroe doesn't mean I don't look out for her welfare. She works for me, and she's a damn good worker," he said, poignantly. "She's been with me ever since I came to Folsom. And while she works for me, it's my charge to assure that the savagery of this town does not come upon her . . . Negroe or not, she is still but a child."

"I understand, suh."

"I don't think so," Roman uttered, through barely parted lips. His light, brown eyes were now visible, and Nicholas could now see that the intensity smoldering within them matched his ever-present scowl. "These are most dangerous times for any man, but for a woman, they're treacherous. Poverty, my young suh, breeds violence. And there is great poverty in Folsom. Surely you know how rampant crime is in our southern states."

Nicholas nodded.

"Friends have turned against friends . . . brothers against broth-ers," Roman continued. "Havin' lost the war, we seemed to have turned on ourselves. We don't even have a mayor here, or any kind of law. Most folk can't even agree whether to hold an elec-tion, because they don't expect Folsom to survive, so what's the point of electin' anyone to anything?" Roman was silent for a mo-ment. "A woman like Maggie Mae caught in that cesspool hasn't a chance. I don't expect her or any of my workers to fall prey to that type of incivility. You do see that," he stated, not asked.

"Absolutely, suh," Nicholas said. Nicholas felt as though he was receiving a lecture not from her employer, but from her father. Ro-man's subdued, yet insistent and absolute need to protect her was most uncharacteristic of a white man toward a Negroe woman, he thought. It stroked against stiff, unyielding southern grain. He knew all southern whites were of not one mind. Not all despised Negroes. He was aware that Quakers, a highly religious and de-vout folk, risked their own lives to help slaves escape by means of the Underground Railroad. He'd learned from his mother and fa-ther, and in lectures at the university, that there were many white, southern abolitionists who fought and died to end the barbarism that was slavery. Yet, it was easier for his brain to categorize southern whites as a single, hate-filled, mindless culture. But what had once seemed so absolutely black and white was now mottled with uncertain gray. Truths now seemed like altered versions of lies. And what were lies, seemed truthful. Nothing seemed to fit well in his head anymore.

"I still have much to learn," Nicholas said humbly.

For the first time, Roman smiled. "Much more to learn," Roman agreed, "but not as much as you might think. Learnin' is the easy part . . . not understandin' what you learned is what keeps a man actin' like a boy."

"And as for learnin'?"

Roman again proved to be far quicker than he assumed. "You still want to speak with my Negroes."

"Yes, suh," Nicholas replied, effectively hiding his enthusiasm.

"Here– at the farm, I see no problem. They'll speak to you freely. But . . . ," The corner of his lip rose. "Venturin' across the river– hmmm? Like I said the other night, I'm not sure how . . . let's say, 'wise', that is."

"I don't fear them," Nicholas announced bravely. "In my experience with them, I've found that the prospect of betterin' their lives stays their hands against those who extends theirs. Besides, it would be foolish– would it not, for them to even think of harmin' a white man? You did say you have good Negroes."

"You've cut me with my own sword," Roman admitted, in mock defeat.

Roman's ruggedly, lined face revealed little to Nicholas. His lack of visible emotion appeared far too polished. "I've been told there's a certain Negroe man who would be of great help to me . . . a man that . . ."

"Lar," Roman interrupted, as though it should be plainly obvious to him.

"Yes-yes! A Laurence . . . Lar Cole?"

Roman leaned back in his chair and placed his hand on the table. "He came highly recommended from Maggie Mae?" Roman inquired.

"She said he was most familiar with all the Negroes."

"She spoke true," Roman admitted. "He's their Negroe preacher – a good Negroe. Hard workin' and honest to the core. I'll vouch for that myself. I suppose you would like to meet him, hmmm?"

"With your permission, suh."

Nicholas followed Roman's lead and rose when he did, and then followed him to the door, all the while gauging the power Roman wielded and wore so comfortably upon his tall, thick frame. Roman's mere presence on the porch caused his workers to pause. Nicholas spotted Maggie Mae sitting on the tailgate of the first wagon loaded with sacks of cotton. She looked in his direction for a moment, but then turned away. If she had seen him, he couldn't tell, for it was a fleeting glance and she was a good distance from him. He could only hope.

Roman called out to one of the Negroes who was loading a wagon. The young, sweaty Negroe he called Eddie, was standing before him, and within moments was off to find Lar. Roman, meanwhile, began inspecting his goods and talking with Mc-Mullen. With stern benevolence, Roman had the caravan of goods reorganized, and within a few minutes, departing down the dusty road, along with Maggie Mae.

It wasn't long thereafter that Nicholas spotted a shirtless Negroe gleaming with sweat walking toward the cabin. He wasn't the tallest Negroe Nicholas had ever seen in his life, though with his broad shoulders and thick chest, he was the most complete package of a man he'd ever saw. The closer he came, the more handsome he became, Nicholas gauged enviously. He never would have pegged the oxen-like man, whose body seemed to have been molded for the sole purpose of hard labor, as a preacher of the gospel. Standing next to Roman, who was towering in his own right, Lar dwarfed him. After a brief discussion between them, they both looked his way and began walking toward him.

Roman made introductions.

Lar was the first to extend his hand.

"Good to meet you, Mr. Cole," Nicholas said, in subdued awe, as Lar's hand covered his own, yet was gentle despite his calloused palm. Nicholas stood as tall as his spine would allow, as he tried to contain the sudden sense of intimidation sweeping over him.

"Mr. Meadows say you wanna find out 'bout Negroe folk 'round here, suh?" Lar's throaty baritone was on full display.

"That– that's correct," Nicholas squeaked. Embarrassed, he cleared his throat and lowered his pitch. "I would very much like to speak with you about the other Negroes . . . perhaps even meet a few others. As Mr. Meadows would agree . . . if I dare to presume . . . industry in the south is reliant upon both white and Negroe if it's goin' to succeed and prosper." Roman nodded.

"And you wanna come 'cross the river, too?" Lar asked.

"That's my intention."

Roman turned to Lar. "I've advised him against it, of course. But he seems determined to do so. He's a northerner," he apologized. "I've told him, my workers have no reservations about speakin' their minds here. Yet, I feel he won't be satisfied until he's done what his mind is set on."

Lar agreed. "That be true, suh. Everybody-somebody know you be a fair man."

Roman smiled as Nicholas had never seen before . . . genuinely. Nicholas was awed by their connection that far surpassed mere civility toward one another. They spoke not like white and Negroe men, but as men . . . just decent men. There was nothing in either one's manner that struck him as false. *Uncanny,* he thought.

"Nevertheless . . ." Nicholas began, but was interrupted by Roman.

"You already have my permission, young man."

To Nicholas' disbelief, Roman then looked to Lar and waited.

"I be down right glad to, suh," Lar offered. He smiled at Nicholas.

Roman raised his head slightly. "I'm entrustin' his welfare to you, Lar."

Lar grinned and extended his hand once again. Nicholas readily accepted it. "He gonna find us to be real welcomin', suh."

CHAPTER 9

Maggie Mae wished that Richard Pullman would just be quiet as they rode in the wagon back to town. But his talking was incessant, and she had to concentrate to block it out. Though there was room on the other wagons that rambled toward town, Richard had chosen to ride with her, much to her chagrin. And though there was ample room on the backend where they were, of course, he had deliberately sat as close to her as possible.

He was trying to work his charms upon her, but talk as he may, Maggie Mae knew the vaccinations her mother had given her against dumb, ugly and foolish were still potent. She had wanted nothing to do with him before Lar, and nothing to do with him after Lar had pushed her away for Mary. Still, Richard was as persistent as a roach, though less welcoming.

"No, thank you," she replied, to his first request to call upon her the following Sunday.

"I too busy takin' care of mammy," she uttered, when he persisted. And then . . .

"I don't eat much."

"I don't like greens . . ."

"Collards either."

"Or sweet potatoes."

"It ain't that hot."

"I alright."

"No– I fine."

"I just tired."

"I ain't thinkin' 'bout nothin'– really."

Bland responses to his thinly veiled complements were not going to shut him up she concluded, so she just stopped answering him. Instead, she recalled recent events she didn't want to think about at the moment, but were far better than listening to Richard go on. Nicholas Barrons . . . she swished his name around in her mind and let her tongue play with the sounds of it for a while. There was no disguising his not so subtle attempts at wooing, she thought. His kind words had disturbed her as much as the fact that he was white. He could no longer claim that he didn't know she was Negroe, she figured. But even knowing that, he persisted. But why? She wondered. She wanted to believe he didn't know what he was really doing. But she couldn't deny that he *did* know, and that he was *not* mental . . . disillusioned perhaps– but not mental.

As she recalled his face from the front . . . from the side . . . when he smiled . . . she couldn't detect any semblance of a lie . . . except his very odd, Negroe-like dialect that rose and waned unexpectedly. But as she put his face in front of her mind's eye again, this time she stopped looking for telltale signs of lies and half-truths, and just looked at him. Maggie Mae guessed him to be a few years younger than she was. His short black hair and brows, perfectly complemented his pale green eyes, she recalled pleasantly, now that she had time to think about it and wasn't worried about him staring at her again.

His warm . . . no . . . his hot hands were firm, she remembered. But strangely, she was surprised that she didn't feel repulsion, as she thought she would if a white man had ever touched her. She hadn't seen lust in his eyes as there was with Richard, who she guessed was at the moment fantasizing that he was massaging her breasts and sliding his crusty hands down '*there*'.

"What on your mind, Ms. Maggie?" Richard smiled.

Maggie Mae groaned internally. She continued ignoring Richard and mentally replaced his annoying antics with the smooth charm of Nicholas Barrons. She didn't sense fear with Nicholas, as she usually did when around other white men. He was like being around Roman, not like the other white men in Folsom who she could feel watching her every move whenever she went to town, and who often hurled crude promises of giving her rapture. Those men . . . those white men were the ones to be feared, she figured. But Nicholas had been different, and that bothered her. It was not proper for a Negroe to look a white in the eye, though that was far from the reason she'd kept her gaze averted from his. No, she admitted, it was for a reason far more disturbing . . . she found him handsome . . . extremely so, as a matter of fact. White skin had never called out to her before or even stirred a fleeting thought of curiosity. Yet, Nicholas had and then some, despite his whiteness.

His smooth talk, warmed with sincerity by his gestures brought back memories and feelings to her that he had nothing to do with. And as he talked and questioned her, she recalled another who seemed so much like him. But all of those sweet memories of Lar were tainted now.

'You ain't safe with me, Maggie Mae,' she remembered him saying, right before he said it was over between them. *'The closer we get, the more white men gonna be after you. They ain't seein' you as a Negroe or white, just somethin' to be taken. And them seein' you with me . . . a big ol' black Negroe, just make'em wanna do it even more. I hear'em talkin' 'bout you, Maggie Mae . . . thangs they wanna do to you. If we stay together, they gonna come for you, and you might not make it out alive. I do this 'cause I love you.'*

Try as she might, she couldn't get Lar to change his mind. To protect her, he had to break her heart, he told her. But her broken heart had yet to ever begin to mend. But Lar had been right . . . the harassment from white men did decrease some when they realized she was not willingly going to give her white flesh over to a black as coal niggah stud. Though in exchange for a modicum of safety, she was now alone, save her mother. And Lar . . . her dear Lar– it was now finished between them. But she was still in love with Lar – and had always been.

Try as she might, still she couldn't suppress the ache and envy that raked at her soul each time Mary's belly was full with Lar's child. Though she prayed with one side of her heart for a child of theirs to live, stalking the chambers of the other side were hopes that it would not, and never be so . . . for if a child of theirs were to live, she knew she would die from a broken heart. But Nicholas Barrons coming into the equation was something she hadn't anticipated. A white man of all men, and a northerner to boot, had stirred her fading embers of hope for a semblance of love to come to her . . . only . . . she realized it could never be. And knowing that it was implausible– she and a white northerner, she savored the essence of the fantasy.

He was so handsome, she bashfully recalled like a schoolgirl, as she pictured him again with his black hair neatly combed back and parted on the side– his curly eyelashes longing to be tickled. His gently angled, prominent jaw was perfect for stroking and holding while kissing. His seemingly genuine concern was as comforting as a thick blanket. If he were hers, she knew she would wish every season were winter. 'A lady!' He had called her. She laughed out loud at the absurdity of it. But, dark thoughts and a familiar sense of wrongness in all that touched her easily slipped back into her consciousness. Without Lar, what was there? She wondered, but the answer always eluded her.

She was childless and had resigned to stay so. She accepted the fact that there would be no husband for her, though she had many suitors, including Richard. She could see death was coming for her mother, and soon she would be alone. She liked to fool herself into thinking that it wouldn't bother her to spend her years watching other women marry and have children. Thinking as such made life a little more bearable. That is, until Nicholas Barrons arrived and awoken what she'd thought she put to sleep years ago.

The cart neared the bridge, which was not far from the Meadows' house. Maggie Mae leapt off and thanked the driver. Richard, still on the backend, waved to her as the cart turned onto the bridge. Maggie Mae ignored him and reluctantly walked to the Meadows' home. She entered the house, and after finding no signs of Lucianna downstairs, she made her way up them. The door to Lucianna's bedroom was slightly ajar. Maggie Mae knocked softly on the door.

"That you, gal?"

"Yes'm."

"Well?"

Maggie Mae entered the darkened room. A hint of ginger was in the air. The windows that stretched nearly from floor to ceiling were open enough to let the heated air in, yet their heavy, lavender drapes were pulled tight. Still, there was enough light to see Lucianna lying on the bed still dressed in her nearly sheer nightgown. She hadn't bothered brushing her hair, and it lay in a tangle of red waves about her. It appeared as if she had done nothing at all but lounge since Maggie Mae had left. Her red, silk dress she wore the night before was laying in a heap on the floor beside the bed– the same one, imported from France that Roman had admonished her for buying at a cost of fifty dollars. Her corset, which Maggie Mae had tightened and loosened on her countless times over the years, was hanging on the back of the chair by the small mirror-table she used to apply her make-up.

Not bothering to raise her head from the pillow, Lucianna spoke lazily. "You deliver my message, gal?"

"Yes'm," Maggie Mae replied, as she picked up the dress.

"Leave it!" Lucianna snapped.

Maggie Mae continued clutching the dress to her chest. She was wise to the ways of her mistress. In one breath, Lucianna would spew demands, and quicker than she could move to act upon them, Lucianna would change her mind or send her off on yet another task. Though as usual, whatever job she performed was never to Lucianna's satisfaction. It always seemed to Maggie Mae as if Lucianna actually preferred it that way.

"Send Aaron up," Lucianna demanded. "Have Bobby water the plants on the east side of the garden. They're nearly dead from that black thumb of yours."

Maggie Mae inched closer to the bed. Even in the murky light, the secrets of Lucianna's pale almost pink body revealed themselves beneath her sheer gown. "I reckon Mr. Aaron and Mr. Bobby ain't comin' today, ma'am", Maggie Mae offered, not sure of what kind of response to expect.

Lucianna stirred. "What do you mean? Explain!"

"Mr. Meadows say he . . ." Maggie Mae stopped abruptly . . . Lucianna was rising.

"Dammit– what did he say!?"

"He . . . he say, he gonna send whoever he feel like sendin'. That what *he* say to tell you," Maggie Mae added quickly.

Lucianna was upright now. She rose to her feet and marched across the room and yanked the curtains open, flooding the room with light. Her gown was transparent in the gloom, but was now practically invisible. Her every curve was now bare as she gazed out the window. "Who are they?"

Maggie Mae went to the window and looking down, spotted two Negroes just entering the garden from the west entrance. "The tall one be Monty and the other be Lucas . . . they brothers," Maggie Mae answered.

Lucianna's nose wrinkled in disgust. She retreated from the window and donned her housecoat, concealing her flesh. "Now he's sendin' me niggahs," she snorted. "Who do you think I am Roman? You son of a bitch! Close those goddamn curtains!"

Maggie Mae pulled them shut, thrusting the room back into a state of near darkness. She waited for Lucianna to issue another command, but she remained mute. Lucianna sat down in the chair by the bed . . . head held high and her legs spread wide like a man. She guessed that Aaron and Bobby must have made a good impression upon Lucianna– well, Aaron at least. Bobby, the pimple-marked one had spent virtually no time with her. But Aaron, Maggie Mae remembered, had stayed in Lucianna's bedroom longer than any of the other men who'd walked up those stairs to be with her. Roman was old enough to be both of the boy's grand-father, and she doubted he could compete with them in quenching Lucianna's never-ending thirst for sex. But Maggie Mae knew, having to change the bed sheets in two separate living quarters each morning, that Lucianna repulsed him . . . but that was no secret in their house or Folsom for that matter.

"Ma'am?" Maggie Mae asked.

Lucianna stared at her with cold, green eyes.

"Send them to work and start your chores." Lucianna stared at the wall. "Niggahs in my yard," she seethed through clenched teeth.

* * *

Breeze-driven clouds finally rolled their way toward Folsom. The impending rain had lifted everyone's spirits. Lar had yet to join in on the celebration, as he was for the second time, on his way back to the Monclair home. He had thought about and prayed for Paul all night and most of the day until the white northerner, Nicholas Barrons, had asked to speak with him that next morning. Meeting Nicholas Barrons *was* a welcome relief and diverted his

270 / ORLANDO SMART-POWELL

attention from Paul, and from Mary, who stayed the night to tend to him. For when he wasn't listening to Paul's screams echoing in his head, there was another boy who cried out in pain who quickly took Paul's place. And though he hadn't heard the other boy's haunting cry in person, he had a good idea of what it sounded like. He'd heard the screams of a man being lynched before– seen it before. Visions of Freda's boy tethered by his arms, hands, legs, and then pulled by horses until his body came apart, sickened Lar to the point where he couldn't think on it any further without calling forth the demon, Revenge, who plagued his dreams so many nights since. And if it wasn't echoes of the boy's screams tormenting him, it was remembering Freda's tears falling from her hollow, dead eyes.

While with a group of Negroes in Meadows' fields loading a wagon, Ollie Cushen, a white worker who had ventured over to Peak Hills to witness the lynching, retold all that had happened to Marky Sloan, another white worker who had been unable to attend. Lar listened intently as they spoke. Ollie recalled the day as though he had been to a fair and didn't bother whispering about it either . . . actually he boasted loudly, as though he meant everyone in earshot to hear what had transpired.

"The Bible say a eye for a eye," Ollie quoted. "Now you don't get no clearer than that! A niggah stealin' be bad 'nough. But rapin' a white woman?! Shoot, boy!!"

"Punishment fittin' then," Marky agreed readily. "They should'a strung up the whole clan of'em. If you breed one like that, you breed 'nother and 'nother and 'nother."

Ollie laughed. "Ho-ho!! They ain't gonna be breedin' no more niggahs now . . . even if they wanted to. Those boys in Peak Hills made damn sure of that!"

Marky grinned. "I know– they killed them bastards."

Ollie spat on the ground. "Aw shit, boy! I ain't talkin' 'bout that, fool. I talkin' what they did 'fore they killed'em," Ollie said with crooked smile.

"Oh yeah . . . yeah-yeah!!! Um . . . what?" Marky asked.

"Well . . ." Oliver paused for effect, and then continued after rubbing his chin, "they got him all noosed . . . he was a big niggah now," he added. "Then a lady in the back . . ."

"A lady was there?!"

Oliver nodded. "Ohhh yeah! Not jus' women, now– boys *and* a few gals. White folk wanna know us men gonna protect'em and make our laws be 'hered to. When niggahs break our laws, white folk need to see what happen to'em."

"You right, Ollie," Marky agreed.

"So then they got'em all noosed and this lady started screamin' . . . 'rapist' . . . 'rapist'! Then soon, the whole lot of'em be sayin' it. So the men started whisperin' back and forth like. Next thang ya know, they stripped the britches and all from that niggah. Then . . . then this black-ass cock fall out. Shit man!– looked like a goddamn snake! When a man's cock get that long, it make'em act like animals and savages like they be 'fore we tried civilizin' 'em. Word be– a whole bunch of niggahs got cocks like that." He waited a moment. "So these good ol' boys had'em a plan . . . and a damn good one. Eye . . . for a eye!" He shook his head slowly up and down until Marky smiled.

"OOhhhhhh," he uttered, as he copied Oliver's head bobbing.

"So they couldn't hold this big ass niggah still . . . he was fightin' boy! I mean he was givin' it all he got! So they went on and pulled'em up and this man with a knife cut *it* off just as he was going up and chokin'." Oliver whipped his left hand down past his crotch. "Just like that!"

To Lar, who heard every word of their exchange, the murder and mutilation of Freda's husband was the furthest thing from justice, and the vilest thing he'd ever heard. Though what Ollie described with such abandon failed to surprise or even shock Lar. Severing a Negroe's penis, before or after a lynching, was the latest fashion not imported from France, but was devised and perfected in the southern states to teach Negroe men that they were not men, Lar knew.

Being called up to the office to meet Nicholas was exactly what Lar needed to get away from Ollie and Marky's gloating. Nicholas seemed pleasant enough for a white man, Lar guessed. And that he was possibly offering an opportunity for more jobs with better wage was a true blessing. There was only God to thank for it, Lar knew in his soul, for such good news couldn't have come sooner with Uncle Matty unable to work the fields any longer. Roman had given Uncle Matty the task of counting loads of produce and cotton, though anyone of his workers could have done the task easily enough. But Roman's word was law on his land: *Long as the crops keep growing he can stay on,* Roman assured Lar. "But if times get any tougher . . . drought like this keeps hangin' on, I'll have to let him go. You understand that right?"

"Yes, suh," Lar responded. "Kinda look like we might be gettin' some rain today though." Blessings it seemed, were coming from where he least imagined they would. Rain was sure to fall, and Folsom needed it badly, he thought, as the sky continued darkening.

And Mary . . . Mary had finally opened up and revealed her true self with unexpected tears, which shook Lar's notion that she was made of iron on the inside too. That was not really a blessing . . . it was a miracle, he concluded. But even the miracles hadn't stopped there for Lar.

After leaving the field's for the day, he went to pick up Mary who was waiting in the backyard of the Monclair home when he pulled up in the wagon. Her eyelids, top and bottom were swollen and spoke of the lack of sleep she had received. Her speech was slurred with drowsiness, and he had to listen intently to understand her. She was only able to mount the wagon with great assistance from him.

"You gonna fall right to sleep even 'fore your head hit the pillow," he assured her. "How that poor boy be?"

It seemed effortful for Mary to keep her head up. "He ain't good at all," she replied mournfully. "He all swollen up in the face and chest and . . ." She stopped abruptly.

Lar decided not to press her any further on the subject. He whipped the horse into motion and turned the cart around. "I get you home and you can sleep for a spell. You feel better . . ."

She stopped him. Then she said the last thing he thought she would ever say. "I need to go see Ms. Enda."

Lar was shocked to say the least. Mary had practically refused to speak more than a few civil words to Enda since their last child had died. "You sho?" He asked, still unbelieving what he was hearing.

Mary nodded. "He gonna end up comin' down with fever if somethin' ain't done. Simeon just 'bout killed 'em," she added. "And Simeon ain't gonna let us take 'em to the doctor . . . he probably just hopin' Paul lay up there and die anyway. I ain't got no choice but to go to Enda."

Lar agreed.

When they arrived at Enda's shack, she welcomed them in warmly, though her gray eyes seemed to say otherwise. "Sit down there," Enda said to Mary, and pointed to a large chair at the table in the center of the room. Enda sat opposite of her, but didn't bother offering Lar a seat. "I surprised to see you come my way," Enda said in her French-Creole accented English.

Lar caught a glimmer in Enda's eye as she spoke and knew it was a lie.

"I come 'cause I gotta."

Enda smiled at her. "No-no . . . you sho' wouldn't come here any other time if you didn't have to . . . would you?"

"No, ma'am," Mary replied without hesitation.

Enda shook her head. "Fair 'nough, I 'spose. I don't 'spect anythin' less from Mary Cole other than to speak what be in her head. I sho'nuff be surprised if you didn't." Enda then looked at Lar. "Why you still standin', boy?" She chided him. "You at home here. Pull up a chair and sit."

If Enda's words bothered Mary, Lar couldn't see it. Mary just began explaining Paul's condition, especially to his privates, which caused his own to begin to tingle and shrink as they made for refuge within his pelvis. Lar could tell there was nothing Mary said that seemed to surprise Enda, who sat there and listened– her face was as pale and inert as it had been when Mary began the tale. When Mary finished, Enda closed her eyes and began to speak, but then her eyelids tightened even more and produced wrinkles atop of the ones she already had.

In a string of words that shunned pauses and breaks, Enda detailed exactly what Mary was to do. It was as though, Lar thought, Enda was sitting right beside Paul and could see each bruise upon his body. When Enda opened her eyes, for the briefest of moments, Lar swore she was still sitting beside Paul. She suddenly blinked and without warning, inhaled forcefully, as though it was going to be her last breath. Enda pushed herself up from her chair, and as she did so, Lar moved to help, but was shooed away. He sat down dutifully.

On the shelf above the stove, Enda retrieved one of the glass jars from the many that were filled with liquids of every shade and consistency. The first jar she pulled down was filled with a pale green liquid. She held it up and then said. "Uh-uh . . . this be too strong. It powerful." She put it back on the shelf and brought down another that was filled with a brown liquid. After opening it, she ladled some of its viscous contents into another bottle with a smaller neck and stuffed a rag into its opening. She returned to the table and pushed the bottle toward Mary and gave her instructions. Half of the solution Paul would have to drink. The remaining contents were to be poured in a bucket of water, and clean strips of cloth were to be soaked in it for an hour. The bruises were to be wrapped tightly– even the swollen testicle, no matter the pain it brought, Enda stated slowly and clearly.

Without warning, Enda reached out and grabbed hold of Mary's arm and squeezed. It startled Mary and she reflexively tried to pull her arm away, but Enda held her solidly. "Like this," Enda hissed. "Bind it all this hard." Enda let her go and continued. "Keep the boy wrapped up like I told you . . . three hours. No longer than that, and no less," Enda said.

"I gonna need somethin' for the pain, too," Mary said, as she rose from her chair, and both she and Lar began walking toward the door.

Enda looked at Mary and shook her head. "I ain't got nuthin' for that kind of pain, chile."

Mary's eyes snapped open wide with anger, as well as confusion. "You ain't got nuthin' or you ain't gonna give it to me?"

"Like I say, Mary Cole– I ain't got nuthin' for that kind of pain."

Lar, knowing Mary all to well, sensed she was gearing up to argue for another herb, or another concoction that could numb the boy's pain, but a mix of weariness on her part and his nudging proved victorious this time, much to his relief. But he couldn't leave until he knew something also. He set Mary walking toward the cart, but he turned around in the doorway. Enda proved to be far quicker than he.

"Yes, Laurence," she uttered. "The answer be 'yes!'"

After arriving back at the Monclair home, Lar waited outside, reflecting upon his unspoken question and answer Enda had given him. But more importantly at the moment, he was curious as to how Paul was faring. He waited a good hundred feet from the house just in case Simeon returned early. There was more than enough trouble about without Simeon coming home and finding him on his property.

Lar had often thought it odd that Simeon would let Paul play with him in the fields next to the house while he waited for Mary to finish her chores. Their sticks could transform into guns and bows and arrows at will. They raced, with he purposefully slowing his pace so that Paul could claim victory as they crossed the huge oak at the top of the hill. And though Simeon had seen them gallivanting about, not once did Simeon ever say a word to him or Mary about it. It was as if he didn't care. Though Lar realized now – he didn't. Simeon's disaffection toward Paul– his own child, puzzled Lar. As a toddler, Paul would run to the road upon seeing Simeon's wagon approaching and wave with joy at his return, Simeon would pass by without so much as a nod of the head in acknowledgement.

But years passed, and with it came change.

In time . . . Paul ventured less toward the road to greet Simeon, until he didn't have to anymore, for Simeon had found other pleasures in town that kept him away late. For a while, it seemed to Lar that as Paul grew older, he'd reconciled that the love he so craved from his father, even in the simplest of gestures, would never come.

But more years passed, and with it came more changes.

The first few bruises Lar had ever seen on Paul had been only slightly alarming . . spare the rod and spoil the child, he reasoned and rationalized it away. He even doubted Mary, who'd swore to him that Simeon was using the rod more than a few times to keep Paul in line, even though Paul was never one to step out of line. But he was a boy after all, Lar thought, and dismissed Mary's concern. But Lar knew how boys were, as he remembered being on the receiving end of Enda's switch more than once himself.

But he was now more than aware that what Paul endured was far more than just the stinging end of a disciplining switch. His pretty face was often purple at the cheeks, if he was lucky. If Simeon was intent on beating the boy's spirit out, Lar guessed he'd succeeded. Within a few short years and many beatings in between, Paul had changed before his eyes from a gleeful, young child, into the solemn, sulking young boy that he was now. Yet through it all, as he waited for Mary, Paul would still venture out to see him– with a smile.

Almost a half-hour later after Mary had went in to tend to Paul, the backdoor of the house opened and Mary exited and began shuffling toward the wagon. He could see exhaustion was winning the battle and was gripping Mary's face and yanking the skin down. He dismounted and offered his hand and she accepted without a fuss. Even helping her onto the wagon, she was eerily quiet. When he asked about Paul's condition, she had little to tell.

"I got'em all wrapped up," she explained. "I don't know if the cure be worse than the pain. It . . . it hurt'em bad, Lar."

"You did like Enda told you to," he assured her.

"I know," she muttered. "It just that . . ."

"Ms. Enda know what she doin' . . . you know that," he said. "You just gotta give it time."

Mary nodded.

The bumpy wagon ride rocked Mary to sleep even before they came into town. They were halfway across the bridge when the first drops of rain began to fall. The sky was so dark it seemed more like late evening. Lar, eager to pick up the pace lest they get caught in the midst of the downpour, whipped at the horse and sent the cart speeding across the bridge and on toward home. He thanked God for the rain and for Mary beside him. He asked God to deliver his unborn child safely this time and to grant healing to Paul. But again, he beseeched God on Mary's behalf.

It warmed him to see her the way she was now, though he hated what had brought her to this point. She was a loving and caring woman– he knew that in his bones. But she was also a stubborn woman who fought hard not to show how much she cared. But today she had, and he loved her even more for it. He didn't have to hear words of love, compassion and caring from her mouth to know how she felt. Having weathered the events of the Monclair home and her tears that she shed freely afterwards, had said it all to him. Compassion and caring was in her refusal to leave Paul alone when he needed her most. Love shone in her touch to his arm as he offered it in aid, which in the past she would have refused, if only to show her worth and independence.

There was so much to be thankful for, he thought, as he raised his head to the sky and bathed his face in a steady shower of heavenly tears for town called Folsom.

CHAPTER 10

The rain had just started when Lucianna was in the midst of stepping out of her washtub. The warm water had cooled, and it would take forever for Maggie Mae to heat another pot of water for it, she thought. Besides, it was getting late, and she was excited about the prospect of being intrigued, *and intriguing* her visitor who was to arrive shortly. The thought of seeing him again sent shivers down her wet, naked body. It had been so long since she'd been in the company of someone she considered to be a true man . . . a real life gentleman. There were a handful of men in Folsom who were satisfactory enough to serve her purpose when required, but as far as she was concerned, they were still little more than gulley hicks, farmers and field workers who were no more than white trash if that. And she had had enough of them in her lifetime to never want another.

But her desires ruled her, and she never resisted them, for they were her treasures to be indulged in without hesitation. There was nothing she could compare to the sensation of having a young man inside of her. The younger . . . more taught . . . the better. The deeper they drove into her, the greater the intensity she felt, ravishing her like old men had forgotten how to. And after they spent themselves within her and lay shaking in the echoes of diminishing pleasure, her own appetite was always far from being sated.

But there were other prizes to be had for her pleasures, she was well aware of. She knew the power she could wield when her sexual prowess . . . her 'gifts'– as she called them, were used prudently. Ironically, it was by the grace of her gifts that she was able to finally climb out of the hole she was born into, one that everyone had told her was inescapable.

She dried off and perfumed the open pores of her skin, and then sealed them with jasmine lotion. She sat at her make-up table . . . nude, and was proud of what she saw . . . delicate, unadulterated white skin . . . fiery red hair still as thick and wavy as it was when she was a child . . . dark, yet piercing green eyes perfect for reflecting envy . . . and nary a hint of a wrinkle at the corners of her eyes and lips.

There were but a few men she could recall that had ever resisted her draw, and those who hadn't succumbed to her invitations, lusted from afar, she was quite certain of that. But upon Roman, her charms that had once dazzled him with desire now ceased to amaze him. She wasn't particularly saddened or hurt by his rejection– far from it. She despised him now, more than ever. 'You knew what I was, Roman,' she whispered.

She applied white make-up around her eyes, making sure that tonight of all nights it was flawless. She recalled that it was Roman's decision to leave their northern home where they'd stayed during the war, and return to the south . . . to a Godforsaken dust-bowl called Folsom. Then he blamed her for it. That infuriated her most of all. She felt no guilt in her actions that had raised the ire of the ever and even-tempered Roman. It was *his* fault, she reasoned, without an inkling of blame on her part. She no longer viewed him as a man, or at least one that she could manage with her feminine wiles as she could his brother.

'So– the great, charming and respected Roman Meadows again fails to see what is plainly evident,' she conjectured, and swooned with pleasure over it. But tonight was not about Roman, she reminded herself. She turned around and eyed the corset on the bed. She called for *the gal*, and counted the seconds it took her to arrive. She glared at Maggie Mae when she entered, and then turned her back to her. "I hope what has taken you so long to get up here doesn't mean dinner is not prepared."

"No ma'am. It all finished. I was straightenin' . . ."

Lucianna sighed, quieting Maggie Mae instantly. "Bring over my corset," she commanded with a flick of her hand in the direction where it lay.

Lucianna squeezed into the tight and very uncomfortable under-gear. She inhaled before each tug and held her breath, while Maggie Mae dutifully pulled and tied each interlacing string. Donning the pale rose dress with white-laced edges was a far easier task and took nary a few minutes. Fully clothed, Lucianna walked to the long mirror at the far side of the room to appraise herself. The dress was old, but still as beautiful as the day she had it crafted. The garment was of French silk she had purchased when she lived in Atlanta before the war. She'd had the bosom of it lowered as far down as possible without it insulting the elite women of Atlanta, whose circle she had snuck her way into. Still, her ample and still quite firm bosom sought to overflow their restraints– a sight she, *and men*, liked very much. With shimmering pink cloth against her pale skin, and her hair swept up and pinned, she saw nothing but perfection. She dismissed Maggie Mae and then judged herself again. "Amazing," she gasped.

The rain that had been tapping on the roof was now drumming. She opened the curtains and was greeted by her ethereal doppel-ganger in the darkened, water specked glass. And then . . . lighting flashed throughout the sky, momentarily brightening the rooftops and all below it, before plunging the world back into an ever dark-ening gloom and growling at her. She hoped the rain would keep Roman away longer than he had planned, but not slow her visitor's arrival. She opened all of the drapes, now that the sun was hidden behind black clouds and was powerless to scorch her fair skin.

She went downstairs. Already in her mind she had the second encounter with Nicholas Barrons planned with exact detail– that is, if *the girl* had followed her instructions properly. She would have before dinner drinks with the handsome, young Nicholas Barrons in the parlor, which as she instructed Maggie Mae, would be lit by as few lamps as possible. She was used to receiving compliments when in dim illumination, which made her skin glow ivory white and exaggerated the depths of her green eyes.

Then, Maggie Mae's sweet cakes would tempt his mouth and only add to the charms of her hospitality. And of course, she planned on offering rum and cognac, which in Folsom was nonexistent if one was not a Meadows or a Monclair who could afford to have it smuggled in, or was friendly enough with either family to secure their own . . . there would be nothing but the best for her visitor. Also, she wanted to be seated and to appear deep in thought when he was escorted into the study. She would react with surprise at his entry. Men loved the feeling of catching a woman off guard, she knew, and she was determined to play the role well.

With a swipe of her index finger, she inspected every other piece of furniture as she sauntered toward the study. She checked the lighting in the hallway by stopping at one of the mirrors and gauging the glow of her skin. Satisfied that she looked not just marvelous, but tempting, she continued on. Her thoughts were now upon how to approach Nicholas. His articulate speech and genteel manner suggested to her that he was from a family of great means. And since he was, she assumed, then he was well educated as well. With that in mind, she knew from experience that her simple charms that drove Folsom men mad for her would not work so easily upon him. Not this one, she thought. This one was no field-boy or factory laborer possessed of a dense mind and wavering will. She figured it would take time to weaken his resolve, as it had Roman years before when she was able to convince him to marry her.

As she admired herself in the next mirror, she paused. There were voices coming from within the study. Had her plan of beguiling Nicholas not been ruined and her anger flaring wildly and quickly, she might have heard exactly what they were saying. But her temper got the best of her. She entered the room stealthily with the intent of putting Maggie Mae in her place, more than impressing Nicholas. But even that was not to be. She felt as if she had just been slapped . . . *twice* . . . first by Nicholas and then by Maggie Mae.

Nicholas was drenched. His hair was adhered to his forehead and dangled right above his dark, black lashes. But she couldn't focus on that now.

He was wearing a gray suit, white shirt and bright red bow tie—she could not help but find him utterly desirable. But even that was of no consequence to Lucianna at the moment.

What was of significance was that Maggie Mae was standing in front of him. *She* . . . dressed in a stained, yellow dress that reeked of wood-smoke and a ratty blue headscarf that was knotted in the rear. Her skin . . . white as ever. Her eyes . . . *those blue-amber eyes* . . . sparkling as usual. Her loathing for Maggie Mae . . . for her white skin, her exotic eyes, and just being more beautiful than she ever was, rose to a new level.

The actual injury to Lucianna's pride came from what she was witnessing Nicholas doing with his hands. All of it formed a leaden lump in her chest, including seeing how her servant, Maggie Mae—the bastard child of a crazy niggah woman, responded to him. Maggie Mae was offering him a towel in her outstretched hand, but instead of taking the towel and drying his hair, he took hold of her hand. "You wouldn't refuse to help a poor, wet pup like me now, would you?" He asked playfully, smiling broadly.

Lucianna felt nothing other than betrayal at the meager resistance Maggie Mae put forth . . . she seeming to widen her eyes as though in fear of his touch and request. Lucianna saw only that Maggie Mae was playing coy, as she herself had done so often when seeking to entice prey. Then he placed his hand on top of hers and brought the towel closer to his head, bringing her hand along with it. As he moved the towel slowly over his hair, Lucianna was horrified when he began caressing her hand and simultaneously raising his other toward her white face, which possessed those damned, beautiful eyes.

"I need to tell my mistress you here," Maggie Mae whispered.

Lucianna figured Maggie Mae's words might have been more convincing had she not began to close her eyes drowsily in anticipation of his touch. "There's no need for that," Lucianna announced. Her only consolation now was that her unexpected presence had startled them both. Maggie Mae quickly bowed her head and skittered away from him. Nicholas took matters less shockingly and greeted Lucianna as though nothing had just occurred. He wiped his hands dry with the towel, and with a flick of his head, sent his hair flying backwards. He walked over to Lucianna and offered his hand. Lucianna wished nothing more than to claw his face– as he was the closest, and then crawl over him and proceed to remove Maggie Mae's eyes from her skull. Quick thinking, however, granted her enough calm to allow Nicholas to take her hand and kiss the back of it softly. She knew men could sense jealously from a woman and despised their kind for displaying such feelings. That it involved a niggah wench only made it worse, she fumed silently, while smiling at him. She vowed never to let him see such an emotion from her. Instead, she decided to turn the tables on them both.

Nicholas assisted her to the chaise lounge in the center of the room, and then took a seat in a chair a respectable distance across from her. "Please forgive my appearance, Mrs. Meadows," he said. "I was halfway here when the sprinkles turned into a torrent."

"But seeing you wet is a good thing, suh. We haven't had rain in Folsom for weeks. And as you can see," she added, still smiling and looking at Maggie Mae who had yet to raise her head, "we are very welcomin' of our visitors."

"I'm very appreciative."

"Do you require another dryin' cloth?" She asked warmly, upon cold air seeping from her lungs.

"No, no. I'm quite fine."

Lucianna looked at Maggie Mae, and then smiled as loving and protectively as a mother holding her newborn child. "Maggie Mae . . . dear . . . come here."

Maggie Mae came instantly and stood by her. Lucianna reached out and tapped her hand gently. "Bring us cognac. That's just the thing to take the chill out of Mr. Barrons' bones. And oh– bring those little sweet cakes of yours also." Lucianna batted her eyes while watching Maggie Mae depart. She then sighed longingly.

"What would I do without her assistance?" She asked, making sure to catch Nicholas' eye as she spoke. "And such a lovely Negroe, isn't she?" She added, and then watched his reply closely. Disappointingly, he nodded meagerly. "She's so fair to be a Negroe, no?" Lucianna pressed. "One would almost think she were white. When Roman first hired her, *I* myself almost took her for white."

"Do you know of her heritage?"

Lucianna purposefully opened her mouth and left it so. "Oh . . . dear God no! Those are Negroe matters. But . . ." she whispered, " . . . one would have to assume that there's been some unlawful miscegenation at play. Why, I've heard her own mother has nearly the same appearance as she."

"You've never seen her?"

"No. She never ventures into town . . . I've heard. She usually sends dear, Maggie Mae," she said simply and truthfully. She lowered her voice back to a murmur. "They say– her mother that is, is insane and is involved in all sorts of ungodly things. You understand? Like those Negroes that were brought from Haiti and settled into Louisiana– *pagans*," she hissed. "Everyone– I hear, stays far from the old woman. It's probably best for all that she *doesn't* come to town. Don't you think, Mr. Barrons?"

"I would agree," he responded blandly. "Sounds tragic."

"Oh, I wouldn't go that far, Mr. Barrons," she said, with a slight uplift in her voice. "Maggie Mae is paid more than a fair wage than one should expect in such dire times as these. I'm quite sure she has the means– with our help, to support both herself and her mother. And that is far more than I can say about the majority of others here in Folsom. We are, all of us, still reeling from that unspeakable war."

Nicholas smiled a little. "If it's any consolation, ma'am, from what I've seen across the south, Folsom is not alone in its condition."

Lucianna looked away from him and was silent for a moment. When she turned back toward him, she gave him her most mournful expression . . . slightly pouty lips . . . batting of her eyes, though not excessively so . . . *one could* over do things, she remembered . . . but a slightly lowered voice could assist in the charade. "Roman works hard to maintain what we have, but these times are so uncertain for all us."

She fell quiet again, but much longer this time. She tilted her head ever so slightly away from him and stared at the wall as though she were suddenly balancing on the edge of despair. As a gentleman, she guessed his sense of chivalry was churning up like a geyser preparing to blow. *What more can a true gentleman give to a seemingly, near hopeless woman than assistance?* She wondered.

As the drinks were poured time and again . . . delivered ever so carefully by a more withdrawn Maggie Mae, Lucianna recalled the legend of the Negroe woman's flesh and its power to seduce white men. How many mulattoes and quadroons and octoroons had she seen about the streets and working in the homes and plantations of Atlanta? She pondered, but couldn't even begin to give an accurate measure to the multitude of them that there appeared to have been. These beings– these things betwixt the shadows of black and white were startling sights to her . . . honey-colored Negroes with eyes of green, gold, chestnut and blues like Maggie Mae's. Some-times their hair was like a white's– it curly, or even absolutely straight, and ranged from coal black to red to shimmering wheat. And sometimes, like Maggie Mae, their skin was as white as white could be, which spoke to the extent of their forbearer's propensity for miscegenation. And who else could have fathered these mon-sters but white men? She thought, and had always wondered why there seemed to be so many of them. That is, until the cause was revealed to her by the well-to-do white ladies of Atlanta. Lust was in a Negroe wench's blood, they told her. A Negroe wench's lust was an inherent part of their savage nature . . . an evil that could drive Negroe men to even greater acts of savagery and illicitness than they were already prone to commit. It was Noah's curse upon his son, Ham and his descendants, which was to blame for it all, the fine ladies assured her. Just as it was the Negroe wench's in-tent to enslave the mind's of white men with their sexual proclivi-ties and reduce them to the primitive level of the Negroe man. And it was a white man's duty to resist it. Though some, the women noted, had failed . . . some time and time again . . . and again and again . . . and again and . . .

In such terms as these, Lucianna *did* understand Nicholas' mis-guided senses and, as far as she was concerned, helplessness, in the grips of Maggie Mae and the Negroe bloodlust flowing in her veins. The call of Negroe blood was making his feet stray from their true white path. Of this she was quite certain and willing to forgive him for being weak as a man in the face of such daunting evil. In fact, she was now determined to help him the best way she knew how. In time, be it sooner or later, she vowed to show him ecstasy unimaginable brought to life and finally fulfilled. With such passions she would give him, it would erase wayward thoughts of the white-skinned, Negroe girl. *I'll consume you as only a true white woman can,* she assured herself and silently promised him.

But she wanted to know more about this handsome stranger before she would act. She chose her words carefully and cloaked her probes in shawls of innocent inquires. When she spoke, she did so as an educated woman, but not one entirely familiar with the world. A woman who was too knowledgeable about the world was not enticing for many men, she knew. "So it's between my husband and Simeon Monclair that you must choose, am I correct, Mr. Barrons?" She asked.

He grinned. "It's not a contest, if that is what you mean. I . . . that is, my father and I are merely lookin' for the best investment opportunity possible."

"Money– they say, does rule the world," she replied. "But, if I may say so . . . it doesn't seem as though your family has much to worry about in that regard. For your father to seek investments in the south at times such as these is a testament, no?"

He seemed uneasy, which was precisely what she wanted. In proper circles, etiquette forbade the inquiry of another's worth. She knew her question would put him in an awkward state. She figured if she kept him off guard, he would have no opportunity to study her while she probed him.

"But the industry would be beneficial to all involved," Nicholas replied, after a moments thought.

"And you have seen the . . ." Lucianna stopped abruptly.

Together they turned in the direction of the door as the pattering of Maggie Mae's footsteps passed by. In the distance, words being spoken were indistinct, but were clearly those of Maggie Mae and Roman. Lucianna smiled proudly at Nicholas, as she fought the urge to squirm as her skin crawled in response to knowing Roman was back. She rose from her chair and met Roman in the doorway just as he was about to enter the room. "Welcome home, darling," she cooed, and then kissed him lightly on his rain-wet cheek. The look of utter shock on his face at her uncommon display of affection was priceless to her. She took hold of his wet hand and led him into the room. Had she not held firm to his wet palm, it simply would have dropped back down to his side like the dead fish it felt like in her hand. *I don't want to touch you either— you old excuse of a man,* she thought. *A means to an end is all you ever were and are to me.*

"You're soaked through and through," she commented. "You'll catch your death in those clothes." *I can only pray you do,* she thought quickly, and then said. "I'll call Maggie Mae and . . ."

"She's layin' out a new set as we speak," Roman replied, albeit dryly. He loosened his hand from hers and extended it to Nicholas.

"A drink, my dear?" She asked.

Roman walked to the small table behind Nicholas where the bottles of spirits were. Lucianna quickly moved to his side and removed the bottle from his possession. "Allow me," she insisted, and then gently stroked his hand.

Lucianna, determined to continue her masquerade as the loving, caring and devoted wife, stayed close to Roman's side. She wanted Nicholas to see and appreciate that which would appear unattainable to him . . . an irresistibly beautiful white wife enamored with her husband. But given the right time and place, which she planned to make accidentally convenient in due time, she would give him what he wanted the most, whether he realized he desired it or not.

At dinner, she occasionally joined in on their discussions on how to revitalize Folsom. She offered unsolicited opinions– though weakly, to maintain her guise of a woman who knew her place in a world where men ruled everything. Though she smiled and nodded at the appropriate times as they two exchanged ideas back and forth, the conversation actually bored her. She had no interest in seeing steamboats puffing back down Folsom's river, or of the hiring of workers to clear fields and ways to diversify crops to replenish the soils nutrients. She could care less about exporting their goods west at a cheaper price but in greater volume, than to the usual northern and southern markets, which paid more but asked for less. And when she thought she could take no more of their man-chatter, the conversation switched to Negroes– again, another topic she had absolutely no love for.

Nicholas wiped his mouth with a cloth napkin and set down his fork. "What of the lands across the river that are heavily forested. In the right hands it would be a great resource."

"That has more to do with politics than rights of property," Roman explained.

"How so?"

Roman finished chewing on a piece of fried, salted pork. After clearing his mouth with a sip of wine, he spoke. "Directly after the war, many mandates came by way of Union generals– many of them being rights to property." He laid down his utensils and pushed his empty plate away from him. "There were two wealthy families here in Folsom at the time . . . the Monclair's, as in Simeon Monclair . . . and the Christianson's, as in his wife, Isabel.

"From what I've been able to ascertain," Roman continued, "Union soldiers destroyed as much of Folsom's worth as they could. Homes . . . lands . . . storage facilities . . . just name it and they did. These union soldiers arrived and saw Folsom not quite as a jewel of the south, but well on it's way to being so. My boy, Folsom epitomized everything the Union soldiers were fighting against.

"Whereas everything south of the river was mauled over, they left virtually all of that land north and across the river unharmed–which is where the Negroes live now. The land had belonged to the Christiansons' who were comprised then of only women. Their men were dead and the southern resistance was in its death throes. The general of the battalion that came here, by his own right, gave that undeveloped land to the Negroes as compensation *and revenge*, they say, and left the Christiansons with the land that was already cleared and developed on this side of the river."

Lucianna spoke up. "What is now the land I and Roman purchased when we came here."

Roman hesitated for a moment. "What few acres of Monclair land that wasn't scorched by fire was all that was left for Simeon, as the sole surviving heir of the Monclair name."

"And so without a choice," Lucianna cut in, "With no more slaves to work the fields and their homes destroyed, they sold their land this side of the river, and Isabel was married off to Simeon . . . with that awful stump of his," she added.

Roman glared at her. "That *stump* is from a battle over his land." Roman refocused on Nicholas again. "I hear tell his hand was severed during a fight with freed Negroes. Still, it is all conjecture. No two people you ask will give you the same answer."

Nicholas sat back. "I thought it impolite to ask him about it. However, I can't say that I hadn't wondered."

Roman sighed. "What man wants to relive his darkest hours . . . eh?" He looked off momentarily. "Isn't it enough that each and every day you must relive what you once had?"

"I suppose," Nicholas responded in agreement.

"Ahhhh." Roman leaned back also. "Don't assume that I have too much compassion for Simeon. He and his people were slave owners after all." He stopped for a moment. "But who am I to pass judgment when I was just as guilty as he? Maybe more so."

"Suh?"

The corners of Roman's mouth turned down, as if he had just detected something rancid on his tongue. The lines of his forehead became mountain ridges– one stacked upon the other, from top of brow to crown. "I have not come by this house and land by mere chance, my friend," Roman admitted. "I was born and raised in the south . . . and as a result, I and my family have had our part in the enslavement of the Negroes also. There's no one with roots south of the Mason-Dixon line that can claim they had no part in slavery or in some way benefited from it. We all did, whether we will admit to it or not.

"My great-great grandfather started an insignificant bank in a small town outside of Atlanta years ago. And it was from that investment that the Atlanta Trust and Banking Company came into being, the one my brother and I inherited. But this institution, Mr. Barrons, not only traded in land, property and loans, but in flesh." Roman took a sip of wine, as if letting his last words permeate Nicholas' mind, then continued.

"How much you know about the slave trade– I won't assume. But I will tell you this," he said. "Slaves were valuable property. In fact, they were probably the most valued of possessions to own in the south. Though my family never owned slaves, we played our own part in their continued enslavement as those who did own them."

Nicholas stirred in his chair. "If I may . . . is that why you moved north, suh?"

Lucianna saw Roman cast a fleeting glance at her. She smiled gingerly at him . . . or smirked . . . or froze. She knew exactly why they had moved north. Anxiety held hands with wonder within her, as she watched Roman's lips start to move again. She wondered how much of the truth Roman would be willing to divulge.

"I had met Lucianna," Roman said. "But there is more to it than just that. There's always more to any story, no matter how well told and detailed.

"Money was a driving force for me . . . for my brother . . . my family. And we made great sums of it. With all sorts of rumblings of secession pointing to the inevitable, I, being the eldest and in charge of the trust company, decided to move my family north against everyone's wishes. I tried to convince my brother that there would be no future for us in the south. I told him civil war was comin' upon us, and it was a war I felt the south just could not win."

"And so you left."

Roman shook his head. "It was not that simple. You see, when my intentions were made known, as it had to be . . . my father's company had to be liquidated and outstanding loans made good upon. It was disaster not only because of the monies involved, but also because of our questioned allegiance to the south. At that time, when the northern states were twisting our arms in regard to slavery and autonomy itself . . . I was branded a traitor, an abolitionist and a coward. And havin' been cast as such, there was no turnin' back."

"But in the end, suh, it appears that you made the correct decision in leavin' at that time," Nicholas offered. "Had you stayed . . ."

"We would have lost everything like his brother and sister who both refused to leave," Lucianna interjected. "All of our money would have been changed over to useless Confederate notes."

"Our home in Atlanta was burned to the ground by General Sherman– I've been told by a few trusted friends who had corresponded with me for a time," Roman admitted.

"And then you moved back south."

"There again," Roman said, "that is another story. Perhaps another time."

Lucianna nodded. "Yes dear, another time."

* * *

The evening ended with Roman and Nicholas returning to the study and Lucianna retiring for the night. The rain, and accompanying lightning and thunder had ceased. With the air cool and its fresh earthy scent abounding, Lucianna instructed Maggie Mae to open the windows of her bedroom before she departed. Lucianna undressed by the glow of two oil lamps that burned softly at either end of her bedroom. She was satisfied with how dinner had gone, though certainly not the moments before when Nicholas and Maggie Mae were touching each other.

A few times over dinner and bread pudding for desert, she caught Nicholas' eye and played coy– immediately glancing away, but only after making sure that he knew she had been watching him. It was simply a game of enticement, arousal and withdrawal. And too, she'd played the devoted wife skillfully, she thought, even if Roman had seen right through it. But she didn't care, for it was not for Roman's benefit anyway.

Thoughts of her younger self in Atlanta came to mind as she removed the thin layer of make-up from her face, and seeing that her skin was still near flawless and supple– for now. Inevitably, she realized blemishes and folds of skin would make their presence known.

She recalled how delicately Roman had recounted their departure from Atlanta to the north. He'd told the truth, just not the entire truth. And what he'd left out was not to protect her, she figured, but more so to hide his own embarrassment. No man that she knew of wanted to admit that they'd fallen in love with and married the daughter of a whore . . . and that the daughter had followed in her mother's footsteps. She laughed softly as she remem-

bered Roman as he *was* then– not the ever-grim, gray-haired, repentant philosopher he was now. Then, there was nary a suggestion of silver in his dark brown hair. His wide shouldered back
complemented his thick frame, and together they presented him as
cocky. He was not rich . . . no– he was wealthy. With his dashing
looks, he was but one of a few remaining unicorns to be snared by
business and statesmen for their daughters. He and his younger
brother, Pilas, had had their pick of young ladies, and they teased
and courted with ghost promises of marriage much to the dismay
of many young girls and their fathers.

No . . . they were far too busy enjoying life that their wealth
provided them, Lucianna remembered. Their love of drink, and of
women especially, was all that they had a care for then. And when
they weren't deflowering less respected ladies, from whom they
would never select a wife from, it was off to the brothels. It was
where they had first met and she desired to have his wealth– and
him– if he had to come with the devil's pact she'd entered into.

* * *

That cool Sunday night in Atlanta, when Roman's coach had
been sent to fetch her from Madame Rochette's bordello, was a
memory Lucianna had never let turn gray in her mind. She never
once looked back or missed those whom she had left, including her
mother who had never been one to her. If there had been one person whom she did have any feelings for in Madame Rochett's
abode, it was the old whore herself. It seemed as though Madame
Rochett was the only one who had the slightest hint of joy for her,
as she had done what all the other whores, including Madame Rochette, had always hoped would happen to them . . . been swept
away to a new life by a wealthy knight.

"You must leave all of this behind you, pretty one . . . the house,
Atlanta, the other ladies . . . your mother especially," Madame Rochette told her, as the coachman loaded her trunks onto the back

of the coach. "In your new life, you'll find many dear friends with your nature and charm that you have so much of. But never," Madame Rochett said sternly, "let yourself be fooled by sentiments of sincerity that can lull you into trustin' these people. Not for a moment! They will as soon as turn on you . . . a whore *and* daughter of a whore. You must never write . . . and only speak of Atlanta in the most vague sense. Remember– everythin' you mention is goin' to be subject to suspicion. If they discover you're not really one of them, they'll love nothin' more than to stomp on you. Now, my little nymph . . . forget this life you've had and everythin' in it, except that I am glad for you . . . *now forget that also*," Madame Rochett told her before closing her door to Lucianna once and for all.

On their way north, Roman and Lucianna were married in a small Indiana town by a minister, and in the presence of his wife and eight children who stunk of the farm on which they worked. Life, for a while was good for Lucianna . . . now lady and wife of Roman Meadows. But with war came eventual despair for southerners, especially Pilas, brother of Roman, who lost everything when he decided to become a slave owner instead of moving north and most of his newly purchased slaves ran away. Pilas' home and lands were scorched by marauders and occupying union soldiers, and his wife, sickened by fever, died along with his only son.

Lucianna had even encouraged Roman to give refuge to Pilas . . . that is, after he suggested that his brother come and live with them after hearing the dreadfulness befallen his sibling. Though Roman and Lucianna's intentions were of the best, it was however, the grand mistake that cracked the heel of the glass slipper she wore.

"And thou, foul beast, shall be cast out of heaven and from my sight for all thy days! So sayeth the Lord thy God."

CHAPTER 11

Serpents and Children

A new day should have held promises of a new beginning. For Enda Sully, it was the same as it was ever going to be . . . she had already seen it come and go. Moving about in a world were she already knew how it was going to end had become tedious for her. Whether she was sitting on her sinking, lopsided porch watching folks walk to and fro or preparing a meal of peas and cornbread; the mystery of who she was going to see walking by, or if the peas were cooked too long or just right this time, had already been revealed to her. She felt no joy in knowing what she was already going to do and then having to do it anyway.

She feigned sleep as Maggie Mae bent over and kissed her before leaving for work. Once alone, with only the chirping of crickets to keep her company, she watched– with eyes closed, as more visions of what was yet to come played over and over again before her mind's eye. She was comforted by the fact that the gift she possessed would die with her. Maggie Mae, from what she could sense, held only a fraction of such power that could easily be chalked up to intuition. And even if she did know how to use such foresight, Enda figured Maggie Mae would never accept it as a gift anyway, but only as curse. But those worries no longer bothered her, knowing that Maggie Mae's blood was far too diluted to possess the true gift that lived in the blood of Negroe women.

Gal got too much white blood for her to see the dark comin', she thought.

Enda's legs kicked and jittered as a new vision passed by. Her heart began quivering . . . threatening to seize up as though it were about to stop. The woman's mouth in the vision she watched curled up in horror . . . not once, but twice. There was pain unimaginable inflicted upon flesh . . . not once, but twice. Enda's breaths came quickly, and only slowed when the vision disappeared into a mist of dark-red, nearly black blood.

The serpent was not lying . . . that she was sure of.

It had given her all she'd asked for and more.

And she promised it all but one thing in return for the life of her daughter. But in saving her daughter, she had condemned others, many of whom she loved as her very own.

The gift the serpent gave could not be returned, she understood . . . what will be was just going to be. The pact had been struck and sealed with blood and an exchange of souls. Death was inevitable . . . *death was already stalking the alleys of Folsom*. It was only the 'where', 'how' and 'why' that remained a mystery to all except her.

Weakened, physically as much as mentally from what she'd just been shown, she lay in bed for a while longer before facing the day she'd already seen. She felt selfish and sad, yet joyful in knowing that her death would be as gentle as a prick of a pin. She understood damnation would claim her now, while others would have to persevere through the pain of hell on earth in order to bathe in peaceful immortality. It was a price she was willing to pay, and if she had to do it all once more from the beginning, knowing what she did now, she knew she would do so without hesitation– even if it meant others would die . . . and die they shall, she saw in the 'tomorrows' yet to come for Folsom, Mississippi.

CHAPTER 12

Mary was just now starting to feel like her old self. Since nursing Paul the past two weeks, she was able . . . almost that is, to resume her usual duties in the Monclair home with a clear head. But even as she welcomed the rest from Paul's daily caretaking, she still found herself busy whipping up a late morning meal of tomato juice and milk, thickened with a couple of teaspoons of flour for him. He was still not ready to chew on food, and the thick soup was easier for him to swallow. She ladled two scoops of soup into a bowl and positioned it on the center of the tray. She was about to leave the kitchen and make her way up the stairs for the fifth time, when she heard an almost imperceptible tap on the backdoor window. She turned around expecting to see Isabel or Beatrice, but quickly remembered that she left Isabel in the front parlor of the house just a short while ago, and Beatrice was already off to school. Instead, she saw David's round face nearly filling the small windowpane.

David had made daily visits for the last two weeks since Paul's beating. Each time, Mary knew, he had waited until Beatrice and her father had left and Isabel was nowhere to be seen in the garden. Each time he'd asked her to let Paul know he had come by, though Mary knew David really wished she would grant him entrance to see Paul. But, Mary just didn't feel right about it. Her apprehension had nothing to do with the *special friendship*, as she called it, the boys had, but more about Isabel or Beatrice deviating from their usual routines and happening upon them. Being put into the position of guard to keep them apart just didn't settle in her stomach right and soured her mouth.

Once Paul had been strong enough to sit up in bed and lucid enough to speak, although much slurred, he began inquiring about David as much as David did about him. Mary tried to give a better name to the *special friendship* Paul and David had, but nothing ever came to mind that seemed to express the sadness and joy both boys were unable to mask when speaking the other's name. As she opened the backdoor, she saw that same expression upon David's face now . . . one that she could only name as 'worry', 'hope' . . . and 'love'.

"Mornin', Ms. Mary." His voice was low and eyes sweeping about the room.

"Ain't nobody here 'cept the Mrs., and she be up front, chile," Mary assured him. She grinned as his meaty, round shoulders dropped in relief.

"I just swung 'round to see how things goin' with Paul," he said.

Mary nodded. "I know . . . I know. He doin' much better than the day 'fore and one 'fore that. The swellin' creepin' back here and there. I reckon I can get'em a'walkin' a step or two if he up for it today."

David smiled. "It'll be good for him to get up, right?"

"Sho'nuff," she replied. "It help get all that fever and mess movin' out."

"That some darn good news, Ms. Mary."

She saw his excitement quickly vanish and replaced with melancholy as his head drooped. As with Paul, she tried to deny her empathy for David, knowing that it could only lead to deeper feelings that weren't accepted or expected between a Negroe and a white. With Paul, trying to bury how she felt about him was fruitless. She loved the boy. That was just undeniable. If she had had any doubt of her love for Paul, Simeon had erased it completely with his fists. Seeing Paul barely able to move or breathe, and being swollen-up like a tick on a dog assured her that what she felt for Paul was as real as the baby in her womb. And now . . . *again* . . . with David, echoes of those same feelings grew so loud she wanted to cover her ears and start singing to drown it out. Without his white skin, he was just a boy, she thought . . . a boy like her Paul, and another who would be hated for what he was and not who he was.

Lord know I can't hate such a sad lookin' thang, she thought, staring at the chipmunk-cheeked boy who was as broad as she was. She couldn't deny that he was brave either. He came day after day to the Monclair home knowing that his presence would only heighten suspicion about him. Yet, came he did. He was fearful . . . yes! He was always twisting his hands over the other, then moving them behind him, and then to the side, and back again rolling them over his protruding belly. Rarely did she ever see his close set brown eyes dead on, as he rarely looked directly at her, as if he feared revealing his secret that she already knew.

"So, he lookin' a hair better now?"

Mary groaned softly. Her right hand rested on what used to be her hip, which was now just muscle and fat. She could think of no one who would approve, or even come close to understanding what she was about to do, not even Lar, and he was the most reasonable person she knew. But Lar wasn't here. And even if he were, she knew not even he would be able to change her mind. "Come take a gander for yourself," she told him.

David's eyes locked onto hers. Seeing his face flush with excitement, she knew her decision was the right one. *So hush-up white man and woman . . . Negroes and all you preacher folk . . . you ain't gonna tell Mary what be right and what be wrong . . . no suh and no ma'am! I got my own good book that tell me better than ya'll ever can!*

"Really, Ms. Mary?"

"Just for a spell now," she made clear. "I get in more trouble than you, if you get caught."

David nodded hard and desperately.

She walked to the kitchen door leading into the dining room as stealthily as her weight would allow upon the wood floor. Listening first and hearing nothing, she parted the door slightly and listened again. She motioned for David to follow as she crept into the dining room and down the hall, pausing every so often to listen for the slightest creaking of wood from doors being opened or footsteps falling upon them. When they arrived at the stairwell, she paused the longest, as the landing would be in Isabel's direct line of sight if she unexpectedly left the parlor and looked to her right. With silence still abound, she furiously waved for David to go up the stairs. He did so with the grace of a baby elephant.

Mary followed him, though was much quieter, as she knew where every loose and squeaky board lay. When she reached the top step, David was standing in the middle of the hallway– bewildered he seemed– not knowing where to go and panting as much from exertion as from nerves. She walked to Paul's room that David had passed right by and rapped lightly, even as she was turning the knob with the other and pushing it open. She could tell Paul was doing much better by the decrease in the room's rancid aroma. He was awake and had already pushed himself up in the bed. His hair was heavy with oil and tussled, as though it hadn't been combed in a week, even though she had bathed him just the day before. But his eyes, which had swelled shut and temporarily blinded him, were open and once again beaming their brilliant, though weathered blues. Paul smiled when he saw her. Both upper and lower lip were still slightly enlarged and scabbed over. He tried to move, but grunted and winced, and then gave up.

Mary silently thanked Enda for the healing herbs, which she knew without a doubt had saved Paul's life. Still, she couldn't forget the pain Paul endured as she followed Enda's directions exactly as she was told to. It appeared at the time as though the cure– tightly wrapping his swollen parts in rags seeped in Enda's malodorous brew, was actually worse than the insults themselves. He'd cried until he could produce no more tears and was reduced to yelping, until even what was left of his voice finally gave out and all he could manage to do was shake and shudder in agony. 'He be livin', though,' she reminded herself.

"Stay still now, Paul," Mary urged. "You need to be real quiet . . . hear me?" She told him. "Someone here to see you." She stepped to the side and revealed David who had been completely obscured behind her. Unconsciously, she turned and took hold of David's shoulder and pulled him forward. When she turned back to Paul, expecting to see his face full of joy and gladness, she saw sorrow instead. She couldn't remember seeing such sadness since that Sunday Freda recounted her dreadful tale of losing her husband and son to a lynch mob.

Her heart wept as Paul began to cry and was unable to wipe the tears from his face. David was crying also, and though he could, did not attempt to shield his sorrow. He, still standing next to her, looked up at her. His face was red and eyes even redder, as if waiting for permission to go to Paul, which she gave with a nod of her head.

David bumbled toward the edge of the bed and awkwardly went down on both knees. Paul managed to reach out a quivering hand, which David immediately took and placed on his cheek. Both boys seemed oblivious to her presence or the impression they gave. Their sobs grew louder and spoke a language that was unknown to anyone else but them.

As they clung to each other, Mary felt like a prying stranger in their midst. What she could sense between them, she could not hate, but only love. She immediately swore never to give them a disapproving eye or word, no matter what Simeon, Isabel, Beatrice and Lar too– or anyone else thought about them. *So hush up white man and white woman! Same go for you Negroes too! Ya'll just stay outta my head and ya'll stay the hell away from them . . . both of them! 'Specially my Paul . . . that child . . . my . . . my lil' white boy. Ya'll best stay 'way!*

Mary backed out of the room and closed the door. She could still hear their sobbing and trembling voices echoing out. The madness and sorrow of it all hit her in the form of her own tears coming unexpectedly. Even the baby, suddenly restless, squirmed about as though it was feeling what she did. Suddenly, it kicked hard, *or* something moved that shouldn't have. But regardless, it was like a knife burrowing into her gut right above her pelvis. She leaned against the wall and wrapped her arms around her belly and stood quietly until the pain passed. Though as the pain eased, it was replaced with a familiar panic. She had felt this kind of pain before. She knew the telltale signs when a baby inside her was not well. The pain– like the sharp one that had just hit her, would soon start coming in waves and increase in intensity until she bled away the child's life within her. Holding her womb, she crept over to the stairs and sat on the top one. She leaned against the wall and closed her eyes. A silent prayer quickly formed on her lips asking help from a God she had no love for. 'Do it for Lar, Lord . . . please let this chile be born alive," she begged of her unseen nemesis, who had so often denied her a woman's greatest joy.

Guilt and anger became fresh in her mind for a god Lar always said was loving and merciful. She understood, and even in some ways accepted her own punishment from God. But she was perplexed why he would punish Lar, who loved God like no other, and was faithful to the God even when God didn't seem faithful to him. And as his duty as a preacher dictated, he spread the word of God to all who would listen, and even to those, including her, who didn't always want to hear it. 'Don't strike out at him Lord 'cause of me and my ways. Give'em just one chile. Just'a one be all Lar need from you. If you want me, then take me. But give him a chile if you do.'

Mary opened her eyes.

The pain was gone, but still she needed to check things below. Quickly appearing and disappearing pains had fooled her into a false sense of security before, only to return unexpectedly with a child murdering vengeance. She leaned back slightly and listened for any sounds coming from underneath Paul's door, but heard nothing. She walked down the stairs slowly and made for the parlor. She took in a deep breath and exhaled, then cleared her throat before rapping on the door and entering. Isabel was sitting in a chair with her crochet needles idle in her hands and yarn in her lap. She didn't respond to the knocking or Mary's presence in the room.

Many times . . . *no* . . . since marrying Simeon . . . *no, not quite*– since Stephen Allister, Isabel's beloved, was killed, Mary had grown accustomed to Isabel's trance-like daydreams. But since Paul's beating, Isabel had retreated into her delusions and illusions, more often than not. And during those times, Mary would have to physically awaken her, only to be met with a look of confusion, as if Isabel truly didn't know her or where she was for that matter. This time, Mary decided against interrupting Isabel's date with Stephen Allister's ghost, who most likely had come by to remind her of what was, should have been and could have been, but alas

was not. Chances were, she thought, she could make it to the outhouse, check her drawers and make it back upstairs to shoo David
out and on his way, and still find Isabel unmoved.

Once outside, she glanced up at Paul's bedroom window before
slipping into the rancid smelling hut. She hurriedly pulled her
dress up and underpants down almost simultaneously. Her under-
garment was spotted with a dollop of gelatinous blood along the
center. Horror froze her in the sweltering heat of the outhouse.
The thought of losing yet another child– *this child*, was unbearable
for her to even contemplate. What God was there, she thought angrily, that would punish her so many times . . . or even punish Lar
with such a loss once again? She couldn't understand why her
body, far stronger than any other woman in Folsom was too weak
to give life.

At the moment, she didn't love God.

Lar would be devastated even more than she at another loss, she
knew. He'd seemed so certain that this one would be the child that
he could finally hold in his arms, and with unbound, fatherly love,
look into its living eyes instead of squinting to see his reflection in
dead ones. This would be the one that he would cradle upon his
curly-haired chest and lull to sleep on warm and chilly nights. And
as the earth, moon and sun aged, he would hold its hand as they
walked into their newly-built church.

She pulled up her underpants and sat on the crudely cut hole
behind her. She tried not to cry, but did. Shielded by the outhouse,
her tears– fueled by anguish and a stomach sickening fear,
drenched her face. She cradled her womb and rocked back and
forth. "You gotta live, chile," she whimpered. "For your pappy . . .
jus' for your pappy. Live chile!" She commanded.

What began as a quiver in her left foot quickly turned into
stomping. She banged on the door with her fist. "Lord! Lord Jesus–
don't you do this thang. You let it live for Lar. Let it be livin'. I
tellin' you! Don't curse it 'cause of me, or I curse you right back!"

She spat. She looked up to the blades of light slicing though the slats of the ceiling. "You hear me?!" She shouted. "You be damned if you kill this chile of Lar's. Damn you . . . damn you . . . damn you," she muttered, until her throat became clogged with phlegm. She squeezed her womb. "You hold on, chile," she whispered. "Your mammy gonna see 'bout thangs and make it right."

Mary opened the door and strode toward the house. Her legs suddenly forgot they were tired and her feet couldn't remember that they were swollen. She mounted the stairs with only a cursory glance down the hallway toward the parlor where Isabel was. She burst through Paul's room without knocking. David was sitting on the bed and cradling Paul's head between his chest and belly. Paul, who had apparently fallen asleep, startled awake at her entrance. Their hands, which had been intertwined, suddenly parted. Both stared at her with wide, frightened eyes and mute open mouths.

She didn't have time to explain that what she'd just seen didn't matter to her. She simply walked over to Paul and laid an open palm on his forehead and shook her head in relief that he was cool to the touch. "I gotta leave for a spell, chile'– alright? But I be back to see 'bout you soon– Lord my witness," she promised. "So don't you fret none if I ain't 'round and 'bout for a spell."

Paul nodded.

"David– I need you to do Ms. Mary a thang."

* * *

David had the horse and wagon nearly hitched by the time Mary made it out of the backdoor. She was about to help him finish, but he gently shooed her off. "I do this every day for my pappy. Just go and get on, Ms. Mary," he told her.

Mary acquiesced.

She hadn't told either boy of the cause of her urgency, or Isabel either for that matter, only that she had to leave and would return shortly– she hoped. Isabel had barely acknowledged her . . . just smiled, all the while looking through her. David however, seemed to sense that something was amiss, and once outside, he sped off to hitch the horse for her as asked.

After lunging up on the wagon, she took the reins in one hand and cupped her belly with the other. Looking down upon David's round face– his wide chest stretching the dingy brown shirt he wore to its limits, and his trunk stuffed into man-sized pants that were still too small, he reminded Mary a bit of herself. She knew what it was like to be a big child all around, whether in the face, stomach or even hands. And it always seemed to her that no matter how little food she ate, she remained the same size, if not bigger. She guessed the same was true for David.

He finished checking over the hitch. "You go on and move over, Ms. Mary."

Mary shook her head the moment the words left his mouth. "Uh-uh, chile. You can't come where I fixin' to go."

David remained where he was. "Ms. Mary, you can't get on like that . . . handlin' this horse with one hand and holdin' your tummy with the other."

"I can manage jus' fine."

"But you won't be fine if the reigns slip and the horse go and get sassy on ya," he countered. "Wearin' this wagon on top of your head ain't gonna help ya none." He shrugged his mountains that made do for his shoulders. "And I want to anyway. It's the least of all I can do for all you done for Paul *and me.*"

Mary knew he was right. Trying to steer a wagon across Folsom's rocky, hole ridden roads was difficult enough with two hands and one's mind straight, but with one hand and a head full of fret could spell trouble. "What folk gonna say 'bout a white boy trekkin' through town with a Negroe woman?" She asked weakly. "And you 'spose to be off at school learnin' your numbers and words anyhow."

He looked down. "My pappy say I can't go no more 'cause . . . 'cause of . . . Well– school ain't my best thing anyhow. But don't fret none, Ms. Mary. Ain't no one gonna be 'round town 'cept a few old folks who ain't gonna care here or there 'bout you and me gettin' on in a cart."

* * *

No more stabbing cramps had come since the first.

To her relief, the baby was moving, telling her that it still lived. But blood *had* come– old, familiar jelly-blood oozed out of her. To her, there was no agony that compared to bearing down to deliver a dead child. What should have been the most painfully joyous time in her life was always the darkest. She wished her mind was stronger than her body, making it easier to leave all those memories on the road called 'despair'. But those memories . . . faces of her dead babies who resembled Lar, hunted and haunted her like a vengeful spirit taken from the world of the living too soon.

Instinctively, she knew that instead of crossing the bridge as they had just done, the right thing would have been to have David veer right and take her to Meadow's farm to get Lar. Lar was going to have to know sooner or later. But it was later that she chose. At the moment, she couldn't even fathom facing him with such familiar, dire news when she couldn't bear to think upon it herself. Neither she, nor David had spoken since leaving the Monclair home. David finally broke their silence as they ventured into an area white children were not supposed to go.

"Everythin' alright with the baby?"

Mary saw nothing but compassion upon his face, which seemed as troubled as hers. His lower lip, slightly larger than the top one, fought and lost the battle against gravity . . . like hers. "I don't know," she replied, in a softer voice than usual, which had become weak from worry and fatigue. "That be what I gonna find out."

"I hope everythin' is alright– I do, Ms. Mary. Your baby is all Paul talks 'bout. I guessin' he wantin' you to have a boy. Ya know, someone to play with at home."

"I didn't know he feelin' so strong 'bout it."

David's eyebrows rose. "Oh yeah! He thinks the world 'bout you, Ms. Mary– your husband too. I can see why. You the only one who seem to give a damn 'bout makin' him well. And he is, only 'cause of you."

Mary felt her face grow fiery as blood rushed to it.

Never in her lifetime, or five or six of them, had she imagined ever feeling such warm thoughts toward whites . . . white boys especially. And then to discover the feelings so genuinely returned was most shocking of all. It made her head dizzy. The love she felt for Paul, and now a burgeoning caring for David did nothing but validate God's love, just as she remembered Lar preaching about. Though erasing her hate for whites wasn't so simple. She felt as though she needed to hold on to hate if she was ever going to make sense of her world, where whites ruled by the knife, gun and noose.

By the time they arrived in front of Enda Sully's shack, any and all of her lingering thoughts of not trusting David had all but evaporated. It didn't even bother her that he helped her down from the wagon and took hold of her elbow as they walked up the rock-laden path. And as any decent gentleman would do for a lady, he stepped on the rickety, wooden steps first and carefully brought her up each one, as his eyes studied her footing and balance for the slightest waver. David raised his hand to knock on the door.

"Wait!" she called.

"Huh?"

"This be Ms. Sully's place. You know who she be right?"

David's eyelids shuttered for a moment, and then quickly popped open wide. His hand dropped to the side quicker than his jaw dropped. "The witch!" he whispered.

"I be mighty careful sayin' that, boy . . . 'specially here," she warned. She knocked on the door herself.

Moments passed, compounding Mary's growing anxiety, as it seemed no one was there. Maggie Mae was already at the Meadow's home, she knew, having seen her earlier that morning walking toward town. But Enda had to be home, she thought. Where else would Enda be if not at home? Mary wondered. She never ventured too far away, and it was too early in the morning for her to be out in the woods behind her house scavenging.

Mary tried peering in the window to the right of the door, but it was covered with a brown sheet from the inside. The window was as old, if not more so, than the shack it was set in. At the bottom of the window, she spied a long, narrow crack where the window frame and wall should have met, but didn't. "Over here, David," she said, pointing at the crack. "Take a peek in."

David left the window on the left side of the door and came and over to the one right of the door where Mary was and kneeled. But as he did, the door creaked behind him. Mary touched his shoulder and gestured for him to move away from the window. She positioned herself in front of him, then turned and said. "Don't speak to her unless she ask you to," she warned. David's face blanching was quite sufficient in telling Mary that he understood well.

"I swore to God I done heard somebody callin' ol' Enda a witch?" Enda sung out. "That what folk callin' me nowadays?" The door swung all the way open. Enda's hair was as white as her skin, and cascaded past her shoulders to her narrow waist.

David pressed up against Mary as Enda hobbled out onto the porch. Still holding her belly, Mary reached around with her left hand and took hold of his. She squeezed it a few times, though that failed to subside his quivering. Enda was staring with the intensity of the cold variety, that only grey eyes such as hers could give. But Enda was not looking at her.

"Ms. Sully," Mary said, trying to draw attention away from David. "I think somethin' be wrong with my chile."

Enda was silent, but her eyes were on the prowl for who stood behind Mary.

"I done had some bleedin' a spell ago . . . pains too. But it ain't like the other painin' I felt before."

Enda looked down at Mary's belly. "I can't tell you anythin' 'til I take a look for myself. You get on in. But you . . ." she said to David. "You come 'round here and let Enda take a good look at ya."

David's trembling turned to shaking. "It be alright, chile," Mary reassured him. "Ain't nobody gonna hurt ya." Despite promises of Enda's benign intent, Mary still had to pull him away and step to the right in order to expose him. She squeezed his hand again. It was only then that he returned the gesture and tentatively moved one step closer. Enda moved quicker than her age suggested, and within a few quick steps, she was within a breath's distance from him. Mary held David firm. She could almost smell fear oozing from him, begging him to run, and quickly.

"Ye . . . yes, ma'am?" He sputtered.

Enda's mouth rounded playfully, as her eyes widened in faux surprise. "Ma'am– is it now? Which it be? Ma'am or witch, boy?"

"Ma' . . . ma' . . . ma'am? Ma'am!"

"Look at ya!" Enda croaked. "Big-tail, white boy standin' there afraid of itty-bitty, Enda. You think she be a witch and gonna put a spell on ya?"

David gasped, and then quickly shut his mouth.

"One day– long, long time from now, you gonna tell folks 'bout me and how you met me. You gonna tell them folk who make steel, meat and cloth, how you came face to face with a real, walkin' and talkin' witch . . . the witch of Folsom, Mississippi . . . a Negroe witch who look white. But they ain't gonna believe your tale 'bout me, or this– or that– or the other. They gonna say thangs turned out to be the way they was meant to." She backed away, though her eyes never left his. "You go 'round out back there and wait for, Ms. Mary. T'ain't good for a white boy be standin' out in front where folks can see ya. You go on out back and take a good look 'round. See if you know those woods far back from here. If you don't, you learn'em."

David didn't move an inch. Mary shook his hand and prodded him on. "Go on now, chile," she told him. "I be out soon, and then we be on our way." Mary followed Enda inside. "Go'on, David," Mary commanded and closed the door behind her.

Enda was hobbling and teetering without assistance of her cane. Mary followed her to the back of the house, which was a most familiar area to her. The house smelled of earth– old dirt that had been rife with worms and what worms left behind. Despite the heat and humid blanket of misery outside, she felt cool. Enda motioned to the bed– her bed. It was the same one Mary almost died upon trying to give birth the last time. She sat down and was about to swing her legs up on the bed. But to her surprise, Enda sat right next to her, and she realized Enda was the source of the earthen aroma that infused her nostrils.

"Spittin' blood out happen now and again when you be with child," Enda explained softly. "It ain't much to fret over, unless you want to."

Mary shook her head. "But this be me, Ms. Enda. You know how I carry chillin', better than anybody."

"Of course, I do," Enda shot back, and then smiled with her thin, pink lips. She stood with great effort, and shook like ragdoll being whipped as she struggled to steady herself. "Go on and show Enda the blood."

Mary wasn't the least embarrassed to scoot to the edge of the bed and remove her undergarments. She slipped them from around her tattered, lace-up shoes– that were too small for her swollen feet to lace, and studied them before handing them over. She didn't see any new spotting . . . just the jelly-blood from before beginning to crust over.

Enda studied her underpants, as only Enda would have dared to do. If Allie Mae– a good midwife in her own right, had done as Enda was doing, Mary would have snatched her underpants back and tore out of the shack like snakes were biting at her heels. But this was Enda, who possessed a certain knowledge no one else around had. She had even heard rumors that Enda knew of the skills used by the Indians who used to live on the lands where they were now, that is, before white folk drove them out west and into despair. No . . . if she had witnessed Allie Mae rubbing at, and smelling the crusty blood of her underpants, she would have thought her friend had gone mad.

Enda shook her head and looked down at Mary. "Ain't nothin' wrong. The chile be fine."

Mary sighed, but the comfort was short lived. In her heart, doubt still lingered. She reached for her undergarments, but was refused.

"Go on and lay back," Enda instructed. "Scoot up ya legs so I can take a peek up in ya."

Mary was confused. "But you said every thang be fine."

Enda hobbled toward the end of bed. "I know what I said, gal. This here what I doin' be for your troubled mind. It make ya feel a whole lot better later rememberin' I took a peek down there instead of just sniffin' some ol' bloody mess– won't it?"

Knowing she was right, Mary complied.

After reaching her hand half way into Mary, and poking around for a bit, Enda said, "Nothin' wrong down there, chile." She pulled Mary's dress back down and patted her knee twice.

Mary pulled herself upright. "Where the bleedin' come from?"

"You tight as boil, gal," Enda cackled. "You done stretched your-self out 'til you can't no more, is all. Look at ya! Skin done split 'cross ya belly. Your body can only take so much. Blood that came, come from you, not from what the chile needin' inside."

Mary looked down at her baby-filled belly and massaged the waters encircling her child. "Tell me," Mary said, but refused to look Enda in the eye. "Just for Lar . . . touch the chile again and look into the 'tomorrows' . . . *and tell me the truth.*"

"You mean for you!"

Mary shook her head. "No ma'am– for Laurence Cole."

Enda took hold of Mary's hand. "Look here, chile," she said, and then waited for Mary to look up. "What you want me to look for, I done already seen the last time you was here with the dead one– *I saw it then.*"

"'Don't have one more chile here', you told me. Those be your words that night," Mary reluctantly reminded her.

"And you didn't listen to Enda, did ya?" Her eyebrows, which were once black as tar, but now were all white, rose up in condem-nation. "I never once lied to ya, and ya did it anyhow. Now you wantin' me to tell you somethin' different. You want everythin' to be alright, but in your heart, you know it ain't. Don't ya?"

Mary turned away from her. "Why it be too much to ask for a chile of my own? The Lord done turned a blind eye to me, Ms. Sully. He punishin' me and my chillin' . . . and Lar too."

"Bah!" Enda spat. "You the one blind, Mary Cole. Here you be reachin' and searchin' and grabbin' for what already right in front of ya. Look at ya! You hollerin' at the Lord 'bout wantin' somethin' you already got. You already got more than most– you ol' selfish thang! But keep on listenin' to ol' horn-head whisperin' in your ears and danglin' what *you think* you want the most in front of your face."

Mary stood and covered her face to hide the tears of anger that started to flow. "How can I not feel pain, Ms. Enda, when he tryin' to take this one from me, too?!" She retorted. "All my chillin' layin' out back of my house under dirt, 'cause big, black, man-ish Mary Cole can't give'em breath to live. Uh –uh!!! The Lord got a hand in this mess. I ain't done a thang to deserve it! And you and God, and every Negroe that say Folsom be home, give witness to the good, godly man Lar be."

Enda grasped her hand and held tight, even as Mary struggled to pull away from her. But Enda held fast and pulled at her. "Sit down, chére. Come on down here and listen to what Enda has to say to you, like your mamà would've," Enda urged her.

Mary reluctantly sat back down upon hearing Enda strip off her Negroe dialect and replace it with one she'd only heard educated whites, like Isabel and her sisters use. Though whenever Enda spoke as such with her French infused English, she never did so with other Negroes other than Lar, Maggie Mae and herself.

"I'm going to tell you what nobody knows except for me. And you won't tell it, because I've already *seen it!*" She stressed upon a heavy breath. "You and other people think I'm crazy– and you're right! I'm crazy as a blind, coon dog only because I've *seen it all!* Right up to the very end.

"I'll tell you something right now," Enda continued. "Nothing is wrong with that child of yours. She's going to come into this world healthy and living. But that's not important, even if you think it is."

Mary's expression was a mixture of anger, sorrow, self-pity and now hope.

"Ahhhh," Enda sighed. "You have more sense than any Negroe or white in Folsom, but you don't use it.

"Lord God will keep his promise, Mary Cole . . . just like when he splits this world in two. I've seen the golden chariots roaring out from the sky and swarming this earth like locusts. Angels will follow beside them– burning and cleansing this land we're standing on right now. The Lord Jesus himself will descend from the sky. His skin will be burned as black as yours from heavenly fire and the love of God.

"With holy words carved into left hand, he's going to raise the dead, *and they will walk this earth again.* With his right, he's going glean the repentant from the unrepentant . . . separate the chaff from the wheat. No longer will it rain upon the righteous and wicked together– oh no, chére! Mother and father . . . brother and sister will be separated by his final words. All sins will be weighed. And then the end will come. What is flat will become a mountain of fire. What people say can't be burned, will melt and flow like a river."

Mary started to turn away, but Enda grasped her chin and brought her face back, forcing her to hearken to her prophetic words. "Your soul is heavy with worries, Mary Cole . . . just like mine."

Mary wrestled her head free from Enda and stood. A dizziness that no physical malady could explain swept over her as she walked to the door. She looked back, but instead of seeing Enda still seated on the bed, Enda was directly behind her. Mary expected more words as dark and eerie as before to come . . . but none did. And of that, Mary was thankful– her soul felt cold enough already. She did have comfort in the fact, as she believed Enda's words as truth, that her child would be born alive, and Lar would finally have his child, come end of the world or not.

Enda shuffled past her and navigated the drop off from the crooked porch, and went around the back of the shack. Mary followed suit. When she caught up to Enda, amidst a plot of ripe, ready-to-pluck tomatoes, purple-hull peas, and off to the left, a chicken coop, she saw David hurling stones out into the field of tall grass. Enda came up behind him, and with a touch to his shoulder, caught him by surprise. David spun around and dropped the remaining rocks from his hand. "What you throwin' at, boy?" Enda asked.

"Jus' the . . . the grass," he replied nervously.

She scanned the dry, sun-bleached grass beyond them. "You done seen somethin' out there?"

"No, ma'am," he replied.

It was though Enda didn't believe him, Mary thought, as Enda continued looking as though *something* indeed was out there. "You see somethin' move out there, you better run quick. You might think it be a snake, but it ain't. There somethin' worse than snakes sneakin' 'round here," Enda warned. She pointed over the grass to the edge of the forest slumbering in the distance. "Lookit there, boy. Learn those trees straight on and the ones beside'em. Look on further west," she then moved her finger toward the other direction, "and east." David did as he was told. "Learn'em good, like you *used* to learn your lessons in school," Enda told him. "Know how to get back here to the front of my house if you get lost in the woods one day. Understand me, boy?" David nodded.

Enda limped forward and into her garden and kept on until she was near the field. "Get on, now . . . the both of ya," Enda called out. "You done got what you come for, Mary Cole. You too . . . big ol' fat, white boy, David. Time for ya'll to leave Enda in peace."

David was already past Mary and mere steps away from the wagon before Enda even finished speaking.

* * *

"She really a witch, Ms. Mary?" David asked. "Ms. Mary?"

Mary was busy staring at the Negroe shacks they were passing by, which were no more than boxes of wood and rusty sheet metal. Subconsciously, she could hear David, who had been talking for most of the way back, but his voice was being drowned out by Enda's last words still resounding in her head. His repeated calling of her name finally drew her back to him.

"Ms. Mary?"

"What say, chile?" She asked lazily.

"Is it true what folk say 'bout her– Ms. Sully . . . that she a real witch?"

Mary sighed, though not in exasperation. "I guess she be what she be. But I don't rightly know for sure what the truth be, chile."

"Folk say she can curse ya if ya get on her wrong side," he stated.

"Who these folk be that say all that?"

He shrugged. "Just folk. That's what my pappy said folk say."

"Well," Mary replied, "seem like it all be gossip to me. One person get scared of the ol' woman and start talkin'– next you know, everybody tellin' the same story like it happen to them."

"Not me!" David protested. "I ain't gonna tell a soul. I don't wanna get cursed."

"And 'cause you ain't never came here neither," Mary told him. "You don't tell no one . . .," she paused a moment and rethought her words. "'cept Paul . . . don't tell no one else where we been or who we spoke to. Folk ain't gonna understand."

"Oh, I won't, Ms. Mary!" David promised.

"You do, and you might get your answer 'bout whether she be a witch or not."

David's eyes began to well with tears again. Guessing she had scared him sufficiently enough to keep him quiet, she smiled at him. He tentatively mirrored her. For a brief moment, seeing such innocent ignorance, she forgot her troubles, but only for a moment.

She'd lied to Enda when she said having a child meant more to Lar than herself. The child was as much for her as for Lar. Foolishly, she thought by imploring Enda on Lar's behalf would make

the difference between her child's life and death. But it was no ordinary Negroe woman she spoke to who could be tricked by a simple twist of carefully crafted words, she knew– it was Enda Sully–
the witch . . . a real witch. Enda could spot a lie as easily as
smelling the funk of a skunk on her upper lip.

You a damn fool, Mary-girl, she thought. Her attempt to deceive
Enda made her realize how far she was willingly to go for the life
of her child. But then again, she remembered, it *was* also for Lar's
sake that she wanted the child to live. Though not being able to
give Lar a child was only part of the problem. Being with Lar had
never been easy . . . even from the beginning. Though, she always
put a great portion of that blame lay at the feet of the Witch of Folsom.

It was less troubling for her to recall childhood memories of her
mother or Uncle Matty, though in truth, it was actually neither one
of them that was easiest to remember. It was always a beautiful
white face that smiled back at her when she remembered the past.
Sparkling, cold grey eyes were the ones most memorable to her. Of
course she remembered her own mother's weatherworn, sun-
blackened face quite well. Sarah had such large, dark eyes they
seemed almost black. But Enda's face was still the easier of the two
to recall. She loved Enda, and as difficult as it was to admit, in her
heart she always felt the tug of a mother-daughter bond with
Enda, but at the same time cursed her.

Mary knew early on that growing up Negroe *and female* was
not going to be easy any way she looked at it– the world belonged
to whites and men. But growing up next to Maggie Mae with her
white beauty made childhood so much worse. The more man-like
she watched herself become, the more beautiful and womanly
Maggie Mae turned out to be, it seemed. Whereas Maggie Mae's
skin was white and soft, she was always in a constant battle trying
to soften hers, which was dark, rough and always ashy. She had
come to accept that her hair would always be black, thick, and as

Negroes were taught by whites to call it– nappy, not like Maggie Mae's whose dark gold hair was silky like white folk's and never stopped growing. Learning to despise Maggie Mae had been the easiest lesson she never had to study in order to master, as everyone tutored her that 'Mary' stood for . . . coal black, tar-baby, pick-a-ninny and mannish . . . while 'Maggie Mae' meant . . . just-like-white, pretty, fair, womanly.

She never wanted to dislike and later hate Maggie Mae, as her friend had never done anything against her that was worth feeling that way toward her. It was simply hard not to feel that those complementary words lavished by other Negroes upon Maggie Mae, meant that she was the opposite of what beauty and being a woman was. It came as no surprise to her, though the hurt was certainly greater than she expected, that everyone just assumed that Lar, the good-son of their beloved preacher, Agmus Cole, would marry the lovely and very white, Maggie Mae Sully.

She remembered how handsome Lar was even in his younger years. When he walked past white women, even they would hesitate to look at him before feigning disgust and quickly turning away. And oddly for a Negroe boy– the bane of the white man's existence– the older he grew, the more gentle and caring he became. He followed in his father's footsteps and spread the word of God, and with all his heart, believed it could conquer anything. It was his love for God then, as it was now, and his genteelness toward Negroes and whites alike that both drew and repelled her.

But no one, not even she expected what was to come. Mary knew she wasn't beautiful, or even handsome in a womanly way. And no Negroe ever expected her to marry such a handsome man like Lar Cole, but more likely– if she were lucky to get married at all, to a man twice her age who was equally unattractive and had exhausted all of his other prospects.

But if her family of Negroes had sought to break her spirit with their talk of what beauty was– Maggie Mae . . . and what beauty wasn't– she, then they had failed miserably. She turned the hurt and constant reminders of her physical unattractiveness into a strength of mind, willfulness, and to the shock of all, a blunt feistiness that was unheard of, and certainly not welcomed from a woman ... especially one that was big in the hips, black as night and had a wide nose to boot. In addition to being built like a man anyway, she was determined to work like one ... chopping wood, patching leaky roofs, plowing fields and seeding them ... worrying ... struggling ... persevering ... *hitch the mule ... grab that hoe and bend yo back. Tired you say? Ain't no bein' tired when floors need washin', and britches and shirts need mendin', and beans need pickin', and hogs need sloppin' ... and ... and ... and ...* What any man was capable of doing, she learned to do the job just as well and sometimes better. What any woman could do, she did with as much care and fineness as the next, but with a better rise to her biscuits and cakes to boot. Her back thickened and spread wide as her prowess swinging an ax grew. Her arms doubled in size from lifting and pulling what needed to be lifted and pulled ... dragging and carrying what had to be dragged and carried. Life became that much harder once her mother passed away, after spending her last few days coughing up blood before slipping away in her sleep to the next world. It was then Mary saw what life she was truly meant to live.

She still spoke to Lar every time they encountered one another, though the love she held for him was still unrequited. His bits of free time from working Meadow's fields was spent with Maggie Mae Sully, whose skin didn't know what scrapes and bruises were. She had no doubt a love-root had been buried somewhere in Lar's backyard by Enda.

Of all the Negroe men, with the exception of Uncle Matty, Lar was the only one who actually enjoyed bickering back and forth with her. She questioned his views of whites, Negroes, women, men, and of course, their greatest debate– God ... all of which were practically the opposite of how she viewed such matters and people. She loved the seriousness that would quickly form on his face when challenged to substantiate his arguments . . . she loved him even more, knowing that he could. But the fire between them always cooled as quickly as it ignited. Back to Maggie Mae he always went. It stung seeing them together, for her love for Lar as more than a friend grew before she even realized it. Even without Uncle Matty constantly reminding her, she finally realized she would be better off not to torture herself over Lar. If only her mother had still been with her, she knew Sarah would have known the right words to say to heal her heart, or at least harden it toward Lar. But her mother was dead, and her heart continued pining for Lar's love that he had promised to another.

Finally, after no longer able to bear wasting her years watching the love deepen between Maggie Mae and Lar, she decided to find another. She was determined to marry a decent man, have his children and raise them with all the love Lar didn't want from her. And at night, she would give herself to him freely, though her passions were red for another. And in the end, having raised her children that were not Lar's . . . loved a husband only half as much, but as much as she could, she vowed to smile, knowing that she had made her life as good as it could be without Lar. But such a chance at a life of mediocrity and complacency never materialized, much to her overwhelming joy and Maggie Mae's sorrow. The love between Lar and Maggie Mae died a swift and awful death, much to the surprise and shock of every Negroe, and even some whites in Folsom.

Even to this day, no one knew what happened between them, other than Lar and Maggie Mae, for neither of them spoke of it. What Mary *did* know, was that Lar's love for Mary changed from sisterly to lover. Within a matter of weeks, Lar had professed his undying devotion and his desire to marry her, but . . . Mary was Mary as Mary was ever meant to be. She refused his love at first.

She wasn't willing to fall so easily for his innate charm or his handsomeness, especially after having waited years for him to notice her as a woman instead of a tomboy-sister. And that he refused to say what had happened between him and Maggie Mae didn't help sway her either. Though the secret to the end of their relationship soon became of no consequence to her, she was determined not to yield so easily to Lar.

After two years of courting, *and* him meeting her demand that he come and live in her home with Uncle Matty, which she refused to compromise on, they were married in Folsom by Cyrus Jones, a Negroe preacher from Peak Hills. Life and marriage for them then became such as it was . . . for the time being.

CHAPTER 13

The Rising

Simeon Paul Monclair realized early on in life that he had been born during a very precarious time. Though life then was good . . . unlike now. Now, it seemed to him, as he sat in his study with liquid spirits for company– as usual, life had become a vile and distorted caricature of what it should have been.

He mourned the days of his youth, which was spent dreaming of the kingdom promised to him. As a boy, he'd seen his future self, family, wife and children far differently from what they turned out to be. Even the idea of living in such a house as he did now seemed only possible in horror-drenched dreams. Such an insignificant abode was for lesser people, not for Monclair's who were meant to live in southern castles. Monclair men married beautiful, elegant women like his mother and his brother's wife, Andreas– daughter of a state senator, not daughters of dirt farmers, who only by chance acquired a modest fortune and had no pedigree to prove it had ever been justified.

He believed Monclair children were supposed to be the best a man and woman could produce– Monclair ladies would have their pick of the wealthiest men near and far, and young Monclair men would serve as bait for respectable ladies from respectable families.

Monclair men and women were to assure that the Monclair name not only became greater with each generation, but also would endure for years upon years to come. But again . . . alas . . . the right to such a way of life for Simeon became a dream long since dreamt and drowned in a sea of Confederate and Union blood.

He was sitting in his study, examining the wall, the floor, the ceiling– anything to preoccupy him from having to walk out and look at the family he never wanted. The taste of bourbon on his lips was no longer sweet– and had not been for years, but was bitter, though still tempting. He saw no future for his bloodline with that 'It', as he referred to Paul. He wished It would have simply just died that night after the beating and made life better for all. There was no place for It in a world of men, he thought. It served no purpose for the Monclair name except to sully it.

But It lived, despite his wish that it hadn't.

It had once again slowly began to eat and drink and move about, and had recently reappeared at the dining table, though It was careful to avoid his gaze and disappeared from his sight quickly after each meal. When he looked at It struggling to pass its spoon and fork between Its slowly mending lips, he wished that he had struck It harder that night . . . that he hadn't stopped when It lost control of Its bowels and bladder . . . that he hadn't withdrawn when he saw It helplessly laying on the floor and with blood seeping from it.

It was still pretty despite his best efforts to destroy it. Why could It not just have been a girl, with those sad, blue eyes and feathery black lashes? He was relieved there were no other Monclair men alive to witness his failure as a man and father. But he still couldn't help feeling humiliated knowing other men in town could see It– his progeny . . . a Monclair, as less of a man and more of an aberration for ridicule.

But It was not from him, he was certain. There was no sickness in his line that could have made a *thing* like that. He was sure the weakness and depravity in It had come from Isabel, another 'It', as far as he was concerned, who masqueraded as a wife. It was all because of her and her pining for that weakling, sissy-man, Stephen Allister, who she had wanted to marry, he figured.

Though Isabel was from a wealthy family, he still considered her bred from inferior stock. He'd had no love for her when he married her, but it was better than the repulsion he felt for her now. In his eyes, he hadn't married a woman, but acres of farmland, real estate and a few coins that the Christianson's had managed to hold on to after the war, unlike he, who at the time was the owner of the valuable Monclair name and a vanished fortune.

And then, there was of course the stump– where his right hand had once been.

He touched the red, inflamed and swollen looking flesh, though actually it was not tender, as it appeared to be. In actuality, it was like cured wood . . . calloused a quarter of an inch thick. Over the many years, some of his true color had slowly crept back into the burnt, rectum looking puckered stump that was crudely cauterized with a torch after his hand was hacked and chopped and hacked at again until it snapped off and lay on the ground before him . . . the fingers even twiddled their goodbye before going limp. Though the stump looked raw, it was now, as he rubbed it, dead to the touch.

But there were better times before his hand was severed, he recalled, with assistance from another shot of bourbon. He remembered when he was just fourteen and being groomed to be co-master of the growing Monclair fortune with his brother, Egan. Even at such a young age, his mother, Lillian, had already begun to search for the best marriage prospects for he and his brother. He fondly and jealously recalled his brother, Egan, that same year marrying the wealthy and comely Andreas Willstock in a lavish ceremony in their garden. In attendance were local, state and federal dignitaries who had come to pay respect to the daughter of their fellow lawmaking colleague. It was Egan's successful joining with the Willstock's that had encouraged his mother to start planning for the next marriage for her youngest prince.

But at fourteen, try as he might– and hard he did try many a night, he couldn't recall having any interest in the female sex, unlike other boys. He had already convinced himself long ago that it was a moot point anyway, regardless if it wasn't. He took a deep drink of bourbon to remind him so . . . another gulp . . . and another . . . and one more for good measure.

Regardless, bitterly he recalled carefree, overly imagined and heavily colored whimsical days spent riding through the miles of woodland he was to inherit and swimming in the Folsom river for what seemed like hours. But unknown to him, though he could feel it and sense it with every part of his privileged unconsciousness, his position in society had already been cast in gold from the first moment he took his first breath at his birth.

Niggahs had no place in his life other than to serve him. He had been taught and fully believed, for there was no dissenting opinions around him, that niggahs were just merely child-like animals who were solely dependent on the whites who were Christian enough to feed, clothe, care for and discipline them. But it was the niggahs, he remembered, who had changed the course of his life into an ever deepening cesspool that could not be drained free of its contagion.

Never were they meant to be as they are now, and no one could convince him otherwise. In the world that he still dreamed of and longed for, niggahs still worked the lands for whites without expectations of payment. They were obedient and caused no trouble, except for their inherent shiftlessness that any whip could correct. There would be no fine dresses and suits for them to masquerade in as intelligent whites. And if that was so, as it should have been, he believed with all his heart that he would still be master of his father's hard earned fortune. But the world continued spinning and would never again spin in the opposite direction, no matter how hard he and his stump wished it would. The niggahs had been given their freedom and the world was worse for it, he thought and preached to every white that gave him a moment's time. He reasoned that he was a prime example of their hate for whites, he who had saved them from a life of depravity.

His head swam inside and out; bobbing up and down as the bourbon once again took control of his thoughts and swept away carefully placed dividers. To that same night the bourbon always took him, as if by force. It never let him forget the insult upon his hand. Back again to that same memory . . . to the same faces of murdered friends and unpunished foes . . . to the rusty hacksaw . . . *to her!*

Even without the bourbon, his stump– hard, reddened and raw appearing . . . lifeless– never let him dispel that memory. The faces of the slaves who'd taken his hand had never dulled in his thoughts. The names of those former slaves of his father who had done it were unforgettable . . . Richard . . . Abel . . . Oliver . . . or were they really called Beelzebub, Asmodeus and Lucifer, he wondered. They were field-slaves he'd seen as a child. Before, when they were still property of his father, they were just one of many black, sweaty face niggahs to look down upon as he'd strode through the fields perched high upon his white horse. But in their vicious act of revenge, they became more than just nameless, faceless niggahs that night to him. The stump they left him with, he realized, was a constant reminder of what his life would never be.

But . . . Beatrice.

She would eventually marry, but not well, he figured. Her choice of suitors had dwindled considerably to a few sons of middling businessmen in towns near Folsom. In the end, it would be what her bridegroom was to inherit. Marriage wasn't going to provide an upward lift in society for her or for the Monclair name, not in these times, he thought.

But at least in her there was hope, his drunken mind thought and brightened his mood for a moment. Beatrice was strong willed and feisty, like a Monclair woman should be– sly as the devil too. Though he would never admit it to her, he respected her ruses. She was a mirror of his own sinewy, leathery heart pounding away, he saw. He knew her lies all too well. And when it suited his fancy to play along with her, as happened to be the case with Paul weeks ago, he was more than eager to indulge her.

It didn't bother him at all that much that she wasn't pretty– barely plain was a stretch, he appraised. She wasn't thin or charming, but she was female, crafty and most importantly– white. The color of her skin would assure she fared better in this life than *It* ever would, he was certain. What mattered was that she was born wrapped in her best asset. Notwithstanding her appearance, she was a true Monclair lady in his eyes.

She would survive the worst adversity come her way. And during times of calm, which he couldn't see coming anytime soon with niggahs running wild and demanding rights meant for whites, she could advance herself by way of her white skin, cunning and cunt, if she learned how to use it judiciously.

But the boy? It? 'Never!' he grumbled.

It would fall before It even stood, he predicted. The world would despise It even more than he did, if not more so– he wished. The only direction in Its life would be down. Fate, he was certain, would see that It fell into flames and Beatrice was lifted into the clouds . . . and the Monclair name could slip into obscurity instead of ruin.

Simeon laid his liquor-laden head on the desk. The blurriness of reality became thicker as his strength waned. He relaxed and answered the call that beckoned him to sleep . . . a restless dream swept over him . . . one full of niggahs, hacksaws and naked handsome men.

CHAPTER 14

Mary was wary of the handsome man standing on her porch
early on a Saturday morning– he was white after all. She'd seen
him once before from a distance at the Monclair store. Now close
enough, she was able to verify with certainty that her first assessment of him was absolutely correct– he was indeed nice to look
upon. Had his thin nose been a bit wider . . . his thin, pink lips
fuller, and his olive skin a nice cinnamon hue, she would have
judged him almost as handsome as Lar. But despite all of his short-
comings, she understood why white ladies, *and Paul*, swooned at
the sight of him.

He tipped his black-banded, white hat at her. "I'm lookin' for
Lar Cole, ma'am," he inquired.

Mary recalled Lar mentioning a white northerner might be coming to look at the Negroes he needed for a business, but he hadn't
mentioned it was *this* white man. But then again, why would Lar
bother describing him? Mary reasoned. To Lar, he was just another
white man, she figured. To a woman, Negroe or white, he was a
wee bit more than that. He was like Paul, she thought, so uncom-
monly striking, it was impossible *not* to notice him.

Mary brazenly looked him over from brown shoes to sun-
tanned face. He wasn't in Folsom proper, and that made all the difference to her. He could expect to command respect in the dusty,

white haven across the bridge, but she felt he forfeited his white-right to slave-like respect from her the moment he stepped onto her porch. "Lar comin' 'bout shortly," she replied. "He work up at the church every Saturday mornin'. He expectin' you?"

Nicholas smiled. "Yes, ma'am."

Ma'am?

"This is the time we agreed upon," he explained.

"If Lar said he be here, then he be here," she replied.

Nicholas nodded. "I'm sure, Mrs. Cole. If I'm not imposin' too much, may I have a drink from your well– if you have one?" He pulled at his sweat soaked shirt.

"It 'round back here," she told him. She moved past him and carefully stepped down the two stairs of the porch. She could hear him following close behind as they went around the shack to the backyard, which was a tapestry of green been plants, collard and mustard greens, tomatoes and black-eye peas.

Next to her clothesline, she pointed to the iron pump sticking out of the ground. Though it was askew– as if someone had tried yanking it out and finally given up– it had more than served its purpose for years. She reached down for the tin cup next to it, and then paused before standing back up empty-handed. "I ain't got no other drinkin' cup . . . you gonna have to use your hands if you want a drink," she said unapologetically.

Nicholas picked up the cup. "If you don't mind . . . I don't at all."

Mary searched out his eyes as he raised his cup of water and drank. They– two white-washed emeralds, sparkled back at her. There were only a few times in her life she could recollect being unable to find words to speak. Not even Lar's proposal of marriage so soon after his break-up with Maggie Mae had rendered her mute. But today . . . this Saturday, out back with this handsome white man drinking from a cup that he more than knew at some point had had a Negroes lips on it, did what Lar had been incapable of doing. She closed her mouth and stared at him. She debated whether or not to lower her wall lined with spears just a hair lower.

He pumped from the well again and refilled his cup. "Are you all right, Mrs. Cole?"

Mary's brows rose. "I fine as can be. *You* feelin' right?"

He wiped at the drops of water that had escaped his mouth and hung on his chin. He held up the cup and studied it, as though he'd never seen such an object like it before. He looked at her and smiled. "Of course– of course . . . you mean this?" He asked, and held the cup in front of him.

Mary barely managed to blink.

"I do hope you might judge me for me . . . ma'am."

These white folk liars, Mary-girl, she warned herself. *Don't be no fool, now! Watch yo'self!* But he showed nothing of his whiteness– yet. Even the way he walked back to the front of the house and casually sat on the broken down porch was as if he was sitting in a place of familiarity and comfort. She wished he would show something of his evil, white nature so that at least she could dispel the doubts that lingered– a raised voice . . . even a stutter when he said 'Negroe' but was really about to say 'niggah'. *Give me just a bit of somethin'*, she pleaded silently.

Nicholas stood and nodded towards a figure approaching in the distance. "Might I inquire if that is Mr. Cole?" he asked.

Mary followed his gaze to the heat hazy-figure approaching with the hat. At this distance, it could be anyone. But Mary was more than familiar with her husband's sturdy gait and the slight bob of his head to either side when he walked. "That be him," she said. Nicholas clasped his hands together and smiled, which made Mary even more suspicious of him. The baby stirred in agreement with her.

Lar smiled at her, and then at Nicholas, which she didn't like at all. Nicholas' hand was the first outstretched in greeting, and Lar responded likewise, though Mary could tell he, like her, was a bit taken aback by the gesture. Once again, this Nicholas Barrons– this white man, had done the unexpected, she saw. White men in Folsom or Peak Hills, or any other place she knew of wouldn't dare touch a Negroe in such a way. Yet, Nicholas did just that. And it wasn't just his willingness to shake Lar's hand, but doing so in such close proximity to him, as if they were . . . were . . . *friends?*

"Mr. Cole," Nicholas said, still holding on to Lar's hand, "so glad to see you again. Your wife has been kind enough to bear with me."

They both looked at her and smiled. Mary hated moments such as these. They expected a smile from her, which she didn't want to give, though did so reluctantly while chiding herself for having done it. She wasn't pleased with why Nicholas had come in the first place– but Lar obviously was. Lar was far too trusting of people, Negroe and white, she thought. Her memories, and those given by her ancestors told her that a white face– especially a white face, could never be trusted. It was just their nature to lie and cheat, beat and murder, destroy and steal, and then once what was good was no more, they would claim innocence and point accusatory fingers to anyone who wasn't white to justify their rise from the ashes they left behind.

She turned away from them and released her mouth from its forced smile. She returned inside the shack and to thoughts that had been weighing upon her before Nicholas knocked at the door. However, her attention was now divided. Muffled talk outside from Lar and Nicholas mixed with more pressing issues in her head. There was no use in constantly reliving the last visit with Enda Sully, she figured. Picking apart Enda's words still gave her no more insight about her child. No matter how she repositioned Enda's latest words . . . *She's going to come into this world healthy and living*, she couldn't forget Enda's previous warning after her last stillborn child, . . . *Don't you have one . . . more . . . child. You hear me, Mary Cole?*

There had been no more blood in her drawers since the last time, though she couldn't help but feel the chill of death nearby. She knew Enda's very words could be as potent as the roots she boiled in her pots and salves she kept inside jars on the shelf. She tried convincing herself that if she wanted the child bad enough, then she and Lar *would* have a living child. But a thought lingered in the corner of her mind, and one she absolutely refused to ponder on for very long, for she had heard and seen it countless times with her own ears and eyes . . . Enda Sully, the Witch of Folsom, had never been wrong yet.

The door creaked open and Lar poked his head in. "We goin' out and 'bout now, Mary. You wanna come with us?"

Mary pushed herself up from the table. "I 'spose I needin' to fetch Uncle Matty. He ain't got no business out in that heat no way. I shouldn't have let him went with you in the first place."

Lar came into the room and closed the door halfway. He smiled at her, which was all it took to calm her. "He ain't done nuthin' all day 'cept sittin' in the shade. He just wanna be a part of thangs and feel useful is all."

"All in all though, Lar, he needin' some food in his belly and rest in a bed. Soon as I find my headscarf I be ready."

Lar snickered and pointed to the top of her head. "If it had been a snake, it would've bit ya."

Mary stopped, turned and then stared at him in confusion. He smiled and jiggled his eyebrows up several times. Mary touched the top of her head. "Dammit!" She whispered, feeling her headscarf already on her head and knotted in the back.

* * *

Nicholas walked to the passenger's side of the wagon and offered Mary a hand up. Mary paused and stared at his white hand,
and then at his white face. She couldn't remember *ever* having
touched a white man's hand except for the boys– Paul and David,
or Simeon's by accident when serving him food. And now here
was this white hand offering to touch hers purposefully.

"It is *your* wagon, Mrs. Cole," he offered. "Even if it weren't,
you're in a delicate condition– please." He edged his hand closer.

She studied her hand as it took hold of his. Rarely had she ever
paid much attention to her own hands other than to notice that
they looked as if they belonged to a man who worked laying railroad tracks. The contrast between the two was more than just dark
brown and white. Her hand on his– it was a gnarled branch lying
upon fresh fallen snow. But the snow her branch lay upon was not
cold, but was warm and exuded vitality in its firm grip.

She rode along without speaking . . . Lar and Nicholas were carrying on well enough without her opinions, she guessed. Her eyes
soaked in what was already familiar to her as the men spoke. She
looked at what she had seen thousands upon thousands of times,
but from a far different perspective this time.

Lar was enlightening Nicholas about the Negroe men and
women who lived in Folsom . . . their hopes and dreams, and willingness to work as hard as need-be to attain such. What Mary saw
through pessimistic eyes was clearly different. Underneath the
smiles of the little ones who played with sticks and ropes in the
road, which at times was little more than a worn path, she saw
only a life of despair for them. She knew they smiled and giggled
because they weren't yet aware of the hard life that lay ahead
them, nor of the grueling life of slavery that preceded them. As
children, they had the luxury of living in a blissful dream-state–
for now. In time, as they aged and became a vested Negroe within
a white world, they would then understand how innocent and
foolish they had once been to have dreams at all. They laughed,

she thought, because thus far, they had only known the sting of a switch from their mother or father, not the backhand or whip of a white man. They skipped along gingerly and waved to her and Lar, and stared awkwardly at the white man sitting in the rear of the wagon, only because they didn't yet know they had to run from white men who were always searching for sturdy trees to hang them from.

"This be where most of us live," Lar said. "This the first section we carved out when we got here– that why it be so crowded."

"But you and Mrs. Cole live further out," Nicholas stated.

"Yes suh, that true," Lar said. "My family been in these parts for a time since the war, but Mary's people come later. That how come me and Mary live out by the river."

"Its Mrs. Cole's house then?" Nicholas asked.

Mary turned around to face him. "It be our house now." Nicholas smiled at her, which made her quickly turn away.

Lar slowed the cart and pointed off to the left where a row of shacks stood. The light of day showed them for what they truly were ... large boxes made of mix-matched wood and sheets of rusted tin. Most leaned one way or the other, while very few stood in a semblance of uprightness. "These be the first Negroe homes here– right Mary?"

She nodded.

"But if you look over there, Mr. Barrons," Lar urged, and pointed in the opposite direction to larger plots of cleared forest-land. "Some of us is buildin' new homes with better pieces of lumber so they won't leak when it rain, and can keep the hot and cold out. As folk can get the wood chopped and cut, we all help build it bit by bit. But you know times be real tough."

"'Specially if you be Negroe," Mary added, without looking at either one.

But Lar did look at her. "*Mary!*" He scolded, and lowered his eyelids at her.

She let his voice pass by her ears as benignly as a summer breeze, when it's summer and breezy.

"But you're right, Mrs. Cole," Nicholas replied, as though neither surprised, or offended. "I've seen it firsthand. We cannot deny the obvious, can we?"

Mary saw that Lar was wearing the same expression as she . . . utter surprise. Peripherally, she eyed Nicholas while looking back at the semblance of a town she lived in. Brown, black and light-skinned bodies were in motion all around them, as it was on any given Saturday morning. Some were plowing their fields or picking vegetables for supper, or ones they could take to market. Men were patching holes on their shacks and women, holes in britches. The ghostly black faces they passed by gave and returned cheerful waves of greeting. But the smiles they had for Lar and Mary quickly disappeared when they spotted the white man in the wagon with them. Grins soon turned to lips pursed in suspicion. Eyes that had momentarily widened and sparkled in greeting, hid under shuttered eyelids.

Jonnie Ray and four of his eight children in tow like ducklings were on the opposite side of the street by Pete Baker's black-smithing shack. He and Michael, his oldest of almost twenty, called and waved. As Mary and Lar returned the greeting, Johnnie Ray's eyes darted to Nicholas in the back of the wagon. His hand immediately dropped, as did his lower lip.

Mary could see the confusion in all the faces of the people they passed. The same question seemed to be poised on everyone's lips – 'What they be doin' with that white man? Who he be?' Women she'd grown-up and shared lifelong secrets with, suddenly shunned her. Men that Lar worked with shoulder to shoulder, mixing his sweat with theirs day in and day out, looked the other way.

Mary couldn't resist the urge to smile just a little. She glanced at Nicholas. In her smirk, she wanted him to feel what it was like to be stared at with repulsion, or even worse, not regarded at all. *She wanted* this *white man* to feel– if only for a short while, what she and her Negroe people felt every time they were in Folsom around white folks. *She wanted* the feeling of being despised to stab at his heart and blot his soul with a cancer. *She wanted* him to feel as though he was suffocating on the very air meant for living. *She wanted* him to feel like they did . . . that if they suddenly dropped dead in the center of town, no one would notice it, lest care about it, that is unless the body was in their way and they had to step around it.

Mary, however, didn't get what *she wanted* from Nicholas.

What she got was the opposite of all that she hoped for. His head was turning from one side to the other– smiling and nodding to all whose eye he could catch before they looked away. She saw no disappointment in his face when they refused to return his silent good wishes. Still, he seemed as content and comfortable now, as he was while sitting on her doorstep just a short while ago. He looked up at her and showed his beautiful, toothy smile. She was staring at him, but only realized that she was when he spoke to her.

"I know exactly *who I am* and *where I am*, Mrs. Cole."

* * *

"Uncle Matty . . . wake up now. Time to head on home," Mary told him.

Uncle Matty stirred in his chair. His wrinkled eyelids fluttered to let his eyes adjust to the light of sun that was peeking through the willow's lazy arms. "Chile– I was gettin' but some good sleep, huh?"

"Yes, suh. Just'a snorin' away," she responded warmly. She saw herself in him, only it was he bending over her, grasping her chin and waking her gently. *"Up-up-up, chile,"* she could still hear him saying, yet his voice was stronger then. *"Gosta get goin' now and feed them chickens 'fore they starve and we along wit'em,"* she re-

membered him joking with her every morning. And though she
called him uncle– as did everyone, her heart never did, for he was
far more to her than that.

Even before she could attempt to assist him out of the chair,
there were two men quickly on each side of Uncle Matty to
assist . . . Frank Clipper and Sam Latter. Both men were slightly
larger than she. Each was equally sweat drenched from hauling
and sawing lumber for the church no more than thirty feet from
them.

"Uncle Matty . . . here we go now," Frank warned.

"On'a 'three'– right?" Sam instructed.

Uncle Matty growled as he was lifted, and groaned as they carried him over and sat him in the wagon. Frank offered and then assisted Mary into the wagon. "Want me to ride back witcha, Ms.
Mary and help get Uncle Matty off?" Though Frank seemed to lack
cheekbones, the lack of contour to his face was somewhat handsome when taken together with his near, true black skin, tiny nose
and pure whites of his eyes.

"No, suh," Mary responded thankfully. "Gettin' down a whole
lot easier than gettin' up. He be strong enough once we get home."

"You come back quick now, Uncle Matty," Sam said, as he wiped
the sweat from his rather large forehead. "These shiftless Negroes
here needin' a push and shove to keep'em movin'."

Uncle Matty smiled sleepily. "I bring my switches next time.
Whup some rump if I need to."

Frank laughed. "You do that then."

Mary smirked. "Alright ya'll . . . he been done did it too."

Mary steered the wagon toward the shell of a church. Lar and
Nicholas were standing near the wood-line. A couple of Negroes
had gathered near them, but not too close, she noticed, as they obviously were feeling apprehensive about Nicholas like she was. But

Lar was with the white man, and that, she knew, meant a world of difference. If Lar trusted Nicholas, the others would follow suit eventually.

"Who that mulatto next ta' Lar?" Uncle Matty asked, squinting harshly through his cataracts. "I ain't never seen that niggah round here before. He be from Peak Hills or somethin'. And why he all dressed up for Sunday when it ain't . . . or is it?"

"Naw– it still Saturday, uncle," she replied, while motioning for Lar to come over. "That just some ol' white man from up north come sneakin' 'round."

"Sneakin?" Uncle Matty asked. "Why he sneakin' 'round us for?"

"Not sneakin', Uncle Matty . . . I meant just nosin'– kinda."

Uncle Matty huffed. "All the same in my book."

Lar reached the wagon before Mary could explain further. "You goin' on home now?" he asked.

"Just to drop Uncle Matty off and settle him in 'fore I head in to see 'bout them Monclair's."

Lar was smiling. "When you comin' back?"

Mary sensed anxiousness. "When I done . . . same as always," she said dryly. "Isabel wantin' a big supper tonight. Guests or fam-ily stoppin' in . . . I don't know and really don't care a lick. I be as quick as I can, 'specially this bein' my Saturday."

"Alright," he said, and then looked behind. The two men who had ventured closer to Nicholas were actually speaking with him now.

"Mary said that white man nosin' 'round," Uncle Matty said, breaking the silence. "What he nosin' for, Lar?"

"I said he ain't nosin'," Mary interjected, somewhat perturbed. "He just . . ."

"He *is* nosin'," Lar said, his voice edging with excitement. "And for a mighty good reason, too."

"What you mean?" Mary asked.

Lar grinned and began walking backwards. "I can't explain it right now. I tell you 'bout it when you get home."

"Lar . . . Laurence Cole! Get your tail back here. What you talkin' 'bout?"

Lar kept walking and smiling. "Justice," he called out.

"Lar."

"Justice, Mary," he sang.

Nicholas waved to her. She responded with a snap of the reigns to the horse's back.

"What ya'll talkin' 'bout?" Uncle Matty demanded. "Ain't nobody give me a answer yet."

"When I get one, I tell you all 'bout it," she huffed.

* * *

Uncle Matty had only eaten a little of the black-eyed peas and cornbread she fixed for him, and then pushed the tin plate away. Goading him into eating a few more morsels was of no use. She knew he was as stubborn as she was, just as he refused to lie in bed for a nap and insisted on sitting on the porch. She could see his last days drawing near in his eyes . . . see it in his parched skin . . . hear his recognition of death following him in his voice. Her hope of Uncle Matty holding her child dimmed even further.

Once Mary had Uncle Matty seated in the rocking chair on the porch, she took off for Folsom. She passed by a few Negroes on her way to the Monclair home . . . Marcus Holley, Larry Addams, Jeffy Marks and his wife Aba Mae. They all inquired about the health of the baby, so she lied in reply. "Just fine . . . thank ya." Their carts were already empty of crops they had sold to Monclair's market, yet there were no smiles on their faces as they passed by. Their pockets were only slightly heavier now than when they'd come, she was sure.

She arrived at the Monclair home, and surprisingly she saw Paul with sickle in hand chopping down brown, dead grass out front by the gate. He looked up as the wagon approached, and then stopped and leaned on the handle. Even at a distance, Mary could see the pain he still carried. His breaths were angry waves rolling up and down his chest and stomach. Though he smiled, it seemed forced, but genuine. And as she drew closer, she could tell that the bruises on his face were all but gone, but she knew pain lurked beneath the surface and had settled into a new home called the heart. Without being asked, he guided the horse and wagon through the side-gate and secured it to the post by the shed. He postured to help her down from the wagon. "I can manage fine, Paul– thank ya," she told him. "You well enough to be out here workin'?" Mary asked, as she walked toward the rear of the house. Paul was no more than a step behind her.

"Well enough for my father," Paul responded, with a dead tone he used whenever he referred to Simeon.

The backyard was full of sunbathing felines. Two were on the small wooden bench near the entrance to the garden; another was on its back in the grass, and still two more were stalking the back-door waiting to enter. Plyus darted from under a shrub near the door and wrapped his body around Mary's leg. He purred when Mary looked down at him, as if he was waiting for her to pick him up.

"Shoo now!" Mary demanded, as he began inching his tail up her leg. Plyus simply looked at her in bewilderment. Paul stepped around her, gathered up Plyus and gently pitched him away. When Paul stood back up, he quickly grabbed at the side of his chest. "What be wrong, Paul?" Mary asked, already knowing.

"Just a twang," he said, through clenched teeth. "Good thing is that . . . it feels . . ." he stopped and caught his breath, " . . . better than it did yesterday."

Right then, Mary desperately wanted to pull him close to her chest. He was being as brave as he could be, but it was not enough, she knew. He was always a frail child in mind and body. She had figured the beating and discovery of his secret was probably more than he could bear. Yet, he still stood, she thought proudly. She guessed Simeon hadn't beaten *all* the strength and will from him yet.

"Come'on and have a seat with me," she told him. "I wanna rest my feet a spell 'fore I get messin' 'round in this kitchen. Then I gotta up and leave quick-like and fix some food for Lar and Uncle Matty 'fore the sun decide it comin' on down. How I gonna do it all, I don't know, chile. But I know right now I gonna rest my feet." She glanced at the empty chair by the wall and then back at Paul. He accepted her invitation.

"Mother didn't tell you?" Paul asked.

"Tell me what?"

Paul looked down.

"What you sayin', chile? C'mon now."

"Mother needs you to stay and serve," he said sorrowfully.

Mary chomped down on her lower lip. "Well, I know your mammy asked for a big supper, but she ain't said nuthin' 'bout stayin' and servin'. Where she be?"

"In town with Beatrice . . . father took them."

Mary sat down in the chair opposite of Paul. They looked at each other in silence for a while before she stood and pitifully shook her head. She took her apron from the hook on the back of the kitchen door leading to the dining room and secured it around her waist. Paul walked into the small storage room adjacent to the kitchen and returned with two buckets full of split wood. "I gathered these up this morning for you."

"That was mighty nice of you, Paul," she replied, and then smiled at him. "You best run and finish up that front yard now. *You* know your pappy as well as *me* if it ain't finished."

He shrugged. "A few more whacks and it'll be done. I can stay and help you if you want."

Mary had her back to him as she retrieved a cast-iron skillet from the cabinet. "You got somewhere to be?"

A telling moment of silence followed before he responded. "Kinda."

She began putting wood into the stove. "Alright then . . . alright. You be back well ahead 'fore suppertime so you can wash-up and comb your hair right. *Well ahead*– hear me?"

"You sure, Ms. Mary?"

"Sure as sure."

"I . . . I mean . . . you know . . ."

"No, chile– I don't know." She was looking for the long handle matches, and then huffed, realizing she had already put them in the pocket of her apron.

"It's just that . . . that . . . David said you went to the witch . . . Ms. . . . . Ms. Sully's place? You went to see about the baby."

"Everythang be fine," she assured him, with a raised brow in hope of ending the matter right there. "I be just fine," she growled.

He looked at her. "Really?"

She admonished herself for having raised her voice at him, knowing that he asked only out of absolute concern. "Come here, boy," she said. "Hurry! Give me yo' hand!" Mary took it and placed it on her belly. "You feel it?"

Paul's face went slack. *"Yes!"* He gasped.

Without warning, he placed the side of his face on her belly. She was shocked, but not alarmed. In fact, she found it delightfully comforting. Only Lar had done such a thing. Yet, here was Paul in the same position as Lar was every morning and night. Another sigh escaped his lips, and as it did, his arms moved up and wrapped around what used to be her waist, though he was far from encircling her. She returned the gesture and stroked his hair, which Paul responded by squeezing her even tighter. As suddenly as he came to her, he pulled away and turned around. She knew he had just shared the same feeling she did. When he spoke, as he walked to the back door, his voice crackled. "I'll be back soon, Ms. Mary."

Mary didn't respond, knowing her voice would also waver.

* * *

The baby squirmed inside of her and Mary loved it.

The sharp, acrid scent of boiled collards and steamed cabbage would have been choking if it didn't smelled so appetizing. The chicken she'd butchered was in the oven sizzling in its own juices and spices. The batter for the apple-spice cake was whipped smooth, poured into a pan and ready to bake once the oven was free. And Mary, now sitting and resting her heels upon a chair, wrapped her arms across her belly.

She dozed in the chair. But her brief moment of rest was just that. Her ears picked up the sound of a wagon . . . one that failed to pass on by. Half asleep, she could hear its wooden wheels grinding the rocks into the dirt beneath them. She didn't bother peeking out the back window. She figured, whoever it was would have to be seen sooner or later, whether it was Isabel and that brat of child, Beatrice or the old bastard Simeon himself. But at that moment, she didn't care who it was. Finishing up at the Monclair's was all she wanted now. The thought of a soft bed– though hers was any-thing but soft, it was close enough– to lie in with Lar pressed up to her backside suddenly made her all the more anxious to get home.

She got up and shuffled to the front door, but it was already opening. Isabel popped through first, obviously delighted for some reason. She looked at Mary and smiled. Mary hadn't seen her beam so much except when she was daydreaming that Stephen Allister hadn't died in the war and she didn't have to grit her teeth and say 'I do', instead of 'I will not!' marry Simeon.

"I'm so glad to see . . .," Isabel stopped abruptly. "Oh– the food smells so good." She closed her parasol and handed it to Mary. "Are you making a sweet cake too?"

"Yes'm," Mary replied unenthused.

"What kind, Ms. Mary?" Beatrice asked, slipping past her mother's ample hips and handing Mary her parasol also.

Ms. Mary, is it now? Mary thought suspiciously. In the weeks since Paul's beating, she'd noticed quite a change in Beatrice. Per- haps it was guilt that was driving Beatrice to seemingly mend her ways. Mary wasn't certain how genuine it was and she really didn't care. The damage to Paul had been done and was irreparable now. In Mary's mind, what she did was out of pure hatefulness. And no second act on Beatrice's part could make her think other- wise. *I hate her more than I hate father. At least Father has a reason for hating me,* she recalled, Paul saying one morning as she cleansed his wounds. *I don't have a sister, Ms. Mary . . . no father . . . and no mother either.*

"Apple-cake, missy," Mary finally replied. Her tone was far from welcoming, nor was it perturbed. Just flat.

Beatrice beamed anyway. "Ohhh– my favorite. This is turning out to be a wonderful day, isn't it mother? First we're in town shopping and were surprised that Allie Mae had finished not one, but two of my dresses. And then . . ."

Isabel couldn't contain herself any longer. "*And then . . . ,*" she gushed. "We were walking out of the store and unexpectedly, we ran into . . ."

"Mr. Barrons," Mary finished her thought for her. Both women stared at her in wonder.

With Isabel and Beatrice practically bursting in and full of schoolgirl chatter, initially Mary hadn't noticed Nicholas pulling boxes from the back of the wagon. While the women were busy inundating her with their ramblings, Nicholas had balanced the boxes in his arms and was making his way up the front of the porch.

"Good evening," Nicholas said to Mary. His head was barely visible above the neatly tied boxes he was balancing in his arms.

"Evenin', suh," Mary responded coldly. She wasn't able to generate a semblance of congeniality while suspicion about him still lurked in her mind. Beatrice and Isabel's delight returned at Nicholas' presence, and they parted, allowing him to pass between their gauntlet of smiles.

"Where shall I put them?" He asked.

Mary stepped forward. "I take them up to missy's room." Nicholas stepped backed. With her back to Isabel and Beatrice, Mary held his gaze privately.

"If you will allow me," Nicholas gently urged, "I'll take them to the top of the stairs." He nodded ever so slightly at Mary.

"There's a blue chair right outside of my room!" Beatrice offered quickly.

"Then– my young miss, that is where you shall find them," Nicholas said, all the while his eyes still locked on Mary's.

Beatrice's face reddened. As Isabel directed him to the stairs, Mary once again assured herself that her initial thought about Nicholas Barrons had been correct ... he was a white woman's dream made flesh, especially for a white woman that was young and very white– inside and out, like Beatrice. Isabel returned shortly. Her approval of Nicholas was evident in her flittering steps, but more so in her moon-shaped face which displayed a smile complete with upper and lower teeth on display. She was about to speak when the back door opened and closed, turning the heads of all three women around. Mary knew who it was and waited for him to appear in the hallway, which he did in a rush, obviously realizing he hadn't come home soon enough. Seeing the women gathered near the front door, he stopped ... his breaths were shallow, his clothes damp and his hair even more so. Beatrice spoke first. "Paul, you're late." Mary expected some additional criticism to follow, as was Beatrice's modus operandi, but to Mary's surprise, none did. "Our guest is already here. You best hurry!" She urged excitedly.

Paul looked at Mary, who nodded in agreement. "You best get washed up quick now," she told him. "Your pappy comin' home soon, I reckon."

"He stayed in town to finish up some business," Beatrice offered. "And Mr. Barrons so kindly offered to take us back home. Isn't that wonderful?"

Isabel's smile, once prominent seconds ago, was nowhere to be seen now. "*He is* on his way here, Paul," she added.

Paul quickly made way for the stairwell. "I got held up," he admitted, but was looking back as he spoke and wasn't paying attention to what or *who* was coming toward him. Mary only glimpsed Nicholas' shadow rounding the corner, but it was too short of a time to warn Paul to stop. She only managed to open her mouth as Paul ran directly into him.

"Whoa there, young man!" Nicholas blurted, as he gently caught Paul by the shoulders and moved him backwards. "Ah-ha," he said approvingly, "you must be the young master of the house . . . Simeon Paul, is it?"

Paul didn't to respond.

With only a view of Paul from behind, Mary knew it was not the run-in that stole Paul's voice, but likely the shock of gazing into a set of eyes nearly as beautiful as his own. She spoke quickly to break Nicholas's spell over him. "Everyone call him Paul, suh. *Ain't that right, Paul?*" She asked loud enough to gather Paul's attention.

Paul turned and stared at her with glassy blue eyes. It seemed to Mary as though minutes passed before Paul spoke. He stepped back and offered Nicholas his hand. "Paul, suh," he said finally.

Mary silently sighed in relief.

Nicholas grinned. "A fine, handsome young man," he announced. "I can see your father in you. I'm sure the ladies bicker and fight amongst themselves whenever you're near."

"Yes, suh. Thank you, suh," Paul responded, and displayed a toothy smile before quickly turning it into just a tight-lipped grin.

It was the first act Mary had seen Paul perform that gave her hope for him out in the world. A simple misspeak could have reignited embers of suspicion about him, but Paul extinguished them before a glow could start.

"Please proceed," Nicholas insisted. He stepped to the side and let Paul pass by.

"I can show Mr. Barrons to the sitting room if you want, Ms. Isabel," Mary offered.

"We can do that," Beatrice piped up. "I'm sure Mr. Barrons would like a drink before supper. I always prepare one for father when he returns from work." Which was a lie, Mary knew. Even Isabel widened her eyes momentarily, but eventually smiled and nonetheless agreed.

Mary waited until the trio was down the hall and out of her line of sight, but instead of returning to the kitchen, she maneuvered up the stairs to Paul's room. She walked in without knocking and caught him completely bare and bent over his washbasin sponging under his arms. He spun around in alarm at first, but seeing who it was, turned back around and continued washing.

Mary didn't care either that all of his personal business was exposed. To her, he was still just a boy . . . a child, and no matter how old he became, would always be so in her eyes and heart. Only, today she sensed something different about him. She detected the budding of a man within him, not the toddler who begged to be snuggled so that he could suckle her milk on his way to sleep.

She crossed the distance, took him in her arms and pulled him in tight. "Yes . . . yes-yes!" She whispered.

"*Ms. Mary!*" He whined playfully, embarrassed at the praise.

She held him tight for a few moments more. "You *do* got mo' sense than a rattlesnake."

* * *

One thing Paul felt he'd just learned was that he too had the power, like Beatrice, to fool people. Though it had been just one person– Nicholas Barrons, who was now sitting across from him dining on herbed chicken, he still claimed it as a monumental feat. If there was one person who had the ability to take his breath away, it was Nicholas– and he had . . . just like the first time Paul recalled seeing him outside of the Monclair store.

He was certain after the run-in earlier, and then reassured by Mary shortly thereafter, that Nicholas saw nothing more in his stare than a startled boy. He was confident he'd masked the heat emanating from his eyes, for Nicholas was not hard to look at or stare at in wonder, like he saw Beatrice doing at the very moment. But for all of Nicholas' physical beauty and gentlemanly charm, Paul knew his heart only held love and passion for David.

Beatrice on the other hand, he saw, was almost comical in her desire to mate. Yet, his reason for craving men was far, far different than hers. In David's *male flesh* . . . he found warmth, acceptance, comfort, and strangely, a sense of invulnerability, as well as a vulnerability that produced an achingly, peaceful love that was impossible to explain. In men, it seemed to him that Beatrice saw only opportunity.

He dismissed her chameleonic change toward him since the beating. Her empathy filled voice meant nothing to him. Her heartfelt apologies, complete with tears, seemed more like lines she was reading from a script. To him, she was but their father . . . only female, younger and more conniving. He knew she still didn't understand that her teasing and threats of revealing who he was were as painful as any blow their father had given him. Though now, a true 'sister' she claimed she wanted to be to him. But past the blues of her eyes, he saw only his father staring back, attempting to lull him into a false sense of security before the next strike.

For the time being, at least, her aim was directed toward another. Nicholas was who she had in her sights . . . his good looks and worldly charm, as well as his unspoken of, but assumed vast amount of familial money *and status*. Throughout dinner, he listened intently as she peppered Nicholas with questions about his past, his family, all to discover if there was a possible beloved who had his heart. But of all the questions answered, Paul noticed, the one of a lover was never divulged. The evasion of that question only seemed to embolden Beatrice's desire to probe further. He knew she wouldn't cease until the answer was to her satisfaction, one way or another.

But there was much more on his mind at the moment than his sister's shameless flirting. He now knew he could be sharp, and even witty when he had to. Nicholas had not only included him in the dinner conversation, but even asked his opinion on topics to his father's displeasure and Beatrice's jealously that she hadn't been asked hers. Though he felt emboldened by the earlier encounter, he was thankful Mary was nearby. As she served each course of the meal, occasionally he would catch her eye. Though she remained like granite, he deciphered the messages conveyed by her dark brown eyes, saying what her mouth was unable to. *Don't look down or away when the man talks to you . . . look him dead in his eyes, but don't stare . . . answer strong! You're a man now, Paul . . . a real man! Act like one. He's not going to know about you unless you give him a reason to start wondering. Fool him like you did before . . . fool them all! Be a good boy for me—my good boy.*

And he did his best to obey. Even with the hateful glances his father sent his way, who refused to even look at him since the beating, he forced himself to smile and answer Nicholas' questions. Of all the questions asked though, only one gave him pause.

"And how do you feel, young suh, about the Negroe situation here in Folsom?" Nicholas asked. He wiped the crumbs of apple-cake from his lips. He turned to Simeon and Isabel, and then back to Paul who was sitting across from him next to Beatrice. "I'm always so interested in the views of our youth– those yet untouched by the ways of this uncertain world," he added.

Paul felt as though his skin was shrinking on his bones as Simeon glared at him. Nevertheless, he remembered and did as Mary's eyes told him to. *Sit up straight ... look him in the eye.* "There's no *Negroe situation* here, as far as I know, suh," Paul responded. "There's no discord between white and Negroe." He then looked to and away from his father before Simeon could show his displeasure for him even existing, let alone daring to give his opinion on such a matter.

Nicholas nodded. " *'Discord'* ... I like that, young suh. Nicely put. So far, your opinion has also been mine."

"I think trouble finds those who go looking for it," Paul continued, with a budding pride in his tone. "Folsom Negroes are good folk."

Simeon dropped his fork on his plate, one of the few of his family's heirlooms that wasn't looted during the war. The 'clink-clang' startled all but Nicholas who simply looked in the direction of the sound. "And what of those lyin', cheatin', thievin' and rapin' niggahs," Simeon spat, gargling the last word in his throat, "the ones over in Peak Hills?" He asked of Paul.

Paul looked directly at Simeon for the first time since they sat down to eat. Simeon had issued a challenge. It was unspoken, but clearly written upon his forehead, in the folds around his eyes and mouth, and in the leathery wrinkles of his neck. Paul fought the urge to shudder. Out of sight, underneath the linen covered table, his right foot tapped furiously in remembrance of the stumped hand descending upon him that night weeks ago . . . the blows to his face and groin . . . the hate in his father's voice as he swung . . . swung . . . and pummeled his flesh to mush.

When Paul spoke, his voice trembled. He was embarrassed, but nevertheless, he was proud that it still worked. "I've-I've . . . heard a few different stories about what happened in Peak Hills . . . father. The boys at school claim they knew. Only . . . father . . . each story about what led to the lynching was different than the next. First they said the father was the rapist, and then the son, and then they were both rapists . . . or-or . . . or it was because the boy stole something . . . but-but then it was the father who was stealing. And then . . . and then . . . I heard it was because the father was arguing with a white man over the price of crops he was trying to sell him. The only part of the story that stayed the same was the lynching itself."

Simeon leaned back in his chair and then placed his stump– red and angry as it was, on the table for all to see. Paul's left foot joined his right in a nervous dance. "You think *them* innocent of *anything*," Simeon stated. "What you fail to see is that there's truth in the many versions you've heard. Regardless, a crime was committed and punishment was doled out to match it. As it should be."

Paul looked down for a moment, yet as his head rose, so did his voice. "Torn apart, father," he retorted. "*Everyone* agrees they tore the boy limb from limb. *No one* agrees why they did it."

Isabel gasped. "Dear God, Paul! Did you really have to say that . . . and at supper?"

"It really isn't polite conversation, Paul," Beatrice added, and then quickly covered her mouth, as though she was about to regurgitate.

Paul's head snapped to the side. His blue eyes locked on Beatrice's. "That's the kind of world we live in. It's not polite. It's anything but."

"And what do you know of the world?!" Simeon growled. He leaned over the table and wiped his plate free of cake crumbs with his shirt. "You know nothin' other than Folsom and Peak Hills– if that. All you know is that food appears at the table and clothes appear on your back. You haven't tasted the world, but you sit there and criticize those who protect it to make sure you're provided for."

"Yes, father," Paul agreed. His eyes once again studied his cake, which he hadn't touched yet. Momentarily everyone was silent. But Paul wasn't finished yet. "What my father said *is* true," he said to Nicholas. "I know nothing of my father's world. But what I do know about it, I don't care for. It's an evil place with lots of evil people. And those who are good– or at least try to be– are punished for it . . . it seems."

Simeon's face blanched. He began tapping his stump on the table. "You're finished and excused . . . *boy!*" Simeon uttered, with a tone more akin to the crackle of a tree's branch slowly snapping off in the dead of winter.

Paul left the table. Only to Nicholas did he bid a good evening. Isabel and Beatrice kept their heads down, unwillingly to show him any sign of solidarity. But he expected that.

In his room, at his desk facing the window, he looked out into the retreating light and looming darkness . . . and then looked out into the retreating light and looming darkness *that was coming*. He had no idea if tonight he would be totally alone, or if his father would visit him again with his stump raised at the ready. Regardless, all that mattered to him at the moment was David, Mary, Lar and the little one who was yet to be born. All were of no blood-kin to him, yet in his heart, they felt more like family than his real family ever had.

Despite his father's insistence that he knew nothing of the true world, he did know that because of his love for Mary, Lar and especially for David, the world would never accept or even tolerate

him. He understood very well he would always be considered an
'other' . . . a 'this' or 'that' . . . an 'outcast' . . . a *thing* . . . but
never a man.

No less than a few hours before dinner, covered by the thick-
ness of trees and cloaked in their shade . . . safely as he could be
with David in his arms, he recalled asking David to run away with
him, and then listening to David's nervous response. "What would
we do?" Paul remembered his answer well. It came solely from the
heart without hesitation. "Be together."

They were lying on the ground with only their clothes laid beneath them separating them from the ground. Paul was behind
him, caressing David's hair with one hand and with his arm
wrapped around his waist. In sex they found rapture, but both
knew they had merely scratched the surface of what pleasure
could be shared with one another. But true pleasure for Paul came
from just being close to David. In David's eyes he saw love reflected back. To him, David's voice was not a boy's, or a man's or a
human's, but a virtuoso's magnum opus of longing and lament
crafted for his heart alone. The feel of David's hand was merely an
extension of his own. *'Together'* with David, he felt more fully
awake than he'd ever felt before, and he vowed he would die before he ever slept again.

But life, he felt, had moved past just being bearable.

Life was wonderful when *'together'* with David. Though being
together was a painful joy.

He realized what a fluke it was to have found someone that was
considered as much of an abomination before God as he was. But
he'd already ceased caring about a God who would allow his father
to beat him like he did. He'd already damned God, and damned everyone else who would consider him anything other than a human
being. He figured, if loving a man made him a freak, then he would

be the happiest freak in the world. If the raw scent of a man was more enticing to him than a woman's perfume could ever be, then so be it.

One thing he felt Mary and Lar, and all the other Negroes taught him, but didn't know they had, was that it was possible to survive in a world that didn't want them to survive. 'Blind to the real world,' he remembered his father accusing him of being. Paul laughed. He felt his eyes were more open than most. Just knowing that despite being cheated, beaten and murdered at a whim, the Negroes still went on, gave him hope that he could also. If they, after all they had been through and still faced, were able to find a way to smile and laugh and celebrate and persevere, he knew he and David could also. The Negroes had found a way to keep on living– he was determined to discover their secret. They were alive! *And so am I,* he thought proudly.

"Don't cry no more, Paul." He could still hear David saying. "I . . . I don't like it when you cry. I know you're feelin' mighty sad."

"No . . . not sad," he told David. "They're happy tears. We could just go away, you know. We're going to eventually . . . if . . . if . . ."

"We want to be together," David finished.

"Yeah . . . . It's too dangerous here. And we aren't boys anymore," Paul said. "We're not going to be able to sneak over here for too much longer. The Negroes are going to stop thinking these woods are haunted and start chopping it down for lumber. We're going to have to get away soon."

"What would we do?"

'What would we do?' But the answer for Paul was so much simpler than the actual action of it. There was never a question in his mind or heart, and he vowed there never would be. The ache of hating who he was had been soothed. The pain of never having love was comforted. It was David he loved.

'What would we do?'

"Be together," he replied.

* * *

Paul was nearly asleep when he heard a knock at the front door. It was too late in the evening for anyone respectable to come calling, which was why he quickly rose from his bed. From his window, he was only able to catch a glimpse of a man with a hat walking toward the house. But rumbling on the porch beneath his window told him there were a few men wanting entry. He crept out of his bedroom and to the top of the stairs, and saw that two other men had accompanied the man with the hat.

He tried listening, but was unable to hear what they were saying. He was able to distinguish his father's drunken, slurred voice from the others. As the voices became fainter, he knew they were headed down the hall toward his father's study. An ill feeling suddenly swept over him. It was more than just that his father was being cordial to them, which in his mind, was reason enough to know they were not good men at all, but there was something else he couldn't quite put his finger on. He had no doubt that whatever they were up to in that room was of no good. The world, he knew, was full of evil men.

CHAPTER 15

Though Mary had picked and snacked on food while she was serving at the Monclair's, the collard greens and slice of cornbread Lar set in front of her was too appetizing to resist. With her swollen legs now resting on a chair Lar had pulled up for her, and the bowl of food nestled precariously on her baby-belly, she ate gingerly. The food, however, didn't settle well with her. She could feel something just wasn't right. That female, Negroe sense Enda had always cautioned her to attend to was nagging at her.

She looked across the table at Lar. He hadn't said a word since she began eating. She scooped a spoonful of cornbread drenched in green collard juice into her mouth and then set the bowl on the table. "What the matter?" She asked, to which Lar smiled in reply. "Lar Cole . . . what you grinnin' 'bout?"

Lar shook his head, but didn't stop smiling. "It be some real good news, Mary. Only thing is, you gotta let me finish when I start talkin' – alright. I don't want you fussin' 'bout it . . . least not 'til you done heard everythin'."

Mary put her legs on the ground just in case she needed to steady herself. "Do Uncle Matty know?" She asked, glancing toward his closed room door, though his snoring made it seem as if he was in the same room as they were.

"Naw."

"So if this be such good news, how come Uncle Matty don't know and I ain't 'spose to get mad 'bout it?"

Lar frowned. Mary quickly sat back in her chair. She pursed her lips to demonstrate that she would comply being silent . . . for now. She studied his face, as though it would tell her what the supposed good news was before his mouth did, but nothing could have prepared her for . . .

. . . *Nicholas Barrons . . . not a business man . . . reporter . . . writer . . . lynchings . . . he foolin' them white folk . . . justice and injustice . . . murder . . . Negroes . . . true to us Negroes—not to white folk . . . articles . . . stories . . .*

After Lar's first words, all that followed seemed more to her like the cornbread and greens in her bowl– one big, green blobby goop of mess. Yet through the pounding that had started in her head, she clearly understood what Lar was saying, only, she didn't like any of it one bit.

"He a good man, Mary," Lar insisted. "I know it in my soul. I done prayed and prayed, and prayed some more 'bout this whole thang. White folks been lynchin' Negroes more and more nowadays, and ain't no one done a damn thang 'bout it. No one! Every time the congress get set to outlaw lynchins', these southern white boys knock the head right off of it. But it gonna change with help from folk like Mr. Barrons. When more folk up north, like Mr. Barrons, get wind 'bout how white folk down here goin' 'round killin' Negroes willy-nilly, thangs gonna get movin' to put a stop to it. The Lord seein' to it . . . Now– it may not be the way we want it to be, but it be the Lord's way."

"You can't believe anything he say, Lar. He a white man!" She reminded him, as though he had forgotten.

"They ain't all the same," Lar countered. "He ain't one of them stump-jumpers who ain't ever heard tell of a Negroe, 'cept one who can't read and write. This man know 'bout us as a people who be good and God-fearin'."

Mary shook her head. She couldn't believe what she was hearing, but could believe that Lar was nearing the edge of insanity, if not already having taken the plunge off its cliff. "It be a trick. What kinda trick it be, I don't know– but it be one."

"He true, Mary."

"He white!" She snapped back. "And if he white, that tell you right there he ain't for us Negroes. None of them is. It a trick, Lar. And it gonna get you and me, and everybody else talkin' to him in a whole heap of mess we ain't gonna be able to get out of." She closed her eyes and slowly drew in a lung-full of stagnant air heavy with the scent of boiled greens. Woozy feeling and now seething at Lar's foolish trustworthiness, she felt more nauseous than she had during the first few months of her pregnancy. "Say it all be true," she offered, while pushing her supper back down to her stomach where it refused to settle. "What you think them white folks'll do to all us if they find out? Huh? Hmmm? Ain't no article in some northern paper gonna stop'em neither."

Lar bowed his head. Mary felt as though she had finally struck some sense into him. In silence, she couldn't help but feel as though she'd won the argument, though she didn't feel victorious. She'd always thought his trust and blind faith in God was his greatest weakness, but best virtue. To leave things be as they were was for the best, she thought.

Lar pushed away from the table and stood with his back to her. "Mary . . ." he began.

"Lar– I know you want this," she said softly. "I know you do . . . real bad. But it be the right thing not to do . . ."

"Mary, stop it! *Right now!*" He faced her. His eyes shimmered in the soft glow of candlelight. "I ain't a dog. I'm me . . . a man . . . Laurence Cole . . . and the decision to do this be mine, not yours. You ain't gotta talk to him"

"Then you gonna end up bein' a dead *Laurence Cole*," she sassed.

Lar sat back down and crossed his arms. "If it be the Lord's will, then I just be dead when all is said and done," he told her. "But I don't believe it gonna be that way." He leaned over the table toward her. "Folk gotta know 'bout all this mess one way or another – murderin' and the rapin', and the stealin' and cheatin' they do to us. We can't even get a decent job, 'cause they give it to the lowest white man 'fore they even look at the best Negroe. White folk'll burn your crops to ash 'fore they see you doin' a hair better than them. This be somethin' I have to do."

Mary refused to look at him. His words were drowning her. She attempted to halt his raging waters with the one thing she knew he cared about the most. "Say white folk find out you done gone airin' their dirty laundry," she said. "If they come for you, who gonna be pappy to this child in my belly?" She raised her brow. "What gonna happen to this child then? What gonna happen to me? You even think 'bout that?"

The gleam in his eyes was undiminished. "Mary . . . *woman* . . . that child of ours be the reason why I have to talk!" he told her. "If you had a chance to do what's right, and know years from now it gonna give someone a better life than what we got now– well I say that be worth my life. And I ain't the only one neither. I dare you go and call out to the river and see what bones come poppin' up . . . white bones that used to have black and white skin on'em is what you gonna see. Those bones gonna tell you the truth 'bout how they died so you can be sittin' where you sittin' right now, and not in your bed prayin' that ol' massah or his boys pick some other woman's legs to spread tonight."

* * *

It was always Mary . . . she was always first, Lar thought.

She had reacted to the *good* news just as he figured she would. In time, he thought, she would come to understand the 'why'. In time, he knew he would also.

Negroe voices rose up around him . . . ghosts wanting to talk to him. Yet suddenly, he realized that they had always been there. For a moment he saw himself back home with Mary, watching her reaction as he told her Nicholas' plans, and then seeing the fear and anger in her eyes which had almost made him change his mind. Before she got off in front of the Monclair home for work, though she had smiled, he knew it was not her usual smile, but one of acceptance of his decision, not approval of it. That, he thought, was good enough for now.

He felt there was no way he could refuse to help Nicholas and his own people. Not when he sensed the Lord God tugging at his heart to do so– like the Lord was actually speaking to him . . . *'give unto this man the news of vileness and hate that hath been put upon thee and thy kin. Sing, my child, the sorrow that hath walked for so long with thee. Let thy dead voice rise up and live once more! Know there is no death or life without my will. For it is I, your Lord God, who hath given both to man. And it is only I that may giveth and taketh both away'*.

A tear of joy fell upon Lar's cheek.

Hidden away in Meadows fields near the woodland, it was easy to group the other Negroe men around him without attracting undue attention from the white foremen. Some who had met Nicholas at the church the other day knew what he was going to say, whereas others listened like children with wide eyes, open mouths and suspicion. He realized the moment was most critical. He wanted them to believe . . . knew they had to believe like he did, that what Nicholas was planning was in all of their best interests, and for every Negroe living with the specter of a lynch mob one day knocking down their door.

Doubt parried faith . . . faith countered by feigning defeat, before advancing with a series of quick unrelenting strokes.

He wondered if he would hear Mary's own words come from the men? How strong was their faith? How far past their own face could they see? Could they too, like himself, hear God's own voice calling them to rise, walk and testify? Silently, with eyes open, as if he were actually looking at the crowd of twenty black and sweaty men, he prayed for the right words.

"I know some of ya'll done heard 'bout the white man that come 'round the other day. Some of ya'll met him, too. And if you met him, then you know he ain't here for no business with white folks – he here for us Negroes." Lar assessed the faces looking at him. Some seemed as though they wanted to hear more. Others, he could already tell, were dead set against talking to Nicholas. A few were waiting to follow the largest herd.

"The man be here 'bout the murders of our people," Lar continued, undeterred by the growls of some of the wolves stalking his flock with dissention. "Lynchins' be the proper name for it, but we all know they be just murders." He paused for barely a moment. "But whatever you wanna call it, you know you can't stop it . . . not here in the south and being Negroe you can't.

"That be why Mr. Barrons, the white man, done come here," he told them. "He be a reporter for a northern newspaper, you see. He gettin' as many stories 'bout lynchins' from Negroes as he can, so he can write 'bout it and let northern folk know just what be goin' on down here. And then just maybe, ya'll . . . just maybe folks gonna start givin' a damn and put a stop to it all. The congress gotta listen for real this time once everyone know the *real* truth. We need the congress to put a stop to it for good and punish those who do it." The men grumbled as they looked at one another. Some heads nodded '*yes*', while others fiercely shook '*no*', yet a small minority still remained undecided . . . just like the United States' congress.

Papa Joe, one of the eldest Negroes, lifted his voice up from the lazy river of discontent flowing around him. "What we gonna do if white folks find out 'bout this 'porter man and that we been workin' wit'em. We ain't gonna have no job, Lar, 'cause we all be lynched." A small, like-minded chorus quickly sang Papa Joe's praise.

"You look at a white woman or man the wrong way and you be hangin' from ol' dead glory center of town anyhow," Eli Sharp countered, who was just twenty years of age. A few men, including Lar nodded.

Dicky Marks, whose head was as white as cotton had his say. "Papa Joe be right, Eli," he said, in his unmistakably, sand-scrubbed voice. "Ya'll youngin's just a few summers off your mammy's titty don't know the kinda mess this can stir up. I 'member my own pappy tellin' us 'bout his massahs jus' gunnin' down niggahs 'fore he let'em go free. It didn't matter none to him 'bout who won *or* lost the war."

Cross Jenkins, a childhood friend of Lar's who was a mirror reflection of his half-Choctaw, half-Negroe mother, with plump cheeks and black lips, spoke up. "You think they need an excuse? Ya'll men think they gonna stop killin' us 'cause we walkin' 'round sayin' '*yes'suh-yes'suh-yes'suh . . . you right, yes'suh!?*'" He shook his head before he'd even finished speaking. "Ain't a goddamn thing stoppin' them from killin' us all, 'cept they needin' us to work the fields, clean they homes and see to they hard-headed chillin'. And the ones that speak to ya or smile at ya . . . ya'll know what I'm sayin' . . ." he pointed to the crowd, " . . . the ones thinkin' they be *real good* Christians by being nice-like to niggahs . . . Shit! They be the same ones sayin', 'I got some rope' when it come time to hang ya'll black asses!"

"But they ain't doin' it now– *is they?!*" Dicky Marks retorted. "If they catch wind of this ree-porter man, and us for talkin' to him, they sho' will then."

"Then lay down," Lar told him. "That what you wanna do, ain't it? Lay'on down– your youngin's, too. Be sure to lay'em down right next to ya. Tell yo' woman, Jessa, lay down too, Dicky."

Dicky Marks looked to the others for help in understanding Lar's words, but they all seemed just as confused as he was. "What you talkin' 'bout . . . 'lay down', Lar?"

"If you ain't gonna stand," Lar told him, "then lay down. 'Cause when the white man come for ya', or your youngin's, or yo' Jessa– and they just might one day, you gonna be too busy layin' down to stand-up for'em. White men can use your 'ol broken down body to step on while they gettin' your family.

"Or is it gonna be you and your chillin, and grandbabies, Papa Joe?" Lar pointed at him. "Or you, Richard– back there shakin' your head. I ain't askin' all ya'll to stand up and speak. Ya'll gotta do what be right for you and your family. But I tell ya'll now . . . if . . . or be it *when* white men come a'callin' at your doorstep, who gonna stand up for you? Ya'll just thinkin' 'bout how things be right now, not later. What 'bout your chillin' and they chillin after them? Huh?! What 'bout them?" He dared. "It ain't but by the grace of . . ."

"Shush, Lar!" A heavy, but cautiously whispered voice rose from the rear of the group.

Lar fell silent. In the absence of his own voice, he soon heard what had caused the alarm to be sounded. The snapping of twigs tickled his ears. The other Negroes quickly scattered like naughty children at the sound of their father's footsteps approaching. A horse's unmistakable grunt sent shudders through their souls, reminding them they were not just men, but Negroe men.

Lar spotted the dusty, brown hat of Marty Schulgg emerging through the brush before actually seeing his aged face of twenty-four, that seemed more like forty. Lar stood his ground while the other men who'd scampered away feigned work with hoes, shovels and axes. He'd known Marty for years, and also knew he was on the slower side of dim-wittedness. It might have taken him some time to copy three strokes to draw a capital 'A'– crookedly so, but he always managed to eventually. Marty looked around at the other Negroes and then to Lar. Lar sensed suspicion in Marty's eyes as he drew his horse straight to him. He kicked the stallion's tail-end around, but even as his head swiveled, his eyes never left Lar's.

"What say there, Lar?" Marty's drawl was deep and characteristic of backwoods, hill-speak that was foreign to Folsom denizens.

"Not much, suh. How you farin' today?"

Marty again took measure of the other works and then turned back around to Lar. The corner of his mouth crept up. "Jus' fine . . . keepin' an eye or two on thangs. Jus' makin' sure you boys doin' what you should be."

"Yep . . . yep," Lar replied, as he too eyed the other Negroes. Not one dared to look up.

Marty spun the horse around again. "A wagon waitin' for ya up at the office, Lar. It gon' carry you up to Ms. Lucianna's to work for the rest of the day."

"Suh?"

"I ain't talkin to this here cotton, is I?" Marty smiled. "Yeah you!"

"Anybody else, suh?" Lar asked.

"What it to you?"

"It ain't a matter, suh."

"Mr. Meadows called for you 'specially. That all you needin' to know, ain't it?"

"Suh," Lar answered.

With a yank on the reigns, Marty spun the horse and began trotting off toward the brush from where came. "Don't dally now, boy. Ya'll done did enough chitter-chatterin' today. You hear me good?"

* * *

The Meadow's home was the last place Lar wanted to be. He was sitting next to Richard Pullman, who seemed happy just to be going to wherever Maggie Mae was, unlike himself. As Harry Wilson, the white driver of the wagon turned the corner, the Meadows' home lunged into view.

Lar figured he'd convinced a few who were initially opposed to talking to Nicholas right before Marty came along. But men like Papa Joe, who Negroes respected and Dicky Marks . . . who was at times too loud to ignore, even if Negroes didn't respect him all that much, could poison the well.

'*Separate and alone*' . . . the idea came to him. Without Papa Joe and Dicky countering his every word, he figured he could take each man off alone and plead his case. With calm and time, a man could form his own opinion, he thought. And then, if they still wanted no part of Nicholas' plan, then at least it would be their own uninfluenced decision.

One problem was no sooner solved before another arose, and one that had been whispering from the shadows of his mind ever since the wagon started creaking along the road toward town. She was dressed simply– a white head-rag and dingy white cotton dress, although there was nothing simple about her. It was no wonder, he thought, why men lusted for her. He caught a glimpse of her in the rear of the Meadows' home as they neared; yet that was all it took to paint his mind with memories of what once was between them. Although the desire for her flesh had since waned as his love for Mary grew, the memory of what could have been was a mountain that rose higher than water, wind, lightning, and was a day older than time infinite.

As they entered the garden in the back, Lar turned and looked at Richard, whose mouth was agape as he stared at Maggie Mae. Fearing the corners of the Richard's mouth would start glistening with saliva, he nudged him in the ribs. "Act right, fool!" He whispered none too kindly, though not quiet enough not to draw Maggie Mae's attention to them.

When she looked over, Lar expected a smile, or at the very least, a fleeting glimpse of happiness sparkling in her brown-speckled blue eyes, before lowering them as she usually did. This time, she held his gaze, giving him neither a smile nor anything that said she was in some way glad to see him. In truth, her lips pursed, as though she was actually displeased they were there. Richard seemed oblivious to her present state. "Hey there, Ms. Maggie! Fine day it be, ain't it?"

Maggie Mae ignored him. "Where the other men be?" She asked Lar . . . and only Lar.

"We be it. Ain't we enough?" Richard volunteered, placing a hand on his hip and giving her the most charming smile he could with what few teeth he still had.

Lar walked toward her. Richard was no more than a step behind him. The closer he came to Maggie Mae the more he realized something was wrong, as he saw her turning her hands over the other. "Mr. Wilson just carried us here, but he already left. We all Mr. Meadows sent today."

"Jus' us," Richard added proudly.

Lar grimaced at him. The 'boy' was simply just that . . . a boy, he thought. A boy smitten with what he would never have. Lar was embarrassed by Richard's antics, which had bypassed foolishness and was now bordering on irritating. To rescue Richard from himself, Lar forcefully suggested he go down to the river and start retrieving water.

"How you know we needin' water?" Richard asked, blatantly perturbed. "Ms. Maggie ain't even told us what needin' to be done yet, and Ms. Meadow ain't neither."

"'Cause we do," Maggie Mae answered before Lar could, though she still refused to look Richard's way. There was only Lar in her sights at the moment.

Richard glared at both of them before stomping off toward the riverbank. "I 'spose *I* get to work now," he announced, to which he received no reply from either Maggie Mae or Lar.

With Richard away and his grumbling now almost inaudible, Lar asked . . . "What be goin' on here, Maggie?"

Maggie Mae was facing the rear of the house. She glanced upward and then quickly back to Lar. "Don't turn 'round," she cautioned.

"She watchin' us?"

"Like an ol' black bird sittin' in a tree."

The urge to turn around and look up was nearly irresistible to Lar. "Why?" He asked.

Maggie Mae was pulling at her sleeves now. She whispered, "You askin' 'bout what you already know. You ain't white and neither is Richard. Now you understandin', Lar?"

Lar nodded.

"Even Mr. Meadows know 'bout it . . . or seem like he do. I see he done sent ya'll this time instead of those ol' nasty, white boys."

"And I know which boys they be, too," Lar said. "Everybody do."

Maggie Mae moved closer to Lar. "You know I would leave if I was sure no harm would come tramplin' after me," she said in a hush. "I would have left years back when . . . when . . ."

Lar began to protest, but Maggie Mae wouldn't even let him begin. She placed the palm of her hand gently and fleetingly upon his chest. Such a simple touch gave him pause. "I know that be over between you and me. I know that, Lar. Lord, I know that," she sighed. "This here . . . right now is 'bout what the missus can or can't do. She done let me know what she can do many times. Just like when her and Mr. Meadows be fussin' 'bout these white men comin' 'round, he scold her– but don't ever say what it be by name. It the same way she be with me. She never say what gonna happen if I go, but she say it with other words that let me know somethin' will."

Lar looked down upon her. In a fleeting moment, he glimpsed their past and present, but within her two oceans, he saw nothing of their future– of that he was thankful. Still, he couldn't help but empathize with her predicament. He laid his hand on her shoulder as only a brother. She shivered in reply.

"If I knew a way to get you away from here, I would help you," he said earnestly. He tilted his head back toward the house. "She be like an ol' devil. And once the devil done got a'hold of you, it real hard to break free. But you gonna have to get her off your coattail somehow, one way or be it another. You need to have God on your side, Maggie."

Maggie Mae smiled halfheartedly. "You know I love God with all my heart. Only thing is, I don't know if he love me the same." Just as she was about to continue, she stopped abruptly.

Lar turned in the direction Maggie Mae was staring at behind him. Lucianna was on the back porch. With skin like ivory, her body was nearly washed out by the white dress she wore. But her hair was fire and her green eyes shone like beacons in the mist. She was a statue, yet her stoic presence demanded and received silence from Lar, Maggie Mae, and even Richard, who paused to look at her also. Her eyes settled on but one person and only one . . . Maggie Mae. From the side, Lar saw Maggie Mae quickly lower her head.

"When I say to Roman that you're about the laziest creature in all of God's creation, he dares to have a mind to disbelieve me," Lucianna said, finally cracking her marble mouth. "And here I find you cacklin' with a man . . . again," she added, "as though *you* were mistress of the house and have nothing better to do."

"Sorry, missus," Maggie Mae uttered, as she scurried toward the house.

"No need to stop your yappin' now," Lucianna told her. "Your chores won't be finished by day's end now anyway."

"I be quick 'bout them, missus."

Lucianna waved her hand dismissively. "Never you mind, gal," she uttered. "Just . . . just show that boy over there which of my plants have the most need for water. And tell *it* to be careful. These aren't cotton plants and beans out here . . . God only knows if *it* knows the difference. He looks quite simple."

The entire time Lucianna was speaking, Lar had averted his eyes from her, but had not once lowered his head. But now, in the momentary span of silence, he saw Lucianna shift her gaze from Maggie Mae to him. "Tell *It* not to forget to water the plants out front sufficiently. You do know what 'sufficiently' means?"

"Yes'm."

"And you . . ." Lucianna said.

Lar looked at her. "Lar Cole, ma'am," he said respectfully.

Lucianna looked up and over him toward the garden. "I know who you are, boy. You're but the biggest man here in Folsom. How could I not know who you are? You were to have married Maggie Mae at one time, were you not?"

Lar glanced at Maggie Mae, but her wide eyes replied 'not guilty."

"Whites do talk amongst themselves," Lucianna informed him. "I know you're now married to some big, Negroe gal, and that you call yourself a preacher."

Lar lifted his chin. "That be correct, ma'am."

Lucianna's face once again took on the life of a stone, before she turned and began walking toward the door. "I was stating a fact, boy," she hissed. "Now come along– there's furniture to be moved about inside. I'm sure it will barely be an effort for something your size."

"Yes'm."

"Maggie . . . see to the tasks as I've told you. And . . . and tell that odd Negroe boy to keep his mouth closed. Every time I see those horrid teeth of his I become ill."

* * *

Lucianna knew she had led an unconventional life . . . from working whore to wife of Roman Meadows. The road having led her to where she was now, she felt, was riddled with uncertainty, though one thing she was clearly certain of, now more than ever, was that she detested *that* girl. She realized she could never break Maggie Mae with such weak and useless words such as 'half-breed', 'mutt', or 'mulatto'. Nor would calling her homely, a bitch, or a darkie suffice, for none of those terms applied to her. 'Nigra' and 'niggah', people she bore no resemblance to, wouldn't suffice, Lucianna figured. A whore she wasn't either, but the opposite . . . or at least that's what she'd assumed until finally seeing Lar Cole up close, which made her question whether Maggie Mae's hymen was indeed still intact.

"This way," Lucianna directed, feigning irritation as she led Lar down the hall toward the front of the house. She turned and looked at him for a casual, brief moment, assuming that he would take it as her making sure he was following. But, it was solely for a glimpse of him once more. Again, after looking him up and down quickly, she questioned whether Maggie Mae was still a virgin, and if so, it was her loss.

She wondered how Maggie Mae ever resisted his slightest advances, when he– this Negroe . . . *this niggah*, excited even her? Even the word 'excited' was too weak, she mused, as a familiar warmth began spreading from her chest directly south to her groin. This Negroe was no ordinary man, simply because if there was one thing she knew well, it was men . . . plenty of them. No white man in Folsom had stirred her so like he was doing– they were just convenient. And Negroe men– she went out of her way to not even look at them. Even the dashing Nicholas Barrons, as handsome as he was, didn't exude such raw maleness as this dark-skinned behemoth, or was as fine looking, she figured. Even his thick forearms bulging from his rolled-up sleeves were enticing.

Lucianna turned, her wavy locks followed a mere second later. Once again glimpsing him, she couldn't help but think that of all the Negroe women available to him, he'd married the most homely one of them all. 'Ah yes', she thought, recalling the face of that creature he called a wife. To call her a beast was to insult every swamp rat and coon in all of Folsom, she contemplated. Seeing her from a distance had been more than enough for her to discern that the tar-faced woman had no beauty to speak of at all. And her size, Lucianna recalled, as she glanced upward at Lar's towering height, was near his or damn close. And if the beast's shoulders were not as wide as his, she'd be surprised.

"Ma'am?"

His deep, smooth voice broke her day-nightmare of what she saw as a wide-nosed, black ogre Lar called a wife and quickly sent her back into fantasy of who stood near her now. His large, soft lips were daring her to touch them. She walked over and opened the door to Roman's study and pointed to two large, leather bound chests by the wall. "Those two I need upstairs," she directed. "And in the next room are tables that I want brought up also. Not that you would know– or care, but they certainly don't go with the mo-tif here. And with the rain finally falling steadier, Roman can surely afford to buy new ones . . . ones that are actually worth visi-tors looking at without sneering. It's not as though he doesn't have the funds for it. He has enough money to pay you Negroes almost as well as whites. I've never heard of such a thing myself, but, that's Roman for you, I suppose."

"He a good man to us, ma'am," Lar responded respectfully.

Lucianna's lips became perfectly horizontal. "You people would say such a thing." Lar smiled and displayed a set of perfectly aligned teeth. Again, a wicked wind fanned the embers of Lucianna's firebox.

"Don't mean nothin' by it, ma'am," Lar said. "I just mean we Negroes ain't never had nothin' to complain 'bout with Mr. Meadows, is all. It ain't nothin' to give a hard day's work when the pay be fair."

"And when the pay isn't?" She asked, lifting her brows that were meticulously arched around her green eyes. "Do you Negroes then do only half the work or just mull about?"

"No, ma'am," Lar replied adamantly. "Some other folk may act like that, but we don't."

Lucianna pointed to the chests on the floor. Lar lifted the first one with ease and balanced the bulk of its weight on his stomach. She led him to the stairs and let him ascend first, then followed at a safe viewing distance. "By *'other folk'*, you were referring to white men workin' for Roman?" Lar had made it to the landing and turned toward her, showing not even a hint of sweat upon his brow, much to Lucianna's disappointment.

"I don't know what white men be doin' on the farm, tell you the truth, ma'am," he replied. "We be out in the fields . . . the foreman just ride through now and then tellin' us what needs pickin', choppin or loading. Then they leave us be 'til they need somethin' more."

"Roman trusts you all to work steadily without proper supervision?" She asked, with genuine surprise. Before he could reply, she answered her own question. "Ahhh . . . my dear Roman," she sighed. "Such faith he has in you Negroes."

"Yes'm," Lar responded in neither agreement nor disagreement.

Lucianna looked him over again. This time, however, she didn't bother feigning that she wasn't. Her eyes found their way back to his meaty, black forearms. The weight of the chest he carried had caused his already thick muscles to swell and bulge, and where they did not bulge; they sank and creased at their connection to hearty bone and sinew. And yet, not a hit of sweat or strained breath was evident as he held the chest that would have been a struggle for most men to lift.

After carrying up two chests, two tables and a barely walked upon rug, Lucianna was finally rewarded with a damp shirt clinging to Lar's chest. As he mounted the landing with a rust colored chair, she actually saw him pause briefly, before striding down the hall with it as though it were simply a bag of cotton. She had him place the chair in the room at the far end of the hall that was used for storage. He turned and began walking back towards the landing where she was standing.

The shadowed hallway made his moist, dark skin glisten like wet glass. It had been such a long time since she could recall what real desire looked like. That such desire was a Negroe only seemed to increase the heat below her waist. Her left hand . . . her most secure and trustworthy one . . . began to quiver. The battle over what was right versus wrong was short lived in her mind. The corners of her mouth became wet and swept up in victory for wrong.

The thought of him filling her, which she had no doubt he could, made her woozy. She imagined his thick arms holding her down as he thrust roughly and carelessly into her. And if she managed to free one arm, or both of them– which her fantasy did allow her to do, instead of struggling to be free, she would caress his face and massage his lips with her own. And when his thick member began pulsing to share his seed with her, she imagined crying out and . . .

"Ma'am– there be sometin' else you wantin' done now?"

The sound of Maggie Mae's voice was like a chilled ice pick scraping at her flesh. *It was always her!* Lucianna seethed silently, as venom flooded her mouth. She longed to make Maggie Mae pay for usurping her rightful place on the throne of what was considered beauty. *It belongs to me!* She cried silently. *Am I not the one who is beautiful and white?! Truly white! Not some mutt, bastard daughter of a mad Creole woman.*

"You have no mind of your own, gal," Lucianna uttered. "Must I instruct you on every matter?" She sighed dramatically. "The weeds are poised to take over the very garden you and that *thing* out there just watered, and you ask me what else needs to be done? The grass is near knee high and you look at me as though you're lost. You have clothes to wash and hang, but here you are looking at me like a fool." Lucianna didn't miss Maggie Mae quickly glancing at Lar. She was now certain how best to strike. "Don't come to me until my garden is as fit as it should be. The same goes for the front of the house. Roman is the most important man in this town, yet his home . . . *my* house, looks as though we live in squalor– like you people." Maggie Mae kept her head bowed. "What are you waiting for, gal?" Lucianna asked gently, as though she actually did care to know. Maggie Mae looked up and shook her head. With her back still to Lar, Lucianna brandished her most crooked smile at her.

Maggie Mae turned and descended the stairs without so much as a fleeting glance back. In the stillness that followed Maggie Mae's departure, Lucianna waited until the creaking of the door sounded twice– one open, and one closed. She turned back to her prey– a black unicorn, she likened him to. In his eyes, she thought for a brief moment she saw a glimmer of weakness. But it didn't matter. In fact, she hoped that there was, for it would only make what was to come all the sweeter and more satisfying.

She approached him slowly and was glad that her dress hid her legs, which were shivering as much from nerves as from excitement. Her hands were behind her back, each grasping the other to the point where their mark would still be evident a day from now. *Do you know what's coming, my black Adonis?* She wondered.

"What is there not to adore about Maggie Mae?" She asked him. Her lips formed into a pretended, sorrowful smile. "Is it true . . . Laurence Cole . . . that you still pine for her? No one would blame you if you did. Why– I think it is almost expected that you should."

Lar shook his head. "No ma'am . . . I ain't and I don't."

The hint of a quiver in his voice encouraged her. She figured he hadn't expected such a thought to cross her mind, let alone her lips. She was close enough now to smell him . . . a tangy, moist smell men exuded at the first break of sweat. She inhaled deeply. Her eyes mapped him slowly and deliberately. *She wanted* him to see that she was doing so. *She wanted* him to watch her as she studied his angular, black face and thick shoulders. *She wanted* him to see her admire his narrow waist, which extended to his round, meaty derriere. *She wanted* him to see her eyes resting right below the waist of his pants. *She wanted him.*

And she knew he now understood her ultimate intent– for he said . . . "I can help them downstairs now, Ms. Lucianna."

Lucianna stepped closer to him, as if he had just bid her to come hither. "They have no need of you right now . . . Laurence Cole. Not like I have," she hissed.

He began walking toward the stairs. But there was no need to chase her quarry. Here, in her home, she knew her net was ever reaching and inescapable, even if he didn't find it as appealing as Maggie Mae's.

"You leave without my permission?" She asked lightly, almost giddily.

Lar took another step backwards. "No disrespect, ma'am. But it best if I do for somethin' that ain't 'spose to happen– happen."

"Happen to you or to your child?" She struck!

Lar stood still. *"What!?"*

Lucianna turned her back to him and walked to the end of the hall toward her bedroom. "I know what they say of me . . . whore . . . harlot . . . Jezebel– I'm not deaf," she told him. She opened the door and stood to the side of it. Still, her back was to Lar. "But be assured, regardless of what they think of me, my word will trump the word of the holiest Negroe, even if it be said that he can walk on water."

Lar was silent.

"You know what they will do to you with one word from me?"

"Ain't no worse than what the Lord God give me if I do what be wrong," he responded.

Lucianna laughed. "Oh– you say that now. Listen to you! Laurence Cole, the holy niggah speaking so boldly and with such conviction. Praise be to Jesus . . . no? Believe me– holy man, your voice *will* go weak when the noose tightens around that strong, black neck of yours. Your eyes will go black and your hands will never again fold in prayer. And your God won't be there to help his black lamb down from the cross either."

"Why you doin' this!" Lar demanded. His voice was devoid of any and all contrived respect. "Why you doin' this to me? Why?!"

"Because you're a man," she replied simply, as though it should've been evident at the start of the game he had no idea he had agreed to play.

"I'm Negroe," he countered as quickly. "And I married, too."

Lucianna turned slightly to the side. Peripherally, she could see his outline at the landing. She could smell him even at their distance apart. "The first is of no consequence to me," she replied blandly. "No one will ever know . . . or believe it for that matter. The second is the same. You're a man . . . a Negroe– yes, but a man, nonetheless. A ring and a promise have never stopped a man from entering my room before. It won't now."

"You ain't thinkin' right, Ms. Lucianna," he told her. "Things gonna look a lot different to you come tomorrow."

Lucianna had had enough. 'A Negroe dares to refuse me? My beauty . . . my womanhood?' She fumed. It was about *her* also– that wretched, half-white bitch. Lucianna was determined to take what Maggie Mae, with all her beauty couldn't. "You will come here . . . now! Or you'll never live to see that child of yours born. And then I'll see to that thing carrying it, too!"

The echo of her voice seemed to linger in the hallway. Would the sound of his approaching steps come quickly or slowly? She wondered. Would he again have the audacity to refuse me? She couldn't understand his hesitancy in the matter. Many men had made fools of themselves to have her passion. Still, under threat of death and loss of child and wife, a Negroe . . . a niggah, was fighting against her will.

* * *

Lar felt his right knee bend and his leg move forward. He knew he was alone and trapped. Maggie Mae wouldn't return. And Richard, who was far too simple to figure it out on his own, couldn't help either, he thought. No . . . he was certain he was utterly alone with her. Even God was gone– the same God he'd ran from weeks ago. And as before, in the absence of God when he baptized himself in the river, the snake had come for him . . . just like it did now.

'She waitin' for me.'

His left leg followed his right.

Years ago, when he first saw Lucianna when she moved to Folsom with Roman, he didn't deny she was beautiful then. But he saw none of that beauty now. What lay behind her façade was finally revealed. He saw only evil now.

His right foot moved forward.

Lar now understood that what Negroes always said about white women was the gospel truth. In the company of their own, they pretended to be frightened of the male Negroe . . . injury, death, or even worse– a savage rape would surely befall them . . . but it was a lie! A damn lie! He realized what they feared and wanted the most was one in the same. How many Negroes had been killed after being put in the same position he was in right now? He won-dered. Whether they were seduced or forced made no difference. It always came down to what the white woman felt afterwards– pleasure or guilt, which determined a Negroe man's ultimate fate.

'Swing-swing from that tree, you rapin' niggah.' And Lar knew he would.

The idea to pray fleetingly crossed his mind. *But why? Why pray now, boy? Who gonna hear you?* He asked himself.

She moved into the room and waited for him. Her lips parted into a crooked smile. Lar glanced behind hoping to see a savior walking up the stairs. But no one appeared. He knew there would be no salvation here . . . the cross and spikes were set out and wait-ing for him. His slow march inside the room was him accepting his fate. Her closing the door behind him was the sound of impending doom.

"Ms. Lucianna," he sputtered, but couldn't think of any other words that could reach her sense of morality, if she had any at all. "Ms. . . ."

She was still behind him. Her hand came upon his shoulder like a freshly sharpened blade, only there was no pain. She was as evil as evil ever was . . . loving and gentle in illusion. Her hands moved down the sides of his torso to the center of his back before rising once more to his neck. Lar began to shiver. He changed his mind and decided to pray.

Her hands moved under his arms and up to the first button of his shirt. Slowly, one by one she undid them all and pulled at the back of it, until it came free and floated to the ground. The hands then returned under his arms and spread out like tentacles moving up and down his chest. Sometimes they moved in the same direc-tion. Other times, they moved opposite of the other.

He couldn't look down nor find the will to speak. And see? No . . . he couldn't see through his open eyes, so he shut them. He inundated his mind with thoughts of Mary and his child. He conjured visions of dirt, wood, mules, the sun, stars . . . anything and everything . . . nothing and something. But her hands were far too deft for his body to resist! As blood began filling his penis, he knew he'd lost the battle against his own body.

At the first taste of his own tears dripping on his lips, he knew at that moment he was no longer a man . . . no longer a husband . . . no longer a servant of God . . . just a toy for her with strings on his arms, hands and legs, and his mouth sewn shut . . . muted and subjugated as if he was wearing shackles.

But her hands were no longer satisfied. They moved south and unbuttoned his pants. Though loosened, but didn't fall. Nature's wanting propped them up. He wanted to yell until his lungs burst, and take one fist and knock both of her faces inward. But he did not . . . could not . . . dared not. *Swing-swing, niggah!* He remembered.

She freed his britches from their hook and let them drop to the floor, and just as quickly, she pulled his underwear down to his ankles. Standing there naked and his penis at full girth, he sobbed. If she heard, and there was no way she couldn't have, for the sound of his weeping was thunder to his own ears, she didn't seem to care. Her fiery breath on his back told him what she did care about.

She pressed her breasts against his back. Her hand lowered until it found his penis. She grasped . . . Lar gasped, and prayed that the burst of air he released was from revulsion to her touch and not the silkiness of it. But the pleasure it caused . . . as evil as it was, he couldn't deny. Her hand, untouched by toil felt like velvet. The rhythm of her hand was a devilish spell. He couldn't resist any longer, and began spraying violently on the floor.

But there wasn't absolute silence in the room. He could hear her panting, as though she had been the one succumbing to pleasure. And now . . . there seemed to be true silence, though he knew she was speaking to him. And like an apparition, startling and unexpected in presence before vanishing, she was gone and he was alone.

He couldn't move. He didn't want to. He wanted to die. He wanted to rush down the hall, or to wherever she had slunk to and strangle her. But he couldn't stop there. Manically, he dreamed of killing Richard and Maggie Mae also, for he had no doubt that they now knew his shame. The spirit of God had departed him, he was certain. He had sinned and sinned greatly. There would be no flock for him to lead, for if he did, it would only be to slaughter, he realized.

"Clean it up."

Yes, that was what she had said, he remembered now.

But his thoughts were still muddled. *Clean it up?* He wondered. *Clean up what? Where . . . where I be? Who I be?*

He looked down and realized he was still naked. His eyes moved past his body out along the floor. In some spots, the wood floor gleamed more than in others, and he realized now what she meant. The sight of his seed forced from him and splattered on the floor was all it took to destroy the damn holding back all of his tears. He used his shirt to wipe away semen and tears, but there were far more tears to be cleaned than semen.

He pulled up his underwear, pants and put on his semen-sticky shirt. In a brash moment of anger and guilt, and a wish for death, he rammed his fist into his testicles, immediately bringing him to the floor in agony, but only producing a small sense of contrition. It was not enough for him. Guilt thrived in his thoughts. He grasped his sinful parts and squeezed until numbness and a blinding light replaced the pain.

Minutes . . . hours . . . days . . . moments . . . they all seemed the same to him as he lay on the floor. How he was able to pull himself to his feet and walk to the edge of the stairs, he didn't know, but he found himself there. Down the stairs and out the backdoor he went until his was at the river's edge. He dipped his hands in the murky waters and washed them.

A voiced called out to him– one that he recognized, scorned and loved all at the same time. All he knew right now was that he didn't want her near, for she too, in his mind, was as evil as Lucianna. Seeing her coming toward him . . . and oh how beautiful she was– made him react.

She cried out and fell.

Only when he was past the gates of the Meadows' home . . . past Richard who was calling out for him, did he realize he'd shoved Maggie Mae to the ground. But they were both only memories now. The bridge leading from Folsom to his home was near. But home was a place he had no desire to go to right now. 'Ain't no home in hell,' he thought.

CHAPTER 16

Nicholas was confused, to say the least, but now was at a loss for words. Hadn't it been Lar's wife, Mary, who'd been so unwelcoming and not Lar? He recalled. That she and Lar had now traded places was bewildering. He posed his question in a different way. "Beggin' your pardon, Mrs. Cole . . . I . . . I . . . just don't think I understand what's going on. Is it that Lar doesn't want to speak with me or wont? I thought we understood one another."

"He just feelin' poorly right now– if that'll suit you," she replied, blocking his view of the inside of the house with her wide shoulders.

"And he hasn't been to church, either?"

"No, suh."

Nicholas shook his head. "Is he still willin' to talk to me?"

Mary shrugged her shoulders. "Maybe, suh . . . I don't know and can't tell you rightfully."

Nicholas detected truth in her voice, but it seemed tinged with an errant chord that suggested he wasn't being told everything. He wiped the sweat from his forehead before placing his straw-hat back on. As he made to leave, he stopped and turned back to her. "Is he alright, Mrs. Cole? Truly– is somethin' a matter?" She stepped back in the house and shut the door.

Realizing there was no more to gain from Mary, even if he wanted to, he walked to the road in front of the house. A group of Negroe men were just passing by. He waved and spoke, and put on his most innocent smile. But his charm wasn't enough to seduce even an involuntary response from them. If anything, it elicited the same wary glances he'd been given when he first came to their side of town with Lar.

"If the men say Lar's ill, then he is," Roman had told him, when he asked him about Lar's absence from work. "Any other man I would call a liar to his face, but not Lar Cole. He's not that kind of man."

Lar had been his greatest supporter and had rallied some of the other Negroes to open up to him. But without Lar's presence and influence, the other Negroes had quickly closed ranks. That left but one Negroe, he figured, who just might say a word to him.

It was Sunday afternoon and he guessed she would be in her home, or if not, somewhere about the shantytown. He figured there was nothing left to lose by going there. Even if she refused to speak to him, he could at least have the consolation of seeing her again. That thought warmed him . . . calmed him, and reminded him of the time when he first sat next to a Negroe girl in grade school and thought then she was the most beautiful girl he'd ever seen.

He found her house easily enough, as though he'd been welcomed there a thousand times. Every visit to the Negroe side he'd made thus far, he'd made it a point to spy her home, whether he thought her there or not. As he neared, he saw a woman on the front porch, but it was not Maggie Mae rocking in the chair– it was the old woman. A woman he'd seen from a distance . . . one who was staring at him as he walked up to the porch.

He removed his sweat soaked hat and placed it behind his back. With a slight nod and a more pronounced bow, he presented himself to her. "Afternoon, ma'am," he said, with as much cordiality as he could muster. He finished it off with a blaring smile. She barely nodded in reply.

"My name is Nicholas Barrons, ma'am," he offered. "I'm a traveler amongst other things. I'm not sure if you've heard of . . ."

"The white boy from the north, are ya?" She replied before he could finish. "You come down here to talk to Negroes and Nigras, huh?" She paused a moment. "You what they call a brave man."

"Perhaps brave is too strong a word, ma'am," he replied, doubting her praise was truly a compliment, but more a statement of his own foolhardiness.

"I say you brave 'cause you ain't come to see Enda, have ya?" She smiled.

Nicholas was caught off guard. "Ye– yes, ma'am," he replied nervously, "with your permission, of course."

Enda turned her face to the side and smiled again. "You already know what I gonna say, don't ya? But *I* knew that before you knew to think it." Again, she didn't wait for his reply. "Ain't like I can stop ya now. If you don't talk to her here, you just gonna wait 'til she in town. But it good you come a'askin for my say-so. Make ol' Enda feel jus' a little better 'bout the whole thang."

"The whole . . ."

Enda moved forward suddenly, as though she intended to hop out of the chair. "Don't make me turn 'gainst you, Mr. Nicholas Barrons– *Mr. handsome white boy*," she whispered. She settled back in her chair and snickered. "I know why you here . . . just like you do– most of the time. I know you ain't come to some old, white Negroe woman who can tell you just 'bout everythin' 'bout Negroes and whites you ever wanted to know . . . and about things you never should find out."

The full-fledged heat of summer did nothing to stave off the chill Nicholas felt creeping into his bones. He looked away from her, but still, it seemed to him as if she were standing next to him . . . and even closer than that. *Stop being paranoid*, he thought. *She's just an old woman.*

"She 'round back yonder in the garden pullin' up some peas," Enda told him. "I already got a kettle full boilin' now. Gonna have some cornbread wit'em, but we ain't got no meat to go with it though, but you can have what we got."

"Thank you, ma'am . . . Ms. Enda," he blurted.

"Go on back 'round there. Folks gonna talk bad 'bout 'ol Enda if they see some white boy out in front of my home . . . *a handsome white boy, too.*" She cackled at her own words. "Yes'ah . . . Lord they will! You gonna give 'ol Enda a bad name." She laughed loudly. "*A baaad name!*"

"Ma'am," Nicholas said, as he departed, but she wasn't listening to him anymore. He glanced back at her as he walked around the house, and still, she hadn't ceased talking and laughing to herself.

The closer he came to the garden– maneuvering around hoes and shovels, and a black kettle full of clothes simmering in white, foamy lye-soap, he finally heard movement within the greenery. His heart quickened. He knew why . . . for he remembered his mother had once told him, as she soothed his broken heart from a woman who had left him for another man: . . . *Nick, my darling boy . . . let her go her own way. You don't have to worry about looking for love . . . love will find you. And when it does, you'll know it inside and out without a doubt. Because it'll make you do the most brave and foolish things you've ever done in your life to keep it forever.*

His heart was thumping, not solely because he knew Maggie Mae was near, but because for the first time . . . truly the first time, he was going to be alone with her. The thought of her aroused feelings that excited, as well as confused him. It was dangerous, too, he knew, but he felt incapable of reining in his feelings for such a woman as she was. He caught sight of her– her honey-blond hair was pulled back and woven into a single braid– her skin was even whiter than his own. A man would be flogged for even suggesting she possessed an ounce of Negroe blood. But that idea only encouraged his fantasies about what could be.

Her small, red lips were pursed and her eyes squinting from the sun's glare. Her look of sorrow and worry only made him want to be that much closer to her. She stopped and turned toward him. With the sun in his eyes, he couldn't tell exactly what her face was expressing upon seeing him ... repugnance or joy. He hoped for the latter.

"You shouldn't be here," Maggie Mae admonished.

Nicholas made a visor with his hand to block the sun. "Do you mean here in Folsom or here with Negroes?"

"Here with me," she corrected him. "It ain't right."

Nicholas moved closer. "Who's to say what is and isn't right when no one can see us?"

"I do," she answered. "And my mammy knows, too. It ain't like you got back here and she ain't seen you."

He circled her so that it was he who now had his back to the sun, yet he was tall enough and close enough to shield her eyes from its glare. He was more than willingly to let the back of his neck scorch if it meant seeing her clearly. But sun heat wasn't enough to bother him now. In his shadow, her face belonged to him. Suddenly, he felt mad with desire. He ached to reach out and stroke her cheek, and touch her lips with his own.

"Your mother didn't seem to have reservations," he offered. "She's the one who told me to come back here ... *and* invited me to stay for supper."

Maggie Mae began pulling at the peas again. "Will you?"

Nicholas chanced his words. It seemed as though when his lips moved, it was his heart, not rationale thinking that commanded them. "Only if *you* want me to." Her eyes widened, he saw. Again, his words seemed to flow involuntarily. "We're hidden, Maggie

Mae. No one can see us," he nearly whispered. "So don't see me as a white man– just a man . . . like I see you as a woman, but . . . but . . ."

Her lips parted. In all his years hearing about the frailty of women, he finally knew what it felt like to feel faint. He reached for her and prayed she wouldn't recoil . . . and she didn't. His fingers found her hair. "Dear God," he uttered, as his eyelids grew heavy and then closed.

"Mr. Barrons . . . *please . . . don't . . .*" She wasn't pulling away, but leaning into him.

What words were left for her to speak was lost upon his lips, as they daringly found hers. And it was everything he'd hoped it would be. He stroked her cheek and held it there as his mouth explored hers. He separated his lips from hers, though it was only to look upon her once more. Her eyes were closed. When she opened them, he prayed he saw the same passion he was feeling. But her head dropped.

"They'll kill us both if they knew 'bout this," she confided to the ground, her steady companion.

Nicholas shook his head, knowing she meant white folks. "You're so very wrong. They'll have to kill me a thousand times over before they ever touch you," he promised.

She laughed, albeit nervously and condescendingly. "*You!?* You gonna stop these white folks? These men 'round here done killed off whole families and gone'on home and ate supper like ain't nothin' ever happened. What you gonna do? Huh?"

"Take you home with me," he said, without the slightest pause. His words were not spoken hastily or without thought. In fact, it had been his wish ever since he first saw her that day he stepped foot in Folsom. He was in love with a woman he barely knew, yet felt, as his mother said it would be, that he was meant for and she for him. And he would take her away from this wretched town plagued with idiots and bigots if she dared say '*yes*'. Jeopardize his inheritance from his grandfather who would disown him if he knew she was Negroe . . . absolutely! And why not? He thought. Was she not herself a treasure beyond measure!?

"I . . . I . . . my mammy!" She finally blurted. "I can't just up and leave her." She shook her head. "No-no. She old now . . . and . . . and . . ." Maggie Mae seemed bewildered. "I don't even know you! And you white, too! And I Negroe."

"You're whom you choose to be," he told her. "Let's be perfectly plain, Maggie Mae– no one would even know. You look whiter than me!"

She backed away from him. "Well I ain't white!"

He stepped closer. "Again I ask– who would know?" For a moment, Nicholas thought she was actually considering the possibility of leaving with him. She had fallen silent, yet had not looked away.

But slowly, she shook her head again. "I can't leave her."

"Then we'll bring her," he said, unwilling to be deterred. He was upon her once more. His hands caressed her face, as he kissed her deeply and she responded in kind, emboldening him. "I'll move this entire house north, if it means you will come with me."

He backed away from her, but before he could say another word, Enda called out for her. "I'm comin'!" Maggie Mae responded, still looking at Nicholas. She bent over to retrieve the wicker basket, but Nicholas was quicker and held it to his chest, like he had out in front of Monclair's store the first day they met.

"Am I still invited for supper?"

"I 'spose it too late to send you away, now."

* * *

"It ain't gonna bite ya if ya taste it," Maggie Mae told Nicholas.

Maggie Mae watched his expression change from pleasure to confusion, as he sat at their small table with a tinplate of food set before him. The boiled peas and cornbread had already disintegrated and melded into a thick, yellow-brown soupy mush. Though there was no meat in it, it was a simple and filling meal that had sustained them for years.

She watched him raise the spoon dripping with pea juice to his lips and slurp it in. She knew he wasn't accustomed to their type of fare. In her mind, she pictured him seated at the table of his white mother and white father– all proper in their manner of dress, style, speech, and eating like anorexic, aristocratic birds . . . steaming, golden brown bread roll filled silver platters on either end of their beautiful table in their magnificent house that kept out air, rain and wind, no matter how fierce God turned up the weather.

She watched for his reaction, as did Enda, who she could see peripherally to her right. His brows raised and his mouth began to move slowly. With his head still lowered, he nodded. "This is delicious!" Maggie Mae's mouth popped open, which she quickly closed. He took another, larger bite of the pea-cornbread mush.

"That's Maggie Mae's fixin' you eatin' there," Enda told him. "'Course now, I done showed the gal how to do it."

"She has certainly done you proud, ma'am," he said, grinning at them both.

Maggie Mae looked down at her plate of food, but saw only Nicholas staring back at her. It was his eyes, she thought. Those green eyes and black lashes of his worried her. They seemed, she felt, to see through her to those things she kept secret. She was embarrassed to admit to herself that whenever she looked at Nicholas, it was as though Lar was peering at her.

She had loved how he touched her face so gently. And his kiss . . . she had wanted to reach around his neck and seal the hold he held her in. She wanted to say 'yes' when he asked her to leave with him. In the garden, she felt his eyes were telling her he would protect her always. The heat from his body said he would never leave. The thundering of his heart vowed, *"I will love you until the end of time."* His hands moving alongside . . .

"Maggie–chile! You listenin'?!" Enda snapped at her.

"Ma'am?" Maggie Mae replied. And no, she hadn't heard a word spoken around her while busily dreaming with eyes open.

"The man here talkin' to you," Enda said.

Nicholas smiled. "I was askin' if you knew what was goin' on with Lar Cole."

Maggie Mae stiffened at the sound of Lar's name. "No . . . can't say that I do," she lied.

"He's not been at his job for days or even at the church preaching," Nicholas stated, in a voice steeped with concern.

"I don't know," Maggie Mae uttered. She moved her peas from one side of the plate to the other before scooping up a few on to her spoon. She paused and pondered whether her hungry, yet sour stomach could digest it. She knew what Lucianna was capable of doing. When she saw Lucianna afterwards brandishing a smirk that she showed only when something was done to her satisfaction, which was not often, she knew something devilish had been done to Lar.

"I just don't understand it," Nicholas said in frustration. "It seemed as though everything was goin' so right and then now, all so wrong. The other Negroes were just beginnin' to open up to me . . . and now nothin'."

"They have families to see to," Maggie Mae told him. "You think its just a little thang– us talkin' to you 'bout what it be like bein' Negroe down here. It ain't simple like that, Nicholas. A skinny sow worth more than we be to white-folk 'round here."

"I don't think so," Nicholas disagreed.

"Ain't nobody give a damn 'bout what you think," Enda piped in. The sting of her words silenced Nicholas. "What you know 'bout Negroes anyway?"

"Beggin' your pardon, ma'am, but I have two journals full of histories that I've collected in just a few short months, not countin' the ones I've already sent north," he said proudly. "I don't claim to know an ounce of what I need to in order to understand the plight of your people, but I am tryin' . . . and . . . *I do care.*"

Enda's eyes shifted from Nicholas to Maggie Mae. "Oh, I don't doubt you care. You just don't understand a lick." Nicholas began to speak but Enda shushed him. "Maggie-chile, go on and light a few more candles. This be a special time tonight, 'cause Enda need to talk to ya'll– right here and right now."

Maggie Mae did as Enda asked. She knew something was about to happen . . . something unexpected. They never lit candles unless they had to. Who could afford them now in these times? *Why now?* That was the question. The answer, she wasn't quite sure she was ready to hear.

* * *

Enda waited until Maggie Mae sat down before she spoke again. She knew how lovely her daughter was– of course, but in the glow of candlelight she was absolutely heavenly. Maggie Mae was that beauty that only comes about every moon-shadowed sun. How could this white man not love her? Enda thought. But that was that, Enda told herself. She knew there was no turning back from the course she'd begun. And so, she decided to begin with that which was not the most obvious.

"I gonna be dead in a few months time," Enda said plainly and simply, as if telling them both its about to rain, while rain clouds hovered above.

Nicholas gasped.

Maggie Mae stared at her. Suddenly, as if she couldn't take one more ounce of ill fortune, her eyes quickly welled with tears.

"Are you ill, Ms. Sully? I-I didn't know," Nicholas sputtered, looking from mother to daughter. Enda's reply was a curt smile.

"She ain't ill, Nicholas," Maggie Mae mumbled, raising her head and looking at Enda. "But she ain't lyin' neither."

Nicholas' brow lowered in confusion.

Enda laughed, though she knew she shouldn't have, but she couldn't help it, for she had glimpsed this very moment– exactly the way it was now. Just like she'd seen Nicholas months ago walking up her path with that same straw hat on, though she had never seen him before today . . . at least not in the flesh. He was as handsome then as he was now.

Doubt of what she'd seen sometimes did cross her mind.

White and Negroe folk all said she was crazy anyway. Or . . . they called her a witch because she could do things Christian folks used to burn people for doing. Yes– she sometimes did wonder if she were indeed crazy, and all of the things she'd seen before they happened was just her mind playing tricks on her, or . . . if the serpent that lay just outside the door listening to them talk right now was even real.

But she'd seen this moment. Just like she'd seen what had happened to the Monclair boy and had prepared a salve for him days before his father beat him. And oh– poor Lar Cole . . . there was nothing to be done for *him*, and so there was no need to even try and intervene, she figured. Her first duty, she was aware of, was to protect that which was most precious in all the world. That was the deal she had struck with the serpent. There was no going back on it now.

"I know I'll be dead soon, 'cause I done already seen it, boy!" Enda told him. "I done seen a lot," she said with a grin. "You done come here wantin' to hear tales 'bout Negroes and lynchins' and beatins' and thievin'. But I gonna to tell you another story tonight. Maggie Mae gonna finally know a few thangs too. So listen-up good."

"I didn't bring paper to write with," Nicholas said apologetically.

Enda cackled. "Chile– you ain't gonna need no paper for this here story. You ain't ever gone forget the tale of Enda Sully . . . the witch of Folsom. You'll remember every word to the day you die."

CHAPTER 17

"You– Nicholas Barrons– see and hear what I want you to.

"You think you know who and what I am– what *we* are?" Enda asked, glancing quickly at Maggie Mae, and then back to Nicholas. "You don't! We're not ignorant, but far from it.

"As you can hear, my manner of speaking has changed– no? No more slave-talk for right now, for I was never a slave and neither were my people as far back as I can remember," she informed him. "Quite the contrary, chére. My father was white like you, but you already assumed that. It's who my mothers were that's most important to all of us sitting here right now.

"My father provided me with nothing but his seed and freedom, which was white skin. I was part of Les Gens de Couleur Libres," she said in perfect French, "'The Free People of Color' of Louisiana. But again, my mothers are the most important in this tale of tales.

"My mother was given to a Frenchman, Aubert-Louis Dozois to be his mistress by my grandmamma, Elodie. *Ahhh*– but she was a woman possessed of mysterious beauty rivaled only by you– my angelic daughter. But more importantly, she was the possessor of the *great gift* that I now have and Maggie Mae has so little of, and will never pass on to her offspring." She stopped for a moment, sensing that Nicholas was puzzled about what gift exactly she was talking about. "It's in the blood, my boy," she told him. "Passed on to my mother from those who gave her life . . . Indians and Africans who knew other gods and spirits before the Christian English, Irish, French and Spanish came with their God and Christ nailed to the cross. The gift is in the blood.

"Its grown weak over many, many years as we've become whiter," she continued. "My mother, Clarice-Marie, knew this would happen. I knew this! Maggie Mae knows this. But all in all, it's for the best. Yes, yes," she murmured, for her ears only.

"However, it is as strong as it ever was with me," she boasted. "I made it so, because I knew how to. I know what moves amongst us that can't be seen. I hear the one who crawls in the grass. I know far, far too much and much too little. And it will all stop with me. The gift and curse that it is will end in two month's time. The fear of that gift stays the hands of whites toward Maggie Mae and me– for now.

"But I confuse you– Nicholas Barrons. Don't I?" She smiled. "Say that I'm a mad woman or witch even, it doesn't matter. But when I tell you that every grandmother of mine has seen this . . . *our time* . . . this very moment . . . *believe it!*"

Enda clenched her fists and narrowed her eyes. "Maggie Mae will be the first female child of our line to love for love's sake. But for Maggie Mae, who possesses little of the gifts of my mothers, once I'm gone, there's nothing to hold white folks back from doing her harm," she told him. "As white as she is . . . more beautiful than any here in Folsom," she added, "she's still just a Negroe to them."

Enda suddenly became silent. She felt wearier than she had in all her long years that were finally, and she thanked God, coming to an end. Recalling the past always physically and mentally drained her. She had done it twice before. Once for Matthew, whom she had told the story to in explicit detail . . . the other time was for Lar, who she gave an abridged version to, like she was doing for Nicholas and Maggie Mae. There were some things they need not know. Some things, she realized, had to remain secret for all time. Though there was one who knew it all . . . Matthew, Lar's Uncle Matty by marriage, he had already promised to take it to his grave.

If they did know it all, they wouldn't believe it anyway, she figured. They wouldn't understand what pacts she had struck with the Indian and African gods of old . . . ancient beings slumbering in myths and tales of fantasy. They didn't need to know that she knew how to wake these forgotten gods, nor that once woken, these dark gods were difficult to put back to sleep, for in a world of Christian men and women, they had become jealous and angry gods.

The years masquerading as a white woman would remain secret also, she vowed. Her white lovers who never knew of her African lineage and who begged her for her hand in marriage would too forever remain obscured in time. And yes– she had killed. The ability to curse was her specialty. She remembered how proud her mother was of that. And oh, it was so easy. The fear of the white-skinned witches of Faubourg had become so great and legendary; just fear that they had been cursed was enough to sicken their minds, which in turn destroyed their bodies.

In having cursed someone without ever cursing them, the fame and fear of the Faubourg witches had grown considerably, she recalled. Her remaining mothers . . . grandmama Elodie and Auntie Fayance sensed this was not a good thing for any of them, as did she herself. The influence of the Christian God had grown considerably as the fear of the old gods waned. It was then they had decided to scatter to the winds of unknowing.

Grandmama Elodie to the north.

Auntie Fayance, her Creole husband and mixed brood of children to the west.

Herself to the east . . . to Mississippi.

"I made it to Folsom a few years after the war had started," Enda said abruptly, breaking herself free from the spell of the past. "By the time I came here, I wasn't a young girl anymore, but I was still pretty enough and white enough to pass when I needed something to eat and a place to sleep."

Nicholas nodded.

"When I encountered union soldiers, I knew enough about slave life and could speak like one to gain their sympathy and protection. To Confederate soldiers, I was just one more white woman who was driven from her home after my slaves revolted. I played this game very well.

"There was always a side to play, especially for myself who could pass between both worlds of white and Negroe at a whim. But it was a dangerous game, Nicholas Barrons," she told him, with a voice that had suddenly grown cold. "As a white woman courting favor of Confederate soldiers and whites, I had to bear witness to atrocities against my own people in order to survive. Lovers of the Confederacy lynched and burned Negroes at a whim, because their hate and animosity was just that great.

"And so they killed Negroes when they wanted to . . . hung them . . . burned them . . . hacked them apart like slabs of meat on a butcher's block. No opening a Negroe woman possessed was safe from a white man's groin. Negroe men and boys were castrated. And if they were lucky, they weren't forced to eat their own parts while white women and men watched on."

Nicholas began gagging.

Enda smirked. "Oh . . . you haven't seen that yet?"

Nicholas shook his head and covered his mouth.

"If you stay down here long enough, you will. You have yet to witness the true brutality of a white man who had it all, but now has nothing. You think you know what evil has descended upon the Negroe– well, you don't. Not yet!" She spat.

"So when I finally made it to Folsom, Mississippi, I encountered freed and escaped Negroes from the nearby plantations. They were just starting to think about scratching out a life on this side of the river, which was all but a forest. It took some time to reassure them that I was Negroe also, but after they realized that I knew about the spirits who moved in and out of shadows, they no longer had any doubt about my white skin and knew I was a part of them. So now, without a blood family of my own, I'd found one that was just as strong, if not stronger. And I came to love them as my own – especially one. But that's what made me finally realize who I truly was . . . a Negroe . . . an African . . . no matter how white I looked. The life of a white woman I then left behind forever. And I don't ever what to see that woman again.

"One particular night I ventured alone from our makeshift camp in the woods to look for fresh roots, even though I knew I shouldn't have. I should have taken one of the Negroe men with me. But nevertheless, I did so– foolishly.

"You see, my children, a woman there with us was with child and was sick. I knew she was going to lose the child if something wasn't done. I knew what ailed her and how to remedy it. I knew what herbs to look for and what prayers to use, and spirits to call on to heal her. I was going to be gone for just a few minutes, but it took longer than I had planned, and I walked further into the woods. The ones right behind this very house. And . . .

"I didn't see them before they saw me," Enda whispered. "Of all that I have seen that has come to pass, I was blind to *them* that night.

"But you say, 'who are *they*?'" She continued. "Young white boys headed off to save their way of life, they were. Only, I figured they were sneaking, because they looked too young to be ready for a grey uniform. They were making their way out of Folsom under the cover of the woods and darkness. They were off to war!

"I had ventured into town a few times in the company of Negroe men with a few pennies we had all scraped together. I was a shock to white-folks . . . a white woman in the company of Negroe men? But they soon learned who I really was, and those that hadn't seen me, heard of me quickly enough and came to know me as a Negroe, regardless of how I appeared. But it was how I looked that made the other Negroes and me aware that I would never be safe in Folsom alone.

"And those boys, knowing I was a Negroe when they saw me that night, they were upon me before I could run," she said, slowly and softly. "The larger of the four forced me to the ground and pulled my arms back above my head. Two others ripped away my dress and pulled my legs apart."

Maggie Mae gasped. Nicholas slung his head low.

"They prodded the youngest of them to take me first," she continued. "But he didn't want to do it. Even as I fought and yelled against these evil white boys, I could see he was afraid. He was as afraid as I was, though it was I who was about to be raped. But he did so nonetheless. So I screamed. I yelled. I cried like all the other Negroe women before me who had white men take from them what was not theirs to have.

"Though he was just a boy to me, he was old enough to put his seed in me. I knew this because I saw his eyes when he did . . . big and wide, and as blue as any ocean put on this earth by God," she said. "I could tell he had never laid with a woman, because he seemed more scared of what his body was doing and feeling than what he had done to me.

"He was silent as the devil when he finished. I knew he was ashamed," she said with a firm nod of her head. "Um-hmm! Ashamed *and* sorry– his blue eyes said so. But I didn't care at the time, because the others were yelling at him to take one of their places so that they could have a turn. So I screamed louder, because I knew they wouldn't stop until each one had. But the boy with the large blue eyes wouldn't move. The others yelled louder and I screamed harder.

"I screamed for help from the ancient gods and the new Christian God. I cried out for the ancient devils and the new one. My soul be saved or damned that night, I didn't care. I cried for help from anyone.

"However, my saviors were not spirits or ancient gods that night, but Negroe men who followed my screams. To me, they were black gods . . . African warriors . . . kings of righteousness. When they saw what those white boys were doing to me, they fell upon them with knives, axes and sickles they carried. Their hatred for whites that night was greater than a thousand whites' hatred for an uppity nigger who could read and write.

"The ground drank much blood that night!" She whispered.

"But I yelled for them to stop when they turned on the youngest . . . the one who raped me. I told them not to kill *him*. But they were afraid he would run back and raise the white folks up against us. I knew he wouldn't.

"I knew that if I became pregnant . . . which I did," she paused only momentarily before continuing, "that I would have murdered the father of my daughter. So I told the men to let the white boy live and assured them he wouldn't tell what had happened."

Enda stopped speaking. She looked at Nicholas and spoke as though the words were meant only for him. "In doing good or evil, there is always a price to be paid. I demanded and received compensation for his evil, as well as a promise from him for saving his life that wasn't worth saving."

Maggie Mae had yet to move.

"What was the price?" Nicholas asked. "And the promise?"

"The price has already been paid. But what it is, I cannot say . . . yet," Enda responded. "I have yet to ask for the promise. Though I think that time is not too far off."

"He's still alive then?" Nicholas' skills as a reporter were once again emerging.

Enda smiled at him. "Oh yes, my boy. Alive, but not well."

Again Nicholas. "He's ill?"

Enda leaned back. The stiff bones of the chair felt good against her own. "You don't have to be ailing in body to be ill. An ailment of the mind can affect the body just as well. Haven't you been listening, Nicholas Barrons? All you have to do is look hard enough and you will see what's true," Enda told him. "I can see in Maggie Mae's eyes . . . my own daughter who is beloved by me, that she has seen him and can see him now. Isn't that right, chére?"

Maggie Mae nodded reluctantly.

"Despite her father," Enda continued, "who he was or who he is, Maggie Mae is innocent. I could've ended her life the moment I knew she was in me, but I didn't. It was meant to be. Just like you, boy, sitting in my house right now. Some things are just supposed to happen, Nicholas Barrons. It wasn't by chance that I encountered those boys that night of all nights. And what of my child? Hmmm?" She asked. "The child is of me, just like she is of him, but she is forever all mine.

"I raised her without a thought of who her father was, because it didn't matter then, like it doesn't matter now. The only thing is that her blood has too much white in it. The gift of my mothers is but a memory in her. But that's a good thing. It's not good to know what's going to be."

* * *

Nicholas left under the cover of darkness. Enda figured she'd given him more to think about than to write about. But hadn't that been the point of it all? She wondered. She liked that he was as adventurous and brave, as he was naïve. He was going to have to be equal parts foolish and heroic, if he was going to survive the coming weeks, she thought.

Knowing that Maggie Mae would never broach the subject, Enda did instead. She sat on the edge of the bed and watched as Maggie Mae cleaned up the kitchen. In Maggie Mae, she saw no traces of herself or of her mothers. The color of her skin was so white . . . far whiter than her own skin was, which had slightly darkened as years passed.

Even so, she was proud Maggie Mae had always claimed the title of Negroe. Though her miniscule drop of African blood was dominant and always would be, outwardly, white skin and features held dominion . . . narrow, uplifted nose, blue-hazel eyes and silky blond hair. Only her slightly puffy lips showed what was truly in her. But those lips set upon such a heavenly face only made her more appealing, Enda noted.

"I know what he wants of you," Enda said in a hush.

"It ain't polite to eavesdrop, mama," Maggie Mae replied, as she gathered the crumbs off the stove into a rag.

"I haven't heard a thing you two said."

"Then you done already seen it," Maggie Mae remarked. "Right?"

"I've seen his face when he's near you. That's all I need to see to know what I know."

"To know what?"

Enda giggled. "That he loves you, chére."

Maggie Mae was unfazed or at least pretended to be. "He don't even know me."

"Enough, gal! Enough!" She spat. The crackling of her voice was enough to cause Maggie Mae to stop and turn. "It's time for you to be done with all this denying and lying. And stop that ignorant talk, too. You've been schooled to speak as well as any white woman, so start doing it! At least around me– and him! Start remembering and practice what I've taught you!"

"Ain't no reason . . ."

"There *isn't*! There *isn't*!" She snapped her fingers. "Goddammit, girl! There is . . . there is a reason to use what I've taught you." Enda was nearly panting, and had to force herself to breathe deeply to catch her breath. "You've been fortunate all these years, you have. Who I am has given white men pause so far, but it won't last. You're no longer safe here and you know it. That pretty face of yours is as much a curse to you as a Negroe, as it is a gift as a white woman. And a Negroe as beautiful as you will never be safe down here with white men running around doing whatever they like to whomever they choose. As a white woman, a white man will kill any man who dared to even *think* of touching you. But they will come for you sooner or later. Unlike me, you may not be lucky enough to walk away, except as a ghost. You aren't safe in a land where whites celebrate killing Negroes."

"Mama . . . mother . . . I can't leave," Maggie Mae responded. "I can't leave you or my home."

Enda shook her head. "You're saying you can't leave *him*. But he's lost to you, child. Can't you see that?" Her voice became soft, almost motherly. "Even when Lar was yours, he was never *yours*."

Maggie Mae walked over to the bed and sat on the floor. She took Enda's hands in hers and stared into her grey eyes. "Look into yesterday and tomorrow for me. Something horrible has happened to Lar. Something happened in that house that changed him. I . . . I . . ."

Enda squeezed Maggie Mae's hands. "You're a liar," she said, raising the corner of her mouth until a mischievous smirk formed.

"What!?"

"I was wrong. I told Nicholas Barrons a lie," she said. "The gift *hasn't* died with you. You don't have much of it . . . but you have enough of it." She nodded. "You sense something is coming– like I do. Something bad. *Real bad.*"

"*Yes*," Maggie Mae whispered.

"Which is exactly why you must leave," she told her. "Leave with that boy."

"Tell me about yesterday– and tomorrow."

"So you can do what? Try to change something?" Enda asked, this time raising a grayed brow. "You think you can help Lar Cole?"

"If I can," Maggie Mae replied. "I still love him. But I know I'll never be with him again. But that doesn't mean that I can't try and help him."

"Don't you think I would help him if I could? I can't."

Maggie Mae pulled her hands away. "I don't believe you."

"That doesn't matter anyway." Enda replied flatly. "You're falling in love with this Nicholas Barrons . . . I do see that. You see it. And he loves you more than you know."

Maggie Mae began to stand, but Enda grabbed hold of her shoulder. "I don't even know him, mama."

"Child, that don't matter," Enda replied. "It's how you feel when you see him and when he's not around. It's how his touch makes you warm inside. And when you don't feel it, the cold that grows in you until he's near again. That's what matters. That's what gives love a steady leg to stand on."

Maggie Mae stood up. "You want me to leave you to die alone in this hell?"

"Alone?" Enda asked. "Child, I've never been alone here."

"Because of me," Maggie Mae stated.

"No!" Enda huffed. "I loved before and I love now. And when you're gone, I'll love until my last breath is gone."

* * *

At first, Maggie Mae was confused about who Enda was talking about, until what had always been right in plain view became so, so very clear, if not downright obvious to her. She remembered

Enda always saying, if you want to hide something, put it out for everyone to see and act as if it isn't there and no one will ever notice– like mason jars sitting on a shelf for everyone to see.

"I never knew you . . . you and . . ." Maggie Mae whispered. "All these years?"

Enda nodded. "Ever since the day he saved me from those evil white boys and killed all but one of them."

CHAPTER 18

In the few hours before the sun was set to rise, the air had just begun to cool right before the furnace was about to be stoked once more. Those living near Enda slept, albeit more peacefully than she. Soon, she knew, a small army of Negroes would soon awake and begin their day anew, which was no different than any other day of toil and perseverance, and then later, back home to sleep and rest weary bones before awakening to another day of the same. In a great procession, Negroes would march down the road in front of her house and she would watch them . . . study them . . . rejoice for some of them and prematurely mourn for others . . . *because she knew.*

She had seen all of their tomorrows, as well as her own.

She didn't regret lying to Maggie Mae, when she'd told her she couldn't see what lay down the road for Lar. She *had seen* what was beyond and over the hill awaiting him! There was just nothing to be done to save him.

She knew if she had told Maggie Mae so, she would try to stop it. So she lied without hesitation.

In the tomorrows to come, she'd seen salvation and redemption that was to follow . . . but they came at a steep price.

It knew this also.

Oh yes– *It* was close by again. She could feel *It*– hear *It* . . . almost smell *It.*

"You ain't won yet," she said to *It* . . . *It* somewhere hiding in the tall grass across the road in front of her home.

A wind sprung up suddenly and cooled the morning air more than it should have, which sent chills along her thin-skinned arms. A small section of the grass seemed to shiver in defiance to her bravado. And as quickly as the gust of air came along, it was gone.

In many, many tomorrows to come, she saw the end of all things coming.

Enda closed her eyes and smiled. She thought she might even try to sleep a spell before the day came.

CHAPTER 19

Dreams of serpents and fire creeping upon a burgeoning horizon . . . Enda was not the only one who stirred restlessly in the land of Negroes in the early morning hours.

Sleep was not Mary's friend either.

She lay next to Lar who was softly snoring. The last few weeks had been difficult for all of them, beginning that Friday evening when he returned home from work without his cart, and Frank Clipper came along with it later that evening. Only, Lar didn't seem like the same Lar to her then . . . or even now. This doppelganger of Lar's was short-tempered and easily angered over the smallest incident or comment from her. He seemed enraptured with irrationality.

For weeks he hadn't worked or preached, or dared to venture past their yard for that matter. And while he spent his days out back staring at nothing but fields of waist high grass, she busied herself with work at the Monclair's or picking beans out in their garden, or while in bed before falling asleep, working on a new lie to tell everyone why he was acting the way he was. Even Uncle Matty, who no longer worked the fields and had been home with Lar since Lar stopped acting like Lar, had heard nothing more than an occasional "yes suh" and "no suh" from him, despite many attempts to crack his nutshell.

"He still farin' real badly, suh." She'd lied to Roman Meadows, hoping that whatever respect and sympathy Roman had for Lar would stay his hand from firing him for a few more days. So far, the ruse had worked. Roman seemed genuinely concerned and had sent best wishes. How much longer Roman would believe the tale, she wasn't sure. But the sooner Lar was back to work, the better for all of them, she thought hopefully.

The Negroes, however, were another story. They were lost without him. What were they to do without their preacher . . . their brother and friend . . . their guide in this life made bitter by white men? She wondered. Their love for Lar came in the form of food from the women and exhausted muscle from the men working their field out in the backyard at night. Mary was full of pride to see that her people loved Lar as much as he loved them. Their ongoing presence around their home made all those visits Lar had made to theirs to minister, sometimes in the midst of the night, all worth it.

However, upon Lar's third week of absence from the world, Mary could tell the other Negroe's were beginning to believe that something more than just an illness had befallen him. Her word that Lar was ill was no longer satisfactory. "*What* ailing a tree of a man like Lar so bad?" Which was basically the general consensus of Negroes who constantly inquired about his welfare. More importantly, they were perplexed why they couldn't see or speak to him. "He dyin', Ms. Mary?"

She understood exactly why they felt the way they did, for she had her own questions that remained unanswered. She knew the day in which whatever had occurred had happened. But that was all. His dark brown skin had the glow of ash when he walked in late that night. She knew if she had noticed his face, she would have known something was amiss with him . . . but she hadn't. Had his clothes, which stunk like river water caught her attention, she would have paused picking the greens at the table . . . but she hadn't. What *had* caught her attention was that he hadn't touched her or the child inside her, which he never failed to do since they'd been married and ever since she'd told him she was with child–again. That something was powerful enough to draw his affection away from her and the child troubled her greatly.

She rolled over to the edge of the bed and propped herself up by the arms, which had finally regained most of their former strength. It seemed with all of the weight she had gained, they were actually larger and stronger. Well, that was just fine, she thought. She figured the way things were with Lar a mess, she needed every extra bit of strength now more than ever. She quickly braided her hair into two cornrows on each side, put on her tattered red headscarf and dressed as quietly as she could. *What sense be there to make a racket and wake him up just so he can sit and don't talk?* She mused sourly.

She hitched up the horse and wagon, and pulled herself up on the seat. She drove slowly through their small section of land as Lar had done since getting the horse and wagon, picking up those who had risen early enough to catch a ride into town . . . if they hadn't already hitched a ride on Picken's wagon, that is. As usual of late, greetings were quickly replaced by inquires about Lar that she was already weary of hearing after the second passenger asked. But now there were five aboard in the back, and one Ms. Allie Mae up front next to her. When the non-answers she gave were not satisfactory enough, six questions became twelve, then eighteen, then twenty . . . then . . .

"All of ya'll just hush-up now!" Allie Mae snipped, swinging her head around and giving her best glare from pea slit eyes. "Ms. Mary done said he fairin' a bit better now, and ya'll still actin' like chillin' . . . yippity yap-yap-yap! Lord help!"

"We just askin'. Damn!" Jimmy Franks barked back. "Mary ain't said it botherin' her none . . . *Ms. Allie Mae!* We just tryin' to see 'bout Lar is all."

"Well it be botherin' me!" Allie Mae retorted, and then turned back around and faced forward.

All was silent for a while until they neared Enda Sully's home and Maggie Mae stepped out onto the road. "Ya'll scoot on up and make room," Mary commanded, as she slowed down the wagon. Allie Mae looked at Mary, but she ignored Allie Mae's suddenly widened eyes and wrinkled up nose.

"S'okay, Mary," Maggie Mae sputtered, pulling her white scarf securely down on her head. "It ain't too far a walk."

"But it be a walk still, chile," Mary replied. "Might as well save your legs a little now. Lord know white folks gonna have us runnin' all day anyway."

"Amen!" Missy Morgan replied from the back end. She was a maid much like Maggie Mae, only she worked for the Bowmans cleaning up after their six children in addition to being a cook . . . gardener . . . nanny . . . servant . . . *heel-dog.* She smiled at Maggie Mae as Jimmy Franks slipped off the cart and lent her a hand up.

"I gotta see 'bout Naper's grown-tail boy still peein' the bed at night," Willa groaned. "Chile sixteen goin' on seventeen in a bit!" She said incredulously. "Whole damn room smell like piss even after I clean it down and good!"

Missy Morgan wrinkled up her nose. "Lord have mercy."

"And the Mistuh and Missus just as nasty as they boy," Willa added. "Hell . . . I'd rather *be* 'round hogs than them."

"How things be with that ol' thang you sees 'bout?" Missy Morgan asked Maggie Mae.

"'Bout the same," Maggie Mae replied.

Jimmy, who was sitting on the rear of the wagon with his feet dangling off the edge, turned and laughed. "With that ol' nasty woman? Gal, ain't nothin' the same when it come to her!"

Missy Morgan sat straight up. "And oooohhh!" She half-whispered. "I hear she just as loose as she wanna be."

"Ol' Jezebel she be– if'n you believe what folk be sayin'," Willa added.

"Believe it, woman!" Jimmy assured her. "I see who she get ol' man Meadows to send up there to see 'bout that yard– same white boys– and they always justa' smilin' when they come back, too. And it ain't 'cause they happy 'bout the work they done done."

Missy Morgan wiggled her narrow hips. "*Oh, they done worked alright!*" Everyone erupted in laughter.

Jimmy Franks was close to tears. "You right! You right, gal! They done worked it, chile!" He bellowed, and began thrusting his own hips. Even Allie Mae, who never joined in such crass behavior had to turn her face to hide her smile.

"Ya'll can say what ya'll want," Mary spoke over the laughter, "but as far as I know, the mistuh be a better man as far as white folk go."

"Girl, that ain't sayin' nuthin'," Missy Morgan croaked.

"What be goin' on in that house, Maggie Mae– really now?" Jimmy attempted to ask with a straight face. "'Sides *workin' it!*" He added quickly, once again rousing up another row of laughter from everyone. "No ... no, seriously, chile." He wiped tears from his eyes.

"I don't know to tell you the truth, Mr. Jimmy," Maggie Mae replied. "I keep my head down and my mouth shut so I can keep food on my table . . . just like the rest of ya'll."

"Preach it, gal!" Allie Mae piped up.

"Well, whatever been goin' on there done stopped cold," Jimmy informed them all. "Ol' man Meadows ain't sendin' young white boys up there no more. He only sendin' Negroes with one of his white foremen to keep'em in line ... well, now he do since Lar ain't been 'round."

"All right, Jimmy! Don't start now," Allie Mae warned.

"I ain't gon' start, woman!" He snorted, and then rolled his eyes. "*I just sayin'!* He trust Lar to keep Negroes in line, *but since . . .*" he spat, "he ain't 'round, Roman send a white foremen up there . . . fat boys he know ol' *Loosy-Anna* ain't got an eye for."

"And speak of the devil!" Willa announced, turning her head around in the direction of the Meadow's home as the wagon crossed the bridge.

As it was, Maggie Mae was the first to dismount near the Meadows home. In the center of town, near the park with its dead tree slumbering silently in its midst, the others finished hopped off and continued the last leg of their journey by foot. The men headed out toward the roads leading to Meadow's and Monclair's fields, while the women sought out the direction of the homes and families they tended to. The lone occupant who hadn't followed suit was Allie Mae.

They were directly in front of the Monclair store where Allie Mae worked. "What be wrong?" Mary asked her.

"That be my question for you," she replied, with wide eyes as brown as her skin. "I know I done talked down the rest 'bout askin' 'bout Lar 'cause I know you sick of it– but it me, girl . . . Allie Mae. You know we done shared everythin' since we been knee-high. If'n you ain't gonna tell me, then I know Lar in a far worse way than you lettin' on."

"I don't know," Mary replied stoically.

"You don't know?"

"Lord my witness, Allie Mae– I don't," she insisted.

Allie Mae looked down for a moment and shook her head. "You ain't gonna like what I say then."

"I know what you gonna say, and I already thought 'bout it."

"Then take him to her!" Allie Mae insisted. "I know you don't care for her, but she is who she be, and you know she can fix jus' 'bout any ailment if she be in the right mind to do it."

"I already asked him."

"And . . . ?"

"He say 'no'."

"Why?"

Mary heaved her thick shoulders. "Maybe 'cause what ail him ain't in the body."

"That don't matter a thang!" Allie Mae shot back. "Not to Ms. Sully it don't anyways. She heal the body *and* the head . . . you know that!"

"He still won't go."

"I don't see why not. Ms. Sully done jus' 'bout raise Lar from knee-high . . .

"Allie!" Mary whispered suddenly . . . alarmingly. She moved her eyes slightly to the side of Allie Mae's head.

Quickly catching the hint, Allie Mae became silent, realizing who was behind her without needing to turn and see. "Mornin', Ms. Ford," Allie Mae offered.

"You comin' in today, o' you just gonna sit out here and flap yo' lips all mornin'?" Delilah Ford snipped.

"No ma'am," Allie Mae replied, as she rolled her eyes. It was all she dared to do.

Mary knew of Delilah's hatred more than most Negroes. It seemed to her that Delilah always went out of her way to be utterly unpleasant to her, not that she was ever kind or even cordial to any Negroe. Even now, Delilah dared Mary with her usual look of repulsion, to which Mary looked away, albeit slowly and only after having looked directly in her eyes. It was a subtle gesture that would be difficult for Delilah to prove as disrespectful and easy for Mary to prove as unintentional. And she knew Delilah knew it.

"I see you in the evenin' if I finish early 'nough and give you a ride back," Mary told Allie Mae.

Delilah spoke before Allie Mae could respond. "Just like a Folsom niggah . . . already plannin' to get home 'fore you even got to work."

Mary let Delilah's bait just dangle, though her hands did tighten about the reigns as she imagined it was Delilah's scrawny, leathery neck she was strangling. Both Delilah and Allie Mae were staring at her, both hoping for opposite reactions from her. "Yes'm" Mary replied, and went on her way to the Monclair house.

She tethered the horses to the post out in back of the house and entered though the kitchen door. It was going to be a scorcher today, she knew. The humidity already clung to her like fresh paint on wood. The door creaked as she entered. In the darkness, she saw several eyes staring back at her. She found the oil lamp and matches on the table where she always left them, and within moments, she had the room flooded in a pale, yellow light.

But she and the cats were not alone.

"Paul!" She exclaimed, half-shocked and half-frightened, and wholly glad that he was there.

Paul jumped up so quickly from the chair, it appeared as though he hadn't been sleeping at all. His startled expression vanished as quickly as it came when he saw whom it was. Only clothed in his underwear, he relaxed once more and plopped back into the chair. "Only you, Ms. Mary" he whispered, and then closed his eyes. Mary moved in closer with the lamp held high in one hand and her other taking hold of his chin and moving his face from side to side. A sickening sense of déjà vu swept over her, but dissipated as she saw he was in the same physical state as the last time she saw him.

"Chile . . . what you doin' down in my kitchen," she whispered, all the while listening for a scuffle or scrape of a footstep from above. She studied his face, which had gone back to being as lovely as it was before. She lowered the lamp to his chest and revealed bruises that had now faded to a pale orange.

He stirred for a moment, and then quickly fell back to sleep after her examination. With his arms folded in his lap, his head leaned back and resting on the wall, he looked finally at peace to her. And if there were anyone who deserved a bit of it, it was he, she figured. What he'd been through . . . and she wasn't only re-membering the last beating, though it had been the worst . . . but with all the beatings before that one, she could only imagine how he felt inside.

Mary let him sleep as she got breakfast started. Even as pots banged and pantry doors shut, Paul never stirred for more than a few seconds. It wasn't until the eggs were waiting in their bowl, the grits indignantly puffing steam, and just out of the oven bis-cuits oozed their *'I'm brown, flaky and ret' to eat'* aroma, that Paul finally roused.

"Mornin'," he croaked. His eyes were half-shut from sleep and an aversion to the sunlight now flooding the room.

Mary was stoked the fire and prepared to fry the eggs. "Why don't you go on up and get change now? I done already heard some stirrin' above like they fixin' to get down here."

Paul yawned. "He was at it again," he sighed.

"After you?"

Paul yawned again. "No . . . well . . . I don't know. I didn't take a chance," he replied. "I heard him as he was coming in. He started yelling at mother about something. I figured I better leave. When he went to his study, I snuck down here."

"'Spose it worked then," she commented. "But you best leave the house all together next time. Ain't no tellin' . . ."

"I'm going to."

Mary nodded. "Good then."

"No, Ms. Mary– I'm going to leave," he clarified. Then in a whis-per he said, "*Leave.*"

She was about to beat the eggs in the bowl cradled on top of her belly, but paused. "Goin' away now, is you?" She uttered, and slowly began whipping the eggs.

Paul nodded affirmatively.

"By yo'self?"

Paul shook his head.

"Eh-hmmm," Mary grunted. She had always wished he would leave Folsom, but now, unexpectedly and selfishly, she wanted him to stay. She *had* raised him, and despite her disdain for white folk, she loved him. If there was one thing she needed right now, it was love, for she knew he loved her also. But it was because she loved him that she would never try to stop him from leaving.

She punished the eggs some more. "Good thang you won't be out there by yourself. When you leavin', chile?"

Paul was on his feet unsteadily. "I'm not sure . . . few weeks maybe? We're still trying to sort out where to go and what we'll need to get there."

"'Spose anywhere be better than here."

"That, Ms. Mary, is dead right," he replied. "I think I know how slaves felt now."

"Say what?!"

Paul quickly moved next to her. His head was almost at the top of her shoulders. "Don't be mad, Ms. Mary. I . . . I didn't mean it like you think." He paused for a moment. "I guess I don't really know how I meant it. It just came out. It was just a feeling I had."

"What you mean?"

His eyes searched the ceiling that was now more yellow grease than white paint. When he looked at her and spoke, she heard not the words of a boy, but those of a man. "Its like . . . like . . . I feel like I'm finally going to be free," he said in wonder, as his blue eyes danced behind black lashes. "With father, I try to do as I'm told. I try to be the son he wanted, but he still beats me. And now . . ." his lips trembled, "I think he would kill me if he . . ." The strength he'd seemed to have found was gone. His arms became flaccid and hung at his sides. Then, with little warning, tears sprang forth.

She set the bowl of eggs on the table, and before understanding why, brought him into her arms. To her, it seemed he was right where he should be . . . close to her other child and close to her heart. She understood his tears now. She realized why he spoke of a connection to her people who were once slaves in shackles, but were now just slaves. She could see how Paul felt imprisoned by who he was, just because of what he was.

Paul pulled away from her and wiped the tears from his cheeks. He managed a smile. "I've got to stop that," he groaned, reaching out and touching the tear wet spot on her apron. Before Mary could respond, he was back upon her and gently laying the side of his head on her belly. His hands rose to either side and caressed it. "Hey, you in there. You're so lucky, little baby," he whispered. "I'm going to miss you. But I'm not leaving until I see you."

Mary bit her lip. *Go on and stay in hell, devil,* she thought. *And you join him too, God, if you don't love this here white boy.*

She laid her hand on Paul's head.

"Your mammy love you too, chile," she whispered to him. "She just ain't . . . strong enough sometimes to show it. I sure protect you if she could."

Paul pulled away from her. "Just because she gave birth to me doesn't mean anything. That doesn't make her my mother."

"Pa . . ." Mary started, but he wouldn't let her finish.

"No, Ms. Mary . . . no!" His eyes welled with tears again. "My mother was never *my mother.* I have her blood and that's it. It don't mean nothing to me, and it never will. It's *always* been you," he whispered, turned, and was through the kitchen door and into the living room before she could even blink.

* * *

As it turned out, Mary was having one of the best days she could remember in weeks. Paul's aunts– Isabel's sisters, had come soon after lunch and gathered Beatrice up for a week's stay with them, who was of course delighted to leave dreary Folsom if only for a short time. There was no doubt that she would return with a bounty of new trinkets and bows and perhaps even a pretty dress if she were lucky and whined enough.

Simeon disappeared soon after breakfast, much to Mary's delight. That left only she and Isabel, as Paul had quickly performed his chores and set off up the road with company. Yes, the day had been good to her, but it wasn't just because Simeon and Beatrice were gone, or that Isabel had finally left her alone to finish preparing supper on time, and mop and dust and change sheets and do laundry . . . it was Paul.

When he was splitting wood out back, she'd watched him struggle to lift and swing the axe against the lingering pain of the last beating. With his shirt off, he looked so frail to her. She could easily see that if he were to strike the wood too hard, he would be the one that splintered instead. Yet, his frailness suited him. His sweat heavy, black ringlets bouncing off his forehead as he swung and chopped; those wondrous blue eyes buried beneath black brows and lashes prettied him so. Mary knew he would never be a thick-limbed, hearty man. But despite that, she realized he'd been teaching *her* a lesson in strength all along. Through beating after beating . . . blackened eyes, swollen jaws, fractured ribs to name a few . . . and just recently the smashing of his manhood, he still persevered. She wondered how could she do any less?

Though she didn't have the foresight of Enda Sully, she didn't need it to know that the road ahead for both of them would be wrought with strife and adversity . . . she, for just being a Negroe woman . . . he, for loving men. She knew hard choices would have to be made in order to survive in the world they lived in. But give up? How could she if *he* hadn't?

When she left . . . after supper was served, the clothes folded . . . floors cleaned, the rooms dusted . . . she was determined to pull herself up and Lar along with her. And she thanked Paul for it . . .

for the lesson he gave just by waking up one more day and breathing ... walking ... living, even though hurt and pain haunted his footsteps, waiting for him to stumble.

There would be no passengers carried back today on the cart, she thought. There was something more important to see to. It was time for answers that only one person she knew of could give her.

It was time to see the witch of Folsom once more.

* * *

Enda's ramshackle house seemed deserted. Mary had no doubt she was in there. It was almost as if she could sense the old woman's presence behind the wood boards. She knocked hard, rattling the entire door that barely clung to its rusted, crumbling hinges. Scarce moments passed before she heard scuffling, and then the unlocking of the latch. The door opened.

Enda's snow-white hair was unbraided and cascaded over her shoulders. "C'mon in, chile," Enda told her, as though she knew this meeting would not be short. She waved her hand about the room. "Sit on down anywhere you like."

Mary plopped herself in the chair next to the table in the midst of the room.

Enda sat across from Mary and began tapping her bone-thin fingers on the table. She looked down briefly and then up, but not at Mary. "Somethings," she began, "somethings ain't worth knowin' 'bout. Somethings is." She shrugged her frail shoulders. "But sometimes answers just lead to more questions that don't have answers at all."

"I ain't rode up in here for some riddles, Ms. Sully," Mary snipped. "For once it be good if you just say thangs like they be."

Enda locked eyes with Mary. "All those years I raised you ... what I done done for you just lately ... this is the respect you come to me with? You talkin' to me like *I* owe *you* somethin'."

"You owe me the truth!"

"I owe you not a damn thing, chére," Enda whispered coolly.

Mary scooted her chair closer. "You done played with my life–Lar's life . . . hell, even your own chile's. You been doin' it ever since we been babies and you still doin' it now."

"That what folk call '*an opinion*'."

"That be the truth . . . old woman!" She growled.

Enda smiled. "You always had a choice, Mary."

"Like gettin' with child when you say not to have any more chillin'?" Mary asked, as her hands instinctively covered her baby-filled belly.

"*Yes!*"

"And tryin' to keep Lar and Maggie Mae together."

Enda's face relaxed. Mary thought she detected a faint smile that was unmistakably motherly and kind, yet mixed with a hint of sorrow. "No, chile. That had nothin' to do with me. None of it at all."

"I still don't believe you."

Enda's fingers began rapping anew on the table. The softness that had soothed her face moments ago was now completely gone. "It don't matter whether you believe what I sayin' or not," she replied, in her usual matter of fact manner. "The truth be starin' you right in the face, gal."

"Then tell me 'bout Lar," Mary demanded. "Give me the truth 'bout what be wrong with him. He ain't got no fever, no sweatin' . . . ain't cool . . . it be somethin' else. And what it be he ain't sayin' to no one . . . not me or Uncle Matty. But I know you know what it be."

"What you gonna do if you know the truth?" Her white brows jumped. "You gonna march 'round and see the wrong be made right– even if it mean crossin' white folk to do it?"

Mary defiantly straightened her spine. She returned Enda's stoic gaze with a frigid one. "If I have to? Yes'm!"

"No."

"No?" Mary asked. "No what?"

"I *don't* know what happened," Enda replied. "I *do* know that it be his God-given soul that be stricken. And there ain't nothin' in these old, white hands and black soul, or anythin' in my jars up on these shelves here that can fix that."

Mary shook her head. "There be somethin' that . . ."

Enda stopped her with a snap of her fingers. "That boy be more my own chile than he ever was his mammy's! If I could fix him right, I would have been down to your place first thang whether you wanted me there or not. But, Mary-chile, I can't. And neither can you. It be up to Lar now to heal that wound . . . or . . ."

Mary asked, almost afraid to know. "Or?"

"Die," Enda whispered. She leaned back in her chair and shook her head affirmatively. "You wanted the truth– well now you got it, gal. He either goin' to heal himself or die."

Mary was speechless . . . but Enda wasn't.

"Oh yes, chile!" Enda closed her eyes and never opened them again until Mary had left. *"I've seen it!"*

* * *

Lar still felt the darkness all around him, but at least it was no longer within him. He now understood there was no way to exorcise the evil that haunted his world. He was sure it would either drag him down to the depths of hell or raise him up to heaven, but only if he let it. He felt as though he had already been to hell once, and once was more than enough.

Hell, he'd found, was not a rocky wasteland whose midst was split by a boiling lake of fire and filled with souls that burned for all eternity. No! Hell was cold and icy. It was a place of loneliness without light enough to cast a shadow from his own body, which would have at times been a welcome companion. Hell was walking amidst the living, yet being unable to feel life. Hell was the loss of his pride and soul, and what it meant to be a man. Hell was the shame that he could not forget or reconcile with. Hell was the need to reach out for help, yet be unable to, no matter how close it was.

Yet, help did finally come.

A voice, he realized, had been calling his name all along. Even when he'd thought he was alone, he wasn't. Prayers he thought that had been blown away by black winds *were* heard. Not slowly, but with great speed and strength, he felt drawn forth from the nether regions of his hellish soul and into the light . . . back in the land of the living who were damned– though this they did not know, yet still they wanted him back amongst them.

Though the memory of what had sent him to hell remained, and still the thought of it tortured him, he grasped hold of the handles of forgiveness. The strength to open his living eyes and to move his living limbs was his once more. To touch and taste were once more under his control. He rejoiced at being alive again.

But memories of that day in that room with *her* refused to fade. He could still see her face . . . smell her . . . feel her touch. Every memory of that moment made his stomach threaten to revolt against him . . . his manhood shrank at the thought of her taking what was not hers to take and reducing him to nothing but an animal.

Mary . . . his strong, beautiful Mary . . . he loved her like no other . . . but even her touch sent those vile memories creeping back into his thoughts. Her touch, which had always warmed him, now felt cold. He knew it had nothing to do with Mary, and everything to do with Lucianna. Still, he couldn't shake the feeling that his sense of manhood was being taken by force every time Mary reached out to him. It was just easier to remain mute, uncaring and numb, rather than be vulnerable to attack and experience it all over again.

So what now? He wondered.

The right to control his body had been taken from him. His seed had been spent upon the floor and he made to clean it up like a dog. Humiliation and helplessness were constantly snickering at him. *What you gonna do now, Lar-boy?* He asked himself. *You back in the land of the livin'.*

He walked to work alone after hearing Mary leave in the wagon. He went through the motions in Meadow's fields as though he had not been gone for weeks. Questions from the other Negroe men were answered with smiles and polite assurances of his return to good health. Even when Roman called him in, the face he put on was one of happiness, though he couldn't feel anything at all. In truth, what strength he possessed to return and interact with the world, he knew wasn't his, but God's, for his true strength he felt was now just dribbled stains on floorboards in Lucianna's bedroom.

That evening on the porch, with only a sliver of the moon to give light, he saw the wagon approaching from the west with so large a figure on top, he couldn't mistake Mary for anyone else. At that moment, every fiber of his being begged him to go back inside, and once there, back to the nether region in his mind where it was safe. Why? . . . because when Mary looked at him, it was as though she knew what had happened . . . that he was no longer a man, but a boy . . . a Negroe boy . . . a niggah boy.

Despite his fear, he stood his ground with a silent prayer upon his lips.

"What say, Mary?" Lar asked, as the wagon rambled up beside him. Mary pulled back hard on the reigns.

She smiled. "Fairin' middlin' I 'spose," she answered almost happily. "Done let the moon beat me home."

Lar wanted to run from her as fast as he could. He grabbed hold of the cart to steady himself. "Long as you back, I don't care who beat who home," he said. He took hold of the reigns from her and helped her down. Again, she smiled for him.

She moved in closer to him.

He knew what she wanted.

He gave her what she needed.

Her lips were as soft as he remembered. Her touch, as she placed a hand about his waist, was as firm as ever. Her scent was that of a woman. He needed this to hold his ground and not turn away from her. With eyes closed, he was assured that it was Mary's . . . not *hers*, whose touch he was feeling. But it was *her* that he remembered now and wished he could forget. When they parted, he forced his lips into a grin. It must have seemed genuine enough, for she returned his gesture.

He held her hand until they reached the door. Once inside, he fed her the meal he'd prepared earlier that he and Uncle Matty had already partaken of. And as he expected, after she finished eating and washing her face in the small bowl of water beside the bed, she laid next to him.

Making love to her was difficult to say the least.

Twice he lost his fullness while inside her. Then, when it finally felt as though it would finally stay engorged, it became a struggle to reach the pinnacle of desire that held no desire for him, but was simply an end to a process. It was as though his body fought against releasing his seed again. Instead of every thrust taking him one step closer to exploding pleasure, it was like a step backwards.

Focusing on how warm, soft and wet she was did nothing to excite him. Seeing and touching her milk engorged breasts failed to fill his manhood with even more blood, as it always had before. No . . . his only pleasure was himself.

With his eyes shut, he increased the speed and intensity of his thrusts. He shut his mind away from everything but the sensation he was feeling, and not who provided it. The sweat coursing down his back and buttocks was coming from desperation not lust.

With more effort than it took to lead a donkey, he spilled inside of her and wished he hadn't, for a sense of helplessness flowed into him as his seed flowed out, as it had in Lucianna's bedroom. It was as though what should have been given freely had once more been stolen from him. When he withdrew, the smell of his seed made vomit quickly rise up in his throat. He quickly lay on his back so that it only seared his throat, and he could then swallow and push the acid back down.

When she pulled at him, wanting him to snuggle, he had to force himself. *Away* is where he wanted to be now . . . away from her feminine touch . . . away from Folsom . . . away from his life as a Negroe man.

CHAPTER 20

It was David who made the first move– taking hold of Paul's hand and pulling him close after slipping into the woods away from prying eyes. Paul welcomed David's firm, yet soft lips . . . cherished each and every callous of his hand, and swooned as he looked upon David's face, for what he saw in David's eyes was something he'd never had. *Yes*– he'd felt love before. His aunts loved him . . . his mother, he guessed, if Mary was to be believed. But there was something different that moved him about David's love. They loved each other because they chose to willingly give away their hearts to each other.

Hand-in-hand, as they walked deeper into the bowels of the woodlands, Paul thought of how circumstance had brought him and David together. Both were despised and ridiculed by the other boys because they were attracted to men. But loving men . . . loving David was his secret, greatest pleasure and sorrow. Being free to love David made him feel alive, but it was that same love, he understood, that could also shorten his life if the wrong someone were to find out about it. Funny though, he pondered, that his father seemed to have always suspected such a thing that he never had a name for himself– until now, that is.

But the others . . . his mother, Mary and likely Lar, he guessed, had his secret forced upon them, thanks to Beatrice. The moment she hinted at his attraction for David in front of Mary and his mother, he vowed to hate her forever. The beating that followed made him promise himself to never forgive her. Only recently, he was able to let David caress him 'down there' without flinching in pain, but the ache wasn't entirely physical in nature. It was something that he couldn't touch or see. What he did know was that thinking about the beating that caused it hurt worse than the beating itself.

"What got you all far and away?" David asked, gently squeezing Paul's hand.

Paul scrambled for a reply that could masquerade as the truth. Remembering the beating his father gave him was one thing, but talking about it was something he wasn't quite ready to do yet. He knew if there were one he would eventually speak to about the vile assault, it would be David and David alone. Who else could ever understand that someone wanted to pound his flesh, tear his soul asunder and attempt to take his life, all because he desired the touch of a man and could only admire friendship from a woman? But it was still far too raw for him to speak of right now. The ache was still too deep.

"Just thinking about Mary and the baby, is all," Paul half-lied. "It should be coming about any day now."

David smiled at him. "She *is* a good niggah."

"Hey!" Paul snapped.

"What?!"

Paul's brow furrowed. "Don't call her that."

David's eyes widened . . . his chubby, already ruddy face turned even darker red. "Call her a niggah? Ain't that what she be, Paul?" He uttered in defense.

Paul slowed down and reined David in by the hand. "Look here," he told him. "Who says she's a niggah? Your pappy and mine? Those bastards at school? The reverend?"

David looked up to the treetops for answers. "Well . . . yeah. We all do. All white folk say it. What the bother with it?"

"Alright then," Paul snipped. "What do you think they say about us then? You and me– the way *we* are?"

David was silent. Then suddenly, as though enlightenment was his . . . "It ain't the same, Paul," he said almost teasingly, attempting to lighten a darkened mood that had descended upon them. He tugged on Paul's hand to continue, but was met with resistance.

"It is the same."

"How so?"

"Then what are you?"

"What? You mean . . ." He fumbled for words. "Well, I a boy . . . I . . . I mean a man, if that what you askin'?"

Paul let go of his hand, stepped back and then jumped toward him. He jammed his index finger towards David's face. "No . . . no! You're sick! You're an abomination and a cocksucker! *You're not even a man!*" He spat. "A thing like you needs to beat and hanged from a tree," he seethed.

David's mouth fell and hung open, as though he'd been slapped with an open palm. It was the precise response Paul wanted and did not want. He loved David, but at the moment, he could think of no other way to show David how he felt, other than yanking at his guts and twisting them until they bled.

"How do you think everyone would feel about us if they knew?" Paul asked. His eyes all but disappeared beneath the cover of his black brows. "They *would* hurt us, David . . . you know they would." He took hold of David's hand and squeezed softly. David looked away as tears began to well in his eyes. "I'm not going to say sorry for telling you the truth."

"You didn't have to say it like that," David mumbled.

Paul turned his face so that they were eye to eye. David's lips were trembling. The lids of his eyes were red. "You . . . we've gotta be tougher than this. We can't fall apart and cry, and get nervous like old women when people question us. Believe it or not, someone somewhere will. We have to learn how to hide it."

"I know," David whispered. He quickly wiped away a tear that had escaped.

"Don't you want to just be left alone to live in peace?" Paul asked.

"Of course."

"Ok, then," Paul told him, "then why not Negroes then? They don't want to be left alone? Mary has always been nothing but kind towards you . . . but are you gonna say to her and Lar, and the baby they can't live without being bothered?"

"No!" He protested vehemently. "I like Ms. Mary a lot."

"But when you call her a niggah, you say that she's different," Paul said. "You tell her and all the other Negroes they can be treated like shit. Each time you say 'niggah', you say that it's alright to do anything bad to them." Paul kissed him and then wiped the tears from David's face with his sleeve. David smiled weakly, but resisted looking at Paul.

"I . . . I guess I jus' don't get it all, ya know," David apologized. "It the way things are . . . with the Negroes, I was sayin'."

Paul shook his head. "And with us, too. People have always hated people like us and always will, just like they hate Negroes and always will . . . but David, listen. Are we goin' to be like them? Now that you know what it feels like to be hated for just being *you?* Do you want to do that to someone else?" David shook his head. "Then don't! If you want someone to treat you fair, treat them fair first. Not that *anyone* is going to treat *us* fair– but that doesn't matter. You and me are on the other side of other folks. We're *not* like other folks anymore. We can hide who we are, but Negroes can't."

But for a while they did hide in the dense thicket away from the riverbank and made love. And afterwards, asleep next to David–

the one place he felt safe, secure and loved for what *and who* he was– the world and lives of men and women . . . whites and Negroes . . . what was considered good and evil, seemed not to matter so much.

* * *

"It's getting late, Paul," David said.

Paul opened his eyes to find David's smiling face hovering closely above his. Before he could fully awaken, he felt David's lips upon his and momentarily fell back into a quasi-dream trance. Innocence is what he saw when he looked at David. Within David's large eyes, Paul could see the truth of his feelings for him.

"Ready then?" Paul asked hesitantly. The idea of returning home quickly iced every warm thought that had just coursed though his mind.

David growled. "Yeah and no," he droned. "But we gotta go somewhere first."

"Where?"

"Well . . ." he started, unable to resist a smirk. "If I told you, you probably wouldn't want to go."

"And why's that?"

David smiled this time. "'Cause where we goin'."

Paul's eyes became half-moons. "And that is . . . ?"

"Just come on."

"You're not going to tell me?"

David rolled his eyes and sighed playfully before turning and lumbering off into the woods. Paul grumbled the entire way, but teased David into continuing to play the bothered, frustrated role. When words no longer sufficed to produce a reaction from David, Paul poked and prodded him, causing him to reply with faux grunts and threats of retaliation. Paul then began jabbing his fingers at David's back. "You'd have to hogtie me first, 'cause I'm not stopping until you tell me," Paul told him.

"You gonna be really sorry then," David warned, "'cause once I got ya, I ain't gonna let ya go easy."

"Who says I want to escape?"

David turned around and pecked Paul on the lips. "Who says I ever gonna let ya go?" David took hold of his hand and began leading him toward the clearing. "Almost there I think."

He was relieved that David had resumed walking so that he could quickly wipe his eyes. "Ah-ah . . . are we?" He stuttered.

As the number of trees thinned and waist high grass thickened, in the distance there stood a lone, tiny house. David pointed at it. "You see it?"

Paul looked at him quizzically. "That house?!"

"Yeah," David replied.

"And . . ."

"It's whose house be why we're here."

"And . . .?"

"It's the witch's house," David whispered reverently. "Ms. Enda Sully– the witch of Folsom."

Paul knew who she was. He'd seen her in town years ago, but her daughter, whose name he couldn't remember at the moment, he'd seen more often. Ms. Enda Sully was the woman people always said not to bother with, unless you want her to cast a spell upon you . . . well at least that was the rumor, he remembered.

"So why are we here?"

"She told me to come," David replied simply.

"*She!?* Ms. Sully told you to?" Paul asked unbelieving.

"Yeah."

"Liar!" Paul snorted.

"God's truth," he said, with large, earnest eyes.

"When?"

David was silent for a moment. "When Ms. Mary and me rode out here that day I told ya. The witch came out and talked to me after they was done doin' what they was doin'."

"And what did she say?"

"To remember this place."

Paul's brows rose.

"Here. Where we be right now," David explained. "She said to remember how to get to her place from the woods."

"Why?"

"Dunno," David replied. "She told me to. I was afraid to ask her why. She's a witch, ya know."

Paul rolled his eyes. "She's not a real witch, David. It's just a story made up so we don't get hurt nosin' around where Negroes live. But that's not true either. Negroes haven't ever done anything to us. It's the other way around."

"Well, I think she is," David protested. "If you see her up close, you gonna think the same thing, too."

Paul sighed. "She's not a witch, David– just an old woman."

"She told me to come here," he replied, as though he just gave Paul verifiable proof.

"You came because she and everyone else have filled your mind with nonsense. Witches aren't real," Paul insisted. "Neither are boogeymen or vampires, or the ghosts they keep saying are in the woods. They're just stories people make up."

"Well, if she ain't a witch, then how come Ms. Mary felt right as rain after seein' her then?"

Paul slapped his head and groaned.

David ignored him. "All I know be that Ms. Mary was feelin' poorly when we came and felt better when we left."

"And she didn't say why she came?"

David's mouth parted, but no words came out.

"There shouldn't be secrets between us," Paul told him, obviously perturbed. "We're risking our lives to be together. You know people would just as soon lynch us as they would a Negroe." Paul paused. His own words sent a chill through his body. He saw that same sense of unease course through David, as his eyes grew wide with fear. "What I'm saying is that, if we're going to do *this*, we have to be honest with one another– completely. Being together means we're going to have to realize that we'll only have one another to depend on. We can't have that if we keep secrets– o.k.?"

"I ain't doin' it on purpose," David protested. "I just promised Ms. Mary not to tell anyone. That the only reason why. I don't wanna keep thangs from ya. I may not be quick like you is . . ."

Paul shook his head. "David, I'm not trying to . . ."

"It true, Paul," he interrupted, passively shrugging his shoulders. "I do think 'bout thangs a lot . . . 'specially 'bout you and me. One thang I think 'bout a lot and don't need no one to correct me on is that . . . I love you."

Paul went numb from head to toe.

"I know I ain't 'spose to be sayin' that to another boy, but I do," he said. "I know men 'spose to love only women the way I love you. But if you want the truth of thangs then, that how I feel inside for ya. Maybe I'm just a . . . a . . . abolition like the bible say. But that just how I be, I guess.

Paul smiled and then cupped David's chubby cheeks in his palms. Its touch was warm with hints of stubble– it all seemed so natural to Paul. "But we aren't abominations, or sick or deviants. For all I care, they are . . . every last one of them who says so about us. I used to pray to God to make me like other boys, but it didn't work. And it *ain't* gonna work!"

"Me too!" David gasped.

"And it didn't work, did it?" David shook his head "I used to pray to God that he would stop my father from beating me, and guess what? That didn't work either. I did what God said to do, and still I'm just me. From what the reverend says, folks have the right to hate me for being who I am. Well you know what, David? I love you just the same as you love me. And if folks hate me for it . . . then they just do. But I'm never going to stop loving you. They'll have to kill me first."

"But they ain't ever gonna find out– right?" David asked and urged.

"Never ever-ever," Paul promised. "And you know what that means we have to do then? We can't just go around saying we're friends . . . people will suspect something."

"Well, I ain't gonna miss Folsom none. Are you . . . *brother?*" David smiled.

"Like I miss a beating . . . *brother.*"

"Who get to be older? We'll never get by sayin' we twins."

Paul shrugged. "Doesn't matter I guess. Not as much as choosing names to go by and sticking to them."

"Oh– I hadn't thought 'bout that. I reckon we should, huh?"

"We can't leave any doors open . . . first and last names for both of us. No one can ever be able to track us back here. We have to forget Folsom and everything about it."

"Ms. Mary, too?"

Paul sighed deeply. "In here," he said, pointing to his head, "but never here," he tapped his chest. "Truth be told, that's the only reason I haven't come a'tappin' on your window to sneak out of here. I want to see the baby before I go. I have to know what he looks like before I leave so I don't ever forget him."

"Really?"

Paul sighed again, but this time more from frustration than anything. "I'm tired of folks telling me what's right and what's wrong . . . especially when my mind is telling me, no matter how I look at things, *I'm* the one whose thinking right about stuff. How can loving someone . . . Negroe or white be wrong? Love is love, isn't it?"

David smiled.

"Is loving a Negroe wrong because they're a Negroe? Just because they're a man? Just because some idiot preacher says so?"

"No!" David resounded.

"How about we start doing things our way and say to hell with everybody else?"

David nodded eagerly.

"Alright," Paul said. "C'mon then." He took hold of David's hand and led him out into the field of grass.

"Where we goin'?"

"To see *her.*"

"Her?" David replied, the tremor in his voice gave away that he already knew who 'her' was. He shook his head. "Uh-uh. She said just to know the way, not come and see her."

"Well I want to see her. I want see your witch of Folsom with my own eyes," Paul announced, with mock grandiosity.

* * *

The lingering light of the day reminded them exactly how long they had been gone from their homes. With each step, waist-high grass receded to worked over black fields bursting with dark green vegetation. And then slowly, Enda Sully's house came into plain view.

"We best hurry up," David urged.

Paul peeked over toward the falling sun. "My father won't care if I'm late or not, as long as my chores are finished. It's not like he has to have a reason to get hateful anyway," he added.

"No. Just your big mouth sister is all," David replied.

Paul snarled. "If I never have to look at *that* fat face again . . ." David nodded in agreement. They passed by the outhouse and chicken coop . . . pigpens and the smokehouse, until they were finally at the rear of Enda's shack. "Well, here we are," Paul announced, turning to David who was attempting to conceal his ample size by crouching. Paul shook his head at him. "*What* are you doing?"

"Whaaaat?!" David whispered innocently. His eyes swept the lay of the land as though something were about to jump out at them at any moment. He straightened his body slightly before his spine turned to rubber once more.

"It doesn't even look as if anyone is here," Paul said, as he took measure of the ramshackle house. A mulatta was what he remembered folks said she was, though he didn't exactly know what the word meant, other than it was used with Negroes who had some white blood in them. But her daughter, he'd seen in their store from time to time. *She* did appear white. So white, it was nearly unbelievable that there was anything African in her. But that was the least of what he remembered that made her unforgettable. He'd seen how men looked at her and why, for it was men that he himself was admiring openly, whilst they were distracted looking at her.

But of Enda herself, he had nothing more to go on but rumor and innuendo. And it was more than an end to the speculation and dark whispers about her that he sought. It wasn't just to prove himself right or show David that she was just an old woman, but he wanted answers about Mary and the child, and not of the hocus-pocus kind. It was the need for those answers that drove him closer to the house, and at times, having to tug a most hesitant and twitchy David until they were in Enda's backyard surrounded by a cadre of bug-pecking chickens, who surprisingly ignored their presence amongst them.

"We shouldn't be here," David warned. He was stuck to Paul's side. "I know ya don't think its true what they say 'bout her– but what if folks be right? She could have us dead in a week."

"Or maybe not," Paul challenged.

Paul took David's hand and pulled him along. They skirted the perimeter of the house, both looking downward occasionally at the crumbling wood foundation for snakes that were known to enjoy the cool shade underneath. At a window that was centered in the middle of the house, Paul popped his head up quickly and looked in. Before David could say a word, he did it once more but with less caution.

"I don't see anyone," he reported. He stood upright and pulled David up with him. He looked inside the film-coated window again. "Not a soul."

David reluctantly peered inside. "Whew!" David uttered, with a relieved smile.

Paul prodded David toward the front of the house. At first he peered up and down the road, which they were now much closer to. He found the road to be like he saw Enda's house . . . deserted. "Clear," he announced. Less cautiously, he snuck a glance around front of the house and then walked out into the opening. He turned around and flashed a victorious smile, and then quickly, before David could resist, he took hold of his hand and pulled him out from the side of the house. He raised his other hand as if presenting his next miraculous feat of wonder to David. "Nothing but a rocking chair," he said, almost disappointedly.

David looked at the front porch. There was a rocking chair with a mason jar full of some brown liquid next to it, as though who ever had sat there had forgotten to finish their drink, or simply grown tired of its taste. The two windows on either side of the door were like the one on the side of the house they had looked into . . . coated with a fine film of dirt, and hidden from the outside world by yellowed, ratty cloth from the inside.

Paul tugged at David, turning his attention away from the house and toward the road. "Nothing up this way either," he assured him. "I'm kinda disappointed though. I wish old Ms. Sully were here. Then I could show you that she's nothing but a woman."

"Well, I glad she ain't," David replied. "Ain't no use of stirrin' up thangs when you don't have to– be it true or not."

The simple wisdom of David's words shocked Paul. David may not have the sharpest of minds, but what he loved about him, and made him so endearing was that his words were always truthful and from the heart. He felt awful for having scolded David for calling Mary a niggah. He realized it was done innocently, because David just didn't know any better at the time, and Negroes to whites had always just been niggahs. Paul knew it was becoming too easy for him to see hate in others, even when it was just ignorance.

But not David.

My David. Well—we'll be gone from here soon enough. He smiled at David. Impulsively, Paul leaned in close to him. It felt like such a natural thing to do . . . to be close to his lover . . . to let him know that he loved him and would so forever.

But . . .

Like a jolt of electric fire surging through his spine, a sense far keener than intuition disrupted his love-dream. So strong it was, it cautioned him to pause before he could touch David. His gut screamed danger. His rational mind tried to reassure him that there was no one around, that they had just surveyed their surroundings and found it barren, save for the chickens and hogs out back. But the alarm from this novel sense would not relent.

You are being watched!

As Paul turned around, it was as if he knew where to focus his eyes. David did the same. As if on cue, as though they had instantly read one another's mind, they released each other's hand in the presence of Enda Sully, who was sitting dead still in the rocking chair on the porch.

Impossible! Minutes . . . no, Paul thought, seconds ago, there had been no one there at all. He knew this to be true because every one of his natural senses had told him so. Yet, despite what his senses had told him, there she was, as though she had been there for quite some time. He watched her reach down with a hand as white as his own, grasp the Mason jar and slowly bring it to her pink lips and sip at the brown liquid. His mind could no longer deny her existence.

He saw that she was indeed as old as everyone said she was, and as white also. *No*, he figured, had he not been told about her, he would never have guessed her to be a Negroe. Her gray eyes also said, *I am not Negroe*– yet she was. But now with his senses awry, he began to wonder whether she really was something more than just an old Negroe woman who didn't look at all Negroe.

"I see you done come back to see Enda, boy," she said. Her eyes were fixed on David. "You done found your way through yonder woods– hmm?"

"Yes'm," David croaked in reply.

Did she see us holding hands? Paul wondered. He couldn't read her stony façade. Her eyes seemed lifeless, even as they swayed in his direction and settled upon him . . . watching him . . . studying him. What she'd seen, she'd seen, he relented. And there was no turning back from it with a lie. "Eve . . . evening, Ms. Sully," he uttered. "We . . . I . . . I'm . . ."

"I know who you be, chile," Enda blurted. She picked up her jar and sipped at her drink. "I know Simeon Monclair's eyes anywhere . . . *Simeon Paul Monclair*." She smiled. "The Monclair boy-chile. But you ain't got those pretty black curls from your pappy."

"No, ma'am."

"Your manners either," she added.

Instinctively, Paul knew he should have been insulted had his father been anything of a father, but instead he felt pride.

"What you two white boys want?"

Feeding on Paul's strength, David spoke up. "Umm . . . you told me to learn this way . . . Ms. Sully. I 'membered it– *see*," he said, as if waiting for some praise or reward.

"True now . . . true-true," she replied. "But I said 'member it, not come sneakin' 'round near dark. I didn't tell you to come 'round this day or that day, did I?"

David inched closer to Paul. His need to hide 'who' they were, now seemed superseded by his need for safety. "No-no-no, ma'am."

"But you came anyhow. I guess why you came be what I should be askin' the both of you two, white chillin'." Her eyes danced from one to the other, yet once again they decided to stay on Paul.

"We came to see you," Paul explained.

"Why?" She crackled.

He looked at David, as if preparing him for what he was about to say. The words were already upon his tongue; he just had to speak them. But when he did, another voice echoed his very, exact words. But it wasn't David who said them.

"To see if you're a witch or not," Paul and Enda said in unison.

Whereas Paul's mouth hung open in horrified wonder, Enda's rounded as she hooted. She stopped abruptly . . . stared at him, and then patted her knee and laughed again. David lost all sense of caution and grabbed the back of Paul's shirt. Paul welcomed his proximity.

"Why you boys lookin' like a couple of chickens done seen a coon run by?"

Neither one answered. Neither one dared to.

Her brow rose slightly, as her voice lowered. She scooted toward the edge of the chair and placed a hand on each knee. "You two ain't the first that done come 'round askin'. It don't take bein' a witch to know what two white boys want when they come sneakin' 'round here."

Paul sighed . . . but only a little. "But . . . but . . . you weren't . . . I mean, we . . . we looked. There wasn't any . . ." Paul stopped and took a breath. "You weren't sitting there before and now you are. We looked!"

"'Maybe you was blind . . . Simeon Paul Monclair," she said. "I been sittin' right here all afternoon long. You ain't seen me 'cause you ain't want to see me. But you see me now, 'cause now you want to."

Paul didn't believe her. He knew what he saw, but her words were befuddling his mind. Actually, everything was. What he knew for sure was a lot of things weren't making any sense at all.

"You figurin' I be a witch now, don't ya?" She asked David, who shook his head like a mouse nibbling on the corner of a cracker. "But you– Simeon Paul Monclair, thinkin' 'no', 'cause witches ain't real. But still you thinkin' you saw what you saw, so now you ain't for sure what Enda be after all." She waited a moment, as though letting her words fully digest in their heads. "So I tell ya'll both what . . . come on up here."

David gathered more of Paul's shirt into his hands. Paul didn't deny he felt the same sense of apprehension. "Ain't no sense 'bein 'fraid of Enda if she ain't what you think she be . . . is there?"

"No . . . ma'am," Paul squeaked.

"Come'on up and ask Enda a question then," she invited, and then settled back in her chair. "If I be a witch, then what I say gonna come true, but if I not be one, then it won't . . . and then you know that Enda just be a crazy Negroe."

Paul moved forward, and with each step he took, David was adhered to his side. Though he found the courage to move closer to her, he stopped short of the porch.

"Ms. Mary came and saw you a while back," he began. Enda nodded her head. "With David here," he added. "Is she . . . is Ms. Mary's baby alright?"

Enda looked out toward the road and stayed there for several moments before saying . . . "The girl-chile be fine."

Paul smiled. "It's a girl!?"

Enda returned his smile with a mischievous smirk. "If I be a witch, then I guess I know these thangs. If not, then ain't no tellin' if she have a girl or boy-chile, or if it be well at all."

Let her be a witch, Paul thought quickly.

"What 'bout us?" David asked, instantly waking Paul from his dream of Enda flying on a broomstick with a black cat.

"David!?" Paul whispered in alarm. He darted his eyes to the side where David stood glued to him, and then back at Enda to gauge her reaction, which had not changed at all. Did she know what David was truly asking, he wondered nervously? If she were truly of the supernatural, then she would already know, wouldn't she? And if she did, then what would she do with what she knew of them? Did David know what he'd done?

This time, Enda's gray eyes stayed on them. If anything, they seemed to darken just a bit. "Believe or don't, Simeon Paul Monclair . . . and you too, David Greenlee. Follow your minds, like you done already set to. Ya'll linger 'round this place here and ain't nothin' good gonna come 'bout it. Now– if ya leave, you gonna find what you lookin' for, one way or 'nother. Death comin' for both of ya. Ya can't escape it, chillin'. It just be a thang how you gonna get there is all."

Believing she was a witch or not no longer mattered much to Paul. Within her icy vibrato, it seemed as if he could hear a pulsing vein of truth echoing in his ears, so much so that his own caution dissipated like steam, causing him to remove David's hand from his shirt and join it with his own. The sweat from David's hand mingled with his so much, they had to entwine their fingers to keep their hands from parting.

"If you two remain as you be right now," she continued, "your days will be as long as promised to blessed men. You part . . ." she paused but a moment, "and what days you been given will chill your bones like a frost come too early."

Paul was already cold after hearing her foreboding words. It was this paralysis that made him immobile when the front door opened and the loveliest of women– unmistakably Enda's daughter, came rushing out. Her blond hair was a bounty of waves crashing upon her shoulders as she darted toward her mother. Her bluish eyes, which Paul saw flash at him briefly, and then at Enda, crackled with yellow fire. "Stop it now, mama!"

"I can't stop what gonna be, chile . . . no matter how bad we want to change what be," Enda replied nonchalantly.

"You can't keep goin' 'round sayin' these things," Maggie Mae whispered in warning, though Paul heard her clearly.

Enda huffed. Paul thought she might spit at any moment.

"Can't?" Enda's voice rose. "I don't know *can't*, gal. Hell . . . don't you know by now I be too damn old for *'can't'*." She pointed at Paul and David. "They came to me! They asked and I told'em!"

Maggie Mae looked at them. In that instant, seeing her up close for the very first time, Paul truly realized what everyone who'd spoken about her meant– she was unearthly beautiful. Even as she scolded them, her voice nothing like her mother's raspy, forbidding echo, she seemed gentle and caring. "What you two boys doin' up 'round here anyway? Comin' 'round here stirrin' up the devil. Ya'll need to get on back to ya'll side of the river. Ain't nothin' here but an old woman, ya hear? An old woman! So just leave her be."

"Yes'm," David answered quickly and was reflexively voiced by Paul also. They both stepped backwards in almost perfect unison.

Enda rubbed Maggie Mae's arm, "Just settle it down, gal. These youngin's ain't meant no harm to Enda."

"They ain't got no business 'round here."

"You 'spose to say, *'they don't have any business around here . . .'*" Enda reprimanded her. "I done told ya 'bout that slave talk, now ain't I?" Maggie Mae began to reply, but as if unable to find the right words to challenge Enda, she simply sighed in exasperation. "I told the ol' chunky one standin' there," she pointed at David, "to know how to get here from them woods out back."

"What for?" Maggie Mae asked.

"'Cause they got secrets like you."

It wasn't just Maggie Mae's look of confusion, but the words that Enda spoke next that made Paul feel as if his foolish need to calm his curiosity had tumbled him into a web he couldn't escape. "They," Enda continued, "gonna have to hide who they be for the rest of they lives. Just like you."

"Mama!" Maggie Mae threatened.

Paul had no doubt Enda now knew about he and David. With one glance at David, whose eyes were wide in fear, he knew David realized the same thing also . . . and the danger it could bring.

"Ain't no sense hidin' chillin'," Enda told them. "Seem to me like ya'll in this thang together. Liars, all of ya!" She blurted. "But lies gonna keep ya'll alive, 'cause white folks'll kill ya dead if they knew. Ain't that right in there?" Her voice rose up and past Maggie Mae.

Maggie Mae's response was as quick and sharp as her turn toward the door. "Stay in there!"

Even as words suddenly began colliding and erupting into chaos between mother and daughter . . . beauty and witch . . . Paul saw that Maggie Mae's words of warning had gone unheeded. The shadow that emerged in the doorway appeared familiar to him, however the voice was undeniable as to whom it was. "It's alright Maggie," he called, before walking out on the porch. Nicholas Barrons walked to her and took hold of her hand. Paul observed how at first she resisted his touch, but soon seemed to welcome it . . . she moving closer to him, as if she were chilled in the balmy night air, yet warmed by him, and all the while cursing Enda with her eyes.

"Don't worry, Paul," Nicholas reassured him, "you either–David, is it?" David nodded sheepishly. "I've got . . ." he glanced at Maggie Mae and smiled, "we've as much to lose as the both of you. There's no judgment on my part about the two of you, if you both have none against us?" He asked, almost pleadingly so.

Paul wasn't sure what to think of his proposal, except maybe he was in danger of falling prey to some trick. Who then, he asked himself, was this man who'd befriended his father not so many weeks ago . . . this man he'd swooned over when he first saw him? His first thought was to grab David by the hand and make for home, but not linger. His gut told him they could leave this very night, prepared or not if need be. But it was her . . . the beautiful demigoddess standing next to Nicholas who looked so forlorn, yet so in love, that planted his feet in the dirt beneath him.

From Maggie Mae to Nicholas, Paul looked once, twice and back again. Two beautiful creatures side by side, yet that was not all he saw, nor the most important facet of either of them. It was the subdued fright in both their eyes as they watched the road for prying eyes, and the strength that was evident in that they both fiercely clung to each other's hand.

"We better go inside if we're going to speak frankly or at all," Nicholas urged, as he guided Maggie Mae to the door. "Paul, come in . . . I promise you both, you have nothing to fear from me or anyone here. Please," he added. "I'll tell you both what all of this is about. And then, you'll have one more secret up on me if you still have fear that I will divulge yours."

Paul turned to David. In his eyes, where Paul hoped to see an opinion one way or another, there was but fear, and he knew their decision would be entirely his own. He desperately wanted to believe Nicholas and trust the women with him. "I think it'll be alright," he whispered to David.

"You sure?" David asked softly.

Paul shook his head. "No– but I won't let anything happen to you no matter what." David smiled.

They gave a wide berth to Enda as they climbed the stairs and entered the house. Nicholas greeted each one with a firm nod of his head, and then began to close the door. "Ms. Sully . . ."

"I stayin' out here. Ain't no one comin' this way if they see me."

"In boys, in." Nicholas' voice was laden with urgency as he shut the door behind them. "It's getting late and I have much explaining to do."

* * *

Paul felt that in the short span of an hour, he'd been taken across the entire south and then back, as Nicholas recounted tales of atrocities he'd witnessed against Negroes. His hope was that he could tell their story and compel . . . or embarrass at least, those who had the power to stop it, to do so. Paul was relieved when Nicholas eventually brought them out of Hades' grotesqueries and led them to his heavenly reward, which was Maggie Mae Sully.

Time, however, had advanced far faster than his tale. David was fairly sure he could sneak in his house by way of his bedroom window. Nicholas was certain, had anyone come looking for him at the motel, he could concoct a believable tale. "I've actually been doing it for the past few weeks," he told them, "It's my only way to get to see Maggie Mae without raising suspicion." Paul, on the other hand, knew he would just have to take his chances and try slipping in without detection.

The three of them left by way of the woods, as strongly suggested by Enda who had remained outside the entire time. Paul and David were certain they could retrace their steps in the dark. They all walked in silence for a while before Nicholas broke the uncomfortable silence. "What exactly did you mean, that you have to take your chances sneaking in?" He asked Paul. "Does someone suspect, um . . . something with you two?"

Paul looked away and nodded.

"His pappy'll kill him this time if he knew for sure," David offered. "Last time he almost did, and that was just 'cause Beatrice was teasin' him over it."

Nicholas was incredulous. "Simeon Monclair? Your own father beat you that bad?"

"Almost killed him!" David spat.

Paul walked in silence as David recounted what he knew of the beating, and then every step of his recovery. Though David did a fine job describing all that *he* knew, which was bad enough in and of itself, still it paled in comparison to what really happened, Paul thought. Were there actually words to describe the vile pleasure his father received from beating him until he urinated and defecated on himself? *No*, he thought. *They haven't made those words yet.*

"What the hell is wrong with these people down here?!" Nicholas growled. "God, I'm so sorry, Paul."

Paul was at a loss for words. It was strange to hear, let alone accept such genuine compassion. "It's o.k." he muttered, though in his guarded heart, he screamed, *Thank you! Thank you for understanding! Thank you for not hating me for being me! Christ! Thank you for giving a damn . . . even if you're just pretending to.*

"No, its not o.k., *dammit!*" Nicholas thundered. He stopped abruptly, causing them all to knock into one another like an accordion being squeezed. "You both have to follow through with your plans– like you said, and get the hell out of here," he insisted. "Get out of Folsom . . . the south . . . Christ Almighty! You must promise me that the both of you will leave as soon as you can."

"We will," David said hastily.

"We are," Paul corrected. "We . . . we just have to wait for . . . "

Nicholas grabbed Paul's arm. "No! No– you don't wait for anything. Maggie and I are leaving here soon . . . and that in itself poses many risks. But if the both of you aren't gone by then, you must come with us. If your father doesn't kill you, or even both of you, and someone here finds out– trust me boys . . ." Nicholas sighed and shook his head, "I've seen men do such vile things . . . more so than you know." Nicholas shook his head again, as if try-ing to dislodge whatever wicked images had crept inside. "Promise me right now." They both did so. "Come on then, let's get the hell out of these woods. And Paul . . .?"

"Suh?"

"Don't worry about your father, I'll see you home myself," Nicholas told him. "He won't be touching you ever again if I have anything to do with it. Next time he wants to fight, he'll fight someone who can give him back more than he can ever give."

CHAPTER 21

To anyone else, the day could have been the same day as any other day, had it not been Lar who'd awoken to *this* very day. However, he wished it were not he. Ever since that dreadful day he felt himself die in the Meadows' home, the days were no longer the same for him. Sunlight rising in the east no longer emboldened his spirit into thinking that on one of *these* days he might just wake to find that the world, through the grace and blessings of almighty God, had changed for the betterment of every Negroe man and woman. His hope that the unseen shackles his people still wore would slowly begin to fade from memory like iron in water . . . *for nothing is forever* . . . all seemed a fool's dream to him now.

The Negroes of Folsom were already lost, with or without him . . . this he now knew. Their fate had already been carved in stone and sunk to the bottom of the sea of hope. He cursed himself for preaching that salvation would be theirs, literally and figuratively, if only they could persevere through these dark times that were their lives. Ever clearer, he saw the doom of his people in their weary eyes, their too soon aged faces, their scars gained from the stoves they slaved over, fields in which they toiled and the ever thickening whip of white supremacy on their soul. What was to be Uncle Matty's reward in this life, he wondered, as he'd left him slumbering in his bed, field-broken and near his final days on earth? He wondered what he would say about his beloved Uncle Matty as they lay his cold body into hot southern dirt. Should he say that the old man lived most of his life like a tethered animal, and the rest like a broken down mule forced to work even harder to survive? Or should he just tell them what they wanted so very much to believe . . . that Uncle Matty was now resting in the arms of the Lord as his just reward for a life of pain, which was his cross to bear? It would be so easy to convince them of the latter, he guessed. It would be as simple as extending his hand to the men and shaking theirs in the firmest of grips, and holding the women who wept upon his chest as he whispered the word *'sister'* between words of comfort.

Yes . . . these days were no longer the same, he felt.

Even as he looked skyward to cloudless blue skies in the midst of Meadows' fields and remembering the face of his Mary and touch of the cocoon wherein his child lay, he felt no joy– only sinking despair. The chatter of the men around him, which had so many times strengthened his sense of brotherhood with them, only reminded him of the manhood that was taken from him. Baritone-sung spirituals that had once moved the day along, now only seemed to stretch each hour, pulling down what little of his spirit he had managed to pull up.

Of course he spoke with his Negroe brothers, but only when he had to. He managed a convincing, caring and sympathetic smile when needed, as someone it seemed, always had a dilemma swirling around them, or just needed a bit of spiritual advice to make life tolerable enough to continue living. Oh, but how he wanted to run when they sought him out. It seemed that his absence had caused a backlog of problems needing to be solved, which only made matters worse for him . . . his tongue felt raw by mid-afternoon.

He wanted to tell them . . . scream at them with all of his might, *"I leavin' this Godforsaken place, and if you know best, you do the same, too!"*

He had no idea where he would take Mary and the child, only that it would be somewhere up north and away from anyone who'd ever heard of the hell called Folsom. He knew, or at least felt, that finding some job wouldn't be a problem at all for him. He figured a Negroe who looked as though he could carry an ox on each shoulder would quickly be put in a field or factory. Mary, being stout and big-boned would be fought over by a multitude of lazy white women to clean their homes and see to their children. Times, he knew, would be tough for a while, but at least, and most importantly, they would be away from Folsom.

But . . . Uncle Matty.

The old man was the only father Mary had ever known. He was the only tether to Folsom Lar didn't have strength to sever. *He* was what kept him in the fields instead of at home this very instant busily packing their things. Uncle Matty wouldn't leave with them, he knew this already, and even if he did, he was too fragile to survive half the journey to wherever they were going. They would end up having to bury him somewhere on the side of the road if he forced the old man to come with them now, he thought. But that was an option he refused to even consider. *Right be right,* he thought. He stopped the swinging of his scythe, giving the encroaching weeds a momentary reprieve. He promised himself that he would honor the old man by burying him here in Folsom– his last home.

Though, it wouldn't be long before Uncle Matty passed. A few weeks, a month, a year at the most, he guessed. The light in Uncle Matty's eyes was already past dim. He'd seen this gradual loss of life many, many times before having ministered to the sick and dying. He already knew what was coming, just not exactly when it would come. And when it did come, he knew he would do right by

Uncle Matty– that he would give him all that he deserved, even if that meant standing over his grave and speaking the Lord's words that no longer gave himself comfort. And then he would leave Folsom. Get away from the memories of that day, for the memory would not release him as much as he tried to release it.

The rumble of horse hooves approaching shook him from his thoughts. In a flash, it seemed he could already sense what news the pale rider was bringing. He wondered if what was happening to him now was how it felt to Enda when the future momentarily became present. He picked up the swinging momentum of his scythe in an attempt to dispel his paranoia. But as the messenger, Tom Reechy, a young white man barely out of childhood reigned in the horse beside him and spoke, Lar wondered if indeed he'd truly glimpsed a sliver of the future, for Tom had spoken the very words he thought he might, and ones he didn't want to ever hear again. His reply was words he'd never expected to say to a white man, but nevertheless, meant from the depths of his dead soul.

"I aint goin' down there . . . suh."

Tom's reply was as wretched as his acne-scarred face. "Wha . . . ? *Boy!*" The word sizzled on Tom's tongue as much as it stabbed at Lar's dwindled pride. "If you don't get yo' ass up there!? What da hell you mean tellin' me . . . 'no?' I wasn't askin'."

Suddenly, Lar felt that even the thought of having to call the pock-faced white-boy 'suh' was like being poked in the eye with a needle. It had never bothered him that much before, as it was simply a part of the way things were . . . another battle to be lost to eventually win the war. But his vision seemed clearer now, though not necessarily wiser, for if it were, he knew he would not have responded with . . . "I ain't goin'. But I can give you two others." Every Negroe within earshot stopped and turned with their mouths pried open in disbelief and a hint of pride stirred up in their souls.

Tom, whose jaw too was unhinged, put his back into position with a vicious snap. "Get the fuck up there, boy!"

Lar knew he'd started something that wouldn't end without some vindication on Tom's part. But it was too late to change any of that, and he wouldn't, even if he could. Going back to 'work' at the Meadow's house was no longer a possibility for him. The boy could scream at him. Hell, he thought, even have him beaten if he wanted, which he knew *was* a real possibility, before he willingly went back to that house.

He knew that by once again refusing to go up to the office and then to the Meadows' home– which he did, what would happen. His indignation would rile Tom and tumble them both into a shouting war, which of course it quickly did. He realized every word he spoke could add an additional strike of the whip to his back. Yet, he was certain he was relatively safe . . . at least for the moment. Every brown eye that was near and staring in incredulity could see the anger pouring forth from Tom, yet even he was not fool enough to dismount from his steed. As superior as this boy-man thought his white skin to be to any brown or black skin, Lar knew he was not brave– or foolish enough, to stand toe to toe with a Negroe holding a scythe who dwarfed him in size, width and strength, and could snap his neck before he yelled '*help*'. None of those considerations however, had lessened Tom's rage. Everyone knew what was at stake for the young, white master of the field, for it hath fallen many men far greater than he . . . that which is known as 'pride'.

A welcome or unwelcome . . . depending on who was interpreting it at the time . . . hasty and thunderous symphony of new horse steps approached. Even before Wentworth, Roman's right-hand foreman came bustling into view, the small circle of Negroe men gathered around Lar and Tom parted to allow him entry. Wentworth pulled his steed to a halt. A whirlwind of dust followed in his wake, but had little time to settle before his voice cracked like a whip. "What the hell's all this commotion about?" He glared once at Tom and twice it seemed at Lar, as if not expecting *him* to be involved in it.

"This fool, actin' niggah here– that what's a matter, Mr. Wentworth," Tom seethed, determined to get the first word in. "He needin' some of that black-ass, sass took off his back!"

"Shut your damn mouth, Tommy," Wentworth replied disgustedly. He inched his horse between Lar and Tom, blocking the young man's view of his prey. "Mr. Meadows' the only one who can say who gets whipped on his land . . . not me, and certainly not *you!*"

"But– but you ain't heard how this niggah done talked to me," Tom cried, as though asking for just a sliver of his authority back.

"Anyone a mile 'round could hear you screamin' like you done lost your goddamn mind, boy" Wentworth shot back. "And why is everyone standin' 'round gawkin'?" The men quickly scattered back to their respective places and feigned working. As though knowing that the bodies had left, but ears were pricked up, Wentworth lowered his head near the height of his horse's before he spoke. "What goin' on here, Lar?"

"I told Mr. Tom I was goin' to send some of my boys to Mr. Meadows place so I wouldn't have to go," Lar replied.

Wentworth looked at Lar quizzically. His gaunt face drew tighter as he resisted what looked like a smile. "Why the hell not? All she want is some flowerbeds and that garden tore up . . . again," he added sassily. "It a whole lot better'n bein' out in this stove choppin' weeds! Hell, you can do what she wants in an hour or two, and be on back home 'fore the rest of us."

Had it been a different day, other than this day, Lar might have studied the ground and did what he was told. Alas, it was not such a simple, benign day, for Lar looked him squarely in the eye, just as he had Tom. "I rather work the fields– suh. If it be alright with you." Lar knew he was testing the man's patience.

"Listen, Lar," he began, "I didn't ask for you to go . . . it was Roman. He asked for you 'specially. I was there when he said it. And you know . . ." he stopped suddenly and turned to Tom. "Get on up to the office, Tommy, we'll be there directly." Tom stood his ground in defiance. "*Tommmmmy*," Wentworth said his name slowly and deliberately. "If I have to repeat myself to you one more fuckin' time, so help me God . . ."

Within moments, the gallop of Tom's mare was but a memory.

"Lar, look here," Wentworth began. "You *know* why Mr. Meadows wants you to go. I ain't gonna to say anymore than that, 'cause it wouldn't be right if I did . . . but we both know . . . don't we?"

Lar was as emotional as a widower burying a wife who had born him eight children who looked nothing like him.

"Just go on up and do what you gotta do and go home," Wentworth continued. "I'll take care of Tommy." His voice then became more poignant, "Watch how you speak to him from now on . . . for yo' sake, Lar. He may be a knuckleheaded boy, but he a white one. We ain't never had a problem with you. And Roman relies on you 'specially. But boys like Tommy ain't got no qualms makin' trouble for you Negroes– hear me?" Lar nodded.

As he watched Wentworth make his way back through the fields, he wondered what words he could use to sway Roman's mind. Like Wentworth, he too had respect for Roman and knew him to be fair-minded. But what words could be used, other than those that might reveal to Roman what he already knew occurred in his house, he wondered? It wouldn't matter that she was the attacker . . . that she had used her white *magic* to kneel his will before hers. It would be of no consequence how 'what' transpired happened, for one simple and unchangeable fact remained that he could not change . . . she was white and he was Negroe. He made for the office with haste, only because he could hear his fellow Negroes calling out his name in a cautious whisper, now that Wentworth was gone. Yet, as he drew closer to the office and could see Wentworth standing on the porch talking with Roman, his footsteps slowed even before his mind could tell them to.

"I know Wentworth here has spoken to you Lar, but I want you to hear it from my own mouth," Roman said. "And I must say I'm very disappointed that it's you I have to say this to, especially since I've always been on you and your people's side . . . *always*." Roman stepped down on the first step, but still high enough to keep his height above Lar's. "I don't have to tell you that Tommy is piping hot over how you spoke to him, do I?"

"No suh."

"I don't know if he's going to let it rest here either," Roman said apprehensively. "You know what kind of times your people live in down here. You know damn better, Lar!"

He could see Roman was expecting something more from him. But still, Lar gave him the same reply as before. "Yes suh."

Roman sighed. "I'm telling you to go because I can trust you, Lar. If you don't think I know what goes on in my own home, you're mistaken then. I know Lucianna all too well. I may have to deal with it, but not on her terms."

Wentworth's mouth became a flycatcher.

Roman dismissively flicked his hand at Wentworth. "For God sake, Wentworth, don't stand there as if you don't know about Lucianna. Everyone knows!" Wentworth was speechless. "That woman has already dragged what bit of a name I have left through the mud and back. Hell, I can't even walk down the goddamn street with my head up without people staring . . . and they hardly pretend to whisper about her anymore. And don't think I don't know which of your boys you sent to my house have helped her disgrace my name. And you can let this be your boy's first and *last* warning about it!"

"Absolutely suh," Wentworth replied. "It won't happen again under my . . ."

"It shouldn't have happened in the first goddamn place!" Roman barked, causing Wentworth to back up. He, who was the picture of what a true southern gentleman was thought to be– well spoken and wise, suddenly transformed into a hurt, bitter and betrayed man. "Just get out of my sight," Roman muttered. "Both of you."

Of all the words that he'd thought he could say to Roman, he had not the chance to even say them. Whether his words might have even persuaded Roman, he didn't know. What he did know for certain was that once again he was stripped of his own free will just as much by Roman as by Lucianna. Of the two, in that respect, he could see no difference, for neither of them saw him as a man, just a Negroe who was some mindless child who should be treated as such.

He arrived at the Meadow's house and hitched his wagon to the rear gate. He was relieved that the first face he saw was one he was actually glad to look upon. He watched as she rang out clothes in her delicate white, Negroe hands. When she looked up at him, a pout formed on her lips. Her blue eyes widened, as if saying how sorry she was. Such a vision of loveliness as she was, swept him back to a time when he cherished her touch.

It was a bittersweet reunion.

She let the clothes she was rinsing drop back into the metal bucket with a plop and came over to him, as she dried her hands on her dress that was already soiled by the Meadow's filth. But there was something different about her, he sensed. Her spirit seemed emboldened . . . some new strength peered through the veneer of beauty, weakness and helplessness– the very things that had driven him from her arms and into those of Mary's . . . true womanly qualities she'd always lacked and Mary possessed in abundance.

He saw this new Maggie Mae not in what she was doing, but what she had not done . . . her head didn't droop nor her eyes ever leave his once, as they usually did. If she cared about the prying eyes of her mistress, she didn't show it. If she cared what Lucianna might think, as she took his hand in hers, he couldn't see it. This new courage she displayed so boldly in such a small gesture swelled him with pride for her, causing him to momentarily feel joy despite himself, which was polar opposite of the concern she was expressing so desperately in her actions.

"I . . . we've all been so worried about you," she said. "It's good to see you moving about."

Lar nodded his appreciation.

"But not here," she added just as quickly, as her voice deepened in alarm. "You shouldn't be here, Lar."

The momentary spark of joy he felt for Maggie Mae vanished. The specter of humiliation that had been haunting him, once more descended like a morning fog and wrapped around. Though what he saw was concern in her eyes and lips, which were tightly pressed upon one another. He couldn't help but sense that she also saw his shame and loss of self as a man. "I ain't got no choice," he replied, unable to look at her directly.

"Just go," she begged. "Lucianna probably already saw you any- way. But you can't go up in there again."

He looked at her. "So you know then?"

"Know what?"

"What happened in there– to me," he mumbled. "You know what she . . ."

Maggie Mae shook her head. "I know somethin' terrible hap- pened in there to you to make you feel the way you've been feelin'. Somethin' scarred your soul deep, and it happened in there." Her eyes darted toward the house. "But that thing in there that calls herself a woman hasn't said it to me. It's just like when those white boys come here, she doesn't say anything to me except don't let anyone in the house and to keep my mouth shut. That's all."

"Cause nobody gonna take a niggah woman's word over a white's," he finished, what they both knew to be true. "I caught too, Maggie. Mr. Roman done sent me 'round here 'cause he know what she be up to with those white boys."

Maggie Mae moved closer to him– so close, if one were to spy them, they would have appeared in an embrace. So close, he could nearly taste her sweet, sweat-tinged scent and feel the warmth from her breath. "But she's hurtin' you in there somehow, Lar– I know it. She's changin' who you are inside. I can see it in your eyes . . . the way you can barely move about . . . she crushed some-thin' inside of you."

For the first time in years, the yearning he once had for Maggie Mae was again set ablaze, though it had nothing to do with lust for her flesh, but for her soul and mind. She completely understood the pain he was feeling without knowing *the why*. In that moment, she was more than just a beautiful woman, but a woman of love and fortitude and understanding . . . a balm that his soul needed. He wished he could hold her and release his pain to her, and expel the darkness that had taken hold of him. But he realized he was trapped in his own prison, just as she was with Lucianna, who held the sole key to their freedom. What happened in that room with Lucianna would stay locked in that room, and would be sealed in the coffin with him when that time came, he vowed.

He pulled her close and trapped her within his embrace. Memo-ries of happier days they shared came flooding back. Days when they were still but children playing under the watchful eye of Enda suddenly seemed like the present. Oh, how he wished that he could stay in that moment of youthful ignorance . . . a time when the worries of his mind seemed small and the world about him even smaller. But some things, it seemed, were just not meant to be. Lucianna's shrill call was like scalding water upon his backside.

Maggie Mae had her back to Lucianna, but from his position, he could see over her clearly and to Lucianna. She had just stepped

464 / ORLANDO SMART-POWELL

down from the back porch onto the ground, and was dressed in a shimmering, red nightgown, which peeked out from under a white, virginal robe. "I said– how is it that my gal and Roman's mill-boy are out here in *my yard* nearly fornicating right before me ... and you both are supposed to be working *for me*? Must I speak to Roman about this ... you two carrying on at his home?"

Once again, he bore witness to Maggie Mae's newfound strength. She neither answered Lucianna, nor turned to show her any semblance of respect. Her eyes, however, were screaming at him to disobey Roman's edict and leave.

"I am waiting," Lucianna said, her voice deepening even further in agitation.

"Yes'm," Lar answered, and stepped away from Maggie Mae. "I . . ."

Maggie Mae spun around and moved directly in Lar's path before he could advance any further. "He just slipped on by to ask if I need ride home."

For a moment, the thought of letting Maggie Mae's ruse lay as it were crossed his mind. He knew he could simply walk away no matter what ... it would always be his choice. Within his soul of souls, he knew he couldn't. For simply having the ability to make a choice didn't guarantee that he could choose the consequence that might result from it. For both he and Maggie Mae ... Negroes ... he was all too knowledgeable of the fact that their choice against a white's could end in disaster. And though he no longer loved Maggie Mae as a lover, today his cup of brotherly love for her runneth over.

He laid a gentle hand on Maggie Mae's shoulder and moved her to the side, stepping around her and now blocking *her* path. "Mr. Meadows done sent me down here to work, too. I just askin' Maggie here 'bout ridin' home later– like she said."

"Is this why you're busy molesting my Negroe instead of working?"

"No . . . ma'am."

"Then why are you just standing there– both of you?"

Maggie Mae slipped from around Lar. "There's this old woodpile around the shed that needs picking up here, Lar," she volunteered.

"I get started out here then, Ms.," he said.

Lucianna quickly stepped in front of Maggie Mae, and advanced toward her until they were no more than a foot apart. "It's funny– my little, Negroe gal . . . how you think that white skin of yours makes you think you're mistress here and *I'm* the niggah. You're nothing here, you niggah bitch!" Lucianna spat. "*I* say what is or is not here, not you! And you are this close . . ." she measured with two fingers pressed tightly upon one another, "to being where we put your kind . . . woman or not, nappy-headed or not, white-skinned or blue-eyed or not . . . *you—are—still—just—a—niggah!*"

Lucianna kept her pose, as if daring Maggie Mae to give her cause to enact her threat. But . . . Maggie Mae was a statue of freshly carved ivory. And as if having won victory, Lucianna took her white robe, wrapped it tightly around and spun away from Maggie Mae. "You!" She snarled at Lar. "Get inside!" She then looked back at Maggie Mae, daring her to speak to the contrary, or at all.

Shockingly to Lucianna and especially to Lar, she did. "Don't go in there Lar."

She had stepped over the line Lucianna had drawn. He knew this was as clear to Maggie Mae as it was to himself, for when Lucianna sped toward her, her arm raised back in a gathering of strength, Maggie Mae didn't twitch at all, though he knew she could have simply side-stepped and avoided the impending strike.

Alas, she did not.

He watched helplessly as Maggie Mae's face reverberated from the open-handed blow before falling to the ground. "Get out of my sight, you bitch! You niggah!" Lucianna screamed, as she hovered over a visibly stunned, though not shocked Maggie Mae. She cocked her hand back again in preparation for another blow.

"Maggie go!" Lar growled. She pulled herself up and dusted her dress off. Blood was coursing from Maggie Mae's left cheek to her lips.

"If you have a mind, gal," Lucianna warned, "you better listen to your niggah lover, and do as he says."

"Get outta here," he whispered . . . prayed . . . begged.

Maggie Mae at first slowly backed out of reach of Lucianna's still outstretched hand, and then more quickly, as if reason had finally slapped her as Lucianna had.

Lucianna lowered hand. "Don't ever come back, you ungrateful bitch!"

Maggie Mae wiped her face and looked at the blood on her hand. She casually wiped it on her dress, as if refusing to give Luciana the pleasure of it startling her. "Lar," Maggie Mae called again.

"Maggie, just go now. Just go," he begged.

"Then come with me. Come away from this place . . . *and her*," she added.

"You'll come away from all of this a dead niggah if *you* don't leave," Lucianna threatened.

Lucianna's threats no longer seemed effective against Maggie Mae. "You'll be the one who's dead Lar, if you go in there."

"I be all right. You just get on outta here!" He pleaded, knowing she was possibly writing her own fate that she would be powerless to write the last words to.

"Well then," Lucianna said calmly. "If your niggah woman can't seem to listen, I suggest you do and get inside like I said. I'll see to it that she gets exactly what she deserves and more . . . personally. If you don't want the same, then I suggest you be the smart niggah and do as you're told."

Lar walked up on the porch, opened the door and went inside her lair without once looking back at Maggie Mae . . . for her sake. Her grave seemed quite deep enough already, he thought. Even as Lucianna followed him inside and shut the door behind her, he could still hear Maggie Mae– her voice trembling with desperation, calling for him.

"She will forever rue the day she crossed me," Lucianna vowed.

What Maggie Mae had said just moments before was true . . . he was ensnared in Lucianna's trap now. But even that was not entirely true, he thought. From the moment Roman had given his command to come to this place, the die had been cast. But even more so, he realized, it had all began the moment he was born with black skin.

"Now . . ." she began.

"She just a child, Ms. Lucianna," he piped in before she could finish. "I speak with her later and have her apologize right for you. Ain't really no sense risin' up folks over some old silly Negroe gal, is there? I make damn sure she apologize right and don't come 'round this place no more."

"Would you do all that?"

'Yes'm, missus."

"For me or for your pretty, white lover?"

Lar could feel the web being spun tighter about him, though for Maggie Mae's sake, he knew he had to at least try and convince Lucianna to show some compassion, if only this one time. "I married. Maggie ain't nothin' to me but just an ol' silly gal."

Lucianna inched toward him. "Really, boy? From what I saw from my upstairs window just moments ago, it seemed so much more than that."

"It ain't so."

"Funny. Last time you were here, I couldn't tell you didn't give a damn about that half-white, niggah gal by the way you were looking at her . . . like you wanted her then– hmm?" She smirked. "And I saw how she was looking at you."

"Ain't nothin' done ever happened between me and Maggie Mae," he countered sharply. "We been brought up together since babies, is all there be to it."

"Oh, well then," she said, moving closer . . . as he moved back. "This thing between the both of you has become incestuous."

Lar felt his body-heat begin to rise, but it wasn't from the heat trapped in the kitchen, but from within his blood. Suddenly, rage coupled with bitterness as his eyes mapped her angular face, which only served to exponentially intensify the rage sweeping through him. She was a thing of vileness and wickedness, whose only agenda was to wreak havoc and destroy all that she touches, he felt. Oh, indeed yes– he wanted to kill her! And it would be so very easy to do.

He wanted to make her pay dearly for the defilement of his soul. He knew the moment his hands encircled her neck, the devilish smirk she wore with such indignation would instantly turn to one of horror. The last thing she would ever hear would be the snapping of her own neck. And after she went limp, he could see himself breaking the bones of each of her fingers that had dared touch him. And in fair turn, for having made him submit, he would find the cruelest of phallic-like objects and take from her what she'd taken from him . . . choice. Then and only then, he fantasized, would they be squared. But he could see that she had no idea of how close she was to death, for she moved closer yet. Her green eyes began to dance and dazzle in a spin of sorcery.

"I can see why she fancies you so," she murmured. "I'm sure you're every Negroe woman's dream."

"I their preacher," he replied solidly.

"Who are always the first to fall from grace," she quipped. "As though your types were ever in grace to start with that is."

The tethers on his anger began to loosen. "Your men of God may be like that, but I ain't."

Lucianna laughed. "Please boy, you supposed *men of God* are the most willing. And you ... I can't imagine you not being so with that thing hanging between your legs. Why, half the length of you would shame most men. Don't you remember? I know what God has *blessed* you with. I'm sure it's made many a Negra thank Jesus."

"What need be done 'round here," he droned.

She moved closer, daring to make forbidden contact. Her hands moved toward that which she had just spoken of as if she owned it, and had every right to do with it as she pleased. "I want you to help me thank Jesus, too," she whispered.

Suddenly her pupils dilated to pinpricks. Lar, at first wondered why. To him, he was just an observer, questioning why he was doing what he was doing. He wanted to shout to himself to stop, and then run. But in the midst of what was unfolding, he found himself enjoying watching her receive what she deserved. His intuition had been right– the flesh of her neck was indeed as soft as lamb's skin, as were the fragile bones of her neck . . . just as he was right about the look of fear that would suddenly replace her smirk once she was unable to breathe. After he lifted her and tossed her against the wall, and she then crumpling to the floor, did he realize what he had truly done? He knew that he would never see his child born, and except through stories told by Mary, the child would never know who it's father was.

"You're a dead niggah!" Lucianna screamed. "A dead niggah! You hear me!"

But Lar already knew that.

It was the moment her hands once again touched his genitals that he felt yanked from his body and fury took over. And when his pent-up vengeance pounced upon her, he felt incapable of stopping it. In fact, he cheered it on and reveled in its ferocity, as she was powerless against its raw, unfettered and unstoppable wake. But what was done now, could never be undone, he realized. Just as he knew he would pay the ultimate price for having regained a sliver of his manhood. "I sorry, Lord . . . dear God, I so sorry," he said.

She pulled herself up by the knob of the backdoor. "You think God is going to stop you from hangin'?!" She struggled for the door and finally swung it wide open and stumbled outside and away.

Maggie Mae entered the kitchen as abruptly as Lucianna left it. Lar was in the midst of sitting down on a chair he'd found in the room. Maggie Mae was frantic– yes. He could hear it in her voice. What words she spoke only came in pieces as his thoughts were far, far elsewhere. From what he gleamed from her, was that she had not left after being banished by Lucianna. And then there was something about her seeing Lucianna run screaming from the house, passing by her and talking about a dead niggah.

"You gotta take my wagon and get over to Mary," he told her, barely able to raise his head.

"What have you done!?" Maggie Mae cried.

"I done killed myself," he said simply.

"Did . . ."

"You know I ain't touched her in that way. I tried to knock the devil outta her when she tried to . . . to . . . touch me. But we both know what she gonna say happen."

Maggie Mae knelt at his feet. "You gotta run now, Lar."

"I ain't runnin' nowhere."

"Don't be a fool!"

"That why I aint goin' nowhere," he insisted.

Maggie Mae stood up and ran to the door. She swung her head side-to-side and listened. "Go, you damn fool!"

"Peak Hills," he said softly.

"What?"

"I said Peak Hills. If they can't find me, who you think they gonna come for then? Just like they did over in Peak Hills. If they can't find me, then any niggah will do. They gonna get someone, and you know who, too."

"Mary," she said slowly.

Lar nodded. "And who to say they won't come for her anyhow? That why I ain't runnin' from here, but you is. They find you here and you a dead woman after the men done had they way with you!"

"Lar." Her voice was quivering. "They're going to take you to the black tree– you know that. They're going to make you suffer before they kill you." Maggie Mae went to the counter, her hand shook violently as she reached up and found the object she knew to be there, for she had placed it there this very morning. She laid it on the counter. "Don't let them get you."

"Get on over to the Monclair's and get Mary back home before they come and get me. Knock her stupid if you have to, but get her outta here, else I be seein' her far sooner than later." He looked at what she'd laid on the counter in front of him, and then back to her. "You know I can't do that."

"If you won't, they will."

Lar nodded. "Get on now, Maggie, 'fore you can't. And tell Mary that I love her . . . and you tell my baby the same when it be born, too."

"You know I will."

"And I love you too," he added. "I always have."

"I know."

"And you hide yourself 'til it all be over," he said, just as she was halfway past the door. "They might not just stop with me."

From where he sat, he could see the top of her head as she ran toward the wagon. Within moments, he heard the horses' hooves trampling the ground and fading away. But no sooner had he heard Maggie Mae took off in the wagon, when he heard a new rumble of hooves approaching– and white men's voices accompanying them. It was tempting to do as Maggie Mae suggested. He had no idea if he could endure what was to come. But what Maggie Mae wished was something that he couldn't do. He picked up the knife she laid on the counter and walked over to the wall and hung it back up.

Already he could hear the voices of white men drawing near. The sound of a shotgun being cocked told him they were far closer than he'd thought. They were already in the yard . . . hiding from him . . . waiting for him.

He lifted his hands in the air and prayed for the first time in weeks. "In your hands, Lord, I sendin' you my soul," he said . . . right before the blast of the first rifle rang out.

* * *

The sound that suddenly rang out caused Maggie Mae to yelp. She prayed the shot she heard– which she had no doubt came from the Meadows' home– had struck only a dead body still spewing blood from its cut throat, but in her heart, she knew it hadn't. Lar would never take his own life, no matter what. What was in store for Lar was almost more than she could imagine. It was the look of acceptance of death in Lar's eyes that kept her feet moving forward. It was fear that sharpened her senses, allowing her to command the horses into a dangerous full-gallop as she made her way to the outskirts of Folsom without drawing attention to herself. But as she soon noticed, she was of no consequence to those caught up by the spreading wildfire, *who* at first trickled, and then began pouring out into the streets. No one, except Negroes paid her any notice, but they were struck mute. Even they sensed trouble had come to Folsom.

* * *

As she stood in the dining room, Mary wasn't sure which door to answer first, as both front and back seemed close to being dislodged from their hinges by whoever was pounding on them. She could hear Isabel near the front door asking exactly what she was thinking. "I don't know what goin' on either, Ms. Isabel. Someone back here just knocking away like a fool, too!"

She started for the front door, but just as she did, the back one burst open and slammed against the wall. She ran into the kitchen and was confronted by . . . "Paul!? What the hell . . ."

But she didn't have a chance to finish her words, let alone her thoughts, for right behind Paul . . . wide eyes, panting and all, came an equally breathless and red-faced Maggie Mae. Her dress was dust covered, as though she'd been rolling in the dirt and not bothered to brush herself off. "What . . .?"

It was as though Paul had sprouted six extra arms as he reached for her, she could barely bat them away quick enough before grabbing a hold of him and violently shaking him until he went still.

"Mary!"

Everyone it seemed had lost their senses, Mary thought, as Isabel was now screaming for her from the front of the house.

""You gotta come now, Mary! Right now!" Paul begged.

"*No!*" Maggie Mae screeched at both of them. "*They'll kill you, too!*"

Paul paid her no heed. "You gotta go get him!"

"What done happened?" Mary demanded. But again she was interrupted as Isabel burst into the room, hands flailing about as though she were on fire. Like Paul, she snatched hold of Mary. "Mary, they're going for Lar. Men are gathering all over to get him. And– and they . . . they just came looking for Simeon . . . but – but he's at the store I think . . . and . . ."

"Oh Lord– what the hell's goin' on!" Mary screamed at all of them– again and again, from one to the other.

Maggie Mae then told her.

And then . . . there was silence . . . before the thunder boomed.

Mary was out of the door and running for the wagon hitched out back. Later . . . much later, she would remember peeling away the hands trying to restrain her, and sending their bodies flinging to the side of her. She would remember Maggie Mae's mouth moving as she spoke, and her feeble attempt to block her path with her slight body. She would recall Maggie Mae's body hitting the ground after absorbing the full force of her backhand.

And after that, as she fumbled unfettering the wagon from its hitch, she would remember only two other things . . .

One . . . that the back of her head suddenly hurt, and two . . .

. . . that darkness soon followed.

CHAPTER 22

Indeed the near boiling hot coffee did a fine job scalding Nicholas' chest, not to mention his genitals . . . and yes, the front of his pants were now covered in an whitish-orange blob from the eggs cooked over easy, just as he liked them. He was now a mess on the outside, but that paled to what was going on inside his head. And right now, he hadn't the taste for anything. He grit his teeth as he'd spilled his steaming coffee and sent the plate of half-masticated eggs onto his lap as he struggled away from the table.

As he ran out of the motel, he was nearly swept away by the tide of bodies rushing past him. For the first time since coming to Folsom, the town had truly come alive. Young . . .old . . . woman . . . man . . . and even children, it seemed had crawled out from their recesses– that is, every white townsfolk. There wasn't a brown face to be seen, and he hadn't expected there to be, for if there was, then surely they were a fool, he thought.

He stayed close to the buildings as the majority of those stream-ing toward him were headed in the opposite. He'd seen this type of event happen one too many times. The look of vengeance on their faces– smirks, scowls and grins, pushed bile up his throat and resurfaced memories he just as soon forget. Pops and blasts of guns and rifles mingled with coarse voices hurling accusations. Others, he heard in passing, professed they knew about what was happening and why, and where, and on . . . and on . . . and on, though most knew little and few knew even less than that, he figured. But all of that was an inconvenient, minor detail, as there was now blood to be had and the thirst for it primal.

Nicholas was certain *they* knew nothing, for *they* were no longer '*they*', but an '*It*' . . . a single-minded organ formed by two elements– white skin and hate. And in it, he knew . . . as he'd witnessed before, one's status in life was no longer a factor, as was one's gender or age of no concern. If he stayed and watched, 'It' would grow into a collective of hundreds of legs, feet and arms, with one sole purpose in mind . . . to kill a Negroe.

But it was all based on a lie, he knew without doubt. If the grimy-faced white boy who had run into the motel to spread the news had said any other name but Lar Cole, he might have paused and briefly entertained the possibility that a misunderstanding with another Negroe and Lucianna Meadows had occurred. But he knew enough about Lar Cole and Lucianna Meadows to vow to give his soul to the devil if a miniscule of any of the accusations against Lar were true.

He ran with all the power his legs could muster without bumbling over one another. All he could think was that she . . . his beloved . . . his Maggie Mae, was still in that house. In the wake of a growing and uncontrollable lynch mob, she would be in certain danger, for men, he knew, were wont to destroy that which they coveted the most . . . Troy . . . Rome . . . Egypt . . . yes!

He was dizzy by the time he reached the Meadow's house. Over the roar of his gasping for breath, he could hear glass breaking, furniture dancing, and a woman screeching inside. The sound of pain emanating from the house made him forget his lungs burned, and propelled his body forward. Once upon the porch, he reached for the pistol he usually tucked into the waistband of his britches, only to realize that today of all days, he'd left it under the mattress of his bed. "Goddamnit!" He growled. He had no choice but to proceed unarmed.

He prepared to ram his shoulder into the door and force it open, but before he charged ahead, he glimpsed at it and saw that it wasn't shut. He slipped inside the foyer, and after quickly scanning the entryway; he found a thin, wooden cane that would just have to do as a weapon.

Another scream from the woman above bounced from wall to wall and tumbled down the stairs to his ears. A thud from above followed, and made him crouch instinctively. The sound was blunt, like flesh and bone slamming against an immovable object, he conjectured. Next, a man's voiced howled from upstairs . . . angry . . . accusing . . . strangely tormented it was, but obviously belonging to the one doling out the punishment. Nicholas realized now was not the time to stand, dither and ponder, but to see, intervene and rescue. He glided up the stairs two at a time with feline ease, yet with elephantine softness. His grip upon the thin cane threatened to snap it into two, as both his arms cocked it to the side to stun whoever was demanding womanly flesh be punished.

As he neared the landing, a serpentine body coiled and uncoiled on the floor toward him. The muscles in his arms ceased twitching and became like pine-boards as he prepared to strike. But as the snake's form revealed its true self in the dust riddled light of the hallway, he realized that all he had assumed was wrong. Maggie Mae– his beloved he expected to rescue and whisk away to safety was not the woman who grabbed his legs and almost tripped him, had he not quickly placed a hand on the wall to steady himself. Terror marked her green eyes. Blood was trickling from the corner of her mouth onto freshly bruised, porcelain skin.

"Mr. Barrons! *Nicholas!* Dear God, help me . . . *he's going to kill me,*" Lucianna cried, through swollen lips. She reached up for him while glancing backwards, as though her menace was nearly upon her.

Nicholas kicked and connected with her soft bosom. She shrieked as much from agony as from insult. In desperation she reached for him again, but he stepped back until he teetered on the edge of the landing. "Murderer!" He seethed at her.

Roman stepped out into view from one of the rooms at the end of the hallway. His fists were clenched and his stony face cracked, nearly unrecognizable in fury. He approached them. Nicholas spotted blood splattered on his white shirt, and knew immediately it was not his. Having obviously given up hope of being saved, Lucianna crawled to the wall and achingly pushed up to her feet. She lifted a hand in surrender and closed her eyes. "For God sake, Roman– no more . . ." she whimpered.

"You fucking whore!" Roman's voice threatened to shake the foundation of the house. "If I kill you, God will only thank me for it."

She clasped her hands together in the most desperate of prayers. "It's the truth," she professed weakly.

It was though those few words were all Roman needed to completely crack his remaining seals. The ferocity in which he lunged at her created an unseen force that pushed Nicholas down the stairs and away from the approaching juggernaut. The first blow Roman delivered was to her cheek. The next, before her body could fall to the floor was to her gut, which briefly brought her off her feet before her body plopped on the floor.

"Liar!" He screamed at her, with a voice that no longer belonged to a human male. "*Do you know what you've done?!* They're going to kill him . . . you hear me!? Kill him over a lie!"

At the moment, Nicholas wondered if another murder had just been committed. Lucianna was lying motionless on her side. Her legs were splayed and a milky-white breast lay exposed from her nightgown. After what seemed far too long to have gone without oxygen, her chest once again began to move slowly before suddenly heaving for air. Alas, he felt no sympathy for her pain. At her weakest, he still sensed evil emanating from her. For what she'd done, he more than felt she deserved Roman's fists and more.

"Why are you in my fucking house?" He barked, as though he'd not even been aware of Nicholas' presence until now. Roman's breaths were as quick, if not more so than Lucianna's, but for entirely different reasons. He pointed a finger at Lucianna. "Have you too come for this thing, too!? This whore. If you have, then take the bitch with you!"

Nicholas quickly waved his hand in innocence. "Roman wait. I came to look for . . . I thought . . ." He stopped. How could he say her name without raising suspicion about he and Maggie Mae . . . but just as quickly, he wondered how he could remain silent? "I came looking for Maggie," he declared boldly. He vowed the rooster could crow all he wants and never hear him deny his love for her . . . once, twice or three times– he loved her. He waited and watched for Roman's response.

Roman glared at him. Nicholas didn't back down, but advanced until they were face to face. Roman moved, but not toward him. He crouched in front of Lucianna who unsuccessfully tried to move out of his reach. She pushed against the floor with her arm that no longer seemed to function properly, and when that did not work, she turned her face from his. Roman simply and unkindly grabbed hold of her chin and snapped it back around, ignoring her whimpers and muddled pleas. He smiled at her.

"Look at me," he said, while jamming his thumb into her chin. "You have one chance to walk out of here alive. Tell me where that gal is, right now."

Lucianna quivered. "She . . . she's . . ."

Roman shook his head. "Uh-uh-uh-uh . . . don't lie, my little whore. You see– if I don't find her safe and sound, I'm going to come lookin' for you and rip that forked tongue right out of your pretty, little red-head. Mmm-hmmm . . . so help me God." He nodded. "So you're going to tell me where she is right now. Right?"

Lucianna nodded weakly. "I-I-I made her leave. Be . . . before all this. I don't know where she is . . . I swear to God, Roman, I don't . . . but . . . but she's not hurt, I swear it. *I swear!*"

"You better pray she's not hurt," Roman threatened. "That gal's never done a damn thing to you but be your goddamn slave, and you've done nothin' but treat her like the whore *you are!* And Laurence Cole . . ." Fury rose again in his voice. "He's a good Negroe. He's more of a man than any white man in this damn town and that's the God's truth. For what you've done this day, the devil's going to welcome you with open arms and make what I've done to you seem like a blessing. You're gonna burn, bitch!" Roman stood up. "Now get the hell out of my house."

Lucianna turned to Nicholas, then back to Roman. "What?" She cried. Suddenly realizing her breast was exposed, she pulled it back in.

"Ooooout," Roman said louder, as though he were speaking to a child who was unsure why they had just received a spanking for starting a fire. "Now! And don't even think about taking a damn thing with you except the clothes on your back. Get . . . out!"

"I –I'm your wife for Christ sake! Roman? *Roman!* Where am I supposed to go?"

"Go fuck everyone in town if you want. You should be more concerned about Maggie Mae being all right, not where you're going to lay your snake-head. If that gal's got one mar on her, I'll choke the life out of you and burn your worthless corpse at the black tree myself." He pointed at Nicholas, directing him down the stairs. "Now get out, before I have a mind to do it anyway."

Nicholas stopped and turned to Roman. "You're respected in this town . . . is there nothing you can do to stop it– tell them the truth? Drag Lucianna down there and make her recant in front of everybody?"

Roman put a hand upon his shoulder and nudged him on. "Come on, boy. Let's go find Maggie before she gets caught up in this hell."

"But Lar?"

"There's nothing I can do about that," Roman uttered in defeat.

"The truth, Roman! What about telling them the truth?"

"Are you thick-headed or somethin', boy?" Roman spat. "Do you really, really think Folsom gives a damn about the truth right now? I barely got here and already they'd stripped Lar as naked as the day he was born, dragging him up the road right past me. And you know what? Lar asked me exactly what you're asking right now– but with his eyes, because they'd already broken his jaw and knocked out every one of his goddamn teeth." Without warning, Roman grabbed Nicholas by the collar of his shirt and shook him until Nicholas cried mercy. Roman pushed him on. "Wake up, suh! *You . . . are . . . in . . . the . . . south!*"

Nicholas knew Roman was right . . . absolutely right. The truth had no voice in Folsom. He knew lynchings had more to do with whites maintaining their supremacy than righting a wrong. With such a horrible accusation placed upon Lar's head, he realized there was no saving him, for he was accused of the most horrific of crimes . . . the rape of a white woman. True or not, he would die this day. Save Jesus Christ himself descending from the clouds and intervening, there was no saving Lar.

"I have to find Maggie Mae," Nicholas told him. "I have to know she's safe."

"We'll find her, boy," Roman assured him. "My wagon is already hitched-up out back. Let's hope she ran across the bridge to her home. But we're going to have to go through town first and make sure she hasn't got caught up in this mess. And let's make sure we don't get mixed up in it either."

Nicholas agreed. "We'll have to swing by the motel. I have a pistol there."

"Uh-uh. That's way too close to the tree at the old park– where they'll all be. I got pistols here that work just as well."

"Fine then."

Roman sighed. "I should have known somethin' was stirring when I saw the two of you walking up to my office."

"It's . . ." Nicholas fell speechless. He figured whatever Roman thought about he and Maggie Mae would have to wait. If there was a consequence to come of it, then so be it, he thought. He met Roman's eyes and raised his head proudly. "I'm not going to deny what I feel for her," Nicholas said. "I love her."

"You think I'm not a man?" Roman asked. "You think if any other white man had a chance with her in a different place and time, they wouldn't? The only thing stopping them is that we live in the south. That's all. That's it! Hell, if I hadn't thought I could change the spots on that whoring wife of mine, and I'd met Maggie Mae sooner, I'd be right where you are. Only . . ."

"What? What is it?"

"Don't be a fool," Roman warned, "like leaving your pistol behind and running off like you're Lancelot to save your Guinevere. Think– and then act. This isn't a fairytale, boy . . . you're in a nightmare. If she is what you want, then you get her and take her as far away from Folsom *and the south*. There are particular rules down here. You break the wrong one and they'll break you. You hear me? They'll lynch both of you . . . to applause."

"I know."

"Well, you better know good and well for both your sake," Roman admonished. "Now let's go get her. And pray, boy . . . pray to God she's not caught up in that lynch mob."

* * *

As Nicholas and Roman neared the center of town, the wind was beginning to stir, and spread the stench of burning flesh everywhere. Nicholas felt as though his already knotted stomach was on the verge of emptying the bile that had pooled in it the moment he'd heard Lar was accused of rape. As they drew closer, the blasts of gunfire, shouts and jeers from those gathered around the dead, black tree was nearly deafening.

With the mob gathered on the north side, Roman steered the wagon south to circumvent the macabre gathering of men, women, boys, girls and even babies who were snuggled to their mother's chests. Nicholas was repulsed by it all. He couldn't think of a word to represent such an inhuman sight, perpetuated by humans that had no humanity. He gripped the gun Roman had given him all that much tighter, wishing he had an opportunity to use it.

He watched young boys fighting for a closer position in front of the black tree where Lar had been mutilated, hanged and then burned, as though a vagabond magician had come to town to amaze and dazzle them, not to witness and participate in the murder of a fellow human being. Women pointed at what smoldered before them, as though they were appraising new hats just displayed in a storefront window. Further back from the crowd, a man busily attached an accordion camera to a tripod in preparation to immortalize the event. But it was the boys and men gathered closest to the spectacle that were the loudest and seemed most pleased by their work. Amidst that group, he spotted the gray haired woman with the bad teeth from the Monclair store stepping to and fro, like a pagan celebrating winter and summer solstice combined. And then there was Simeon Monclair who stood off to the side as though he was supervising it all. Nicholas prayed that Lar's death had come quickly and that he was already with God.

"I don't see her around there," Nicholas said, anxiously and with relief.

" Me either. Thank God, man," Roman, replied.

As they were halfway around the park, Nicholas glimpsed a sight he wished he hadn't. The black tree obscured the majority of Lar's body, but still, like a crooked branch jutting out near the base of the tree, he saw a burnt, smoldering limb that was once Lar's arm. In front of the corpse, the mass rejoiced, as though Moses was dead and Baal, the god of gold, would save them if they reveled enough. He turned away, though it was too late, for the charred image of Lar slid next to all the other images of Negroe men, women and children he'd seen lynched. And like other lynchings, he knew the photo that would soon be taken would be copied and given away as souvenirs, along with pieces of Lar's hacked off flesh as reminders of what once was the right of a white man and woman.

They sped on westward at Roman's suggestion. "We head out to the Monclair place where Lar's wife works," he said. "If Maggie Mae isn't there, then we can assume she's across the river, right?"

Nicholas bobbed his head in agreement. He was just glad to be away from the carnage that raged behind them. The stench of burnt flesh was infused in his clothes and nostrils, and in his head, where no rag or bar of lye-soap could ever scrub clean.

The road was deserted as they expected, since most of Folsom's citizens were busy celebrating in town. But not long after they rambled on in silence, a wagon with two riders at the helm came into view. Roman took hold of his pistol at the very moment Nicholas did.

"You know how to use that thing?" Roman asked, never taking his eyes from the oncoming wagon.

"Well enough."

"Then be ready. If you hesitate . . ."

Nicholas looked down at the pistol gripped firmly in his shivering hand. The closer the wagon came, the closer he felt to losing control of the weapon. That is, until he realized he wouldn't be in need of it. What once was a blur moving toward them slowly began to coalesce into something recognizable . . . two frightened young boys.

Nicholas sighed in relief. He looked at Roman and smiled for the first time since the entire ordeal had begun. "It's the just the Monclair boy and his friend."

"Who?"

"Paul– Simeon Monclair's boy and . . . and . . . David," Nicholas said, anxiously. "They're good boys."

Roman scowled. With one hand on the reigns and one still gripping the pistol down and out of site, he slowed the wagon to a crawl. "Monclair?! I don't trust a damn one of them, especially a spawn of Simeon's. You saw the old bastard up there with the rest of them."

"Well I know the boy and I *do* trust him . . . and his friend," Nicholas replied. He jumped down and raced toward the oncoming wagon.

"*Nicholas!*" Roman yelled. He dropped his gun, and with both hands free, yanked on the reigns and brought the wagon to a halt. Nicholas had made it to the other wagon by the time he reached for and retrieved the pistol. "Dammit, boy!"

"I told you its' alright," Nicholas snapped. He didn't blame Roman for being wary, especially now when the entire town had gone mad for blood. Though he'd known Paul and David for a short time, he knew *about* them, and they about he and Maggie Mae. That evening at Enda's and during the walk back to Folsom, they'd bonded, he felt. He could see in their wide, frightened eyes that the feeling was more than mutual.

David, who was sitting on the passenger's side, was shivering as much as Paul's hands were on the reigns. Both boys spoke simultaneously as he approached. Their voices rose and sank in anxiety and fear. He waved his hands to stop them, but it only seemed to make them talk that much faster over the other. Paul's face was red blotched and his blue eyes glassy. "Calm down . . ." he urged, reaching up and laying a hand on Paul's arm. "We know about Lar," he said softly, as the words caught in his throat.

"Say he's ok," Paul begged, shaking his head slowly before tears began to roll down his cheeks.

Nicholas wanted to lie, if only to stop the pain that was slicing through Paul. It was hard to watch such an angelic face be in so much agony, but his silence gave Paul the answer he was reluctant to say. The howl that came out of Paul was something he knew he would never forget. Paul had told him that he was close to Mary and Lar, but he now realized just how deep that love ran. That a southern white boy, who was born and bred to regard Negroes as animals held such love for them, swelled his heart with pride. David was sobbing also. Nicholas stepped up on the wagon and grabbed him, yet had not really, for Paul was already collapsing in his arms. He looked at Roman, who had raised his pistol at the ready, but slowly lowered it and looked away.

Nicholas placed his chin on Paul's head, and in doing so, glanced at the back of the cart. Heaps of blankets and sheets were carelessly piled upon one another. He was glad that Paul and David had finally made the decision to depart Folsom. He figured now was just as well, for he and Maggie would make a similar journey once she'd been found, which was all it took for him to pry Paul away from his chest and shake him gently. "Look now, Paul," he said. "Things are worse now than before. Folsom's gone mad. They want blood– lots of it."

Paul nodded, as did David.

Nicholas hushed his voice so that only Paul and David were privy to his words. "You're both men now and have to look out for one another . . . you know what I mean?" He asked and told them.

"Now I need you both to help me." He paused. "Maggie Mae has gone missing. Do you know where she might be? Down with um . . . um, Mary . . . Lar's wife? No?"

Though neither replied, Nicholas immediately knew something was afoot. David, who was far more readable than Paul, suddenly looked as though he'd been tortured and was ready to confess to anything. "David– if you know something tell me now," he said firmly at first, and then softly begged. "Please."

It was Paul, however, who spoke up. "Is that Mr. Meadows over there?" He asked, squinting and squeezing out more tears in the process.

"Yes."

"Why's he here?" Paul whispered.

Nicholas glanced at Roman. "To help me find Maggie Mae. That's all we want. That's all *I* want. You know how I feel about her– you too, David. You both know I love her!" His voice began to tremble. "And if you don't know that I'll kill anyone who even looks at her, then you haven't believed a word I've told you."

But . . . Nicholas realized he was wrong to assume that Paul and David were making their grand escape. Clothes and food were not the cargo the boys carried, for the sheets moved, and whatever lay beneath them suddenly began struggling to be free. A voice called his name. To him, it was the most beautiful, wondrous and sweetest sound to ever caress his ears.

He jumped down and ran to the rear of the cart. Seeing Maggie Mae emerge from underneath cloaks of secrecy, he didn't know whether to smile, laugh or cry . . . so he did them all as he pulled her straight out of the back, not for a second letting her feet touch the ground. He kissed her hard. The magic she commanded over him swept the stench of death from his senses and replaced it with sweet ether, making him lightheaded and weak, and causing him to slowly set her down on firm ground.

"I . . . thought I'd lost you," he whispered.

Maggie Mae had to struggle from his embrace to pull her head up. "You didn't and you won't, but . . . we've got big trouble, Nicholas."

He stroked her cheek. "Shhhhhhh . . . no– no. Everything is fine now," he assured her.

Maggie Mae shook her head. "No, its not." She began pulling the rest of the sheets from the wagon and revealed a most unsettling, though relief-giving sight.

Nicholas looked from the rear of the cart to Roman, who had since made his way toward them with a foreign smile on his weathered face . . . which was all for Maggie Mae. "You're alright," he heard Roman say to Maggie Mae.

But all Nicholas could say was . . . *"Dear God!"*

Roman was by his side within moments and looked at what was in the rear of the wagon. "What the hell happened?!" Roman exclaimed.

"It was me," Maggie Mae volunteered.

"It was all of us," Paul added.

"Yeah– all of us . . . and it wasn't easy neither," David said.

All eyes studied the contents of the wagon, which contained a seemingly peaceful sleeping, and very pregnant Mary Cole. Had there not been a small pool of blood around her head, it would have appeared as if she had just laid down for a rest. The tale of how Mary came to be in such a state came in spurts and pieces from all three . . . Maggie Mae, Paul and David, each cutting into the other's story when it seemed as though an important detail had gone unspoken. Nicholas and Roman listened speechlessly and in eerie wonderment as the tale unfolded . . . how, after Maggie Mae was knocked to the ground by Mary, that she had found strength enough to right herself and quickly find a shovel by one of the sheds and gone after her. With both hands and one swing, she told them, she caught the back of Mary's head and rendered her unconscious.

"But that ain't the hard part. I didn't reckon we ever get her in the back of the wagon," David huffed. His voice was heavy, as though it had just occurred.

"It took all five of us to pull her up and in," Paul added.

"Five?" Roman asked.

"Um– Mrs. Monclair and . . . what's her name?" Maggie Mae asked David.

"Beatrice," David spat.

"It was the only way to stop her from going into town," Maggie Mae continued. "I promised Lar I would before . . ." Her voice died within her throat.

Nicholas pulled her into his arms. "I know, sweet one . . . I know."

"Ain't none of it true what they said he did," David announced.

"It's not, Mr. Meadows. I swear on my God-given soul," Maggie Mae added. "I saw and heard everything. It's . . ."

"Lucianna . . . believe me, I know," Roman interrupted before she could finish. "And she'll reap hers one day. But now isn't the time to wait until she does. We have to get off the road is what we have to do before someone comes along. Folsom is rabid as a coon right now. Don't think they'll stop with Lar if they see whites and Negroes acting like we are."

Nicholas turned Maggie Mae so that they were face to face. "He's right. If you could have seen how they were acting . . . *Jesus!*" He gasped.

"We have to get Mary out of here and keep her away until she's able to think straight," Maggie Mae told him. "She wants revenge. She wants their blood, Nicholas. And if she wakes up now, she'll fight everyone of us to get it."

"And she'll be a damn fool then. They'll hang her right next to Lar if she tries it," Roman countered.

"Lar was her husband!" Paul snarled at Roman. "She loved him and I did too!" Paul pounded his frail chest. "And if she wakes up and wants to kill them all, I'll help her myself."

"Paul . . ." Nicholas whispered, attempting to calm him.

"They killed him, Mr. Barrons! Killed him!" He shouted.

"Look, boy," Roman said, "I didn't mean anything by it– just that she would put herself in danger if she walked in there trying to avenger Lar."

"It's going to be alright, Paul," Nicholas lied. "I promise." Paul glared at him. Nicholas knew the hate brimming in such beautiful eyes was not meant for him, but for the white skin he wore that represented everything that Paul had come to hate the most. "Where are you taking her?" He asked Maggie Mae.

"To my mother," she answered. "Her head is going to need tending, and the baby, too. Then someone is going to have to talk some sense into her. She's not likely to listen to any of us. And my mama's home is the last place whites are going come to because they think she's . . . you know."

"I'm coming too," Nicholas insisted. "I'm not risking you passing through that– that mob . . . without me." He turned to David and Paul, and then lowered his head and raised a brow. "And you boys need to get back home and get to doing what you said you were going to do."

"Not until Mary is safe," Paul uttered defiantly. "I'm going with her."

"Me too!" David added quickly.

"This ain't a game, boys," Roman, none too kindly reminded them.

"We know that, Mr. Meadows," Paul growled back. He reached behind his back and retrieved a pistol from the waistband of his pants and brandished it for all to see. "That's why I borrowed this from my father's drawer. Does it look like I'm playing cowboy to you now, Mr. Meadows?"

Roman flinched as Paul waved the pistol in his direction. "Be careful with that thing, boy!"

"So'kay, Mr. Meadows," David said nonchalantly. "I done already show him how to use it. I been huntin' coon and squirrels and shootin' pistols since I could hold one in my hands."

"Well, you won't be shooting any rabbits and coons around here," Roman snapped back, cowering David into silence.

"Everyone just settle down and be quiet for a moment!" Nicholas boomed. He turned to Roman first. "You have to get into town now. Like it or not, people will come looking for you– they'll want their thanks . . . and you'll have to give it."

"Wha . . .?" Paul croaked.

"It's what I've been trying to tell you two *boys*," Roman said. "What they did to Lar was to avenge the honor of my wife . . . that's the lie. Nobody gives a damn about her. We . . . we don't have time to explain it right now. You'll see what I'm talking about when you boys get older."

"What I'm saying is that if he's not in town, they'll come looking for him, which won't be hard seeing that were sitting here with our necks out," Nicholas added. He turned to Maggie Mae. "As for the rest of us . . . seeing that Mary's bound to wake-up at any moment, and you won't be able to handle her if she does means I'll have to ride in the back with the both of you. You boys," he continued, "are going to drive straight through town to the bridge and on to the other side."

"And don't stop for a goddamn anybody," Roman added sternly. "Or else you just might get to use that pretty pistol of your daddy's."

"Exactly," Nicholas concurred. "Not even a friend . . . family . . . someone you think you can trust. Right now we trust no one but each other. Agreed?"

Both boys shook their heads.

"Alright then," Nicholas said, refusing to let anyone's eyes stray from his gaze before receiving some verbal or non-verbal sign of assurance. "If anyone knows any prayers, say them now."

* * *

Nicholas had never felt more vulnerable than he did lying between Maggie Mae and Mary, and covered in sheets and blankets. Every wagon that passed by started his heart pounding anew. Celebratory gunshots boomed near and far, as those who were returning home sought to share their triumph over a defenseless Negroe with Paul and David. A few passed on news that Roman, who'd scurried ahead to put distance between them, was not the only one being searched for. "Boy– your daddy been lookin' high and low for ya," a man called out to Paul. Then from another on horseback, "You best get up there with your pappy . . . son of Mr. Monclair 'spose be standin' by his side. Ya gotta learn these niggahs 'bout what happen if ya go touchin' a white woman." But each encounter passed without incident, except verbal bravado. Nicholas was just thankful Paul hadn't slowed their pace one gallop.

Then came voices– young ones who must have been walking, for he hadn't heard their approach. They called out to both Paul and David. "Well, looky– looky. If it ain't the two faggots sittin' together so pretty-like," a boy said.

"Hey, Paul*yanna*," another said, in a croaky falsetto. "You wanna suck my peeter?"

"Sure he does. He a cocksucker, ya simpleton!" Another added.

As quickly as the voices had grown loud, they began to wane as the wagon rumbled onward. But the taunting wasn't over yet. Something hard suddenly struck the side of the wagon. And then quickly thereafter, a succession of strikes peppered the cart. But not even the barrage of pebbles and rocks cast was successful in producing the slightest rise out of Paul and David. Even in the face of scorn and derision, Paul and David were relentless in their mission.

"Sissies!" A boy screamed at them.

"Faggots!"

"Hey! Hey David!" A voice yelled from a distance. "There a big, black nigger dick layin' up on the ground there for ya!"

"Yeah ... you can stick it up your ass, ya fat sissy!" Another yelled. Laughter erupted from all before eventually fading away.

Nicholas finally released the air he'd been holding the entire time. He was proud of David and Paul. He had no doubt the words hurled at them had cut at their souls; for he felt his own was now bleeding. He had wanted to rip away the sheets and take each one of the boys and smash each of their faces in, especially after hearing Paul say to David ... "It's o.k. They're nothing to us. Just ... just don't cry. Not right now, David ... o.k.? Not until we're safe."

"They ain't ever gonna leave us be. I just hate'em, Paul," David gurgled.

"So do I," Paul replied. "But we can't let them get to us right now, alright? They're not worth even one of your tears."

Again, there was nothing Nicholas could do except remain silent and hold tight to Maggie Mae and keep a hold on Mary, who had begun to stir more and more. He knew immediately when they reached the town proper ... the stench of death and smoke had returned even before the gaggle of voices around them did. There didn't seem to be as many still around, but without being able to look, he was unsure. Still, even one was one too many for his peace of mind.

"Paul! Paul!"

Nicholas knew without question who was calling out for Paul, even before he heard David say to Paul that his pappy was running for them. "Damn you boy!" Simeon's voice grew louder and closer. "Stop that fuckin' wagon right now!"

"Don't!" Nicholas whispered. "Keep going, Paul."

"*Yeahuh!*" Paul responded with vigor. The wagon surged. Simeon's belly-bellowing quickly became a distant howl, but his threats of what was to befall Paul when he returned was clear and unmistakable.

Rumbling of the wagon on wooden planks assured Nicholas they were finally somewhat safe. The vibrations from the bridge sought to unhinge every joint he had. It was already too late for his head, which had been spinning ever since Paul snapped the horses into a hasty gallop. But what had made him loopy had the opposite effect on Mary, who began moaning louder and was becoming ever more restless.

Nicholas chanced a peak from under the sheets. "How close are we?"

"Ms. Sully place is right up the road here . . . just a quick step," David replied. "I think ya'll can come out now. Ain't no one 'round."

"You can say that again," Paul added. "It looks like every Negroe has left."

"And there's not likely to be one out and about," Nicholas said. "At least not tonight. If you're Negroe– you're hiding right now." He pulled the sheets from their heads a little further. "How you doing?" He asked Maggie Mae.

"Fair," she replied, squinting from the sudden blast of light in her eyes.

Mary moaned again, signaling she was beginning to win the battle and was close to waking. Her arms slowly began moving about. "Hurry up, Paul!" Nicholas cried.

"I'm pulling in now!"

"Get up as far to the house as you can," Nicholas directed. "We have to get her in as quick as possible." He squeezed Maggie Mae's hand.

Maggie Mae reached over Nicholas until she could lay fingertips on Mary's belly. "Sshhh, Mary– calm down, girl. You just lay still. It's Maggie Mae here with you."

Mary mumbled incoherently.

We're here!" David cried.

Maggie Mae began pulling back the sheets, but Nicholas shook his head at her. "You boys sure it's all clear?"

"Ain't a no one," David answered, as he climbed down from his perch. "Well . . . Ms. Sully on the porch."

Nicholas looked up at Paul, who'd turned around and was looking down at him with distant eyes. "Just Ms. Sully, suh. No one else," Paul assured him.

Nicholas extracted himself from the wagon and looked around. The world this side of Folsom was bereft of any signs of life save their own. Maggie Mae's feet were already spinning before Nicholas lifted her out and her feet touched solid ground. She bounded up the wood steps with her arms held out, seeking her mother's embrace– or so Nicholas thought. What he expected to see did not happen. The encounter turned into something that was quite the opposite. Maggie Mae grabbed Enda by the shoulders and began shaking her, but not before a scream barreled from her lips . . . *"YOU!!!"* Nicholas was already in pursuit as Maggie Mae spiraled into a psychotic tirade. "You saw this and didn't do a God-damn thing to stop it! How could you, mama?! *How could you?!"*

Prying Maggie Mae's hands from her mother was harder than he'd expected. Her fingers were curved bands of steel dug into the old woman's flesh. He had to lift Maggie Mae from her feet and completely set her on the opposite side to get her out of reach of Enda. He became a scarecrow to form a barrier between the two. Enda simply turned around, walked over to her rocking chair and sat down.

"You should've told him what his '*tomorrow*' was!" Maggie Mae screamed.

Enda pushed off with one foot, setting the chair in motion . . . rock up . . . rock back . . . rock up . . . rock back . . . "Why ain't you?" She asked calmly.

"I did!" Maggie Mae yelled. "I told him what would happen if he went in that house."

"Ah– but he didn't listen to you did he, gal?" Enda hissed. "Just like he didn't listen to me when I told him he'd never see a chile of his born . . . ever! Ain't but one person he would have listened to, and she layin' right on up in there." She pointed to the wagon with a gnarled finger.

Slowly, Enda turned her head to Maggie Mae. Nicholas swore he could almost hear the bones in her neck creak and snap as she did. Her eyes– grey and cold, seemed to warm the inside of his chest as they looked at him, yet through him. And with a voice that chilled the soul more than any ghost could, she said . . . "More important now– since my boy-chile be dead, is how *you* knew it was gonna happen . . . lil' witch."

* * *

Mary was certain that whatever Enda had given her was to make her feel drowsy and even more uncertain of what she was uncertain of. There were a few things she did know for a fact, even though all she could see were shadows speaking in whispers around her. And her head was hurting something fierce! It was as though every thought she conjured pushed and twisted some unseen knife deeper into her skull.

Some of the hushed voices were familiar to her, though some were not. Maggie Mae– yes . . . a white man's smooth, definitely un-southern speech– no . . . Uncle Matty was near. And there was another male voice that seemed familiar, but she wasn't sure enough to guess. And then there was Paul . . . thank God, she thought.

Paul had been crying. He was holding her hand and speaking to her also. The other voices rose at times, only to fall like pebbles down a gulch. Sometimes they argued amongst themselves, but that too lasted for only a short while. It was too hard for her to separate what was real and what wasn't . . . who was there in the flesh, and who was just a figment of her mind.

She could still taste the sweet, slightly bitter concoction upon her tongue that Enda made her drink before she was conscious and willful enough to refuse it. It soothed her and played games upon her mind in an attempt to erase recent memories. But for all of Enda's so-called powers she was said to possess, she knew the potion would never be strong enough to erase the fact that Lar was dead. Yes . . . dead.

Lar had denied Lucianna Meadows and her response was to cry 'rape' . . . well, that's what she heard Maggie Mae telling everyone in the room. But Lucianna Meadows wasn't the only one to blame for Lar's death, in her eyes. The whites of Folsom held equal blame. They didn't care if Lucianna was truthful or not, only that there was a niggah to be lynched.

'Dear Lord! My head be splittin' apart!' Mary tried crying out, but all she could do was toss and moan.

Paul moved closer and tightened his grip upon her hand. His other stroked her face. There was whispering again . . . telling her to lie back down . . . sleep more . . . telling her it would be all right. Mary realized she was not only moving, but also trying to push herself up.

Her sight was finally coming back. Rage was helping to coalesce the shadows into solid figures. It's sister, *Vengeance*, wet her tongue and her mouth, and started to give her voice back. Her world tipped right and then left, and what was down slowly became up with helping hands. Once erect, she saw those hands belonged to Maggie Mae . . . to David . . . to the handsome man who'd come visiting the Monclair's– Nicholas Barrons, and behind them sitting at a table staring at her was Enda and Uncle Matty. But next to her, refusing to release her hand was Paul . . . my Paul . . . my boy,' she thought.

The time for mourning would come later, she promised herself, but not now, and perhaps not for a long while. She knew her heart would never begin to heal unless she took back what was taken from her. And to make that so, she would have to mourn her loss later so that she could make sure every white in Folsom who took part in Lar's death would always remember this day. 'Oh– and they gonna pay,' she mused silently, as her sight went from black shadows to hazy candlelight to vile scarlet. She stood shakily with Paul's help and leaned on his shoulder. She waved away the others who postured to assist. "If there be a God, he best send me to hell now," Mary said, "'cause I gonna get'em. Every . . . last . . . one of'em."

CHAPTER 23

"You can't, Mary," Uncle Matty told her, echoing the sentiments of the others.

"It won't do anything but stir white folks up," Maggie Mae added.

What you know anyway, Mary thought. It wasn't *her* husband who'd just been murdered– just a lover she's been pinin' for. But seeing the way Maggie Mae looked at Nicholas wasn't lost upon her either.

The energy she'd mustered to stand was short-lived, and with Paul's help again, she sat back down on the bed. Both boys took up residence on the floor next to her. David was staring up at her with glassy eyes, while Paul kept his head lowered. If no one was aware of what the two boys felt for each other before, well– she figured, they knew now ... not that any of that mattered at the moment. Just like after Paul helped her sit and he kissed her cheek, no one in the room flinched ... they had other things on their minds.

"Use common sense, gal."

"They'll do you in too!"

"I want you to come with me and Maggie Mae. The boys are coming with us too!"

"I beggin' you, chile—don't do it!"

Mary ignored them all. She knew what had to be done for Uncle Matty and the loss of a son Lar was to him . . . for the fatherless child within her . . . and for herself. She wanted to scream her grief aloud. He was gone . . . *gone* . . . killed in the worst way a Negroe could be.

Dead . . . *gone.*

His embrace– *gone* . . . his lips– *gone* . . . his touch– *gone* . . . her love– gone.

So– they could beg and plead with her all they wanted, she thought, and it wouldn't stray her feet from her path. There was, however, one piece of advice she did plan on taking, but it wasn't because it offered safety, but because it just happened to fit into her plan. "I *is* leavin' from here," Mary told them. "You best believe I goin' someplace." Heads nodded their approval and lips formed solemn smiles. "But I comin' back!"

Nicholas' brows crumpled upon themselves. "What do you mean, Ms. Mary?"

"I comin' back with the law."

Maggie Mae gasped. "White men?"

"You want to try and bring lawmen to Folsom?" Nicholas asked incredulously.

Mary smiled. "Ain't no trying– just doin'."

Nicholas' head dropped. "Oh, dear God."

"God ain't got nothin' ta do with foolishness," Enda said.

"Ain't nothin' foolish 'bout what I said, old woman!" Mary retorted. "This here be a new south . . . ain't no more slavery! New whites done taken a'hold. Just 'cause ain't none of them here don't meant there ain't some 'round somewhere. If I gotta look high and low for a lawman that'll listen and do somethin', then that be what I do. If I gotta stomp all the way up to Washington to find one, then I gonna do it. Then they comin' back with me to this . . . this . . . this hellhole of Satan, and make right what been done wrong."

"Chile," Uncle Matty puffed, "you ain't hearin' yo'self. You talkin' from grief."

"Uncle Matty's right, Mary," Maggie Mae agreed. She left the company of Nicholas and moved closer to her. "White men aren't going to punish another white over a Negroe. They never have."

"Then I keep lookin' 'til I find the right one," Mary countered.

Nicholas tried his hand. "Mrs. Cole . . . Ms. Mary, please-please-please . . . just listen *to me*. You know what I do for a living and why I'm down here in the first place. And the very reason why I'm here is because Washington hasn't done a damn thing to stop these murders. The white race just doesn't get it, and that's what I'm trying to change. But it hasn't changed yet, Ms. Mary. It's not even close. In fact, it's all going backwards, to tell the truth. They've already pushed Negroes out of politics and are writing laws as quick as they can to put Negroes right back where they want them. Lynching Negroes is just their way of blowing on the wet ink to make sure it doesn't rub off."

"If what you say be true . . . that you just not some old white man like those up in Folsom– then help me. You told me and *Lar* you here to help us Negroes by writin' 'bout it. So you gonna tell the world what Folsom did to Lar?"

"Absolutely!"

"So you help me then?"

"The world is going to know what a good man your husband was, and the injustice inflicted upon him . . . yes! I promise you that," he replied. But his voice lowered as he continued. "But if you're asking me to go with you and then come back here, I . . . I can't, Mary." He looked at Maggie Mae and then said, "*We can't*. It would be suicide for the both of us, and God knows who all else."

Mary closed her eyes slowly, but quickly opened them. She wanted and didn't want to see *him*– not Nicholas, but *him*– for *he* too echoed Nicholas' words. She shook Lar's shade from her mind. "He trusted you. He stuck out his neck for you."

Nicholas knelt in front of her. For a second, it seemed as though he was going to reach for her hands, but instead he clasped his own together and raised them up. "I know that, Ms. Mary. And I am as grateful now as I was then."

Her teeth ground upon one another. "Then help me!"

He turned to Maggie Mae, then back to her. Mary was quite familiar with the look he gave Maggie Mae, as it was the same way Lar always looked at her. He was in love– like Lar had loved her . . . like Paul loved David. One thing she couldn't refute was that *true* love dwelled deep and was ever honest. She knew it was love of her spirit and not of the flesh that drove Lar into her arms and away from Maggie Mae. What made his loss so much more painful than she felt anyone could ever understand, was that a man like Lar . . . a real man . . . such a handsome one, saw so much more to her than two braids of kinky hair, thick hips and big lips . . . midnight black skin and a wide nose. It wasn't just that he loved her . . . but that he loved *her!*

She knew Nicholas' answer even before he could even say it. "I don't need your help then," she told him nonchalantly. "Ain't no one gonna do right by Lar but me! If I be scared, then I just be scared. But I ain't gonna let it pass. If I gotta walk taller than a man to do it 'cause ain't one willin' to come with me, then I will. And if no man gonna come back with me, then I'll come back here and burn this whole damn town to the ground myself!" A gentle touch to her thigh, accompanied by a voice of utmost purity did what no one else present was capable of doing– quelling her rage.

"I'll go with you, Mary," Paul said.

Ragnarok banged upon the door of her burning soul. She knew he would willingly give his life to avenge Lar's death. She squeezed his hand and smiled at him, but shook her head. "No you ain't," she told him. She looked at David also with the same mother bear intensity, ready to cuff them both to teach them right from wrong. "Ya'll two gonna be gettin' out of here and far away as can be."

"But . . ."

She jerked his arm. "Ain't no *but* 'bout it! You ain't comin' with me– you hear me, dammit!? I said do you hear me!?" She knew tears were going to come even before they began coursing down his cheek. But that was a good thing. He shook his head before pulling away and burying it into David's shoulder. But again, that was good. There was no way she was going to let him come close to danger . . . not now and not ever, if she had anything to do about it. He'd already had a lifetime of pain in a life barely lived, she thought. Being who he was . . . loving who he loved, there would be more pain coming his way just for that reason alone. And . . . she loved him . . . as much as she loved the child within her, and was prepared to maul anyone who sought to do him harm.

"That be all to it now, Paul," Mary cooed. He refused to acknowledge her and remained firmly tucked in David's embrace.

"Ms. Mary," Nicholas said, "you wish Paul to listen to reason, but you won't."

"And she ain't ever goin' to." Enda, who had remained silent for so long, spoke up. "Girl-chile been like this her whole life. She just can't listen to folk when she need to."

"Amen!" Uncle Matty croaked.

"You wanna go off and get help– then you do that!" Enda continued. "Go on! What you waitin' on, gal? Go on out there and dance your jig in that snake pit, but don't come back actin' all surprised that you got bit."

Mary stood up. "I didn't ask for *your* help, did I?"

"'Cause you know better," Enda muttered in reply.

Mary shook her head. "No," she argued, as she began drowning in everything she despised about Enda. "It 'cause I know you won't! And if you did, it'll all turn to shit anyhow!" She snapped. "I sick and damn tired of you and all your *tomorrows*. Your *tomorrows* ain't did a damn thang for no one 'cept 'cause everythin' to go wrong."

"Now, chile," Uncle Matty intervened. "You know that ain't true. Enda here care 'bout you like you be her own. Grief be talkin' for you now– we know that . . . we all know that, chile. But . . . but . . ." Uncle Matty's voice faded into whispers. What strength he had mustered dissipated and revealed what he truly was . . . an old man who was sitting next to his closest friend . . . *death*. Finally, as though his strength was finally exhausted, he began crying. No one, including Mary was brave enough to hold their head up to bear witness to his pain. "You . . . you . . . you be all that left of my kin . . . 'cept the chile in yore belly," he choked out.

Mary walked over to him and laid her hand upon his. When he looked up at her, she knew he had no more to give. The life-force that had kept his heart beating this long was waning before her eyes. It would be only a matter of time before his spirit joined Lar's in the hereafter. So when she said to him that it was time to go back home, his answer was not a complete shock to her.

"No," he responded. "This here be the place where I close my eyes for the last time."

Enda smiled at him.

"My bones done gone soft on me. I can barely stand, let alone walk," he said.

Mary saw only good in Uncle Matty's decision to stay. He could have what only a few ever did . . . the chance to leave this world in peace. And there was no one but Enda who could fulfill that wish for him. She didn't have to look at jars lined up on Enda's cupboards to know that what Uncle Matty would need when the time came was up there somewhere. So with that settled, she turned and walked toward the door.

"Stay here with us, Mary," Maggie Mae whispered. "At least for the night so mama can see to you and the chile."

Mary shook her head side to side.

She appreciated Maggie Mae's concern, but at the moment, she wanted to be alone. Though as she peered outside, she realized that would not be quite so easy. A crowd of Negroes had gathered around Enda's house. They were brave, she thought. Had it been any other Negroe than Lar who was murdered, she was certain there would not be a soul present.

"Paul . . . you and David stay put in here and way from the windows . . . you too," she said to Nicholas. "We got some Negroes out here. I 'spose they figure I be here. When they see I done gone, you use my wagon and take these boys back 'cross the river, hear? I'll fetch it back when I ready to do what I gotta do. You just make sure those boys be safe."

"I beg you, Ms. Mary," Nicholas said. "I have just as much hate for those whites up in Folsom as anybody here in this room. *They're* the animals. And maybe it's hard to believe that even though I'm white, I'm on your side. But I beg you, please . . . just think really, really hard before you act on anything." He looked at Maggie Mae. "We already insisted that the boys come with us . . . right, Maggie?"

"Absolutely," Maggie Mae said without hesitation.

Nicholas' words brought a smile to David's chubby face. Paul's eyes showed a hint of a spark.

"Fortunately for *all of us*," he continued, "my grandfather is a very wealthy man. There is basically nothing I can't ask for that he won't give me. But all of the money in the world can't replace your husband. But I can provide you and the child with a new start far away from here. All you have to do is say yes and I'll help you pack your things myself."

Mary looked out to the Negroes waiting outside. As much as she wanted to take Nicholas' more than generous offer, she couldn't leave. She knew they would never understand that her soul would never rest, and Lar's soul could not escape this world until vengeance had been had. Her reply was the same she gave to Maggie Mae.

Mary opened the door and walked out. Silent Negroes with bowed heads greeted the mourning wife of their king. Night had already come, yet an orange beacon in the sky above Folsom marred the darkness. She knew the source was 'he' who had made life as a Negroe woman for her bearable. Her consciousness screamed at her to look away from such a horrible sight, yet she stared at it nonetheless. Though it made her nauseated, she continued to watch that far off glow that emanated from what was left of Lar, for she needed her fury unbridled.

Heads were now raised and faces were staring at her. In the crowd she saw Picken who was held close to his pappy's chest . . . Allie Mae was toward the back on the left . . . Pete Baker, Buck and Lily were in the center . . . Willa was there with her two oldest boys flanking her on either side. Toward the front of the crowd was Bra' Evans, Ms. Ettie and so many more; Frank Clipper, Sam Latter, Jonnie Ray, and on and on and on and on.

The sea of blackness awaiting her parted. But there was no crashing of waters upon themselves . . . no rumble of chariots driven by soldiers with war chants bursting from their lips. There was no crackle from the pillar of fire that swirled up and over town. There seemed to be no sound at all, save her own breaths. The bellow of the wooden step was like thunder as she lowered her weight upon it. No one spoke or moved. And though no one uttered so much as a whisper, grief-laden eyes refused to remain silent. Mary knew what they were all thinking without a single word being said. Their drawn faces told her that old, unforgettable tale of how once again the white man had euphorically driven his point home with blood and fire; that Negroe men were not men and Negroe women not women . . . that somehow the Lord had seen fit to curse their lives with slavery, whips, rape, torture, grief and despair . . . suffering and angst . . . and when that wasn't enough, an inhuman death that only another human mind could invent.

She walked through the black sea in silence, but the waves suddenly fell upon themselves in a vitriolic rage just as she cleared them. To whom their hate was directed was clear from the very first words yelled out . . . *'It Simeon Monclair's boy. Get'em!'* There was no thought to her actions as she cupped her distended belly and spun around. She pushed and swung wildly at anything made of flesh as she fought her way back to where she had started.

"Goddamn whites!" A man yelled as he pointed to the porch. "Git'em!"

"You all devils!" A woman screeched.

Kill'em! Kill'em like they did Lar!" That was Jonnie Ray. Mary knew his voice anywhere.

Trouble was brewing as calls for Paul's death gained momentum quicker than a brush fire in the depths of a draught. The crowd turned mob wanted white blood as much as she did, and Paul, who'd walked outside and onto the porch fit the bill. "Leave him be!" Mary bellowed. She swung her arm into chests and bosoms alike.

That Jonnie Ray was successful in sweeping the crowd into a frenzy so quickly pumped fuel into her limbs. And her sudden burst of strength had come none too soon, for she saw that it had all taken Paul by surprise before he realized what was happening and could flee back inside. She saw and heard him cry out as the men rushed him and lifted him from his feet. And like children were won't to do when danger was upon them, he cried out for the one who was most constant in his life. *"Ms. Mary!!"*

Mary reached the bottom step of the porch just as David . . . foolishly lovesick, David, came barreling out of Enda's home with an animalistic scream of his own. He was quick enough to grab hold of Paul's hand in an attempt to pull him back to safety, but his rescue was short lived, as he too was taken hold of by a group of men and boys whose chants of death were now directed at him also.

Mary finally reached the porch after swatting at faces and punching aimlessly to clear a path. Though it was Paul, and David too, who should have been in her sights as she bounded up the porch stairs, it was neither of them. Jonnie Ray, who was practically drooling at the lips as he held onto Paul's thrashing legs, was the one she focused on. She did to Jonnie Ray what he probably never expected her to do– and what everyone gathered thought she might be capable of, but was not sure she could . . . she cold-cocked him at the temple, not only knocking him down, but completely out. *"Get away from him!"* She screamed at an already unconscious Jonnie Ray lying at her feet. Mary swung again and caught another man in the throat, who immediately fell to his knees gasping for air. The others dropped Paul and ran off the porch.

Mary spun around with her fist cocked, ready to deal with those who were holding David, but he was already being set free. She realized the men were not releasing him out of fear of her, but from another who could stop any man in his tracks with but a look.

Enda Sully– the witch of Folsom now held court. Fear, Awe and the Reaper– her unseen ladies in waiting were present too. She shuffled past Mary and the crowd who edged upon the first step. She turned to the men who were holding David. "Get off my goddamn porch!" The men scrambled over one another in obedience . . . that is, except Jonnie Ray, who was just now waking and looking for the train that had slammed into him.

Paul and David huddled close to Mary, who put her arms around them both. Enda reached out and slowly caressed each boy's face. "These here white boys done been touched by *me* now," she told the fearful mass. "They done saved your Mary and your

Maggie Mae today, and ya'll just bitin' at the bit to do'em harm?"
She waited. Her head swiveled from one end of the crowd to the
other, as if almost daring someone to speak against her. No one
even moved. "First one of ya'll touch these white boys gonna die.
Ms. Enda swear that!" She turned around and gave each boy a lingering gaze. "Ya'll get on now."

Mary had to pull at both boys to get them moving. Whereas she
knew that no one would defy Enda's edict, she could tell that Paul
and David had no such knowledge of the power Enda wielded over
her own people. They clung close to her. Now, instead of carrying
the weight of just her and the baby, her burden was increased by
two more it seemed. "They ain't gonna touch ya'll," she whispered
to them, as they descended the steps. As she knew they would be,
they were given a wide berth through which to pass, for a death
call from Enda could follow them home and into their beds, and
would not be stopped by even the most sincere Lord's Prayer.

The only ones brave enough to speak were the horses, who
yelped after all three were on and Paul tugged at their reins to begin a trot along the road to Mary and Lar's home. Only, to Mary,
when she did reach home, she knew it was now and forever just
hers. The shack of rotting wood and rusted metal only reminded
her of what little whites allowed her to have in this world. And
now the most precious thing she had was taken from her, simply
for being a Negroe. She felt there was no life left inside the shack,
and didn't wish to go in, for she would catch his lingering scent
and it would drive her mad. She would see his shirt, his shoes, a
strand of his curly hair wrapped around the tooth of a comb . . .
and she would go mad. She might even see his spirit sitting in a
chair waiting for her . . . and she knew she would go mad. And in
madness, she knew grief would come for her and steal the strength
she needed to avenge him. In grief, oh– that kind of grief that takes
one by the gut and twists them, she would only be able to think of

one thing . . . that Lar was now and forever gone. She began a slow, uneasy walk to the front door when she was caught by surprise . . . though not actually.

"I'll still go with you," Paul offered. She had no doubt he would. To hell and back and all over again he would go, which was where she knew her path was leading.

"Me too," David added.

That they actually would go was the very reason she vowed they wouldn't. "No, babies. I'll never let ya'll do somethin' like what I gonna do. It ain't gonna be safe for me or anybody 'round me. But it be somethin' I has to do. And I can't do it if I worryin' 'bout both of you."

Paul looked up at her. "But– but . . . what if . . . what if something . . . "

"You boys take that white man's offer and go north with him and Ms. Maggie Mae . . . you hear?" She used her most loving, yet direct voice she could muster at the moment. "What happen just gonna happen. Don't worry 'bout me. But if somethin' do happen, you just gotta know that . . . that . . . I love you. Always have and always will . . . no matter what. I know Negroe folk thinkin' Ms. Mary crazy. White folk done killed my Lar and here I be lovin' you white boys with all my heart and all my soul," she whispered. " You a grown man almost! And don't ever let nobody tell you different, 'cause you be more a man than any of them over there in that town. You more a man than your daddy ever dreamed he could be," she said full of pride. "Now go on now," she told them before turning around. "Ain't a Negroe in Folsom gonna' touch you two– ya'll be safe 'round here. Ain't but one thing be worse than white folk coming for you, and that be Enda Sully comin' for ya."

CHAPTER 24

Paul and David held hands as long as they could, which was, until they spotted the first of many Negroes walking toward them. The first was a woman with two boys around their own age. To his relief, and David's as well, it was exactly as Ms. Mary said it would be, and how Ms. Sully had commanded–they were allowed passage unmolested. But more than that, not only did the oncoming Negroes not even look their way, they vacated the entire road until he and David had passed by. When they arrived at Enda's house, Nicholas slipped out from it even before Paul had pulled the wagon to a stop. He hopped up in front next to David. "You boys alright?" He asked.

'*What do you think!?*' Paul wanted to scream at him. Lar had been murdered . . . he and David had almost been . . . and the one person he'd loved all of his life had just sent him away. '*Alright?*' Paul volleyed the word back and forth in his mind. He couldn't think of a time when he could ever use the word "*alright*" again to describe how he felt . . . not after this day and what they had been through.

He remembered David tugging at him as they passed along the road where the celebration of Lar's death was in mid-swing. "Don't look over there," David had begged. But he couldn't resist. As they made their way around the backside of the old park, he could see Lar's blackened arm sticking out from the base of the tree. Most of his flesh was melted off down to the elbow, revealing bone which remained alight from the oil-accelerant clinging to it.

"There a big, black nigger dick layin' up on the ground there for ya!" Paul sickeningly recalled Payne Hallson, one of his classmates, taunting as he and David passed him and his friends before they began pelting them with rocks. He felt nauseated just thinking of what they had done to Lar . . . stripping him naked for all to see, and then slicing off his penis as if it were a fleshy tumor needing to be excised from an animal. It had taken all of his will not to pull out his pistol and put a bullet in all of their heads. And God only knows, he thought, what else they did to him before setting him on fire.

'Alright?' Paul stared at Nicholas. *'No—I'm not alright!'* Especially not now, he wanted to say, as a sudden queasiness began rumbling his stomach. Before he could warn David or Nicholas, he already had a mouthful of vomit. The first stream landed on all of their feet. With the second and third that came shooting out, he was quick enough to turn to the side and hear most of it on the ground, though the horse on the left did end up having its backside splattered.

"Oh shit!" David yelped at the foot washing, but then a softer, more worried tone came from him. "Oh, Paul," he whispered, and began rubbing his back.

He continued heaving, though there was nothing left in his stomach to expel. The memory of seeing Lar's arm ablaze and the smell of burnt flesh made him began retching again, and brought fresh tears to his already red and sore eyes. The pain Lar suffered seemed unfathomable to him, but no matter how much he wished it would go away, it was a reality to his eyes, his nose, and his mind. He knew how Mary felt, for he felt the same way. He wanted vengeance for Lar that only blood could satisfy– nothing less would do. He fantasized that what they'd done to Lar would only be a prelude of what he would do to them if he had a chance. He wiped his lips and spat out the remaining bits of vomit. "I'm fine," he whispered to David.

"We better get right home and quick like," David said. "My pa's gonna whip me good and red if he finds out I been over here. And yours . . ."

"That was your father– Simeon, who was calling for you?" Nicholas asked, as he innocently tried scraping the vomit from his feet on the side of the cart.

"Sorry about that," Paul muttered watching him. Nicholas smiled demurely at him. "Yeah– that was him alright."

"And mad as hell, too," David added. "You know he gonna beat you for runnin' off like that."

"He's not going to lay a hand on you," Nicholas interjected. "I've told you both that, and I meant every word of it."

"What he gonna do then?" David asked. "You can't be with Paul night and day. Even if you could, that's Mr. Monclair you talkin' 'bout. We ain't got no mayor in Folsom, but if we did, he be it. That what my pappy say. Mr. Monclair runs this town."

"He's still just a man," Nicholas replied unimpressed.

"But he's Mr. Monclair!" David protested.

"He's saying people don't cross my father unless they're planning on leaving Folsom," Paul explained. "Right or wrong, Mr. Barrons, people will do what he says to keep their job."

"So if someone could have stopped . . ." Nicholas paused. "Stopped what happened to Lar– then you're saying your father could have?"

Paul had witnessed men far older and far younger than his father cower from just a look from him. But the people of Folsom had wanted blood from Lar. Whether his father could have stopped it or not, he wasn't sure. What he did know was that his father had not even tried to stop it. But why would he when his father hated Lar simply for being a Negroe? He thought. "I don't know," Paul answered, and then shrugged weakly. "Maybe. But probably not."

"Well, were not staying anyway," Nicholas said, after a moment of thought.

"We're *not* leaving yet," Paul countered harshly. Nicholas sighed heavily in response, and then leaned over and placed a hand on his knee, which he quickly jerked away. "Not yet!"

"Paul– I know you want to help and protect Mary. But these people around here aren't thinking rationally at the moment. They're liable to do just about anything to anyone given the slightest provocation."

"I'm still not going."

"We're waiting on the baby," David told him. "Once the baby's here, then we're going . . . right?" He looked to Paul for confirmation.

Paul tipped his head. "Right!"

"You promise?" Nicholas asked.

"I do," he replied, and meant it.

An ill pause followed as they neared the bridge. The fiery beacon that was Lar's funeral pyre was gone, and just a plume of white smoke spiraling up signaled the location of the man who once was. "Then Maggie Mae and I will wait, too," Nicholas told him. "Mary seems damn close to having it."

"It's a girl. We were hopin' it was gonna be a boy, but Ms. Sully said it's a girl," David corrected him.

"Well, we'll just have to lay low for . . ."

"Why do you even care about what happens to us!?" Paul spat. "We're cocksuckers and buttfuckers and . . . and . . . abominations that are supposed to be lynched, too. What do you want from us anyway? Or-or-or are you one of those men who likes to diddle with little boys or something?" Paul lashed out. Whether it was because they were coming closer to the murder site, or it was the anger he'd been holding back for so long, the damn finally burst, he didn't know. It was as though his mouth had disconnected from his mind and melded with his heart. He sensed an opportunity to release his hurt, if only to make someone else feel just a little of what he was feeling. And it worked . . . Nicholas' mouth was hanging open. He felt ashamed for having said it to Nicholas, who'd been nothing but kind to him. In his wounded heart, he knew Nicholas didn't deserve any of it. Like a scolded dog, he simultaneously lowered and turned his head away from Nicholas and David.

"Mr. Barrons is our friend," David chided. "He a good man, Paul. Why would you say . . .?"

"I-I-I . . ." Paul couldn't find the words to ease the sting of his previous ones. He began choking up.

"It's alright, David," Nicholas interjected.

But Paul knew he'd hurt Nicholas more than he was letting on. He could hear it in his voice, no matter how hard he tried to disguise it. He felt foolish for having succeeded in hurting someone; it was the wrong someone to hurt. He took a deep breath. "I'm sorry Mr. Barrons. I'm very, very sorry that I said that. I-I . . . I don't believe any of what I said to you. Its' just that . . . that . . ."

"That it hurts?" Nicholas finished for him. He reached out his hand once more. Paul quickly met him halfway and took hold of his hand. "If there's one thing my parents taught me, it was to love as much as I can, no matter who that person is. But as I'm finding out the hard way, choosing to love can cause pain, too. My parents chose that path and were hated by whites as much as whites hate Negroes down here. I guess sometimes those are the consequences of the choices we make. My parent's choices made our lives harder than you know. When you're shunned by your own people . . . your house vandalized, you're constantly physically threatened, children aren't allowed to play with you or even speak to you . . .

well," he paused. "But the love you receive back is immeasurable, Paul," he proclaimed, smiling widely. "To love hard and have it returned even stronger? That's the only way I'm going to live.

"But when that love is taken from you, or it's beaten out of you, it's going to hurt worse than anything you know. There are no words David or I can say that can soothe that ache you have in your heart. But I tell you this . . . as your friend," he beamed proudly. "I going to protect you both." Nicholas squeezed his hand. "Now first things first. We can't risk you going home."

"Well, I can't stay with David. My father knows enough about us to look there first."

"Yeah. Thanks to Beatrice's big ugly mouth," David uttered.

"Then you'll stay with me," Nicholas stated. "The Williamses never stay up late. Once they're turned in for the night, we'll slip you inside. But once you're there, you can't leave until we're ready to leave Folsom for good."

David huffed. "I don't like that idea one bit."

Paul was taken off guard by David's blatant expression of jealousy. At first it was a bit amusing, but not for long, seeing that David quickly crossed his arms and lowered his eyelids nearly shut. He knew then that David didn't really understand how deep his love for him dwelled. Even if a handsome man such as Nicholas stripped off every stitch of his clothing and offered himself to him, Paul was willingly to stake his life that his love for David would never allow such a thing to even come close to happening. One day soon, once they were long gone from Folsom, he vowed to tell David exactly why he would never have to worry about such a thing . . . ever!

Don't you know you saved me from death? He wanted so bad to tell David, but not during this whole mess and in the company of Nicholas. But soon, he promised. He would tell David exactly how that afternoon in the forest when they touched for the first time, that he let go of his will to die and found the strength to not only live, but love . . . and it was all because of David. And for that, he wouldn't jeopardize it for anything, let alone some momentary bit of pleasure. Still, even if Nicholas' suggestion was feasible, he didn't think it was a wise decision either. Paul shook his head and said, "I can't do that. Reason being is, I know the Williamses and the Lewis' on the other side of them. It's too risky."

"Yeah, too risky," David added quickly.

"Then where?" Nicholas asked. "Don't even say with Ms. Mary."

"With Ms. Sully," Paul replied, as he pulled the cart to a halt. David and Nicholas stared at him in disbelief. "It's the safest place – you can't say it isn't. Negroes won't bother me, and white folks are just as scared of Ms. Sully as they are. No one would even guess that I would be there anyway. And . . . I'll be close enough so that I can see the baby when it comes, too. It's the best choice. Either there or with my father at home."

"I don't know about that, Paul," Nicholas cautioned, but went no further.

Paul handed the reins to David and jumped off the cart before they could protest. "There's nothing to know. It can only be for a few days at the most anyway. I'll slip on by the house when I know my father is at work or out drinking himself stupid and gather what I need, and that will be that."

"And you think you're just going to walk up to Enda Sully and say, 'let me stay here a few days?'" Nicholas asked.

Paul pondered for a moment. "Yes," he replied plainly.

It was Nicholas' turn to reflect. "On the edge of a knife," he muttered.

"Huh?" David puffed.

Nicholas took the reins from David, but then quickly gave them back to him. "What am I doing? I can't drive this thing. Turn it around," he told David, "and you, get back in . . . now!"

"I'm going back, Mr. Barrons. It's the–" Paul started, but Nicholas cut him short.

"I know, because we're taking you– no argument." His voice was on the rise. "I said I was going to look after both of you. Now get in!"

* * *

Nicholas conceded that Paul was right and had been about many things this night. Enda Sully's house was the safest place for him to be right now. And again Paul was right, for Enda, who was sitting on the porch when they arrived and seemed not the least bit surprised at their return, did indeed offer him sanctuary. He couldn't deny that it did his heart good to see Maggie Mae again, though they'd only departed moments ago. But they didn't linger, as it was well into evening and David still had to work on sneaking into his own home or face consequences.

As he and David drove back to Folsom, and he listening to David's tales about what he'd heard about Enda being a witch, it worried him that he actually began to believe parts of it. In particular was what happened when Paul foolishly ran out to follow Mary and stirred the Negroes into a frenzy. He remembered how he rushed for the door after him. "Stay here!" Enda had commanded, laying a hand upon his chest as she did. But it was just that . . . *that hand*. Through his shirt, the burning cold emanating from her wrinkled hand shot through him in every direction all at once, paralyzing him where he stood.

He wanted to believe that it was simply mind over matter, like the effects hypnotists held over weak, already open and susceptible minds. He wondered if he had fallen for the same trick the Negroes fully bought into as they scrambled away at her command, practically shielding their faces from hers, as if she were Jesus reading their sins from the Book of Life. Whether a witch or not, that people believed she was one was a good thing for Paul, he guessed.

When they came to the circular road in town, they were silent as they quickly passed by the old park. David kept his eyes firmly fixed on the road ahead. A short time later, they passed by the Monclair place, which had nearly every window illuminated by lamplight. Nicholas guessed that whatever was stirring within was not good at all, and felt a wave of relief that Paul was, for the time being at least, safely hidden away. David pulled the cart to a halt. "All right, Mr. Barrons," David announced. "I guess you and me do our partin' here."

Nicholas took the reins as he jumped down. "You going to be alright?"

David shrugged. "Yeah . . . my house is just a bit of a walk from here. I can sneak in my bedroom window like last time."

Nicholas sighed. "Alright. Now you know I'm staying at the Monclair motel. If something comes up, or you need something, you come get me right away– no matter what."

"I will."

"And David? You be ready to get out of here at a moment's notice. If I come to tell you were leaving, then we're leaving right away– no delay."

"Gotcha, Mr. Barrons," he said, before lumbering off into the dark.

Turning the wagon around was tricky, not driving it, Nicholas realized. He desperately tried recalling the movements of the reigns that David and Paul had demonstrated so naturally. The horses seemed to forgive him as they finally settled into a whimsical walk back in the opposite direction. He wished he could ride them all the way back to town. His mind, as well as his body was past exhausted.

He hadn't said anything to anyone about Simeon's new brothers. The Knights of the White Camellia, they said they were that night he met with them at Simeon's house after dinner. A new band of murders for all he was concerned, and hell-bent on one thing and one thing only . . . the genocide of the Negroe race no matter the cost. A price that was always paid in Negroe blood. He had no doubt they had ignited the murdering blaze under the townsfolk of Folsom.

By the time he reached the town, he was sure he could be detected a hundred steps away by even the oldest nose, for he could barely stand his own stench. But it was far more preferable to the smell slowly creeping toward him. Unfortunately, he realized, his senses were becoming far too accustomed to the foul odor of burned flesh. The first few times it had caused his eyes to burn and his stomach to boil with bile until he vomited. That it was just a bother to him now, he took as another sign that he'd lingered in the south for far too long. He wanted to be as far away from this place as possible and never return. He wished Mary solace, though in his heart, selfishly, he wished she would have the baby tomorrow, for that meant freedom for him.

He would never leave Paul and David in this cesspool of a town. That was his vow and he expected to keep it. There was just something about Paul that was so endearing to him. Though he did feel sorry for him, that wasn't it. It was as though he could sense a spark of life in him just waiting to be set free from beneath layer after layer of pain. And strangely, he thought, it never crossed his mind that he should be bothered that Paul and David were homosexuals. He recalled all the words he'd heard used to describe men like them . . . deviant . . . immoral . . . psychotic, but Paul and David were none of those things. Innocent . . . loving . . . brave . . . decent, were more fitting words, he thought. The pure and unconditional love residing within Paul was so obvious, to him. He recalled seeing Paul hold Mary's hand as she lay unconscious at Enda's, and how he didn't hesitate in offering his life to help her find justice for Lar. Paul's love for Mary, David, Lar and the baby seemed almost tangible. Paul's irreproachable moral code and utter valor were the very traits Nicholas' own father had tried to instill in him.

How could I not do everything in my power to protect him? He wondered. Paul was just a mere boy who had already demonstrated the bravery of ten righteous men and still he puts them to shame . . . *me included*, he thought. If Paul was willing to risk his life for those he loved, could he do any less? He pondered.

And Maggie Mae. *My dear, Maggie Mae,* he thought lovingly, yet achingly. Once again, Paul's strength was a stern lesson to him. Her legacy of Negroe blood could mean trouble for them both. But to have her love, just as Paul loved David, he was willing to risk his life once, twice, a thousand times.

Nicholas was thoroughly lost in thought, and didn't realize he'd made it right into the town's center, where the now thoroughly fire scorched tree stood with its newest branch. He dismounted and hitched the horse and wagon out in front of the Monclair store. Without thinking, he turned his head away from what was left of Lar before he could catch a glimpse of Folsom's macabre handiwork, only to come face to face with Lucas and Arthur, the men he'd met at Simeon's weeks ago . . . the same men who were trying to recruit Simeon into their order. Both were stumbling toward him. Both reeked of booze and tobacco. He hadn't realized it right away, but the townsfolk had not yet settled down. The tavern next to the motel was still quite lively.

"Goddamnit boy!" Lucas yelled at him. "You done missed a fine ass show!"

"Where the hell you been anyway?" Arthur asked. "We tried lookin' for you a second, but things 'round here got goin' quick . . . as you can see," he slurred proudly, and pointed to Lar's corpse behind Nicholas.

"I heard," Nicholas grunted, as he continued walking toward the motel, hoping that his few words would suffice the murdering drunkards. But it was not so.

Lucas grabbed him by the shoulders and spun him, not completely around, but far enough for him to see what he had no desire to. And again, another image of a lynched human was seared into his mind. He turned away as quickly as he was turned toward the ghastly visage, but it was too late. The body, or what was left of it was on the ground, as if the legs had been taken off and it was resting on what was left of its waist. Blackened bones that were once arms were outstretched toward the dark heavens. The head was now just a skull without eyes, and was nearly separated from the body, as it rested far, far too low from its shoulders than a head should. But worse of all, Arthur walked over and stood right by it, lit a cigarette and grinned.

Nicholas' head began to spin.

Though Lucas' breath repulsed him, he was glad for his hands at his shoulders keeping him steady, for he knew if they weren't there, he would already be on the ground. "You all right there, Yanky-boy," Lucas snickered.

"He probably ain't never seen nothin' like this we got here," Arthur commented. "We made sure this one got it done right for what he done. Though, by the time we got to stringin' his ass up, damn niggah was already dead."

"But we got'em though."

"Damn good too. And made sure we cut that donkey dick off while he still tryin' to fight us off," Arthur continued. "You go 'round and rape a white woman . . . hell, don't let us catch your niggah ass– right Lucas?"

"Yeahup! You do, and you ain't gonna be walkin' around with that thing between your legs," he said, slapping the back of his hand to Nicholas' crotch.

"You should've seen that niggah's face," Arthur said.

"His face?!" Lucas squealed. "His holler be what you talkin' 'bout. That niggah screamed like an old woman when those boys ran up there and sliced off that donkey dick and that thang goes . . . boing-boing-boing . . . *bawwwwwk!!!!*" Lucas retelling was abruptly halted, for already, it was more than Nicholas could take.

In Lucas' still moving mouth, on his lower chin and top of his shirt, Nicholas spewed; projecting a vicious stream of yellow vomit that he had no idea was rising up in his throat. While Lucas' expression turned from jovial to horror, and it seemed as if he was going to regurgitate also as he spit Nicholas' vomit from his mouth, Arthur bellowed in laughter.

"Son'a bitchin' Yankee!" Lucas hollered.

Nicholas was already running– dizzily for the motel, stopping twice more to vomit horrendously on the plank-board walkway before nearly busting through the door. The room was in complete darkness, until his bumbling, crashing into tables and chairs, and God knows what else lurked in the dark awoke the Williamses.

Edgar and Deborah came running from their bedroom, which was behind the counter. Nicholas knew by the solid, metal click that Edgar was armed and ready. "It ... its me, Nicholas ... Nicholas Barrons!" He cried quickly. "Don't shoot!"

The darkness was suddenly illuminated by the glow of candle-light from behind Edgar. "Who is it?" Deborah asked.

"Just that northern boy stumblin' 'round in the dark. Drunk like the rest of the idiots next door," he replied. "And you! You damn near done got your head blown clear off. You know that Yank?"

"Uh ... uh, yes suh," Nicholas replied, thoroughly nauseated, and now his knees banged up something terrible. His eyes were finally adjusting to the dark. He spotted the stairwell to his left and made for it. "Sorry to have woken you."

"Damn town down went nutty," Edgar spat. "How in da'hell am I 'spose to run a business with that mess right outside my God-damn door. It's sickenin'! Who in the hell gonna rent a room when that niggah got the whole damn town stunk up? These niggahs better clean that mess up good."

Nicholas could still hear Edgar blathering on about his imaginary losses as he wound his way up the stairs and into his room. He trudged over to the bed and fell upon it, seeking the pillow and covered his face to muffle his crying. His body curled up involuntarily, as though it forgot he was a grown man. And it felt good to him to be his true self. *True* in the essence of being repulsed by the sight of what remained of Laurence Cole. *True* in knowing there was no justifying the evil done. *True* in knowing that another innocent soul had been taken from the earth.

Had there been no Maggie Mae, or Paul, or David, who were sparks of light in the darkness, he was certain he would have already packed up and left Folsom weeks ago. He was sick of the south and its depraved white people who terrorized Negroes every chance they got. Not only had they killed a good man, but they castrated him alive, burned him alive, and were disappointed that he'd died before they could hang him. And then after, that they could drink and carry on though as though the smoking corpse was not but a turn of the head away, astounded and confounded him. Yet, as horrendous as the lynching was, it all seemed to them as though it was the best celebration they had been a part of in years.

It took him awhile to finally cry himself to sleep, which was only somewhat restful and hardly welcome, for he had a visitor come by to see him. Lar Cole came and sat on the bed next to him. It seemed so real to him, even the bed seemed weighed down from the apparition's weight. Lar smiled at him, as though at long last he'd found the peace that had eluded him his entire life. But before he vanished into smoke and whispers, he said . . .

"Don't forget me, Mr. Barrons . . . Laurence Cole, husband of Mary . . . slaughtered in Folsom, Mississippi, because of a white woman's lie."

CHAPTER 25

Paul finally decided to open his eyes, though he had been awake for quite some time already. Not far from him on the floor was Maggie Mae, who too had slept on a pallet of sheets and quilts after having given her bed to Uncle Matty. Though she did nothing for his loins, he knew that was not the case with Nicholas Barrons, or any other man who loved women for that matter. Her face gave him a strange sense of comfort, which he hadn't felt for quite some time. He studied her closely, trying to figure out exactly what it was about her that made her so much lovelier than other women. Her blue eyes spritzed with honey were of course just one. If he hadn't been so lost in his study of her beauty, he would have realized that those very eyes were at the moment staring right back at him.

"How'd you sleep, child?" She asked.

Never in his wildest thoughts did he imagine a day that he would be sleeping next to a Negroe– in a Negroe's home, and on the side of town that was filled with nothing but Negroes. But also, he never thought that he would finally follow his heart and love a man either. Everything had changed, he realized. Some things had for the better, as he pictured David's chubby face . . . alas, some for the worse, as he remembered that Lar was no more.

"Sorry," he said finally. "I don't mean to stare."

"It's alright."

She stood and stretched, and then walked over to the table and sat. She adjusted her gray nightgown over her pale bosom . . . the color her gown had once been. Paul followed suit and sat across from her at the wobbly wood table, which seemed destined to fall apart at any moment. Even half-asleep, she seemed a wonder to behold to him. He'd seen his sister Beatrice in the same drowsy state, but was always shaken by what he saw . . . her blond hair a mess dangling in front of her face, and her blue eyes held up by her constantly puffy lower lids. But Maggie Mae's wavy hair shimmered in the dim light they were in. Her eyes, even in sadness, shone with an almost ethereal brilliance. And her skin . . . he'd never seen such a marvel of unblemished, milky perfection. Sans the layers of powder and cream white women wore, and which usually cracked like dried earth after a few hours, she was even more lovely up close than from a distance.

"Do you know how beautiful you are?" He asked. "I mean . . . you are really, really beautiful."

She stared at him for a moment before responding. "I guess if you've been told that so many times, you have to start finding some truth in it."

"Right. But you have to know that you are," he told her. "Really, Ms. Maggie– there are some things you just can't say isn't so. When you see yourself in the mirror, how can you not see . . . you?"

She smiled and shook her head. "Boy– you'd be surprised how wrong you are."

"Why haven't you ever left Folsom, if you don't mind me asking? I guess . . . I mean . . . you could pass for white if you wanted to. Actually, you wouldn't have to pass. You just look white. I guess I'm wondering why you stay and get treated how they treat Negroes around here if you don't have to?"

"Why have you stayed?" She asked instead.

"Just scared, I guess," he responded. "No . . . there's no guessing to it. I was scared. Well, I still am. But I'm leaving whether I am or not. I can't stay here in Folsom anymore."

"I was scared about leaving, too," she said softly. "I don't want to leave my momma in this place, but . . . but, I guess I don't have much of a choice now with whites running around like they are."

"Don't get me wrong when I say this . . . I mean, I like Nicholas a lot, but . . . you could have found a man easily to help you and your mother get outta here together."

"Well, I wish it was that simple." She smiled. "You're a nice looking boy yourself. Just as pretty as . . ."

" A girl," he interrupted her, and then sighed. "I know– I know. Pretty like a girl. Pretty– pretty– pretty . . . I hate that word. I'd like to be *handsome* like Mr. Barrons if I had my way."

She tilted her head and grinned at him. "So you find Nicholas handsome?"

Paul felt his face begin to grow hot.

"Don't be embarrassed. He is very good looking."

"Sorry, I . . ."

She shrugged. "Sorry for what? Either he is or he isn't, hmm? Like you said, there are some things you just can't deny."

"I mean that, I . . . I don't think about him in that way."

"So what if you do? They're just thoughts." She was silent for a moment. "You asked me before if I knew how beautiful I was. Well . . . I know how men look at me, and it doesn't take much to know what they're thinking when they look at me in that way. But– don't think we women folk don't have our own thoughts about men." She laughed. "We're just better at hiding it."

"Did you have feelings for Mr. Barrons when you first saw him?"

"Absolutely not!" She exclaimed. "A white man?! No– no– no– no– no."

"How about just as a man? If he weren't white?"

"No," she replied again. "Did I think he was handsome? Of course. It took time, Paul. Just like it probably did with you and . . ."

"David."

"David– yes. I didn't want to be in love with Nicholas even when I was already in love with him."

"I didn't want to have feelings for another person like me," he said, cautiously, but then wondered why. She already knew he was attracted to men and hadn't hated him for it, just as Nicholas hadn't. It was just so automatic for him to protect his secret. From clergymen, to the boys at school, to his own family, he knew a man loving another man was something he was supposed to be ashamed of, despised and punished for. But with Maggie Mae, he knew he was safe; they were brother and sister in deception now. "I didn't want to fall in love with a man," he said louder . . . stronger. "I've always felt this way. I prayed and prayed and prayed that it would just go away, but it didn't. And when I met David, and we knew we were alike, it was like . . . like being trapped in a prison you know you can never escape and someone walks up to you one day and hands you the key. And– and once I walked out of that prison, I knew I was never going back in it again. I'd rather be dead than live like that, Ms. Maggie. And if David and I are ever caught, and it might just happen too, but . . . well– I'll take my chances."

Maggie Mae reached over and took hold of his hands. "You just said what I've felt all these years. It's funny that a little white boy way across town has been feeling the same way as me– a Negroe. You're something, Paul– something special. I see why Mary loves you so much."

'I wish she had been my mother,' he thought wistfully. To him, Isabel was only 'mother' in name. There was simply no instinctual mother-child bond when they touched, which was rare– just cold and distant flesh. But Mary's touch made his heart slow and beat softly. Within her arms, he felt safety and warmth draped over him like a thick blanket, so much so, that it hurt when she released him. Even now he could see her moving about the kitchen while he would be sitting on a stool watching her. Two, three and four different pots of beans, meats, greens– a cake or pie in the oven too, all going at the same time while she slipped in and out of the back to wash and hang clothes, and then back again to stir each pot before passing through on her way to clean floors or change bed sheets, and then back into the kitchen to take out the food. And during it all, he was guaranteed that she'd always find time to listen to him rattle on about his day.

Leaving Folsom, and thereby leaving Mary would be excruciatingly difficult, he knew. It was hard for him to even think about it without crying. That he couldn't be with her now was painful enough. But knowing that he would never see her again would be almost unbearable, if not for David who was going to be by his side. Contrarily, leaving his own family would be a blessing, he thought. It would be a happy goodbye to all save Mary and the baby . . . and poor Lar, who he knew without a doubt was now safe in heaven. He had David now, and that was all from Folsom that he wanted. But . . . now there was Maggie Mae. It was like she said. They had been connected all along by such similar grief and pain, yet were figuratively worlds apart because he was white and she Negroe . . . until now.

"Ms. Maggie," he said. She looked at him, but slowly and strangely, he saw her expression changed from curiosity to something akin to fear. "What's wrong, Ms. Maggie?"

The bedroom door behind Maggie Mae creaked as it opened. Uncle Matty's wood-sawing snores filled the outer room as Enda came out. She quickly shut the door behind her. Her white hair was in waves that were remnants of the braid she had worn the night before. She seemed just like any old woman in her tattered nightgown, though after the last few weeks and especially last night, Paul knew there was far more to her than just rumors of her being a witch.

"Go on and answer the boy, chile," Enda told her. "And don't you lie 'bout it neither."

Maggie Mae's trance broke. She focused her eyes on him once more. He had no idea what she'd seen, but he didn't like the way she was looking at him. "What is it?" He asked.

"You can't bury Lar, Paul," she said. "The body has to stay where it is for now."

She was right– not that he wanted to bury Lar, but that was exactly what he was thinking about. The idea that Lar's body was still hanging from the black tree unnerved him. Lar, he felt, deserved to be buried properly and with honor. But it seemed even that was not to be.

"Why can't the Negroe men just go and get him? Haven't those murderers already got what they wanted?!" He asked. "What do they care anymore?!"

Maggie Mae looked to Enda and said, "Because it's not over yet."

They knew something– both of them, he thought anxiously. He'd already accepted that Enda was something otherworldly. Now he wasn't entirely sure that Maggie Mae wasn't either. "Tell me! Please," he begged.

Maggie Mae shook her head. "I . . . I don't know for sure, Paul. It wasn't very clear. It's still not. But . . ."

"What?"

"Tell him," Enda commanded.

"Death is still around here!" She proclaimed. "It's a feeling though . . . just a feeling, but it's around you. It's all around you, Paul."

He choked up. "Me? I'm going to die?"

Maggie Mae took hold of his hand. Her face bore a beautiful ferocity like the cherubim in Eden wielding its flaming sword. "You can't leave this house, Paul," Maggie Mae warned. "Not until we all go. And we should leave now."

He snatched his hand back. "No! Not until the baby's here. I'm not leaving!"

"Paul, please . . ."

"I said I'm not leaving!" He shot back. Having lost so much already, and having accepted that he would lose Mary too, seeing the child before he left was all that seemed worth anything to him now. "You and Mr. Barrons can run off if you want, but David and I are staying until the baby comes."

"We're not going to leave you," Maggie Mae whispered. "Nicholas promised you . . . I promise you. But right now, it's not safe for you. I just feel it."

He knew Maggie Mae was right. Lingering in Folsom was putting his life at risk. But he could already feel another hole expanding in his heart. Mary promised him that this baby was going to live. And after waiting for so long, and so patiently, he knew only a chasm of grief would remain if he weren't able to see the child at least once.

"It a bitter taste, ain't it boy?" Enda asked.

"Momma, stop it! Just leave him be."

"Oh no, gal," Enda whispered, "It too late to be pretendin' 'bout this and that. His eyes be open now."

"I don't understand," he said.

Enda came over and laid her hands upon his shoulders. Her touch felt like ice, but also, it seemed to lessen the weight of grief and loss bearing down on him. "But you do understand!" She told him. "You feel it now, don't ya? In your bones . . . your heart . . . deep in your soul?"

"Yes," he murmured.

"You fallin' deeper and quicker and can't stop yourself. You want life, but you know death is waitin' for you to move wrong so it can snatch you up." Her hand crept down until it was on his chest, and then patted it lightly. What breath he had rushed out in one long gasp. "And what you hope to grow in here seem not worth growin' at all if it be taken away with a snap of a finger. Sorrow be your bread and pain be your water . . . both be bitter and poison, but you needin' them both to live."

She clamped her thin, red lips together in a smile. Her hand on his chest grabbed hold and jerked him, but strangely, he hadn't moved at all, at least not his physical body. Her face came close to his. If she moved one inch closer, she would be kissing him. "See for yourself," she commanded.

And in those cold, grey eyes, he saw his reflection. But . . . what was, was not. It was another of Enda's tricks, he thought at first, as he watched his skin turn gold and then to a dark bronze. The vision was so vivid; he could even see the irises of his eyes go from blue to dark brown. And his hair . . . it retained its black hue, but the large curls that swept his brow grew tighter, coarser, and receded past his forehead until they were tiny springs. He had changed before his very eyes into another . . . almost. Something remained the same, despite the Negroe him he saw staring back. From the table of his Negroe mother and father, he saw himself being schooled in the protocol needed for a Negroe boy to survive in a world ruled by whites.

You say, 'yes, suh' and 'yes, ma'am' . . . to every white man, woman and child, no matter how old they be or you be.

See or talk to a white . . . then you best know how much dirt be around your feet while you do.

Don't back talk a white . . . well– just don't talk to'em if you ain't got to . . . you live longer that way.

Be out of town by six in the evenin' and on your side of the river, or you might not make it back in one piece.

Don't even think 'bout lookin' at a white gal or woman . . . hear me, boy! You end up like Lar Cole with your wanky cut off.

Get used to workin' hard for little or nothin'.

Pray hard for mercy . . . maybe you get it in the hereafter, but not here with the livin'.

You hear your stomach a'growlin'? Get used to it!

With each 'you can't do this or you best do that', Paul thought he would feel some part of his soul being chipped away, but he remained now and forever, the same Negroe-Paul. Enda pulled back from him and took the vision with her. But he knew now that all he just saw was really none of her doing. There had been no mysterious magic used upon him, just simple, powerful commonsense. He could tell from her crooked smile that she knew he finally understood why there had been no pain, no clawing at his chest for the plight of the poor Negroe-Paul, for he was already that Negroe-Paul. Just like the Negroe-Paul who couldn't scrub his skin white to spare himself a life of strife and anguish, he couldn't stop his feelings for men, it being such an inextricable facet of his being, like his heart, his blood and mind was. And like the Negroe-Paul who looked to God and gospel for salvation but was ignored, he realized so was the white-Paul who loved men, who too was denied such reprieve from a life of strife.

"Your life be bound by hardship, chile . . . if you choose it to be," Enda said. "I done chose mine long time ago. Been days when I was young when I could walk and talk like a white. Wasn't no backdoor for me and my white skin, and my white eyes, and my white lips and white nose– uh-uh. But there's powerful blood flowin' in these here veins beneath this white skin. It be the blood of Africans . . . potent blood, boy, like you ain't ever gonna know. And I always be African, no matter what people see me to be . . . and you too, gal," she said to Maggie Mae, and then to Paul, "live your life with a white gal if you want . . . choose boy. Live your life with a white man if you want. But with each come a bitter drink you gotta swallow and can't spit back up. And it gonna turn your stomach raw, but only one gonna kill you dead as a doornail."

"I'd die before I stop loving, David. That's how it already felt before I did," Paul responded achingly. "You ... you know then, right? How it feels to not feel at all? To hate yourself and wish you were just dead, don't you? To hate being alive because you're alone, and nobody cares, because if they knew about you, they'd want you dead anyway, because they hate you more than you already hate yourself." He shook his head defiantly. "I won't, Ms. Sully. I can't."

"And neither could I," Enda confessed. "That be why I gonna stay here with my African people and let ya'll go on and make ya'll lives what they be."

"What about me, momma?" Maggie Mae asked. "Your African blood flows through me too, but you want me to pretend that it doesn't."

"You love that white man and he love you. He risked his life for you! You found a man who'll give his life to be able to love you. Don't be a fool and throw away somethin' most folk look for all they life and can't find. You do what you gotta do to keep it and protect it . . . like this white boy here be willin' to do to keep what he want the most."

"Even if that means lying?" Maggie Mae asked.

"'Specially so," Enda replied. "You got everythin' you need to do it too. You look white. I done taught you how to talk white. And God done seen fit to make you so damn pretty. And you, boy . . . " She smiled at him. "You a white, boy-chile, and that alone be enough to see you through most messes if you smart 'bout what you say and do . . . or don't do."

Paul nodded.

Just as Paul felt he was beginning to see some light within the darkness around him, which was naught but death and the harsh sting of more loss, a vicious rap upon the door gave the darkness strength and shut off the light yet again. Ah– but he knew it was not good . . . he could feel it in his bones . . . he could sense it in the energy that reverberated the wood plank door. He glanced at Maggie Mae, whose expression of fear told him he was entirely correct in his assumption. Enda's look never changed, as she held up her hand to him and Maggie Mae to stay where they were.

Another series of raps came as Enda reached the door, but this time they were accompanied by a distressed voice. "Ms. Sully! Ms. Maggie!"

Enda had barely cracked the door open before he was squawking again. "It be Ms. Mary!"

Paul was out of his chair and at the door. "What happened to Ms. Mary?"

The shirtless, dark skinned boy of his own height stared at him open mouthed. That is, until Enda reached around the back of his head and smacked him smartly.

"Owww!"

"Pickens! Wake up, boy!" Enda commanded.

"Uh– uh . . . she headed inta town, Ms. Enda," Pickens said. "She said she gonna go get . . ." his voice fell to a whisper, " . . . get him."

Maggie Mae pressed up behind Paul. "Momma, you can't let her go there. They'll kill her!"

"Where she be now?" Enda asked him.

Pickens turned and pointed down the road. "Folks been yellin' at her to stop, but she ain't. Lar's wagon be gone, and she just helped herself to mine and didn't even ask me. Men-folk tried grabbin' her and she done knocked Jonnie Ray out flat again and took out two of his teeth too! That be when Ms. Allie told me to run up here and get you, 'cause Ms. Mary too big even for men-folk to handle."

"What I 'spose ta do, boy?"

536 / ORLANDO SMART-POWELL

"Put a hex on her," Pickens told her, as though it was obvious.

Enda lowered her eyelids. "How 'bout I take your eyes out and throw'em in my pot here? Ya' li'l fool!"

Pickens froze.

"Go tell'em ain't nothin' I can do," Enda said. "If Ms. Mary dead set on goin' on in to town, then that be what she gonna do. This day or the next, her mind already set. Now get on." Pickens quickly turned tail and began running back from whence he came.

"Ms. Sully . . ." Paul began, but stopped. He looked down, knowing it was useless to ask her for help, as it would be for him to try and stop Mary. Both requests would be a resounding 'no'. Mary would do what Mary was going to do, Enda had already assured him that was so, and he believed her.

She walked back into the house. "Close the door, boy."

But alas, he couldn't resist seeing Mary coming. And during a span of long nervous minutes– two, five, ten and then twenty– he was rewarded by her sight . . . full-bellied as she drove the stolen wagon on alone with a stone-faced scowl on her face that he knew only meant one thing . . . she was ready to kill.

* * *

Mary realized she had fallen asleep on the floor after returning home last night. There was no way she was going to crawl into a cold, empty bed by herself. Regardless of being stiff all over as she rose, she figured she might as well have been in hell . . . for she remembered Lar was gone. All that was left of him, she guessed, was hanging from a tree like a slab of burnt, rotting meat for crows to ponder which piece of him to start on first. White folks had taken his life, and now, she wanted revenge. An eye for an eye and a tooth for a tooth, she figured would settle the score. One way or another, she was determined to make it so.

Wave after wave of waxing and waning strength took a mighty toll on her. In one moment, she found the strength to pull herself up from the floor, march about the room and plot in exact detail how she would quench her thirst for vengeance, and the next, without warning, she was kneeling over her bed, drenching the sheets with tears and not knowing how she could ever go on living. While weak, she prayed to God moments before she accused God of abandoning her and not existing at all. No real God would have allowed such a thing to happen to Lar, she thought. Not to her Lar. This couldn't have happened if there was ever a Jesus Christ who walked the earth. Where was this God that Lar loved so? She wondered. Where is this Jesus Christ? This Holy Ghost? Hah!

She raised her fists to the ceiling and screamed, "Where you be, damn you?!" She dared him, his son, or the Ghost to show their faces. "If you be God, then strike them white folk down! Lay'em dead! Give . . . me . . . back . . . my . . . Lar . . . if you be so damn almighty!"

And then . . . knowledge of what should be done . . . what must be done, became what will be done. Her cascade of tears slowed and then abruptly stopped. If death and damnation were the consequences for what she had to do, then it would just have to be, she figured. "On my soul– they ain't gonna get away with it," she whispered to her child.

She walked to the door and greeted unwelcomed, waiting Negroes outside. They had already given up knocking on the door and begging to come in. What for? She wondered. She hadn't the urge to kneel and pray like they begged her to. Pray for what? They couldn't raise Lar from the dead, she thought. They couldn't undo all that's already been done. They couldn't speak a word that could ice her fire. 'Stay where ya'll be,' she fumed silently. *Go on run and off to that church that ain't got no walls and no God, and leave me be!*

But they didn't.

They were waiting for her . . . Pickens, Allie Mae, Perry, Buck and Lily, Jonnie Ray, Jeffy Marks, Ms. Ettie, and on and on . . . lost sheep mourning their shepherd who was hanging from a tree in Folsom. She felt sorry for them, for they still believed in not just a God, but a righteous God. She could see on every face that they realized their savior who was going to lead them to the Promised Land was gone. And with him gone, they knew nothing else but to camp out in front of her home and pray.

"But I do," she whispered.

"Chile . . . we been just a'prayin' for you and the baby all night," Allie Mae called out. She stepped up on the porch and moved in close enough to whisper, and close enough for Mary to see that if Allie Mae had slept at all last night, it was not for long. The wells of her red eyes were quickly filling. "I been worried so 'bout you, girl. And the chile . . . the chile be okay?"

Mary nodded.

Allie Mae sighed. "Thank you, Lord Jesus." She reached out her hand. "Come on back in, Mary and rest girl. The mens already done talked and figured thangs out, now. Alright? They gonna see 'bout gettin' to town in a few days from here and . . ."

"And what?!" Mary snapped. "Bring back what's left of him? I can smell the burn from here!" Allie Mae cowered, as did all of those. "You brave men, huh? Brave niggahs gonna crawl on over to Folsom and beg the white man to give you the body, huh? What if they spit in yo' face and say go home niggah? You gonna lick it up like a dog? What 'bout Lar? We just bury him and go 'bout like ain't a thang happen, 'cause we scared? What 'bout you, Jonnie Ray?"

Jonnie Ray acted as though he suddenly forgot his own name.

"You so ready to kill li'l white boys last night. You were runnin' your big ass mouth talkin' 'bout wantin' to go over to Peak Hills when they lynched that boy and his pappy. You show me what kinda big, bad man you be now and go to Folsom with me then."

"You know they kill me, Ms. Mary," he muttered.

"Oh . . . " Mary smirked. "So you be just another loud mouth man that ain't gonna stand behind a damn word he say then."

"Ain't nobody need to be goin' in to Folsom," Perry cut in, and then turned around and repeated it for all to hear. "Those white folk done gone mad! Ya'll playin' ball with a hornet's nest if you do." The crowd of Negroes agreed silently, and some not so silently.

"I didn't think any man here had it in them anyway," Mary accused. "And for all ya'll information, those two white boys ya'll was ready to do in were the only ones who said they would come with me. Two li'l ass white boys got more courage than all ya'll." She scrunched up her lips. "Two li'l ol' white boys."

"Goin' where, Mary?" Allie Mae questioned.

"To get the law," Mary replied, and then said, "but first, to get my Lar."

"Girl– don't you step foot in Folsom," Allie Mae warned. A chorus of likeminded voices quickly joined hers.

"They kill you, Mary."

"We gonna get him once thangs simmer down."

"Don't do it!"

"Please, chile."

"White folks crazy up in there . . . you know that!"

"You gonna bring those peckerwoods back here!"

Mary raised her hand, not unlike the way Lar was wont to do to command silence on Sunday in the Lord's house. "Lar ain't ever been 'fraid of no white folks ever! If he was, then he be standin' right here with me now, but he ain't. No! He up in Folsom, strung up like a hog. And you want me to let him sit there . . . after all he done done for ya'll . . . hummpf!" She left the porch and pushed her way through the crowd. At first, everyone was silent, but then like one bee, then two, then four and five and fifty and a hundred, their voices rose up.

"Somebody gotta stop her!"

"Perry . . . Jonnie Ray grab her," a woman cried frantically.

Allie Mae's strained voice could be heard above them all. "Mary no! Mary!? Mary!? Don't do it. Mary!?"

"Somebody grab her for she get us all killed!"

Mary suddenly found herself face to face with Jonnie Ray, who stood as straight and tall as he could to block her way. Only . . . they were not face to face per se, for Mary had to look down at him and he up at her. For the first time this morning, she found reason to smile. *Good ol' Jonnie Ray . . . the biggest mouth this side of the river,* she thought. She easily had five inches on him. That and the weight she'd gained in pregnancy, which on most women would have made them appear more motherly, gentle and delicate, made her look dense, masculine and more monolithic than she was before.

Mary stretched out her trunk of an arm at him, and with her index finger now a branch made for whipping, tapped his chest none too gently and teetered him off balance. "Boy– if you don't get yore nappy-headed ass out from in front of me, I gonna knock you out!"

He caught his balance and moved back toward her. "You ain't goin' in there, Mary!"

When she struck his face dead-on with a clenched fist, she knew the next time he would remember to be scared of her. She had to step over Jonnie Ray's limp body before she could spin around and ready herself for the next in line. She hoped his unconsciousness was warning enough to all the men gawking at her and Jonnie Ray alternately. She resisted rubbing the knuckles on her right hand, though they did sting something fierce. Without having to look down, she knew she'd taken some of the skin off of each them. But if more came, she was ready with both fists clenched this time. "Who next?!" She dared.

Not another moved toward her, but from the corner of her eye, she did spot movement . . . Pickens's little head bobbed and weaved through the crowd. He took off running up the road. She knew where his destination was going to be. *Best raise up every devil you got to stop me, ol' woman,* she thought, before marching over to Pickens's wagon and hopping on board. "Heyah!" She yelled. The horses were not nearly as stubborn as Jonnie Ray and quickly did as they were told.

It wasn't long after she was on the road that for the second time she saw Pickens running, but this time in the opposite direction . . . away from Enda's home and back to hers. As she came closer to Enda's home, she saw that the front door was open. As strong as she was, she knew physical might was useless against Enda's mind when Enda had a mind to use it. But it was a different, and unex-pected white face that appeared in the opening.

"Stay inside, chile" she pleaded, as Paul's head came into view. What he was doing there didn't matter, she was just grateful that he was anywhere his father wasn't. She wondered . . . hoped, that it meant that he, David, Maggie Mae and Nicholas were preparing to leave. If things went wrong, it would get bad and in a hurry. And the quicker and farther Paul was away from it, then all the better. She was thankful he had not spoken or waved, or made any gesture toward her, but simply shut the door. If there was anyone other than Enda who just might be able to stop her, she knew it was Paul, with his big, sad blue eyes.

The journey into Folsom seemed long and not all that long. She was anxious to retrieve what was left of Lar, but not so to have to look upon what was left of him. She followed along the road where the Meadows' house was. Roman, the husband of the woman who'd caused it all, was standing out in front.

"This whole thing is partially my fault, Mrs. Cole," Roman told her as she pulled up next to him. His suspenders were down and dangling by his legs. "You may lay blame at my feet if you wish . . . if it makes any difference to you at all. I am sorry."

She stared at him, wondering if his drooped mouth, sunken eyes and pale face were just another white man's ruse. "Blame be spread all over Folsom," she replied.

"Yes– but she was my wife."

"Was?" Mary growled. "She still be if you ain't divorced her."

He approached a little further. "In that sense, yes– but as it is for me– no. She's gone and good riddance. She'll never show her face in Folsom again if she has any sense."

"If she do, she best not let me catch her," Mary snorted. "She end up bein' one dead white woman."

Roman looked up and down the road. "Shhh! Mrs. Cole . . . please. I'll kill her myself if I see her, but . . . but you," he lowered his voice to a whisper, "you can't go around saying that about a white. You know that, Mrs. Cole."

"It be exactly what she deservin'– you know that!" She mocked.

"Don't think for one minute they'll give you leeway because of your condition– they won't!"

"They white folk, ain't they?" Mary sassed. "I ain't 'spectin' them to be anythin' other than what they be– liars and murderers."

"Exactly, Mrs. Cole . . . cold-blooded murderers, plain and simple. And you risk everything you have going in there," he said, gazing at her baby-filled belly.

"I takin' my husband back with me, Mr. Meadows," she said adamantly.

He lowered his head and sighed in frustration. "I see now why they had to knock you out cold."

"I would have killed them all– Lord willin'!"

"And so you might have tried. You going there right now?"

"Yes, suh."

"Well . . . if you're going, you better go fast then. Most are probably still sleeping or just waking, so if you're quick, you can slip in and out before anyone takes notice." Roman held up his hand. "Mrs. Cole– hold on. Don't go anywhere just yet."

Roman quick-walked back to the house and slipped in. When he returned after a few minutes, in his hands he held a long handle knife used for slicing the necks and bellies of hogs come butchering season. He turned the knife around by the blade and thrust the handle in her direction.

"You'll need this– unfortunately, to free him up," he said, releasing the gutting knife into her possession. "I wish I could go with you, but . . . but . . . Well, I guess there just isn't a good reason at all. I already know what they'll do to the both of us if they're in the same mood they were in last night. I guess I'm just a coward." He lowered his head and shook it. "No, Mrs. Cole . . . I am a coward," he corrected. "You won't find any justice here in Folsom if that's what you're looking for. The closest lawman is fifteen miles past Peak Hills, and if he gives a damn about a Negroe being lynched, I'd fall over dead in shock. If you don't see that now, you never will."

"Did you really know Lar?"

"Not as well as I wish I could have."

"If you did know him better, you would understand why I doin' what I doin'."

"He was an honest, good hard worker– I know that. I heard tell he was a righteous preacher."

Mary smiled. "Hah! He was more than that! He was the best thang God ever gave two legs, two feet, two arms and a mouth to. It be the very reason why he was taken from me. Good men die young, Mr. Meadows. A dead niggah may not mean much to white folk, but every hope and dream I done ever had is over yonder hanging from that ol' black tree." Mary snapped the reigns and took off, leaving Roman Meadows behind without another word said between them.

For a while it seemed to her as though it was just she, the child, the horses and the constant grittle-bang of the wheels against the road as she drove past house after house, until homes became less and less, and stores and shops became more frequent. As she rounded the apex of the circular road between the storefronts and the park, she had no idea what to expect, and began wondering if she could take what was to come. The last memory she wanted of Lar was of him laying next to her in bed, or his face beaming with his toothy smile at her. But leaving him strung up from a tree was unthinkable. Lar's burnt face haunting her thoughts was far preferable to her than letting another white hand touch him, or another white jeer at what was left of him. If there were nothing else she could do for him, it would be this. And in that moment, when his body . . . what was left of it, slowly came into her sights . . . two things were made certain and known to her . . .

One . . . that Lar no longer resided on earth, but in heaven amongst the celestial hosts. Two . . . that there was indeed a living and almighty God, whose son was Jesus Christ, who all should bow and tremble before, for his vengeance is great and his might unimaginable.

She realized both of these things, for she knew her own strength would not have enabled her to leave the cart, stand, and face the devil himself. It was only by the Lord's will, she was certain, that she hadn't screamed in horror at such a sight, but was able to reach behind her and fumble on the seat of the cart and take hold of the butchering knife. It was the Holy Spirit that moved her forward, she knew. And it was only by the grace of God that she was able to sever the ropes that had melted into the flesh of his neck, where his head once was.

With every move of her hand she prayed. She grasped the torso and lifted it, ignoring as much as she could his crisp flesh scraping along her skin and both of his legs that snapped off like twigs and rolled toward her feet. With every step as she carried the rest of his pieces back to the cart, she asked God for even more strength. Finally finished, she walked back to the black tree. Though charred, it stood as solidly as it always had. She pointed the butchering knife at it while she damned and cursed it for existing at all.

"Lord, forgive me," she whispered so low, she wasn't quite sure if He'd heard her, so she said it again. "It done took this for me to believe in you, and now I do. You ain't gotta teach, Ms. Mary no more, Lord. I done seen what no woman or man 'spose to and still be walkin', talkin' and livin'. You hear me, Lord? I still livin' . . . and I thank you for that. And I thank you for all those years with Lar. I thank you, for lovin' me, when I hated you." She closed her eyes and silently said the Lord's Prayer.

"Holy shit!"

Mary's eyes snapped open, but she turned around even quicker to the sound of a screeching, yet familiar voice. Mary knew that tone so often used by white men– faux shock with a double dose of superiority. On the other side of the wagon by the tavern was a shirtless, bone-thin white man with scraggly hair. She quickly walked back to the cart. But as she fast walked to the cart, so did he towards her.

"What the fuck you doin' cuttin' that boy down and I ain't said you could!"

Almost there! She thought.

"Bitch! You hear me talking to you?!" Arthur blurted. "Mother-fuckin' niggahs takin' Goddamn hold of this place! I knew it . . . and ain't a Goddamn one listenin' to me neither. Bitch!" He sprinted toward her. "You best answer a white man when he talkin' to . . ."

But Arthur never got to finish his last word. Mary quickly raised the butchering knife. They both knew that had he not skidded to a halt, more than just the tip of it would be piercing the flesh of his neck. He backed up slowly, but Mary advanced, keeping the tip in solid contact with his neck.

"Now you listen here, white man," she seethed, knowing it was again God's grace alone that kept the blade still in her hand, even as her heart battered its bone cage. "This wagon and what be in it be my property, not yours. I takin' my husband with me one way or 'nother, but how I go 'bout doin' that be your choice right now."

"Nig ... nig ... you-you-you gonna hang for this." His eyes crazily swept side to side. "You-you-you see this?! Anybody!" He yelled. "This– this niggah got me by a knife, ya'll!"

Mary kept her eyes fixed on him, though peripherally, she could tell that they were not alone. What she knew was that, if whoever the person was standing by the Monclair store decided to make a move for her, the white man in front of her would lose his life, and the one charging her would be next.

"You know who-who-who, I am!?" Arthur sputtered, trying to backtrack, but stopped as Mary moved with him tit-for-tat.

Mary's brow rose. "I 'member you, alright. You that buddy of Simeon Monclair. But you be a dead man if you don't leave me in peace. Both of you," she said loudly. "Folsom gonna pay for killin' Laurence Cole, and I'll see to that. And I thinkin' now, you one of the main ones up in it."

"Damn right. I got that rapin' niggah. And-and, he deserved what he got ta– ta– too!" Arthur challenged, until the blade suddenly pressed deeper. "Noooooooooo!" He howled.

It was the Lord, Mary was certain, who held the blade from going in any further. "He innocent ... like me!" She screamed at first, then suddenly lowered her voice. "You come for me, then you comin' for a innocent, just like Lar was. Innocent! I ain't done a damn thang to whites 'cept live and breathe. You want my blood?

Innocent blood? Then you gotta take it then, 'cause I ain't givin' it free. Now you back away and leave me be, or you come for me and be a dead man."

Arthur took a tentative step backwards, and then seeing that Mary stood her ground, he ran to the safety of the walkway in front of the tavern. Mary wasted no time mounting the wagon and commanding the horses into motion. It was in that moment that she caught full view of Delilah Ford in front of the Monclair store watching her with a crooked smile on her face.

"Niggah bitch!" Arthur hollered, with his hands still about his throat. "We gonna come for your black ass!"

Mary was already rounding the curve of the road when she heard the white man scream out, and knew what he said to be true. She saw him running toward Delilah Ford and could hear his anger spiraling higher. "Get'em up!" She heard him say. The next call was directed up and outward. "Wake your asses up, Folsom!"

They would rise up indeed, Mary knew. She had threatened the life of a white man . . . in Folsom . . . in Mississippi . . . in the south, where there was only one consequence for that! How they would come and when they would come, were the only questions needing answers now, not if they would.

In a way, she felt it was always just a matter of time before they came for her anyway. A Negroe woman could never be safe in a land of whites, she knew. Whether she kept her head down or head up in front of a white, if a white wanted to have a problem with you, they were going to have one with you. And today, more than any other day, she was determined to keep her head held high, for she knew she had to do what she did.

As she crossed the bridge, she wondered how long it would take white folks to come looking for her. Even if she left for Peak Hills now, she knew she would get no further than a quarter of the way before they caught up to her. And if she did leave, and by some miracle was able to escape and hide, it was almost certain that all the other Negroes would pay for her having not just stood up to a white man, but threatening him. She realized her fate was sealed, just like everyone said it would be. More importantly, so was the child's, she understood, as she caressed her swollen belly.

She was surprised at her calmness in the brewing storm that was waking up, putting on drawers and pants and shirts, and heading in her direction. What she did not expect to see come running toward her as she neared Enda's home was Maggie Mae, grasping and pulling at her dress to free her legs from their constraint. Her hair swirled about her head as she picked up speed. "Mary!" Maggie Mae cried. "Mary, stop! Stop the cart! It's Paul!"

The sound of his name was all it took for Mary make the wagon cry out in agony as it slid to a halt. "What be a matter!?"

Maggie Mae grabbed her arm. He's gone!"

"What?!"

"Gone! He took off!" She cried. " We were in the other room dressing Uncle Matty . . . and . . . and when we came out, he was gone– the door was wide open and everything. He's gone, Mary!"

Mary slammed her foot on the floorboards. "Goddammit! How in the hell he done took off and ya'll don't know where he be? Dammit it all!"

"I'm sorry, Mary . . . you know we . . ."

"You gotta find him now!"

"I already checked out back and . . ."

"No . . . now woman! White men comin' and they comin' hard. They comin' for me, 'cause I took back what be mine and had to walk over a white man to get."

Maggie Mae ran to the rear of the cart, but couldn't see above the side panels. Her nose twitched and she quickly covered it, and then began coughing. Realizing what the smell was coming from the back, her mouth gaped open. "Oh– oh . . . oh God . . . Oh, my God!" She shrieked.

"Don't look. Lar be in there, and you ain't wantin' to see how he be now."

Maggie Mae gasped as the muscles of her face went slack. "Your baby," she whispered.

Mary rubbed her belly. "This chile and me and Lar, and all my other babies be together forever, no matter what white folk do to me. It be without sin, and can't nobody take that away from it."

"But . . ."

"Ya'll gotta find Paul 'fore white folk get up in here," Mary warned. "Then tell every Negroe to stay put where they be and let me deal with them. I be who they want."

Mary took off, hoping that Maggie Mae could do what she was unable to do herself . . . find Paul, while she looked for another boy . . . Pickens. Though as she made it further into the land of Negroes, she found a suitable substitute . . . Negroe men. A few were gathered with Pete Baker at his blacksmithing shop. Around him were Richard, Satchel and Jonnie Ray with his shirt full of blood and his lip twice its normally plump size, thanks to Mary's rock solid, right fist. All heads swung her way as she came barreling toward them. Seeing who it was, Jonnie Ray began backtracking and looked as though he were about to fly away at any moment.

"One of you get in here!" She yelled, before she could stop the cart. "One of you fools get up here, now!" She screamed. Jonnie Ray stepped back, though Pete Baker did the opposite.

"You get'em?" Pete asked.

Mary tried slowing her breaths, but it was useless. "He be . . . he be . . . in the back here," she blurted. "But ain't no time– white men comin!"

"What you done, Mary Cole?" Jonnie Ray asked, accusingly from a safe distance away.

"What none of you men folk had the guts to do ya'll selves. That be what I done did– boy!"

"And gonna get every one of us killed too," he shot back.

Mary wished she had knocked Jonnie Ray harder and broken his jaw. She had little time left and wasn't willing to waste it on someone whose skin may be black, but inside was yellow through and through. "They comin for me, Pete, but I got to get home and somebody gotta get Lar's body away from them. They can have me." She turned to Jonnie Ray and then looked back at Pete, "I ain't 'fraid of no white man . . . but they can't have Lar again—ever!"

Pete placed his hands on his hips. "You a fool of a woman, Mary Cole. Brave, but a fool," he told her. He went into his shop and returned with an oil stained tarp. Satchel and Richard followed him to the rear of the cart until he spun around on them. "Get ya'll asses back!" The pups cowered and complied. "Ya'll ain't needin' to see Lar like he be," he said mournfully. Pete closed his eyes for a moment, and then looked at what he was about to cover up. "Lord Jesus!" He gasped, as the tarp slipped out of his quivering hands. For a moment, he was transfixed at what was before him. He reached down slowly and retrieved the tarp. When he looked over at Mary, his eyes unashamedly leaked his sorrow.

"Satchel . . . Richard." Pete could barely choke out the sounds through his quivering lips. The tenor of his voice was now but a shadow.

"Yes, suh?" They answered in unison.

"Ya'll get on over to every house and tell'em white folk comin' and to stay inside! Stay . . . inside!"

"Yes, suh," they replied.

"And if one of ya'll find tappin'-head Pickens, tell him to do the same. But if you see a white man comin', ya'll run ya'll tails home." Satchel nodded and took off around the corner. Richard, who was headed down the road, yelled back that he understood also. "We gotta hurry, Mary."

"I know, Pete."

They took off, leaving Jonnie Ray behind with an even grimmer look upon his puffy face. "You done did it now, Mary Cole," he yelled at her, once he was sure she was out of striking distance. "You and your damn pride gonna kill us all. You hear me, Mary Cole?! Your damn pride!"

"Don't pay that boy no mind, Mary," Pete told her. "You know he ain't got a lick of sense anyhow."

"I ain't. But he might be right."

"I ain't never known that fool to be right. Poppin' him in the head ain't done a lick for him, but Lord know he needed it good."

"Pete– there be one more thing," she said, spotting her home just a ways off in the distance now.

Pete shook his head in knowing. "I gonna hide the body 'til we can get him buried right. Don't worry 'bout that."

"And I thank ya', too. It be all I want for Lar, but . . ."

"What?"

"The li'l white boy that was with me last night . . ."

"Monclair's boy . . . uh-huh. What 'bout him?"

"He done gone missin' somewhere and . . ."

"And what?" His voice rose suspiciously. "Don't think 'bout askin' me to go find some white boy . . . 'specially not Simeon Monclair's boy. Mary– white folks 'bout to come rushin' up in here and you worried 'bout some white boy, now? A white boy?! I thinkin' you really done lost yore mind, gal."

"I just askin' if you see him, knock his head and get'em over to Enda Sully."

Pete looked out toward the road and stared blankly. "You have lost your mind. Knockin' Monclair's boy upside the head? Take'em over to Ms. Enda? Wha? Wha? Ha! Ha-ha! I ain't goin' over into Folsom . . ."

"He be here with us Negroes somewhere."

"What the hell he still doin' here?!"

Mary slowed the wagon to a halt in front of her shack and had already spied what she needed next to the house. "He hidin' out." She jumped down from the wagon. As Pete slid over and grasped the reins, she took hold of his arm.

"Monclair gonna burn this town down lookin' for that boy!"

"Monclair don't even know the boy here. But they might kill him if they find him."

"And me too, if I touch him."

"Please, Pete," Mary begged. "Lar loved that boy and I do too. On my soul that 'bout to leave here, I swear he ain't like them white folk over there in Folsom. He everythang but that."

Pete waved his hands crazily in the air, like the Holy Ghost had just caught him. "Alright– alright– alright . . . damn you, Mary Cole! You just can't take a man tellin' you no, can you?" He seethed. "If . . . I see him, I'll ask him to come with me . . . but ain't no way in hell I touchin' that white boy."

Mary snuggled her distended belly and made toward the side of the shack. Pete circled the wagon and headed back to his shop. He waved at her. She didn't return the gesture, as she was too busy removing the axe from the stump they used to split logs . . . exactly where Lar had left it the morning before. She walked up the porch stairs and then into her home, and prepared for hell to arrive and take her kicking and screaming . . . but not without a fight.

CHAPTER 26

Hail Mary

Hail Mary, full of grace, the Lord is with thee. Blessed are thou
amongst women, and blessed is the fruit of thy womb . . .

Hell may have been coming for Mary, but inside her shack, she found a single piece of heaven. At first she was furious, and then was nearly overcome with joy that he was safe . . . sound and secure– for now. She had barely closed the door and propped the long handled axe beside it, before Paul ran to her from seemingly out of nowhere. He wrapped his arms around her and began weeping.

"I knew this would be the last time I could see you before I left. I can't stay here for you and the baby," he sobbed. "I want to, Ms. Mary– I do . . . but . . . but . . ."

She pried him from her waist, though truly, it was truly the last thing she wanted to do. "Listen to me, now. Paul . . . my Paul . . . *my sweet, baby boy.* This time listen– you gotta leave now!" She told him. "I done riled them white folks up by gettin' Lar's body back home, and they comin' for me– soon I think. And you can't be 'round when they get here!"

Mary had witnessed Paul's spirit being broken by his father's beatings, the constant taunting at school and struggling with who he was and who he loved. But now it seemed as if his tipping point had now been reached. He howled like a wounded animal in its death throes. His face drained of blood. He began pawing at her crazily, and then tried pushing her back toward the door. The more she fought to push him away, the greater his struggle became.

"I won't let them!" He screamed.

But . . .

. . . the faint, erratic beat of horse hooves made Mary's ears prick up. With choices running out, she shoved him back. Before he could return and attach himself to her bosom once more, she slapped him across the face, sending him tumbling to the floor. He lay there, motionless from a blow that had nothing to do with the physical assault, but from the emotional power behind it.

He pulled his legs to his chest and wrapped his arms around them, and began moaning. She couldn't fault him for finally crumbling under the weight that was his world. But there was no time for such pondering. The rumble of death was marching near. Making him safe was her only priority now. She pulled him up with only her strength, as he was now more like a well-used ragdoll ready to be discarded.

"I sorry, baby." She turned her head and listened. *Kalump . . . clump, kalump, clump.* "Dammit," she whispered.

"I'll die now too," he whispered.

She kissed his lips and shook him gently. "No, you ain't! Hear me? You gonna live– for me . . . live for this child and for Lar. Right in here," she told him, while rubbing his chest.

"I can't, Ms. Mary. Not anymore," he whimpered.

"You can, chile," she told him. She pushed him back until he was against the door to Uncle Matty's bedroom. "It all bad right now, but long time from here, things gonna be a whole lot better for you. Ms. Mary promise you that. You gonna see– but not if they find you."

His tears flung to either side as he shook his head in protest. "Why didn't you just leave him there? Why?! Now they gonna take you away from me too!"

Mary cradled his chin in her hands. "Why baby?" She looked down. "It hard to explain if you ain't ever been me. I ain't never thought someone would ever love me like Lar did. White folk say don't love Mary 'cause she a niggah. Negroe say don't love Mary 'cause she big, black as tar and ugly. I say to me, don't love yourself, gal, 'cause don't nobody 'spose to love you– but Lar did. Lar saw who I be inside, and you know what? He loved it. He loved it with all his heart and soul. And him lovin' me like that made me feel more beautiful than . . . than Maggie Mae can ever be. His love reminded me to keep my head held high because I a good woman. Now that be a real man . . . somebody who can see your soul and love it . . . like you, Paul! And I can't have this here chile grow up and know I left a man who walked hand-in-hand and step in step with the Lord, hanging from a tree like a dog, when he should be layin' right in the Lord's arms gettin' his crown– *Amen!* I know Lar, chile . . . and I know he loved and forgave those folks who killed him– that just be how he be. He was love through and through. He loved me and this chile. He loved you too!"

Paul was weeping. He looked up into her dark brown eyes. "I love you too, Ms. Mary."

Mary covered his mouth and turned her head toward the front door. Footsteps had now replaced the sound of hooves. She turned back to Paul. "Now you go in there." She nodded toward the room at his back. "You get under the bed and don't make a sound– hear me? Not a sound! No matter what you hear or think you hear, you stay put. If you love me, you stay hid and quiet. One day, baby, after you done lived a good ol' life, you gonna see me and Lar and this chile again. Now that a fact."

Boots trod on the steps of the porch. Paul began to shiver and so did she. She turned the knob of the door behind him, opened it and backed him inside. She kissed his lips once more and then closed the door softly. More footsteps joined those already on the steps. A metal click echoed. She didn't have to see its origin to know what had made the sound. A shadow then began creeping along the sheet-draped window, and one sneaking in from under the door, close to where she had left the axe.

She sneaked toward the door, watching out for the floorboards known to squeak and howl. With the handle of the axe almost in hand, a horrible knock, like Satan's own fist shook the door. "Mary Cole! Come on out, gal!" A man's voice called.

She grabbed the axe and began inching backwards.

"Come on now! Don't make us break down this door."

Her hands were shivering– her baby was still.

She turned her head toward Uncle Matty's room. Through the gap, which was the entire length of the ill-fitting door, she saw one blue eye staring back at her. It was *then* that her quivers ceased. It was *now* that her left hand joined her right upon the axe's handle and gripped it so tight, her flesh became one with the wood. Effortlessly, she raised it up and back. *Splittin' wood be a man's chore,* she remembered Lar telling her every time he caught her doing it, and she continuing on; she liked that she was stout enough to do it better than most men.

"You done cut up a white man," the man continued. "That husband of yours done went and raped Mrs. Meadows and paid for it . . . like you gotta for what you did to Artie. Now you come on out so we can deal with this mess and set things right in this here town."

"You niggah bitch! I told you we was comin' for your black ass. So what you gonna do now, huh?!"

She recognized the second voice and regretted not cutting his throat when she had the chance. *I gonna die today,* she thought. They came looking for blood and wouldn't be satisfied until they had hers and her child's. She suddenly realized, and of all times to finally put a line between point A and point B, that she had been so very wrong and Enda Sully so very right when she said, *Don't you have one mo' child here, or you both be dead.*

"Mary Cole!" The man called out again.

"I innocent and you know that," she yelled back.

"You cut a white man, gal!"

"And tried ta' kill me!" Arthur cried. "Niggahs rapin' white women and now tryin' to kill white folk! I told ya'll. I been sayin' ya'll Folsom niggahs gonna turn on ya'll . . . and now ya'll see it with yo' own eyes. If we can't teach these niggahs what they place be, they'll come after every one of us and our youngins too!"

A series of shotgun blasts boomed in the air and rattled the door in full support of Arthur. A chorus of inhuman whistles and howls followed them. Then, the glass window to the right of the door exploded into hundreds of shards as a large rock came barreling through it. The voices outside now came through clearer. Three, four, six of them? She wasn't sure how many were out there, but she vowed that whoever chose to be brave enough to come through the door first was going to be the unluckiest of them all.

"And yo' wives," Arthur continued, riding his wave of support. "These niggahs gonna rape ya'll wives and daughters, too." His voice then became a screechy falsetto. "Next thing ya know, they'll be sayin' they have souls and be wannin' to sit right next to us in church!" There were no exclamations of agreement this time, just laughter at such a preposterous idea.

"Last time, woman!" The first man said, as the laughter faded. "Come on out!"

Mary raised the axe a hair higher. "You come get me if you want me," she whispered, just as Arthur cried the charge.

"Now!"

But another man said, "No!"

And another, "Wait . . . wait-wait!"

But before the voices of caution had even faded, the door exploded open. With only a moment to blink her eyes and block the splinters sprayed at her, she saw the unlucky one coming at her, and in his hands a shotgun, but he was losing his grip on it as he struggled to gain his balance back. But all Mary really had eyes for was his red neck, which her mind transformed into a thick log that needed splitting. Then, with almost three hundred pounds of man-like muscle behind her, she swung. At first the blade of the axe caught bone, but kept on going. Before Arthur's body dropped to the floor and began dancing, his head hopped once on his shoulders before falling to the floor. Her shock at the force she wielded was only surpassed by the satisfaction that it was Arthur's neck now spewing blood on her clean floors. She looked down at the decapitated body and thought, *I gonna die today, but you'll never see it.*

The white men and boys stood on the porch with open mouths and bugged-out eyes that were no longer blue, brown, green and hazel, but all black. In the brief seconds that they were gawking at the headless body, Mary had already cocked the axe back above her shoulder. She knew that her life was already lost. The men would get her no matter what. Knowing that as a fact, she hurdled Arthur's twitching, soon to be corpse, and bolted for the closest body to her. She screamed like a woman and swung the axe like a man. The boy she hit was holding a rifle. Had he not been so transfixed in looking at what was left of Arthur, he might have pulled the trigger and killed her. But he hadn't. And it was a most unlucky day for him also.

The snap and crack of the boy's breastbone broke the silence right before he screamed. The horrified eyes that looked up at Mary belonged to Payne Tressen, Beatrice's hopeful paramour . . . the same boy, she remembered, who was mocking Paul and David at the bridge the day she went looking for Paul. Archie Tressen, his father, was standing one step below his dying son on the porch. He began screaming as he played tug of war with Mary . . . he pulled for his son and she pulled to retrieve her axe from his chest. Payne, however, wasn't doing anything at the moment. The axe had split his heart asunder and he was already dead. But then, Mary heard a shotgun blast from so close her ears rang, and suddenly she couldn't feel her right ankle anymore.

* * *

The headless body was the most ghastly and most pleasing sight Paul could remember ever seeing. That was, until he saw Mary's next victim. Seeing Payne Tressen, who for so many years had done nothing but torment him, now with an axe in his chest brought a momentary smile to Paul's lips. But then, Mary had dropped from his sight as he peered through the crack between the door and frame. And then it was as though hell had erupted outside.

Over the frantic screams of Mr. Tressen, who was trying to hold Payne with one arm and pull the axe out with his other hand, the men began screaming like women on fire. A woman had swiftly and deftly killed two white men, and that she was a Negroe woman only added further insult to their egos. Paul knew exactly what the white men were thinking . . . if fewer of them had come, or had they not brought guns, the niggah woman would have hacked them all to pieces– patted her hands and walked back inside her house. The white men needed their masculinity made whole again, Paul knew. Mary would have to pay dearly to give it back to them. It was why Paul wished they would just shoot her dead, right here and right now.

Alas, that wasn't to be her fate, for one of the men yell out, "Get'er ass up!"

And another. "You, fuckin' niggah . . . **you . . . you bitch . . . you gonna die!"**

"Kill'er!"

"Shoot that *black* bitch in the face!"

"Somebody help me!" Archie Tressen begged. "Please . . . someone help my boy."

"Get Artie!"

"He dead. That boy's dead. They're both dead! Artie . . . Artie ain't got no head," one droned in disbelief.

"*My boy ain't dead!*" Archie screamed at them. "Payne? C'mon, Payne . . . Payney-boy, move some. Just move a li'l. Please ya'll . . . Somebody help *meeeee!*"

"Hack that bitch up!" Another demanded.

"No! No!"

A shotgun went off and silenced them all, except Archie who was still sobbing and begging for help. And then someone said, "Tie her up and load her on the wagon. We gonna show this niggah and this whole fuckin' town a show today. And I guarantee you, ya'll niggahs ain't ever gonna trouble ya'll again."

"Mary, no," Paul whispered, as she was pulled to her foot– the other was no more than mangled bone and dangling raw flesh.

From the sliver of the crack he looked out of, he saw her fall twice on the way to the cart. The first was after a butt of a rifle was slammed into her temple. The second was when a pistol was cracked against the back of her skull. And through it all, never once did he hear Mary cry out . . . moan yes, but she never screamed.

"Somebody help carry Archie's boy, and somebody grab that dumb-fucker in the house– and don't forget his head. And you . . ." Paul couldn't see who 'you' was, "Get on in the house and see if there's anyone else up in there."

That was all Paul needed to hear to scurry under the bed and thank God for having made him slight of frame. A few pounds heavier and an inch or two longer, and he would have been bulging up the bed or sticking out from it. By the time he had completely squeezed underneath the bed, footsteps were already approaching the other side of the door.

He stopped breathing when he heard the shotgun being cocked.

And then he remembered to stop breathing.

The doorknob squeaked as it turned, and then . . . it suddenly stopped. Without warning, the door flew open, followed by a blast of the shotgun that said, this white man had no plans on being hacked to death like the others. Then . . . Mary screamed. Paul knew it wasn't out of pain, but to draw attention back to her and away from him.

"Grab her!" A man yelled.

"Stop that goddamn horse!"

"She's tryin' to bolt!" Another cried.

"Knock her head!"

Paul's lungs were searing as the dust-covered boots in front of him began to move forward, but the commotion Mary was causing seemed to give the man pause. The right boot lifted again and then stopped, and returned to its original position. The boots spun around and bolted out of the shack. "Ain't nobody in there," the man announced.

Paul finally dared to let some air leave his lungs, as well as a bit of pee that he could no longer hold. The voices, sound of hooves and gunshots began fading into the distance. But still, his joints felt fused. He dared not move, fearing that they were only pretending to have left. Ten minutes passed . . . or was it twenty? He estimated. Without the sound of men and gunshots, there were only the hens out back clucking their pride over newly laid eggs. But no longer able to hold his swollen bladder, he slid out from underneath the bed and scampered to the corner of the room. Not bothering to unbutton, he pushed his pants off his narrow hips down to his knees and began urinating in the corner of the room and angering the black spider whose home it was.

Paul finished up. It was then that he noticed that the wall to his right was peppered with buckshot, which had it hit flesh, would have shredded it. He tread lightly to the door that now hung by one hinge, and dared a peek past it before quickly moving his head back. He chanced another glance, but this time a moment longer, and was assured that he was alone.

He walked toward the door, but his eyes were fixed on the porch. It looked almost the same as when he'd first came . . . a rotted porch leading out into a dry, rocky yard and even rockier road. The difference now was that there was blood everywhere. There was an enormous pool of black blood inside the house that he jumped over. As he ventured further, there were more puddles of it . . . red and dark, nearly black splatters of it on the steps and on the ground. As far as his eyes could see, there was no trace of Mary or the white men who took her– not even a trail of dust over the road leading into Folsom.

He wanted to just sit and cry . . . or scream . . . or all three at once.

First Lar . . . now Mary and the baby– gone just like that, he grieved. "They're all dead," he whispered. "All dead. They're dead . . . dead . . ." he repeated, trying to convince himself of what he knew to be true. But then . . .

"No," he peeped. "She's not dead. Not yet! Think Paul, think." His mind swam in a sea of dizziness trying to figure out what to do next. He then began walking . . . then running . . . and now faster. One thought did grasp him, though he was sure it would fail and called himself a fool for even thinking it could succeed, but he knew he couldn't live with himself unless he tried. His dreams were already haunted by 'the now', and he had no intention of adding a new specter of 'what if's' to the menagerie of horrors that took center stage in his thoughts every night.

He was already out of breath even before he made it close to Pete Baker's shop. He knew he couldn't run all the way into Folsom and wasn't planning on it. He searched for a horse to steal, not like there was anyone to borrow one from. There was not a soul stirring about, but he expected that.

He looked. He listened.

He peeked behind one building . . . nothing. The next place– one that looked like some sort of a store . . . nothing . . . someone's house . . . he heard movement within and then silence, but behind it– nothing. A blacksmith's shop . . . *yes!* Two horses were already hitched to a wagon. "No time," he said breathlessly, forgoing un-hitching one and decided to take the whole thing. *"Yeaahhhh!!!"* He screamed, with a snap of the reigns, demanding the full strength the beasts possessed.

He was down the road as quick as the wagon would allow without overturning, which it almost did twice. As he approached Enda's home, the last one on the road before crossing the bridge into Folsom, he spotted her on the rocking chair, but Maggie Mae was running for the road. He slowed the wagon not to listen, but to instruct.

""We gotta go tonight! No-no!" He yelled, changing his mind. "As soon as I get back!"

"Where the hell you going?!" Maggie Mae cried. He could tell she already knew they had Mary– it was all over her tear soaked face. "Get off that wagon and get inside . . . now!" She commanded.

But he was already goading the horses back up to full speed. "Just be ready when I get back," he yelled behind him.

"Paul!!!"

And then, over the horse's huffing and the board-rattling wagon, he heard Maggie Mae scream again, but not at him. 'Mama,' it sounded like she said. He turned around and saw Enda walking out onto the road. He checked his bearings before turning around again. It seemed as if both women were grabbing at one another. He looked back one final time before starting onto the bridge and then saw only Enda. In her hands she was holding onto something, but he couldn't tell what it was. Focusing on what was ahead of him, he saw what looked like everyone who lived in Folsom streaming toward the town's center and the black tree therein . . . and so was he.

The gathering of adults and children had all of the makings of a town picnic, only instead of carrying baskets full of food, they brought cans of oil, torches and rope. Smiles and greetings were replaced with trading tales of *Mary Cole* and the dastardly acts she committed. And again, Mary protected him– first by crying out and distracting the '*bootman*' who came looking for others within the house, and now, with the whites of Folsom so engrossed and in shock upon hearing about Arthur's decapitation and Payne Tressen's open-heart surgery, no one paid him more than scant attention.

The crowd became so thick, he could get the wagon no closer than a block from his family's store, which was where he knew he had to get to and quickly. 'Please let him be there,' Paul prayed, and truly couldn't believe that he was actually wishing on such a thing. He made his way through the crowd of familiar faces, and ones after tonight, he never wanted to see again. Though, as all of his energy was focused on locating one face, he couldn't help but be barraged by the chatter of those around him.

"*Took his head right off they say.*"

"*With an axe . . . right at the neck!*"

"*What? I thought it was Bobby Taylor . . . its' Archie's boy? He dead?*"

"As a doornail."

"But she cut up that fellow from Alabama first I heard, then went right for the boy!"

"A Nigra did all of that?!"

"Have you seen that big ass heifer?"

"They say she was possessed!"

"I heard she was trying to cut his heart right out of his chest before they could stop her."

"They animals, I say."

Closer to the store, the hundred legged, hundred-headed monster with a hundred hands crowded upon the wooden walkway, pushing and shoving against itself. All heads stretched their necks to see the spectacle across the road, which swarmed with an even larger beast with hundreds of arms, heads and legs.

"Mary Cole, did it?" A woman asked.

"She wanted white men arrested over that niggah of hers. You believe that? After he raped, Mrs. Meadows?"

"What she expect?"

"Niggahs expect to get away with everythang," a man added. "That poor white man she killed been tryin' to tell us they would do this mess. He done gave his life to protect us white folk."

"Albert's dead, did you hear?"

"No, not Albert—she cut Archie Tressen's boy's head off . . . Payne. And chopped that boy's arms and legs off, too."

"A woman?" Another said.

"Delilah Ford said that niggah gal always actin' like she was 'bout to go crazy. That what Delilah said."

"She strong as an ox, too—I heard."

"So was that niggah last night!"

"That was her niggah man!"

"I know that!"

"Paul!"

The desperate call of his name immediately caught his attention, but distractingly so. It wasn't coming from the one he was listening out for. He looked around for the caller of his name, but being knocked from side to side and nearly completely around at times by the surging beast, was making it more and more difficult to maintain his focus as well as his balance. Without warning, his shoulders were grabbed and his body spun around again. At first Paul thought it was simply another gawker determined to get a better view, but it wasn't . . . and it wasn't who he expected it to be, though he was relieved to see him nonetheless.

"Are you crazy!? Get the hell out of here!" Nicholas fumed, in as low of a voice as he could while driving his point home.

"Ms. Maggie will be waiting for us when we get there . . . but . . ."

"But nothing!" Nicholas scolded. He pulled Paul crushingly to his chest and whispered in his ear. "Get back to Ms. Sully's now before this mob turns on someone else, namely us. Don't you see what's happening? They want this town back like it was. That means Negroes in their place, and no people around like you and me. And your father . . . he's around here somewhere– I just saw him." Nicholas tilted his head forward and bore his eyes directly into Paul's. "It looked like he was looking for someone . . . and I'm guessing its you."

"Good," Paul said dismissively. "Because they're about to kill her and . . ."

Paul stopped as he spotted his father closing in quickly, but not upon him. Before he could warn Nicholas he was in danger, for in his father's hand was a metal rod raised high, it was already falling down toward the back of Nicholas' head. But some fortune was abound. Whether Nicholas saw the warning in his eyes, or from his jaw suddenly dropping, he turned to see what was coming for him just as the blow struck. Instead of the rod catching him squarely upon the back of his head, it struck the side of his face, but still, the force knocked him stupid and to the ground.

"Goddamn, Yankee sodomite!" Simeon swore, as he hovered over Nicholas, who had lost movement in his arms and hands to even grasp his cheek that was gushing blood. The beast around them shuddered and became silent. Slowly it broke apart into separate faces and bodies, and again became individuals. "You stay the hell away from him." Simeon then turned on Paul. "And you– you little bastard."

"Father please, they . . . "

"Shut your fuckin' mouth!" Simeon placed the metal rod under his other arm and took hold of Paul's shirt. "Mr. Barrons– I want you out of Folsom now. If I see you around here again, I'll have *you* strung up too, you sick fuck!"

"Father– please just listen."

Simeon ignored him and began dragging him toward the park. Realizing where his father was planning on taking him, Paul struggled to be free, but the grip of his father's sole hand on him tightened and refused. His dilemma was, he could escape his father's clutches, but if he did, all of his efforts to save Mary would be for naught. Although not getting away meant seeing a sight he prayed he wouldn't have to look upon. The memory of Archie's headless body and Payne's chest being cleaved, were more bearable to live with than seeing Mary at the mercy of the reconstituting beast.

He begged Simeon to stop and listen . . . pleaded, even as he turned his head away from what lay ahead of him. To the beast, it looked as though he was crying into his father's chest as he was dragged closer to the black tree. The beast parted and made room for their unloved benefactor and his son. "Look!" Was his father's only response to Paul who was unashamedly crying.

His plan was foolhardy, Paul realized now. But it was the only one he could think of that had a chance of saving Mary's life. If there was anyone who could save Mary now, it was his father, as the people– the beast that was now Folsom, belonged to Simeon. Anyone with common sense knew better than to move against his father . . . that was clearer now more than ever, as the beast waited for Simeon's next move. With a final swing of Simeon's arm, Paul was slung backwards and fell. He gazed up just as Simeon took hold of the rod from under his arm.

"Stand up, boy."

Paul climbed to his feet. He knew Mary was close behind him, not just because above him the black tree's leafless branches extended overhead, but because he could hear Mary moaning. "Father . . . just let her go. Make them take her to Jackson and let the law there deal with her," he pleaded.

"Turn around," Simeon said, in an unexpectedly soft voice.

Paul shook his head. "I can't."

"Turn . . . around."

Paul looked out into the swarm for one helpful face, but the beast was whole once more. It smirked at him. "No," Paul managed to utter, realizing he was alone against his father and the hungry beast. He knew what was coming even before it came. He realized it when his father's already doughy white skin paled ever more, making even a corpse's waxy sheen appear lovely. Paul prepared himself for the inevitable as his father struck his arm with the rod, sending a searing pain up and down it. Simeon drew the rod back again and paused. "Turn around!"

"No."

Simeon struck again. This time Paul squealed. Mary moaned even louder. Albert, a schoolmate of Paul's who had wiggled his way to the front began chuckling. Simeon turned to Albert and silenced him with one look.

"You see what you are to them?" Simeon seethed. "Don't think I don't know what you are. You're supposed to be a Monclair and look at you," he sneered. "This is your last chance to be a man. You turn around now and face that niggah bitch and leave all that other sick shit behind you, boy. All of it! Stand upright and be a man right now . . . *a Monclair man.*"

Paul lowered his head. He knew this was his last and only chance to claim or reject who he was. But not for a moment did the thought of denying who he was and who he loved ever cross his mind in those dead, brief moments while the beast and his father eyed him and waited for his next move. All that mattered to him was what Mary and she alone thought. In that reaffirming moment that he truly knew who he was, who he wanted to be, and never wanted to be like, he turned his head and looked at her. He gazed upon the woman his heart has always known as mother. Three white men were gathered around her. One he knew to be the man who'd came and met with his father many times as of late. And of the three, it was he who smiled the broadest.

Mary was stripped from head to the toes of the only foot that was still attached . . . the other was a dangling mess of sinew and bone that dripped blood on Lar's ashes below. The noose was tight upon her neck, though loose enough to keep her struggling for air while the tips of her toes danced on the ground. Her right eye was black and swollen nearly shut, and her left eye completely closed. Blood from the top of her head oozed down to her lips that no longer resembled lips, but split open, raw pieces of flesh that drooled red-tinged spittle on her breasts and black-blue bruised womb.

Unable to take the sight of her suffering one moment longer, he turned back toward his father. His legs were weak now. The pulse in his veins was diminishing. He hadn't turned to look at Mary because his father wanted him to, but to show Mary– if she could still see him, that his love for her could never be diminished, but only made stronger. It was his love for her that gave him the power to kneel before his father.

"Please . . ."

"Get up!" Simeon barked. His hand was quivering and threatened to lose hold of the rod.

"Father . . ."

Simeon tightened his grip on the rod and raised it. *"I told you to get up, boy!"*

"Please let her go," Paul begged.

The rod came down in fury of successive blows. Even with his hands quickly raised for cover, the rod still rocked his head. His brain felt like it was being rocked back and forth on its way to becoming jelly. The strikes only ceased when he could no longer remain kneeling and fell over, and even then, he was given three more blows. "Get her done with, Luke!" Simeon yelled, to the overweight man standing and grinning by Mary.

The beast surged around Paul. On its way to Mary, the beast spit upon him . . . some of its feet kicked him . . . it called him niggah-lover . . . sodomite . . . pervert . . . cocksucker . . . all the while his father encouraged the physical and verbal onslaught against him with his silence.

Paul turned his face to the side just in time, unfortunately, to see Mary being lifted from her feet by two men pulling on the rope around her neck. Her hands and legs instantly spread out and waved crazily like a marionette in the hands of a child.

* * *

Mary's breaths were fading and so were her last sights of this world. And for that, she was thankful.

What was still visible was Paul. He was lying on the ground below her and barely moving. *You a brave boy,* she thought, *just like my, Lar. And I love ya'll both.*

And then . . . she felt herself suddenly lighten, and heard why. Over gasps from men, women and children, and even Paul's piercing scream, she could hear it.

She smiled, though she had no lips to truly smile with. A final satisfaction that no man could give or take away was what she felt as she left her body hang where it was. She was finally free from pain and hate and anguish, as familiar, strong black arms wrapped around her . . . and her own hands reached out for one more innocent soul yet to come.

* * *

Paul struggled to his feet and scrambled toward Mary's still flailing body when he saw Luke, who stood next to her, produce a long blade from behind his back. He knew what Luke intended even before he saw him hold the blade across Mary's stretch-mark riddled belly. But never . . . ever did he think any man could contemplate an act so evil, let alone follow through with it.

Paul dropped back to his knees. Everything around him seemed to stop. The beast gasped and then fell silent also. Paul felt as though he was teetering on death's doorstep, for he too felt death's blade plunge deep. As assuredly as the knife sliced Mary from flank to flank, so was the last piece of innocence carved from him. He felt his soul drop into a dark pit, as did the girl-child crudely released from Mary's womb drop on the ground. Amazingly, the last miracle Paul witnessed was that, through lungs that had emptied of amniotic fluid by the bouncing on the ground, the infant began wiggling and then crying.

But the devil had yet to truly show itself in Folsom, Mississippi. *It* saved its best act for last.

Luke moved forward and looked at Paul and smiled, just as he raised his boot above the infant's head.

And for Paul, nothing thereafter was ever again the same.

* * *

The beast that was Folsom, Mississippi, disintegrated into a multitude of bodies as it scattered when the gun went off . . . that is, except Luke, who slumped to the ground and fell over from the bullet that pierced his eye and scrambled his brains. The next shot that rang out, close to Paul's head, hit the man next to Luke in the chest and took him off his feet.

With his ears ringing from the shotgun blast, Paul scrambled to the screaming infant and cocooned her with his body. Who had given him the chance to save her, he didn't see, but he heard. He knew then that when David bragged about being good at shooting coons and squirrels, it wasn't just bravado.

"Mistuh," he heard David say to the lone man standing by Mary, "You raise up yo' gun and I'll blow yo' head off too! You best drop it and step back."

Paul raised his head and saw not only David, who had a direct bead on the man behind him, but Nicholas holding a smoking shotgun in his hands standing next to Roman, who too was armed with a pistol. He looked around and saw the man next to Mary drop his pistol and take off running. David was then quickly at his side, as was Roman and Nicholas, who pointed their weapons at the mystified mob staring at them.

"Niggah lovers! All of you!" Simeon berated them, as he raised his rod. "You can't stop us all, you cocksuckin' Yankee," he spewed at Nicholas, and then looked at Roman. "Or you– you turncoat bastard."

"You'll be the first of these murderers to see your maker if any one makes a move for us," Roman dared him.

"Heh-heh-heh! Ain't no need for that. Devil already be here!"

The mob that was Folsom gasped collectively and began backing away, not from the sound of the voice that had called out, but from the one it came from. Enda Sully stepped from out of the mob of whites, who she was as white as and had blended into without anyone noticing. She walked over to the black tree with a cloudy mason jar snuggled to her breast.

She set the jar down and picked up the gutting knife that had sliced Mary open, and cut a lock of her waist length hair from the root of her scalp. She bent down next to Paul and tied off the infant's umbilical cord with the hair and then severed it. After snuggling and kissing the child's bloody forehead, she handed her back to Paul, and then grabbed her jar and stood.

"It be over Folsom!" She called out. She held the Mason jar out for all to see. "The witch of Folsom be here, and I brought powerful magic with me. Ya'll got the blood ya'll wanted, and that be that. Go on now . . . God and the devil gonna see 'bout ya'll sins later. But right now, ya'll come for us, and I'll show you what a chile of the devil can do to folk who walk an unrighteous path."

"Get . . . get . . . get outta here, old woman," Simeon gurgled.

"Why?" Enda croaked. "Just 'bout everybody here owe you money . . . Simeon Monclair . . . but you owe me– 'member?"

Simeon raised his rod to her, but Roman swung and pointed his pistol no more than an inch from his face. "Don't be a fool, Simeon."

"Fuck you!" Simeon spat.

Enda scuttled next to Roman and brought his arm down. "Oh– you ain't gonna be needin' that. I done told you I got powerful magic with me." She turned to Paul, David and Nicholas. "Ya'll get on now to do what you need to do– mmm-hmm. Paul-chile, your sister waitin' for you. She help you take care of Mary's baby." Paul was the only one who didn't look bewildered. "Yes– yes, Paul's other sister . . . the pretty one. Right Simeon Monclair?"

The rod slipped from Simeon's hand. He began backing away. "You– you– you bitch!"

Enda raised the Mason jar above her head. "And you dead, Simeon Monclair." She threw the jar at his feet, which shattered and spattered him with its milky, noxious contents and something solid, that he was the first to recognize.

Simeon wailed as he dropped to his knees and scrambled for his severed hand, which after many years was nothing but stinking, rotting flesh falling off bone. He looked up and screamed again, and again, and again . . . until he was alone, rocking back and forth in a puddle of filth, cradling his hand while sitting next to the corpse of Mary Cole.

The beast that was the mob, that was Folsom, that were the people of a town in Mississippi, went back to their homes from whence they had come and waited for the words of Enda Sully, the witch of Folsom to come to pass . . . *"God and the devil gonna see 'bout ya'll sins later."*

EPILOGUE

PART 1

Life was never the same for Paul, David, Maggie Mae, Nicholas and baby-girl Cole– who Paul named Angel . . . after they left Folsom, which was that same afternoon Mary was murdered in the very spot her husband, Lar was.

But time had a strange way of healing the heart. Paul, or Andrew Anderson as he went by now, discovered this after many years which had given him a full-beard and twenty extra pounds. Working in the great city of Chicago, Illinois, and each night going to the home he shared with his fellow 'bachelor brother' David, now Robert Anderson, provided a peaceful monotony he'd never had before. Raising Angel Mary Cole as his charge, gave joy to him in the days when the dark memories of Folsom came back and seemed never ending.

His half-sister, Maggie Mae, now Mrs. Barrons, lived with Nicholas in North Chicago in a sprawling, secluded estate, courtesy of Nicholas' generous inheritance from his grandfather, who instantly was smitten by the beauty of his grandson's fiancé. As the years passed on, so did some of the pain of what had brought them all to these new lives.

Paul still awoke at times in a sweat and screamed in the dead of night. But he was always unable to remember what had been so frightening . . . at least that's what he always told David, who would then cradle and rock him until he fell back to sleep. But Paul did remember his dreams– vividly. Mary was always there . . . Lar was a frequent visitor also. Other times, it was Enda Sully who came by to talk about more tomorrows to come. But more often than not, the dreams were just memories of that last day in Folsom . . . the knife slicing across Mary's womb . . . and then next, he was upright in bed screaming until David grabbed hold of him and soothed the horrors away.

They were all euphoric at the publication of Nicholas' article, "Legalized Murder: Southern Lynchings and the Blind eye of American Justice," and the small swell of outraged to stop lynchings that resulted from it. Years later, even some senators and representatives in the nation's capital would quote from Nicholas' piece in an attempt to pass a federal law having lynchings declared illegal– it failed . . . time and time again. But Maggie Mae, Nicholas, David and especially Paul, were not surprised it had not passed each time it was put to a vote. It simply reaffirmed what they all knew justice was for Negroes . . . no justice.

But together they persevered. Life had tested them and dearly so. It had taken them all to the brink of oblivion and then jokingly, tried to cut the wispy tethers that stopped them from dropping off. But each time they saw one another, they realized they were still 'there' . . . and that they loved freely now . . . and that they could go on as far as they wanted, if they chose to . . .

. . . and they did.

EPILOGUE

PART 2

THE LAST DAYS OF ENDA SULLY, THE WITCH OF FOLSOM

Enda spent the last day of her life on earth out on her porch in a rocking chair, which was exactly two days after walking into and out of Folsom to give back to Simeon Monclair what Uncle Matty had hacked off years ago. Word did come to her by way of Pickens that Simeon Monclair had died in his study the day after Mary Cole was murdered. But that wasn't news to her . . . she had cursed him. 'I be a witch– ain't I?' She told Pickens, who then wet the front of his pant and ran off down the road fearing for his own life.

Uncle Matty was already dead by the time she returned from Folsom. She was disappointed that he would never get the chance to hear about Simeon Monclair's death while he was alive . . . but he already knew that when she told him about his 'tomorrows' years ago. She knew when her time came; she would not be joining Uncle Matty where he was, but seeing Simeon Monclair far too soon. She and Simeon Monclair belonged to the serpent now . . . that was the deal. She'd always loved Uncle Matty for saving her that night. And as long as he was determined to stay here in this shantytown next to Folsom, she had promised to raise and watch over his niece, Mary.

But as much as she loved Mary and Lar, she knew there was no changing of their fate. The serpent had given her the skill to change minds, but not hearts. And Mary's heart even as a child, was bigger, stronger, more willful and more full of love than any one person, man or woman, she had ever known . . . until the serpent showed her Paul's tomorrows . . . Mary's child who God decided to make white, who was as full of love as his Negroe mother.

And so she waited until the serpent came, which it did the next day.

* * *

For a very short while *It* was nearly sated by the generous offering of blood Folsom had given it. But just as quickly, its hunger resurfaced with a vengeance. "Foolish men," *It* spat from its forked tongue. "Thou are so easily corrupted. So easily fooled. So easily damned!" *It* loved every minute it had spent in Folsom. *It* was proud that so much blood could flow from one little town that was willing to give it freely with but a few simple suggestions to their minds.

Knowing there was so many other towns just like Folsom so close by made *It* attempt to twist its rubbery mouth into a smile of glee.

It slid off the old, dead black tree and slithered down the road and over the bridge to collect what belonged to it. *It* had fulfilled its promise to show the witch 'tomorrows', now it was her turn. *It* found her waiting . . . willing . . . sitting in her chair on the porch. She did not resist. Instead, she leaned her head to the side and bared her neck fully.

And *It* bit deeply . . . taking the life of the witch of Folsom.

* * *

"And now," *It* thought, "I must be even more clever . . . more bold the next time– for I am who I am. In the mist of men I must come so that he knows not that I have come amongst him. He will trust me, adore me, love me and listen to me, even when he knows it is a lie, for I shall promise to feed his hate, envy, passions and jealousies. So now, I must renew my subterfuge."

At first, *It* thought, perhaps a butterfly. 'No-no . . . far too beautiful, someone will suspect me.' Then *It* wondered about shaping itself as a Negroe woman. 'Alas no– for she is already discarded by man. Far too obvious.'

"Ahh," the serpent hissed. "That no one shall suspect, but come willingly to me, even if I say . . . 'Abraham, take thy son's life if thou love me above all others'."

The serpent . . . *It* . . . was no longer a beast of the ground, but stood tall upon two feet. *It* gave itself a slim waist, a smart suit, a tie, and a bible that it tucked under its arm. But before its walk northward, *It* adjusted the reverend's collar about its white neck, for *It* knew appearances meant everything to man . . . and what resided in the soul– nothing . . . except for the ones who truly escaped from Folsom that day . . . the Negroe woman, her husband and child . . . the quadroon and her lover . . . the boys. But they, *It* knew, were the exception, not the rule.

'Foolish men,' the serpent thought. *It* knew men's souls had many tomorrows yet to come and far more than it could ever count, for their tomorrows were infinite, but its were numbered. But in that day that man discovered this knowledge, just as they once did when *It* beguiled the woman to take fruit from the Tree of Life . . . in that day man would surely die.

But men had many more tomorrows for *It* to play with in the meantime. There were many more towns like Folsom that were begging to be set on fire.

Folsom on Fire is dedicated to all of the named and nameless people who were lynched in the north and south during those dark years following the Civil War.

Author Biography

Orlando Smart-Powell is a Speech-Language Pathologist and the owner of a Consulting Service and Special Needs technology company. He holds a Masters Degree in Communicative Disorders and is a veteran of the United States Army. Currently, Orlando is finishing his next novel, "Gods of Egypt", a dark fantasy exploring the rivalry between God and Lucifer. He has also begun work on another literary novel, "American Messiah" about a man who dares to give voice to the unspeakable truths about race, gender, sexual orientation, money and politics, and starts a grassroots movement that those in power, politicians and heads of corporations, want silenced.

As an avid reader, writer and staunch advocate for those who often do not have a voice in literature or society, Orlando Smart-Powell dedicates his prose to elevate all voices. If this book has stirred you to reflect inwardly upon how you feel about yourself and others, and you feel it can make a difference for someone else, would you take a few seconds to let your friends and family know about it? I'm sure they will be grateful. As will I.

Sincerely,
Orlando Smart-Powell

Visit me at:

www.smart-powell.com

Facebook: Orlando Smart-Powell – Author

Twitter: @SmartPowell